Maxim Jakubowski is a Lo[...] born in the UK and educate[...] publishing, he opened the w[...] London. He now writes fu[...] has edited over twenty bestselling erotic anthologies and books on erotic photography, as well as many acclaimed crime collections. His novels include *It's You That I Want to Kiss, Because She Thought She Loved Me* and *On Tenderness Express*, all three recently collected and reprinted in the USA as *Skin in Darkness*. Other books include *Life in the World of Women, The State of Montana, Kiss Me Sadly, Confessions of a Romantic Pornographer, I Was Waiting For You* and, recently, *Ekaterina and the Night*. In 2006 he published *American Casanova*, a major erotic novel which he edited and on which fifteen of the top erotic writers in the world collaborated, and his collected erotic short stories as *Fools For Lust*. He compiles two annual acclaimed series for the Mammoth list: *Best New Erotica* and *Best British Crime*. He is a winner of the Anthony and the Karel Awards, a frequent TV and radio broadcaster, a past crime columnist for the *Guardian* newspaper and Literary Director of London's Crime Scene Festival.

THE MAMMOTH BOOK OF

Best
New Erotica

Volume 11

Edited by Maxim Jakubowski

ROBINSON

RUNNING PRESS
PHILADELPHIA · LONDON

Constable & Robinson Ltd
55–56 Russell Square
London WC1B 4HP
www.constablerobinson.com

First published in the UK by Robinson,
an imprint of Constable & Robinson Ltd, 2012

A copy of the British Library Cataloguing in Publication Data is
available from the British Library

UK ISBN: 978-1-78033-441-7 (paperback)
UK ISBN: 978-1-78033-442-4 (ebook)

1 3 5 7 9 10 8 6 4 2

First published in the United States in 2012 by Running Press Book Publishers,
A Member of the Perseus Books Group

US ISBN: 978-0-7624-4600-1
US Library of Congress Control Number: 2012938749

9 8 7 6 5 4 3 2 1
Digit on the right indicates the number of this printing

Running Press Book Publishers
2300 Chestnut Street
Philadelphia, PA 19103-4371

Visit us on the web!
www.runningpress.com

Printed and bound in the UK

Contents

Acknowledgements

THE BOILING SEA © 2011 by Angela Caperton. First appeared in LIKE A VORPAL BLADE, edited by Jen Blackmore.

WHAT ARE YOU WEARING? © 2010 by Matt Thorne. First appeared in SEX IN THE CITY: LONDON, edited by Maxim Jakubowski.

CTHULHU'S TOAD © 2010 by Robert Buckley. First appeared at the EROTICA READERS AND WRITERS ASSOCIATION.

MY TWO HALVES © 2010 by Alana James. First appeared in RED HOT READS, edited by Miranda Forbes.

A WASHINGTON SQUARE ROMANCE © 2010 by Maxim Jakubowski. First appeared in SEX IN THE CITY: NEW YORK, edited by Maxim Jakubowski.

JOHN UPDIKE MADE ME DO IT © 2010 by Donna George Storey. First appeared in CLEAN SHEETS.

THE PURPLE GLOVES © 2010 by Gala Fur. First appeared in IN/SOUMISES, edited by Gala Fur & Wendy Delorme.

CHECKPOINT CHARLIE © 2012 by N. J. Streitberger. First publication.

THE RED BRASSIERE © 2010 by EllaRegina. First appeared in SEX IN THE CITY: PARIS, edited by Maxim Jakubowski.

THE ANTIDOTE © 2011 by Lisabet Sarai. First appeared at the EROTICA READERS AND WRITERS ASSOCIATION.

SKINHEADS © 2010 by Jacqueline Applebee. First appeared in BEST WOMEN'S EROTICA 2011, edited by Violet Blue.

NEW YORK ELECTRIC © 2010 by Cara Bruce. First appeared in SEX IN THE CITY: NEW YORK, edited by Maxim Jakubowski.

SALVATION © 2011 by Jordan LaRousse. First appeared in OYSTERS AND CHOCOLATE.

HER FIRST THURSDAY EVENING © 2010 by M. Christian. First appeared at THE EROTIC WOMAN.

THAMES LINK © 2010 by Justine Elyot. First appeared in SEX IN THE CITY: LONDON, edited by Maxim Jakubowski.

FREEING THE DEMON © 2011 by Sacchi Green. First appeared in DREAM LOVER, edited by Kristina Wright.

RIVER © 2010 by Catherine Leary. First appeared in SLIPTONGUE.

GOING VIRAL © 2010 by Helen E. H. Madden. First appeared at the EROTICA READERS AND WRITERS ASSOCIATION.

LEOPARDESS WIFE © 2011 by Debra Gray De Noux & O'Neil De Noux. First appeared in INDECENT PROPOSALS, edited by Miranda Forbes.

ANONYMOUS © 2011 by Daisy Danger. First appeared at DAISYDANGER.COM

OF COCKLES AND MUSSELS © 2010 by Stella Duffy. First appeared in SEX IN THE CITY: DUBLIN, edited by Maxim Jakubowski.

SAVING THE WORLD © 2010 by Thom Gautier. First appeared in LUCREZIA MAGAZINE.

ONE LAST FLING © 2010 by Kristina Wright. First appeared in THE MAMMOTH BOOK OF THREESOMES AND MORESOMES, edited by Linda Alvarez.

JEWELS OF THE TIDE © 2010 by Alice Gray. First appeared at the EROTICA READERS AND WRITERS ASSOCIATION.

BOSTON. BREASTS. BOHEMIANS. © 2010 by Jeremy Edwards. First appeared in THE COUGAR BOOK, edited by Jolie du Pré.

LET'S DANCE © 2010 by D. L. King. First appeared in FAST GIRLS, edited by Rachel Kramer Bussel.

AN UNUSUAL LEGACY © 2011 by Anya Levin. First appeared in MASKED PLEASURES, edited by Jennifer Levine.

ROOFTOP HUNGER © 2012 by Aimee Herman. First publication.

WHITER THAN SNOW © 2011 by Zander Vyne. First appeared in her collection WEATHER GIRL AND OTHER KINKY STORIES.

THE PEANUT BUTTER SHOT © 2011 by C. Sanchez-Garcia. First appeared at the EROTICA READERS AND WRITERS ASSOCIATION.

DR MULLALEY'S CURE © 2011 by Delilah Devlin. First appeared in CARNAL MACHINES, edited by D. L. King.

DARK SIDE OF THE MOON © 2010 by Kristina Lloyd. First appeared in BAD ASS, edited by Alison Tyler.

THE AMAZING MARVELLA © 2010 by Elsie McGraw. First appeared in CLEAN SHEETS.

OBIT FOR LYNN © 2010 by Tsaurah Litzky. First appeared in SEX IN THE CITY: NEW YORK, edited by Maxim Jakubowski.

I WAITED FOR YOU BY THE RIVER OF TIME © 2010 by Remittance Girl. First appeared at the EROTICA READERS AND WRITERS ASSOCIATION.

PICKING APPLES IN HELL © 2010 by Nikki Magennis. First appeared in SEX IN THE CITY: DUBLIN, edited by Maxim Jakubowski.

BARNACLE BILL © 2010 by Angela Caperton. First appeared in her collection DARKNESS AND DELIGHT.

BELLEVILLE BLUE © 2010 by Carrie Williams. First appeared in SEX IN THE CITY: PARIS, edited by Maxim Jakubowski.

AQUA SUBCULTURE © 2010 by Lee Ee Leen. First appeared in THE BEST OF SOUTHEAST ASIAN EROTICA, edited by Richard Lord.

GET UP! STAND UP! © 2010 by Madeline Moore. First appeared in THE COUGAR BOOK, edited by Jolie Du Pré.

YOU GET WHAT YOU PAY FOR © 2011 by Robert Buckley. First appeared at the EROTICA READERS AND WRITERS ASSOCIATION.

Introduction

Welcome to another entertaining, sexy and – who knows – educational cruise in the shimmering waters of erotica.

The Mammoth Book of Erotica series has since the early 1990s been at the forefront of what I would term "literary erotica". Literary as opposed to merely stories full of sex scenes in which the characters are not made of flesh but second-rate cardboard, and of course miles away from what I would consider pornography. Now I know that there are still people out there who would wish to taint anything that describes sexual acts and represents the complicated world of the senses we live in in all its often crude reality as pornographic, but it has always been my contention that erotic writing should answer to the same standards as any popular form of writing (think crime & thrillers, SF & fantasy, romance ...) and not only entertain the reader but also make him or her think, speculate, or at any rate leave a mark on their memory and stimulate their imagination. Mere titillation is never enough.

Trawling through the myriad anthologies, magazines, websites and blogs of the previous 18 months (the periods covered by this volume are somewhat extended due to the publication of our recent *Best of Best Erotica* volume, before we revert to an annual selection again with volume 12) is both a pleasure and a duty I undertake on a regular basis with a heavy but trepidating heart. Sturgeon's Law (named after the renowned speculative fiction author) states that 90 per cent of any body of work, irrespective of genre, is rubbish, and my task has always been to uncover the gems, the 10 per cent that justify my faith in the healing, exciting powers of erotic writing and, once again, the writers I've been privileged to collate for this 11th volume in our series have delivered with bells ringing.

Not only have they proven madly inventive, but always deeply provocative, sensual, literate, intelligent, and the adventures and dilemmas in which their characters swim will make your heart beat just that little bit faster and, I daresay, even see many of you partly identify with them. Because, after all, we all have sex lives and wonder endlessly about the lives of others, don't we? Be honest.

For the past few years, there has been a veritable deluge, a sheer avalanche of erotic tales being issued in new mediums like the Internet and as ebooks, which I fear has been to the detriment of our beloved genre, as a distinct lack of quality control has often been sadly in evidence outside of print publications, but the nuggets we have managed to pick up from these murky streams are always worthwhile. To the extent that this volume welcomes ten writers who have never appeared in our pages before, some totally unknown to me previously (including our first ever contribution from the far shores of Malaysia) and others who have been active in other pages or genre areas. As a result, a handful of regulars to the series have not made the grade this time along; there are only so many pages available to me!

As always, not every story will be to every reader's taste. But diversity is paramount and demonstrates yet again how varied literary erotica can prove to be. You will be delighted, you will be shocked, you will be puzzled, you will on occasion be both scared and aroused, but I am certain you will keep on reading, knowing all along there is always something intriguing and sexy around the next page.

This is the best erotica of the year without a shadow of a doubt and your life would be poorer without it.

Savour slowly!

Maxim Jakubowski

The Boiling Sea

Angela Caperton

I met the Walrus in July 1969, my first full day back in the world. Sometimes I think that everything that happened after that was only a dream, all the decades just fantasy or hallucination, but I know better. Everything changed, but it's all as real as flying pigs, as certain as cabbages.

I came back from Nam that summer and, after my discharge, I went home for a bad afternoon and evening, just long enough for my parents to remind me why I'd enlisted the very moment I turned eighteen. Around four a.m., jacked up on white cross and thermos coffee, I took my old Ford and headed for the nearest coast, through lowland fog, to a crackling soundtrack of Top Forty radio and clear channel preachers. I wanted a taste of what I'd been reading about in magazines back in-country: hippie girls, California pot, and loud, beautiful music. I had nearly three thousand dollars and no ambition but to have a dangerously good time.

Not long after sunrise, I rolled up in a little resort town called Waling. You probably know a place just like it. Two thousand souls in the winter and ten thousand in the summer. The citizens complain about the tourists while they sell cases of beer and suntan oil. I parked the Galaxy in a dusty lot, near a hippie bus painted in psychedelic colours, and walked down to the waterfront.

Speed and sleeplessness broke golden sunlight into jagged pieces on the ocean. A boardwalk ran several hundred feet along the shore and I saw a café at the end of it. I walked in that direction, first on the sand and then the boardwalk. Both seemed like clouds beneath my feet. I was a free man. No one was trying to kill me. I was exhausted and frayed, but deliriously happy to be alive.

A few early shop workers watched me pass, probably marking me as a tourist or trouble or both. None of the shops were open yet and I didn't pay much attention to them, but I stopped outside the big, stucco building beside the café. The peeling marquee read Theatre de Fantasia, and a banner painted in Day-Glo heralded a show called *Alice, Baby!* Below it, I saw a sign: "Help Wanted. Maintenance and set construction. See Julian."

I headed on to the café, a place called Red's. Most of the booths were full and I saw a lot of young, friendly faces, some of them female and beautiful.

I thought Waling might not be so bad a place to spend some time, so I took one of the last seats at the counter and ordered toast and coffee from a pretty, middle-aged woman who called me "hon". Even buttered bread sounded like too much food, but the ache in my gut said I needed to eat. The waitress must've seen the crazy look in my eyes, because she hovered over me and smiled when I'd finished. The food anchored me enough to smile back at her. Her name tag said "Velma".

"Saw the sign next door," I told Velma. "You know Julian?"

"Oh, hon, everybody knows Julian. He'll be along any minute." She sized me up. "You going to work for him?"

I looked around the diner. Everyone else had resumed breakfast and morning chatter. "Maybe. It's a theatre? He shows movies?"

"Other kind of theatre. Julian writes plays, and his actors perform them on summer weekends. The tourists love them. The kids, you know?"

"He owns the theatre and writes the plays? Is he rich?"

"Must be," Velma said, taking my plate and refilling my coffee. "Anyway, you'll like it here. Lots of folks your age this summer. Hippies." She said the word with amusement and no animosity at all. "Some of them live in town and lots more stay at the Marlin, on East Thirty-Eight. Some of the kids call it a commune, but it's just an old motor court. You need a place to stay, maybe they can help you out. I'd rent you a room but Ronnie'd kill me." She winked at me and sauntered off to wait on an old man at the other end of the counter.

I watched her walk away and when I turned back around, the Walrus sat on the stool beside me. Dark hair pulled back in a tail, he looked like that guy in The Byrds, David Crosby, but bigger and heavier. He was older than me too, maybe ten years older, and he had the biggest, darkest eyes of anyone I ever knew.

"I'm Julian Brightstar," he said. "What's your name?"

"Tom," I told him. "Tom Rimer."

"You know which end of a hammer to hold onto?"

"I do, for a fact. Army construction and summer jobs before that."

"Ten bucks a day and a place to sleep." Julian grinned at me. "No hassles at all, man. You in?"

"Sure. When do I start?"

"Right now. I need a set built by Friday night. And you need to meet the players. You ever do any acting?"

I shook my head but when I followed Julian out of Red's Café, I felt the gaze of every eye in the place, like I was already on his stage. As we stepped onto the boardwalk, I saw a bearded man the colour of ashes skulking in the little alley between Red's and the theatre, a beach bum in the last stages of bumming before he becomes a corpse or a guest of the county. Half in shadow, he watched us pass with shattered eyes, and I wondered what hell had given him such a stare.

The Theatre de Fantasia smelled like incense and mildew, but I caught the sweet scent of weed in the mix, so I wasn't surprised when Julian offered me a twisted, yellow joint. He locked the door behind us as I lit up, drawing the spicy smoke deep in my chest. I'd smoked a few times in Nam but over there, even in Saigon, it made me so paranoid I couldn't stop my hands from shaking. Home on leave, when I blew a number with the guys, I was fine. Julian's pot tasted strong and my head turned nicely into muted Day-Glo mush by the third hit.

Julian led me through the little lobby and into the theatre. Built for movies back when movie theatres still had stages, the place might have held two hundred people, except most of the seats in back had been pulled out by the roots. The only light in the cavernous space came from backstage, flickering orange, red and yellow, like a fire.

The pot spun my head and each step took me further from all the things I wanted to leave behind. We walked carefully up the steps to the stage and then back into the wings. The light came from a big room behind the screen, lit by a lamp hung with a slowly rotating shade that scattered flame colours across the walls and ceiling. Almost a dozen kids, boys and girls, sat around a little table or sprawled on mattresses. Flats and decorated set pieces lined one wall. A vivid ocean and a painted beach stretched into a false forever.

As my eyes adjusted to the whirling light, I saw some of the girls in the room were naked, maybe some of the guys too, but my gaze glued to a redhead stretched out on one of the mattresses. She lay there, bare and open, like the most natural thing in the world, and I saw the whirling fire in her eyes, the long, straight mane of her hair, and the tangled flame of her bush.

My cock grew three sizes in my jeans and Julian laughed. "Welcome to Wonderland, Tom," he said, and everyone laughed, joyous and inviting. Someone clapped me on the back and I looked around to see a tall, dark kid, maybe nineteen, shirtless and muscled like a lifeguard. He offered me another joint and I blew away the last shreds of my sanity.

I remember laughter and dancing, everyone crazy happy. Two of the chicks stayed naked and we took turns, blindfolded, exploring them with our hands, trying to guess who was who. I learned their names. Sheena, the redhead, and Cowgirl, a brunette with wide hips, nice tits and a wild giggle.

Then the girls had their turn.

"Get naked, Tom," Julian told me, and I remember thinking, *what the hell*. This was everything I wanted. "Lorina, Sheena, Beth, Cowgirl, make him feel welcome."

Two of them held me down with tender force: Lorina, a beautiful blonde, the youngest girl in the room, surely no more than eighteen, wearing a long, blue, simple cotton dress; and Beth, a black girl who smiled but never laughed, dressed in a T-shirt and short shorts. They gripped my bare arms and held me while Sheena and Cowgirl worked me over with their hands, not quite touching my aching cock, but massaging every muscle in my arms and legs, my back and my hips, their touch soft as feathers but firm as coarse leather. Everything fell away from me, the blaring, bloody days in Nam, the rough ride home, home itself, until I lay in a pleasurable coma of lust.

"Okay, Sheena," Julian commanded, "blow him."

All that remained of my tension was in the seven plus inches of heat she took between her lips. She cupped my balls, pulled me deeper than the girls in Saigon, fearless. She worked for only a moment, slow but insistent, and I came in an endless explosion of fevered dream, the rushing road before my car, the passage out of darkness and into the dawn, into the here and now.

Into Wonderland.

After a while, people drifted away and I slept a little on a mat in that dark room. Sheena, dressed now in jeans and a stomach-baring, fringed top, woke me with a kiss.

"Get dressed. We're going to have rehearsals on the beach." She ran her hands over my shoulders and hips, finally catching my hardening cock in her hand and caressing the head. "Cannot wait for you to fuck me," she purred. "But Julian wants us now." She released me and I pulled my jeans on, my thoughts a tumble of fog and lust.

"No shirt, baby," she said and licked my right nipple. "So I can touch you."

We traipsed out of the theatre and down the boardwalk to the bus I had seen in the lot when I drove in. The front of it had been painted with the face of a white rabbit, the hazy headlights its eyes, front bumper flocked with stiff wiry whiskers, long cartoon ears airbrushed all down both sides of the vehicle. Beautifully painted flowers scattered before the rabbit's charge, every petal detailed and beautiful.

Under a scrubby tree, at the edge of the parking lot, I saw the ash-faced bum I had seen in the morning. He watched as we boarded the bus. No one paid any attention to him, but I felt a stab of empathy. I now recognized the look in his eyes. I knew it from men in-country, men who had seen bad things, or who had done worse things. I wondered who he was.

Aboard the bus, I wanted to sit with Sheena, but Julian had saved a spot for me in the seat just behind the driver, an enormous Nordic kid named Lars.

"Everyone is in the play," Julian said, not looking at me, but staring out the window as the bus manoeuvred out of the parking lot full of families, children running seemingly everywhere, bright, summer chaos. "I'll give you a role too," he said. "Maybe more than one."

"It's a play for kids?" I asked. Out of the lot, the bus bumped down State Sixty, past trailer camps and motel crossroads, everything sun-bleached and holy to my shattered eyes. "Called *Alice, Baby*?"

"For the kiddies, yeah," Julian said and laughed. "But the mamas and papas have to dig it too. You ever read Alice?"

"Like in Wonderland? No." I knew the book was regarded as cool, even trippy, but I didn't read many books. I'd heard the Jefferson Airplane song.

"I saw the movie," I said. "And one pill makes you smaller."

"That movie was a mindfuck," Julian said. "All that heavy shit right there in the heads of a whole generation, man. Even Walt Disney couldn't fuck that up."

I had no idea what he meant but I nodded and focused past Julian on the seats across the aisle, where Sheena and Lorina sat, the baby blonde on the aisle. I stared – I couldn't help it. She was pale as white porcelain; the afternoon light through the bus windows was warm on everyone else, but she looked like snow, her hair fair as sun on glass, too bright to look directly at.

Julian followed my gaze and grinned.

"She's our Alice," he said. "Every tale of Wonderland has to have an Alice, the wise innocent who falls into strange days, brother. Alice is like America, dig?"

Once again, I had no idea what he meant but I nodded and said, "I dig."

We rode in the rabbit bus a couple of miles down the coast, by bait stands and bars, then we took a narrow turnoff to a desolate stretch of beach, a shore of grey sand sloping to choppy surf, too rough for swimming or surfing. The sunlight capered on whitecaps and kissed my bare shoulders with wellbeing as I helped unload the bus, blankets, and crates of food and drink.

They rehearsed with the sea as a backdrop, a lot of giggling at first, but then the players fell into their work, and I listened and watched awhile. Mostly Julian made them dance, repeating the steps of a complicated reel, critical but funny as he corrected the steps and timing.

"If you can dance on the sand," he told them three or four times, "you can dance anywhere. Today you are nothing but a pack of cards. Shuffle and deal, brothers and sisters."

I watched, hypnotized. Cards, of course. I saw it the way Julian wanted it to be, the dancers' choreographed movements suggesting dovetails and overhand shuffling, mixing and separating again. "When they wear the costumes, the effect will be perfect," Julian said with a triumphant smile.

They were certainly not wearing costumes now. Most of the kids had initially worn T-shirts and bathing suits but the shirts had all come off and they all danced nearly naked on the shore of the sea, all except Alice – Lorina – who wore her thin, blue dress, translucent when she moved against the slanting sun.

At the end of the rehearsal, Alice danced alone at the centre of the pack, the whirling treys and tens not quite approaching her, but others, Sheena and Lars, grew bolder, and began to pull at her arms, spinning her among the cavorting deck. The dance became a riot of flailing arms and kicking legs, sand like powdered diamonds in the merciless sun, and the pack of cards fell, almost naked, glistening with sweat, onto Alice, all of them laughing like children.

We ate rice, drank tea, smoked hash, and watched the sun burn in a slow crawl down the sky to the juncture of sea and sand. Waling was barely visible around the curving coast. Sheena sat close, leaning on me, her bare breasts a constant heat against my arm or my chest, her hand always on my thigh or my back, fingers firm and warm as brands.

Everyone seemed lost in a mellow fog and Sheena's voice startled me when she asked, "Did you know Julian is a magician?"

"Stupid," I grunted. "Magic is lies and tricks." The collective, stoned consciousness of the group focused on my words. They laughed at me. My breathing quickened and I pushed back a surge of anger.

Julian eased himself out of Beth's arms, stood up and loomed over me, his shape dark against the red sky.

"No," Julian said. "It's not." His tone was light, gently mocking. "We're all magicians, Tom. We turn food to shit and time into garbage, wasting our lives with trivia when the real world is only waiting for us to see it."

"Real world?" I growled. Sheena scooted back as I staggered to my feet. "You don't know what 'real' is!" I tried to punch the air to make my point but my arms remained immobile at my sides, too heavy to support my message.

"You think you know what is real?" Julian asked, grinning. "The only reality, Thomas, is the one we make of dreams and numbers. Lewis Carroll – Charles Dodgson – had genius for both. He knew how to open the door behind the laughing knob, and I, I am learning how too."

"That's a load of crap," I spat. The whole troupe held its breath. I imagined them falling on me, swords and spades, cutting me to pieces. But Julian only watched with a smile until his smile was all I could see.

"Where are you going?" he asked.

"Nowhere," I answered. "Everywhere."

"Then it doesn't really matter which way you go, does it? Walk with us awhile. *You can leave whenever you want to.*"

"Tom," Sheena said and I turned to where she half-reclined on the sand. She had shucked her shorts so she lay entirely nude beneath the stars and moon, the dark red-golden bush between her legs a shadow that concealed amazing things. I forgot my anger, forgot Julian's bullshit. In the dark, Sheena's eyes glowed and her lips shone like blood petals. I dropped to my knees, hardly daring to reach out and touch her, but needing to fuck her just as much as I needed to breathe.

Her eyes, her lips, the dark-tipped moons of her breasts, her hands reaching out to pull my shorts down . . . I saw each of her charms in isolation: total, divine. I forgot everyone in the troupe, everyone in the world, except the girl who stretched beneath me. As I moved onto her, Sheena faded away unless I looked directly at her, her eyes suspended in the darkness, her lips, her tongue . . . then I was in her, our bodies gritty with sand, hot enough to become glass, fused like my cock in her pussy, grinding, and I neither knew nor wanted anything in the world but her cunt, her core, and I would do anything to have her.

In that moment, I knew only Sheena's sweet pussy, but later, when I thought of the beach, I remembered Julian watching us.

Grinning like a cat.

I woke with sand between my teeth and mud in my brain, sprawled on one of the mattresses in the back of the Theatre de Fantasia, naked, with Sheena wrapped around me, sticky and hot. She rubbed against my thigh and I woke up a little and then she rolled to straddle me and ground her crotch against mine. I was only half-hard when she caught my cock and tucked it into her pussy, but the motion of her hips brought me to erection and she rode me in slow waves, her fingernails sharp in my shoulders, her eyes wide and hungry. We came together in a slow, rolling rush of sensation and she settled atop me, her hips still working just a little, milking me.

Some of the others in the troupe were already awake and pretty soon we got up and dressed too. Julian led us down to Red's and we filled three booths with spillover. Julian insisted I sit with him at the bar.

Velma smiled at me and winked. "Found a job, eh?" I wanted to talk to her, but Julian caught me by the shoulder and turned me to face him.

"Serious question, Tom," he said. "Who are you?"

My head hurt, but Sheena had left me with a sweet edge even Julian couldn't temper.

"I'm a free man," I told him.

"That's not what I mean," he laughed, his moustache twitching and his jowls shaking. His eyes sparkled kindly, but very dark. "Who will you be in the play? You must have a role."

"I don't know. Can't I just be a carpenter?"

"Oh my word," he said and laughed. "It is so obvious I didn't see it. You shall be. You will be the Carpenter."

We ate our breakfasts and Julian paid for them. I left a two-dollar tip for Velma and winked at her. She didn't wink back. I saw something in her eyes that might have been worry, and I told myself I'd come back and talk to her soon.

Back at the theatre, Julian showed me the workshop, a padlocked shed behind the theatre with a bench and a decent set of tools. He handed me a rough sketch of the set he wanted made from plywood. I needed to shape it and join it so it could be assembled. Some of the others would paint it when I was finished.

"It's for the trial of the Knave of Hearts," he explained. "This will be the jury box and the queen's throne."

"Maybe I can be the Knave of Hearts," I said.

"Lars is our knave for now. Maybe for you, a knight. Just now, you're our carpenter. Get to work!" He passed me a fat joint and left me alone, which was more than fine with me.

As I measured the wood and cut it, I fought with the urge to walk away from Julian and his craziness. I'd never heard of Charles Manson then. I didn't even know the word "cult", but I knew Julian had some kind of hold over the troupe that was spooky. The other kids obeyed his every word. But why not? Julian had endless supplies of good dope. He treated the girls well and every guy had a girl whenever he wanted one, sometimes two of them. If Uncle Sam had offered as good a deal, I would never have left the army.

I figured I'd stay with Julian a little longer. I wouldn't let his horseshit drive me away.

I could leave whenever I wanted to.

I worked till past midday then knocked off to look for the others and found the theatre empty. I was starving. Julian hadn't given me the key to the shop's padlock and I hated to leave it open, but I figured it would be okay if I grabbed a quick bite at Red's. The worried look in the waitress's eyes had nagged me all morning, so I closed the door tightly and made my way to the diner.

Velma came straight to me. She was pretty and maybe not as old as I had first thought, like the lines around her eyes and mouth came more from smiling than from age. She smiled now as she took my burger order, but I saw the same concern in her eyes. When she brought the food back, I took the plunge.

"Something on your mind?" I asked pleasantly.

She looked around the sparsely occupied room, gave a nod to the other waitress, and plopped down on the stool beside mine.

"None of my business," she said, "but I'm kinda surprised you've taken up with Julian and his bunch. You don't seem like an actor or a dancer."

"I'm the . . . a carpenter," I said. "I took that job."

"I figured, but his last carpenter was an actor too, and a singer. He sang really pretty."

I saw she was holding back, so I asked, "What happened to him?"

"He's . . . You might've seen him. He's still around. The local cops don't have much use for panhandlers, but I guess he doesn't really ask people for money and they haven't gotten sick enough of him to run him off. I think they feel sorry for him."

I knew she was talking about the grey-faced bum I had seen a couple of times since I hit town.

"What happened to him?"

"Can't say for sure. One day he seemed fine, then I didn't see him with the others for a few days, then next time I did, he was like he is now." She smiled when she looked away. "He had a really nice singing voice."

An overdose of something, I thought, but I just nodded. I'd done enough dex to know what being strung out felt like and, of course, I had read all the stories about LSD and what it could do to your head. One pill makes you smaller, another makes you crazy. "Do you know his name?"

"Bill maybe, but Julian always called him Brilly. You seem like a nice guy. I'd hate to see you get in trouble with . . ." She didn't finish the sentence, but I understood well enough.

"I'll be careful, Velma," I told her, and smiled as reassuringly as I could. She patted my hand and went back to waiting on tourists. When she brought my burger, it was world class, though I hardly tasted it. I left her a dollar tip and gave her a wink and a smile as I headed back to finish my work.

As soon as I closed the Fantasia door behind me, I relit the joint Julian had left me, wondering if the troupe had returned. Listening as I passed through the theatre, I heard nothing besides creaks and stage ghosts. The pot turned my legs a little rubbery but I knew I'd be fine once I got to work.

Where were the others? On the beach, I guessed, with a little pang of lonely anger. Was this Julian's way of making me take a part in the play? Or maybe he really needed the sets done that day so they could be painted before the weekend. I didn't have more than another two hours' work and I was already planning the cuts and joints as I walked out of the theatre towards the work shed, opened the door, and stepped into darkness.

Someone kicked the door out of my hand, slamming it. Combat instincts came back in a stoned rush as I swung into the absolute black and missed.

"Don't," a voice hissed, rasping and desperate, but not threatening. "I just want to talk."

I reached for the light switch, but the voice repeated, "Don't."

I smelled him then, over the cut wood tang and the stale dope smoke. He stank like cat pee and rotten fruit.

"Brilly?" I guessed.

He grew very still and, as my eyes adjusted to the darkness, I saw his shape and knew I'd guessed right.

"Not Brilly," he corrected me. "Brillig. 'Twas brillig, and the slithy toves . . ."

I waited for him to start making sense. I remembered the knife rack and my hand found the handle of a big carving knife. The hair at the base of my neck stood up and I sensed the imminence of blood.

Brillig sang, his voice just as nice as Velma had described it, "He took his vorpal sword in hand: long time the manxome foe he sought . . ." Then he watched me in the near darkness. "You don't know the song." He sounded disappointed. "But you will, one way or another. Julian will *show* you."

"Not me, man. There's nothing Julian can show me."

"I thought so too." Brillig giggled. "And here I am."

"He didn't make you a bum. You did that to yourself."

He made a grunting, growling sound. "Now I can't be too near people," he said when he found his voice. "You don't know what it's like, but you will. One way or another." To punctuate his words, he opened the shed door, startling me with how close he had crept in utter silence. I gripped the knife, more than ready to use it.

I let him go, leaving a rank wake behind him as he shuffled across the courtyard and into the alley. Just as he reached the shadows, he looked back over his shoulder, and called out, "Beware the Jabberwock, my son."

In the sudden afternoon light, I saw his face gone almost to bones, skin stretched and pitted, his eyes dancing mad foxfire when they caught the sun. He smiled and I must have hallucinated, because it seemed like he had double rows of teeth.

I finished the sets in an anxious blaze, focusing my tensions into the saw and the drill. I worked warily, facing the open door of the shed, but Brillig didn't return. When I finished, barely an hour later, I closed up the shed and locked it. I figured if Julian didn't have the key, he could break the fucking door down.

Just to be on the safe side, I took the carving knife with me, wrapped its blade with cloth, and stuck it in my pocket. I'd get a clasp knife soon, or maybe a gun, and if that fucker Brillig came near me again, I'd be ready. The theatre still echoed emptily, so I headed down the boardwalk, rigid with nerves. Julian's pot had done nothing to calm me. I vibrated with paranoid intensity, trying not to look at the tourists as I passed them, afraid of what I would see in their eyes, or what they might see in mine.

When I got to the end of the boardwalk, I remembered what Velma had told me that first morning, that a bunch of the local kids lived at an old hotel, the Marlin, on East Thirty-Eight. I started the Galaxy and sprayed sandy gravel as I hit the blacktop, weaving eastward among the Winnebagos and Airstreams. Past the town limits, I saw the Marlin on the right side of the highway, behind a broken neon sign with a tailless, smiling fish, and an asphalt parking lot full of sorry cars and Julian's rabbit-branded bus. Behind the motel, a line of low, grass-spotted dunes marked the edge of the beach.

When I climbed out of the Galaxy, I saw, past the parking lot, a line of weathered, coral-pink cottages and, beyond them, a swimming pool shining under a couple of sunburned palms. Laughter and music swelled from the cottages and hippies cavorted in primeval abandon all around the pool, tribal dancing to amped whoops of electronic noise, feedback from a tormented Gibson. I followed the siren's call and saw Julian's troupe at the centre of the orgy, a dance of naked frenzy.

It was more than just Julian and the Fantasia players. There must have been twenty or thirty kids in the dance, most of them bare-assed. Sheena spun out of the sweaty storm and caught me in a hard hug, rubbing her breasts against me, licking my neck. She tore my shirt and bit me just under my nipple; she drew me with her teeth into the dance.

Someone gave me a joint and the pot bloomed, scattering my fear, rendering it irrelevant. I felt the music throb, my cock hardening as Sheena stroked it through my jeans, her lips red with the trickle of my blood, her tongue teasing my nipple.

We danced, vertical fucking to the crazy noise and then she pulled me breathless and insane, out of the dance, to Julian.

He handed me a glass of crystalline liquid. "Drink me," he said.

I drained the glass. Sheena's hands worked in my pants now,

jacking me. I tried to meet Julian's gaze, but he smiled and looked away. The dance had disintegrated into knots of people sprawled around the pool in inventive patterns of mutual orgasm.

Sheena's hands insisted and all my anger and tension melted under her touch, the extremity of sensation burning new fire as she pulled me down to the ground, stripped away my jeans and took my cock in her hands. I had never been so hard.

She sat on me sure and fast, impaling herself and riding wild, until she came with a scream of pure abandon. I stayed hard, the world beginning to shimmer, my breath bright light, the space above me arced, the sky a ceiling and Julian's face looking down, beatific, his cock hanging over me, until Sheena leaned out to take him between her lips. She ground down on me, gripped with the wet heat of her cunt, pulled me up into her, until she came in shattering colours, Julian's spunk on her chin, then all of us together, in the moment, the golden glow of perfect orgasm.

Wonderland.

My anxiety uncoiled slowly, like a snake in winter, and Julian must have felt it because he kissed Sheena and told her to leave. I sat up, aware of how close I was to him. He was heavy but the weight of his naked body appeared solid, not flabby. His cock must have been eight inches long, even spent. I reached for my pants, stood up and slipped them on, carefully checking to be sure I still had the knife.

My heartbeat shook my ribs and the sky turned entirely to shades of gold and brown. What had he given me? LSD? Something stronger?

Julian put his pants on too and ordered quietly, "Come." My feet moved like he was pulling their strings, like I was nothing more than a tripping marionette. I followed him away from the moans and the cries of the kids, all of them fucking and high.

We walked past the cabins, afternoon sun turning everything to crystals, the weedy grass on the dunes twitching and pulsing with the rhythm of wind and my own blood. As we cleared the last of the buildings, I saw Lorina – Julian's Alice – waiting for us, wearing a short white skirt and a bikini top to match. Her eyes were black saucers and her smile was sweet and open.

Julian kissed her cheek and said, "Come and walk with us." He gave me her right hand to hold and then he took her left and led us both into the dunes, towards the laughing splendour of the sea.

"This has been a good day," he told me. "We rehearsed the play for the brothers and sisters who live here and now they see with new eyes that Wonderland is all around us if we want it, that the hang-ups and hassles of the world don't matter unless you let them."

"You got them high," I said. "That's all."

Julian laughed, his bare belly shaking with amusement. "Oh what will it take to convince you?" he said, as much to the wind as to me.

The three of us walked barefoot through the sand, up the sloping warm dune to its crest, then down towards the beach. A nearly flat surf sparkled in breaker lines, foaming on the shore, washing soapy white, then gone again.

"Paradise is ours for the taking, Tom." He embraced me, his bare, sturdy flesh against mine, still holding Lorina's hand. She broke the grip and put her arms around both of us. I saw the moon like a faded ghost on the horizon, a pale, hopeless sphere. Lorina smelled like honey and roses and my cock grew hard when she laid her hands on my shoulders and back. Julian turned me towards her and I drowned in the dazzling gold of her hair, in the depthless pits of her eyes.

Alice kissed me and her lips were life itself, the promise of the world that I had earned by my survival, as precious and arousing as any kiss I ever knew, her tongue tasting me and pushing deeper, inviting a duel. I crushed her to me. She felt as ethereal as a woman in a dream, a spectre of infinite desire.

I loved her more than any woman I had ever loved and I wanted her with my soul.

She drew me down, Julian helping me because the sand beneath my feet felt treacherous as slippery glass. Together they removed my pants and Lorina lifted her skirt to show me a tangle of golden hair and the glistening cleft of her cunt. I moved over her, intending to fuck her, but Julian put his hands on my shoulders and pushed me down.

"With your mouth," Alice said and she widened her legs so I saw her pussy lips and the wetness between them.

I had never gone down on a girl before that night. She smelled sweet, a little like vanilla, as I touched my nose to the ash-pale curls above her pussy. The afternoon light glowed golden around us and I pressed my lips against her cleft, then the tip of my tongue, tentatively at first, until I tasted her. Sweet as honeysuckle, slippery. I pushed deeper, opening her, finding complexities, folds of flesh, an evasive knot I knew was called a clitoris.

Her scent and slick heat amazed me. I had a lysergic vision of the first ocean pouring out of the cunt of a mother goddess and I drank it from Alice, even as Julian reached under me and took hold of my cock.

I'd never been touched by a guy before but it seemed right and natural. Julian handled me with rough expertise, jacking my shaft and lifting my arousal to new heights. Alice – Lorina – moaned, and I echoed her when Julian's thumb brushed my asshole.

Lorina was the lush land below the earth and Julian the sky god manifest in the wizard, the mathematician, his lust measured and ruler-exact, and his touch upon materiality hot and irresistible.

Lorina began to cry out as my tongue and lips attacked her clit mercilessly. The rhythm was mine now, the same as the sea, the wind, the pulse in the sand, reverberations all the way to the heart of the world. Something cool and gooey creamed my rectum, then the thick head of Julian's cock penetrated me, the sky god claiming the red horizon. Of course he knew the rhythm and he fucked me, sliding in and out of my ass in glorious, pulsing strokes as he worked my cock with his hand. Alice came, her legs wrapping my head, her hands tangled in my hair as my senses burned between gifts and giving.

She moved against me until she lost the breath to scream and, beyond her, I saw the sea turn to fire, felt the gush of my own orgasm over Julian's relentless hand and felt him claim me, wet and hot, as he came.

We collapsed and shifted, then lay in the sand together, Lorina between us. My mind whirled and spread upon the dusk, but there was no shame, no regret, only wonder.

"Remember what I have showed you," Julian whispered against my ear. "We are gods, all of us. We can be whatever we allow ourselves to be. Now, there is an important question I must ask you. Consider your answer carefully."

I waited, watching the ocean whitecaps trace sunset fire.

Julian began to giggle. He seemed to suppress the laughter at first then gave way to it, merry and open. Lorina laughed too, until I couldn't help myself and laughed with them.

We laughed until the sea stopped burning.

Then he found his voice and asked, still breathless. "So, Carpenter, how did you like the oyster?"

Thing about acid is, sometimes you can't sleep for hours. After we left the beach, I wandered away by myself. The cascade of colour and sensation faded into grey and pearl. I embraced the encounter and accepted. I believed Julian and I thought I understood the lesson of his wonderland. So simple and so hard.

Julian had shown me true freedom.

I found a mat in one of the old motel rooms and stretched, watching the shadows crawl in pastel patterns until flickering darkness claimed the ceiling and then my eyes. I slept deep and without dreaming.

On Saturday, I watched the matinée premiere of *Alice, Baby!* from backstage, numb and placid with hashish. I had not seen the costumes before, had not seen the troupe in its glory, razor sharp in the delivery of their lines, each dance step perfect and professional. Every worn seat held a tourist; pudgy parents and wide-eyed kids. Sheena told me the evening crowd would be hippies, teenagers, and younger couples and there would be joints passed down the rows. When I wasn't mesmerized by the vibrant motion on stage, I watched the faces of the audience, frowns on some of them, but most as entranced as I felt, caught in the glamour of Julian's vision.

Alice danced better than anyone else, animated and innocent. I remembered how she'd tasted and how she'd screamed. I couldn't wait to be with her again.

Near the end of the performance, two of the Waling cops, a big one and a little one, came into the theatre and stood at the back.

"Stuff and nonsense," Alice said on the stage. "The idea of having the sentence first."

"Hold your tongue," cried the queen.

"I won't!"

"Off with her head!"

The two cops looked at each other.

"Who cares for you?" Alice shouted. "You're nothing but a pack of cards."

The dancers whirled in a hallucinogenic rainbow, catching Alice and the queen up in their frenzy, spinning them, then all collapsing in a heap as the liquid, psychedelic lights dimmed to blackness absolute; even the exit signs extinguished for a moment.

Alice's voice, Lorina's voice, amplified and muted into an enormous whisper that settled on the hall like a veil, "Oh! I've had such a curious dream!"

Then the lights came back up and the tourists clapped and whistled before they shuffled to their feet and out into the afternoon sun, but the cops stayed until the audience had gone. As they came towards the stage, I looked around and realized everyone else had split too.

"What's your name?" the big cop asked.

"Tom Rimer."

He had a few more questions and I answered them honestly.

"Soldier, eh?" the little one asked. He was older and I wasn't surprised when he said, "My boy's over there. Don't suppose you knew him, Danny Breshca? He's an MP."

"No sir," I told him. "I was mostly in the boonies."

After that, both officers treated me with polite respect. I wondered if Julian had left me to talk to them because he knew they would.

"You know a guy named Bill O'Daniel?"

I started to say no.

"They call him Brilly."

"Yeah," I said. "I've met him. Why?"

"He's wanted for almost killing a woman this morning. Velma, waitress at Red's next door."

"Damn." My chest constricted. "Is she OK?"

"She will be. She's at the hospital up in Ludville. Lost a lot of blood. Looks like the guy tried to take her head off, but she fought him and some fishermen came along. She was lucky."

"He cut her?" My pot-bemused glow had blossomed into an adrenaline rush.

"No, Tom. He used his teeth."

When the cops went away, I looked for Julian, but he'd left the theatre. Most of the troupe avoided me, like the aura of cop heat had rubbed off on me. I told Sheena what the officers had said and she shivered and hugged me.

I understood that all of them were afraid, but whether of Brilly or Julian, I couldn't say.

The evening performance played to a half-empty house and we all knew why. The whole town buzzed with evil rumour. Two fishermen had vanished from a secluded cove; a little girl had been attacked.

Already the boardwalk seemed deserted.

After the late show closed, we sat in the big room behind the stage, drinking warm wine. No one passed a pipe or joint because we all knew the cops were watching, probably sniffing at the doors eager to make a bust.

Julian sprawled on one of the mattresses. "It's all right," he said. "Maybe we'll move along and come back next summer. We'll give it a few more weeks."

I spoke as calmly as I could. "What did you do to him, Julian?"

The room tensed. Sheena caught my arm with sharp nails.

But Julian answered, calm and thoughtful, "Hmm? To Brillig? We did nothing to him. He is what he wants to be. Jabberwocks are the price of Wonderland, you see?"

As usual, Julian's words made no sense.

"What are you going to do about him?" I asked.

"Me?" Julian asked. I heard chuckles and suppressed giggles. He reached down, under the mattress and drew out a knife, the carving knife from the shed. My knife. He handed it to me and I accepted it from him. He hugged me and I felt a sweetly painful ache when we kissed. "There's your Vorpal blade," he said. "Now go kill the Jabberwock."

The hilt felt good in my hand. I thought about Velma, how frightened she must have been. I saw myself stalking Brillig in the darkness, almost smelled his stink there in the room with us. I stood up slowly, more aware than anyone else of just how closely their Jabberwock lurked.

I held the blade and studied my reflection in its steel. The army gave me a gun and orders to kill. My family and town constructed conventional walls to cage me. Julian gave me choice.

I tossed the blade lightly, so its point stuck in the old wooden floor between me and Julian. I loved Julian with all my soul and I would thank him every day of my life for what he had shown me.

But I was a free man and I wouldn't kill for him.

"Not me," I told him. "I've done that. You kill your own goddamn Jabberwock."

Then I walked out of the Theatre de Fantasia and I tried with all my soul never to look back.

Of course, it wasn't that easy.

They never caught Brillig, but I had to go back to Waling three times to answer questions. The second time, well into October, the Theatre de Fantasia stood empty, its marquee blank. Officer Breshca told me that the bus had rolled out a week earlier, the troupe headed for Mexico. I thought a long time about following them, but I went home instead.

A year later, I was living in New Orleans and a package came in the mail. Even before I had peeled the wrapping away, I recognized the contents. My knife. The Vorpal blade, and a note, "You may need this yet. Love, Julian."

I owe Julian a debt I can never repay. He freed me and, for almost forty years, I've lived just like he showed me. I've loved men and women and embraced colourful ecstasy and bright hope. I cherish the wonderland that is this world. He opened my mind and I live every day free in my heart and my soul.

I saw Julian all through the eighties, late at night, on high-numbered cable channels, selling his vision for a penny less than twenty bucks. Brightstar Ministries. Now he's on the internet. Thousands of people follow him.

Sometimes I think about going to him, telling him how much he did for me, offering to give him my freedom like a sacrifice, but then I remember I *am* free.

And I keep my Vorpal blade sharp and near.

What Are You Wearing?

Matt Thorne

We've gone out four times when he asks me.

I've already decided I'll have sex with him, if he wants me, but I'm wrong-footed by his suggestion. He claims it's research for a screenplay but I know he's lying.

The name of the auction-house – Greasby's – seems fitting. They hold the viewings on Mondays between two-thirty and six. If you don't go you have no idea what you're buying because the details are so vague. It might say something like "Green Case containing 25 × New Knickers", but nothing about whether the panties are La Perla's finest or polyamide horrors from Littlewoods; for Damien's purposes it's too risky to take a gamble.

It used to be only the most dedicated scavengers who showed up at auctions but the downturn has removed all the embarrassment from the process, especially with all the new booty arriving from Terminal 5. There's good money in suitcases if you're prepared to itemize and have the patience for eBay. Not a fortune, though: most times they take out the valuables and sell them separately. Damien isn't interested in the laptops and iPods, but he does get upset when they remove the shoes. Shoes, he believes, should be part of the deal.

"I'm no retifist," he tells me at the end of this fourth date, after he's explained what he wanted us to do, "but when I'm checking people out on the Tube it's always the footwear that clinches it. That's not just a male thing, right? Women feel that way too."

"Nothing worse than a sexy man in cheap shoes."

"Exactly, right? And when you see a woman in fucking Crocs it's like she's given up on ever wanting to get fucked again."

"Well, maybe not ever again, but certainly not that day."

"You agree. Now I'm not saying women should totter round in high heels the whole time, but there are plenty of other comfortable yet attractive options. What's wrong with gladiator sandals?" He strokes the inside of my arm, our first physical contact aside from kisses of greeting and farewell. "*You* never wear ugly shoes."

I stick my feet out from underneath the tablecloth and examine my shoes – white patent Escada sandals I should've retired by now but wore tonight because I knew Damien would appreciate them. "Yeah, but that's different, I get sent mine for free. Maybe you shouldn't be spending so much time on the Tube."

He doesn't like it when I criticize him, especially when I point out that his life is less glamorous than he wishes. His mouth gets anxious, amplified by his thick black moustache. He looks at his watch and changes the subject. "Can I tell you about something I watched on YouPorn today?"

This is his attempt at regaining the upper hand so I just smile and say sweetly, "Isn't that why you like me?"

He returns my grin. "Cum-shots. A goth couple. Well, the girl was a goth, I'm assuming the man was too although you never saw him, just his helmet occasionally and most times not even that. You heard the fucker though. Every time he ejaculated on her, he started sniggering. At least I assume it was him. It would be just too perverse if he invited a giggly mate round to film him every time he jizzed on his girly. I mean, can you imagine that?"

We both take a moment to consider this.

"Anyway, there were about fifty splurges edited together into a five- or ten-minute film. He came on her face, between her toes, up her back, in her shaven armpit, in her hairy armpit, in her ears, on her shaved cunt, on her hairy cunt, on her tits, on her bum, up her bum, in her anus, in her hair, in her mouth, on her teeth, down her legs . . . and every time he bust a nut, that infernal sniggering. It was an amateur film but I felt more sorry for this woman than any professional porn actress I've ever seen. Aside from Sabrina Deep and anyone who's ended up at the wrong end of Max Hardcore." He looks up and makes one of his mental leaps. "Did you have sex on your wedding night?"

I don't know why, but this question startles and embarrasses me much more than the porno talk. "No. I was too full."

"So when was the first time? The next morning?"

"No, we slept late and nearly missed the flight."

"On the plane?"

"Don't be ridiculous."

The waiter delivers our coffees, smiles and backs away.

"When you arrived?"

"No. We were jet-lagged and the complimentary champagne sent us to sleep."

"So when you woke up?"

"No, we were hungry and we went for dinner and then we were tired again."

"When then?"

"The next morning."

"Wasn't your husband anxious?"

"No. He knew we'd get round to it."

Damien takes a moment to consider this. Then he says, "I had some friends. The first time they made love after they were married, he kept saying, 'I'm fucking my wife, I'm fucking my wife,' every time he thrust inside her."

I find this less profound than he does. "Shall we discuss your proposition now?"

He smiles. "You're up for it then?"

"It's not what I expected, but yes, Mr Joy, I believe I am."

"Good. There's something else. It's a story, OK? We're characters. I want you to go to the Jury's Inn in Islington and check in under the name Victoria Coles. When you go to your room you will find a suitcase waiting for you. I want you to choose some clothes from the suitcase and then go to The Castle, which is a pub more or less opposite the hotel. I'm not going to give you any back-story aside from this . . . you've come to The Castle because you are horny and you need to get fucked as a matter of supreme urgency. Do you understand?"

"I understand. But . . ."

"What?"

"I know this probably isn't what you want but I'd appreciate it if we could have a safe word."

"Why? Don't you trust me?"

"I'd trust you more with a safe word."

He seems reluctant. "Like what?"

"November shovel."

When I arrive at Jury's Inn, I'm expecting the front desk to request a credit card for extras and wondering how I'll explain why I'm checking in under a different name to the one on my Marbles card, but instead they simply say, "Enjoy your stay, Ms Coles," and hand me the keycard.

There are three suitcases in the corner of the room and a note from Damien:

AS THIS IS OUR FIRST TIME, I THOUGHT I'D EASE
YOU INTO THIS GRADUALLY. HERE ARE THREE
CASES FILLED WITH WOMEN'S CLOTHES. I
HAVEN'T LOOKED INSIDE THEM AND YOU ARE
FREE TO CHOOSE WHICHEVER YOU WISH. AS THE
SHOES HAVE BEEN REMOVED I HAVE PURCHASED
A SELECTION OF FOOTWEAR IN YOUR SIZE THAT
YOU WILL FIND ALONGSIDE THE CASES. WEAR
WHICHEVER PAIR BEST SUITS YOUR CHARACTER
BUT <u>YOU MUST NOT WEAR YOUR OWN SHOES!</u> THIS
IS <u>VERY</u> IMPORTANT. ALSO, BECAUSE I THOUGHT
YOU MIGHT BE SQUEAMISH ABOUT WEARING A
STRANGE WOMAN'S DIRTY UNDERWEAR, I HAVE
FILLED THE DRAWER NEAREST THE TV WITH A
SELECTION OF BRAS AND KNICKERS. PLEASE DO
NOT MAKE A CHOICE TO PLEASE ME BUT SELECT
THE UNDERWEAR THAT BEST SUITS YOUR
CHARACTER. IF YOU DO FEEL COMFORTABLE
WEARING A BRA AND KNICKERS FROM THE
SUITCASE SO MUCH THE BETTER.
SEE YOU VERY SOON,
DAMIEN.

I read the note twice, wondering whether I'm going to get annoyed.
I decide against it and lift the first suitcase onto the bed. Whoever
originally owned this suitcase was clearly a stylish woman – it's full
of expensive designer gear. But she's also a slob: the clothes smell
bad and the first two dresses I pulled out were marked with off-white
stains. I find myself wondering whether I believe Damien's claim
that he hasn't looked inside the cases – what if all the clothes belonged
to fat women, or old ladies? I brought some safety pins with me and
I am, it's true, an average size 12, but it still occurs to me that maybe
this would force my decision and I'll have to wear these designer
duds after all. I consider this a moment, then open suitcase two.

The clothes in this case clearly belong to a poorer, and somewhat
conservative woman. I'm relieved to discover that, once again, she is
my size, which means I do at least now have a choice of outfits. While
the other case had been cleared of anything that might identify the
owner, in this one there's a plastic wallet containing a temporary
paper ID – no photo – to get her into a Greek hotel nightclub. (The

club's logo, bizarrely, is a lime-green iguana performing fellatio on an electric-pink dildo.) The name has been filled in with a pink pen and I'm amazed to see it is the alias Damien has given me – Victoria Coles. Is he deliberately toying with me? Or did he purchase this case first and decide to widen the choice later? I'm not sure how I feel about being given an identity along with the clothes and wonder whether there was anything else in this case that might fill out this woman's character.

I dump the contents onto the bed. Among the clothes are three spectacles cases, an asthma inhaler, a toiletries bag, a make-up bag and an alarm clock. I open the spectacles cases first. Ms Coles has taken three pairs of glasses on holiday: one pair of sunglasses and two pairs of glasses: one stylish and modern with Prada frames, and a far more dowdy pair she presumably only wears indoors. I'm short-sighted myself so I go to the bathroom, pop out my contacts, and try them on. Her prescription is much weaker than mine but not so much that I can't wear them, at least not for the few hours it'll presumably take Damien to get me into bed.

It's started to rain heavily. I unbutton the blouse I wore to the hotel and let it fall onto the bathroom floor. I study my body through her glasses, imagining I'm observing myself through her eyes. I still have another case to sort through, but I want, just for a minute, to imagine myself as Victoria Coles. I look at my bra and wonder whether Victoria would wear something like this. It's not particularly stylish or elegant, just a purple and nude bra from the Elle Macpherson range, but somehow it doesn't seem right for Ms Coles. I go back to the clothes heaped on the bed and discover my intuition is spot on – all her bras are either black or white. I take off my bra and drop it onto the bathroom floor.

I suddenly find myself with an overwhelming desire to know whether Victoria ever wears G-strings. And as this curiosity sweeps over me I remember how quickly I confessed my voyeuristic tendencies to Damien. Even before we'd gone on our first date I'd told him how I'd persuaded my brothers that the only way to secure their diaries was to entrust them to me, and about the time my first female flatmate kicked me out of our shared accommodation when she found my fingerprints on her secret snapshots of her boyfriend's stumpy cock. Maybe it was reverse psychology; by telling me I didn't have to investigate these ladies' underwear he guaranteed I would.

And yes, there is a G-string in the suitcase. I knew it! Out of character, but that's why it's here – the contradictory detail that makes a person real. Plain girls are always kinkiest. Not that G-strings are necessarily kinky – I know lots of women find them practical – but I can't help associating them with rappers and encouraging men to put their fingers up your anus once they've stripped you down. I have to acknowledge that Victoria's solitary G-string is tasteful, a rather pretty blue Cosabella brief with pink flowers and a matching lace trim that makes me think of the icing on birthday cakes. I gingerly open them up and look inside, expecting the prettiness to hide dried secretions and crap tracks, but they're the freshest item in the suitcase, so I take off my jeans and knickers and slip them on. Then I go back into the bathroom and as I'm looking at myself in the mirror something extraordinary happens.

I metamorphose.

At first I assume it's the glasses I'm still wearing, but when I put my hands down to my thighs I feel the muscles lengthening beneath my fingers. My whole body is tingling and stretching, the most immediately diverting development being the way my inverted nipples right themselves and pop out like the teat on a baby's bottle. My fingers go up to touch them and I remove Victoria's glasses. Unable to see without them, I have to move forward and squint in the mirror. When I'm that close I see my face has changed completely. My formerly blue eyes are now hazel, my cute button nose has become long and straight, my eyebrows have thickened considerably and my pretty, angular face has filled out.

I am someone else.

But I am not unattractive. I misjudged poor Miss Coles. My hair is my best new feature. My own hair looked great backcombed when I was a teenage goth – not something I copped to as an adult, one of the reasons I felt embarrassed when Damien told his story about the sniggering ejaculator and his girlfriend – but since then it's always been thick and hard to manage, with too much grey I can't be bothered to hide.

All of these thoughts come quickly, of course, soon swamped by fear. But before I can panic I hear a voice – not my own – inside my head telling me, *Relax, you can stop this at any time. Do you remember your safe word? Don't say it. Just nod if you remember what it is.*

I nod.

When you say your safe word aloud you will return to normal. Would you like to practise now?

I nod again and put my glasses back on, wanting to witness the transformation. "November shovel."

For a moment I am transfixed by the sight of my pubes shrinking
and vanishing back down my thighs and inside the G-string as Miss
Cole's untended thatch turns back into my neatly maintained muff,
but as I stare at my knickers I feel transformations in my fanny that
I didn't notice when I was changing before. I stick my hand down
the front of my G-string and clutch myself.

Ready to change back? the voice asks. I nod and feel my labia
changing shape beneath my fingers. My clitoris swells beneath my
fingers in an entirely new way as it becomes *her* clitoris. I have a very
small clit, the glans, shaft and prepuce mostly hidden inside my
labia, but Victoria's is much bigger, protruding above the majora. It's
full and thick – not one of those freaky ones you sometimes see in
weirdo porn films that look like a miniature penis, but big enough
that I doubt any of Victoria's boyfriends ever struggled finding it. I
pull down my knickers and shuffle closer to the mirror, wanting to
get a better view. *Are you sure you want to go see Damien tonight?* the
voice asks me. *We could enjoy ourselves alone.* And I have to admit she
has a point. But I'm too curious. I want to know if Damien has
changed too. And if he is somehow responsible for what's happened
to me. I can't believe this is possible, but I need to find out.

It's a different receptionist when I go back down and she doesn't
comment when I hand her the keycard and head out. The rain's got
much heavier while I've been in the hotel and I find myself wishing
that Victoria had packed a raincoat. I cross the road to The Castle,
still absorbing the changes in my body. *Her body.* I can't stop myself
from fingering the extra weight at my hips and wondering whether
Damien will find the transformation sexy. I walk up to the bar and
order a Southern Comfort without thinking, even though it's a drink
I've never had before in my life.

I sit at a table in the corner by the window and look around the
other people in the pub, wondering whether Damien's already here
in disguise. There are two men drinking alone, one of whom is sitting
at the bar chatting with the barmaid and another at a table at the
back drinking a pint of Guinness and reading. I don't think either are
my secret lover.

There wasn't a watch in Victoria's suitcase so I'm not wearing one,
but he must already be at least ten minutes late. Damien's always
arrived early before so I wonder if this is also part of his new
character.

The door opens and a tall man in a black suit and white shirt enters. He looks round the room, sees me and grins. It's definitely Damien, albeit in someone else's body. The person he's inhabiting is nearly a foot taller, and has a sharper edge to his physical appearance, especially his face. Inside this stranger, Damien looks smug and excited, like a man test-driving a Porsche. He walks towards me. "This is going to sound cheesy, but I'm sure we've met before."

"Really? I don't think so."

"Are you sure? Sometimes you see someone and you recognize them and you don't immediately know why but you definitely know them. Are you here alone?"

I nod.

"Would you mind if I joined you? We could work out whether we do know each other. If that isn't going to annoy you . . ."

"Are you confident? I'm only interested if you're confident."

I can see he's surprised by this – doesn't fully understand the new me yet – but hides it well, taking a seat opposite me and saying, "I think you'll find I'm very confident."

Fifty-seven minutes later we're back in the Jury Inn, standing outside my hotel-room door. He kisses me for the first time and as exciting and bizarro and unique as this all is, I can't help feeling wistful that our first kiss should be through other people's mouths. The kiss becomes a passionate snog and Damien – who tonight is a man named James – dips down and scoops up the material of my long skirt as he strokes my thighs and brings his fingers up to my crotch. Victoria's fanny feels much more active than mine – I've been feeling new internal wobbles and twinges all night and she's already much wetter than I normally get until at least ten minutes of full-on foreplay. I turn away from Damien and push my keycard into the slot.

The door opens and James backs me towards the bed. I turn away from him and crawl across the duvet towards the banked pillows and cushions, pretending I'm trying to escape. He lifts up my skirt and throws it up over my hips as if uncovering an artwork. He stares at my butt for a moment, then reaches out and stretches the damp G-string back from my ass-crack. "Oh," he says, "I like this."

I assume he's referring to Victoria's underwear rather than her anus and I smile, about to reply, *I thought you would*, when I catch myself and manage to avoid blowing the game. I gently move away from his attentions and take off his jacket. Then I unbutton his shirt and unzip his fly. When I pull out his cock it's one of those agaric mushroom kinds, with a thin stalk and a large helmet that is so shiny beneath the hotel room lights that it looks like it's been polished. He whispers, "I'm bigger than him. Wider. Uncut."

I laugh. "Was it worth breaking character to tell me that?"

"I am, I promise. Take me in your mouth and I'll prove it."

Since it seems to mean so much to him, I kneel down on the floor in front of James and put his cock in my mouth.

"Now, be careful," he tells me, "I don't want to choke you."

"Stop boasting."

"November shovel," he says, and it turns out he's telling the truth. The cock in my mouth swells in an entirely different way to a penis growing harder from oral attention. But his body changes shape too and I have to suck hard to stop the cock getting away from me as his body shrinks. I give it a couple of licks, trying to judge how he's feeling, then put my hand around it and gently slip it out of my mouth. "You know what I'm thinking? I'm thinking this opens up lots of possibilities . . ."

He grins. "And I want to explore them."

"Damien," I say, feeling able to talk about this now he's paused the fantasy, "I have to confess something . . . as fun as this is, I am a bit disappointed that you didn't want to see me naked first. I mean, as myself . . ."

"Oh, I do want that, more than anything. But I needed to test you first . . ."

"Test me?"

"I needed to know whether this would freak you out. I probably shouldn't admit this and I can promise you that you're the first woman I've done this suitcase thing with, but this isn't the first time that I've had one of these weird experiences and in the past, well, it's been hard to find a partner-in-crime. I knew you were open-minded, that's what all the porno talk was about, testing your barriers, but there's a difference between being sexually adventurous and being able to cope when the usual rules of the universe no longer hold—"

"Damien, wait up, you're going too fast. Do you mean that you're the one who's making us change? That you can control this?"

"No, not that. It's hard to explain. Ever since I was a child I've occasionally had these incredibly lucid dreams where I see myself able to do extraordinary things. And I've found that if I follow what happens in these dreams . . . if I go to the places I see when I'm sleeping and re-enact what I do in the dreams, then I gain the ability to do these things in real life.

"Three months ago I had a dream where I went to an auction house, purchased a suitcase . . . I didn't even know such a thing was possible . . . took this case home, dressed in the clothes and then . . . you can see how hard this would be to explain if you hadn't experienced it . . . turned into the person whose clothes I'd bought.

"Now a normal person probably wouldn't think anything of such a dream. But because I've had these sort of weird experiences before, I went on the Internet and looked up where these auctions take place, went and bought a suitcase, took it home, and *transformed*. The experience was fun, and trippy, but there's only so much you can do in someone else's body. I went to a club, picked up a woman, took her home and fucked her. And it was interesting, but creepy, because I knew I couldn't tell her what was really going on without freaking her out.

"So I decided that the best way to enjoy this would be to find someone I could share it with. Of course, I had no idea whether it would work for you, but then I had another dream where I was inside someone else's body fucking someone who looked like you do now."

"That's not fair," I say petulantly, "you've had this experience already."

He smiles. "Not exactly, but I must admit, I didn't realize you'd be quite so chilled out about this."

"I was scared when I changed," I tell him, "but now that I know that the transformation's not permanent . . ."

"But aren't you frightened that such things are possible? Doesn't it challenge your belief system?"

"I don't have a belief system. And I've always been open to having my consciousness expanded. Maybe this'll seem weirder to me once it's all over, but right now all I want is your cock up my cunt."

He's gone a bit limp while he's been talking so he wanks himself as he advances on me once more. "November shovel," he says again, becoming James. I go to pull off my G-string but his fingers halt mine. "Take off your skirt but leave your knickers on for a moment. I do want to fuck, more than anything, but what you said before, about wanting me to see you as yourself. I wonder if we could try something. Take off your skirt."

I unzip it and kick it to the floor. "Shoes too?"

"No, there's something about those shoes that is just so fucking sexy."

I laugh, pleased that I made the right choice. They're just a pair of ordinary flat brown shoes, but somehow perfectly complement Victoria's G-string and cunt.

"Get up on your knees," he tells me. I do so. "Now," he says, "show me your holes."

I do as I'm asked, slipping my finger under the material of the G-string and pulling it back, allowing him a full rear view of my cunt and ass.

"Spread it a bit," he instructs. I do so. "Now change back."

"November shovel," I say, and there's something wonderfully exposing about returning to my normal self.

He groans. "I don't think I could ever explain how erotic this sight is."

I make the transformation back and forth a few more times, letting him enjoy himself as he watches the movements of my asshole and pussy. Then he gets up on the bed, holding the G-string to one side as he enters me. I let him take me as Victoria – she's bigger and wetter – then, once he's inside, I turn back.

"Oh God," he moans, as the transmogrification of her cunt into mine provides his penis with a squeeze more intense than any amount of Kegel exercises would allow me to furnish. "Now you do it," I say, while he's inside me as me, and the swell of his cock inside me is not painful at all but more divine and intense than anything I've experienced before. I let him fuck me for a while and then ask, "Are you thinking what I'm thinking?"

He withdraws his penis from my vagina and I have an anxious moment wondering whether this is going to work or if it will do some terrible trauma to my insides.

But it has to be tried, so I let him finally remove my sopping G-string and lick my asshole for a while and then grease me up with some lubricant he's brought before sliding inside my butt as James.

"Are you ready?" he asks.

"I am a little scared."

"I won't do it if you don't want me to."

"No," I tell him, thinking about James's cock swelled in my mouth as it turned into Damien's and deciding my rectum can take it.

"November shovel," he says.

It does burn badly to begin with, especially as I think he's up to full size but then he swells again, but then his fingers find my clitoris and the pain turns to pleasure. I stuff my hand into my mouth and bite down.

"Is it too much?" he asks.

"No," I say, "but don't move for a moment. November shovel." I transform into Victoria and her rectum must be wider than mine or more used to getting it this way as the pain from before immediately lessens. He continues to finger my clit as he sodomizes me without mercy.

When it starts to ache just a little too much, I ask him to turn back and he does so. After feeling the full force of Damien's wide cock in my arse, James's smaller penis feels much more manageable and I relax enough to let him fuck me until he comes.

He's feeling bad because I haven't orgasmed yet. "Is it the situation?" he asks. "Is it too weird?" It amuses me that even in this situation his ego remains healthy. "No," I tell him, "I just find it hard to come when I'm being assfucked. It's too intense or something. Besides, our clits need more attention."

I roll over and just for an instant I'm not even sure who I am any more. Then it comes back to me. I'm still Victoria. He crawls up on me and puts his hands on her thighs and begins to kiss and lick me. I have this strange sensation in my head where my brain keeps trying to force me to acknowledge that it's not my clitoris he's expertly stimulating, a distinction that our body is finding it increasing hard to make. I transform back to myself and he takes a moment to locate my now much smaller clitoris with the tip of his tongue. But when he does find it, it's suddenly so much more intense, and I stay as myself until he brings me to the greatest, most oddly guilt-free climax I have ever experienced.

"You want to come on us, don't you?" I ask him afterwards, remembering his talk about cumshots on our date.

"Do you have to keep saying 'us'?" he asks. "It creeps me out."

"Really?" I reply. "It turns me on."

"I definitely chose the right person for this, didn't I? And yes, I do."

He arranges himself on top of me and starts masturbating. I change back and forth as he's doing it. He may not like me talking about it, but he certainly likes the reality of it, my face turning into Victoria's and back again, and with every transformation he grips his penis and wanks faster.

It's a game for both of us, the suspense being whether he'll come on my face or hers. As he's doing this I remember reading an online confession by an American teenager who said that something similar to this was all the rage at high school and college parties – ten girls would kneel in a circle while ten men would wank and rotate around them, so that you never knew whose face would get whose load. The game seemed delightfully inclusive, in a twenty-first century way, as the teen had written that the game wasn't any fun unless there was a mix of attractive and ugly women and men.

The whole point was that the girl geek might get a face full from the quarterback, or that the boy nerd might get to shoot his sperm over the homecoming queen's perfect features, and afterwards these people would feel closer to each other than anyone from my generation ever did. Call it sexual networking.

He didn't transform as he wanked, staying as James the whole time. It was Elizabeth's face he shot over, a relatively small payload but still impressive for his second time of the night. "I wonder if his spunk tastes different to mine," he says, and then to my surprise, licks some from my cheek. "Turn back," he tells me, "I want to see what you look like with my jizz on your face."

I do so, and he kisses me, the sperm sticky between our lips.

Later that night, before leaving the hotel room and returning to my husband, I ask Damien, "So how long do you think this is going to last? Is it a one-time thing? If you get more suitcases will it happen again?"

"I can only go on the past," he says, "and when this sort of thing has happened before it's generally lasted for two or three months. And when it stops it's usually about a year or so before I have another dream."

"OK," I tell him, "I will carry on doing this for as long as it still works. When we stop changing, it's over . . . agreed?"

He doesn't say anything for a moment. He seems to appreciate that I'm offering him a "Get Out of Jail Free" card, but at the same time is unable to quite accept it. "But if this hadn't happened . . . how long would you have continued seeing me then? Would you have left your husband for me?"

"Never. Maybe our affair would've lasted longer, but who knows? Maybe this time will be different to your past experiences. Maybe we can keep transforming for years."

"Maybe," he says, "but I doubt it."

"Agreed then?" I ask.

"Agreed. But just in case, in the meantime, I think we should make the most of it. How soon can you get back here?"

"Next week," I say, looking at my watch, "but I still have another couple of hours tonight. He's used to me coming back very late."

"So what are you saying, the other suitcases?" he asks, and we both look at them.

"Well, I've already looked in one of them, the designer one, and I don't want to turn into her, but the third one . . . I haven't looked in there yet . . ."

He smiles. "Oh," he says, "I think we're both going to find what's in there very exciting."

"Really," I ask, getting out of bed and walking, naked and achy, to the third suitcase and unlocking it, "let's see."

Cthulhu's Toad

Robert Buckley

The Essex Street pedestrian mall throbbed with a swelling bustle of souls crowded within its confines, some in costume, some in warm-weather street dress. Girls in short shorts or even shorter skirts, skimpy tops, bare-chested young men sporting war paint, it all became a pulsing carnival of flesh and frippery bathed in warm October sunshine.

Making their way through the maelstrom of humanity a man in puritan dress dragged a similarly dressed woman bound by the wrists. Eddies of human beings swirled after them towards the Old Town Hall where they would re-enact the trial of Bridget Bishop, and where the modern-day audience would most likely vote to condemn her to the gallows for "sundry witch-crafts".

Swept within the swirl, the Revd Walter Wright took his wife Adeline by the hand, towing her against the current like a tugboat until they neared an area roped off with tables and chairs outside a tavern and grill.

"Addie," the minister said. "Let's sit down. Are you hungry?"

"A little, but mostly I'd just like to sit a while."

They entered the open air café and emphatically planted their behinds in the chairs. Adeline wiped away a fall of light brown hair from her forehead. "Whew! I thought we were going to be pulled apart."

"Amazing, isn't it?" her husband agreed. "All this revelry, and all in the service of the devil. Revd Hanson had warned me, but I had no idea. We can do some real good here, Addie."

"Oh, Walter, I don't know. It seems such harmless fun. The young people especially enjoy it."

"Addie, it's the young people we are most in danger of losing. Of course they think it's all fun, but it's subversive fun, it undermines the message of the Lord. This city is entirely in danger of losing its soul."

"Amen to that, sir."

Neither of the Wrights had noticed the young man sit at the table next to theirs. His eyes were dark, set back deep beneath his black brows. His hair was long and loosely curled; his beard black as his mane.

"Forgive me," he said. "I couldn't help overhearing. I've been saying the same thing since I moved to Salem, but no one wants to listen. My name's Tovan."

The reverend glanced at his wife. "Revd Walter . . ."

"Yes, Pastor Wright . . . I know, and this must be Mrs Wright." The young man nodded at Adeline who responded with a smile.

"I read about your visit to the Enoch Baptist Church, all the way from Iowa. I've been looking forward to listening to your lectures."

"Are you a member of the church?"

"No, sir, in fact, I haven't made up my mind which church to join, but Enoch is one of those high on my list. It has a good, consistent message."

"Well, it's very refreshing to meet a young person so concerned with his spiritual welfare, uh . . . Tovan?"

"A very unusual name," Adeline added. "Is it your first or last?"

"My only," he answered as his eyes narrowed. A smile, more like a smirk, subtly creased his face.

Before either of the Wrights could respond, he twirled his finger in the air then aimed it directly at Adeline's chest.

"I had no idea your wife had such full and lovely breasts, may I see them?"

Adeline's hand went to her throat. She began to say something, but hesitated.

"Revd Wright?" Tovan pressed.

Walter's words also backed up behind his teeth. Then he looked at Adeline.

"Well, go ahead, dear. We don't want to seem rude."

Adeline smiled, a nervous tic twitching her cheek.

"Um . . . of course . . . I don't . . . that is, I suppose . . ."

She unknotted the little tie at her throat and began to undo the buttons of her dirndl blouse.

"I'll have to reach back," she said, as if in apology. Then she unfastened the clasp on her bra. Hesitating a moment, she lifted blouse and bra and exposed her vanilla-hued scoops of flesh to Tovan. Some passersby stopped and pointed; chortling rang out in the crowd.

"Very nice, Adeline." Tovan nodded. Then he turned to Walter.

"You enjoy your wife exposing her breasts to others' eyes, don't you, Revd Wright?"

"I . . . but . . . well . . . yes, I suppose."

"And why not? They're such awesome tits; they should be shared."

"Yes, yes, of course," the Reverend nodded, but his expression was that of a man who was struggling to remember something.

"Adeline, you like to exhibit yourself, too, don't you."

"I . . . I suppose . . ."

"Nothing to suppose, it makes you feel good. You're such a slut, Adeline."

Tovan pointed across the mall. "See that young man there?"

The Wrights peered towards a hulking, shirtless man tugging at his crotch.

"Adeline, that big healthy teenager has been watching you, wanting you. Won't you please give him some relief? There's a van parked around the corner. Go with him; ask him if you can suck his cock."

"I . . . I . . . well, of course, I suppose I should . . . cock?"

"Penis . . . you stupid cunt. You like being called a stupid cunt too, don't you. Your pussy is drenched, isn't it?"

"My . . . my . . . ."

"Don't pretend you don't know what a pussy is. Now, be a good Christian and go with that young man. Walter will be along soon."

Adeline smiled and stood, her breasts jostled unfettered behind her dishevelled blouse. Her eyes fixed on the young man across the pedestrian mall.

Tovan and Walter watched her as she spoke to the young man, who put his arm around her waist and guided her around a corner.

"Well now, Walter, does she often fuck other men?"

"I . . . well . . . I can't remember . . ."

"You enjoy it though, don't you?"

"I . . . yes . . . Yes, I do . . ."

"Have you ever wondered what a smooth, pale teenaged cock like the one your wife is sucking on right now would feel like in your own mouth, Reverend?"

"I . . . that isn't . . ."

"And to play with young, virile balls?"

"I'm so . . . what's happening?"

"Come with me, Walter."

Walter followed Tovan around the corner where a nondescript white van was parked. They approached and Tovan flung open the door. Adeline was on her knees sucking the young man's cock. She was naked, her clothes piled in a corner.

A tall blond man stood behind her.

"Walter, this is Lars. Lars's prick is as smooth as porcelain, just delicious. You want a taste?"

"Yes . . . yes!"

"Lars, may Revd Wright suck your lovely dick?"

"He can, after I fuck his slut of a wife. I'll need a cleaning then."

"Is that all right with you, Walter? Ask Adeline."

"Addie, please, I must have some of this beautiful young man's cock. Please, let him . . . let him . . ."

"Fuck her, Walter."

"Yes, please let him fuck you."

"Yes, Walter, of course he can fuck me. They can all fuck me. Walter, see, I'm a whore, they said I'm their whore."

"Yes, yes, Addie."

"Watch me fuck this bitch's cunt," Lars ordered.

"Yes, yes, please, fuck her . . . . fuck her!"

Tovan hopped outside and slammed the door of the van.

"Too easy," he chortled.

"Ladies and gentlemen, the captain has indicated we are making our final approach to Boston's Logan International Airport, please place your trays in the upright position in preparation for landing."

Lois squeezed the hand that had tumbled into her skirted lap when her companion dozed off more than an hour ago.

"Hey, we're landing soon."

Locan groaned and stretched. "Damn, I hate sleeping on these things. I don't usually."

"You had quite the strenuous night," Lois said and squeezed his hand again. "But I didn't mind."

"Oh?" He grinned.

"Even if it did kinda make me feel like a thief."

"Huh?"

"Locan, it wasn't me you were making such amazing love to last night."

"What are you talking about?"

"You know, I was going to take another night before I headed back to DC. Maybe shack up with you in Boston one more time, but . . . dammit, I'm so envious. Who is she?"

Locan frowned. "No one I'm ever likely to see again."

"Somehow, I think you'll find a way. Just for my own ego, I'd like to think she's some skanky alley cat."

Locan chuckled. "She's definitely no kitten."

"Hmm, well, I guess I'll always have Rome, even if I was just a stand-in."

"Lois, look—"

"Shhh, it's okay. It was a romantic weekend in the Eternal City, and all paid for by the State Department. This girl's got nothing to complain about."

"Don't sell yourself short, Bouncy."

"Bouncy? I heard you had a penchant for bestowing nicknames on people, but 'bouncy'?"

"Uh-huh, and I'm the trampoline."

"Oh? Yeah, I see what you mean." She shrugged. "It must have been the chianti."

"I didn't mind," he said, and kissed her hand. "At least you're cushioned."

"I guess I'll take that as a compliment."

"You should. You are a very lovely, very sexy . . . civil servant."

"Hmm."

They parted with a kiss at the airport where Lois hurried off to make her connecting flight to Washington. Locan gathered his one bag and stood outside the terminal. The nondescript, but official-looking car soon pulled up and he got in.

"Ever been to Salem before?" Special Agent Mullens asked.

"Yup, plenty of times."

Mullens laughed. "I suppose I shouldn't be surprised, in your line of work."

Locan's grin was wry and crooked. "I used to visit that town long before all of that Halloween shit took hold. It's a pretty fascinating place. That whole witch trials episode was a brief hiccup in its history."

"If you say so, but that's all anyone ever remembers about the place."

"That's too bad."

"Anyway, Rome talked to State, which talked to Justice, which talked to the bureau, and so here I am watching your back again. Just try to keep a low profile this time; it gets tougher bailing you out of shit."

"You're my own guardian angel, Mullens."

"Angel, my ass."

"So what does the bureau have on this guy?"

"Not much. He has no record. His name is Marshall Conway, but lately he goes by Tovan – just Tovan. Ex-seminary school student, left before he graduated and never got his DD. Could have been something concerning a girl, another student. Some rumours it was even a rape or sexual assault, but no charges brought. Then he shows up as an asterisk in a bank heist in New Jersey."

"Why just an asterisk?"

"It wasn't actually a heist . . . at least nothing he could be charged with. He said something to this little girl teller who filled up a couple of bank bags with cash and walked outside to the kerb and waited there as if she was expecting someone to pull up and scoop the loot. Probably no one would have paid any attention to her except, before she went outside, she stripped down to her bikinis. He was questioned because he was the last one who talked to her before her *episode*."

"Hmm."

"Oh, another thing I'm supposed to tell you."

"What's that?" Locan said, as he rolled down the window and took in a lungful of ocean air along Lynn Shore Drive.

"They've partnered you up on this one."

"No. What the hell for? I work better by myself."

"They didn't tell me why; I'm just the messenger."

"Shit. Did they at least say who?"

Mullens tried to avoid traffic by detouring off Route 1A through Marblehead, but as they came abreast of the state university he could see it would be a long chug into the city. They sat and stared at the bumper of the car in front of them.

"It's a bitch getting into this town this time of year," Mullens said, as if trying to spit a seed from his mouth. "Shit!"

"Yeah, it's that time of year."

"So, is your guy some kind of Halloween freak, or something? And why is the Vatican so interested in a guy who has no record? Must be some kind of spook if they've sic'd not one but two paladins on him. Why Salem, of all places?"

"Because this is where the landmarks are."

"Landmarks? What landmarks?"

"The school here."

"The state university?"

"Arkham University."

"Huh?"

"Ever read any horror stories, Mullens?"

"I read some of King's stuff when I was a kid. I get enough real horror tossed my way on the job."

"Yeah, I suppose you do at that."

They inched along Lafayette Street and turned right onto New Derby.

"Headed for the Hawthorne?" Locan asked.

"Nope. You guys are putting up at a little bed and breakfast off Derby Street."

"A B&B?"

"I checked it out. Little place in an old house. Don't worry; you have your own shower and a-c."

"Won't need the a-c at night. No matter how unseasonably warm it gets in October, the nights are always chilly on the coast."

"Your partner's already there. Oh, and your name for check-in purposes in Sumner Osgood."

"Where the fuck they come up with a name like that?"

"You're tracking your genealogy in case anyone asks. That's why you came to Salem."

"Not the Halloween festivities?"

"That too."

They passed the maritime site and the old Customs House, then Mullens turned hard down a narrow street that paralleled Derby Wharf.

"Kosciusko Street?" Locan said, noting the street sign.

"Polish neighborhood. Practically on the water. You know that Seven Gables joint is just up the street."

"I know."

"Oh, yeah, you said you'd been here before."

Mullens stopped the car and indicated they had reached their destination. Locan stepped out and retrieved his bag from the trunk.

"Stay in touch," Mullens said. Locan nodded.

A small white wooden shingle affixed to the house indicated it was built in 1800 by Joshua Briggs, sailmaker.

Inside Locan was greeted by a cheery blonde girl he guessed to be about fourteen.

"Hi, I'm Jeanie. My dad'll be back soon. I can check you in." she said. Her grin seemed to brighten the dark-wood interior from a tiny pulpit of a desk wedged into a corner.

"Hi, yourself, Jeannie. Sumner Osgood."

"Yes, Mr Osgood. Mrs Osgood checked in two nights ago."

"Good. I suppose I would have had to be a bit flummoxed if she wasn't here."

"Well, she isn't here right this minute, sir. She took the ghost tour; it came by to pick her up about twenty minutes ago."

"You don't say. Hey, would you have a copy of their itinerary?"

"Yeah, sure. Gonna catch up to her?"

"Gonna try to head her off at the pass . . . maybe here: Howard Street Burial Ground."

"I bet she'll be surprised. If you don't mind my saying, Mr Osgood, your wife is really pretty. Kinda younger than you, huh?"

He nodded. "Kinda."

"Well, nice to have you stay with us. Here's your key."

"Thanks."

"Oh, and Mr Osgood?"

"Yes, Jeanie?"

"I hope . . . I mean, when I said you were older than your wife, I didn't mean . . . well, truth is, I can see why she married you, if you don't mind my saying."

Locan grinned. "Don't mind at all. You are a refreshingly candid young woman, Jeanie."

He made her blush.

She wasn't dressed for the season, but the translucent pale yellow sundress and floppy white hat were perfect for the weather: 80 degrees and breezy even as twilight approached. The breeze teased its way around her ankles, lifting the hem of her dress just fleetingly to reveal an enticing view of her knees and calves. Locan sighed, then admonished himself. But his cock twitched too. Had he missed her that much?

She meandered between the tourists who disembarked from a bus made out to look like a trolley that was made out to look like a big hearse. The guide led his charges through the gate of the burial ground. The kid looked to be about eighteen and was dressed in a crypt-keeper's cowl. Locan thought he must have been sweltering.

"Now, folks," the kid began, "there isn't much to tell you about this dumpy old graveyard except one very important thing . . . it's haunted."

"Excuse me, son," Locan called out. "Would you mind where you're stepping? You're about to trip over Mrs Peabody."

The kid did a slow turn and a slow burn. Locan grinned widely from the granite tomb cap he sat upon.

"Sir?"

"Mrs Eliza Palmer Peabody . . . Nathaniel Hawthorne's mother-in-law. Mom to Elizabeth the transcendentalist who introduced kindergarten to America, and Mary, who married the great educator Horace Mann, and Sophia, Nathaniel's wife. She was an artist, you know. Anyway, you're stepping on her, Mrs Peabody, I mean."

The kid cocked his head like a confused mutt.

"Her gravestone is pretty eroded already; I'd hate to see someone accidentally damage it."

A collective mumble rose among the tourists. Some snapped pictures of the tombstone.

The kid forced a chuckle. "Everyone's a historian in Salem, folks. Sir, maybe you should wait for the literary tour to come along."

"You don't have one. Shame. There's a lot more to Salem than witches and ghosts."

"Well, for the moment, I'm working the hauntings tour. Think I could continue?"

"Oh, pardon me, son," Locan grinned and nodded. "Didn't mean to interrupt. Please, carry on."

"Thanks." He turned towards his group. "As I was saying, this is where the ghost of Giles Corey appears whenever there is an impending disaster facing the city of Salem. He was crushed to death right here." The kid waved his arms, indicating Giles met his end right behind where the kid was standing.

"Oh, sorry, hate to be a pest," Locan interjected again, "but more likely old Giles was pressed over yonder in the parking lot of the Catholic church there. It would have been right across the street from the old gaol."

The kid was seething now. A familiar sweet giggle erupted among the tourists.

"Is that so?" the kid challenged. "Well, I've been conducting this tour all summer and—"

"Well, glad I could set you straight. Wouldn't want to misinform all these good people who paid to get the accurate story. Especially since there's nothing else to recommend this old bone yard. Except perhaps that I'm sitting on Mrs Hawthorne, Nathaniel's mom, and his sisters and grandparents. And just a few yards away lies one of the most celebrated marine artists of his day, and a stone's toss from Mrs H. is Colonel Carleton, who raised his own regiment and served under Washington at Valley Forge. Hey, folks, has he shown you where Captain White was murdered yet?"

There was an emphatic acknowledgement from the group.

"Good. Well his nephews are buried here too, the first defendants to be convicted of accessory murder in the United States. They were both hanged right over there at what used to be the county jail . . . looks like they've turned it into luxury apartments."

The crowd was losing its cohesion with individuals snapping photos and talking excitedly.

"Folks, we really got to shove off now," the kid pleaded, "got to get to the next haunted stop."

Like a frustrated border collie he tried to herd them back onto the bus.

She didn't follow the group, but instead slowly approached Locan, a careless relaxed roll of her hips with each step. He had missed her, even more than he realized.

At last she stood in front of him, the breeze carrying her scent into his nostrils. He resisted the urge to lay her down on the tomb cap and screw her senseless.

"Have a seat, Mrs H won't mind."

She slid her behind onto the tomb cap, her dress moulding to the valley between her cheeks.

"Planning on becoming a tour guide when you retire?"

"I didn't know you could retire from the Palatinae. Only *they* can say when your penance is up."

"Hmm, that poor kid."

"He'll probably get laid tonight; he'll get over it."

"You think that solves all problems?"

"The only ones worth solving."

"Locan . . . I missed you."

"Missed you too, Rachel."

"Racey."

He grinned and pulled her towards him, kissed her, and deftly turned her onto her back.

"Here?" She asked, feigning wide-eyed surprise.

"Uhmmm."

"It isn't even dark yet."

His hand slid up her thigh.

"Stop! We have a room."

"Too far," he said, and kissed her neck.

"I'll shift."

"Nooo, c'mon."

"I mean it. Screw me on a nice soft bed, not a table of bumpy granite."

"But I don't know if I can walk," he whined.

"I'll help you; maybe we'll get back before you get an ingrown erection. That would be a shame."

"Ohhhh!"

Their walk back to the B&B was more like a pursuit as she fended off his hands and endured his pinches. They greeted Jeanie and almost fell up the stairs as the teenager blushed and giggled.

Once inside the room Rachel kicked off her shoes and tossed the hat. He lifted her dress to her shoulders and held it a moment. Her body was so pale.

"You don't get out in the sun much, do you?" he said.

"I prefer moonlight. Complaining?"

"No, no, no . . . it's just . . . a guy could go snow blind looking at you." He lifted the dress over her head and let it fall. Her chestnut hair tumbled over her shoulders, veiling her unfettered breasts; she wore only a flower-print bikini panty. He began to back her towards the bed, but she sidestepped him and worked at his belt buckle, zipper, and took hold of his trousers at the hips. Then she had them off and his boxers with them.

He was on the bed, naked. She had lost the panties and had straddled him. It seemed she was about to forgo any preliminaries. But he wanted to kiss her, even more than fuck her. He reached up and pulled her onto his chest, lifting her so her lips could reach his.

She kissed him back, a long, lingering, lip-licking kiss.

He trailed more kisses and nibbles along her neck and over her shoulders, and let his hands roam down her back until he squeezed palmfuls of her round derrière. Still kissing, kissing every inch of her he could reach while on his back. His hands coursing over her cool skin, he couldn't feel enough of this girl.

She clasped his cock in her hand, lifted herself and plunged herself onto him. Her cunt clenched him as her buttocks pounded his pelvis. Her eyes were closed, her wet lips parted in an "O". A high, musical note was building into a wail. She was fucking him, taking what she wanted, impatient, rapacious.

A thousand blue fireflies cascaded down her arms.

She cried out in mid-thrust and plunged down, squeezing his thighs between her knees. His eyes rolled back and his fluid rocketed out of his cock. Every bit of tension drained from him. He went limp.

She refused to release his cock, even as it retreated, and began to swivel her hips, lazily swirling his cock inside her.

"God, that was good," she said. Her eyes were half open, sleepy, and her mouth slanted into a sloppy smile. "C'mon, I'll fuck you slow now."

His cock was responding, but he thought it had a long way to go before making a useful recovery. He sighed, thinking how wonderful it was to be used and abused by her. He closed his eyes, a languid smile playing across his lips.

"Oh, my God, did I do that?"

"Huh?" he tried to sit up.

"Your pelvis is all bruised . . . wait a sec. Those bruises are . . . a few days old." Her eyes lost that sleepy aspect and narrowed sharply.

"Bouncy," he sighed.

"Bouncy? Sounds like one of your patented nicknames. Who is she?"

He sighed again. "A wonderful woman who granted me the privilege of pretending she was you."

Her eyes softened again. "Oh . . . should I send her a thank-you note?"

"C'mere. I want to kiss you some more."

She slid off his cock and snuggled into his shoulder, granting him her lips and kissing him deeply. When she broke their kiss she shook her head. "What is it about you, Locan, that girls just naturally want to be on top?"

"Hmmm, just easy, I guess. Or lazy."

Later as she delicately played her fingers along his recovering cock and he swirled his hand across her ass, he asked, "Wasn't there anyone else for you?"

"Sure . . . you can't let an itch go unscratched for long. It was a girl, though."

"That's right; you had a thing for girls too."

"I like girls . . . a lot. I like cock too."

"And I'm glad you do."

"She was a girl they partnered me up with. Her name was Daphne; she was nice. She'd had a run-in with a pooka . . ."

"Was she the girl with Dex O'Leary when—?"

"Yeah, she said that was her last partner. You know her?"

"Know about the pooka run-in she and old Dex had. It's legend among the Palatinae."

"Anyway, she was scared to death she'd run into another one. She used to sneak into my bed at night. We'd cuddle, and then we'd try other stuff. It was just girlfriend sleepover stuff, but it was nice to share a bed with someone."

"How come they didn't keep you together? Someone get wind of the 'sleepover stuff'?"

"No . . . she saw me shift. We had a thing cornered in an old church. Jacoby told us it was an elemental – really dangerous. Turned out to be a fucking run-of-the-mill serial murderer, except he was a really hideous-looking dwarf. He got the drop on Daphne; only way I could get to him fast enough . . . anyway, it freaked her out a bit. She asked to be transferred. I couldn't blame her."

"How many times have you had to—?"

"Twice . . . there was just one other time."

"Dealing with it?"

"Yeah, sure. I am what I am. Sometimes though . . ."

"What?"

"The sensations are so . . . incredible, so intoxicating . . . sometimes I'm afraid I won't want to shift back."

He held her head close to his chest. They dozed off.

They slept and screwed for the rest of the evening, not even bothering to have dinner. In the morning they awoke famished. The temperatures had fallen overnight. She slid into a pair of jeans, not bothering with panties, and pulled on a roomy sweatshirt. Locan watched her dress, then used his imagination to undress her again. No bra, no panties, just the ankle holster cradling a Beretta. He liked her sense of fashion; he pulled on his own jeans and a hoodie bulky enough to disguise the Bulldog revolver tucked into the small of his back.

The breakfast room was small and accommodated only one other couple, who looked to be a long time retired. Jeanie again seemed to be on her own as she waited each table.

"My mom's coming home next week," the girl said and grinned.

"She's been away?" Rachel asked.

"She had a tiny stroke a few months ago and she's been in the rehab hospital. That's why my dad hasn't been around much. But she'll be home right after Halloween."

"Glad to hear it," Locan offered.

"Yeah, I'll be glad for my dad; he really misses her being around." She refilled their coffee cups and returned to the kitchen.

"Nice kid," Locan said.

"Yeah, a really sweet personality. I was such a moody bitch when I was her age."

"You were being fitted out for the convent. Hell, I'd be moody too."

"So, what are we doing here?"

"They didn't tell you?" Locan's brow wrinkled.

"They were in too much of a hurry, I guess. Plucked me right out of Prague and put me on a plane."

"Well," Locan said, leaning his elbows on the table and forming a chapel arch with his hands. "I gather it's a big panic over nothing. Silly really."

"Rome doesn't dispatch a pair of Paladins over something silly," Rachel said, emphatically biting a bagel and smearing her upper lip with cream cheese.

"Oh?" Locan replied, shaking his head and making a face. "They do it all the time. But this time, I don't know, it's amazing what some people believe."

"Well?"

"OK, ever read any horror fiction?"

"Stephen King."

"Of course. Well, back in the day, pre-World War II, Stephen King was a guy named Lovecraft. He used to write some densely weird shit about ancient immortal monsters who every so often showed up and made some people's lives a nightmare. Anyway, he concocted a whole mythos about these beings, and he very craftily let other writers expand on it, even to the point of citing allegedly genuine ancient texts as their source. You ever hear of the *Necronomicon*?"

"Yeah, during training, that's one of the books Brother Theodosius told us to look out for. He said it was full of spells and was 'extraordinarily evil'." She mimicked the monk's sonorous voice.

"Doesn't exist. It's bullshit, entirely concocted by Lovecraft and other writers."

"But, why would they tell us about—"

"Lots of people believe it's real because Lovecraft and his acolytes did such a good job of promoting it. The Vatican isn't taking any chances, so here we are."

"You mean they sent us after a book that doesn't exist?"

"No, we're after some nut job who believes it exists and who thinks he can summon these old monsters. About a year ago the Vatican began receiving odd emails. They read like Lovecraft stories, except the author isn't calling them stories; he says they really happened and that he has the key to the whole mythos. Well, shit, there's a general call to battle stations over this; it's absolutely ludicrous."

"So what are we supposed to do?"

Locan leaned over and wiped the cream cheese off her lip. "They know who sent the emails. It's a little douche bag who's calling himself Tovan. He's here."

"Why here?"

"Lovecraft set a lot of his stories in a group of fictional towns on Massachusetts' North Shore. One town he called Arkham, but anyone with any knowledge of the area would know Arkham is a stand-in for Salem. They figure he's going to summon these creatures forth at Halloween. We're supposed to stop him."

"How?"

He gazed at her a moment. "The guy's a crackpot, but it doesn't matter, they think he's a threat to humanity and, by extension, the Church. Either way, he gets a one-way ticket to hell."

"That . . . that's not right. I mean, if he's just a nut."

"Maybe, just maybe there's more to it, but that's the basic story."

Locan's cell phone rang. Rachel shuddered. It rang for only one reason.

"Yeah?" Locan answered. "No shit? When? What the hell . . . ? Where? On our way."

He snapped the phone shut. "We're taking a walk to the police station."

The heat had dissipated overnight and an autumn chill had settled in. Tourists filled the streets wearing jackets and sweaters, or bulky fleeces. It was an axiom of New England weather that held true: if you don't like the conditions, wait a minute.

Locan proceeded to give Rachel the nickel tour as they made their way along Derby Street.

"That's Derby Wharf over there, juts about a half-mile into the harbour. The guy who owned and developed it made a fortune in the Far East trade. He became America's first millionaire. That's the Custom House directly opposite where they used to tally up the cargo of every ship that came into port and levied an excise on it. It was the federal government's sole source of revenue for a long time and Salem accounted for about half of it. See the corner office?"

"Yes."

"Once occupied by Nathaniel Hawthorne. Had enough time on his hands to imagine *The Scarlet Letter* there. Lost his job when the administration changed. Used the prologue to get back at all the life-time hacks who kept their jobs. Real catty stuff, ever read it?"

"No. Never read any Hawthorne, except what I had to in high school. Don't really remember any of it."

"Hmm, but you read Stephen King?"

"Sure."

He pointed out a mansion that figured in a Lovecraft story as well as the Old Burying Point and the Witch Trials' victims memorial.

"And that's why all these people are here celebrating and wearing costumes and having a great time," he said. "Because three hundred years ago a handful of people got their rights trampled over and paid for it with their lives. I wonder if three centuries from now some little town in Poland will have itself a little month-long festival like this, and folks'll be walking the streets in striped pyjamas and having a gay old time."

"Isn't Halloween *supposed* to be fun?" Rachel said.

"Yeah . . . sure it is."

They approached the police station, which was set kitty-corner beside railroad tracks. It looked like a redbrick Norman fortress. The lobby was bare; a pair of officers sat behind a counter separated from the lobby by bulletproof glass.

"Yes, sir, can I help you?" The officer was blonde, her hair tied back in a short ponytail.

"Sumner Osgood and wife to see Lieutenant DiLeo."

He watched her eyes dart left to her male companion.

"He's expecting us," Locan added.

"Sir, would you and your wife please step through the metal detector."

"That won't be necessary, officer." Mullens appeared out of nowhere.

The officer nodded and buzzed them into the inner sanctum of the station.

Mullens guided them to an office and hustled them through the door. A dozen eyes had watched every move they made.

The officer who stood behind the desk eyed them warily. Locan at once noticed the decoration on his lapel: The Order of St Peter. They didn't give those out with a can of beans.

Mullens made the introductions: "Lieutenant DiLeo, Mr and Mrs Sumner Osgood."

"Nice to meet you," the lieutenant offered. "Now, let's see some ID."

Mullens nodded towards Locan and Rachel. They each proffered a leather hip wallet. The lieutenant took them and looked through Locan's first.

"Garreth Locan and Rachel McDaniel . . . Palatinae . . . Paladins.

I've seen Interpol, Scotland Yard, even Moscow Militia. First time I ever saw one of these. They talk about you guys at cop conventions, you know, like you're some kind of legend or maybe fairy tale. God's cops, they call you."

"Hardly," Locan said.

"Agent Mullens wants you to see the rev. and his wife. There's a lot of chatter going on about why the FBI is nosing around this thing. If anyone ever got wind that you two were here . . ."

"We'll try to keep a low profile, Lieutenant DiLeo. What can you tell us about this couple?"

"As much as the local paper printed today. The minister was stopping kids as young as ten on the streets offering to pay them twenty bucks to hump his wife. Some parents tipped us; we got a warrant and ran their motel room. Found a couple of sixteen-year-olds with the missus. Busted them on a few dozen charges. You know, this guy's known throughout the country as a conservative evangelical. He was in town to give a lecture at one of the churches. Can't figure it out."

"No bail?" Mullens asked.

"It looks like all that juice he used to have dried up real fast. Their own people in Iowa aren't returning our calls. The pastor of the Enoch Baptist washed his hands of them. Right now, they don't have a friend in the world, and Revd Wright didn't have enough money on him to make bail for him and his wife. Spent every dime trying to get his wife laid."

"Anyone ask them what they were up to?" Locan asked.

"They're talking some ragtime about obliterating innocence at the behest of Cthulhu. Know who that is? Some half-assed god or something from one of Lovecraft's stories."

"Lieutenant, you've read Lovecraft?" Locan nodded towards Mullens and Rachel.

"Yeah, we had a crew of graffiti vandals a few years ago spray-painting Cthulhu all over town. Had to read up on it to get a handle on who they were."

"What did you think?"

"I like Stephen King. Lovecraft was just too weird."

"Hmm."

"Another thing they kept saying is how they were guided by Tovan. We put the name out on the wire and that's how we got the bureau hit."

"Well, Lieutenant, can we speak to the reverend and his wife now? In fact, I'd like to interview Mrs Wright first."

"Follow me. I want to avoid as many people as possible on the way to the cells. We'll put her in an interview room for you."

Mrs Wright was serene, a slight smile playing across her face. Locan thought the forty-something minister's wife was attractive enough to draw a man's attention without the help of her husband and a fistful of twenties, but teenagers? Her attire was sensible, even demure, but her figure indicated she took care of herself. Locan put himself in a teenager's mind. Mrs Wright looked like the average high-school teacher. Then maybe, if a guy was paying you and your hormones were raging, why not screw your teacher?

Locan sat directly across the table from the woman; as Rachel sat off to the left, so Mrs Wright would have to turn her head to talk to each of them.

"Hello, Adeline, do you think we could have a little chat?"

Mrs Wright's smile widened and her eyes slid to her left.

"She's pretty," the woman said. "I could lick her pussy for you. Make her scream when she came. Want to hold her down?"

"Um, no thanks, dear, we just . . ."

"I'll suck your cock; get you all hard. Fuck her in the ass; I'll hold her head between my thighs while you rape her asshole." Mrs Wright licked her lip and grinned.

Locan reached over the table and took hold of Mrs Wright's hands. "Look at me, Adeline, right here."

He briefly let go of one hand and with two fingers indicated she look straight into his eyes.

The woman's lasciviously childish demeanour faded as quickly as a shadow crossed her face.

"What's going on in there, Adeline? Who's telling you to say such things? Look at me; it's OK, it's not your fault, dear. Someone put some nasty ideas in your brain. What happened?"

The woman's chin trembled; her eyes filled and spilled over in an instant. He could see the wail building from a deep dark place in the back of her mind; he braced for it.

The woman's sob when it surfaced made Rachel flinch. She wanted to talk, wanted to tell him, but the spasms of remorse were just too much to control at that moment.

"Tov-tove-tove . . . mum-ma-made me . . ."

Locan glanced at Rachel who hurried to hold the woman as her sobs broke upon each other like waves crashing on a rock. He stood and left the interview room. Lt DiLeo and Mullens had been watching through a one-way window.

"That woman is in a state of deep hypnosis. She's coming out of it now, but we're going to need a shrink to stand by."

"Hypnosis?" DiLeo said. "I didn't think anyone could hypnotize you to do anything against your will."

"That's not quite true. Everyone has dark little what-ifs floating around in their heads. A skilled hypnotist can zero in on them and pretty much suggest a 'for instance'. Like, 'Mrs Wright, say for instance you thought once or twice what it would be like to be an insatiable nymphomaniac slut with a liking for young men?' "

Locan looked towards the room holding Revd Wright. "Or maybe he said to the reverend, 'How can a man have sex with another man, have you ever tried to imagine what it's like to suck another man's cock?' The truth is, of course he can imagine, everyone makes themself imagine such things, even fleetingly. Is there a guy alive who hasn't wondered what it's like to be a girl?"

Locan stepped past them into the other interview room.

Wright stood and looked at him up and down. "Wow, you're a big one. Bet you have a big dick too. I'll let you fuck my wife's big ass if you let me suck it first."

Locan said nothing, but slammed his open hand into the side of the reverend's face. Before he could fall, Locan took him by his lapels and lifted him up level with his eyes.

"Wright! Snap out of it. Look at me. Come out of there!"

Locan watched the panic build behind Wright's eyes.

"Oh, dear lord Jesus! My wife . . . Adeline! No-no-no! I'm sorry . . . I'm so sorry!"

"Hang in there, Wright. You didn't do anything."

"I . . . I sold my wife like . . . like she was . . ."

"Tell me about Tovan."

"Tovan? Tovan! That . . . that . . . that . . ."

"Fucking?"

"Fucking bastard!"

Locan chuckled. "Now you're talking, Rev."

"That poor woman cried for a straight hour. I thought she was going to have a heart attack, she cried so hard."

Locan, DiLeo and Mullens nodded with no comment as Rachel recounted her efforts to interview Mrs Wright before she and her husband were transported to a psychiatric hospital in Boston.

"I couldn't get a lot out of her in the state she was in," Rachel continued. "I got that Tovan has a gang of lackeys, young guys, and that they think he's some kind of magic man, a regular rock star."

"Why not?" Locan said. "The guy can literally charm women out of their clothes. It's every adolescent's fantasy: hypnotize girls into having sex with you. No fear of rejection."

"I never heard of a hypnotist who could do that," Rachel said.

"Neither did I," DiLeo said, "but I caught a show at one of the Route One comedy clubs with an 'R-rated hypnotist'. I saw one show where they had a group of people thinking they were having sex; I figured they were just faking or maybe they were weak-minded. Then one girl – she looked like the shyest of the lot – got on the floor on her knees, lifted her behind up, and you'd swear she was taking it up the . . . um."

"I get the idea," Rachel nodded, suppressing a grin.

"I saw a show in Vegas once," Mullens added. "This guy really did get people to take off their clothes and think it was the most normal thing in the world. I think he could have gotten them to have sex on stage, but that would have been pushing the legal limits even for Vegas."

DiLeo's phone rang. "Yeah. Aw, shit. Stall him . . . Shit!"

"Problem, Lieutenant?" Locan inquired.

"We have an assistant DA on his way up here. Talbot. Very ambitious, he's looking to make his bones prosecuting the rev. and his wife. Hell, those people didn't know what they were doing, did they?"

"Yes, they did, but they couldn't do anything about it. Not to worry, I'll handle this . . . Talbot?"

Before DiLeo could answer, ADA Talbot barged into the office without knocking.

"All right, Lieutenant, just tell me you Mirandized those perverts so there's no surprises when I prosecute their twisted asses."

"Mr Talbot."

"Who are you?"

"Sumner Osgood."

"Are you friends of these . . . people?"

"Just an interested party."

"Suppose you take your party the hell out of here."

"You're very rude, Mr Talbot."

The ADA hooked his thumbs into his waistband and puffed out his chest.

"Your boss, the district attorney, he's very involved in the Catholic League, Knights of Columbus. He's about to receive a very prestigious decoration from the Holy See, means a lot to him. I understand he's going to Rome to receive it from His Holiness himself."

"What's that go to do with . . . ?"

"No grand jury, no indictment, no charges against the Wrights."

"What? Are you kidding . . . ?"

"Try it and your boss will be left standing in St Peter's Square in his silly knight's get-up with both his hands up his ass, because no one at the Holy See will even know who he is. And he *will* be told who is responsible."

"But . . . who . . . ?"

"*Dominus vobiscum*, Talbot. Don't let the door hit you on the way out."

After the door closed, Locan lowered his voice. "Wright told me Tovan had put the whammy on some young kids, teenagers. I'm not sure what his fixation on young teens is other than rewarding his toadies with underage quail. I'd like to find out what went on between him and that girl at the theological school."

"She's being interviewed right now by our guys in the Minneapolis field office."

"Let me know what you find out. In the meantime – Don – your guys will have to keep their eyes out for any lascivious behaviour out of the norm."

"Out of the norm? Locan, this is Salem; we're right at the windup to Haunted Happenings. We see all kinds of crazy shit out there. Every year, I swear, the city pays to put up billboards all over the country advertising 'Free Proctology', because every crazy asshole in America shows up here, including plenty from overseas."

"Nonetheless, Don, you're likely to come across folks who've been hypnotized like the Wrights, but especially keep an eye out for younger kids acting like sex-crazed demons."

"Let's just nail this guy Tovan," DiLeo insisted.

"Listen guys, we've got nothing on Tovan."

"What do you mean?" DiLeo said, shaking his head.

"What are you going to charge him with: felony hypnosis? There's no such thing. Maybe, just maybe facilitating the endangerment of minors, but it'd be damned hard to prove, even for Talbot. I can tell you this: this guy's got it into his head that he can summon Lovecraft's übermonsters."

"That's fiction," DiLeo insisted.

"No shit. You wouldn't believe how many fools on this planet believe it's all real, the granddaddy of all urban legends. Anyway, I think this guy is going to try to bring them to earth with some ritual, probably on Halloween. Most likely in one of the city's graveyards."

"Which one?" DiLeo asked. "I'll have them staked out."

"No, Don, we can't have anyone near them except whoever Tovan expects to be there, like his toadies and maybe a bunch of mesmerized teenagers for whatever reason. Besides, your guys'll have their hands full that night. I'll keep you posted."

"Mullens, you need to contact Professor Helen Girolf; she's at Harvard Medical. Mention the Palatinae; she'll be more than glad to help. Have her set up at the local medical centre. Don, have your guys pick up any kids, or anyone, who acts like they're in heat. Bring them straight to Girolf."

"Maybe we should alert the public that someone's been hypnotizing tourists," DiLeo suggested.

"Who the fuck is going to believe that, Don? It sounds like a Halloween joke. No, you're going to put out an alert that someone's been dropping acid on unsuspecting people. In fact, that'll be our story for the Wrights. Anyone can believe someone was slipped a drug."

"The mayor and the Chamber of Commerce are gonna be pissed," DiLeo sighed. "Shit, one more night to Halloween."

"God, it's like Mardi Gras, only chillier," Rachel said as she and Locan weaved through the throngs of people, most of them costumed or sporting face and body paint.

"Look at the cleavage on that witch," Locan said, pointing.

"Padding," Rachel insisted.

"What a mob. Everything is happening on a weekend too. It'll be nuts. Trying to find that freak in this sea of souls would be tough anyway. We'll nail him tomorrow night. Want a drink?"

"No, but speaking of nailing someone, how about we go home and you nail me."

"Have I ever mentioned to you how much I admire small breasts?"

"Shut up."

He lifted her off her feet and kissed her amidst the swirl of humanity. Blue lightning crackled around her head. They heard someone say, "Cool, did you see that?"

"Ooops!" they said.

Locan put her down and they made their way as best they could through the crowd.

A man greeted them at the door of the B&B.

"Hello, Jake Sprague, Jeanie's father."

They shook his hand.

"Sorry I've been so scarce."

"That's OK," Locan assured him. "Jeanie told us about your wife."

"She'll be home Monday. Poor Jeanie, she's been terrific helping out. I gave her a break, let her go out with her friends tonight, but I'm getting kind of worried. I asked her to get home by ten and it's nearly eleven."

"She's probably having too much fun," Rachel said. "I can remember being her age. She's a sweet girl."

"I know; she's never given me any grief. But I still worry; hell, some nut's been dropping LSD in people's drinks downtown. They think that's what happened to that poor couple, the minister and his wife."

"You don't say," Locan said, shaking his head.

"Yeah, cops just put it out over the radio, and they dropped off a bunch of leaflets. I'll give you one."

"We can grab it on the way in," Rachel said. "We're really tired, been doing the tourist thing all day, you know."

"Sure, well, have a good night. Glad I finally met you folks. Jeanie is quite taken with you."

"She's a terrific kid," Locan nodded.

Once inside, Rachel snagged a bright orange leaflet from the desk. "Wow, it didn't take long for DiLeo to get the word out."

"Good, people might be a bit more circumspect about who they chat with."

"You know," Rachel whispered. "I'm naked under all these clothes."

She grabbed his hand and towed him up the stairs. They tumbled through the door and Locan hooked his thumbs into her jeans and began to tug them off her hips.

"Whoa, you're gonna rip them. Hey . . . what's wrong?"

Locan's hands had frozen. He turned Rachel around to face the bed. Jeanie sat right on the pillows, her back against the wall.

"Jeanie," Rachel said. "What are you doing here? Your father—"

"I listened to you last night, I heard you . . . fucking." The girl licked her upper lip and giggled.

"Jeanie?" Locan inched closer to the girl.

"Let me come to bed with you . . . puhleeeeze. I'll be good. I can suck pussy and cock. Make me your dirty little whore, oh, pretty-pretty-please?"

"That fuck!" Locan spat.

"Please, Mr Osgood, be my first. I got a juicy cherry just for you. You can fuck me while I suck out her cunt."

"That wouldn't be a good idea, hon."

She pouted, "Then I guess it'll have to be my dad. The dark one wants me soiled."

"Who, Jeanie?"

"Cthulhu of course, when he brings him to earth. We'll be his first meal. Can you imagine what a come that is, to be devoured by Shub-Niggurath?"

"Oh, sure, old Shub, used to have him over for dinner all the time. And when is this supposed to happen, honey?"

"I'll tell you if you let me lick your dick."

"No . . . tell first."

"Okay . . . promise?"

"Promise."

"Well, of course on the feast day, silly. We'll be the feast, me and all the dirty little sluts, and the little cocksuckers, and the vile priests. Yum-yum, eat us up." She stepped off the bed.

Locan stood between her and the door.

"Aw, sweetie, I'm really sorry for this, but . . ."

He slammed his open hand hard across the girl's face, grabbed her and shook her.

"Come out of there, Jeanie. Look at me, look into my eyes."

The girl's eyes refocused. "Oh, God, Mr Osgood . . . Mrs Osgood . . . I'm so sorry, I didn't mean . . ."

Rachel took the teenager in her arms. "It's okay. It's not your fault."

"Someone's been screwing with your head, Jeanie. Do you remember?"

"He said . . . he said . . . I thought he was nice. My friends, Sally and Toni. Oh God!"

"It's OK. We'll take care of them. Now, you need to see a doctor."

They summoned Mr Sprague and explained that Jeanie had fallen victim to the serial acid-dropper. Locan called DiLeo directly who had an ambulance sent to pick up Jeanie and her father, and a cruiser to the homes of her friends.

Later, Locan called Mullens.

"It isn't going to happen on Halloween," Locan told him. "I should have figured, Halloween night, too many people floating around, goofing in the bone yards. He's going to do it on All Saints' Day, the night after Halloween. The town will be dead then, crowds gone, tumbleweeds blowing down the streets."

"OK, if you say so. I got the Minneapolis field report on that girl's interview. Her name is Mercy Tramwell, comes from a very wealthy, very conservative family."

"Don't they all? Fax it to me, OK?"

"Done."

Locan and Rachel lay naked together in bed as Locan thumbed through the FBI report. She nibbled his shoulder, reading each page in turn as he turned it over.

"That's all?" she asked. "He slapped her around because he found her in bed with another guy?"

"I think I'm beginning to understand this guy. Those agents in Minneapolis were good getting her to admit to this stuff. Ah, the lead agent's first name is Denise. OK, use a woman to coax stuff out of a woman."

"Whaddya mean?"

"You know that shit you girls pull with each other, 'You can tell me, it's just between us' type of baloney."

"Oh, guys don't do that," she said, a sarcastic inflexion in her voice.

He laid the report on the bed table and pushed his head back into the pillow. "Shit," he sighed and closed his eyes.

"What's the matter?"

"Jeanie."

"She'll be fine. Didn't Mullens say Girolf pulled her out of it? She doesn't even remember—"

"She *will* remember. It'll pop into her head when she least expects it. Lousy thing to do to a kid. I'm glad she came right home before she offered herself to some freak on the street."

"Well, sure, she has a crush on *you*."

"You too."

"Maybe. You really smacked her. You scared the shit out of me when you did that."

"Had to snap her out of it fast. Goddamn it, kids today are so casual about sex, they're getting and giving their first blow jobs while they're barely into their teens. If you're that casual about a BJ, where the hell's the magic in your first kiss?"

"You remember your first kiss?"

"Better than I remember my first fuck. Mary Therese O'Toole, she had the longest, silkiest, dark brown hair."

"So, you always liked brunettes, huh? First fuck?"

"Her name was Barbara, she was blonde. She cried the whole time. Geesh." He shuddered.

"I think Jeanie's growing up just fast enough," Rachel assured him.

"Yeah. She was."

"Locan, I want to be the one to take this prick out . . . for what he did to Jeanie."

"He's yours, kid."

"Something else is eating at you, isn't it?"

"Fucking guys, we're so hard-wired, you know."

"When she was coming on to you, you were responding?"

"Yeah, I'm loath to admit it, but damn, all the bells and whistles went off."

Rachel shrugged. "You'd never take advantage of a girl like that."

"I'm not sure that's the point."

"Of course, that's the point."

She threw the covers back exposing his growing cock, took it in her hands and licked its length from base to tip and back.

"Want me to be an innocent little girl; want me to cry?"

"Rachel?"

"Please, don't hurt me . . . you're so big, I'm so scared. Are you really going to rape me?"

"Rachel!"

She slid underneath him and coaxed him on top of her. His cock dangled at her gate.

"Oh, you're going to . . . please don't tell my parents. Oh, please, I'm scared." She began to weep.

Locan's cock was steel. He slid it into her cunt.

"Owww! Please, oh no, don't rape me . . . don't . . . oh God; no, don't make it feel so good. I don't want it to feel good. I'm a good girl . . . noooo!"

She was sobbing now, he couldn't tell if she was faking or not. He increased the pace of his thrusts as she wailed for mercy.

"Urrrgh! Bitch! You want it!"

"No, please, don't make me . . ."

"Slut! You're a slut!"

"Don't . . . don't make me say it."

"Cocksucking whore!"

"Don't . . . I'm so ashamed."

"Slut! Say it!"

"Slut!" she sobbed. "I'm a slut! Oh, please . . ."

She cried so sweetly.

"Jesus!" His fluids rocketed out of his cock. The release was so sudden it hurt, but it felt so good.

He held his cock inside her as it deflated. He felt wicked, cruel, giddy. Rachel lay beneath him, still weeping.

He lay beside her and scooped her into his arms. Her tears wet his shoulders.

"God, Racey. Are you, did you really . . . ?"

"Shhh, I can't just break character like that, you know. Let me cry a while."

"Yeah . . . sure."

She quieted, then she began to snore.

"Mr Osgood, it's none of my business, but that fax that came in for you, well, I noticed it was from the FBI. I wasn't snooping, mind you, but I noticed."

"Yes, Mr Sprague."

"I think maybe there's more going on in Salem than some punk moron dropping LSD on unsuspecting people; I think maybe that's why you're here. I don't want to know, or need to know anything and I ain't asking. Just one thing I want to say to you."

"Yes, sir?"

"That son of a bitch that screwed around with my girl, you get that bastard."

"You have my word, sir."

Locan and Rachel left the B&B after breakfast and walked a block past the House of the Seven Gables to the Salem–Boston ferry dock. The high-speed catamaran had just discharged a full load of tourists. They waited for the crowd to thin and for the vessel to back out into the harbour fully loaded for the return trip to Boston. Mullens and DiLeo approached from different directions. They all gathered at the quay.

"Where do you need us to set up tomorrow night?" DiLeo asked.

"Nowhere. Like I said, I don't want him scared away. He's not expecting anyone to show up except whoever he told to be there."

"What are you going to do with him? You said no charge would stick."

"Don, you don't need to know that."

"We'll take care of it," Rachel said. Her tone was so flat, cold. No one said anything for a moment.

Mullens cleared his throat. "Which graveyard? You figure that out?"

"Not the Burying Point; it's the one all the tourists flock to, and even if Halloween will be over, there'll be a few stragglers around. He wouldn't take the chance. Broad Street would be a good choice, just outside the central downtown area, and the Corwins are buried there."

"Who?" Mullens asked.

"Jonathan and George, judge and sheriff during the witch trials. George oversaw the torture of Giles Corey. So their graves give the place a certain creepy cachet."

"OK," DiLeo nodded.

"But I think it'll be Howard Street. It doesn't get much attention except from bums and vandals. It's a big dark patch in the city. I think he'll show up there, and that's where we'll be. We'll wrap it all up. It'll be neat."

"Guy should get a trial," DiLeo said.

"He's had one," Rachel said.

Rachel and Locan sat with their backs to the wall of the old brick lighthouse at the end of Derby Wharf. Except for a few couples who strolled to the end of the pier and back, they remained mostly alone in the dark. Behind them and all about them they heard the sounds of a city in revelry. Halloween in the trick-or-treat capital of the world. They were good sounds mostly, people having fun, laughing, shouting.

"A ship would push off from this pier and wouldn't come home for a year or maybe three, but when it did, people got rich overnight with the cargo it brought home," Locan said. "Can you imagine the adventure, the risk and the payoff? Did you see those mansions lining Chestnut Street?"

Rachel snuggled into him in the chill air.

"What about the women?"

"They stayed home, took care of the kids, and prayed to God their man came home."

"And if they didn't?"

"They had their little social safety nets. But it was do or die, boom or bust."

"The stars are brighter out here," Rachel mused. "It's the kind of night I could run naked through."

He squeezed her hand and tried to put the idea of ever losing her out of his mind.

The feast of All Saints dawned as a grey November morning. It was Sunday, a day to recuperate from a particularly immense party. The crowds were gone, leaving their trash and detritus behind. The city wasn't about to pay overtime to clean it up. It could wait until Monday.

The streets were empty. Now after a celebration of all things weird and unnatural, the city genuinely felt like an eerie place. Sunset seemed to linger close by even at the height of the day.

"I always hated Sundays," Locan said as the gloom grew deeper. "I could never enjoy a day knowing I had to get up for school the next day, or work."

"I liked school," Rachel said.

"Figures."

It was after 10 o'clock and they had scoped out the burial ground.

"I want you to wait by the copse of trees by the old jail," Locan said. "I want you flanking me when I confront this guy. I'll try to convince his toadies to run along; if not, they go down too."

"I hope it's not a long wait."

"Rachel . . . stay dark."

She nodded and they separated. Locan spotted a tomb cap in deep shadow, sat down upon it and waited.

He heard Tovan's toadies first, still a distance away, young guys' stupid bluster. They followed behind Tovan along Howard Street. Locan studied his body language and compared it with the careless antics of the group several steps behind.

"He's cutting them loose," Locan whispered to himself.

Tovan entered the cemetery and strode towards a tabular monument; it could have been an altar.

A tall blond kid peered into the dark corners. "Shit man, where are all the little cunts? You must have spelled a few dozen."

The rest of the group of five young guys mumbled. One said, "Yeah, weren't we going to have one big fuck party first?"

Tovan didn't answer. The blond acted as his mouthpiece.

"Fuck it! After tonight, we're all gonna be kings." He spun around and faced Tovan. "That's right, isn't it, magic man?"

"You're nothing . . . but food."

"Huh . . . what?"

"Here it comes," Locan whispered.

"Food for the old ones. Just like the little bitches, and they'd be here too. But someone's been working against me. It doesn't matter though. It all changes tonight. You'll know the terror of his jaws."

"But ... but you said ... Hey man, you're the man, the magic man. You said we'd rule—"

"Fucking Neanderthals ... I don't need you anymore."

Locan thought the tall blond guy was going to cry. Then he turned to the others. "Shit! Let's get out of here."

They ran like hell was chasing them, tripping over tombstones, stumbling through the gate.

Tovan laughed. "There's nowhere to run, idiots!"

Locan let him have his last laugh before he stepped out of the shadows.

Tovan's back stiffened. "You!"

"Yeah, me. The guy who's been gumming up your little party."

"LSD? You couldn't tell them the truth, could you? You couldn't tell them their phony world and all their false beliefs were going to end in horror. They'd panic just like those fools."

"People can understand being the victim of a malicious twerp dropping acid on them. That way there's nothing to excuse or forgive. It'll help some people regain their good name."

"Who the fuck ... ? Ah, it doesn't matter. When they come ..."

"No one's coming, chump."

"I will call them down ... you'll digest for eternity in the belly of Shub-Niggurath."

"Shub-shlub. This isn't about mouldy old gods that some fruitcake from Providence dreamt up." Locan chuckled. "What did that town ever produce besides nerdy writers and low-level Mafiosi?"

"You'll see, I can call them; I will call them."

"That girl really fucked up your head, didn't she?"

Some of Tovan's bluster escaped him.

"Poor Marshall. Poor nerdy Marshall. You couldn't buy a date with a girl, could you? I'll bet you prayed and prayed one day that some girl would give you the time of day. And not just any girl, a beautiful blonde, with lots of money and all the class you'd never have."

Tovan stumbled back as if reeling from Locan's words.

"You better shut up!"

"Or what? Is Marshall going to call on some dumb fuck of a god to slap me down? Jesus, why the hell would anyone want to venerate Azathoth? Even Lovecraft said he was an oblivious idiot stumbling around the cosmos like a big retarded baby. What the hell did you expect a god like him to do for you, even if he did exist?"

"He does!"

"No, Marshall. I understand the kind of kid you were, creepy, awkward. All the nerds got into Lovecraft, at least the saddest ones did. Meanwhile, you still expected God to hand you sex on a platter. And why not? You were smarter than everyone else; you deserved it. You thought you had some special arrangement going with God. You enrolled at the theological college and that's where you met Mercy."

Tovan's face soured as if his stomach had regurgitated.

"We talked to her, Marshall. She told us how she felt sorry for you, how maybe if she gave you a simple hand job you'd be satisfied and stop pestering her."

Locan laughed out loud, grabbing his belly.

"Jesus!" He laughed, trying to wipe his eyes. "You didn't even rate a sympathy fuck; all you got was a sympathy hand job. That's just too funny, too . . . fucking . . . sad.

"Of course, you misinterpreted the whole thing. You thought she loved you. What the fuck did she say to you when you barged in on her and her boyfriend? Really, what could a girl say to someone like you that would leave you even more fucked up and twisted than you already were?"

Tovan couldn't reply. Locan could hear his breathing laboured by rage, his teeth gnashed into a snarl.

"Did she tell you that you were a pathetic creep? That she'd die before your pokey little worms ever had a chance to swim into her belly?

"You caught her alone a few days later; you hit her. Got your ass booted out of school in exchange for no charges brought. It was worth it to her and her family that the world would never know that you even briefly darkened her day with your shadow.

"So, what did you do then?"

"I studied, I searched, I acquired the power!" he roared back. "I'll turn their virgins into whores, their shamans into filthy, carnal pigs!"

"What power? You've done nothing a decent stage hypnotist couldn't do. Oh, I'll grant you, you've got some talent. I figure you met someone in your wanderings, someone who showed you how it was done. An entertainer, maybe, maybe even a clinical hypnotist. You had a real knack for it. And then what? See, that's what I couldn't understand."

Tovan's fists clenched at his sides.

"You see, Marshall, that's the primo Nerd Fantasy, being able to charm women out of their clothes, hypnotize them into wanting to give you all the sex all the ways you want it. But you weren't satisfied with that. And then it came to me, how Mercy so unmercifully fucked you up. Her tirade was so traumatic, you can't get it up, can you Marshall?"

"Shut up!"

"God, that's it, isn't it? Now you can have any woman you want, but you can't do shit about it. You poor slob."

"It all changes tonight; they'll all see . . ."

"Mercy was your idea of an innocent Christian girl sent to earth especially for you. Then it turned out she wasn't so innocent after all. So you set out on this bizarre revenge mission; you were going to soil the very notion of innocence, turning young kids into crazed carnal idiots. You were going to take it out on the churches too, target any clergy you came across; the Revd Wright and his wife, they were just going to be the first . . . or have there been others?"

"They marinade in their own hypocrisy. The old ones will nosh on their bones. Just like you, look at the ooze; watch it seep out of the putrefaction of this ground. Sink, drown in it!"

Locan took a look around. "You know, Marshall, I'm just not seeing what you're seeing. No ooze, just solid ground."

"No, it's sucking you under."

Locan took a few loping strides towards Tovan and drew his revolver from the small of his back. Without any hesitation he swung the pistol up aside of Tovan's head and fired. Tovan reeled from the report going off in his ear. He rolled on the ground and shook himself. He stood slowly and looked around.

"What do you see now, Marshall?" Locan taunted.

Tovan frantically scanned the darkness. Over on Howard Street a few lights had gone on in the darkened homes. He stamped his feet on the ground.

"You poor dumb shit," Locan said, his voice even. "You hypnotized yourself . . . hypnotized yourself into thinking this Lovecraftian nonsense was real."

Tovan stepped back and sat down hard on the tomb cap. "I . . . I didn't do anything. You can't prove . . . you can't prove anything."

"I'm not here to prove anything, Marshall. Except what a worthless piece of shit you are. Lots of people get handed the shitty end of the stick; they aren't so smart or good-looking. They suck it up and get through life, lonely as it is, maybe no one ever notices them, but they get through life with dignity. Then there are the mewling little shitheads like you who take what little you have going for you and try to get back at the world. You selfish, self-centred little creep. You think the world owes you an apology."

"I didn't do anything!"

"Marshall . . . yes you did. You damaged lives. You had no right to do that. And now you gotta pay."

"I . . . you can't . . ."

"You wanted to bring horror down on this world? You don't know what horror is. I'll tell you what horror is, and I'll tell you what eternity is. Horror is fangs . . . fangs you see in the split second before they close around your neck and squeeze like a vice until they puncture your arteries and snap your spine. And in the billionth of a second after your head separates from your body those fangs are the only thing you'll remember; and that, for you, you pathetic shit, will be eternity."

"Racey!"

Tovan turned his head towards the darkness and then all he could see of the world shone with a lurid blue luminescence. He was blind to everything except the fangs coming at him at an impossible speed. His neck was in their vice.

Locan had looked away from the flash. Now he turned in time to see Tovan's head launch off his body, arc through the air and then land with a thump. His lifeless body was being shaken, twisted and worried like a rag. Then it was left draining on the sod.

The animal was dark and sleek, its eyes glowing, its fangs whiter than marble on a tomb and blood-streaked. It began to drag the body away. Locan followed, stooping to pick up the head. He followed it across Bridge Street to the railroad tracks along the North River where it had left Tovan's body. Locan tossed the head a little further along the tracks.

The animal turned and loped back towards the cemetery. Locan found it pacing amongst a row of tombstones.

He knelt and held the animal's glowing blue gaze with his own.

"Please, Racey, come back. Come back to me."

She hopped onto a stump and raised her head. Her howl echoed about the silent city, haunting all its dark corners.

Locan closed his eyes. The blue light shone through his lids and then subsided.

Rachel lay naked on the grass.

It started to rain, a cold, soaking rain. His practical mind told him this was a good thing. It would obliterate the blood trail.

Locan covered her with his jacket and lifted her into his arms.

"I forgot to bring a change of clothes," she said in a hoarse whisper. Raindrops trickled like tears off her face. She laid her head against his chest. He carried her out of the graveyard and down the dark-shadowed streets, bereft of any other soul. Through the common and down to the waterfront, along Derby Street past the maritime site. He was drenched to his skin. At the B&B he fumbled for the key and pushed open the door. The tiny lobby was dimly lit. He carried her upstairs.

Inside their room he placed her on the bed, retrieved some towels and patted down her naked body, and then dried himself. He slid beside her and pulled the covers up to their necks. She lay on her belly. He began to kiss her shoulders and her back, and all the while his hand coursed gently over her behind and the backs of her thighs. A contented moan escaped her, then her breaths became regular, feathery. He continued to kiss her; he would kiss her until he also surrendered to fatigue and slumber.

"Mr Osgood, a fellow left a car here for you. Here's the keys."

"Thanks, Mr Sprague." Locan took the keys. "Your wife is coming home this afternoon?"

"Yes. Jeanie's getting out of school early so she can come with me."

"That's wonderful. I only regret we'll not be able to make the lady's acquaintance."

"It was good to have you, sir. There'll be no charge."

"No, no, no, sir. I'll have none of that. My employers have very deep pockets. You were a wonderful host."

"Well, it's just, I'd like to give you something, me and Jeanie, that is."

"No need."

"You got him . . . didn't you, Mr Osgood?"

"We got him, Mr Sprague."

Rachel came down with her one bag and kissed Mr Sprague. "Say goodbye to Jeanie."

"Sure will, Mrs Osgood."

Locan fired up the car and pulled onto Derby Street, navigating the narrow streets on the way to the Interstate.

"Where to?" Rachel asked.

"New York City. We have a new assignment."

"What, don't we get a break?"

"We're driving. We'll put in to some delightfully cheap motel halfway through the speed bump between Boston and New York."

"Speed bump?"

"Connecticut."

"Oh. So, what's next?"

"A simple recruiting assignment."

"Recruiting? We don't recruit. That's what the big black monsignor is for."

"Occasionally we recruit. These must be very special people; a lot of bigs are going to be there."

"Who are they?"

"Not sure, a young Jewish couple."

"Jewish?"

"When it comes to the Palatinae, the Vatican is very ecumenical. All they're looking for is talent and merit."

"Hmm, I don't know any Jewish people."

Locan looked at the old town in the rearview mirror and smiled. Behind them a dull, grey-steel sun lingered low in the sky over Gallows Hill, impatient to set.

My Two Halves

Alana James

I sit in the dim room of the private members' club, eyes fixed on the illuminated platform in front of the audience. The Magician moves lithely over the stage, like a snake uncoiling. He gives no name other than The Magician, and hides most of his face behind a black mask. "Ladies and Gentlemen!" he says, and much more.

The Magician goes like this, like that, reading minds, conjuring tricks. My lover, Alexander, sits beside me forsaken. This is his club, he brought me here, into his exclusive world, but I am no longer here with him. My body is stirring with desire for this faceless Magician. His deep brown eyes are hypnotic; they draw me in, deeper and deeper so that I have the sensation of falling.

I objected when Alexander told me his surprise date was a magic show. I thought it childish, another sign that it is time to fly free of our relationship. Alexander had insisted we go, that his friends at the club would be disappointed otherwise. Alexander is older, more commanding than my previous lovers, and I've enjoyed surrendering to him sometimes. The sex has been decadent and uninhibited, though lately I've begun to feel constrained by us, by him. Now, however, I am glad I capitulated, as I find the magic show is stirring very adult, X-rated, feelings within me.

When The Magician calls for an assistant for his next trick my hand twitches. I realize Alexander is nudging me, encouraging me, "Go on Laura . . .", and soon the people sitting around us are joining in. I hesitate, then submit.

The last thing I see before the box shuts over me is the masked face of The Magician; his eyes shine intensely and then all is darkness and sensation.

At first I feel nothing except my own nerves. My body is shaking silently. I tell myself, this is just a trick, it isn't real. From outside the box I can hear the muffled tones of The Magician, explaining the trick to the audience. He is going to saw me in half.

Lying on my back, fully enclosed inside The Magician's box, I wish I were wearing something less flimsy. The satin of my skirt is making me slide over the smooth velvet as I struggle to stop trembling. The strapless corset exposes the pale peaks of my breasts, giving me a vulnerable sensation. My red hair has fallen in waves around my head, as though I am an unseen sleeping beauty about to fall asleep for a thousand years.

I am not sleeping; instead my body is pulsing with excitement and I long for The Magician's attentions. I lie here, drifting into fantasies about The Magician's touch, how it would compare to Alexander's tender yet forceful advances. Then, suddenly, hands start to come through the holes along either side of the box. The box is lying on top of a wheeled table and is made up of five wooden sections, which fold up and close with latches at the top. Each section has a round hole on either side, and panels at each end with semi-circular gaps cut out for my body. I force myself to stay calm. The Magician explained that he would ask members of the audience to come and check that I really was lying fully down in the box, that there were no hidden compartments. No trickery in the magic trick of course.

Softly, fingers begin to roam the sides of my body. They prod into my flesh, as though checking that I am real. Then they move further inside. Hands grasp my wrists and ankles, other hands are sliding over the material on my thighs. I squirm a little, as if to say yes, I am all here. They don't desist, instead foreign fingers reach the mounds of my breasts over the top of my corset. I'm not sure if any lines have been crossed, or if it is just that my senses are heightened because I can't see anything.

Then one hand pushes hard, pushing its fingers under my corset, and I know this shouldn't be happening but still I lie here doing nothing. I feel . . . electric. I want to see where this will lead, how far it will go. As the fingers finally find my nipple, others begin to rub between my legs. Ashamedly my thighs part as much as possible within my confines to give them more access. I can feel my pussy growing wet and eager. I realize I have been holding my breath, and release it now in a low groan. More, I'm thinking, give me more. Both my nipples are being twisted, the pain balanced by the sweet sensation as my clit is rubbed. As the strangers' hands caress me I think of the mysterious Magician, of his slight yet powerful body. The dark box smells of my pussy now, and I think I might actually come but then the hands withdraw.

Did someone realize what was happening? Did Alexander understand this infidelity, hidden yet right before his eyes? Or was one of the hands his? I wonder how he will feel about this possession of my body by others. I am too turned on to know what I think about it yet. No one releases me from the box though. Again I hear the sound of The Magician speaking to the audience. They are poised on his every word, laughing on cue. A brief moment of silence and then The Magician raps on the top of the box; this is my signal that the trick is about to begin.

He never explained how it would work, I realize. He only told me not to worry, that I would be put back together again in the end. I remember that he winked at me and I didn't think to ask any more. I surrendered once again.

The box starts to shudder, and there is a loud, roaring noise above me. The saw! This isn't real, it isn't real, I repeat to myself, but I'm not sure I believe me. Before I lay down, The Magician showed me the electric saw, let me touch its teeth, feel how real it was. It is supposed to saw halfway through the middle section of the box and me, splitting me in two. I see it in my imagination now, the long metal prong coming towards me. The horrible sawing noise continues and I feel so frightened I am crying. It goes on, getting louder until at some point I pass out.

When I come to I feel queer, but very much alive. The top two sections of the box, around my head and upper body, have been opened and The Magician is standing over me, gleaming proudly. "Ladies and Gentlemen," he announces, "I reveal the two halves of my glamorous assistant!" The small room applauds thunderously. The Magician takes two steps back from my head, into the middle of the stage. I can't believe my eyes but I see now why the applause is so great. When I roll my head to the side and look across the stage, I see the box that I am in. Rather, I see the lower half of the box; the two sections below my waist have been opened so that my body, from my hips down to my feet, is revealed. The spotlight is no longer on The Magician. Instead the two segments of my body are illuminated. My two halves now command attention.

It is impossible. I know that what I see cannot be real. There is no pain and I know that the saw did not touch me. To test this strange reality, I wiggle one of my legs. The leg across the stage likewise wiggles. I lift it up, cross my legs, and watch as my body obeys at a distance. The audience laughs at my dismay, as does The Magician. He calls for volunteers to come and test for themselves. Slowly people start moving out of their seats and onto the platform. I notice how different they are from me; they are more self-assured, like Alexander. I cannot see my lover in the milieu.

The audience begin walking back and forth from my torso to my legs, marvelling at the trick. Someone grabs one of my legs, I gasp, and the crowd laughs. They remove my shoes and tickle my bare feet and I laugh too, though I feel quite uncomfortable. A woman bends down close to my head.

"Is it real?" she asks. "You can feel that?"

"Yes, I can feel the rest of my body. It is my body."

"How spectacular." This is not what I would say if I was her, I would be too astounded and would probably want to leave. I don't have that option though. The woman doesn't seem afraid, instead she leans closer and kisses me on the lips. She smells of flowery perfume, and faintly of cigarettes. When the shock fades I try to move my lips away, but she, or someone else, holds my head in place, pinions my arms to the bottom of the box. The kiss is long and deep. I have kissed women before, but none have been this forceful and it rekindles my desire and frustration. My body begins to throb again, yearning. This woman's lips are replaced by another's.

At the same time I can feel more hands on my lower half. The crowd are no longer tickling me, they are caressing me, my feet and legs. When I am no longer being kissed I see my body across the stage, my skirt being slid up, at the same instant that I feel it happening. I try to sit up, to object, to say I am unsure. I feel I could go one way or the other, withdraw in fear or submerge into pleasure. The Magician appears above me, flanked by Alexander. Their eyes are smiling wickedly and I know now that this is all part of the show. That perhaps I was the only audience member who didn't know what would happen to me. Momentarily I am surprised that Alexander has given me over to The Magician, to the audience, like I were his property. I am a plaything for these people, but as much as this enrages me it excites me too. The two men shift and fade out of vision, leaving me to the mercy of the crowd.

I watch voyeuristically as a group of men and women pull my skirt up above my legs, see my lacy underwear on display, and feel the sensations all at once. Their touch is gentle yet insistent. The people surrounding my upper half have unbuttoned my corset, and I feel cool air on my breasts and lips teasing my nipples. I feel in all ways torn in two; I want to drown in the attentions being given to me, but I can't tear my eyes away from the spectacle of me across the stage.

My pussy, though removed from me, feels slippery and aching. I see my hips twitching, thrusting my gash towards the crowd. Fortunately they see the sign that I am ready, and pull my underwear from me. Fingers begin to circle my labia, tugging at my curls of pubic hair.

Pulling my awareness back to what is happening around my upper half, I see that several men have undone their flies and are masturbating over me. I yank my arms free and gesture to them to give me their cocks. Soon I am being kissed again by strange faces while I pound their shafts. I feel, not see, the first cock that enters my pussy. It is rough and hard, and I can feel the smooth texture of a condom. My body stretches to take it in. I move my hips in motion with my unknown lover, feeling but not seeing his hands around my hips. I increase the speed at which I jerk the cocks in my hands, even as the one inside me speeds up. My groans mingle with those of the crowd around me, watching intently. Then, too soon, hot liquid spurts over my palms, and then over the top of one thigh. I moan, this time in frustration because my body is still too turned on for this to stop.

The men who have finished move back, making way for new ones. The group at my upper half shift so that I can see across to my lower half once more. I feel and watch a blonde-haired woman lick the come off my leg, then she turns and passes it from her mouth to another. My legs are pulled wide, for a brief moment I see my own pussy spread open as I never have before. Then someone else, a man who may or may not be Alexander, begins to fuck me. I grunt with satisfaction at the movement I can feel and see, and the heat inside me starts to build again, coursing through my body.

Before I lose myself completely, a woman with her short skirt hitched up lowers her bare pussy over my face. She grinds her wetness over me, journeying up and down before bringing her mound to my lips. It is hard to breathe like this, and I am overwhelmed with her sex juices, the cock still driving into me and the stiff members being pushed into my hands. But I ride it out, thinking again more, more, I can take more. Still I desire one more. Where is The Magician who rent me asunder? He is obscured, his whole body masked now by the crowd.

All around me is sweat and confusion. I lose track of how many men come over me, of the women whose hands twist my nipples, who offer their nether lips to my mouth, of the number of times my sex is consumed. There are too many hands touching me for me to distinguish each stranger's touch; they hold my legs open, knead my breasts, cup my ass, slide along the thin layer of sweat coating my body. I am unable to orgasm through penetration and this means that I can exist in this flush of arousal for a long time. In all of this I feel passive yet powerful. I did not set out to be the object of desire for these people, but I find myself in the thrill of it, my body and mind responding in equal measure. I am the star of this show now.

But slowly there is a parting in the throng of people, a tunnel of vision, and I see The Magician pushing the lower section of the box on its wheels across the stage to me. I cry out in despair, I am not ready for this to be over, I crave The Magician still. The Magician doesn't respond, his jaw is set in determination. The two halves of my body are being reunited, but I see now that they are topsy-turvy. My head lies below my feet, staring into the passageway between my legs.

I see my own sex now, see my sexual desire before me like it is a secret entity I am just discovering. How many women truly know their own pussy? I view my own hungry maw clearly for the first time; it is mine yet it is a stranger to me. I gaze in awe now at the puffy red folds of flesh, the soaked sets of lips and the hard, pulsing bud of my clitoris. I reach out to touch myself, enthralled and intensely aroused by my own body. The crowd around me are once more just an audience, watching silently as I penetrate my pussy with one finger, then two, three, four. And I too watch myself, see how my gash expands to receive my hand. This vision raises my arousal to fever pitch. I groan unabashedly, caught up in the moment, but then my hand is withdrawn by another, replaced by the leather gloved hand of The Magician.

Yes, this is what I want. My body responds in crescendo to The Magician's touch. He remains masked, leaving only his eyes and mouth visible to me and this makes me want him more. I close my eyes, choose to only feel and not see. I sense heat, and his mouth closes around my clit, sucking on it until I can scarcely breathe. His fingers continue to drive, deep; the leather is supple and I feel it sliding easily along my insides. It is like a symphony is being wrung from me, the notes getting higher until I am singing out. The Magician is using his other hand to pull my skin taut above my pussy, increasing the intensity of his touch. He twists his fingers inside me as he fucks me with them, and tugs on my pubic hair with his teeth, teasingly, before biting softly on my clit. The bittersweet contrast of this pain with the pleasure of his tongue lapping in circles around my clit brings me close, closer, until I'm climaxing at last. I open my eyes again and watch as I come in shudders around The Magician's hand. He pulls his mouth away, letting me see the full glory of my pussy in orgasm. Spent, I close my eyes and darkness descends once more.

When I open my eyes, I sense that time has passed. The spotlights have gone out, and I am shrouded in silence. I am lying, still on the box, but all the sections are open now. My body is whole again and fully clothed. I sit up tentatively, fearing I could break in two. The Magician is gone and the room is empty, save for Alexander who is sitting in the front row watching me. He gets up now and helps me down from the table. I let him put my shoes on as I readjust to being whole.

We do not speak. I am grateful to him for this night, but I know now that I am ready to leave him. My body, its power, has been re-awakened and I want to savour it, reclaim it. I kiss him briefly and then walk away.

A Washington Square Romance

Maxim Jakubowski

On Broadway, he bought her an *I LOVE YOU* rubber stamp, which would never be used.

At Ground Zero, peering at the monstrous hole in the ground and the early signs of reconstruction, he held her against him and tried not to cry. It wasn't because of sympathy or compassion with the victims of the tragedy, but because he felt he had never been so close to her than he was now.

Under the arch in Washington Square, he kissed her.

She had reached Barcelona Airport early and gone through security and passport control with more than two hours to spare before her flight left for New York, and had spent the time sipping coffees at one of the multitude of shiny bars in the duty-free zone, leafing soporifically through some of her Catalan literature textbooks and daydreaming. When her plane was called, she had been in no rush to make a beeline for the gate, only to realize to her dismay, once the back of the queue where she had been standing reached the final control point, that she could not find her passport. Her heart stopped. Where could she have mislaid it? It had been in her hands when she had checked her lone piece of luggage in.

She had run back breathlessly to the duty-free zone and the café. There was now someone else sitting at the table she had occupied. She felt her heart jump, her stomach convulse with anxiety. She asked the man if there had been anything on the table when he sat down. He looked at her with a puzzled look. She had automatically asked him in Italian, which he visibly couldn't understand. She switched to English. No, the table had been empty. He suggested she walk over and ask the attendant at the bar.

Which she did.

The young girl on duty had only just begun her shift. She completed the order she was working on and finally moved to a back door to enquire with a colleague. A few minutes later, an older man with grey eyebrows and leonine features walked out with a broad smile on his face. Giulia's attention was immediately drawn to his right hand. In which he held her passport.

Immense relief swept through her whole body. She felt faint. Held her breath.

"Thanks, thanks, thanks, so much," she said, in Spanish this time.

The man grinned back at her, and silently handed her the lost passport.

She thanked him again a dozen times or more in her joyful haste and began to run back to the final control checkpoint. However, when she reached it, she was informed that the plane's crew had already locked the aircraft's doors and that she had missed her flight. Her solitary suitcase had already been unloaded. She pleaded her case, began sobbing uncontrollably, but it was to no avail. An airline attendant escorted her back sympathetically to the luggage area where the bag could be retrieved and then to the American Airlines desk.

There were no more flights to JFK today, but in view of the circumstances and even though they had no obligation to do so, they agreed to put her on the same flight the following day, which fortunately still had some empty seats.

Tears still drying across her hot cheeks, forlornly pulling her bag behind her, Giulia found herself once again in the departure and check-in area of Terminal A. She pulled her mobile from her handbag, checked the printouts of the emails they had exchanged and rang his hotel in New York. He wasn't in his room. Why would he be? She left a message for him to call her back.

By the time he did, she was back in her dormitory north of Plaza Catalunya, and she had exhausted all the tears a human being could expend in the space of half a day.

Hiccupping between words, stuttering, crying out of control, she informed him that she had missed the flight.

She could almost feel the weight falling like a hammer across his own heart all those thousands of miles away.

But his voice remained calm and soothed her once she had managed to explain that she would still be coming, arriving on the same flight tomorrow.

"It'll be all right," he said. "It's just a day, a night less. The main thing is that we can still be together. Just try and get a good night's sleep and be at the airport nice and early, and don't linger over coffees this time," he said, a hint of affection and humour in his deep voice. "I'll be waiting for you."

"Yes."

"And don't forget to take a cab from JFK to Washington Square," he added. "I'll pay for it. Don't want to waste any more time, do we?"

"I want you so much."

She barely had time to drop her luggage to the floor before he wanted to undress her. He had been waiting in the hotel lobby for her fifty bucks taxi ride from the airport to reach the city, reading a magazine, distracted by every new arrival. As she ignored the doorman and ran towards him, he smiled broadly. She embraced him, squeezed him against her, and all the pain and anguish of yesterday's disaster faded away in an instant.

They called the lift, and although not alone in it, she felt his hand caressing her arse through the thin white linen skirt she was wearing.

"I want to see you. All of you," he said as he took a step back from her once they entered the fuchsia-coloured room.

She quickly slipped out of the skirt and he pulled the *Strangers in Paradise* T-shirt over her head. She was braless. Had never really needed one. He sighed as he saw those nipples again whose shade he could never quite capture in words, an ever-so-subtle variation between pale brown and pink he had never witnessed on any other woman he had witnessed naked before.

His breath caught in his throat.

She laughed and approached him. Pushed him back onto the bed and straddled him.

Outside, the cold February sun illuminated the recently refurbished arch, like a stone rainbow at the southern extremity of Fifth Avenue, towering above Washington Square while dogs ran loose across the park and small children laughed and shrieked on their swings and hardy squirrels scampered over the sparse grass and the chess players in the southeast corner of the park pondered and ruminated on and on and all was well with the world.

Pearls of his come like miniscule diamonds scattered across the curly jungle of her pubic hair, her inner lips swollen and a darker shade of bruised pink; catching their breaths, the bed a field of lust and sheets creased in every direction of the zodiac.

"Is it your first time in New York?"

The familiar smell of her cunt wafting like a upright fountain towards his nose, reviving his senses, joyful, loose, full of the flavour of life itself.

"No, I came when I was a teenager. My father was talking at a medical conference at Columbia. So he brought the whole family along. I shared a room with Tommaso, my younger brother. He was a pest then. We stayed in a big luxury hotel near Central Park. Did a lot of shopping."

His hand strayed unconsciously towards her nipples, picked one up between two attentive fingers, caressed the rough tip, kneaded her flesh like soft dough, weighed each orb with abominable tenderness, the feather-like compactness of her slight elevations. He sighed. How could skin be so white?

"Look," he said, almost slurring his words, nodding towards the window where the outside light was fading, "dusk approaches. We must absolutely take a walk across the Square before night falls and then we can find somewhere to eat. If we stay in this bed any longer, I'll want to make love to you again, and right now I'm just too raw . . ."

She had been sitting with her neck supported by the bed's headboard. She slouched down, stretched herself lazily across the rumpled bedcovers, yawned languorously, opened her legs in a wider angle. The wetness at the core of her delta shone. He couldn't take his eyes away from her cunt. He silently lowered his head towards her core and systematically licked the drops of come still lingering around her opening.

"You tasted a bit salty, earlier," she remarked. "Where did you have lunch?"

"At Live Bait, a Cajun restaurant near the Flatiron Building."

"Oysters?"

"How did you guess?"

"I had a glass of white wine with my meal on the flight," she grinned.

His tongue dipped into her cunt.

"Oysters and wine," he said.

"I must call my mother, just to let her know I arrived safely," Giulia said. They'd shared split pea soup, pierogi and meat-stuffed cabbage at the open-24-hours Veselka Ukrainian restaurant on Second Avenue. He knew she would like it. She was not allowed spicy food as it badly upset her stomach.

"Do you want me to leave the room while you speak to her?" he suggested.

"No. It's fine, but stay quiet."

Her mother knew she had travelled to New York with her mysterious new boyfriend, but her father had been kept in the dark and she was terrified he would find out she was having an affair with an older man. After all, he had insisted that whilst in Barcelona she stay in student digs supervised by Catholic nuns. But she hadn't even told her mother about the difference in age that stood between them. Giulia was a talented liar.

Midnight was nearing. She threw off her shoes and walked over to the corner of the hotel room and unzipped her luggage and pulled out a deep-blue silk nightie.

"Look," she said.

"It's beautiful," he touched it. "So soft."

They had always been in the habit of sleeping naked.

"My mother bought it for me, when she learned I was going to spend a few days, a few nights with you," Giulia confided in him. "She felt I ought to look nice in bed," she giggled.

"A most understanding mother!"

"She is nice."

"Little does she know what her dear daughter is concealing from her, or does she?"

Giulia gave him a look of protest, as if he were pushing his luck, emphasizing her duplicity. For a moment he did wonder what her parents would make of him. Likely scream with shock, he guessed.

But her parents were not present in this room by Washington Square. They were.

"Come here, let me hold you,"

And again the warmth and softness of her body was intoxicating, releasing waves of terrible tenderness through every square inch of his body, his veins, his brain cells, as if he had lived his whole life until this very moment waiting for her, to fulfil him, to make him a better man.

He undressed her.

She slipped the nightie on.

It ended around mid-thigh and, at the top, its elongated V-neck revealed the quiet onset of her slight cleavage.

He delicately raised the hem of the silk garment and ventured a finger into her cunt. She was wet already. He pushed her gently back towards the wall, and entered her with agonizing slowness.

He was home.

She never did wear the silk nightgown again that week in New York.

Mid-afternoon. February.

They had seen a mediocre thriller at the Union Square multiplex movie house and, sitting in a generic cafe on Broadway just a hundred yards away from the intersection with Houston, were debating the merits and virtues and otherwise of Bruce Willis, who had starred in the film.

"I like it when you tell me stories," Giulia had said.

The waitress who had served them had a piercing in her right eyebrow and wore black from head to toe. He vaguely recognized a tune by Bruce Cockburn amidst the background muzak. When they had walked in, it had been to the strains of The Walkabouts playing Neil Young's "On the Beach". They were bathed in coffee fumes and a reassuring warmth. Giulia could spend her life in cafés; it was that Italian upbringing of hers.

"Will you tell other women stories about me when we are over?" she asked him

He wanted to be truthful and say no, but already she knew him too well. He was who he was, and aware that the temptation would be too strong not to talk about her, to improvise tales of beauty and fury, of lust and longing, songs of adoration and missing.

He lowered his eyes, nodded.

The punk waitress refilled Giulia's cup.

She sipped pensively from the hot cup and watched him.

"I don't know," he answered. "At any rate, not in the same coffee houses. Let's go walk."

Under the Washington Square arch he stopped and took her hand and said, "I'm so happy right now. Kiss me." Her lips still tasted of coffee and her tongue of sugar and her dark eyes shone in the early evening penumbra and his whole body shivered. A band of assorted buskers played ragtime jazz across from the fountain. On the south side of the park, on the pavement outside the massive university buildings, hawkers were selling rag-tag secondhand books on trestle tables and old issues of *Penthouse* and *The Magazine of Fantasy and Science Fiction*. Impulsively he bought her a copy of an old Philip Roth novel about an older man who was in love with a younger woman. A few years later, they would film it and it would remind him of her, even though she looked nothing like Penelope Cruz, despite their common Mediterranean roots.

An anorexic sun was setting in the distance, disappearing in the shadows that lurked around the Empire State Building. Traffic roared down Fifth Avenue as if every inhabitant of Manhattan was in a rush to reach home before dark settled. Coloured and Asian nannies were fleeing the park at the speed of lemmings, frantically pushing cots in front of them as if their life depended on it, returning their charges to their nearby apartments where their working parents were about to return from their offices.

They sat by the dogs' enclosure.

New York.

February.

Early evening.

"I'll write a story about a couple, call them Conrad and Julie maybe, who love each other terribly, obscenely. But they cannot stay together. Too many things separate them. The weight of years, the presence of others, frontiers, past and future adventures, the weight of the world and expectations, different ambitions, a life almost lived and a life that still requires mad adventures . . ." he said gently, as she buried her head across his shoulder. "So they part, as it must be and will be. Years later, his life has fallen apart in bad ways and he is sitting in a bar in Paris in the Latin Quarter, a place he never took her to, when a man, a stranger, enters the joint and tells him he needs his help to find his missing daughter. And passes a photograph of the missing girl to him across the plastic-topped table. And it's Julie. He tries to tell her father he is no detective. But the man won't listen to him, and pleads for him to accept the case. So Conrad reluctantly takes on the job and begins his quest for . . ."

He paused for breath, his imagination running ahead of him into all sorts of tangents and plots and illogical directions.

Looked up at her. There was a tear falling down Giulia's right cheek.

"Or maybe," he changed his tack, "it will be the tale of a man and a woman on a train that takes ages to reach China and she falls asleep with her head on his shoulder, just as they are nearing the border and—"

"I prefer that story," Giulia said. "But you must never give your female characters my name. That would be disrespectful to me. I won't like it."

He interrupted himself. "Please don't make me promise that," he thought, knowing all too well it was a promise he could never keep. But she said no more.

"I could write a thousand stories," he said. "I *will* write a thousand stories. But, right now, we are together and there is no reason to even think of the future. This is a moment out of time, Giulia. Our moment."

She wiped the thin teardrop away.

"Let's go back to our room," she asked. "I want to be with you between the white sheets."

He is watching her shower, her black curls unfurled all the way down to the small of her back, steam rising through the narrow hotel room bathroom, white plastic divider pulled to the side, water splashing against the tiles.

"One day I will go to live in San Francisco," she says, above the muted roar of the jets of water streaming across her skin through the plastic shower head.

The spectacle of her nudity is too much to bear. He pulls off his grey T-shirt and steps out of his trousers and steps into the bathtub and joins her. The fit is tight. Silently she hands him the soap bar and he lathers the foam across her back and spreads the thin bubbles across her, lingering tenderly over her arse. He soaps her crack, his fingers maliciously slipping and sliding down her wet valley, cleaning her, scrubbing her with all the care and attention of a slave attendant. He cups his hand under the shower head, fills his outstretched palms with water and finally washes the soap's foam away from her skin. Unsteadily, trying to retain her equilibrium in the reduced manoeuvring space left by the bulk of their two bodies in the bathtub, she swivels on her axis and turns around. She faces him. Her nipples eerily shine, a combination of dampness and the light from the inlaid electric bulb in the ceiling. He lathers up the soap he was still holding in his left hand and begins to scrub her front.

"I've already cleaned there," she says.

He ignores her and continues. Painting an invisible fresco across her small, velvet breasts, spreading the softness all over her slight hillocks and the imperceptible valley separating her chest into two parallel and identical landscapes. Giulia moans quietly. His hands move downwards, bypassing the mini-crevice of her belly button and its familiar mole and making an assured beeline for her cunt. He kneels down in the bathtub, his face now facing her opening. One pair of fingers part her, while his other hand places the soap bar on the side of the tub and invades the thicket of her pubic hair, travelling through the obstinate curls, treading her jungle, spreading the wetness, massaging the ground below like an alchemist in search of a magical formula. Her dark lower lips open up like a flower to a deep and moist cavern of redness. Her inner lips are still beautifully swollen from the incessant lovemaking of the past two days. He wipes the last remaining bubbles of soap away and his tongue nears her vortex.

"In San Francisco, I will find myself a black ambassador and I will marry him," she says.

He never quite knows when she is joking, or trying to provoke him. He says nothing and begins to lick her. Wetness against wetness. He closes his eyes. A blind man now, worshipping from memory, on automatic pilot, homing in like a bird of prey towards the fountain of life, the taste of Giulia coursing through the bridge that his lapping tongue has now become towards the very centre of him, dragging pleasure and bittersweet tastes alongside, an essence he would never truly be able to explain. In the darkness of his genuflection, his hands wander upwards. Her nipples have the gentle hardness of pizza crust, the beating sound of her heart reverberates through her chest, boom, boom, boom. He is out of breath and realizes that for several minutes now, his tongue planted deep inside her, his nose buried beneath the hard shield of her curls and stomach, he had actually forgotten to breathe. He gets up from his uncomfortable squat. Turns her round. Under the warm waterfall that splashes relentlessly over the both of them, he pulls her arms away from her body and positions her so that they are now both now leaning for support against the wall above the taps. Without being asked, she spreads her legs open. He takes his cock in one hand and guides it towards her and enters her.

"You know," she says. "When I was in Ibiza, Pedro one evening when we were chilling, smoking pot, touched me on the arm, and I knew he wanted to fuck me. And I wanted him to fuck me too. I needed it. That's why I'd let him see me naked on the beach that afternoon. But his hand on my skin just felt wrong, you see, not like yours. So I brushed him away and took another puff on the joint. It was a crazy evening."

Hearing the name of another, he felt a wave of anger and bitterness sweep through him and thrust into her as hard as he could and, entwined as they were, they almost slipped. Fucking in showers looked easier in movies, to be sure.

He withdraws from her.

"This is too awkward," he points out. "One of us is going to slip and we'll injure ourselves. Let's go to bed."

They retreat to the room, swathed in white towels. He hurries to the bed and slides in between the sheets.

"I have to dry my hair first," she said. And stands in the bedroom, facing the mirror, massaging the soft material into the jungle of her hair. The other large bathroom towel tightened around her body slips to the ground.

He watches, his heart beating wildly, his breath taken away yet again by the sheer innocence of her nudity. Walks out of bed and embraces her as he is overtaken by tenderness. Her hair is now less damp and she throws the towel she had been using aside. Both facing the mirror, his face peering across her naked shoulders. An image he would treasure forever, indelibly printed into the back screen of his brain.

On their final evening in New York, she wanted go out. Properly.

She insisted he shave his chin and cheek stubble, wear his black suit, and a clean shirt which she selected from his pack. She foraged inside her untidy suitcase and pulled out a backless evening dress, and shoes with heels. This was the first occasion in all the time he had known her she had ever worn heels. At an open-all-night Korean convenience store on the corner of Third and Sullivan Street, he bought a red rose she planted amongst the thicket of her curls.

They walked down to the restaurant on Bleecker Street they had chosen earlier and Giulia floated on air and heels like a royal gypsy queen proudly taking ownership of the cold night. The lights of Greenwich Village flickered. Pride swelled in his heart. Combined with a sense of impending loss because it was to be their final night here. And he never knew on each trip together whether it would be their last.

"I feel sad," he said to her, picking at his pine nut and asparagus risotto.

"You musn't."

"I know," he replied.

The restaurant was almost empty and the food disappointing.

The evening before he had bought takeaway sushi from a downmarket Japanese on the corner of Sixth and Greenwich Avenue and fed her individual morsels by hand while they both sat upright in bed, drops of soya sauce pearling down across the Antarctica of her small breasts, which he then obediently licked clean, savouring the taste of food and the musky, natural smell of her own skin.

"Yesterday was better," he pointed out.

"Yes," Giulia said, with a hint of a satisfied smile.

"Oh well . . ."

They walked back to their room taking a detour by Washington Square, a crescent moon laced the shadows falling across the facades of the massive apartment blocks on the southernmost side of Fifth Avenue. Under the arch they kissed briefly, but the temperature was falling fast and she had no coat to shelter her naked back from the growing cold. He draped his jacket around her shoulders.

The night porter watched them impassively as they trooped across the lobby towards the main elevator.

They stripped quickly and sought warmth between the cold sheets. The silence that divided them now was deafening. Their hands fumbled in the darkness, seeking each other, their bodies suddenly uncomfortable and self-conscious. His hand grazed one breast. Her fingers grasped his cock and felt it grow under her contact.

On Waverly Place, they made love and wept.

Her limousine arrived a quarter of an hour early the next day to take her to the airport, where her flight back to Barcelona was waiting. They didn't have much time to talk.

He just stood in the lobby watching her walk to the swinging doors of the hotel, dragging her metal case alongside on its small wheels. He was searching for the right words to say, but they just wouldn't come. They never did, did they?

Out in Queens, past Jamaica Boulevard, travelling down Van Wyck Expressway, separated from the Arab driver by the glass partition, Giulia pulled her notebook from her bag, and began drafting him a letter. She would continue writing it in the airport's departure lounge where she had a couple of hours to spare until she boarded the flight. She'd had no wish to have a coffee this time around or spend time in the duty-free shops. The letter spread over nine pages, her handwriting all over the place, sometimes shaken by the tears rolling down her cheeks or that terrible feeling of despair that so often lurked in the pit of her stomach. She used both sides of the paper. During the long flight back to Europe, she made changes, crossing out lines, adding words, erasing others.

It was a love letter. Thanking him for the wonderful time they had spent together by Washington Square. Attempting in bursts of savage hunger to tell him, explain to him how much she loved him, even though the whole essence of their relationship was wrong, could just not sustain itself. She made promises she knew she could not keep.

Tried to understand, as she wrote, why love could also contain so much pain.

By the time she landed, she had already decided she would never send him the letter. It remained at the bottom of her bag for the next six months. Accusing her. Chiding her. But wasn't it him who had one day explained to her that words weren't enough. That they couldn't change the course of things?

One day, by accident, he would read the letter, but by then it was too late. They had both moved apart; only lust kept them together under its heavy cloak of illusions when they took excursions away together from their real lives in other foreign cities or beaches. Ironically, his discovery of the letter coincided with their very last tryst.

Of course, the letter made him cry. Because he now realized that they had both left their hearts behind in Washington Square.

John Updike Made Me Do It

Donna George Storey

Roots of an Obsession

John Updike made me do it.

He definitely deserves a lot of credit anyway.

Because when I think back on that night in Tahoe, it's almost as if he were right there in the hot tub with us, his lips stretched in a patrician smile as he guided my hand over to caress the rock-hard cock of a man who was not my husband. Of course said husband was too busy sucking the rosy nipples of the German woman, Katharina, to notice or care. And Jürgen and Jill were already kissing as if they'd done it dozens of times, which they hinted they had when Jill spent her junior year in Bonn. None of them seemed to need John Updike's help, although no doubt they had his blessing.

Updike had been softening me up for this night for years. Sitting in the effervescent spa water with five other horny married people, the Sierras soaring around us into the star-flecked sky, it was just like stepping into the pages of a steamy novel. In fact, it was the same surreal excitement I felt as I devoured *Rabbit Is Rich* or *Couples* under the blankets as a teenager. Sneaking them from the bookshelves in my parents' room, I instinctively knew I could only read them when I heard the soft click of their bedroom lock at night.

While my parents "did it" the customary way – with each other in their marriage bed, their lust invisible to the world – the couples in John Updike's stories were fearlessly experimental, so they ended up all jumbled together like Halloween candy in a plastic pumpkin. They'd jet off to the Caribbean where the wives would confer to redistribute sex partners for the night. Or they'd fall into affairs, then confess to their spouses who would graciously consent to sleep with their cuckolded counterparts to even the score. Even Updike's memoirs glittered with shocking transgression. I can't tell you how many times I masturbated to the scene of Updike fingering a neighbour's wife through her ski pants as they drove back from Vermont through a starry winter night.

I knew these were just stories, maybe even pure fantasy, but I sensed, too, that John Updike was giving me a glimpse of the hunger and restlessness of the adult world. What were these people looking for in their swaps and affairs? Did they ever find it?

Would I?

The Games Begin

We'd just passed Auburn on our drive up to Tahoe to spend the weekend with Nick's old friend Jill when the snow started falling hard. Before long, Nick had to pull over and put on the chains. I suppose I started playing the "swinging" game because the poor guy was half-frozen when he got back in the car. With the traffic inching along I-80, we were sure to miss dinner at the cabin. He'd need more than Power Bars and trail mix to warm him up.

I explained the rules to him: we'd take turns naming a couple we knew, then describe what we thought it would be like to swap for the evening. I opened with the most obvious couple in our lives. "How about switching with Grace and Jack?"

Nick's eyebrows shot up. Grace was one of the most talented programmers he worked with and he once mentioned casually that he found her attractive. With her porcelain skin and hourglass curves, I doubt he was alone in that opinion.

"I could see that as a possibility," he said cautiously.

"A possibility? Come on, you'd love it. Grace straddling you cowgirl style. Those melon breasts jiggling as she rode you, her pale skin all flushed with arousal. You could grab her nice round butt and knead it while she creamed all over you. Then you'd tickle her ass crack – you're good at that – and when she came she'd probably give that sweet little laugh, like she did when she was drunk at the Christmas party." I giggled in what I thought was a decent imitation of his favourite colleague.

"Jeez, you don't have to get so graphic." It was already dark, but in the glow of the surrounding headlights, I could see he was blushing.

"What's the matter? Am I giving you a boner?"

Nick shifted in his seat. "So what about you and Jack?"

"I don't know. He's not the worst candidate. But to be honest he's too good-looking for me."

"*Too* good-looking?"

"Yeah, blond muscle boys like him are used to being worshipped by women. They don't try hard enough. If I'm fucking someone just for the sex, I want a guy who has something to prove."

"You're hard to please." Nick narrowed his eyes at me, but I suspect he liked me that way. "How about Michael and Heather? He strikes me as the ambitious type."

I shook my head. "He's so hairy. And he is ambitious, but not in a good way. He's bound to be selfish in bed. But Heather? With that limber little body of hers you could do it in all kinds of kinky positions. Maybe push her legs to her shoulders until she was practically bent in half? Her vagina would be all stretched and tight like a warm, wet glove, gripping you with every stroke. She's so light, you could do it standing up, too. You could take her up against the wall, her ass banging against it like you were spanking her. I'd bet you'd make a lot of noise, you two."

Nick laughed, discomfort mixed with definite arousal. "Well, I've always thought Heather was nice. So that makes it two to nothing. Can't you think of anyone you'd like to be with?"

I paused. To be honest, I was having so much fun turning him on with my dirty words, I hadn't even thought about it.

"Maybe Jill's German friend will be right for me. If you believe John Updike, vacations are a good time to do a little swinging. The rules of ordinary life don't apply. How about you and Jill?"

Nick grimaced. "Don't even mention Jill, OK? She's practically my sister." He turned and studied my face. "I know you like Ben, though."

"For his mind, darling. He's a little . . . soft . . . for me."

"True, he's not particularly athletic," Nick agreed. "Hey, what's with all of this swinging talk anyway?"

"I was just rereading Updike's *Couples* and everyone's screwing around and swapping like crazy." I closed up the bag of trail mix and leaned back in my seat. "I always wondered how often it happens in real life though."

Nick glanced over at me again. "Is this something you'd like to try?"

"No, I'm just curious," I replied rather too quickly. "How about you?"

"I guess if the right opportunity arises, for both of us, I'd be OK with it. Not that there's much of a chance, being married to Ms Choosy."

"How could I top perfection?" I said, reaching over to pat his crotch. He was still hard from the fantasy romps with Grace and Heather no doubt. I was pretty damp myself. I knew at least one couple would be having sex at the cabin tonight.

The truth was the idea of trying a swap with another couple did turn me on, but I never thought in a million years it could ever be more than a game.

Aural Orgy

We finally got to the cabin in King's Beach around eleven. Good old Jill was waiting up for us in the kitchen with a pot of cinnamon tea.

"Sorry about the bad luck with the weather, you guys."

"No problem," Nick said, giving Jill a peck on the cheek. "Maria and I had a nice long talk in the car."

"Actually there's another little complication tonight. I thought this place had three bedrooms, but the third queen bed is the sleeper sofa in the living room. Katharina and Jürgen took the bedroom on the other side of the house and they'll be walking through your room to get to the bathroom."

Nick and I exchanged glances. That could put a damper on the sex part of our holiday weekend – unless we decided to live dangerously.

"And . . . um," Jill began with an apologetic smile.

"What is it now, Jilly-bean?" Nick said, in not-quite-mock annoyance. In fact, they did act a lot like brother and sister.

"So, you know how Germans are more comfortable with their bodies than Americans?"

Nick shot me a what-the-fuck grin. We were both a bit punchy from the drive.

"Just so you're prepared, sometimes Katharina and Jürgen walk around the house in the nude."

We held our laughter until we were snuggled together on the sofa bed, snowflakes still battering the windows.

"Beware the naked Germans," Nick whispered as I muffled my giggles in his shoulder. His hands slipped under my nightshirt and he slowly, teasingly inched it up over my breasts.

"Hey, are you sure you want to do this? A naked German might walk in on us any minute."

"We can pull them into bed with us. That's what you want, isn't it?" Without waiting for my answer, Nick scooted under the blankets and eased open my thighs. He knew once he got to work with his mouth *down there*, I'd stop arguing.

Sure enough, the instant his tongue met my clit, jolts of familiar pleasure shot through me. I arched back on the bed, but remembered where we were just in time to swallow down a moan. However, to be honest, the thought of fucking in a semi-public place where a stranger might see us turned me on in a big way. Besides, keeping quiet seemed to increase the sensation, sounds of my pleasure trapped and throbbing in my belly. My mind was teeming with images, too, fragments from the evening all tumbled together like trail mix. Nick fucking Grace, while Heather rode his face, their sweat-slick breasts swaying as they writhed in ecstasy. I watched the lewd scene before me while Jill's faceless German friend groped my nude body, pinching my nipple, twisting it, just as Nick was doing in real life now.

I bit the corner of the pillow to keep from crying out. Every moist click of his tongue, every creak of the cheap mattress as I rocked my ass up for more, seemed to roar in my ears like a jet engine.

They could hear everything. They all knew exactly what we were doing.

Suddenly I heard a soft knocking filtering down from Jill and Ben's room in the loft. *Tap, tap, squeak.* It took a moment before I realized what it was: a headboard nudging the wall, another mattress protesting under the thrusts of joined bodies.

Ben must have been waiting up for Jill. He had to watch the German woman parade around naked all evening and he was desperate for release. Jill was now paying for her friend's provocation as she lay beneath her husband's big body, his dick sliding in and out of her swollen, pink pussy. *Tap, tap, squeak.*

My thighs began to shake. I was close. Nick pulled away and rose to his knees, guiding his cock into my very wet cunt.

He bent forward and his lips closed over mine. We began to move together in our familiar rhythm, making love as we always did. Except tonight we had company.

Tap, tap, squeak.

Now another voice joined the chorus, a low feminine moan, with a hint of Bach. Jill's friends from Bonn were fucking, too. On top of the blankets, of course, their nude bodies fully exposed. The heady mix of sex sounds swirled through my head in an aural orgy, dancing down my spine to gather in my cunt.

We're all fucking. Together. Friends, strangers, fucking, coming.

It was too much.

I climaxed, my teeth biting into the pillow. Nick was right behind me, his face twisted in a mute grimace of pleasure.

A few moments later the knocking above and the moans from the front room subsided. I heard six pairs of lips exhale in a collective sigh of carnal contentment.

John Updike couldn't have planned it better.

On My Ass in the Snow

"The Winter Olympians have descended from the slopes," Ben announced, taking the last swallow of his third Irish coffee.

I was still on my second drink, but was definitely feeling the effect. I aimed a jaunty salute at Nick, Jill, Jürgen and Katharina from my perch by the fireplace in the lodge.

Nick swaggered over to me, with that cool-yet-clumsy gait of a man in ski boots. "Don't you look comfy?"

From his tone, he didn't exactly approve. OK, so I did have my stocking feet resting in Ben's lap, but that was only because my legs were sore from doing the snowplough all morning and Ben kindly offered a massage. At that point it was all completely innocent.

Katharina strolled up and stood close to Nick – too close. They made quite the dashing couple in their ski togs, frosty goggles pushed up on their foreheads. "Your husband is a very good skier."

Her feline eyes twinkled like a German Christmas tree.

"She's being kind," Nick said, giving her a fond smile. "It took me all morning to get back up to speed. I haven't skied in about six years. You were very patient with me."

"On the contrary, I had trouble keeping up with you. You were very daring."

Maybe it was the whiskey but I watched all of this with a detached interest, as if I were observing someone else's handsome husband flirting with another woman. It occurred to me, too, that Nick had stopped skiing when we met. Had he stopped being daring, too?

Jill and Jürgen joined the circle. Amusingly, they made a good couple, too. Jürgen was tall with a close-trimmed blond beard and ponytail and looked every inch the Olympic skier. Jill wore her golden hair in a ponytail, too, and the stylish red outfit showed her long legs to advantage.

Ben and I were definitely the low-rent pair of our happy group in our hired gear. But I strongly suspected we had just as much fun off the slopes critiquing the elitism of winter sports and redefining our sorry performance in the snow as a protest against the tyranny of consumer capitalism.

"How was your day, sweetie?" Jill gave Ben a quick hug.

"Well, I spent most of the morning on my ass in the snow, but things improved considerably when Maria and I decided to hit the bar instead."

"Don't listen to him, Jill. He was the king of the bunny slope. I, on the other hand, spent the *whole* morning on my ass in the snow," I added.

Katharina laughed. "'Bunny slope?' That is very adorable. In German, we call it the 'idiot's hill' ."

Nick grinned at her, as if he found *her* adorable.

Ben's lips shifted into a crooked smile. "I definitely feel like an idiot with those skinny sticks on my feet. Give me food, wine and the hot tub. Those are my gold medal events."

I giggled conspiratorially and drained my Irish coffee, tipping my head back like a floozy in a beer ad. When I rocked back up again, licking the last bits of whipped cream from my lips, Nick was staring at me, eyes glittering, as if he saw the stranger in me, too.

Updike's Hand

Since Ben and I had the easiest day on the slopes, we offered to make the fondue dinner, which also meant the two of us got to loll around in the hot tub in our swimsuits while the others did the dishes.

Fortified by the riesling, I was telling Ben about John Updike and how I couldn't seem to get him out of my mind. That led to a discussion of Updike as the chronicler of a particular moment in American cultural history – the generation who came of age in the 1950s and experienced the allure and angst of the Sexual Revolution after they were married. It was exactly the sort of mildly provocative intellectual bullshit Ben and I had indulged in all afternoon, but when Nick joined us in his swim trunks, he seemed to feel the need to explain.

"Sorry, Ben, my wife has this fixation on John Updike stories. She likes the spouse-swapping."

Ben arched an eyebrow at me. "I didn't know you were a fan of 'the lifestyle' ."

Before I could reply, the sliding doors swished open behind us and Jürgen and Katharina appeared. As Jill promised, they climbed into the hot tub totally nude.

I felt Nick's body stiffen beside me. No doubt he was stiffening in his swim trunks as well. I myself sneaked a look at Jürgen: dark blond pubic hair, an uncut dick, gorgeous thigh muscles. No wonder Jill lingered on the deck in her robe, enthralled at this vision of Nordic male beauty.

"Get in, babe," Ben called, gesturing to the empty place between him and Jürgen.

"I'm not sure I have the nerve to do this," Jill said with a small laugh.

"You've lived in Europe, *Liebchen*. I remember when you were not so shy," Jürgen teased.

Jaw set bravely, she took a deep breath and shrugged out of the robe. She practically sprinted the five steps to the hot tub, one arm over her full breasts, the other shielding her crotch.

"The sky did not fall down upon you, did it?" Jürgen said with an indulgent smile. He smiled at the rest of the bathing suit brigade, eyebrows lifted in a dare.

Nick shot back with a "no thanks" and Ben shook his head.

I'm not sure why I rose to the bait. Maybe I wanted to shatter their image of me as a coward and a prude. Or maybe, on a subconscious level, I wanted to nudge things along. "Oh, I'm going to get naked, I just thought I'd wait until we all start having sex."

Five heads turned to me, mouths gaping.

Jürgen's eyes flickered with approval. "I have no argument with that. Or is this an example of the famous American sense of humour?"

"Don't underestimate Maria," Ben said with his usual I'm-just-joking grin. "She acts innocent, but I'm told she has a wild side. She's into swinging."

"So are we," Jürgen replied matter-of-factly. *He* obviously wasn't kidding.

Katharina's serene smile left no doubt it was true. "It is very refreshing to meet another daring couple," she said, turning to Nick. "I see you agree sex is a healthy adult pleasure also. Like skiing."

Nick and I exchanged a glance. *Be careful what you wish for . . .*

But I saw something else in his eyes, too, a reflection of my own dark urges. The barriers of ordinary life had indeed softened in the thin mountain air. It was as if I were floating, beyond the rules of time and space. This could be Europe or 1968. We could be our parents or grandparents, taking that first sweet taste of sexual possibility, or characters from a novel whose very existence depended on doing something shocking to keep the pages turning.

I'm not exactly sure who actually made the first move, but things progressed quickly from there. Before I knew it, Jürgen bent to kiss Jill, murmuring something softly in German. Katharina took Nick's hand and guided it to her breast, her eyes hooded in lust. This time my husband did not resist the dare. He circled the large nipple with his fingertip then bent to kiss it.

I turned to Ben. We'd been talking all day. This time we spoke with our eyes alone.

Do you want this, Maria?

Do you?

Why wouldn't I? I've had a crush on you forever.

That's funny, just last night I was imagining what you'd be like in bed.

Back when I was dating, I rarely made the first move with a man, but now I curled my fingers around Ben's hard-on. His thick, meaty cock twitched in my grasp and a jolt of forbidden excitement shot through me. At the same time, the odd floating sensation grew stronger, as if part of me were gazing at the scene from far away.

As if the hand reaching out to seal the deal were Updike's, not mine.

Compare and Contrast

John Updike didn't write orgies. His couples retired to separate rooms to explore their new partners and pleasures. So did we. The last to touch, Ben and I retired first, claiming his bedroom after stopping in Jürgen and Katharina's room for a condom.

Stripping off our swimsuits, we crawled onto the bed, again without words, as if we were playing out a script we both knew by heart. When Ben kissed me, it wasn't like I thought it would be, sex for the sake of sex. I always imagined unbridled passion, a desperate, animal coupling. But Ben's lips were surprisingly soft and tender. The strange taste of him took me back to high school, when I made out with many different boys, reminding me that kisses are like ice cream, the same creamy treat, but each with a different flavouring or spice.

I liked Ben's kisses and his satiny skin, the heat of his broad body. He was different from Nick who was sinewy and hard. My palms tingled at the new sensation.

Is this what the swingers in the stories were looking for?

"This doesn't seem real," Ben confessed. From the deck below, I heard Katharina laugh, a throaty, sexual sound.

"It isn't real," I said. "We're in a John Updike story."

"I'll have to read his stuff." He smiled and cupped my breast, brushing the nipple with his thumb.

I sighed to show him he got it right.

"You're beautiful, you know," he said, repeating that pleasurable motion until I squirmed and my breath came faster.

I laughed. "Are you trying to seduce me?"

Ben's expression was serious. "I want to make you happy tonight, Maria." He took my hand and guided it between my legs. "Teach me how you like to be touched."

Under the circumstances, a little hands-on tutoring wasn't a bad idea, but in truth it had taken me a while to feel comfortable touching my own pussy in front of Nick.

So I closed my eyes, touched my sweet spot and started to strum. My clit swelled beneath my fingers, a hard, aching diamond. It was just like masturbating in my teenager's bedroom, biting back my moans while I imagined John Updike rubbing me through my ski pants in the back seat of the car on a wintry night. That is, until Ben's large hand closed over mine, and his very real finger carried on with the task.

I spread my legs wider. Ben was a fast learner. He slipped his left arm around my shoulder to rub one nipple, while he suckled the other. It felt good, very good, but still it seemed more like a fantasy, my old naughty dreams made flesh. A cold winter night, a ski weekend, another man with his hand between my legs, working my clit patiently. I had to come soon, and oh-so-quietly or my husband would be pulling the car into the driveway, stopping the engine, then turning to catch us doing that naughty, forbidden thing.

Before long, I was indeed shuddering and thrashing in Ben's arms.

He kissed my cheek afterwards. "Thank you for that. Tell me what you want next."

"I feel greedy," I confessed.

"Don't. I like pleasing you."

"OK, I want you on top now. I want to feel you all around me."

Tap, tap, squeak.

I almost laughed at his bed's encore performance as we rocked together, my legs clasping him, feet hooked behind his thighs. I didn't come again with him – I actually pushed his hand away when he tried to finger my clit again. Instead I floated somewhere outside my body, drinking in the sounds of his ragged breath, the way he suddenly tensed, then bucked rhythmically, his quivering moan of release.

These are the things I would remember best, my small, shiny souvenirs from the land of Updike.

Answers

"Did you have a good time?" Nick asked when we were back in bed together again. I'd guess it was sometime after midnight.

"Yes. And you?"

"It was nice."

We both seemed to sense detailed descriptions weren't in order now. As if on cue, we rolled towards each other and embraced. I stroked his back and shoulders, filled my lungs with his scent, seeking some change in him, some mark to prove it was real.

"I should be tired, but I want you." His voice was hot in my ear. "I want you naked inside and out."

What happened next was the real surprise of the evening.

Because those words broke something in me, like a balloon blown to the bursting point. A sigh, more like a sob really, forced its way through my lips and I clutched him, squeezing until my muscles burned.

He groaned, too, his lean body pressing against me as if he would crush me to pulp.

When we kissed, it was more like a bite, our lips banging together, stinging from the pressure. Our hands roamed over each other's bodies, grasping, reclaiming what was ours. I wanted him, too, his naked cock buried in my wetness. And I wanted him now.

I rose and shoved him over onto his back – I never knew I had such strength in me. When I yanked down his sweat pants, his cock sprang up like a jack-in-the-box, bobbing against his belly. I struggled out of my own pyjama pants and straddled him. Our genitals met like a head-on collision, my pubic bone jamming onto his belly over and over. There were no questions. We knew just what to do. Nick grasped my nipple and rolled it between his fingers. His other hand circled around to my ass, the territory on which he still had sole claim.

I started to fuck him, angling my hips so I could feel his cock pressing against my front wall the way I liked best.

"Come for me, baby. Come for *me*," Nick growled.

Which is just what I wanted, too. And with his finger invading my ass and his lips tugging my tit, I did, roaring as my orgasm tore through me, not caring who heard.

Only afterwards, when I lay in my husband's arms, my pussy raw and slick with his jism, did it finally make sense. Because the story had two acts: a wandering off to glimpse the familiar in the foreign and to watch the stranger in the man I knew best. And now the rush of bittersweet pleasure you can only know when you come home to real life from a fantastic journey.

Because I never felt closer to Nick than I did that night.

I suppose I had John Updike to thank for that, too.

The Purple Gloves

Gala Fur

Translated by Noël Burch

A cold April wind blew in from the North and through the streets of Paris, whipping the coats of passers-by and the pleated skirt that Elvira was hugging to her thighs. She heard soles slapping the pavement in her wake. Elvira was a long-legged woman in her early thirties and the sensuality of her rolling gait drew men like flies. Intrigued by this new admirer's perseverance, she turned to have a look. A pair of violet ballerinas with matching quilted pocket-book and gloves tapped along behind her. Today, it was a woman pursuing her along the empty sidewalk on Avenue Mozart. Only a few minutes before, Elvira had caught a glimpse of the tweed-suited woman's pallid face as she strolled arm in arm with their dermatologist across his waiting room. Her fellow patient had the face of a collectible porcelain doll. The unhealthy pallor emphasized her thick black hair held in place by two barrettes over the temples and swept up in a high bun. Elvira pointed her magnetic key as if she were switching TV channels. The orange headlights on her Mercedes winked at her. She scrambled into the car and was reaching for the dashboard button that would lock the car when already the right-hand door swung out and a face appeared in the opening.

"We were together in Dr Goult's office. Are you heading for the Left Bank?"

There was the touch of an American accent in the stranger's question. Instead of "Sorry, I have things to do," Elvira heard herself replying: "I can leave you at a cabstand near L'Étoile, if you like." It was those sudden bursts of generosity that endeared her to her own "patients". Elvira was a professional dominatrix. She had the gift of empathizing with the needs of her masochistic clientele. As her psychoanalyst put it, performing services for others was a vocation with her. The pushy American woman sat down beside her, those doll's eyes staring straight ahead, holding that violet pocket-book on her lap with gloved hands. There was something unreal about her mother-of-pearl complexion. Had the dermatologist rejuvenated her? Embalmed her? Elvira had a passion for vampire stories. Driven by a morbid bulimia, she would spend her sleepless nights watching one horror movie after the other.

The Arc de Triomphe was coming into view when the woman spoke again:

"Where do you live?"

"Saint-Germain-des-Près."

"You're on your way home?"

"Yes."

"I have an errand to run in your neighbourhood. Saint-Germain-des-Prés is a lot like the Village in New York. I live on Bleecker."

"Oh?"

"I come to Paris regularly to see Dr Goult."

Elvira had known Pascal Goult for years. Tall and athletic as he was, he liked having his face slapped. In exchange, he took care of her skin. Elvira enjoyed slapping. When she was expecting a client for a slapping session, she grew terribly excited. She had to change her panties afterwards because they were so wet. If she had been a hard-line dominatrix, she'd have slapped this importunate woman. *Only a New Yorker is capable of acting like this, she said to herself.* Instead of pulling over to the kerb and ordering her out of the car, she said nothing: she was consumed with curiosity. Chance meetings always affected her this way.

On Place Saint-Germain-des-Prés, she called out "End of the line!" The woman ran gloved fingers over the dashboard. Elvira reached out to open the door for her and her arm brushed against the woman's breasts. Both were wearing the same perfume, L'Instant Magic by Guerlain.

"Be seeing you soon," said the woman, peering through the glass with a little wave of her hand.

Elvira bought fresh bread, rice, artichokes and fruit at the supermarket. As she turned her key in the lock of her apartment door, she saw the unknown woman again, ensconced in her hallway. Her smile looked as if it were painted on sticking plaster.

"I left my gloves in your car."

The witch has probably bribed the garage attendant to get my address. Elvira suddenly had the feeling she'd seen her somewhere before. In

NewYork, probably . . . A shiver ran down her spine. Was her stormy past pursuing her to her very door? She was overcome by a burst of paranoia, like one of those attacks that cured junkies experience. *What if this woman's been paid to investigate me, do me an injury, kill me?* If she was merely prying into Elvira's present means of subsistence, an expertly applied arm lock should be dissuasive enough: she would escort her out of the building by force. The woman patted her shoulder.

"Doctor Goult's treatment has made me thirsty. Can I have a glass of water?"

Already the clever little vixen had slipped into the kitchen. Elvira turned on the tap and filled two glasses to the brim. She handed one to the woman who took a few sips, pasted on another artificial smile and began questioning her again.

"Did you have our friend the dermatologist touch up your face?"

"A shot of Botox in the bunny lines. And you?"

The woman stood looking around the room and seemed not to have heard the question. Elvira took a sip of water, drew a deep breath and took another sip, gripping the glass, ready to pounce. A Saint Andrew's cross was propped against the living-room wall. The woman gazed at it with empty eyes. Two perforated leather straps with metal buckles hung from the cross-ends. The woman balanced her glass on the edge of the sink and undid one of the mother-of-pearl buttons on her blouse. She fanned her throat with her hand. The trembling silk clung to her full round breasts. *Is Doctor Goult responsible for that perfect pair of tits?* Like Elvira, she wore no bra. Her face took on a touch of humanity, a tint of old-fashioned pink like Japanese greasepaint. She came up to Elvira, took her hands and pressed them to her breasts. Elvira finished unbuttoning the light blue silk blouse and tugged at the cloth, freeing the last button from a fold in the skirt.

She bunched the woman's breasts together and pressed them to the sternum. The woman moaned. Elvira stroked her cheek. Next, she pulled off her own sweater and dropped it on the rug. The woman gazed at Elvira's bare bosom and murmured:

"I took a long time choosing between NewYork and Paris."

"I'm happy to hear you say it. So did I. And I'm glad I made the choice I did. NewYorkers are impossible people, especially the women."

Elvira's voice was no longer the same. It had become sharp, authoritarian. She dug her nails into the porcelain skin, leaving pink streaks on the woman's arm, then between the two breasts which were back in place now, tips slanting towards the armpits. Throwing her weight against the other woman's pelvis, she backed her towards the wall. Step by step, the American retreated towards the cross, quite unruffled. To make it easier for the dominatrix, she raised one arm, hand hanging limp. Elvira attached her wrist to the cross, passing the prong of the buckle through the third and last hole in the strap. The woman held up her other arm. Her head was bowed. In her rolled-up eyes, the white of the iris had supplanted the bright brown of the pupils. Their faces were almost touching. The woman looked straight at her. In her eyes, there was no trace of fear, she did not so much as blink. *Arrogant bitch!* They locked gazes, with the American squinting. Words fell from her lips without a twitch of her facial muscles:

"I've just come back from a trip to Peru. Macchu Picchu . . . Have you ever been there?"

Elvira twisted her ear with wiry fingers.

"No, I've never been up Macchu Picchu."

She gripped both the woman's nipples and twisted them clockwise. Then she dug her nails into them. The woman's gaze began to quaver. A shudder ran through her shoulders. There were creases on either side of her mouth. Her lower lip hung loose and moist. Elvira bit hard into the limp bit of flesh, meanwhile pinching her again and again, at regular intervals. Then she relaxed the pressure but left her nails where they were. The woman rose on tiptoes as if to recoil from another pinch. Elvira rubbed her hands together and, without a word, slapped her twice. *That did it, I'm wet as any slut!* A lock of dark hair danced in front of the foreigner's pale face. The bun was slowly coming apart, the locks of hair like snakes coming to life. Elvira seized one of the barrettes that slipped over the ear and brandished it threateningly before the woman's eyes.

"How long have you been spying on me?"

"I don't understand," the woman said, exaggerating her American accent, and then sucked her lower lip

What an actress, she's doing all she can to excite me! Elvira's cheeks were burning. She dropped the barrette and pressed her sex against the American's thigh, the other woman's body was jutting forward like a ship's figurehead. As she rubbed her cunt up and down on her visitor's firm flesh, cum flowed in little spurts down her own thighs. She ran her hands over the woman's hips, feeling for the skirt zipper. She jerked it open and pulled the skirt down around the knees. The woman wriggled.

"A skirt around the knees isn't very stylish."

Elvira laughed sadistically. She caught hold of lips that still bore traces of purplish lipstick in spite of all the sucking and nibbled on them. They had the sickly sweet taste of tinned lychees. Now and then she would stand back and chortle with glee. The American looked her straight in the eye. *I'm going to teach this one a lesson.* Elvira seized her panties with two fingers, seamless Lycra panties, cut low over the flat hips, violet like the shoes and bag. Her own panties were twisted up inside her vulva and each of her moves deepened her excitement. She pulled the Lycra away from the woman's white skin and slipped her hand inside. Her fingers moved downward one after the other, the way one imitates the footsteps of an imaginary character in a story told to a child. For the first time, the woman's eyelids fluttered. She tried to fend off Elvira with her tongue, gluttonously licking her cheeks and nose. Elvira's index finger entered the plucked slit, followed by the middle finger. Her left hand pulled the skirt down further, leaving it crumpled around the woman's calves. She inserted three crooked fingers and pushed upward. With each to and fro, her wrist rubbed against the woman's bare belly. Another finger entered the gaping vagina, then the thumb and finally the whole hand. Elvira's torso was pressed against the woman's bosom. The woman gave a cough, not a real cough but an imitation meant to contract the belly and eject the churning fist inside her, but it was no use. Elvira leaned forward, took one of the breasts in her mouth and began sucking on it vigorously, as if it were a genital organ. She moved her head back and forth, mouth wider and wider till it touched the rib-cage, engulfing the whole apple of flesh. The woman's closed eyelids quivered. Drops of saliva dribbled from her mouth. She moaned in time to Elvira's fist and mouth and came with a long scream, neck stretched, eyes suddenly open and staring at the ceiling beams. Elvira sighed.

"In my study, there is a plane ticket to Lima. I just purchased a week's excursion up Macchu Picchu. How could you know about that?"

Lips pursed as if to keep from replying, the woman rattled her wrists in their straps. Elvira released her and closed the light-blue silk blouse. The woman pulled up her panties and skirt, picked up the jacket and pocket-book she had laid on a kitchen stool and left. Elvira snatched up the phone and called Dr Goult.

"What was the name of the American woman I saw in your waiting room as I left your office?"

"I don't know who you mean. What did she look like?"

"About my age, dark-brown hair, with violet shoes and matching handbag."

But the dermatologist had seen no American patient that day. Elvira put her hand over her pounding heart, took a deep breath, jumped up and hurried down to the third level of the garage beneath her building. She opened the door of the Mercedes and searched the passenger's seat and the dashboard compartment. No gloves. Yet she distinctly remembered the woman wearing them when she got into the car. The attendant had given out no information about the person renting space No. 353. Nor had he seen a brunette in a tweed suit.

The next day, when Elvira described the incident to her analyst, he told her to stop being so hard on herself.

Checkpoint Charlie

N. J. Streitberger

Charles knew he was in for an adventure when the taxi driver started waving a revolver around.

He was on his way from Tegel Airport and the driver was keen to show what would happen if anyone got "funny" with him.

This was the summer of 1988 and it was Charles's first visit to Berlin. He was on an assignment for *E:Go*, the style-making magazine for which he wrote about cinema. Ken Loach was making a rare foray beyond the shores of the UK for a film about an East German musician sneaking into the West to try his luck. Cannily aware of the influence of the magazine, the producers had invited Charles over for a few days to watch Loach at work and hang out in the city.

While he had a thorough knowledge of the director's work, he had virtually none of Germany, apart from what he'd read and seen in movies. Berlin had always seemed to him like a fantasy city, a place of dark dreams. This imagined city had been built in his mind over the years by several viewings of *The Blue Angel*, in both German and English versions, Fritz Lang's *M*, *Cabaret*, some (though by no means all) of the films of Fassbinder and Herzog and frequent exposure to the works of Kurt Weill and Bertolt Brecht, Isherwood, Lotte Lenya and Dagmar Krause.

Impressionable as he was, even Charles could tell the difference between real and reel life. As he had never had a loaded gun pointed more or less in his direction, it was a nerve-wracking, thrilling experience. By the time he got to his hotel, he was in a state of heightened expectation.

The day on set had gone well. Loach and his small crew had handpicked several local teenagers and punks to appear in the film and Charles very quickly fell in with them.

Although they were almost half his age they took him under their collective wing and promised to show him as much of the Berlin nightlife as possible in forty-eight hours. The fact that he wrote for *E:Go* was his passport into their world as they all read it in the same way he had devoured the *NME* when he was their age.

The director had been generous with his time, talking to Charles between set-ups and allowing him a full hour during the lunch break. He had also included him as an extra, wandering through a party scene in the non-speaking role of a record-company executive. The young punks had strutted their stuff brilliantly, mainly because they were required simply to be themselves.

It had been swelteringly hot, and back in his hotel Charles had shivered under a cold shower just to try and cool off. Down in the lobby, three girls dressed in distressed leather, ripped jeans and Doc Martens were waiting for him; his unofficial entourage. Two of the girls took his arms and marched him out into the dusk. It gave him a strange thrill to be in the company of young gorgeous, reckless and very friendly Berlin youths. Maybe he was too old for this.

Then again, maybe not.

The night proceeded apace. One club after another – some howling with music, the walls actually pulsating with the throb of the bass; a couple of dark basements where people recited poetry and sang little songs. Somewhere around 4.00 a.m. he was sitting on a sofa with the stuffing protruding from one of the arms drinking coffee while the girls danced to Eddie Cochran's "Cut Across Shorty" on the jukebox. It was pleasantly bizarre.

He wondered whether sex might be on the cards later. Would they all come back to his hotel room? It would be impossible, not to say discourteous, to choose between them and he had never before engaged in a group session. These German girls could be very uninhibited. Or so he'd read. After all, wasn't it the decadent lifestyle of the West that the East objected to so strongly? He imagined girls in boots and Nazi-inspired fetish wear, black silk stockings and leather corsetry; he fantasized about slender women dressed in formal male attire, black dinner suits and bow ties, cigarettes in long holders, patent leather pumps, monocles – lipstick lesbianism long before the term was coined. Otto Dix meets Salon Kitty.

By the time 5.30 a.m. rolled around and he staggered out blinking into the dawn, it was clear that it was simply an innocent night on the town. A few hugs and promises to see him later and they left him to find his own way back to the hotel. Nice kids, he thought, with just the slightest pang of regret that he hadn't pushed home his advantage. Ah well. So much for fantasy Berlin. They were just punks past their outrage-by-date. Counter-culture shadows.

What remained of the day was free. A few hours' sleep and he was ready to do what he wanted to do which was to visit Checkpoint Charlie and go and have a peek at the East for a couple of hours. *The Spy Who Came In from the Cold* loomed large in his imagination as he asked directions and then discovered that he was only five minutes away from the infamous crossing point at the Wall.

His first sight of the sign stating, "You are leaving the American Sector" in four languages, was somehow thrilling. It was like stepping into a movie.

Charles approached the white hut in the American sector with rising excitement. He produced his passport and was asked his business.

"Just a look around. I will only be a few hours."

After giving him the standard spiel for visiting foreigners, the bored official waved him through. He walked slowly, savouring the moment as he crossed into East Berlin. Suddenly, brutally aware that he spoke no German and that he was venturing into uncharted territory, he hesitated a little, looking up at the watchtower and the barbed wire and the general accoutrements of the border. On the other side, there was a long zig-zagging barrier which he had to negotiate. He approached a long line of huts and went to the nearest window. A glum guard looked at his passport and went inside. After a while a door opened in the building and he was beckoned inside.

Charles stepped into the building and was greeted by a stern-faced woman with short-cropped blonde hair. Her face was neither beautiful nor unattractive but very square and strong with a jaw you could have hammered horseshoes on. The shapeless dun-coloured uniform gave no clue as to the figure beneath.

She was holding his passport between a finger and thumb as if she had just fished it out of a pile of dung.

"*Bitte*," she said. "It says 'Writer'. What sort of writer are you?"

"I am a film critic," said Charles nervously. "You know, *Kinema*."

"I know what a film critic is," she replied. "Empty your pockets."

Charles did as he was told. Wallet, handkerchief, a few coins, an embarrassingly greasy comb, keys and some extremely ancient ticket stubs for the Odeon West End. In his coat pocket he discovered he had a rolled-up copy of the latest *E:Go* which he had brought to read on the plane. He put that down on the table.

She immediately picked it up.

"What's this?"

"Er, the magazine I write for. See? My name's in there somewhere."

She flipped through the pages of streamlined fashion models and restlessly coiffed young men in clothes that wouldn't even figure on her dream list. She paused at a particularly provocative pose by a very young model in absurdly expensive jeans and nothing else, her androgynous breasts peeking from behind her loosely crossed arms.

"Who is this?"

"Uh, Kate Moss. She's the hot new model. In London."

"She is a child."

"Well, she's fifteen, actually. Or fourteen. I forget."

She folded the magazine and put it in a drawer.

"You cannot take this. I must confiscate it. It is decadent material and we cannot allow this kind of corruption in the GDR."

"Oh."

"How long are you staying in the East?"

"About three hours."

"Very well. Go now."

Slightly discombobulated, Charles left the building and walked on through into the eastern part of Friedrichstrasse. It was like stepping through a portal into another dimension.

Unlike the swarming, noisy roads of West Berlin, the streets were empty and quiet. Instead of the garish posters and lurid colours of advertising hoardings and billboards there was nothing but blocks of grey stone buildings. The silence was uncanny. It was like walking into *On the Beach*, as if all humanity had been wiped out.

But the sun was shining and he began to walk. He managed to find his way to a large square, marvelling at the huge buildings, and the way the magnificent architecture of the old ones jostled with the blank dirty-white Soviet-era office blocks and apartments. Christ, he thought, someone actually designed these.

He looked in awe at a car park filled with Trabants. They were parked in such orderly rows that their square outlines looked like a row of child's plastic bricks, lined up and ready for construction.

He wanted to buy something, a souvenir of the GDR, but wasn't entirely sure how to go about it. There must be shops, he thought. Even communists need to buy stuff.

Eventually he spotted a lone policeman standing at an intersection. He asked directions to the shops. The cop (if that's what he was) ignored him and walked away.

Finally he ventured into what looked like a department store called Centrum. He wandered around the aisles and tables gazing at the mass of dreadfully dull materials and ghastly manmade-fibre clothes on display. The women seemed to be all fat and listless. There were no men. Probably all working, he guessed. He bought a pair of red socks as a kind of joke souvenir for himself. At least I'll have something to remind me of the visit, he thought.

By some miracle, he found his way back to Checkpoint Charlie.

He arrived at the gate and walked through. As he was presenting his passport a door opened at the side and his formidable interrogator beckoned him inside. Oh well, he thought. Maybe she'll give me back my magazine.

She took him along a corridor and into a small office where she closed the door firmly. On the scuffed desk lay his magazine, opened at a fashion spread involving two men and three girls whose limbs seemed to be looped around each other.

"Anything to declare?" she asked. It was odd that she should use the very words employed by Customs people at British airports. It was almost like a parody.

"No," he said, before remembering his socks. "Well, just these."

He took out the crumpled paper bag and placed them on the table. She tipped the socks onto the magazine and moved them around with a stubby finger as if checking they were really dead.

She looked at him.

"Put them on."

"Excuse me?"

"Put them on. Now."

Thrown into confusion and finding his nervousness return tenfold, Charles took off his shoes and the socks he was wearing and slipped on the rough, scratchy red socks. They just about fitted him but he knew that after one wash they'd be fit only for a toddler.

"Now strip."

"What?"

"Off. Everything. Everything else. I must search you."

Oh shit, thought Charles. I'm going to be banged up in some ghastly hell-hole in the GDR and the Stasi are going to torture me with live electrodes and I'll never be seen again.

He stripped down to his gingham M&S boxers. Why oh why couldn't he have worn black trunks?

The woman looked him up and down.

"Those too."

He took a deep breath and removed his shorts, flipping them over his feet. He put his hands in front of his genitals and stood like a schoolboy waiting for matron to administer something unpleasant.

"Turn and face the wall," she instructed.

He did so, fear rising in him like lava.

There was a scuffling and rustling noise behind him.

"Now turn around."

He turned and gasped. She had stripped down to her underwear and stood provocatively before him. Her body was voluptuous and magnificent, her well-formed breasts straining against the material of her brassiere, a cleavage deep enough to get lost in. Below her waist, where her rounded abdomen curved down in a gentle incline, a pair of knickers barely contained the fertile growth of her pubic hair. Even in his confusion he couldn't help noting that she was a natural blonde.

Her underwear was exactly the same shade of red as his newly acquired socks.

"Snap," she said.

Beneath his cupped hands, he felt his cock start to stir. He pressed down hard, trying to hide what was happening. She approached him, her breasts swaying slightly in their flimsy packaging, and gripped him by the shoulders. She pushed him onto the desk and he fell backwards on top of the open magazine. He inadvertently moved his hands to stop himself from falling and his cock sprang up. Lying back on the desk, with his knees dangling over the edge, he was helpless, like an overturned tortoise. His feet encased in his red socks became very hot.

She reached behind her back, unfastened her brassiere and removed it, allowing her breasts the freedom they had so clearly desired. She rolled her knickers down her thighs and stepped out of them and climbed onto the desk above him, placing her knees on either side of his hips.

"Umm," he said. She slapped him lightly across the mouth.

He didn't say anything else.

She held his cock with one hand and guided it into her and seated herself on his loins. For the first time since he had set eyes on her, she smiled.

As she began to ride him, he could feel her cunt throwing off hot wet fluids that made him think he was in danger of being scalded. She bucked wildly and leaned backwards, almost breaking his cock off at the roots, before leaning forward again into a more comfortable position, and continued to ride him until he gave up all resistance and any thought for his immediate predicament and safety. He reached up to take her breasts in his hands and she slapped them away. She gripped them herself and began to squeeze and knead them, pinching the nipples until they glowed dark red.

There was nothing else for it but to allow himself to be fucked into oblivion. Resistance was futile. For you, Charlie, he thought, the war is over.

As she approached her orgasm she squirmed and rode him faster, shifting her buttocks from side to side. He could feel his own climax rising and hoped he wouldn't let her down by arriving at their destination before she did. He didn't want to be shot for dereliction of duty.

Her eyes blazing, she reached down and gripped his neck and banged his head against the wooden desktop as she came, groaning and growling deep in her throat. As she soaked him with her hot, flowing tide he let go inside her and slid into a semi-coma of pure, unfettered ecstasy.

He was in the American Sector when he came to his senses.

"Are you OK, Charlie?" said a voice he vaguely recognized.

One of the teenage punk girls was looking up at him with concern. Her two companions were behind her, chewing gum and giving him quizzical looks.

"Yeah, yeah. I'm fine," he said. His cock was sore and his head ached. But at least he was alive.

"We thought you'd got lost."

"No, I'm fine."

"So we came to meet you," she said.

"Very kind of you," he mumbled.

"You have to be a bit careful on the other side," she said. "We should have warned you."

"Well, I made it back."

"Yeah, and we wanted to show you another aspect of the city."

"Oh?"

"Yeah, we thought you'd appreciate a taste of Berlin hospitality."

"Great," he said. "Where are we going?"

"Back to your hotel room," she said with a wicked smile.

Charles couldn't believe his ears. Beyond resisting, he let himself be led away by the three girls.

"And Charlie?"

"Yes?" he whimpered.

"*Love* the socks."

The Red Brassiere

EllaRegina

Outside Pascal's bedroom window, erect nipples pressed against the glass. They shivered in the early hour crisp, waiting for him to awake, bucking towards the white duvet rectangle with a gentle persistent knock. Pascal's fingers, curved around his morning hard-on, idly synchronized their rhythm to the odd staccato.

As the sun rose over the quartier, a shadow edged across the stone facade of the grey building overlooking Rue de Ménilmontant, then fell through the panes into Pascal's room on the top floor where the patch of darkness landed on his face like a cloud blocking a piece of blue sky.

Pascal opened his eyes and looked towards the sound coming from the window. Paris was always grey to him, even though it was in colour. Now, suspended over the balcony and breaking into the black-and-white image, was a Red Brassiere – a buoyant arrangement of lace curves and negative space, alert and fastened, as if enclosing a body. The garment was animate, not clothesline-limp; it appeared to be levitating, like the velvet top hat hanging from the invisible fishing line above his bed.

Pascal considered himself a fine magician, though he had yet to make a woman disappear. He glanced around his bedroom. Everything was in order. The dove was quiet in its cage, under a canvas night cover. His props were in place near a battered green suitcase – scarves, card decks, a pile of rings. Near the door an arm emerged from the wall at the elbow, dressed in a navy-blue suit sleeve, hand extended as if to shake another, its fingertips holding his velvet cape and black cane.

His performance the previous night had gone without incident; he had been onstage as usual, standing in the dank, ancient, dimly lit Marais subterranea, twenty-five metres directly below a vitrined jelly-doughnut pyramid in a Jewish bakery, correctly guessing the identities of female audience members, prompted by spontaneous appearances of their names – a moving rash of line on foreheads – written slowly in his loopy handwriting.

Pascal got out of bed and opened the floor-to-ceiling window. He squinted up at the next building – a hand and forearm shaking out a grey rag. He looked down at the cobblestones – a black cat curled on the sidewalk, licking its genitals. The Red Brassiere moved aside. It was free-standing, apparently, not a snagged runaway specimen from the nearby *marché volant*.

Pascal stepped onto the balcony. The Red Brassiere bolted out of reach in a wide arc, then came closer, tentatively. It rubbed up against Pascal as if locked in his embrace. When he lunged for a shoulder strap it pulled away again. Not much for teasing, Pascal returned to his bedroom and closed the window, the Red Brassiere quickly following in a silent swoop, slipping inside before it shut.

Pascal returned to bed, unaware that the Red Brassiere was behind him. It flew up to the rafters, under the skylight, and angled downwards as if worn by a woman on a ladder. Pascal's erection resurfaced and he closed his eyes, resuming his morning routine, stroking himself with more than the usual intensity. The Red Brassiere descended from its lofty perch to investigate, placing itself squarely above Pascal's hidden hands. A perfume filled the room – that of Genevieve, an early love; the pungent grapefruit and cumin of her armpits, the private spices between her legs – and with it a distinct vision occupied Pascal's imagination: Genevieve, on all fours, his full cock in her mouth, her wine-stained lips encasing him.

As he pulled at himself the smell grew stronger. Pascal opened his eyes. The Red Brassiere swayed at his face, emitting a heat along with the unmistakable scent. It did a bob and a bounce. The duvet rolled back into a croissant and Pascal's pyjama pant buttons undid themselves one by one. His cock sprang out, shaking off his gripping hand, and disappeared into what felt like a mouth but was just empty space above a quivering piece of lingerie. The length of his penis came in and out of view as unseen lips slid over him. It was as if he were a figure drawing being erased and then re-sketched with the mouth's advances and retreats. His palms grazed the Red Brassiere's pebble-like nipple bumps. The fabric felt warm, inhabited. Pascal's head flushed as if wrapped in a feverish blindfold. His eyelids burned. The invisible mouth took him deeper, containing him completely. He rubbed until his magic lamp released its oil then relaxed, all muscles spent. The Red Brassiere collapsed for a moment, folded at Pascal's feet. He observed the silk and lace. On a shiny white label flattened at the inside, near the underarm area, a size number and style name were written in his loopy script: *90C Genevieve*.

As Pascal's empty cock lay in repose the word vanished from the satin tag along with any traces of Genevieve's fragrance. The Red Brassiere hovered motionless above the bed, as if waiting for a sign, a signal, an instruction.

Pascal enjoyed the company of women. Many many women – each one, one at a time. He was a sexual cartographer, leaving semen imprimaturs in bodies across Paris like inkblots on a map of the city. He had bedded women from every arrondissement, *in* every arrondissement, several times over. His erect cock had been a directional pointed throughout Paris as frequently as a *Vous Êtes Içi* map indicator. He could summon the chronicle of his roving carnal travelogue at will. Its various destinations were also the settings for his fantasies, both daydreams and nocturnal reveries.

To Pascal's highly developed sense of smell each woman was a snowflake – there were no two alike, even when they wore the same perfume. And of all the characteristics women presented to him their personal scent was the thing he found most arousing and the feature most indelible in his memory. He could recall the specific melodies of each one, the way a gourmand has the ability to detail a history of refined meal courses. And, despite the esoteric differences between them, they were linked by an irrefutable underlying aura of femininity as a given, an aroma which also varied but was fundamentally and ultimately similar, exhibiting the entire olfactory spectrum, from highly pitched to low and broad.

Pascal eyed the Red Brassiere intently and rewrapped his fist around his rigid cock. He closed his eyes and concentrated. The first woman to enter his thoughts was Delphine, the private tour guide who had fellated him in the artificial lake pooled beneath the Paris Opéra. Delphine liked to have sex in public or nearly so. She enjoyed being stripped naked except for a pair of high heels and a string of pearls. She favoured wearing a chef's toque during intimate relations and bought them by the half-dozen at a uniform store on Rue Turbigo. She wore Mitsouko – he could always smell her before he saw her.

Pascal tugged at himself with ferocity, conjuring Delphine from puffy hat to pointy toes, filling in more of her details with each hard stroke. He raised his eyelids. He was face to face with the Red

Brassiere, its cups enlarged as if supporting Delphine's abundant breasts, the bedroom smelling like a Mitsouko tornado.

In that moment Pascal understood that the Red Brassiere was both a *tabula rasa* under his control and an object that could hold him simultaneously under its spell.

Pascal spent the entire day in bed with the Red Brassiere as his travel companion. He plugged and played, repeatedly. With each change of character the Red Brassiere assumed specific dimensions and offered Pascal a particular scent; the label changed its size and name information accordingly. He journeyed the entire city without leaving his bed.

Noémie had persuaded the man taking tickets for the Eutelsat tethered in the Parc André Citroën to let them up alone. Once the dirigible halted 150 metres over Paris she bent over and Pascal entered her derrière. Noémie's dark hair smelled like roses. Pascal watched as the Red Brassiere showed its back to him – a narrow band of hook and eye – as he imagined Noémie. The odour of rosewater filled the room.

He and Agnès had visited the Panthéon forty-five minutes before closing. They'd positioned themselves against a column where Pascal could slide himself unseen inside her from behind and fuck her to the rhythm of Foucault's slow-swaying pendulum. All the while Agnès kept a straight face, so as not to betray what was happening. The Red Brassiere tilted almost imperceptibly from side to side like a slow metronome wand as it gave off Agnès' personal fragrance, a mixture of sex and tea tree oil.

Octavie was – appropriately – an accordionist who played beneath the arcades of the Place des Vosges. She and Pascal spoke about the perfect acoustics of the space then went for a pastry at Sacha Finkelsztajn on Rue des Rosiers. Afterwards, Octavie played Pascal's organ in private. She wore perfume made for babies. The Red Brassiere seemed to heave as if taking deep breaths while it replicated her bouquet.

Pascal went through his personal index of intimate sights and smells. He thought of the dark-skinned Sidonie (lilacs), whose long thin nipples echoed the dome tops of the Sacré-Coeur. He recalled Irène, into whose patchouli-cloaked nakedness he thrust until the houseboat on which she lived drifted away from its moorings. He remembered Odile, who had welcomed him inside her on all of Paris's thirty-six bridges (Chanel No. 5, thirty-six times). There was Eugénie, whom he had balanced on his cock for fifteen minutes in an automated street toilet, at her insistence (baby perfume with a hint of bleach). Clémentine gave Pascal a hand job at dusk one summer night in the centre of the labyrinth at the Jardin des Plantes. She smelled not of clementines but of lemons. Vignette took him in her mouth on a rented boat in the Bois de Boulogne, lying flat so that he appeared to be the sole passenger, rowing as slowly as he could to keep the craft – and Vignette – going. She liked the smell of his semen in her hair.

Pascal dressed and left his apartment. The Red Brassiere followed him down the building's spiral stairs in a corkscrew blur like a thrown party streamer. He stopped at the Bar des Sports for an espresso and a brioche. The Red Brassiere clung to his back, protected from onlookers, as he leaned against the zinc bar. He watched the twin peak line of red strap tops, like a child's drawing, reflected in the mirror. A boy of twelve or so was playing a noisy game of flipper, head down. Pascal paid for his breakfast and a few loose cigarettes and was on his way, the Red Brassiere at his shoulder. He picked up a newspaper at the kiosk.

As Pascal walked, the Red Brassiere played with him, evading his grasp when he tried for a strap, pulling a storey above, then falling down like a torpedo to reclaim its place beside him, each time smelling like someone else, a woman whose fleeting image had just made an appearance in his head because of something he noticed on the street, some *je ne sais quoi* suddenly noted, which struck him, awakened him, moved him – an object, a sound, a memory.

It began to rain. As its fabric soaked up the drops the Red Brassiere got richer in hue. Pascal unfolded his newspaper in an attempt to shield the garment from the elements. Before he could fully succeed, a series of umbrellas opened like black flowers, clutched in hands at the ends of extended male arms left and right, one after the other like a choreographed dance, offering the Red Brassiere dry passage. It hopped from the shelter of one to the next, for the three-block duration of the cloudburst.

They passed a lingerie store where the Red Brassiere stopped for a moment of camaraderie with the black and white models in the display window, worn by silently laughing mannequins, until Pascal sensed its absence and walked back for retrieval, firmly hooking his fingers around the elastic straps.

At the flea market the Red Brassiere admired its own reflection in an antique mirror, its nipples brushing the hard surface as if kissing itself.

Back at his building Pascal tapped in the entry code and opened the heavy green wooden door. As he pushed inside, the Red Brassiere broke free and flew to the top storey, hanging outside Pascal's bedroom window until he arrived himself.

The next morning there were already several people waiting at the bus stop near the Rue des Pyrénées. An old woman bumped headlong into the Red Brassiere as if it were invisible but the men stared at it, unblinking, and stepped out of its way.

They boarded the 96 which would deposit Pascal in front of the magic club. The bus driver made him pay two fares. It was standing room only. A man with a white cane occupied the handicapped seat near the door. The Red Brassiere loomed above his shoulder in the last available wedge of space, overlooking a blonde woman in a blue trench coat flipping the pages of *Oh Là!* magazine. The Red Brassiere appeared to be reading over the woman's shoulder.

"Marie-Blanche?" asked the blind man, arching his head in the direction of the Red Brassiere, "*est-ce que c'est toi?*"

The blonde looked at him quizzically. "We do not know each other," she said curtly.

"*Non – pardon,*" replied the blind man, "I was talking to *her,*" again motioning his eyebrows towards the floating garment.

"*Qui? Il n'y a personne içi, monsieur.*"

"*Oui!*" he insisted. "Marie-Blanche!" he continued in a singsong, "I was just thinking of you!"

"Idiot!" huffed the blonde, vacating her seat and pressing the red request button for the next stop.

Several women jostled the Red Brassiere as they left the bus, as if they did not see it. But Pascal sensed the sure and steady gaze of every male passenger – sitting or standing – their eyes, young and old; blue, green, grey, brown and hazel, uniformly fixed on the Red Brassiere, surrounding it from all spots in the bus. Pascal could see their erections, in various stages of angle development like a progressive geometry diagram, pointing at the Red Brassiere from their trousers, a collective of anatomical radii, as if the Red Brassiere were Étoile and the fleshy pointers radiating spokes of the surrounding streets – avenues Victor Hugo, Kléber, d'Iéna, Marceau, the Champs-Elysées . . . Pascal felt cornered. There was a quick change of plans: he would not go to the magic club today. At the next stop Pascal swiftly grabbed the Red Brassiere by a shoulder strap and hurried off, several pairs of men's hands trying unsuccessfully to snatch the delicate fragrant gossamer as it passed – like sticks thrusting at brass carousel rings in the Jardin du Luxembourg.

"Françoise!"

"Adèle!"

"Lucienne!"

"Mignon!"

The men followed Pascal off the bus in pursuit of the Red Brassiere, and with each block more added to the mob, the mass of hands and shouts expanding like a bubble. A dozen Chinese men practising tai chi in the Parc de Belleville got wind of the Red Brassiere, each man smelling a different woman. They tracked their noses and joined the rumble. Pascal broke into a sprint, the Red Brassiere an angel's wing above him, just clear of the men's grasps.

The Boulevard de Belleville was crowded, the market stalls taking up the shaded pedestrian median. The sidewalks on either side were filled with young women in hijab and shawls, men in kuftis and caftans – some of them shopkeepers in long blue smocks over their street clothing lounging in front of their stores, suitcase-sized bags of rice at their backs.

Pascal ran in and out of traffic, on and off the sidewalk. He passed an Algerian patisserie, a Cambodian sweet shop, a kosher restaurant, a halal boucherie, le Marché Franprix. A laughing teenage boy on a motorbike grabbed at the Red Brassiere, almost pinching it. The Muslim grocers in sandals, the kosher felafellers, the Chinese and Vietnamese restaurateurs, the African marketers – all relinquished their posts to follow the Red Brassiere, each one with a massive erection, plainly visible, no matter the type of costume. Some were openly stroking themselves, with one hand or two, under and over their clothing. The men yelled women's names in a Babelous ruckus:

"Minou!"

"Bashira!"

"Habiba!"

"Wei!"

"Hong!"

"Falala!"

"Batool!"

"Odile!"

"Halima!"

"Shoshana!"

"Li Li!"

"Malika!"

"Ming!"

"Haboos!"

"Sultana!"

"Mei Xing!"

"Kalifa!"

"Hua!"

"Tzipporah!"

"Jing Yi!"

"Magali!"

Pascal reached for his mobile phone and tried to ring the police. He managed the 1 button twice but the gadget slipped to the ground and into a sewer grate before he could press the final 2. Pascal kept running, through the market stalls and along the shops on the margins, passing the sidewalk vendors and the crowds browsing their merchandise – sacks of dried lentils and peas, fruits and vegetables, bolts of African fabrics, plastic crates full of mini-Eiffel Towers, flat displays holding cheap telephone cards. A man in front of the "Tout à 1€" store stuck out a foot to trip him, withdrawing it in the last second.

The lanes of the boulevard were filled with cars. There were few taxis, and those present had solid orange roof lights indicating passengers. Pascal crossed the street, dodging the moving vehicles. He found a narrow alley, the width of one person. A man carrying two pillows on either side of him approached from the opposite direction. Pascal managed to pass him but the pillows momentarily blocked the rush of the screaming crowd on his heels. There was a *pop* and a million white and grey feathers filled the alley. The Red Brassiere ricocheted off the walls in a zig-zag with the velocity of its forward propulsion. Pascal spotted a patch of grass beyond a decaying wooden fence matted with movie posters, away from the melee. He checked to see that the Red Brassiere was steadily behind him. It lurched over the barrier while Pascal scaled the structure and for a moment everything stood still.

The voices got louder, closer.

"Galia, I can smell you!" cried one man.

"Kumani, I know you're there!" screamed another.

"Mahmoode, I'm coming to get you!" bellowed a third in a caftan.

It was too late. The gang broke down the fence. The Red Brassiere gave off an odour of pure fear as its strap snagged on a café sign shaped like a top hat. One man scrambled onto the shoulders of another and dislodged the Red Brassiere, yanking it down.

Droplets of nervous perspiration formed on the piece of lingerie. It crumpled and shuddered, then disappeared from Pascal's view, obscured by the drapery of a sea of hands. One hundred erections pointed towards the Red Brassiere like hungry knives. The knot of men released an intense heat. There was the sound of cloth being ripped, and ripped and ripped again. When, finally, there was no more rending to be done, the men retreated, man by man, each with a shard of red lace or silk as bounty. Three had hooks, three more eyes. One man held the small decorative bow from the front, still intact like a perfect unmolested rosebud. Short scarlet threads covered the ground, twitching like organisms under a microscope. Pascal sat forlornly, abandoned by the crowd of men, holding the very last piece of the Red Brassiere, a tiny red sliver, off which hung the tattered label – now a blank scrap without a name – soiled with shoe scuffs, a discarded grape skin. There was no smell.

In that moment, one by one, brassieres were seized from every corner of the city. Women strolling each rue, boulevard and avenue felt themselves coming undone – unravelled – the intimate harnesses drawn out through their sleeves. In thousands of boudoirs, from the First to the Twentieth, drawers slid open, their contents unfolding and taking flight out of windows and skylights. A parade of fantasy lingerie emerged from the department stores. Street-market brassieres displayed on headless mannequins unhooked and dashed away. In Père Lachaise a half dozen Wonderbras were pulled from the hands of young female tourists about to fling the apparel onto Jim Morrison's grave. The gigantic brassiere of Babar's cousin Celeste vacated Jean de Brunhoff's book illustrations and took to the air like a magic carpet.

Women all over Paris stood at their windows – topless and stunned – watching the silent flight of silk, satin, lace and nylon in hues of white, yellow, orange, red, blue and green. One woman tried to loop a strap as it passed.

The brassieres formed tandem rows, filing through the streets and across the Seine, on and off bridges, the march of an invisible, scantily clad army; bounding on cobblestones in a rainbow arc, going up stairs, turning corners in a calico jumble. People seated in cafés dropped their glasses at the sight of the promenading spectacle.

The brassieres headed skywards in Pascal's direction, single file now, making dotted lines like trolley wires above the centres of streets, an airborne queue flanked by pitched rooftops. As they flew, other objects joined the mass in solidarity: a fleet of berets and handkerchiefs from Left Luggage at the Gare du Nord; bows from the hair of well-dressed children in the Parc Monceau and silk scarves from the necks of their nannies; one hundred paper airplanes set into motion by schoolboys in a hundred classrooms; pornographic passages ripped from paperbacks sold by the Seine bouquinistes; a stream of orphaned gloves from the Bureau des Objets Trouvés, forefingers all pointed towards Pascal. Rose petals fresh off the faces of women getting floral treatments at the hammam bundled with others plucked from the garland of florists and gardens woven through the city. Taxidermied birds left their gnarly branches at Deyrolles. Kites were whisked from small hands in the city parks. Braiding, embroidery, fans and parasols trailed from the Musée de la Mode. The stockings of Madeline's Miss Clavel stepped up – in two straight lines, sails detached from toy boats on the pond in the Jardin du Luxembourg and peacocks lost their quills in the Bois de Boulogne. In Père Lachaise, Isadora Duncan's last scarf slid out from her tomb like a long pink tongue while lipstick kisses unpeeled themselves from Oscar Wilde's headstone, hanging in midair for a moment like frightened spots off a cartoon leopard. Glittering in the evening's final light were sparklies from Joséphine Baker's last revue, followed by feather boas from the Moulin Rouge, hose and garters once belonging to Kiki of Montparnasse, and, running to keep up, Edith Piaf's little black dress and tiny shoes.

The various objects filled the skies and soared towards Pascal, sitting long-faced in the grassy lot, staring at the shattered Red Brassiere remains, both spirit and cock deflated. He welcomed the inventory, tethering everything together. Celeste's brassiere formed a hammock underneath him and he fell backwards into it as into a giant open hand. His cock immediately asserted itself, encouragingly resuscitated. Every item found its place as if part of a puzzle, creating a complex latticework. The craft took flight with Pascal at the helm using scarves and straps as directional reins. The toy boat sails spined the ship like dinosaur's scales, acting as rudders. A poufed string of chef toques encircled the assemblage, jewelled with bits of cotton candy from the Bois de Vincennes.

The multilayered, multidimensional sling caught the wind and Pascal was pulled aloft by the cluster, a helix pulled high over the beige-grey city. It began a large path of outward-moving spiral flight, mirroring the layout of the arrondissements below – a beignet, an escargot shell, a coiled snake.

Pascal veered away from Notre-Dame to avoid the low-voltage shocks intended for gargoyle-bound pigeons. Beneath him he saw the City of Light: the twinkling tiaras of the bridges spanning the Seine; the unbroken red and white meandering automobile beam stripe blurring the boulevards – a long slice of the Tricolour; the blinking green neon animation of pharmacy crosses.

From the Fontaine Stravinsky, Jean Tinguely's shiny red puffed lips blew Pascal a kiss. In unison, the light-sensitive windows at L'Institut du Monde Arabe closed their shutters like camera apertures – 240 portals momentarily constricting in a conspiring wink, giving him the gazes of 1,001 Arabian nights from sheathed feminine eyes behind a thousand burqas. The Tour Eiffel grew another six inches – the full extension of its phallic architecture – and spouted fireworks from its tip in a lusty salute.

Birds spiralled around Pascal, now moving like a rapid current, intoxicated by the fragrant tufted cloud trapping him in a tangled skein, a tempestuous tempting agglomeration. He stroked himself in sheer abandon as he inhaled the combined bouquets of the unseen women whose garments surrounded him, cradled him – women from past and future, known and not, spanning the centuries. Female names appeared on the hundreds of fluttering labels, writing and rewriting themselves in endless succession – like magic slates ad infinitum. Pascal laughed and sang while he alternately pulled at himself and guided the barrelling sphere. He rode the edge of light turning to darkness as night blanketed Paris. A golden swirl of shimmering Michelin stars, shot in a farewell booster from the restaurants below, formed a constellation around the flying contraption, raising it still further skywards, pulling Pascal up, upwards over the city – ascending far and away – his cock aimed towards the end of the sky.

The Antidote

Lisabet Sarai

'Yeah, I can get it – well, I can tell you where to get it. But it's expensive."

Merle and I huddled together on the bench in the fifty-second-storey roof garden of the New Sears Building where we worked. Even here, talking was risky. There were certainly cameras, but mikes were less likely out in the open.

"I've been saving. How much do you think it will cost?"

Merle named a figure four times what I had squirrelled away.

"Gads, Merle! It's not gold!"

"No, it's more valuable than gold. What do you expect? People will pay almost anything for the forbidden."

I blinked and looked away, not wanting her to see my incipient tears. After a few deep breaths, I thought I could continue the conversation without embarrassing myself. My friend wasn't fooled.

"You really want this, don't you, Lena?"

"More than anything." It was true. I'd been experimenting on my own, trying to reverse the effects of the government's anti-sex interventions, with no success at all.

No one knew exactly how the drugs were delivered. I went two days eating nothing, drinking only rainwater gathered on our unit's balcony. The fact that Jeff travelled so much for his job had made it easier. I just waited until he was away on one of his trips. Then, physically weak but determined, I hacked through the Net filters to one of the most notorious underground porn sites, hosted, according to Merle, in Kazakhstan.

Nothing. I felt nothing. I watched the contortions of the naked bodies, the penetrations and the climaxes, and felt no desire, only a vague, painful sense of loss.

I was second-generation post-Plague. I knew the history, but I didn't remember the Troubles: the millions of deaths, the riots, the massacres of homosexuals and prostitutes. None of it seemed real to me.

When the Council had introduced its libido-suppression programme to stem the spread of the virus, most people were enthusiastically in favor. Now it had become second nature. Society ran perfectly smoothly without the lubricant of lust. But I resented it. I wanted to know what I was missing.

Not sex. Of course Jeff and I had sex, once a month when our fertility booster package arrived. And our coupling was fabulous, as the Council intended, thanks to the hormone supplements and the stimulants and the fact that Jeff and I had been matched for compatibility long before we'd even met. When he was inside me, it felt as though we were a single being. I loved my husband deeply. That wasn't what this was about.

I didn't want societally sanctioned, procreationally focused, conjugal sex. I wanted to fuck strangers. Nobody used that word anymore, but that's what I craved. I wanted sex for its own sake, wild, extreme, dangerous. Sex with men – more than one man. Maybe even sex with women. And for that, I needed the antidote.

It was strange. My fantasies did not arouse me physically – the drugs prevented that – but I still continued to rehearse scenarios in my mind. I prodded the empty place in my psyche like someone would poke her tongue into the socket of a pulled tooth.

Merle watched me, sympathy softening her sharp features. "There might be a way for you to get it for free," she said, sotto voce. "If you're really desperate."

"How? I'm desperate, believe me. I can't stand it any longer."

"The clubs – some of them will give you the antidote without charge, if you agree to perform."

"Perform? What do you mean?"

"Put on a show for the clientele. Screw strangers on stage while other strangers watch."

I shivered. My stomach did a little dance. Could I do that? Did I dare? It might be the only way. I'd never be able to raise the sum that Merle had quoted.

"Tell me where to go," I whispered. "Who to talk to."

"I can set it up." Merle gave me a conspiratorial smile. "When do you want to do it?"

"Tonight." I swallowed hard. "Jeff will be back tomorrow and his next trip isn't for three weeks. It's got to be tonight."

★ ★ ★

The club was in a crumbling district of deserted warehouses, down by the lake. At some point the government would probably raze them to build modern, hygienic high rises, but right now there was no pressure. The population was recovering, but slowly. This space wouldn't be needed for decades.

I took the skytrain to the closest station and walked from there, my heart slamming against my ribs. I kept an eye out for Inspectors on the prowl, the alibi I'd concocted ready on my tongue. But the streets were empty, dark and silent.

I stumbled over the cracked pavement in my high heels. I didn't really have the right clothes for a sex club. Under my raincoat, I was wearing my shortest skirt, black, and a tight scarlet top with a scooped neckline. I had made up my eyes, painted my lips, and let my hair flow over my shoulders, but I still looked more like the customer service manager I actually was than a porn performer.

The stretchy fabric of my blouse hugged my breasts, massaging my nipples each time I moved. Tiny sparks sang through my body. The mere prospect of receiving the antidote seemed to have awakened my senses.

I stopped in front of a massive steel door at the address that Merle had made me memorize. This looked like it. There was no sign, of course, no lights, no sign of life. No bell or knocker, either. I wondered how I was going to get in.

"Name?" demanded a gruff voice, from somewhere above me. Of course they would have cameras – I should have realized.

"Lena." No one used last names in these places, according to Merle.

"Who sent you?"

"Sigmund."

"Let me check my list." After a moment, the door swung silently open on well-oiled hinges. Behind it was a giant of a man with a shaved head and bushy black eyebrows, carrying an LCD beam. His lips stretched into a grin, but his eyes cut right through me. "Welcome, Lena. I understand that you're part of tonight's entertainment."

"Um – yes, that's right." He closed the door behind me.

"Good. We can always use fresh blood."

My stomach did a somersault. I looked around. A vast dark space echoed above me. My guide shone the torch on a spiral stairway to our left. "Downstairs," he said. "All downstairs. The bar, the dance floor. The stage." My insides started to jitterbug as he took my arm. "Bolt's the name. Don't trip. They're steep."

I could feel his strength and, between my legs, a hint of dampness. No! Not possible! But perhaps the antidote was gaseous, something in the air we breathed together. I sniffed, smelling only damp wood, rust and lubricating oil.

There was another door at the foot of the stairs. It opened onto an expansive, low-ceilinged space, dimly lit with rosy light. Soft jazz played in the background, punctuated by sighs and moans. Couches lined the room. Some were piled with bodies, confusing tangles of naked limbs. Others had a single occupant, usually male, often fondling his penis while watching the couplings around him. I surveyed them, my prospective audience, curious and envious. I wanted to feel what they were feeling.

Bolt peeled off my coat and hung it in an alcove, then led me past an empty dance floor and the raised platform in the middle of the room, to the bar at the far end.

There were a few women, including one whose petite build and sharp features made her look a bit like Merle, if Merle had worn purple spiked hair and a nose ring. She caught my eye as I passed, giving me what I could recognize, even in my sex-suppressed state, was a come-hither look. My heart shifted into high gear.

"Sit."

The hulking proprietor poured me a shot-glass of brilliant green liquid. "Here. The antidote. Drink it in one gulp. It takes effect quicker."

I stared at the slightly viscous emerald concoction. Fear tickled the back of my neck. If I got caught with this, it would mean fines or prison or both. But I wasn't afraid of the Council. No, I was afraid of myself, of what this would do to the Lena I knew.

"Don't worry," Bolt growled, running his hand up and down my arm. "You'll enjoy yourself. I promise."

I closed my eyes, grabbed the glass, and tossed the contents down my throat. It was sweet and tart. I swore I could feel it, sliding down into my belly, coursing through my veins. I felt momentarily dizzy. Then a rush of heat swept over my body. My earlobes burned. My nipples kindled into burning embers. My cunt was suddenly molten.

"Wow!" I opened my eyes to Bolt's fiendish grin.

"Ah! Getting off already. Excellent." He leaned forward abruptly and grabbed my breasts, flicking his thumbs over the nipples. "Some people react stronger than others." Electricity arced from his hands to my pussy. "You've got fabulous tits, Lena." He pulled me off my stool and headed towards the central stage. "You should let everyone else appreciate them."

Before I could think or resist, we had climbed the three steps to the platform, which was furnished with a mattress and a couple of chairs. A spotlight clicked on in a corner, temporarily blinding me. Bolt stood behind me, his arms circling my body. He kneaded my breasts while he worked the crowd. I struggled not to faint from the sensation of his fingers digging into my flesh.

"Ladies and gentlemen, welcome to Club Lust. Tonight we have a special treat, a newcomer enjoying her first taste of freedom." He gripped the bottom of my jersey and pulled it over my head in one deft motion.

All eyes in the room turned to my suddenly bare chest. The heat of their attention brought a flush to my cheeks. My nipples contracted into throbbing bullets of needy flesh. Bolt pinched and twisted them, far rougher than Jeff had ever been. Liquid gushed from my cunt as though he'd turned on a faucet.

"Such fine, round, bouncy tits. Just looking at them makes me want to rub my cock in between them until I come all over her face. Don't you all agree?" The crowd murmured its assent. I don't know what excited me more, his words or the fact that simultaneously he'd unzipped my skirt and pulled it down to my ankles. Underneath I wore the red bikini briefs that had come with our last booster pack. They were soaked.

Bolt's hand dropped from my breast to cup my pubis. I shivered. My cunt clenched at the indirect stimulation as he brushed his palm over the wiry hair underneath the pseudo-silk. My clit swelled, hot, demanding. I arched my pelvis, pressing my sex more firmly against his hand. He wriggled a finger between my lips, pressing the fabric into my cleft. Pleasure shimmered through my whole body. Earlobes, lips, fingertips, nipples, clit, toes, all throbbed in time. I heard myself moan.

"Our little slut is very wet," Bolt gloated. "I think she wants to be fucked. Let's get a look at her cunt."

I heard a click beside my ear, then felt cold steel against my thigh. Fear flickered through me, almost indistinguishable from lust. Fresh blood, he'd said. But his blade sliced only through my panties, first at one hip, then the other. Still behind me, he pulled the saturated fabric out from between my thighs. The friction and the knowledge that I was being watched combined to pull me into the whirlpool of a minor climax. I slumped in Bolt's grasp, twitching helplessly. The audience responded with enthusiastic applause.

I was still shuddering when Bolt pushed me onto the mattress, face down, butt in the air.

"Spread your legs, baby. Show them all your hot, pink twat. Let them see your tight asshole. Tonight we're going to fill you up, kitten."

I obeyed, overwhelmed with shame and yet eager to display my slick lips and hungry holes. The embarrassment made me all the more excited. I wiggled my ass, trying to attract Bolt's attention. The watchers clapped in delight. Bolt landed a stinging slap on one butt cheek. Heat streaked through me, nearly triggering another come. He spanked me again. My cunt clenched, empty, ravenous.

"You need a cock, don't you? At least one. Well, here you go." A fat rod of flesh appeared in front of my face. "Suck this, slut."

I needed no further invitation. I couldn't wait to taste him. Bolt's cock was as monstrous as the rest of him, far larger than Jeff's, but I swallowed him whole. I ran my lips up and down his length, pressing my tongue firmly against his bulb at the apex of each stroke.

He tasted funky, as though he hadn't showered in a while, and a bit bitter. In my aroused state, I found him delicious. The mattress smelled of mould, though the sheet seemed clean. It didn't matter. My clit burned. My thighs felt sticky. My cunt drooled onto the makeshift bed.

My nipples ground against the rough cotton. All my senses were heightened, but they were sending only positive messages.

He swelled and jerked in my mouth and I eased off. I wanted him to come in my cunt, or spurt all over my back. So that everyone could see.

He knew. He pulled his dripping cock from my mouth and circled behind me. Grabbing my buttocks with blunt fingers, he pulled me open. With one jerk of his hips, he buried his swollen dick in my sopping pussy.

I screamed, shock, pain, pleasure roiling until I couldn't tell one from the other. He stretched my poor tissues to the point of tearing. I wasn't used to this. I tried to relax, to open to his invasion. He reacted by pushing deeper.

"Like it? Do you like my cock? Do you, baby?" He punctuated each question with a fierce thrust.

I couldn't answer. I could only moan as he rammed me, again and again. I heard moans from the audience, too, evidence that the show was turning them on. Another climax gathered on the horizon of my consciousness.

A picture of Jeff swam into my mind. Handsome, kind, responsible Jeff, the model husband. The model citizen. He'd never approve. He'd be shocked, maybe disgusted. I pushed away the guilt that threatened to dampen my pleasure. How could I have been satisfied with him? He worked closely with the Council, helping them implement their policies for the good of society. Whereas I was an outlaw, a horny cunt who got off being watched while strangers fucked her.

Bolt suddenly pulled his rod out of me. I clenched around his vanishing bulk. "I'm going to come all over you. To show everyone what a filthy slut you are."

The audience roared. His spunk showered down on me, a bitter, sticky rain. He smacked his cock against my butt, scattering the last drops of semen over my back. At the same time, he reached forward between my legs and squeezed my clit.

My body dissolved in a sea of mindless pleasure. I'd never known anything like this, not in the most ecstatic, intimate coupling with my husband. A thousand sensations flooded through me, washing away every thought. I was nothing but a whirling, trembling mass of flesh, tossed on currents of dark delight.

The convulsions slowly faded. My mind returned. I lay on my stomach on the mattress, thighs gaping, fluids seeping out of my still-swollen cleft. The buzz of conversation in the audience died away as I stirred.

"Ready for another cock, baby?" I would have thought that I was too exhausted, but my nipples peaked and my clit jumped at the question. "We've got one ready for you."

I looked over to the armchair next to the mattress. A wiry man with chocolate-coloured skin relaxed there, naked. His long, slender cock jutted up from his lap, straight towards the ceiling. He grinned at me, a bit shyly. Bolt pushed me in the man's direction. "Climb on, baby, and take a ride."

The spotlight followed me as I approached the stranger. His cock twitched; a drop of fluid welled at the tip. New desire surged in me. My hungry pussy tightened at the thought of taking him inside me.

I needed no lubrication. I simply straddled him and sank down slowly, swallowing his delicious length with my cunt. "Ah!" he moaned. "You're so wet and tight!" I gripped the hard rod inside me, sending spirals of sensation through my sex. He jerked in response, and tried to thrust, but in this position, I was in control.

He let me take him. I eased myself up and down his slippery rod, letting us both feel every inch of penetration. Letting the crowd see him glistening between my thighs as I raised myself above him, before plunging down again. He leaned forward, pulling one of my nipples into his mouth. Every time I ground my pelvis against him, he sucked harder, tightening the cord that linked that nub to the hard pebble at the apex of my sex.

My eyes were closed. I was focused on the sensations sparking through my body, that and the sound of the audience. The watchers were quieter now, only an occasional gasp or sigh. I felt the weight of their gaze, the urgency of their desire. Their lust fed mine. I wondered if I could ever enjoy private sex again.

A new scent reached me, a breath of the ocean in the smoky basement room. I opened my eyes to see the spike-haired woman I'd noticed earlier. She had placed one foot on the arm of the chair. Her skirt was crumpled around her waist. Her pussy gaped in front of me, glistening and bare, smelling of the sea. I could see the red pearl of her clit, nestled in those slick folds. I let out a deep breath and her flesh quivered. Saliva gathered in my mouth. I knew what she wanted, before she asked.

"Eat me, sweetheart. Eat me like you're starving."

I was starving. I had never felt such hunger. Still riding the black man's cock, I leaned sideways and grabbed her thigh for support. Then I stuck my tongue into the moist cavern that beckoned to me.

Her flesh was steamy, smooth, silky under my lips. I swept my tongue back and forth between her lips, swirling around her clit each time I reached it. She tangled her fingers in my hair, pulling my face deeper into her cunt. I heard applause. I gave up trying to ride the man underneath me, but he took over, his thrusts quickening as he began to lose control. I lost myself in the woman's slippery depths.

Every time she quivered under my tongue, I felt a sympathetic vibration in my own clit. I burrowed into her, licking, nibbling, sucking, frantic to make her come. I wanted to drown in her fragrant juices, to be carried away by her convulsions. I could tell that she was coming close. Her clit jerked at every contact. Her labia were plump and tender, trembling under my tongue.

All at once, I felt movement behind me. I heard the watchers stir and sigh. A slippery finger pressed against my anal sphincter.

No! I thought, tightening reflexively. The fingertip circled and massaged, relentless, nudging me open. My resistance dissolved. The pleasure was incredible, beyond anything that I'd felt that amazing night.

"I told you we'd take care of all your holes, kitten. Our clientele just loves a good DP. Don't you, people?"

The audience whistled and clapped. The fingertip vanished. All at once, I was torn apart as Bolt pushed his bulk into my loosened asshole.

I screamed, from the suddenness, the sharp pain of invasion, and the terrible pleasure that welled up in its wake. I could feel the man's monstrous cock, stretching my bowels, filling me to the point of impossibility. The desire to expel him was overwhelming. He would not allow it. Instead he ground himself into me, pushing deeper, augmenting the guilty delight. "Relax," he whispered in my ear. "Let everyone see how much you love being butt-fucked."

He started to thrust, timing his incursions to match the increasingly frantic jerks of the man in my cunt. When both cocks were at their deepest, the sensations were unbearably intense. I thought that I would split open, my body rent by the hard flesh of these strangers using me. The image only heightened my fever.

The man sitting in the chair began to grunt, obviously close to exploding. Bolt rammed into my ass with equal force. I writhed between them, lost in pleasure, a creature of total lust. The woman, whom I had momentarily forgotten, clutched my hair and dragged my mouth back to her cunt. I caught her clit between my lips and worried it like a dog with a bone.

Everything happened at once. The woman yelled, digging her fingers into my scalp. Salty fluid gushed into my mouth. The man below me arched his back with a groan, emptying his balls into the depths of my cunt. Bolt's cock, embedded in my rear, swelled to huge proportions and then burst, searing my bowels with his come. The audience yelled its approval. A whistle shrieked. A loudspeaker barked.

"Halt. Don't anyone move. You are all under arrest."

A woman screamed. A man whimpered. An Inspector's halogen spotlight blinded me. I came as everyone stared at me, convulsing helplessly, the cocks of two strangers embedded in my cunt and ass, the come of a third smeared on my cheeks.

The first thing they did was shoot us all up with drugs. Even before the syringe left my arm, I felt the dullness settle down, quenching the fires kindled by the antidote. I didn't care. They could remove the desire, but not the memories. I would never be the same.

Bolt resisted arrest. He managed to bloody one Inspector's nose before they jabbed him with a tranquillizer. I watched him slump into his captors' arms, almost too heavy for them to handle. My heart ached. The rest of us followed instructions like the sheep that we were. They separated the men and the women, then herded us into the backs of grey transports parked on the fractured tarmac outside the warehouse. There were no windows in the truck, and none in the bright, featureless room where we waited for hours after the raid. I was exhausted, and so sore I could hardly walk. I wore only my raincoat. The nylon clung to the sticky patches on my ass and back.

The purple-haired woman who had performed with me sat on a bench across the room, her face in her hands. I tried to catch her eye. I wanted to tell her not to worry. I wanted to thank her. But she never looked up.

Every so often, a stocky, stern-faced female Inspector would enter and call out someone's name. The people she took away never returned. Were they being interrogated, forced to reveal who had led them to the club? I swore to myself that I would never incriminate Merle. I didn't care what they did to me.

I only hoped that I could keep my resolution.

Time stretched on, monotonous and empty. I thought about Jeff. Would I ever see him again? Or would I simply disappear, the way Merle's husband had? And if I was released and returned to him, would he ever forgive me? Did I want him to? I wasn't ashamed. I couldn't pretend that I was.

I was too tired to worry for long. I dozed, despite the lights glaring overhead. I woke only at the sound of my name.

"Lena Brinks. Come with me."

I limped out after the guard, glancing back once last time towards the woman I had eaten to orgasm. She was watching me, her expression blank. How can they do this to us? I raged silently. We're human beings, not cattle.

The grey-uniformed Inspector led me to a steel door. She unlocked it and pushed me through. "Get out of here, you degenerate."

"What?" I didn't understand what she was saying.

"You're free to go. Someone bailed you out."

Merle? I thought. But how would she know? And where would she get that kind of money? I stood just outside the door, totally confused.

"Are you stupid? Move!"

I hustled down the corridor and through another, unlocked door at the end, into some kind of anteroom. Seated there, waiting for me, was Jeff. My bravado dissolved. Guilt swamped all my other emotions.

"Lena! Are you all right?" He looked genuinely concerned, not upset or angry at all. I allowed myself to feel a quantum of relief.

"Yes, but . . . how . . . ?"

"Hush, honey. We can talk about this later. Let's go home." He put his arm around me, pulling me into his familiar warm embrace. My eyes filled with tears, for the first time since I'd been arrested.

He led me to a rented hover-pod. I was shivering. He tucked a blanket around me and gave the autopilot our building coordinates. In less than fifteen minutes, we were home.

Jeff undressed me tenderly and tucked me into our bed. He didn't seem in any hurry to confront me with my transgressions. But I couldn't go to sleep without clearing the air between us. I wanted him to know who I really was. Who I had become.

"Jeff – I know that you must be shocked and hurt, that I'd go to that kind of place without you . . . It's not that I don't love you, I do – I just had to try it. I had to know . . ."

"You were magnificent, Lena."

"What?"

"I couldn't take my eyes off you. I came twice. I've never seen anyone so abandoned, so totally taken by lust. And you looked so gorgeous . . . so sexy with another man's prick pounding into you . . ."

"You were there? But why? How?"

"I often visit that sort of place. I don't usually participate. But I like to watch."

"What? Why didn't you tell me? Why didn't you take me with you?"

"I didn't think that you'd understand, or be interested." He looked young, sheepish. "I thought you'd be disgusted."

My guilt evaporated in the heat of sudden anger. "You should have told me. That's why you're away so much, isn't it?"

"No, no, my trips are real business, but I often . . . extend them. Add a bit of recreation on one end or the other."

"And the antidote? How do you afford it?"

"The government is not as incorruptible as they would like us to believe. I have connections. Access."

"You bastard!"

"Lena, please . . ."

I sat up in our bed, pushing away the hand that tried to stroke my hair.

"What about me? What about the rest of us? What about Bolt? And that poor woman who was with me? What about her? What will happen to her?"

"That's not my responsibility."

"The hell it's not! You pretend to be Mr Morality-and-Social-Conscience, all cosy with the Council, but do you care what you're doing? What you're supporting? All you want is to get your rocks off."

"That's what you wanted."

"Yes, but I have no power to change anything. You've got connections, or so you say. Maybe it's time for a change. The Plague is long gone. Maybe it's time the Council let us make our own decisions again, about who we fuck, and how."

"Maybe you're right. But the Council won't willingly give up the policy of lust-suppression. It makes us all so easy to control."

He caressed my cheek, then allowed his hand to drop to my breast. Dimly, I felt something stir in my crotch. "Seriously, hon, there's nothing that I can do."

"You can get hold of the antidote, right? For free?"

"Well, for favours. But yes, I can get it. Several of my project sites are at the drug factories."

"Let's start giving it away."

"Giving away the antidote? To whom?"

"Anyone who wants it." I thought about Merle. She'd take some. She'd pass it on.

"The Council . . . the Inspectors . . ."

"They can't arrest us all. They need us." I leaned forward and kissed him, trying to summon a hint of the passion I'd experienced earlier. Something flickered through me, a pale shadow of the lust I knew I was capable of. It was a tiny spark, but real. I thrust my tongue deep into his mouth, concentrating on that spark. Trying to fan it into flame.

Jeff returned my enthusiasm. The rich scent of his sweat tickled my nostrils, overwhelming his aftershave. I broke the kiss, searching his face. "Did you take it again? The antidote?"

"I managed to persuade the Inspectors not to inject me with the suppressors."

"Do you have any?" I wanted to feel it again – the rush of desire overwhelming every other emotion.

"Yes, but you should rest."

"Give it to me."

"Lena . . . it's dangerous."

"You said you like to watch. I'll put on a show for you like you've never seen." Jeff looked tempted. A lump was clearly visible in his crotch. I allowed my hand to rest on his bulk for a moment. He was like stone.

"Let me do this for you, baby." I was already on my feet, twirling my nipples with one hand, lightly brushing my cunt hair with the other. Even without the antidote, I felt the echoes. Maybe it wasn't chemical at all. Maybe it was all conditioning. "Let me perform for you. An audience of one."

His obvious eagerness made my cunt wet and my nipples hard. I began to stroke myself, marvelling at the sensations awakened by my own touch. His breathing quickened as I spread my folds. Now he could see my glistening lips and the dark cavity they flanked. If he looked closely, he might notice my flesh quivering.

"Want to watch me fuck myself?" I bent over, showing him my ass, slipping one finger into each hole. Both my cunt and my anus were sore and stretched and still wet. Memory of my double penetration blazed in my mind. I struggled to stay standing. I needed to follow through with this. For myself. For him. For all the rest of us poor souls.

"Yeah . . ." Jeff could hardly get the words out. I looked at him between my spread thighs. His cock sprouted from his lap, pale and obscene. "Show me, baby. Show me how nasty you can be."

A thrill surged through me. I frigged myself, pushing back the orgasm, wanting to make it last. Wanting to please my audience, my husband and yet a stranger. Afterward, maybe I could convince him that we had to do something. I, at least, wasn't willing to give up what I'd found.

Jeff yelled, spraying his come across my butt. I let go and let my climax take me, not as intense as the fury that had possessed me on the stage at Club Lust, but still enough to turn me into a twitching pile of limbs on the carpet. A good start.

Jeff sank down next to me, cradling me in his arms, murmuring incoherent endearments. I smiled to myself in satisfaction.

The Council had done a better job at matching us than they'd ever guess.

Skinheads

Jacqueline Applebee

I was only a little girl when I started following the fascists home. I didn't know what that word meant back then; I just knew that's what people called the gang of skinhead white boys who walked through Belmont Park, scattering all in their path. I guess it was the power they seemed to radiate that snared me: the lean but muscular legs and arms, the arrogant, sneering faces. I loved the way they used to stare at people, intimidating anyone who came close. North London in the 1970s was not the healthiest place to be a black child. At that age I never appreciated the danger I put myself in every day after school. I didn't know that the white boys I was attracted to hated people like me. In fact they hated just about anyone who wasn't like them. I only knew that my first stirring of desire for the opposite sex sparked at the exact same time when most boys at school wore the worst fashions ever seen. I was surrounded by swathes of beige nylon trousers, polyester shirts and stripy school ties. The skinheads dressed differently. They wore tight white shirts, tighter washed-out denim jeans held up by black braces. But the thing that got me scurrying around behind them, when sense told me to stop, was the footwear. Pairs of brightly polished Doctor Martens would stomp ahead of me, disappearing out of sight to where my little brown legs could not follow. Ever since then, I've hankered after boots with at least fifteen holes.

I heard things. I saw the bruises, the smudges of red over fists. People told me to stay away from them; teachers grew concerned that I would try to exact some kind of childish revenge for the way the white boys treated the black ones. I was a tiny girl. What could I do? Besides, the way the skinheads treated the black boys was no different from how the black boys treated most black girls.

As an adult I still found myself craving skinheads. I'm no longer a little girl – even barefoot, I'm as tall as most guys I know. I soon discovered gay men who wore outfits identical to those that the fascists sported back in North London. I saw people reclaim the look, the tight lines, the shaven heads and the tattoos. But to me, it was always about the white boys strutting around as if they owned the whole bloody world.

My desire led me to Camden, to a warehouse where I had arranged to meet a friend of a friend, called Stuart. I was also to meet his boy, which was the real reason I was hanging around with the tramps and tourists on a hot Saturday afternoon.

Stuart, a tall solid man, met me by the stairs as I sheltered in what little shade I could find. He wore a black leather kilt, and boots the colour of blood. He looked me up and down before he held out his hand. I gave him the agreed money – a clutch of notes in an envelope that he counted quickly in the shadow of the stairs.

He turned to me, speaking in a low voice. "I'll not have my boy marked in any way."

I sighed. "Is this little talk necessary?"

"I know what you women are like with all that cutting business."

"I've got no interest in that."

Stuart looked at me a moment longer before he inclined his head. I followed him. I could see up his kilt as he walked ahead of me, but it was his boots that held my attention.

Stuart's boy stood in a corner of a large dusty room. He looked nervous. Like Stuart, he was tall with a shaven head, in his early twenties I assumed. But unlike Stuart, this boy wore bleached denim trousers that stretched tight over his thighs. Stress lines in the fabric crossed this way and that.

"He'll do just fine." I put my large bag down.

"I'll be over here if you need me." Stuart pointed to a single chair against the wall near the door.

"You're staying?" That wasn't part of the agreement. I blew out an annoyed puff of air. I wasn't going to start arguing about it now. "He got a name?"

"I'm Darren." Stuart's boy looked less nervous now, more pissed off at being addressed like that by a black woman.

I smiled, took a step closer to the young man. He swallowed, looked away for a moment. I ran a hand over his thin belt; I would have preferred him to wear braces, but it would have to do. I hooked my fingers around the leather, pulled him to me. Darren grunted, but said nothing. I held his hand, pressed it to my jeans, to where the harness I wore beneath sat snug against my skin. I knew he could feel the buckles and rings when he smirked at me.

"Are you one of them chicks with dicks?"

He barely said the words before I smacked him hard across the mouth. "Excuse me?" I asked politely.

"Shit!" Darren touched his lip, which was already starting to swell.

I raised my hand once more. Darren flinched, looked to the corner where Stuart was. I felt a stir behind me, saw a shadow move on the dusty floor, but it retreated after a moment. I'd learnt this little dance from years of watching older boys intimidate younger ones. I'd memorized the way that force could be used – not in excess, so as to attract unwanted attention, but just enough to get your point across.

"Take them off." I stroked down his torso for a brief moment before I stepped away. I watched as Darren peeled off his tight top.

All the times I risked life and limb by creeping into the boys' changing rooms at school finally paid off. I was no longer a little girl peeking around corners to see glimpses of flesh. Today, I was getting the whole damn show.

Darren had a smattering of hair over his tiny nipples. Blond wisps collected in a line down the centre of his stomach, down to the tops of his pants where it got darker. He reached for the laces on his boots.

"Keep those on."

"I can't get my pants off if I keep them on," he complained.

"Do yer best, Darren," Stuart called out. I could have done without his input. I wanted the boy to concentrate on me, not his old man.

I unzipped my jeans, and then bent to my bag where my black dildo lay among a variety of toys and tools. It only took a moment to fasten it to the harness I wore.

Darren took several steps away when he caught sight of my silicon erection. "You're never going to put that thing in me!"

I heard Stuart sigh, along with the scrape of his chair on the hard floor. He stood beside me, peering down at my dick. "I've seen bigger," he smirked. I gave him a look, and put my hands on my hips. Stuart raised his hands, stepped away.

I returned to Darren, who was now pouting. I slid his belt out of its loops. He wriggled, looking uncomfortable, embarrassed. I wasn't about to make things any easier for him.

When I shook my head, he visibly drew himself up to his full height, puffed out his chest. It took all my concentration not to laugh at the spectacle.

"Bitch, please," I said with a smirk.

"She called me a bitch!" Darren squeaked in complaint, looking in Stuart's direction.

"Must I put up with this?" I asked out loud. "Do I have to request a refund?"

Darren stilled. His hands returned to his pants, which he pushed down with effort until they lay bunched around his knees. Even with the drama-queen attitude, he was still my living, breathing, wet dream.

"I think I'll take you up against the wall."

Darren shuffled to the nearest wall, his clumsy movements disturbing the dust into little blooms. I followed him, fingering the dildo I wore. I rolled a condom over my silicon length. I could feel the lines of sensation travel up my body from my clit to my breasts; electricity that was so intense and sharp, it was physically painful. However, I tended to enjoy pain – whether giving or receiving, I always lapped it up.

When I reached the boy, I was buzzing, burning up with anticipation and need. I braced my hands on either side of his head, rubbed myself over his back, over his bare arse that had a little tattoo on it: a St Andrew's flag. I lost myself in simply feeling his hot body beneath me. My dildo prodded his thighs, the curve of his arse cheeks.

"I'm ready," Darren said.

"I'm sure you think you are." I stretched around to his front, felt the hot burn of his erection on my palm.

"Go on then, do it," he hissed. "Just do it."

My little bottle of lube sat in my back pocket. I applied a liberal amount to my fingers, and then pushed one between his cheeks. I circled around, enjoying the sight of him writhing against the wall. I stepped back slightly, and then with my free hand, I slapped his arse, making him jump with surprise. I spanked him some more, steady beats that turned his white boy skin a rosy red. When I returned my hand to his cock, it felt harder, hotter.

"Now you're ready."

Darren whimpered. The sound of surrender made my nipples tingle. I wanted to hear him make more noises like that.

The first slide of my cock into his body was a sucking squelch. I breathed out along Darren's neck, exhaling the stored-up passion and want that had stirred inside me all those years ago. I pushed further, implanting myself inside the boy. My feet were unsteady. My hips moved of their own accord. My head span. He didn't have to do a thing to surrender his power. It leapt off his skin, dribbled with the sweat that ran down his back. I licked around his throat, pressing teeth to the flesh that was stretched tight. I wrapped my arms around him, possessively circled his body with mine.

"Please," he whispered into the wall. He arched up against me. I understood of course. I had power of my own. I brought down my hand against his arse once more. He shuddered beneath me, bucking slightly as I slapped him again and again.

A movement to my left made me look up, gasping, into the eyes of Stuart. His kilt was held up by a large pin. He grabbed his cock in his fist, stroking it hard and fast. He nodded at me. Knowledge and power combined into a potent aphrodisiac as I mirrored his movements with my own. I circled my hand around the boy's cock, pulling and stroking in the same way that Stuart touched himself. Darren leant back against me, his weight threatening to push me over. I pressed him back against the wall fully, continued to jerk him off as I thrust inside.

"Shit!"

I don't know which of the men swore out loud, but warm come erupted over my hand a moment after. Stuart squeezed his eyes shut, and then he came too, spraying his boy with thick streaks of white.

I breathed deep. My clitoris sang with pleasure, even though I hadn't come yet. That was something I'd do later when I was alone at home. My orgasm was a powerful moment that I wasn't about to let these guys see.

I slid out of Darren's arse carefully. He winced and squeaked with every movement until I was free of him. He sagged against the dusty wall, sticky and sweaty. He didn't look so tough now, although his boots were still impressive. I pulled the spent condom from my dildo, threw it down on the dirty floor. I felt my own power surge within at what I'd done. Somewhere inside me, a little girl jumped for joy.

"Will you be wanting to make this a regular arrangement?" Stuart's voice was raspy, breathless.

"Make him wear braces next time. I don't want to see the belt again." I sounded hoarse too.

"Yes, ma'am," Stuart said with a smile. "That's not a problem at all."

I straightened myself out, picked up my bag, and left without another word. But as I descended the metal stairs, and strode out into the bustle of Camden on a busy afternoon, I felt like I owned the whole bloody world.

New York Electric

Cara Bruce

I got my very first real job before I even graduated college. I was excited, thrilled even. I was supposed to start right after school ended and I couldn't wait. This was the way it was supposed to be: you went to school and got a job. I believed that my life was about to finally begin. I had new grown-up clothes which made me feel fabulously chic, even though looking back now they were cheap and plain, like playing dress up, and not even very well. That first job was in white-bred Connecticut, proofreading science journals. It was horrible, tedious work. I had to sit in a room, stark white and empty except for a single table which held an imposing stack of reference books, each of them thicker than the last. By the end of the day my head would be swimming with words, thousands and thousands of words, like tiny black ants, marching to a militant beat across my brain. It was boring, and I dreaded it more and more each day. After the first day my eyes were tired and after the first week I was depressed. I could hardly stand it. I felt trapped; walking into that blank white room was akin to suffocating. It didn't take long until I knew without a shadow of a doubt that this wasn't for me.

Each new day sucked another piece of life from me. I couldn't understand why people fought for jobs like this, how they could give forty hours of their lives each week to doing tasks that would only make someone else money. How they could give their lives to doing something they didn't care about, to go through life not creating something, not feeling passionate about something, not loving every moment of every day. I watched them hurry to the bars as soon as five o'clock hit. I questioned a society where alcohol was the biggest thing people had to look forward to; a society where boredom and unhappiness were so accepted, even fought for and sought after.

I suffered through it for almost a full month. I longed to be back in school and missed the freedom of being encouraged to follow creative and artistic pursuits. I already knew that parts of me would die if I continued along this route. And then one glorious day, my friend Dee called. She had been my film partner in college. We had made three movies together, two narratives and a documentary. She called to tell me that she had got a job as a production assistant on a movie set and she was sure that if I came to New York to join her I could get one too. It sounded like a great idea, and even though I wouldn't be paid I had some money saved and Dee and I would share a room and all of our costs. But the best part was that it was outside. It might not have been the most intellectual work, at least not on paper, but I had already discovered intellectual work that looked good on paper could be incredibly boring. And more than anything, that monotonous month had shown me that I hated to be bored.

So I told her I was coming and I quickly gave my notice and packed my things. The next day I took the train back to my parents' house in Virginia to drop off my work clothes and get clothes proper for unpaid grunt work. Dee and I didn't have a place to live yet, but we did have a few weeks until the movie started. I borrowed my parents' car, a crappy Chevy Celebrity, and drove by myself into New York City. This time I was convinced that my life was finally going to begin. No more false starts; even if this didn't work out, at least it would be something worth remembering.

Dee and I got every paper and made call after call, searching for a suitable place to live. We walked for miles, up and down the city, checking out each and every room, of which there were few. We talked up bartenders and waitresses, college students and professors; we woke up at 5 a.m. to be on the street when the *Village Voice* was dropped off, we tried begging and bribery, and we finally got a few leads on possible places for rent. We saw an efficiency apartment in Hell's Kitchen that had the bathtub in the kitchen. It wasn't even big enough for us to be in the same room at the same time. To get any privacy one of us would have to stay in the bathroom, a tiny room with just a toilet; to wash your hands you also had to use the kitchen. But even in the bathroom you weren't actually alone, cockroaches scattered each time the single yellow light bulb was turned on and something scurried across the floor each time it was shut off.

We saw a five-floor walk-up railroad apartment in the Lower East Side. Our lungs and sides stabbing with pain by the time we reached the top-floor apartment but we still considered taking it. At least until we went out that night; walking out of the building we were caught in a fluid stream of junkies. It was like a zombie film, but instead of brains they were searching for dope. Winding lines formed at burned-out buildings. A burly man in a worn leather jacket stood guard at every corner, crossing guards directing the dope fiends to the proper spot, to their own personal place of safety. You got into line, then when you made it to the front you handed one guy your money and he passed it off to another kid, then he would jerk a hanging rope, the number of yanks telling the boy above what you were supposed to receive. The rope was attached to a can which was hoisted up to the second or third floor, they put the glassine baggies of dope, marked with stamps or skulls or names like Redrum, into the can and lowered it back down. Even the drug dealers understood branding. They were marketers as savvy as Pepsi or Coca-Cola, an old drug for a new generation.

We watched as the drug addicts pushed up their sleeves to show their track marks, proof that they weren't cops, desperate badges of tainted honour. We also watched them scatter like rats in the light whenever the cops did appear. Rumour was that once in a while the police would load up all of the junkies into a wagon and drive them around until they were sick or drop them far uptown in Harlem or the Bronx. It was probably true; there wouldn't have been enough room in the Tombs to hold them all.

We watched them slink into abandoned, boarded-up buildings after they scored – dirty shooting galleries where diseases spread like rumours in a high school. It was a bit scary and depressing but it was also strangely thrilling. Simply walking through those night-time streets was a rush of crazy adrenaline, a drug in itself. I remembered books like Burroughs' *Junkie* and I wondered if he too had walked these streets, scored in these same buildings, and in a sad, twisted way, it was almost glamorous to me. Of course I didn't know the truth, couldn't know the truth. That would come years later.

But when we went to look at our apartment we saw rats, large and fierce, crawling out of a gigantic hole in the foundation of the building. We saw a woman, skinny as a rail, her jutting hipbones and pointed elbows poking out of her, squatting on the sidewalk and taking a shit right in front of our front door. We hesitated, but after speaking to a weathered man who perched like a gargoyle on the front steps and learning that the apartments were robbed almost weekly, we finally decided against renting it.

We were staying at Dee's grandmother's apartment, all the way up the East Side at Ninetieth and York. It was a typical older woman's apartment. The plastic-covered couch folded out and we shared it;

by morning we both had rolled into the crack, stuck together in the heat. She had a window air-conditioner unit that she refused to use; instead she preferred shaking her head and complaining about those crooks at Con Ed. We stayed there for a few weeks until a friend of mine from back home called and said she heard I needed a place to stay. She lived in a studio apartment in the East Village, right on St Mark's Place between Second and Third Avenues. We walked all the way downtown and met her that evening. An hour later we had signed her sublet lease and made plans to move in. For almost two weeks we shared a studio apartment on St Mark's. It was a very close fit. Lou Reed used to live in our building and every Saturday morning tour buses would pull up out front and the entire bus would empty, necks tilting, cameras clicking and the entire crowd collectively oohing and aahing, between asking each other who this Lou Reed had been, and if he was famous.

We would sit on the balcony and throw extra eggrolls at the punk rock bouncer of Coney Island High. I loved that apartment. New York in the early 1990s was a much different place than it is now. It was dirty, gritty, real. Today you will see well-dressed people eating at chic cafés, but back then it was homeless kids and heroin addicts, artists and beautiful androgynous boys and girls. It was alive; the very streets pulsed with danger. Every night was like dipping your toe in quicksand, a little too far and you could feel how easy it would be to be sucked in, warm and smooth, enveloping you like a fleece blanket, seducing you deeper and deeper. We weren't there long. During that second week her other roommate came back from her European vacation months early and we were, once again, homeless.

Finally, we lucked into a two-bedroom apartment on Seventh and D when two junkies overdosed and died, their bodies undiscovered and decomposing around the stained vinyl kitchen table. At one point it had been a bright and cheery yellow, the top was now nicked and scarred, gouges had been violently spooned out of it. We got the apartment for a great price, an amazing price actually, and all we had to do was clean out all the shit they left behind – including a drawer full of used hypodermic needles and a closet floor of clothes that stuck together and smelled as if they had never been washed.

My friend, Dee, and I moved in before the place was completely clean. We found old letters, photographs, and a large, brown spatter of old blood behind the bed. Underneath the bed frame was a collection of dried boogers. Rotting food made opening the refrigerator more a dare than a domestic event. It was depressing and disgusting, I had done heroin but not like this. I had snorted a bit here and there but I had never shot up and didn't understand what really being a junkie actually meant. This apartment was my first taste of the reality of that lifestyle, and even with the evidence surrounding me I still neglected to accept it.

Dee and I had already started working on our first film set. Not Hollywood film sets but independent guerrilla-style film sets, the kind with no money. These are the people you see running from transit cops and using stolen shopping carts as dollies. It was guerrilla filmmaking at its finest. To a girl fresh out of college, not yet skilled in the ways of the world or the ways of men or love, was incredibly romantic.

Just as Dee had promised, the first job we got was as production assistants or PAs. We worked our asses off for no money, just paper plates groaning under the weight of all the carb-heavy food from the craft services table. But we had an idea, we would specialize, learn a skill. So Dee attached herself to the grips, putting together scaffolding, and building things, and I began training as an electrician. I loved it. There was a beautiful, tall, thin, mulatto boy named John, who wore T-shirts boasting little-known punk bands, and shorts with combat boots. It took me just a week to convince him that I was worth keeping around, that I could do the job. Finally, he took me under his wing.

He taught me how to put up scaffolding, how to adjust lights, how to create shadows. He taught me how to tie in to live power lines and steal electricity. This was the biggest rush. You attached metal alligator clips onto live electric wires. You were supposed to stand on a rubber mat while someone stood behind you with a thick, heavy wooden board. If you were sucked into the power current they would have to hit you really hard and knock you out of it. I got shocked a few times, but I never had to be whacked across the back with that impending piece of plywood.

My hands were small and I was unafraid. Back then I wasn't afraid of anything. I would walk into the heart of Alphabet City at any time by myself and buy whatever illegal substance I wanted or thought that I needed. I did things that now make me cringe with fear and self-awareness. I climbed down an elevator shaft to lay cables, mice and rats crawling over my feet. I hung off a broken statue with one hand, twenty feet in the air, to hide the thick, black cable. I didn't care. Every day was an adventure, and every new experience a dare to be accomplished.

Strangers pointed at the tiny girl buckling under the weight of the bulky, heavy lights. I squeezed through chained doors and cracked windows to get into locked rooms with beckoning electrical boxes. Often I was the only one who could fit. People were impressed by my fearlessness, my ability to take everything in my stride. I used to have dreams, night after night, about winding cable, feet and feet of black cable, rolling it around my arm until it was a huge, thick roll of dead power.

There was something thrilling about working with electricity. It was alive, dangerous. Electricity always has to be balanced. You have to measure, to make sure that one part of the set isn't using more than the other. That meant you had to lay cable evenly, plug the right paddle cords into the right boxes. If the balance was off you could end up with a power overload, and either no power at all or a fire – the type of fire that wasn't even afraid of water.

Making a movie is all about light. It's about capturing light, manipulating light. You use light to suggest what time of day it is, to set ambience and feeling. Lights on a film set are huge and bulky. They're heavy, you put them on stands and point them at anything that needs to be illuminated, uncovered. Once they are set you can place barn doors on them, a metal box with "doors" so you can close them to cut the light, or keep it from shining on a certain part of the set. Scrims are also used to cut the light; different size scrims allow you to control how much light you cut. Gels are used to change the colours, blues and oranges to create day and night. I'd put on my heavy, insulated work gloves and eagerly climb up the metal scaffolding. I'd be sitting on top, queen of the city, waiting to make the adjustments to my big light as soon as the director of photography, or John, was ready to instruct me.

I also drove the film truck, packed with expensive equipment, because no one else wanted to. It was hard driving a big rig through a crowded city, making wide right turns and avoiding pedestrians. Road construction was an especially irritating and terrifying event.

I was the only girl electrician most of the other grips, gaffers, and crew hands had seen. They laughed at me, running around making sure everything was in place, but they stopped laughing when I lifted forty-pound lights and placed them expertly on top of a stand the size of my finger or moved around a hundred-degree light with my bare hands because the director couldn't wait. I impressed them all, but the only one I really cared about was John.

On a typical film we'd work three weeks of days and one week of nights. Each day was twelve to sixteen hours of work. We worked all summer, sweating under the hot sun and even hotter lamps. I'd get home and wash off a thick, black layer of dirt and grime, the city itself having transferred to my skin. I hated getting stuck sitting on a set when the cameras started rolling because you'd have to be perfectly quiet. It sounds glamorous but it was horrible. If you were stuck in a squat, then in a squat you'd stay, whether your legs began to ache before falling asleep or not. We'd stumble home, backs bent and shoulders burning, shuffling our feet all the way to our beds. Then we'd wake up at 4 or 5 a.m. and do it all over again. Leaving our apartment in the thin darkness of the morning and returning in the thicker, blacker darkness of night. Our lives were nothing but the film. Films we would never see, films almost no one would ever see. The crew members became family, the actors distant cousins who made you slightly uncomfortable every time they walked into the room.

On the weeks that we worked nights it was a mad hurry of doing laundry, going to the bank, and it was the one week that we actually had to buy groceries. The rest of the time we'd simply fill our backpacks and Tupperware containers with lasagna, baked ziti, and everything else in the pasta family that the creative craft services could think of to feed us. We'd say to ourselves that we would have time to spend with ourselves, that we would go to museums, get some culture, read a book, but usually, starting around two in the afternoon, we'd find our way to the Holiday Cocktail Lounge.

The Holiday was the diviest of dive bars. It was always dark in the Holiday, no matter what time it was. Sad, dingy Christmas lights hung year-round over the big mirror behind the bar, plastic palm trees from a celebration that was long since forgotten were still pasted on that mirror, their corners lazily peeling off over the years. The big oak bar took up the entire right side of the establishment, a few cocktail tables littered the left, and in the back were two tattered red vinyl booths, and a jukebox. The same people sat at the bar day after day, lonely men and women who were older than they looked, hands shaking as they lifted that first blessed drink of the day, extras from a Bukowski book, perfectly cast for their own never-ending dramas. The bartender was nice enough; he looked the part with his shocking white hair, passing his days polishing glasses.

John and I would duck in, a dark respite from the brutal heat of a summer in the city. It was always cool in the Holiday; in here, time crawled. We'd stop at the bar to order $2 watered-down vodka cranberries in tall, thin glasses with even thinner straws. We'd stand side by side at the bar, our shoulders touching, and even that faintest touch bringing back the electricity. Then we'd head to the back, again side by side, and each time our legs touched it was a surprise. John would play the jukebox, the same songs over and over. "Satellite of Love" by Lou Reed and "Blank Generation" by Richard Hell were my favourites and to this day they both take me back there.

We'd talk and laugh and make plans for the next movie we'd work on. John always promised to take me with him. It was in the Holiday that we first kissed. John took my hand, running his thumb back and forth over my palm, his touch inspiring me. He pulled my hand close to him and leaned in and kissed me. His lips were strong and his breath tasted faintly acidic like cranberries. We held that kiss for as long as we could and when it was over he pulled back and we looked at each other. We had wanted this for so long, skirted around it for so many days until the tension itself had become palpable, sexy. I bit my lip and lowered my eyes and he lifted my chin with his hand. He smiled at me and we kissed again before we were interrupted by Dee and two brothers, Jorge and Mikey, who worked with her as grips. They slid into the booth with us, unaware of what had just happened.

We were all excited, that night we were shooting on top of the Brooklyn Bridge. I had never been up there and couldn't wait to see a new view of the city. John and I had to pick up the generators so we took off early. Once we had them we met everyone at the staging location at the base of the bridge. It was a strange day, the air was quivering with tension; in California they would have called it earthquake weather but in New York it is a rare feeling for summer. It was more like Halloween – that spooky impending feeling you can't explain yet you can't shake.

The entire crew and all of the actors started walking up the ramp to the bridge two by two, like the animals ascending into Noah's ark or little children attached by that invisible bond of the buddy system. Low conversations drifted back to John and me as we pushed the generators ahead of us. Dee and Mikey each took a corner and, laughing, we made it up the ramp, calves aching as we pushed one leg in front of the other. Finally we made it to the top. New York, alive and buzzing, a million lights each promising a million stories, shone back at us; on the other side was Brooklyn, darker, it appeared almost naked – the strong silent type compared with its dazzling show-offy sister.

Like the starter pistol at a race or the quick snap of a finger, the director clapped and off we went, struggling to get light stands and lights set up, an impromptu make-up station, and the director began preparing the actors. John and I were working as one, passing tools back and forth without asking, exchanging meaningful glances and laughing at nothing. When you work together in a situation like this, where every second counts, and often where one of you can't move, it's important that your partner feels confident that if he asks you to do something it will get done. We had that relationship. We depended on each other implicitly.

We had got off the first shot when the rain started. It was a light drizzle at first, nothing more than a fine mist. By the time we had set up the second shot, the sky opened and the world began to cry. It sobbed, bawled and with the first huge crack of thunder, it was as if Zeus himself was shaking a gigantic rattle in the holiest of temper tantrums. We were out in the open; there was nowhere to go, nowhere to hide. People were screaming, panicking, worried about getting a little wet but John and I were the ones dealing with live electricity. There is nothing like the heaven-splitting strike of that first lightning when you are high above a dark body of water, hundreds of cars racing right beneath you, and live wires at your feet. The director, producer and PAs began ushering people off the bridge. John and I started taking down the lights. The thunder and lightning were getting closer together, and we were moving as fast as we could. Other people were taking our disassembled lights and stacking them on dollies, like lines of dismembered heads on gurneys. I ran over to unplug that last cable and the largest bolt of lightning I had ever witnessed crashed across the sky. The hairs all over my body stood up and I could feel the shock passing through me. It wasn't bad, I was lucky, but I still felt it. I pulled my hand back and John was right behind me, holding my arms. I turned to him, shaking and he kissed me, hard.

"We need to get these generators out of here," he said, stroking my hair.

I nodded but pulled his head back towards mine. John and I were the only two left on the bridge and we were already soaked – my T-shirt was stuck like a second skin, my nipples were hard. It was thrilling; kissing on the top of the Brooklyn Bridge, John pushed me down and rolled over on me. We were kissing as raindrops rolled down my face like tears. With one hand he reached up and held my face, he slid the other hand up my shirt, lightly rolling my nipple between his fingers. I moaned and arched my spine. I put my hands on his strong back and pulled him down closer. He pushed his leg between mine, applying pressure on my cunt. I wanted him, wanted him inside me, filling me, completing me.

The thunder, lightning and rain kept coming. A boat blew its horn, the low and terrible moan of a lost and tortured ghost and the rushing cars blended into the frantic wind. There was something otherworldly about it all. Something so far from normal. I hurried to unhook his belt and pulled down his shorts. His dick was hard, rock hard. I wrapped my hand around it and stroked it, over and over. He unbuttoned his shorts and pulled them the rest of the way down.

I pushed him down on his back and kissed a soft line down his chest to his stomach. He shivered beneath my gentle kisses, slightly arching his back up to meet me. I continued down, breathing hot breath against his crotch, I kissed the inside of his thighs, lightly, and was answered with a happy moan. I kissed up the shaft of his cock, kissing the head before taking it in my mouth. I sucked it long and hard as his feet clenched and his body tightened. He leaned over, trying to yank down my shorts without interrupting my mouth. I helped him, getting my shorts and panties down. His finger found my clit, circling it faster and faster, I could feel my pussy dripping as my body responded to his attention. I pulled my mouth up and slid my hot, wet pussy down on his dick.

"You're so tight," he moaned, as I began pushing myself up and down, faster and harder. He reached up and pinched my nipple, twisting it until I felt the most exquisite pain. Then he flipped me over so he was on top, expertly he moved me around until I was kneeling and he was behind me, his hand snaked in front to tease my clit.

"Yes," I groaned, "harder, fuck me harder."

He did, he was pounding his cock into me, and his finger was working diligently, moving faster and faster until I felt myself beginning to come. My body was tightening, my cunt squeezing and contracting around him. He pulled my hair back, pulling my head up; I opened my eyes and saw the blood black water beneath me and all of New York before me. It was beautiful, being up so high, the entire world laid out beneath us. I wanted to hold on. I didn't want him to stop but I couldn't take it anymore. I pushed back against him. "I think I'm coming," I said. "Don't stop."

He pushed into me harder and faster until I let go, my body exploding into spasms. He pushed once more, deep, and I felt his body go tight before he stopped, collapsing onto my back. We stayed like that for a moment, connected.

We lay naked on top of the Brooklyn Bridge, the rain pouring over us. He took my hand and held it for a moment. Another bolt of lightning shocked the life back into us.

"We should go," he said. Then rolled over and kissed me.

We got up and began pulling on our wet clothes. There is almost nothing worse than putting on clothes that are already soaked. The temperature had dropped drastically. It was now freezing and I shivered each time a new breeze blew. We pushed our generators down the ramp, careful not to let them go too fast or too far ahead of us.

When we finally got down to the bottom Dee and Mikey were there waiting. "Oh, thank God you're OK," Dee said. "We thought you might have been electrocuted."

John and I exchanged smug looks. "Then why didn't you come to help us?" I asked.

She shrugged, "If you had been and there was still live electricity, we could have got electrocuted just walking up there."

We all laughed because she was right; there was no point to all of us dying. Not when there was the promise of so much light.

Salvation

Jordan LaRousse

We lived in a small town in Tennessee in a weathered farmhouse with a brick driveway that wound endlessly between rows of dogwood trees. He was the pastor of the Baptist church. Tall, muscular, a shining bald head, and teeth that flashed as white as the southern sun on a hot July day. The youngest pastor our town had ever seen.

I was the daughter of an alcoholic and I needed salvation.

My reputation at the girls' school all but barred me from setting foot over the threshold of Our Mother Mary Catholic church. I was too ashamed, so they assumed, to repent. They were right. I didn't want to tell Father Ray, confessional screen be damned, about my tryst with his nephew in the bathroom at the diner during our shift break. I didn't want to worry him with the details of how I took his God-fearing nephew's God-endowed cock from his trousers and placed it delicately between my rouged lips and indelicately sucked it sucked it sucked it until he cried out the Lord's name in vain. I would never confess.

Still, I needed salvation; I didn't want to go to Hell. And it was with this in mind that I found myself in the Baptist church on the east end of town. My skin, the colour of fallen snow, my hair, the colour of autumn leaves when they are still gripping with life, stood out among the sea of black and brown. My body didn't fit in. But my soul had found its rightful place. And I could sing, and sing I did.

It was here in this hot, sweaty profusion of almond-skinned bodies. It was here in this glorious worshipful place. It was here amidst the clapping of hands, the Hallelujah cries, the Amens that lifted the rooftop to the heavens. It was here that I met him. Him. My saviour. His name was Darrel Louis Walsh the Third. We called him Pastor Trey.

Pastor Trey was quick on the uptake. He saw the pretty little thing with the voice of an angel, as he called me, and swept me right up off my feet. Took me up right out of my sins and onto his wide, muscular shoulders, took me towards my salvation.

Although we spent hours upon hours with our tongues upon each other's lips, our teeth upon each other's necks, Pastor Trey refused to fuck me under the eyes of his Lord and saviour until we were truly and rightfully man and wife. In my quest for salvation, I agreed. In my quest for love, I agreed. In my quest for his cock, which I had only felt through layers of denim, layers of cotton, layers of corduroy and beneath layers of the fine blue suede of his favourite Sunday suit. I agreed.

Oh lord yes how I wanted to undress him, to lay my weary head on his chest and kiss his heated skin, to drink of his fruits, to bask in his love, to wake up with his horny, glorious hard-on pressed up insistently against the crack of my ass.

Despite the hemming and hawing of old Mr McGee from the general store, despite the piercing glares of several of his admiring parishioners, including the voluptuous Lucy and her slender sister Sue, despite the disgruntled grunts of my father, and the gossiping croons of my co-workers at the diner. Despite it all. We were married.

The ceremony was brief. A cloak-and-dagger affair. A marriage with few witnesses, despite my husband's affection for the limelight.

He didn't marry me for love. He married me because he desperately craved my pussy.

I learned this quickly.

We ate apples dipped in honey beneath the full moon, but there was no real honeymoon. The night we were married he took me to our new home. The weathered farmhouse at the end of the long brick driveway. The air was musky. Wooden. The windows had not been opened for years.

There was a mattress stuffed with straw on the floor. It was here that I first made love to Pastor Trey. It was here that we consecrated our marriage. It was here that I spread my legs before his tongue and let him weep deep and long prayers between the folds of my sex. It was here that he flipped me onto my knees and plunged himself deep into my pink cunt. It was here that I cried out and begged for him to fuck me fuck me fuck me fuck me!

He loved me there in that bed night after night, morning after morning, afternoons too. We spent hours pressed together like a hot iron to a strip of fabric, rubbing back and forth heatedly. We spent countless minutes pressed together like two pages in the centre of a book, comfortable, still and warm.

Outside the farmhouse, though, he grew distant. On the streets of our little town he begged for me to pretend not to know him. He said that he'd been getting threats from the sheriff, threats saying he would lose his pastorship, lose his job, lose his life if he married that white girl. Problem was we were already married. God had consecrated our relationship even if the sheriff had not.

I made exclamations of my dedication to him. I made protestations of my hatred for our bigoted little town. Saving a month's worth of tips from the diner, I bought bus tickets to Atlanta where we could walk the streets, my white hand in his black hand, without consequence. But Pastor Trey did not want to leave his congregation. He did not want to leave voluptuous Lucy and her slender sister Sue; he did not want to leave old Mr McGee from the general store. He told me we had to bide our time and hope that times and sentiments would change.

Between his greedy mouthfuls of my pussy, between my singing his praises, between all of this, but before my orgasm, he told me I could no longer sing. Starting Sunday I would no longer be welcome at his church. It was for my own safety, he said. He breathed his fears between my thighs, said he believed his congregation could read our surreptitious glances, could feel the energy zipping between cock and cunt, could sense the saliva he had left on my left nipple in the moments before the church bells rang. If they knew of our marriage, he fretted, his flock would leave him. They'd flock out of the church's gate and disappear into the Tennessee hills. He'd be left behind, alone, without purpose.

I smiled at the thought. Let the congregation flock. Let them go so we could go to Atlanta. We could be free to be together. We could raise children. We could buy a proper house with proper neighbours and a proper bed. He could become pastor of a city church, preach tolerance and love, we could fill the chapel like a crayon box, thirty-two colours of creation.

His eyes grew as dark as a violent southern storm. A glint of lighting shot through. A menacing cloud washed over his smile, turned it upside down.

"We are never leaving this town," he said.

I sat at home that songless Sunday, wondering. I thought of Pastor Trey preaching in his freshly ironed suit. The one I had laundered after accidentally leaving my fragrant juices on the knee when he had fingered my wetness. The one I laundered after accidentally leaving my lipstick kisses on the collar. The kisses left behind from when he had gripped my face between his palms and professed his undying love for my pussy.

I thought of his praising and healing and preaching and of the huge breasts of voluptuous Lucy and the small pert ones of her slender sister Sue bouncing up and down up and down beneath the taut fabric of their dresses in the front row of the church. Their eyes supposedly raised towards heaven, but surely eyeing the crotch of my beloved husband. If he had married Lucy she would be on stage beside him, singing. If he had married Sue they would kiss in front of the entire congregation if they wanted to. Man and wife showing off their holy matrimony. My green eyes shone with jealousy, my red hair flamed with rage. He was my man I his wife, and our matrimony was holy. I wasn't going to hide it anymore.

I put on my Sunday best. My green floral dress that showed off the colour of my eyes. My wide grey hat. My white gloves and black handbag. It was too hot for a bra and my breasts were small enough to go bare. I rolled on my nude stockings and hitched them to my garter belt. I slipped on the more comfortable pair of pumps because my husband had taken the car and left me out here at the end of a long driveway, at the end of an even longer dirt road. I knew that if I hurried, I could walk that road to town in about an hour and would arrive at the church after the salvation was served, but before the lemonade and crumb cake.

The Tennessee sun was hot on my skin as I walked. My anger made me hotter. My longing for Pastor Trey's hot touch made me hottest of all. I damned the dress, damned the nylons, and damned the pumps that rubbed at my feet in all the wrong directions. Yet I walked furiously, arriving at the church just in time to see the worshippers stream out from the building, mingling on the lawn in their pretty dresses and sharp suits with lemonade in right hand, crumb cake in left, dropping cinnamon crumbs into their white napkins.

And I saw him, my husband, as he embraced woman after woman close and tight, their breasts pressing deep into the muscles of his chest. His hands leaving warm dents in the soft flesh of their backs. His breath close to their ears whispering his encouraging words.

My eyes shone green with envy. My hair coiled in red curls of rage.

I stomped stomped stomped up the sidewalk, stood behind my husband's back as he embraced yet another woman. Watched her hands scrunch into his suit, the one I had freshly laundered. I tapped on his shoulders and he spun around flashing his hot-sun grin.

His grin toppled, left side down, when he saw me standing before him in my green floral dress, my wide grey hat, my nude stockings, my sensible pumps now scuffed with the dirt from the long road in.

His grin toppled, right side down, as I threw my arms around him and kissed him solidly on the cheek, on the chin, on his neck, on his chest and proclaimed him my husband, my beloved, the love of my life.

The sound of crumbs from the crumb cakes falling. The sound of ice clicking against the sides of plastic lemonade cups. The sound of uncomfortable shuffling of feet against grass. Ahems and hahs. Silence but for those sounds.

My exclamations became more brazen. "My husband, let's go home," I announced. "Let's go make babies; this is what man and wife do on a Sunday afternoon. Remember the lovemaking we shared this morning? I want more. I want to take you in my mouth, in my pussy, I want to take your width in the tight space between my ass cheeks."

These announcements flew from my angry lips like a colony of bats taking flight from a dark cave. Without thought for my dear husband's reputation, my words flew haphazardly.

Abruptly he took control of the situation. With a smile that cracked deeply at the edges he grabbed my wrists in one large, strong hand and declared me possessed by the devil. He declared me overtaken by demonic rage. He laid his other hand to my forehead and began a prayer even as my rage spewed forth.

A crowd gathered around us, and soon the shouts of Hallelujahs and Amens rang in my ears. I collapsed in the arms of my husband, completely overcome by heat, by emotion, by the compassion of his flock that he refused to leave behind.

The prayer done, and me subdued at last, Pastor Trey saw his escape. He wished his congregation a blessed Sunday, advised them he would call my father to come fetch me home, and he took me over his shoulder and up the steps into the church. He sat me down on a pew and turned to shut the massive doors behind him. I heard the deadbolt slide locked. I heard his ragged breathing, his anger washing up anew. His footsteps echoed in the empty room and he stood before me with dusty stripes of light crisscrossing his massive chest.

I felt weary from my long walk, exhausted from my jealous rage. Yet his gleaming eyes, his fisted fingers stirred me into arousal.

Wordlessly he pulled me to stand before him. He laid my wide grey hat on the pew and encircled his arms around my waist, brought me deep into his embrace. His hand slid to the back of my dress and a long zip, an eternal zip, sounded as he slowly pulled the metal apart. He worked the flat of his hand into the space made by the parted fabric and gripped me harder still. His searing palm on the flesh of my back throbbed with energy.

After a still moment like this, he dropped his arms and pushed me away, took the shoulders of my dress down and let the entirety of its fabric fall to the floor and pool around my sullied shoes.

"You are beautiful," he whispered. His voice strangely quiet in a room where it usually boomed and rang from floorboard to rafter. "But you have ruined me."

A familiar sense of shame burned deep in my heart upon hearing his words.

I stood vulnerable in my stockings, my garter, my panties, my shoes, my gloves. Yet my naked nipples poked defiantly at him, like two fingers claiming it was his fault that he was ruined. Not mine. All I had wanted was for him to be my husband, proud for me to be his wife.

He knelt before me, wrapped his arms around me and grabbed my two ass cheeks in his two strong hands. He poked his pink tongue into the fabric of my underwear. Poked and prodded and found the nub of my clit beneath the cotton. I felt the heat of his breath, the moisture of his saliva as it seeped through the cloth. His hands kneaded my behind and spread the cheeks wide.

"You have ruined me." He looked up at me and I saw his eyes shining with tears. He released my cheeks and brought his hands to my garter. He carefully unsnapped each snap, until all eight had been released. Then he eased the garter down over my hips and pooled it on the floor with my dress. He slowly rolled my panties down my legs and those too, he left pooled about my feet. He took my left hand, set my pocket-book down and took off the white Sunday glove finger by finger. Then just as deliberately he tugged the glove from my right hand too. I now stood before him in my stockings and dirty shoes, my other clothes discarded at my toes.

He pressed his forehead into my stomach and breathed heavily into my crotch. He breathed heavily and repeated, "You have ruined me." He brought a long finger up and pierced my centre. He pushed it in deep and pulled it back out. Pushed it in deeper still and pulled it back out. Pushed it in as deep as he could and pulled it back out. He leaned forward to retrieve the nectar that he had stirred up and lapped, lapped, lapped at it with his tongue. He dipped his tongue into my cunt and eagerly sipped at the juices that came forth.

I grew dizzy at his unexpected tenderness. I felt as if I would fall to the floor. I held tightly to his broad shoulders beneath that suit, pressed the fabric in as I had seen the women of his congregation do.

He took my left foot and then the other and released them from the pile of clothes that bound them. Then, standing up, he led me to the stage. The stage where he stood Sunday after Sunday and sermonized to the masses about love and salvation. He led me naked up the stairs and once there he had me kneel before him in a position of repentance. It was here that he unzipped his zipper, an eternal ungrasping of metal from metal and at long last brought forth the heavy flesh of his cock.

I pulled his offering deeply into my mouth and sucked upon it hungrily. I let the tip push at the back of my throat while I ran my tongue up and down its underside. I felt the heaviness of his balls in my hand as I sucked sucked sucked. I felt suddenly ravenous. I wanted to be filled with his seed. I wanted to suck suck suck until his cock exploded its nourishment, its love, its forgiveness into my ravenous body.

I imagined his congregation lining up in the pews behind me. I imagined them watching my bare ass as it bounced on the heels of my dirt worn shoes. My red hair, ridden of its rage, cascading down the white plane of my back. I imagined them clap clap clapping and shouting out their praises as I swallowed the preacher's cock deep into the back of my throat.

As if my husband were overtaken by this imagery too he shouted out an unexpected and triumphant "Amen!" One that began at the root of his sex and exploded from the depths of his abundant lungs. It bounced off the barren pews and back into my ears. My heart leaped with joy, elated to have brought forth such utterances from my heretofore angry lover.

He pushed my face away from his cock leaving me starving, leaving me hungry, leaving me thirsty for more. He shed his clothing, first his shoes, then his pants, he wore no boxers, then his jacket, then his white button-up shirt which he opened button by button as if he had all the time in the world. He carefully folded these garments and laid them atop his pulpit.

He took my hand, helped me to my feet and led me to the piano bench. He sat down, his erection pointing towards the heavens, and then he pulled my soaking pussy onto his lap and pierced me deeply. I sat there motionless at first, savouring the way his penis filled me. Savouring the pulse and rhythm of his flowing blood against my walls. Savouring his hands wrapped around my waist, my back pressed to his chest, his lips on my neck, my nipples pointed towards the risers where not long before the choir sang its songs of glory.

And then he began to pump into me. Deep into me. He pumped and dug his fingers into the tops of my thighs and pumped and bit the back of my neck. He pumped and grabbed a fistful of my hair and brought his other hand to my nipple and twisted it as he pumped deep into me.

And I let my body be carried by his ravishments. I let him have his way with me his wayward wife. I relinquished control and let him love me as he knew best.

At the moment I felt my orgasm well up inside me, at the moment that I felt his cock become as hard as it was able, at the moment that my moan overtook the vacant space, at the moment that his grip grew tighter and his breath drew harder. At this moment he crashed backwards onto the piano keys and a great discordant tune clattered about the church. And we both cried out discordantly, yet together in a great and final instant of utter satisfaction.

We sat there in stillness for a moment, but then my husband, he pushed me from his lap. My skin unstuck from his skin and I dropped weary and sated to the floor of the stage. My husband stood and slowly pulled on his trousers, slid his shirt up his arms and buttoned it one by one as if he had all the time in the world. Drew on his jacket and pulled on his socks and shoes.

I sat there and watched him as he put himself together. Watched him as he ran a hand over his smooth, bald pate, wiping off all evidence of his exertion. Once again he stood as before, a man in control, a man who did not want to leave our little town.

Her First Thursday Evening

M. Christian

Weird little flukes rule our lives. Like Starbucks. I normally avoid the place, but that one day the caffeine demon was riding my ass pretty hard and Starbucks was the nearest source of the magic bean. She was behind the counter. That was on Monday. I asked if she'd like to get some coffee sometime, and we both laughed. Weird little flukes: I'm normally quite shy around people I don't know, but with her, the words just came.

On Tuesday, we went to the movies. Something loud with explosions and much bloodshed – or was it something with "hey, dude" jokes and silicon tits? – or maybe something with tears and sunsets? Doesn't matter, because I can't remember. But her arm, bare because of the hot summer days, was against mine and sometime during the credits she moved it to better hold my hand.

On Wednesday, I ran into her on the way home from the post office. Really, honestly: flukes rule our lives. We went out for dinner, a little place full of steam and rattling dishes – or was it someplace quiet and elegant, with artistically placed portions? – or maybe someplace with corporate smiling clowns and plastic tables. That, too, doesn't matter, because all I remember was laughing and listening to her own sweet giggles.

Her place was in the mission, just a few blocks from BART. A shadowed, narrow alley smelling of garbage and piss, a set of winding stairs up to a sloping back porch. Her front door was the back door of the flat, the apartment beyond dark and quiet. I smiled and put my hand on her back as she jingled her keys. That Thursday evening we made love: our breaths mixing in each other's hot mouths, my hands roaming her body, trying to feel what I would hopefully soon see. Her own hands were fixed, immobile on my back, holding me close – almost too close. Eventually the clothes fell away; my coat, her coat, my fingers on the buttons of her blouse, her hands on my still-shirted chest, my hands pushing up her skirt, her hands stroking the hard outline of my cock through my pants, her panties, and then beyond them to the hot wetness, my cock in the cool air, her hands around my shaft.

Her nipples were brown, like old chocolate, and big – which reached down somewhere deep in my body and tugged hard – making my cock even harder. Her pussy was barely furred, just a hint of downy soft brown hair. She was sweet in her very wetness, her clit hard between my lips. Her own lips were firm and quick on my cock. There was a passion about her that put a smile on my face and kept it there. Our Thursday night was a laughing, giggling, hot breaths kind of time. The best kind of sex, where it becomes nothing but play between two people.

After, when I'd come and she'd come and we crawled into her big, crooked bed covered by dozens of cheap, heavy coats ("Better than a comforter and cheaper") she'd cried. It wasn't my first time, being with a suddenly crying girl, but there was something about the quickness of the transition that made me catch my breath, made me put aside the usual tricks of hand-patting, hair stroking, and "I'm here for you" things. I just held her, for what felt like a very long time. Finally, when the sobs slowed to only heavy breathing and slick heat on my neck and chest, I managed to croak out: "Tell me about it. Tell me what I can do to help."

Those words. Those words have got me in a lot of trouble, but for some reason speaking those to her, that Thursday evening, soft voices under musty overcoats, it was right. I didn't love the girl, I barely knew her, but I cared about her – and the words I'd sometime spoken simply to calm troubled seas came tumbling out of my mouth with honest sincerity.

"I was just wishing you could have been around a few years ago," she said, almost a whisper. "My first time . . . wasn't that great."

I kissed her forehead. "I don't think anybody's first time is ever all that great."

She swallowed another sob. "Mine was really bad. There was this boy, Mark Bradley. I thought he liked me. We were at this stupid high school dance, something about Paris in the Spring. You know how stupid those things can be. Anyway, so I asked him . . . you know, to dance, but he said 'no' and gave me this nasty look. That was bad but I didn't want to go home or anything so I just stayed around. Later, when the party was almost over and I was getting my coat, he came up to me, apologized for being such a jerk, and offered to drive me home. I know, the back seat of a car – my life is just full of clichés, isn't it? But I read somewhere that's where most people lose their cherries, so maybe I'm just average." She gave me a look and a smile, but I saw the ache there and kissed her hard instead.

"Nice," she said, her voice softer. "Yeah, Mark Bradley. He said he was sorry and then we did it. He wasn't any good – not like you – but that was it." She was quiet for many heartbeats, which is the only way to measure time during moments like that. I waited, patiently, stroking her hair. Did she get pregnant? Did he beat her? Were her parents crazed fundamentalists who told her she was going to hell? Did she get the clap ... something worse? I waited, feeling the tension rise in my back.

When the answer came, it was like any one of my conjectures – and in some ways worse. If he'd beat her, then he was a bastard, and if I ever came across him I'd break his knees with a five-iron. If she'd got pregnant ... then that was something I could support her with. If her parents had slapped her with the Bible, then there are other religions.

"After, he said that he knew I'd do it with him because I was fat, and so I'd be desperate."

More tears, and I wondered how to get his address out of her – and where my five-iron was. "You're beautiful," was what I said, meaning every word. Her face was cherubic, angelic, with lovely cheekbones. Her eyes sparkled with smarts and laughs. Her breasts were plump and pillow-soft. Her ass was full and round, like a perfect peach. Her belly was silken, the perfect place to rest your head, or sweetly kiss. I didn't see her as fat, though I knew people saw only that about her. I just saw her as a lovely young woman, full of body and big in spirit.

She cried for a little while more, eventually lifting herself from my shoulder to sniffle and snort. Fumbling around for a box of tissues, she loudly blew her nose, bursting into a lovely laugh at the sound. "I'm sorry," she said, "I don't normally do that. It just came up suddenly."

I sat up, kissed her forehead, then her cute little mouth, her full lips. "No apologies. I understand. Well, as much as I can." I smiled. I'm thin, always been that way. "Tell you what. Right now, right here, let's fix that right away."

She smiled, and it was a lovely sight. "I don't think my cherry is something you can put back."

"Let's give you a new story – something nice, sweet, and special.

Come on, it'll be a fun game." I put my hand under her breast, lifted it to kiss her nipple. "Someone as lovely as you deserves a good first time."

It was a nice Thursday. One of those Thursdays that doesn't feel like the middle of the week, but rather just one day short of Friday. [What time of year was it, sexy?] It was a lovely summer Thursday, warm but not hot. You were thinking of the dance, walking across the campus, just daydreaming, when BAM, someone runs smack into you [Yeah, I know it's a cliché but what do you expect, right off the cuff?]. In a tumble of books and legs you both fall flat onto your asses in the grass. "Are you all right?" a young guy says, helping you to your feet. You get up, brushing grass and twigs from your [skirts or pants?] skirt. At first you might have been a little pissed. I mean there's all your [favourite subject, sexy?] math books and homework scattered all over the place. But then you recognize him as someone you've seen around school. Not a jock, not a nerd, not a "perfect" kid, just a nice boy. Maybe a little unusual, but in a good way; like there was something more to him. He laughs and smiles and says something like "Boy, I want to go where you're going – must be fun if you're trying to get there so fast." [Lame joke, I know] So you laugh and stay a little while, just talking. It turns out that he's interested in math as well, but maybe isn't as good at it as you are. But he's curious and maybe a little bit shy, nervous around you for some reason. Finally the bell rings and you have to go, but he asks you – almost blurts it out, actually – if you'd like to go see *The Rocky Horror Picture Show* that night [I didn't know, love; I just guessed]. You stand there for a second, wondering if you should go to the prom with all those stupid paper decorations, watered-down punch and decades-old tunes or go with this sweet – though a little nervous – boy to see one of your favourite flicks. Before you know it, you say "Sure!" and, giddy as all get-out, you float through the rest of the day. PE, Art, English, even your beloved Math all slip by in a haze. Finally, you're home and facing your clothes. What to wear? What to wear? You don't want to be too provocative, but you also don't want to be too dowdy. You finally pick a simple black skirt, a white blouse, and before you head out you check yourself out in the mirror . . . and it hits you so hard you just have to stand there and look at yourself. Yes, you're a big girl, but you're also really pretty. You're pretty – very, very pretty. Something else, too, something you knew about but didn't really understand before: you're damned sexy. And standing there, smiling, you unbutton the top three buttons on your blouse and skip out. It takes you a little while to get to the theatre, and you're nervous all the while, but get there you do – then the young man is nowhere to be found. [Don't worry, girl, you'll see.] But then someone touches you on the shoulder and you spin around and . . . almost burst out laughing. He's not a good Riffraff, but it was the thought that counted, right? He smiles at you and you melt a bit inside. You also notice that he's very fascinated in those undone buttons, which makes you smile a bit more. So you go in and, gallantly, he pays for you both. It's a great night. You've seen the movie before, of course, but this time it's even more fun. The place is full but not packed, but everyone there is into it: rice flies, toast sails, and everyone screams "ASSHOLE!" at just the right moment. Then, right in the middle, you're kissing. There are good kisses and fair kisses, but this is a great kiss. This is a kiss that's so good you feel yourself just melting right there in the theatre seat. It's a kiss so good that one moment your lips are touching his, your tongues – at first hesitant and then with urgency – meet and move together, and then hours seem to have passed; from the rainstorm to the Time Warp in wonderful bliss. It's natural, right, and perfect to be kissing this boy. It also seems right that your hand should be resting on his strong thigh and his hand should be cupping your breast, thumb nervously resting on your hard, throbbing nipple. Then the show is over, the lights are rising, and you both giggle, aware that the real show was between the two of you. Suddenly shy, you both giggle and then you're kissing again, drawn together like two magnets. You would have stayed together that way, it seemed, forever, till a young guy, all white-face and garters, yelled "get a room, you two" with laughter. So you get up, adjusting yourselves as your cheeks burn with embarrassment, and dart out. The night has grown cold, the sky black between blazing summer stars. You know that you should go your separate ways now, but for some reason you can't let go of his hand. Then you're kissing, and his hand falls to your side. Smiling as you kiss him, you take his hand and place it on your ass. He's shocked somehow by this, and squeals and breaks your dance of tongues and lips. A sadness comes over you, almost a prelude to tears [Don't worry, sexy, you'll see] and you mumble something about needing to get home. He looks very sad too, but then says something like, "Would you like a drive home?" Still somewhat quenched by his shock at touching you a few minutes before, you almost back away – but then you remember his hands on you, his lips on you, and, instead, you say "Sure". The walk down the street to his car is long and cold, but he holds your hand and you find yourself warming right up. His car is old and battered, but with a strange kind of character – like the boy. Inside, it smells of paints and thinner, and you smile thinking of him in some art class. He starts the car and after a sweet smile at you sitting there in the passenger seat, he pulls away. As he drives, you notice a kind of tension about him again, until he finally manages to blurt out, "Thank you so much for coming with me. You're so beautiful, I was really hoping you'd say yes." Then there you are, a few blocks from your house. He asks you to point out your place so you tell him . . . but you point to a house far away from your real house. He pulls over and says again, "Thank you so much." His eyes are drinking you in, relishing you, and you understand why he was so shy with you, why he pulled away from you. As you kiss, as you melt together, you take his hand and put it on your breast, mumbling "it's OK". His hands are warm on you and as you kiss, kiss, kiss, he feels the outline of your big breast [just like this] and how hard your nipple is getting. Then, with the heat growing with every second, you unbutton your blouse – and he breaks the kiss to stare at your breasts, your bra. "So beautiful," he says kissing the tops of them, feeling the weight of them, the hardness of your nipple. Then, before you can say or do anything he bravely reaches down and pulls one of them free from your bra, exposing your nipple to the cool night air – but that's not why it's so hard, of course. He kisses it, then takes it into his inferno of a mouth, sucking on it. The feeling is almost beyond words, almost because three of them keep ringing through your mind: "oh my God." Distantly, you're aware that he also has his hand down his pants, slowly stroking his cock. What with his lips on your nipple, his hand on your breast and his hard penis so close, you can't resist and so you mumble "show me." He's shocked and breaks the delicious suction to look up at you, but your hands repeat what you asked: they touch the strong muscles of his thigh and grip his so-hard dick in his pants. Then they are on his fly, then his pants have been pushed down – by you or him you don't know – but then his cock is out. You've never seen one before, but somehow it's still . . . beautiful? Maybe, but beautiful or not, it's something you want to touch. You do, your hands stroking him, running up and down the thick shaft of him [yeah, like that] and relishing in the soft head. You could have stroked that penis forever, but there's something demanding even more attention – something that keeps pulsing between your legs. His hand is down there – and your thighs are wide apart, and you know you're so wet, your clit so stiff – but that's not enough. You don't have a word for it, but you know what you want, so you scoot up on the car seat and finally get rid of the annoying barrier of cotton between his hands and your pussy. Feel his hands really touch you. Gently but quivering with excitement, he strokes your lips, relishing in every inch of you, all the time mumbling "so beautiful, so beautiful, so beautiful . . .." Then you're on top of him, holding his cock down between your quaking thighs, guiding him in. He's stopped talking – his voice having been lost to his quick breaths – but now you speak softly, sweetly. You mumble "yes, yes, yes" as his cock slowly enters you. It's a lot of things to you – a little pain maybe, a little confusion when the act itself has started – but you know more than anything that it's right and damned good. Up and down, up and down, you go, kissing sometimes, his hands on your breasts and nipples sometimes. Your breaths fog the windows, your hands are busy exploring each other, taking in as much of the other as possible . . . until it's all too much, all of the sexy goodness has reached its peak and the come begins – a shattering, jarring orgasm that moans out of you both [unrealistic, I know, but sometimes we need fantasy more than reality]. After, you hug and kiss, slowly crawling into your clothes. Then you realize how late it is and your hand is on the door handle – but his hand is on your shoulder. You turn, expecting words but he gives you something better – another kiss, a kiss that combines them all in one wordless act. Suddenly crying, you step out into the cool night and drift slowly home. You see him again, of course, as many times as you can but then he moves away. You cry, he cries, but no distance can take away the specialness that you shared.

She is almost asleep, eyes closed, breath hot on my shoulder. "And that," I tell her, "my beautiful, sexy, girl, is your first time." She smiles, her eyes still closed, and lifts her head for one last kiss.

Then she is asleep. I'm right behind her, but not before I drop a few of my own tears. Yep, flukes rule our lives: she wasn't the only one who wanted that story to have been what really happened back then. As a lonely, shy, geeky art student with a passion for fat girls, she didn't have a monopoly on crappy first times.

Thames Link

Justine Elyot

I sing the praise of the sleazy man.

The man with the shifty eyes, the man with the floppy fringe, the man with the sensual lips, the man who drinks a little too much red wine and eats a little too much cake. You might see him on the train; his eyes follow you over the top of his paper and you try not to recross your legs too often. He might be standing at the bar so you have to feign enormous levels of animation with your companions. Perhaps he works with you and there is a rota in place among your colleagues so nobody has to go into the photocopier cupboard at the same time as him.

He's a creep, he's a sleaze, he's a perv. He's my kind of guy.

I know, I sound insane. Who on earth likes men like this? I suppose it's his honesty that appeals to me. No "I really like you as a person". No discussion of mutually admired bands and comedians. No number swaps or long waits for the phone to beep. Better than the man who moves in with you before revealing his wardrobe of skintight latex. Better than the man that waits until you have his ring on your finger before asking you if you fancy a pint down the swingers' club. This is a man who wears his cock on his sleeve, and quite rightly so.

He'll speak fluent innuendo. He'll sit too close to you on the bus. He'll walk behind you in the park, watching the sway of your backside. In the ultraviolet light of the disco, he'll try to get a hand up your skirt.

No, he isn't a rapist, it's not about power. It *is* about sex. He wants it. Not you. It.

And there's something about that I find refreshing.

I have a sleazy man of my own, tucked away in my address book for days when I don't feel pristine or perfumed. On days – and they come all too often now – when I feel rumpled and seedy, when my tights are clinging damply to the crack of my arse and my skin is grimy with the London summer, I call him.

I'm going to call him now, actually.

"Morning, foxy. What can I do for you today?"

"When are you free?"

"Hmm . . . it's looking like a late one. Could take a two-hour lunch break, though."

"Lunch sounds perfect. Midday?"

"Blackfriars Tube. Wear the green dress. Hold-ups. No knickers. Got that?"

"No knickers," I repeat, my clit puffing up, my silky scanties already wet. Who cares? I will have to take them off before I leave.

"Don't forget your perfume, Jane," he says softly before hanging up.

How could I forget that? The application of scent is the precious first step in the ritual, setting the tone for all that is to follow.

These are his rules: I must draw back the bedroom curtains and open the window, so that the block across the green is visible to me, and I to it. I must strip naked and lie down on my unmade bed. I must take my vibrator and masturbate to orgasm, plunging it deep inside, juicing it up until it gleams. While I am doing this, I must think of some of the filthy, slutty things I have done for him in the past – easy enough, for there are plenty to choose from. Once I am red-faced and spent, I must take the vibrator and rub it across my pulse points, making sure I am generously anointed before smearing any remainder on to my nipples, breasts, belly, thighs. I must dip the vibrator back in and repeat the process until there is nothing left to apply. Only when my skin is stiff and heavy with the smell of my sex am I allowed to dress.

Today, a sheer white peephole bra, some nude lace-topped hold-ups and the green dress. The dress I was wearing when we met – though that sounds grandiose, as if we have a story or a future. The day we picked each other up, perhaps.

The dress is made of very light cotton in eau-de-nil. It buttons all the way up and has a short, flippy skirt whose hem is only just beneath the lacy bit of my hold-up. The merest breath of breeze is enough to give my thighs a tickle, and on some of the windier Tube platforms I have to clamp it down with my palms flat on my legs, shuffling bent double like an ancient babushka.

Then it is time to slap industrial quantities of gloss on my lips and mascara on my lashes before slipping into strappy sandals and running for my train.

Once again, it is a hot day, humid and dirty, the way it was the first time we met. The station platform is crowded – several previous trains have been delayed – so I know I will stand no chance of being able to hide my sex-drenched self in a corner seat away from the masses. I will have to force it on my carriage-mates, mingling it in with their smells of onions and cigarettes and engine oil and boiled aftershave, all with a sweaty topnote.

When the train arrives and its doors slide open, I look for the least respectable grouping I can find. I light on a bearded bikerish type and his heavily pierced moll, wondering idly who on earth would wear leather trousers in this weather as I push myself towards them. The smell is heady, though, and powerful, almost cancelling out my pussy perfume. Almost, but not quite. I catch them looking at each other, half-winking, guessing at what I might have been up to. If Shaun were here, he might nod at me, indicating that I was to try and get myself felt up by one or both of them. We've done that before. But he is not here, so I hold myself away from them, straphanging and concentrating on the trickle of sweat travelling downwards from the nape of my neck, breathing myself in, not daring to catch any eyes.

The train was less busy when we met. We both had seats, opposite each other. About halfway through the journey, I looked up from my book for the eighth time to find him staring at me. He made no attempt to be furtive about it. He simply watched me with a face like stone and narrowed eyes, from Herne Hill to Blackfriars.

What does one say? "Do you mind?" "Can I help you?" "Is there a smudge on my nose?" I could not decide, so I returned to my book, though I did not read another word. I squirmed inside all the way to Blackfriars, where he alighted.

I watched him walking down the platform. Despite the July heat, he was wearing a coat – a light grey ankle-length raincoat. Every few paces he would stop and turn to look at me and my eyes would dive guiltily back to the page. It was strange, that such a simple gesture could be so very sinister. He wanted me to know that he was watching me, and I had no idea why.

For the rest of that week and a few days beyond, the same thing happened every day. The seating opposite, the staring, the turning and looking. I tried to stand as far away from him on the platform as I could, yet he always hunted me down to my carriage. I had no idea how I should deal with it. Should it be dealt with? I could not even work out how I felt. I thought I should probably be intimidated or something. It was a bit like having a stalker, although he never stayed on the train to my station, or followed me home. I wasn't intimidated, though – I was rather *excited* by the whole thing. It was like a mysterious game of hunter and prey and I was intrigued, speculating on how the situation might develop. Besides, I could handle myself. You had to, when you were a woman living alone in London. Despite the fact that he was not my type at all – too short, too fleshy, not enough cheekbones – I began to think about him while masturbating. He pushed me into a darkened railway arch and ripped my skirt in his haste to fuck me. He tied me to a bed and told me that from now on I belonged to him. He plunged his hand into my knickers and fingered me on the train, right in front of all the other passengers, telling me that he had known this was what I needed all along. When I imagined his voice, it was not deep and manly, but a little bit nasal and whiny. For some reason, this made him seem all the hotter – the idea that I could be taken like that by somebody so ordinary. Only a slut would fantasize about an ugly man who stares at her on the train. Only a slut, whore, bitch . . . yes, yes, yes.

On the tenth day he was reading a newspaper. Except he wasn't reading it – he was staring at me from over the masthead. And the newspaper was the one I worked for.

Even though it was popular enough with the commuters, I began to feel a little freaked out. Did he know I worked there? Had he followed me to the office? Had he followed me home? Was he ever going to talk to me? Was he waiting for me to crack and talk first? Did he fancy me and this was his bizarre courtship ritual? Or what?

On the eleventh day, after an evening of peering through my curtains to check for dark shapes in the bushes, I determined to say something.

He was reading that paper again. I looked briefly around the carriage to make sure nobody was listening in and said, as quietly as I could, "You're making me feel uncomfortable."

He said nothing, just continued staring. Was he hard of hearing? I tried again.

"You're making me feel uncomfortable. Could you stop staring?"

He put the paper down on his lap. "I could," he said, and the sound of his voice made me gush between my thighs – not nasal or whiny, but creepily soft. "But I don't want to."

"Why not?"

"I think you're the most gorgeous thing I've ever seen. I can't take my eyes off you."

"Oh." I was stymied. "Right. You could have just asked me out instead of—"

"Come out with me then."

"I . . . OK." Somehow my sex brain had overtaken my rational one. Surely this was a bad idea.

"When do you finish work?"

"Six."

"Half six, then. Three Kings on Clerkenwell Green."

"That's . . ." I was about to say *very handy for work*, but something told me he already knew. "Right," I substituted lamely.

We engaged in a mutual stare while the sun-dazzling brown Thames glided by in my peripheral vision. Next stop Blackfriars.

"Don't be late," he said, standing and gathering up his belongings. There was more than a hint of "or else" in his tone.

"What if I . . . can't make it?"

"You can. I'll see you there." He smiled, though it was more like a smirk. "I know you'll come," he said.

He knew more than I did, then. All day at work, I contemplated the foolishness of my actions, deciding to stand him up, then wondering what I would say on the train the next day if I did. Maybe I would have to start getting the bus to work. Or rather, buses. No, that was going too far. It was just a drink after work. No obligations on either side. The pub was popular and would be busy. He would not be able to abduct or rape me. What about going home though? We would be travelling in the same direction . . . I decided to tell a friend what I was doing.

"Hi, Mags," I said cheerily. "Just wanted to let you know, I'm meeting someone for a drink after work at the Three Kings. So if he turns out to be an axe murderer . . ."

"Aha. Got it. What's his name?"

What was his name?

"I . . . oh God. I'm not sure. I've forgotten." Somehow this seemed more acceptable than telling her I didn't know.

"He's made a big impression then. So if you aren't at work tomorrow, I'll tell the police to look for a nameless man."

Crestfallen, I mumbled, "Yeah. Oh look, maybe I won't go after all . . ."

"Oh, stop it, woman! Go! You only live once. It's been two months since Paul did the disappearing act – I bet he isn't waiting around for Ms Person with a Name."

"No. You're right. You're bloody right. Thanks, Mags."

He chose his venue well.

The Three Kings is situated exactly where the lane curves round towards the Green, so there is no question of having a quick spy before you approach – as soon as you can see the building, you are visible from it.

The steps of St James's church opposite were thronged with post-work drinkers and foreign students and their pint glasses. I squinted at the bare chests and acres of sunglasses, but saw nobody who looked like my mysterious date. They all looked healthy and sunkissed and wholesome, not pale and full-lipped and surging with perverse lust.

My throat was dry and tight; I hadn't eaten all day and I needed a shower. Perhaps, I thought, I should go home. I turned back, looking unseeingly into the window of the junk shop over the road from the pub. A reflection loomed behind me, quicker than I could respond to, and then there were hands over my bare elbows, clammy hands, and hot breath in my ear.

"Where do you think you're going? I hope you weren't thinking of standing me up."

His voice, thick and greedy, pretending to be jokey but with a deadly serious undertow.

"I'm . . . not sure," I confessed weakly. Now I was in his clutches. *In his clutches.* I liked the phrase. I liked the idea. But would I like the reality?

"I am," he said, dripping his poisoned honey into my ear. "I'm sure. I knew you'd come."

"You couldn't know that."

"I could. Come on, I've bought you a drink."

There was nowhere to sit, so we leaned against the wall. He picked up a glass for me from the pavement – white wine, though I'd have preferred mineral water under the circumstances. All the same, I took a gulp, grateful for anything wet. He watched me over the rim of his pint glass, just as he had done that morning over the newspaper.

"I like your dress," he said, and he leered. A true and unmistakable leer. Behind his eyes, his mind was stripping it off me and pushing me down on the church steps before pounding into me, right here, right now, in front of everyone.

It seemed wrong, somehow, to say "Thanks," in response, but I did it anyway.

"Thank *you* for wearing it," he said, with a catch of something in the back of his throat. For a split second, he sounded self-conscious and it was such a relief. Oh, was he human after all? But then I realized it was laughter. He turned quickly to face me, his eyes vivid, skittering from side to side. "And thanks for coming."

"You knew I would come," I pointed out, somewhat sulkily.

"Oh yes. But thanks anyway."

"So come on. How did you know? You worked it out by the power of your stare? Are you some kind of Sherlock Holmes character, and you're going to tell me what I had for breakfast and the name of my childhood pet?"

He snuffled a bit and moved the toe of his boot closer to my strappy sandal, so that they touched. "No, nothing like that. Just applied a bit of psychology."

"What? Explain?"

"Very curious, aren't you?" He smiled slyly.

"What . . . do you mean?"

"I've given you your answer. And that's all I'm saying."

"You . . ." I was beginning to feel seriously outmanoeuvred. Even more so when he took the glass from my hand and put it on the wall next to him.

"But I'm very glad you came." He took my hand and grazed my knuckles with his lips and whiskery chin. "Like I said, you're gorgeous. My favourite kind of gorgeous. Filthy gorgeous." He flicked out his tongue and licked a knuckle. I tried to draw my hand back, but he was too quick, pulling me closer to him and whipping an arm around my waist. His hand patted my hip while he continued to say weird and creepy things to me. I could have disengaged, I could have looked around for help from the crowds of evening drinkers, I could have told him to fuck off.

I didn't.

"You like the attention, don't you?" he said. "You like men and you like sex. Is that true? Would that be fair?"

"Yeah." It was true. It was fair. "But . . ."

"It's OK, sweetheart. It doesn't make you a bad person. A 'bad girl', maybe, but not a bad person." He grinned at me, then his hand shifted down until it rested on the curve of my arse. I looked up sharply, appalled at how arousing I was finding all this, feeling I should put up a fight, but having absolutely no desire to stop him. He gave my bum a proprietary little smack, drawing a few giggles and whispers from some of the people nearby. "I think you're a dirty girl. I'm certainly no Mr Clean. What do you think?" His hand was bunching at the back of my skirt, drawing it up so the lace of my hold-up would have been visible to anyone watching from the right angle.

"Of what?" I asked, feeling drugged and stupid with need now. My knees felt as if they might buckle and my cunt had sucked all the humidity from the air into it.

"Of me taking down your knickers." His fingers crept under the dress and slipped between my burning thighs. "And giving you what you want and need." They pressed lightly against my gusset, finding it soaked. "And deserve," he whispered, rubbing the wet cotton between my swollen lips and over my clit.

"People . . . looking," I said, my tongue too big for my mouth.

"I can hardly blame them, can I?"

"Might be people from work," I urged, but I did nothing to stop his lazy fingering of me all the same.

"You work near here?"

"Yes." It came out like a shiver; I was so sticky and damp all over I could barely think. "I thought you knew that."

"No. I guessed you might, judging by the train route. I guessed you'd have to be no more than a stop or two beyond me, to make it to the office for ten." A fingertip slid under the elastic. "Christ, you're wet. I knew you would be."

I could see a group of men in suits, ties off, collars open, watching us curiously, making inaudible comments.

"They know what you're doing," I moaned. "We'll get thrown out."

"Let's go somewhere more private then." I could hear the sucking sounds of his finger in my slick heat; in my confusion, I perceived them as deafeningly loud. "Unless you want them to watch. Do you like being watched? I bet you do. I bet they're wishing they had their fingers where I have. Not just the fingers either. Shall I invite them along?"

"Oh, don't," I wailed, having to work at remembering that this was not a good place to start rotating my hips and pushing down, begging for more, harder, deeper.

"Don't invite them? Or don't find somewhere more private?"

"No . . . let's go somewhere they can't see us."

"That's a very good idea. They'll know, all the same. They'll know I'm taking you away to be fucked. You do want to be fucked, don't you?"

"Mmm." My lips were pressed tight, my voice strained and

high-pitched. I nodded sharply to emphasize the importance of the point. Two fingers speared my cunt, holding me in place, owning me.

"Good. I think I know a place."

The fingers sloshed out, he pulled down my skirt and patted my bottom again.

"Come on," he said, taking my hand and entwining fingers so my own wetness was transferred to me. We walked in front of all the people lolling on the church steps and through an arched gateway leading into the churchyard.

Behind us I could hear some whistling and laughter.

"Oh God, you can't be serious! In a churchyard! All those people out there saw us come in! What if we get caught?"

"My erection doesn't travel well," he said grimly. "This place is shady and dark. And if we get caught, we get caught. I'm having you now, no matter what."

"I don't want to be arrested!"

"You won't be."

We walked along the side of the church, through a dense grove of trees. We were only halfway down the path before the illusion of distance from the London crowds descended. The chatter and clink of glasses was muffled by the foliage, even as dry as it was, and the endless traffic drone receded to a mild buzz.

He saw the place before I did – a tree trunk bent backwards at an angle that made it comfortable for leaning against.

"Right, that'll do," he decided. "Knickers off and leaning back on that tree trunk with your legs either side, please."

I was breathing heavily now, desperate for him to use me, but faintly aware that this was my very last chance to back out. Did I want to use it? Should I get out of here and run like fury to Farringdon Tube?

"You've brought a . . . ?"

"Of course. Don't know where you've been, do I?" He flashed a smile, then unexpectedly jerked me towards him and kissed me. "But I know where you're going. Straight on the end of my cock. Go on, then." He nipped at my earlobe, then spun me around and gave me a gentle push towards the tree.

In a dream now, I stepped out of my knickers and left them on the scrubby crackly ground, then I slowly, carefully aligned my spine with the bark of the tree and parted my thighs either side of the trunk, which was slightly thicker than my body. My legs were well spread now, the bottom button of my skirt straining a little, so that I had to pull it up to my waist, exposing my overripe pussy and sweaty thighs.

"Mmm, let me look at you like that for a minute," said my sleazy seducer, folding his arms over his brown and orange striped shirt and standing with feet wide apart to accommodate the obvious bulge in his suit trousers. "God, that's exactly how I've imagined you this past fortnight. That's how I've got myself off every night, thinking of you, spread and ready for me, just like that. Fuck, you're perfect. No, don't shut your eyes. Look at me, sweetheart. Take a really good look around. Because by the time I've finished with you, you won't be seeing straight for a long, long time."

He unfolded his arms and strode towards me with a demonically purposeful air.

"Look at her," he said, running hands up my soaked hold-ups to my even more soaked splayed sex lips. "Lying there with it all on show, just ready and waiting. You really need this, don't you?"

"Please . . . just . . . hurry up."

"Can't wait? Been sitting on the train every day wanting to pull up your skirt like this and show me your hungry pussy? Hey?"

"Yes," I yelped. He lowered his mouth to my hot core and gave it a long, luscious slurp.

"I can tell. You're streaming with juice. You want it badly, don't you?"

"Mmm, oh yes, I really do. Do it, please." By now I was rubbing my spine up and down the tree trunk, feeling everything clinging to me, ready to just grab at him and shove him inside.

"Oh, I'm going to." He stood straight and started unbuckling his belt ruthlessly. "I should have brought some rope. I'd love to tie you up here, keep you like this."

"Oooh." No more words. Beyond that now. Just bucking my hips up, flexing my calves, holding my thighs apart with kneading fingers.

His hands shook as he skinned on the rubber; he had to brace one palm on the tree trunk to keep from falling over. "I can't believe this is happening," he muttered, to himself more than me, before slapping his body up against mine and swarming up inside me to the hilt in one sweet, sharp thrust. "Ah yes," he mouthed blissfully. "Ah yes. You. I've got you." I brought my legs around and tucked them under his bottom, feeling the muscles tauten, preparing for action. "All the way up you," he whispered, wanting to hold on to the moment a while longer. "You're going nowhere, babe."

"No, no, I'm not." His body was heavy and hot on mine; it would not take much for us to start melting into each other, becoming one on the tree trunk. He pushed himself upwards without letting me off his hook and began unbuttoning my dress until it flapped either side of me. He pulled the cups of my bra over my nipples and gave each one a hearty suck. "Salty," he said. He traced patterns in the grimy sweat of my abdomen with a fingertip. "You're hot. I'm going to make you hotter."

He held my arms at my sides and began to slide his cock in and out, slowly at first, excruciatingly slowly – I could tell that he was having to make an effort to keep from coming then and there.

"You don't know my name, do you?" he said conversationally, presumably as part of this endeavour.

"No," I shuddered, digging my heels into his soft pale buttocks to spur him on.

"I know yours. You're called Jane."

"How do you know?"

His pace began to pick up; his chest crushed down on my breasts, one of his shirt buttons chafing a nipple with each stroke.

"Your security pass. You wear it on the train. You aren't wearing it now."

"Oh. Shit. Yeah. I suppose I do. Oh, please, more."

He wedged a hand between our pelvises, reaching for my clit and strumming it. "More? I can give you more. So, you don't know my name. But you're lying here in the open air taking my cock and begging for more. What does that make you?"

"Oh, fuck, a slut, a slut, a dirty whore!"

"Well . . . put," he ground out, ramming me into the tree trunk now, holding me down by one shoulder while his other hand worked over my clit. I was so hot, surely I was steaming, surely I would be a puddle of sweat and pussy juice by the time he was finished with me. The canopy of dry leaves overhead blurred; I even had sweat in my eyes, stinging them shut, so I had nothing more to concentrate on than the burning hot hammering taking place between my thighs and the bunching fingers on my clit and what a whore slut bitch I was to let a total stranger do all this to me without even asking his name and . . . oh . . . when I came, I cried out all kinds of things, things that made no sense at all, things that brought him smashing into his own dark climax, and he fell down on me and sank his tongue into my mouth, ending it all with the most violent kiss I could remember.

"Fuck. Oh fuck," he said when he let my mouth free. "You beautiful fucking whore."

My throat was so dry I could do no more than rasp. "Wow."

"Even if I never see you again, I can die happy," he said, nuzzling my neck, careless of its city grit.

"But you could," I whispered. "If you wanted."

His lifted his head, staring at me again with those shifty blue-green eyes.

"I mean," I stammered, not quite sure where I was going with this, "not like in a heavy sort of way."

"In a friendly fuck sort of way?" he enquired dryly.

"Well, yeah. If you want."

"I want," he said. "I'll make you do things you never imagined you'd do."

"You already have."

"Good. And it's Shaun, by the way."

Perverse bastard that he is, he made me go back to the Three Kings with him for a drink. I had to sit on the steps in my rumpled, sweat-patched, dirty dress. There was a dead leaf in my hair, my make-up was melted to fuck and my legs bore definite tree-bark patterns. This time, though, I enjoyed the attention. I enjoyed the thought that anyone looking at me could see I'd just been firmly and thoroughly shagged by the ordinary-almost-even-ugly bloke sitting with his arm around me, fingers playing idly with the hem of my skirt. We kissed like swooning lovers until dark fell and we took the last train home together, parting at the station.

No spending the night. No acting like boyfriend and girlfriend. Strictly hot, sweaty, horny, kinky, casual sex.

Which is what I'm looking forward to right now. I'm crossing the Thames, my knickerless bottom pressed into the biker's leathery thigh, wondering if he can *tell*, wondering what Shaun has in store for me today. It is difficult not to let my fingers stray crotchwards. Shaun has proved to have the very best kind of dirty mind – an endlessly inventive one – and he has led me down some very peculiar paths indeed since that tree-lined one at the side of the church. Without exception they have been worth the detour; I have discovered tastes and predilections I never knew I had.

At last the train draws in at Blackfriars and I look forward to the prospect of breathing in some slightly less stale air, fighting my way through the crush to get through the door and on to the platform.

At the ticket barrier I spot him, slouching against the wall in an open-necked white shirt, his floppy hair smoothed back against the heat. As usual, he waits until I almost pass him before putting out an arm and dragging me over to him by the wrist. He puts his nose in the crease of my neck and takes a deep draught of my dried-on scent.

"Mmm. Have a good wank, did we?"

"Not bad, thanks."

"What did you think about?"

"I thought about the time you lifted my skirt in St James's Park and spanked my arse in time to the marching band."

He chuckles. "That was a good one. Got another good one lined up for you now. Come on." He kisses me, very quickly but still managing to get a sliver of tongue in there, and leads me around to the station entrance. In a small alcove, away from the main drag, he shields me from view with his body and lifts my skirt.

"Time for a quick check," he says, making sure I am not wearing knickers, and that I am wet, as I am expected to be. Not a difficult rule to obey; I am always wet when we meet, whether I want to be or not.

I shut my eyes and rest my head against the sooty brickwork, breathing in tarry heat, hearing the pneumatic drills that are like the pulse of the City, always there. The thing about London is that, whatever you are doing, you can always bet that somebody has done it here before. Somebody has stood here, maybe before the river Walbrook was built over, being felt up by a nasty man who had nothing but dishonourable intentions towards her. Maybe then he was wearing a tunic or maybe he was wearing a top hat and a fob watch. But I bet he was here, and I bet there was a girl here with him, giving herself up to her dark side.

Once he has slicked up his fingers and given them a sniff, he leans over to kiss me. I used to find his kisses sloppy, but I have grown to love them, love their indiscipline and barrier-breaching, love their careless, breathless adolescent quality.

He takes me by the hand and leads me towards the bridge, but we do not cross it. Instead we take the steps down to the Embankment. At this section of the Thames, it is little more than a concrete pathway, the river rushing busily in front while the Blackfriars underpass road roars behind a wall. With the railway lines thundering overhead, it is not exactly a spot people choose to linger in, but all the same, there is a brief hinterland of scrubby greenery between the path and the road with some stone benches set at intervals for lovers of ear-bleeding urban racket.

He waits until we pass under the railway lines we travel together most mornings, then he pulls me down into the yellow-brown grass and hisses, "Here!"

"Here?" I wrinkle my nose. "People walk past here."

"They don't stop though. People walking down here are usually in a hurry to get somewhere else. They won't look either side. They look ahead."

Already he is pushing me on to my knees, lifting my skirt. The grass is prickly and I am conscious of the midday sun scorching down. If Shaun is an Englishman, does that make me a mad dog? A mad something, at any rate, to let him do this to me in our most public place yet. He has unbuckled and freed himself; he sits down on the grass and pulls me into his lap, making me gasp as I find myself swiftly and inescapably impaled on his hot, hard cock. I am facing forward, kneeling with my knees on either side of his thighs; his arms are wrapped around my ribcage, holding me in place. I am not sure how this would look to a passer-by – I think it might not be completely obvious that I am shafted by a prick beneath my flimsy skirt, but I cannot say for certain.

We sit there like that for a while, getting used to the position, trying to plan how it will work. I gaze across to the Tate Modern and the Millennium Bridge, wondering if our dotty shapes look lewd or innocent from that distance. Trains curve incessantly around the railway bridge, in and out of the station, cutting sparks on the tracks and making that strange piping and shushing noise that they do. Their rumble makes the ground we are sitting on vibrate; their fumes surround us on all sides. And then Shaun lifts me slightly and then slams me back down, and the main event has begun. I have to lean forward, to find my angle. I put my palms on the baked earth and give him the leeway to thrust while I jiggle back and forth, already too hot, already too wet, but knowing I cannot stop this until I have shown my slutty core to the towering London skyline.

"Do you think they can see us from the trains?" asks Shaun, his vigorous thrusting making it clear that he does not care either way. "Do you think they are looking out of the window watching you get fucked in the open air at lunchtime on a workday? They know that this is your idea of a lunch break. You don't get a lunch break. You get a fuck break. That's what you need. A daily fuck break. That's what you're going to get. I might pencil you in for tomorrow as well. You should see my diary, Jane. Meetings, meetings, social, meetings, fucking my slut, meetings, more meetings. Uh!"

He pulls me back up to his chest abruptly and for a second I wonder if he has come already, but then I see that two suited men are wandering up the path, speaking loudly into mobile phones in competition with each other. Shaun buries his lips in my neck, making us look as much as possible like normal lovers catching a quick lunchtime rendezvous. The men barely give us a second glance, though one double-takes briefly and smirks in Shaun's direction before moving on under the railway lines and away.

Then Shaun bends me back over and commences a savage onslaught, hard and fast, until I am dripping and scratched and raw and burning. "They knew I was fucking you, Jane. They knew it," he whispers, and I come, and he comes, and the Oxo Tower shimmers in a heat haze that blankets all of us while we fall forwards, wailing and sighing, on to the hard ground.

Half an hour later we are sitting outside a riverside pub, drinking lager (him) and vodka and orange (me). It is beginning to occur to me that, in the space of six weeks, this sordid arrangement has become an addiction – something that will damage me if I cannot learn to control it. The combination of heat and sex and alcohol makes me lightheaded and bold and I say things I would not normally dare to.

"The men can't take their eyes off you," he is saying, relishing the words. "They can probably smell you. One day I might invite them over."

I raise my damp eyebrows at him. "One day, Shaun. This can't go on forever though, can it?"

His face falls a little. I want to touch his hand, but it seems against the rules somehow. Too intimate.

"I've met someone at work," I tell him. "It's nothing much at the moment. Coffee, chat. We're going to the cinema this weekend. Might come to nothing, or it might get serious. And if it does, I can't do this any more."

Shaun looks away, over the river, for a moment, then looks into the dregs of his pint.

"You want to be a nice girl," he says flatly. He looks up at me squinting against the sun, waiting.

"No. Not necessarily. I don't know. I want to be . . . Jane. Jane who's a slut sometimes, but a person as well."

"There aren't enough sluts in the world," says Shaun wistfully. "Not perfect ones like you, at least. I might have known . . ."

"Shaun," I say, a little distressed. "I'm not saying . . ." I don't know what I'm saying.

He drains the last drops of his drink and bangs his glass down on the table.

"Well, you don't have time to say it now, anyway. I have to get back to work. To the offices of the London Merchant Bank. On Threadneedle Street."

I catch my breath. He has never told me anything about himself before. He is standing up, taking something from a pocket. Paper and pen.

"That's where I work," he says, "and this is where I live. Not far from you, I think." He scribbles down an address, three streets away from my flat, and puts the paper in my hand. "If you want to call round. Tonight. Tomorrow night . . ." He shrugs. "I'll leave it up to you." He dithers, as if unsure how to end our encounter, looking around to the exit and then back at me.

Time to seize the day. Time to also seize his hand.

"Promise you won't ever stop being sleazy?"

He smiles, toothy and broad. "No question of that."

"I'll see you tonight then."

We snog for ages, by the river, ignoring the sniggering remarks of the boozy bankers, then I have to run for my train, all the way back to where it began.

Freeing the Demon

Sacchi Green

In two years of drifting in place Jayne had seldom looked out the window. What was the point? At night, clients came, and went; in the daytime she slept. Sometimes, very rarely, she dreamed.

She might never have noticed him looming just beyond her balcony if a nervous college kid hadn't felt in sudden need of air.

"Hey, terrific gargoyle! French, probably, limestone, taking a beating from acid rain. Not much detail left." He grasped at the distraction. "They say gargoyles are demons cursed with eternal imprisonment in stone. Guess nobody figured even stone might not be forever."

Jayne's stroke on his thigh turned him from the window. Long, pale hair swung with the seductive tilt of her head. Grey eyes looked through dark lashes into his. "You like things . . . French?" He forgot about the gargoyle.

Jayne didn't forget.

On a rainy evening she watched through summer dusk as rivulets washed over the stone shoulders. Thin glistening ribbons of water criss-crossed in ill-defined grooves, giving a sense of layered scales, or feathers; something indelibly winglike.

The massive back was hunched. The twisted, upturned face hurled mute defiance at the heavens, while pointed ears and horns stabbed at the sky. The jaws had once spouted water from the eaves, but the intake had been clogged for years and the torrent spilled haphazardly down the head. The teeth were mere vestigial stumps. Jayne thought of the acid rain, and her own fleeting youth, and mourned for them both.

That night, after a bout with a truly nasty customer, Jayne leaned out into the light rain. Leopold sent such creeps from time to time to scare her, keep her in line.

She gazed at the still, dark figure as mist cooled her skin and a breeze swept the fouled air away. He hulked, blot-like, against clouds lit by ambient city light. "They're wearing us down, *mon ami*," she murmured.

As her eyes adjusted to darkness the stone face seemed to flush with a reddish glow. A dull light pulsed through slanted eyes and gaping throat, highlighting the teeth. At thirteen storeys a connection to the basement furnace seemed unlikely, but Jayne was too drained to care.

In daylight she took a closer look, finding nothing but dry stone mottled by smoke and rain and bird droppings. Some obscure proprietary impulse drove her to take water and soap and a long brush and scrub as far as she could reach. A curse was one thing; debasement was something else.

Over the weeks she watched him in varying lights and weather. Only the combination of night and rain produced the strange effect, as though acidity ate away a thin veneer that resealed in daylight.

Jayne found herself trying to communicate. "Who trapped you? Someone higher up the chain of evil? Or a self-righteous moral bigot? I've known both kinds. There isn't much to choose." His pulsing glow seemed to quicken in agreement.

Her own sense of comradeship surprised her. Since the stone demanded nothing, she yearned to give. Not, of course, that she could think of anything worth giving.

In symbolic sharing she reached up to lay morsels of food on the stone tongue. When she tried this on a rainy night, the offering was sucked into the red cavern with a force that thrilled and frightened her. When she offered raw meat, the eyes glowed hotter and a swirl of smoke rose from the rumbling depths.

She blinded herself to the ominous implications, preferring to think, if she thought at all, that her sanity was slipping. What had sanity ever done for her?

Reality was increasingly hard to bear. Someday soon Leopold would forget, or cease to care, that he couldn't afford to mark her face or body.

On the night he finally snapped, rain splatted against the window and shards of his spittle flecked her face as he shouted and raged and shook her.

"Yes!" she screamed at last. "Yes! I held out on you! I hid money! Why not? I earned it!" The capitulation startled him into releasing her.

"It's out there, in the gargoyle's mouth." She gestured towards the window. "But it slipped down and I can't quite reach it. You get it, if you want it!"

"Like hell! In the fucking rain? In this suit? Get out there and don't come back without it!"

The cold rain slicked her thin wrap to her body. She'd lied about the money being there, though she did have a stash secreted elsewhere, saving for . . . for some other kind of life. Any other kind.

It didn't matter. She wasn't going back.

She looked down. Neon flashed and car lights crawled along the street far, too far, below. To sprawl in their glare, broken and distorted . . . no . . .

She turned to the gargoyle and clung. It felt warm, vibrant, even . . . responsive. If only she had known! Such opportunities lost.

Leopold came cursing and stumbling out the window. He had shed his coat, but rain soaked his silk shirt and rage twisted his face. His cronies on Wall Street would scarcely have known him, even those who knew this source of his money because they had paid for the pleasure of Jayne's company.

Jayne stepped up onto the low balustrade, reached an arm into the gargoyle's mouth as far as she could, and willed herself to oblivion. Heat pulsed from within. Tremors shuddered through the stone.

Then Leopold was tearing and striking at her, not caring that her feet slid off the balustrade, that her arms were slipping from the stone torso.

The void below dragged at her, tried to swallow her – but something enfolded her, something warm and winglike and unseen, holding her safely while Leopold clawed at the stone and crammed his fist into the gaping maw.

Whatever she had hoped for, it was better and worse. His head went last. Hot blood streamed past, mixed with cold rain, and only when all ran cold did she know it was over. Then she was through the window, on the floor, not remembering how she had crawled there.

Dawn showed Leopold's crumpled coat beneath the window. There would be cash in its inner pockets, but Jayne couldn't bring herself to touch it. Yet.

No one would wonder at any extremity of cries from her apartment. Leopold would hardly be missed except by his creditors. If she could just make sure nothing could connect her to his disappearance . . .

When at last she steeled herself to look outside there seemed to be no trace of him, until sunlight glinted on a gold wristwatch dangling from a stone jaw and jewelled rings tilting precariously on vestigial teeth.

She reached out, tentative at first; then her touch became a lingering caress across the rough stone face.

How quickly, she wondered, did erosion wear away the stone? What would happen to the world when the demon, if such he were, broke free? Did she care?

She knew what she cared about. She remembered the embrace of invisible wings, the power summoned by night and rain and her need. Her hands moved sensuously, stroking the folded wings, the breast, the ridged belly slanting away between braced forelegs. She sensed the mounting tension in the rigid stone, and whispered promises, waiting for night, and rain.

For two days it stayed dry. Jayne took the necessary steps to change Leopold's jewellery into cash, and to make the cash secure along with what she'd found in his pockets. Attention to such details occupied a level of her mind that seemed to be waking after years of sleep. She no longer drifted.

On another level, she was willingly swept along on a tide of erotic fantasy, feeling rough stone where there were only plaster walls, seeing slanting, glowing eyes in taxi tail-lights. When the first tongues of rain licked her skin as she hurried home through the dusk, ripples of heat flowed over and through her. Her breath quickened in anticipation.

She started tearing at her constricting clothing in the elevator. By the time she thrust open the window she was naked.

The rain had intensified, and now it blew cold on her skin. The shock gave her mind a chance to catch up with her need.

When Jayne finally climbed out onto the balcony she was wrapped in a deeply hooded raincoat. She knew the allure of mystery, and slow unveiling; she also knew all previous experience might be irrelevant. Could her demon be pleased like human men? Until she knew his pleasure, she would simply please herself.

The light from his depths glowed hotter than ever before. In anticipation of her coming? Or had he gained strength from devouring Leopold? A shiver of fear sharpened her excitement.

She pressed herself against the rain-slick stone and inched the raincoat open. Chill gave way to warmth wherever skin touched stone, and when she stretched upwards from the balustrade a deep vibration pulsed through the rigid mass. She pressed closer, bruising her softness on his ridges, melding pain with pleasure, but when she sensed a desperation in his trembling she loosened her grip and stepped down.

Jayne knew the art of pleasing watchers. They had been her only bearable customers. In any closer interaction it was she who would become the watcher, removed, unmoved, observing with vague repulsion what her other self must do.

She wondered whether he could see her, but when she raised the edges of the coat like dark wings the light beamed obliquely from this eyes to warm the pale flame of her body.

The coat, once released, did not fall but floated above and behind, supported by the light. She forgot the rain, forgot everything but herself and that burning presence, feeding on his hunger as it fed on hers.

Beginning with dance-like movements, slowly, sinuously, Jayne curved her hands from waist to hips, slimness to taut fullness. Her touch was the watcher's touch, but under her command.

Then she drew her fingers lightly upwards, brushing them teasingly around the outer curves of her breasts, catching her breath at the sweet soreness. As she cupped them gently and then less gently, the fullness, the firmness, grew; in her mind her outline transformed from slender to voluptuous.

The ripples of pleasure intensified. Urgency flowed down her body. She throbbed both with fullness and with an aching need to be filled.

Jayne thought fleetingly of pulling back. How could she bear it if this hot tide never flooded into release? But it was all she had to give. And besides, it was too late.

Hard nipples jutted from her round full breasts, yearning desperately for the stroke of hands that could not reach out, for the hot press and tug and bite of a mouth frozen in stillness. Her fingers teased their tips into greater, harder, unbearable tension, while her palms still cupped the swelling fullness. She thrust against her own hands and moaned, again and again, until a deeper echo sounded from the stone before her and she raised her eyes.

Red light pulsed from the depths. A low rumbling sound went on and on. How could she truly touch him, penetrate the shell of dark magic, bring his torment and hers to an ecstatic peak?

She had come to despise men's bodies, but now she cursed the spell, or sculptor, that had shaped the gargoyle, pressing the forelegs together to obscure the loins, leaving her without even a simulacrum of maleness to stroke, taste, press against.

Her hands slipped downwards. Her breasts still yearned with fullness, but a hunger still more intense built in her depths, a pounding pressure that demanded a harder pressure in return, more, and more . . .

Detachment long gone, she could only open mind as well as flesh to him, projecting her own sensations, hoping for him to somehow tell her how to meet his need.

His vision of her flashed through her mind; eyes half-closed, lips full and parted, head twisting from side to side as damp, heavy hair coiled over her shoulders and slid across her thrusting nipples, rising and falling to the ragged rhythm of her breathing. It was his will that raised her hand to cradle and press one breast and then the other, gently at first, then harder, sending hot lances downwards. She no longer knew which sobbing cries and moans were her own, and which reverberated from the stone.

Somewhere in the outer world there were sounds. Pounding on a door? Or her own blood pounding in her ears? The clamour of her body drowned any intrusion. Linked with this being who watched and shared and demanded, she moved in response to his will as well as her own, hips twisting, undulating, arching towards him, hands stroking and kneading and tantalizing but leaving the hot, pulsing void for him, for his filling, if only he would come to her, into her . . .

A sharp crack split the air. The balcony shook. A wave of force slammed her against the building, jarring her teeth into her lower lip until it bled. She forced down pain-sparked anger; whatever she had incited she would willingly accept.

The pressure surged up and down her body. She couldn't breathe, couldn't see, mist swirled before her eyes . . . but the force eased at her struggles. She pushed against it and it eased again, in slight, unsteady increments.

As her vision cleared, distant lights and buildings twisted and wavered, distorted by something not quite visible, something trembling between being and not being. She reached out and felt a throbbing as of air propelled by beating wings, or a pounding heart.

She leaned into the pressure, then fell back as it surged towards her. Forward, back, approaching a balance; "Yes, gently, softly, but not too softly . . . now harder. . . ." He was taking form now, still murky to the eyes but tangible to her hands, her skin, her demanding body.

Wingtips curved around her. Strong arms circled her and hands grasped the soft fullness of her buttocks to lift and press her up against him. Fiery crescent eyes flickered closer and closer as she stretched upwards. He bent his head and with a tongue gently rasping, like a cat's, licked the drops of blood from her lip.

She clutched at his massive chest, iron-hard under deep velvet fur; gripped corded thighs with her own, straining to raise herself enough to meet the tip of the great cock pulsing against her belly. He lifted her higher, and she was there . . . there . . . but in spite of overflowing readiness she thought at first she could never fit him in.

She sobbed in frustration, thrusting frantically against him, and he raised her again until his hardness teased, stroked, licked at her, flooding her with wetness and sensation. When finally, slowly, he slid inside, the demanding fullness was a pleasure/pain almost more than she could bear.

Distant sounds, banging, harsh words, impinged on her consciousness. Then he moved, and drove her to move, and the world receded. Hot surges of sensation wracked her, until they came so close and fast that she rose on the wave and rode it until it crashed, at last, into thunderous release.

Even the ebbing was glorious. She clutched the great body, now solid, dark, completely there, and held him as his wrenching spasms went on and on and on.

At last, when he seemed almost spent, she reached up to stroke his face; but it grew ever more distant as the presence that had filled her receded. She slid down until her feet touched the floor. His form dissipated slowly, like smoke, leaving her a last vision of a wraith-like hand outstretched in supplication.

Cold air chilled her fevered skin. She watched the glow intensify inside the stone and knew he was trapped again, though a thread of fire showed through the long crack newly formed between braced forelegs.

The rain had stopped. She forced herself to move, bent to reclaim the limp raincoat, turned towards the lighted window. Lighted? She hadn't turned on the lamps! Had she locked the door before rushing to the window? Sounds and words she had blocked out came back to her in a rush.

There had been banging on the door, thumping on the window frame, a harsh voice shouting, "For Christ's sake, buddy, get it off already, will you!"

She knew that voice, like oily gravel. One of Leopold's "associates". She had expected to have to deal with him, or someone like him, but not in such a state of vulnerability. The raincoat felt wet and cold and gritty as she hugged it around herself and stepped through the window.

"Kinky bastard, eh?" He waved a heavy arm towards the window. "Isn't coming in? Afraid to be seen? I don't give a shit who he is. Just tell me where fucking Leopold is hiding out and I'll be out of here."

Jayne was shaky, but not as dazed as she sounded. "I . . . who . . . ?" She glanced vaguely around the room. "I'm sorry, Mr . . . Mr Robinson, isn't it? I haven't seen Leopold in three or four days, and that's just fine with me."

The hair was impeccably styled, the skin pampered, but the wide mouth grinned in a toad-like face. "You don't say! Considering new management?" She saw the move coming but couldn't retreat. He whipped her raincoat open and yanked at it, turning her until it fell off. "Rough stuff. Nice." A thick finger jabbed at the bruises on her neck and shoulders where Leopold had gripped her, and the scrapes from tonight's impact of stone and wall. Then he gripped her jaw and squeezed her mouth until drops of blood from her cut lip ran down her chin.

"What does it cost for a piece of that?" His voice had thickened.

"What's it worth to you?" Her purr masked her fury. Keep him off guard, find a way to kill him, feed him piece by piece to the stone jaws . . .

"Get rid of the john out there and we'll see." He adjusted his trousers. "Christ, he's going to freeze his ass off, if you've left him any!" He moved towards the window.

Without any clear plan she moved to intercept him. He stiffened. The toad slash curled into a snarl. "That's fucking Leopold out there, isn't it! Fucking Leopold, fucking! He should have stuck to that side of his business instead of pimping worthless mutual funds." He gave a bark of mirthless laughter and shoved her aside.

Rage coiled through Jayne like a steel spring. He would not foul her balcony with his gross presence, leer at the red glow of her lover's trapped spirit! She launched herself at his back, striking between his shoulder blades with all her weight and fury. His startled cry mingled with a roar from beyond as his upper body pitched forward, through the window . . . and beyond into a spray of blood.

Jayne watched in savage joy. Her demon was so strong now, he could reach out so far . . .

When it was over, though, she stumbled to her bed and sank, shaken and drained, into darkness.

Late at night the demon came to her, in vision deeper than dream.

Jayne saw his true form, merely caricatured by the stone carving; a shape more man than beast, long-limbed, graceful, powerful, covered with a thick black fur whose silken touch made her shiver with delight. The curved horns rose naturally from his proud head, extending the line of the pointed ears. His slanting eyes curled into crescents when he smiled, a wicked grin that showed strong, gleaming fangs. She had to smile back.

He held out a hand, cruel talons retracted, and she grasped it with her own. She pressed against him, but after a moment he swung her gently around.

Only then did she become aware of the surroundings in her vision. Walls of smoothly fitted stones, candles smoking fitfully in sconces, hangings in deep colours with intricate designs not quite revealed by the dim light. An ambience profoundly other, yet vaguely familiar, a scene from a history book, or fairy tale.

He drew her to a small arched window, and she looked through iron bars down into a torch-lit courtyard. She watched, unseen, as a red-robed figure passed by, thick fingers stroking a heavy golden cross; but when she looked for holiness in his face she read only a cruel sensuality she knew all too well.

The demon gripped the bars, bent them with slight effort, then pushed with increasing tension against an invisible field of force just beyond. When she reached through the bars she felt no barrier; it seemed to be devised for him alone.

Ancient magic or future science? She was distracted by the play of muscles across black-velvet shoulders, back, buttocks . . . no wings? But the wings were there, sweeping in and out of visibility as he strained against the unseen wall. They faded as he slumped back and turned towards her, face twisted in anger and despair.

The proud head bent, the tall form folded, knelt, until he crouched at her feet like a great dark knot of wood shaped by a master carver.

A wave of compassion swept her, and, in its wake, a resolve. If he asked for her help, it must be in her power to give. In the world she inhabited (however tenuously) they had already cut a strange and bloody swathe together; she would willingly challenge whatever world held him captive.

She reached out to embrace him, pressing her breasts against his bowed head; the sheltering mantle of her moon-pale hair enveloped him. "Yes," she murmured, "yes," more certain of the answer than the question. A cool breeze stirred the curtain of hair. She saw brightening sky outside the window and, as she watched, a shaft of hazy sunlight came through the window and crept towards them, until, with a convulsive lurch, her lover was gone from her arms and she was left empty, hollow, kneeling on her own floor in her own room in a cold pool of daylight.

Even with Leopold gone there were some regular clients to deal with. Those few who persisted despite her refusal went the same way in due course, each adding to her demon's strength. She began to think he might break free of his bonds while still in this world. It would be disappointing if she never got to follow him to that other place.

Jayne was disappointed as well that his continual gorging appeared to interfere with arousal. She savoured for days the lingering feel of him, like a taste too intense to absorb all at once, but by the end of a week the urge for further tasting consumed her.

It was time for a test. He had devoured the latest victim at the very door of her bedroom, sucking him into that unseen dimension that claimed them all. Could he come in visible and tangible form just a few steps further?

She watched her reflection in the dark window. A long white satin gown caressed her skin, clinging and rippling; she might have been a caryatid, or an angel from a Renaissance artist's erotic dreams.

When she opened the window a stream of raindrops brightened with a reflected glow. He knew she was there.

Jayne stroked the creamy satin; then, deliberately, turned away. The lick of silky fabric over skin already sensitized drove her longing close to pain. If he didn't come she would have to go to him, and soon.

But he was there before her, lounging on the bed, watching with hot eyes and laughing mouth. She avoided his outstretched hand, letting a satin thigh just brush his fingertips. He kept talons retracted, willing to play the game.

When she knelt by the bed and pushed gently at his chest he leaned back onto the mounded pillows. Her hand brushed his erection, making it leap; she felt an urgent pang but kept her movements languorous.

The inner sweep of his thighs, where the fur almost disappeared, shivered under her strokes. Avoiding the most outstanding feature, she burrowed her face into his silk-furred belly, then pulled back quickly. He was gripping the blankets now and breathing faster.

Jayne slipped a white hand between dark thighs and cupped his heavy fullness with gently increasing pressure. His buttocks tensed, his back arched. She slid her fingers upwards, moving along his pulsing cock, trembling slightly as she wondered how her cunt had been able to hold this immensity, and how long she could bear to wait before doing it again.

Too much protraction of this game and she might cheat herself, but to see him like this, to press him to the edge, to bend, taste . . . His head was thrown back, his eyes slits, a low growl rumbling along with each ragged breath.

Her tongue flicked in and out, again and again, tasting the very tip, tormenting him with the lightness of each touch. His talons pierced through to the mattress as he gripped the bed. She pulled back to shrug the satin down over the peaks of her nipples, then leaned forward to brush them against his hardness.

She ached to be filled, but still . . . One more teasing lick, then her whole mouth plunged over him, filled with him, sucked at him, savoured his salt tang, while her hand slid up and down the length that was too much for mouth and throat to hold. The throbbing began, the taste intensified . . . she had gone too far . . .

Great hands gripped her shoulders, pushed her back. Through streaming hair she watched him wrestle for control, a harsh moan grating in his throat, drops of blood welling where fangs clenched in his lower lip.

Then his eyes burned into hers, urging, demanding, sending a message she didn't understand. All she could do was what she did understand, sliding the satin gown up above her hips, moving over him, meeting his hardness with her own wild, wet need, sliding down over him slowly, slowly, until the fullness drove her to rise, and plunge, and rise.

He gripped her hips, stilled them, then grasped her shoulders. She was consumed by the need to move, but he pulled her until her damp hair brushed his face; then his tongue came out to lick at one of the drops of blood gleaming on his lip. She remembered that tongue on her own lip, her own blood . . .

Jayne lowered her head and ran her tongue along the line of drops, then closed her lips around his and sucked gently until her mouth was full of the metallic tang. She swallowed. A tingle spread through her body in a frothing tide, ebbing just as he began to move, at last, in the demanding rhythm she craved.

Then she knew only the driving ache of pleasure, the mounting of the great wave that must break at last into the maelstrom of release. But he held her there, riding the crest, farther and farther, until they spun at last completely out of the world she had known.

The blaze of sensation faded gradually into glowing embers. Jayne became aware of the beat of wings. Still they spun on, ever slower, until at last familiar stone walls enclosed them and all motion ceased. She buried her face in his velvet chest.

He stroked along her hair, and down her back. Her shoulder blades tingled. The sensation grew, swelled – and at last she understood, and felt her own power, and gloried in the unfurling of her own great white sheltering wings.

The red-robed priest might think to hold a demon captive, but he could never resist an angel of seduction, and ecstasy, and death.

River

Catherine Leary

The woman leaves everything behind: home, job, cats, clothes, friends. Armed with only a car and a plastic card she ventures forth into the rest of the world.

I was born in New England and it's a cold place. Raised in the four iron walls of the long winter. Left to brood in the dark. Growing up there made me strange though I never understood how strange until I'd shaken the winter salt from my boots. I drove south and watched the summers lengthen and felt the heat make its home in my skin. The forgotten dream spurred me onwards and some days I thanked it and others I cursed it but I was happy to have the ice melted out of my toes.

The car gets a flat tyre in South Carolina. Riding along on a back road tangled with trees and spooky with Spanish moss when she feels the shudder and blow, the telltale pull of the wheel.

In Pennsylvania the woman picks up a hitchhiker. This hitchhiker is a young woman who calls herself River. River is younger. She is twenty if she is a day and she smells like she hasn't bathed in a while but she's young and has straight white teeth and perky breasts. She never wears a bra. She giggles at everything. She sits in the passenger seat and twiddles through the radio stations and threatens to pee in an empty waxed paper cup when the woman can't find a bathroom. The two of them pick up another hitchhiker in Virginia, a bearded guy who's been hiking the Appalachian Trail. He has pot and he asks politely if he's allowed to smoke. The woman rolls down the windows and says she doesn't care. The windows keep most of the smoke out of her head but not all of it. Before they are even out of Virginia, River fucks him. She does it in a gas station bathroom while the woman is paying for gas.

River is the kind of girl who has to fuck everybody. The woman muses on this while she is driving and eating a fruit pie. River fucked her way out of New York and cemented the allegiance of their wannabe nature bumhead with her cunt and will likely fuck her way to wherever she wants to go. The woman wonders if River will make a pass at her. The night after they leave the mountain man at a bus station in Georgia she gets her answer. They're staying in a cheapo motel with one bed and the woman lies in bed and pretends to sleep and River kisses the back of her neck. River kisses her neck and puts her greedy arms around her waist and the woman cannot bear her need. So she turns her down. Unlocks her hands and pushes them away. She lies in bed and listens to River fall asleep and thinks that if River offers again she may take her up on it.

Fixing the tyre is expensive. Waiting for the tyre costs even more.

One night after showers River makes another try and the woman kisses her and thinks this feels like nothing *and she puts River's fat young nipples in her mouth and thinks* still nothing. *She touches River's cunt and it's full of water. There's too much of it, too much slickness and the woman has no idea what to do with such desire when it's not her own. River is disappointed that the woman is not even moist and gets down on her knees beside the bed but her tongue feels slimy and it's not at all good. River gets petulant. She gets angry and throws a container of pork fried rice. The carton doesn't even break open as it tumbles to the floor and something inside breaks her. River cries. She falls into the woman's arms and the woman holds her. She strokes her hair. River breaks apart with astonishing ease. The woman comforts her and helps her put herself back together again and they go out under the buzzing blinking neon sign in the heat of the night and buy a bag of burgers. They eat fries together under the big neon sign and slap the moths away from their faces.*

River takes her empty cup into the parking lot and drops her shorts. She hovers over it. She pees on the ice and the woman laughs until she is out of breath.

The Mississippi River awed me.

"When we cross this we will be in the west," I said.

River had stolen the mountain man's stash before we got rid of him. She had eaten some of it and was stoned. "Who cares?"

"That's one fucking big river."

"Yep." River knocked a fist against her chest. She burped and giggled. "Can I get an amen?"

"Amen. Fucker."

"Double fucker."

Almost at the Texas line and a tent revival on the side of the road slows them down. There's a little cash now because River sold what was left of the stash to a car full of college students back at a rest area and she carries the money folded up and hidden in her shoe. The woman just wants to get across the Louisiana state line. River is captivated by the idea of the tent revival.

"Come on, man. I wanna get laid."

"You always want to get laid."

"Come on. There's some prime virgin ass just waiting to be tapped. I wanna get Jesused. I wanna get down with the Lord. Who knows, maybe we can knock over the collection basket or something."

"Yeah, right before we get tarred and feathered and run out on a rail."

"This is modern times. They don't do that tarring and feathering thing anymore."

"How would you know?"

"Come on, honey. Let's do it. I'm bored."

"You're always bored."

"So?"

"*You* can knock over the collection basket."

"Does this mean we're going?"

"It means I'm tired of driving."

"Yay!"

The woman is nervous about leaving her car in a place where there are so many people milling around but River convinces her to put all the stuff that anyone might want to steal in the trunk. They get out of the car and clean up the floor and put the trash in the trunk along with the rest of the stuff even though River laughs and declares that no one in their right mind would want to steal a bunch of broken sunglasses and burned CDs. The woman stands with her arms wrapped tight around herself. She looks up at the night sky. The night sky is beaten back by floodlights.

"I'm still nervous."

"Oh come on, man, it's a bunch of holy rollers. How wrong can it go?"

"Plenty wrong if you try to steal from them. Most people don't appreciate it. Including Christians."

"I won't try and steal from them. I promise. Now are you still nervous?"

"Yeah. I'm sorry, River, I can't shake it. I'm just jittery. All these people and this place are making me jittery."

"Maybe you've just been in the car too long."

"Maybe. I don't know. Maybe it's my druid blood speaking."

"Druid blood my ass. You're tired."

"I am that, but I'm also nervous."

"I'll lead you in, OK? I'll even hold your hand."

"Oh Christ don't do that. They'll think we're lesbians and that we are in need of extra saving."

"Well I am in need of extra saving, but not the saving they've got in mind. There are some cute girls here too. Maybe I should run me down some pussy instead."

"God, is that all you think about?"

"Is your druid blood all you think about? Or whatever it is?"

"All right. All right."

"I'm talking you down."

"You're talking me down. You silver-tongued devil you."

River giggled. "Come on, honey. Let's go in."

"I can't help it, I feel like someone's going to lob a rock through the window just for spite."

"But this is a bunch of Christians feeling the love. There's no love in rocks."

"I'm not getting into that with you. Let's go in there before I change my mind for good."

"I'll throw grass at you. Or mud if I can find it."

"I'd feel better if I could see a star or two."

"You know, that makes me want to draw one on my boob with a sharpie just so I can flash it at you. Maybe one on each boob."

I burst out laughing. "All right, then. I'll be OK once we're in there."

"You better be. Though you could blame it on tongues. Or the Holy Spirit or whatever it is that happens at these things. You don't think they'll handle snakes do you? I don't like snakes." She shuddered. "They're cold and creepy."

"If there are snakes I'm getting the hell out and leaving you here if you don't come with me."

"Okey dokey. Deal."

Just as the two of them move into the tent, thunder claps overhead and it starts to rain. Fat smacking drops on the canvas. They wend their way through a maze of folding metal chairs and murmuring disgruntled

*people while the rain quickens from a tapping into a steady growl and
then into a full-on wet-throated roar. River giggles and takes hold of the
woman's hand and glides along, her arm outstretched and looking
backwards as though they are partners in some dance. Between the
pouring rain and the voices they slip through a wall of noise. More and
more people are crowding into the tent just to be out of the rain.*

*There are empty seats in the back. The old ladies in the back think they
are sisters, even when River picks up the woman's hand and kisses her
knuckles and giggles at her own coquettishness. River wants to stand on
the chair and the woman doesn't let her. River wants to sit on her lap. The
woman says no. She sits on her own chair and crosses her legs and rests
her hands on her knee like a polite schoolgirl and this makes River laugh
even harder. River laments aloud that she doesn't have any more dope.
She passes judgement on several of the young men in attendance and not
a few of the young ladies. The old women sitting around them beam
benevolently and the woman comes to the conclusion that they are deaf or
maybe senile and possibly here looking for a laying-on of hands. River is
looking for a laying-on of hands all right. With all these people around she
twitches in her seat like an animal in heat and the woman recognizes that
is what River is, really, just a cat in heat, a pussy on the prowl looking for
anything. The woman wonders what will happen to River when she gets
old. One day River won't have young nipples or young hips and her
giggling won't be cute anymore. It will just be annoying. She'll be old and
wrinkled and unable to get out of bed and won't be able to fuck her way
into anything.*

*The woman looks at River and sees all the way down time's dusty
corridor.*

*The preacher comes out. He can't stand still and so he paces as he talks
into the microphone. He works himself up with each step, words coming
hard and fast and repetitious in places until he works out a rhythm, nails
it down with his words and hooks the crowd with it and all at once the
crowd is surging forward and the preacher is leaning backwards. They're
only words rendered in this stranger's voice but he is seducing them just
the same. Just words. The pitch of this man's voice is escalating and the
breath of his congregation is escalating. It's like fucking. The woman is
amazed. Crowd psychology, she knows it, has seen the same thing happen
at conventions and rock concerts but there is something primitive about
the inside of this tent, being hemmed in by the rain, the very air she
breathes laden with the scent of mud and too much sweating skin.
Fermented zealotry. Or maybe it's the eye of faith.*

"I'd so fuck him," River breathed.

I rolled my eyes. "I'm shocked. Really."

"You think I should try to?"

"No. What would be the point?"

"It's like nailing the top banana. It's serious street cred in the bad-girl Christian world. I don't think I've ever fucked a preacher."

"You probably have. You just don't know it."

"You spoil everything. You rain on my parade."

I looked at the canvas ceiling. "You're right on the rain. But the rain isn't my fault."

"You aren't going to blame that on your druid blood too?"

"Shut the fuck up about my druid blood. Do not piss on my druid blood. It's a real thing."

The preacher's good and worked up now, his forehead gleams with a sweat that puts her in mind of a lathered horse and the people in the tent are agitated and full of moans and sways. A man falls down in the aisle and convulses while spitting out a stream of gibberish. The woman thinks seizure *but the congregants think* holy spirit *and this man is borne up on a sea of waving hands and passed around like an artefact. Every finger in the place touches him. Even the woman puts her hand on his ankle thinking maybe faith is like a virus and it's worth catching a little something, that maybe it will creep up on her and the desire for the Bible will be like a fever and the next time she's busy living her life she'll feel a tickle and instead of a sneeze out will come a big fat hallelujah.*

My toes curled in my sandals and pushed all the blood out of my nail beds. I marvelled at their paleness.

There is a man walking into the tent. He is tall. His coat is long. It is cut to the shape of his broad shoulders and it falls around him in a sweep, the motion of his stride captured in a flap of storm-coloured canvas. He's wearing some kind of old-fashioned pale hat with a black band. A fedora, she thinks, but I'm not sure if that's right, it's the only kind of hat I can think of that men don't wear anymore, and whatever kind of hat that is men don't wear it anymore. It's gone by the wayside. It's been plucked off a corpse. This thought rises out of a secret place and makes her shiver. The man pauses at the head of the congregation and takes the hat off, shakes the rain from it. His water-coloured eyes move across the crowd. The woman feels their sweep and her face feels funny, detached and floating, as though it has risen above the crowd and cried out to be seen. She wants to cover it with her hands but knows it will be hot. There is too much blood in her cheeks.

"Are you OK?" River squinted. "Your face is all red."

"I'm all right."

River straightened up and looked around. "You sure? It is kinda hot in here. We can go and get some air if you want."

"No, I'll be fine. I just saw something."

"What?"

"Nothing."

"What?"

"Nothing!"

He puts the hat back on his head and people are noticing. They see his fine coat and notice. They see his hat and the casual disrespect of it. They are huddled in an itinerant house of God, still a holy place even if the walls are canvas and the fallow ground beneath their feet belongs to a local farmer. There is still sanctity even if it is makeshift.

"Tell me," said River.

"There's nothing to tell."

"Goddamn it you're bullshitting me and I want you to stop it. What is going on? What did you see? Is it that guy we picked up in Virginia? Oh my God it is, isn't it? Isn't it?"

"No. River. Calm down."

"It is. You just don't want to tell me."

"It's got nothing to do with that."

"You're going to wait. I see how it is. You're going to lie to me about this and wait and then when he figures out that I stole his dope he's gonna . . ."

"River, you are freaking out about nothing." I kept my voice a low hiss. "I'm only going to say it one more time: it's nothing. There's nothing. The guy with the dope isn't here."

"What else could it be? Why are you acting like this? Are you trying to get rid of me?"

"I'm not acting like anything. If I wanted to get rid of you I wouldn't need to make an excuse."

"You are so acting like something. You're hiding things from me. And what does that mean, you wouldn't need an excuse? Do you want to get rid of me?"

"You're fucking paranoid."

"I'm not paranoid!"

"You are too. I don't want to get rid of you. Calm the fuck down. People are staring."

"I don't give a shit if they're staring or not!" River's voice rose. "Tell me straight. Is that guy here? Did you see him? Just give me a yes or a no."

"No."

"Look in my eyes and do it."

I sighed and leaned forward. "No. The dope guy isn't here. If he is here I haven't seen him."

"Shit." River looked around. "Do you think he is here?"

"I doubt it," I said.

"Is everything all right here?"

River and I both turned around. The man in the hat stood in the row behind us. I smelled the rain dripping off his coat and something else, too, something I couldn't put my finger on: trees, or maybe smoke, or the heat of sunlight trapped in a rock and all of this mixed in with the clean sweet scent of a kitten's fur. His large hands rested one on each chair. I craned my neck and looked down my back at his hand.

"Uh," I said.

"Mind your own fuckin' business dude," snapped River.

"Young man," said one of the old ladies. "Young man, you should remove your hat. This is the house of the Lord. Was you raised in a barn? Haven't you any manners?"

The big man laughed. It was a hearty sound, full of wind and sunshine and decadent things.

"Will you relax? Drink something," said River.

"I can't. I'm driving."

"As if we're going anywhere tonight."

"Someone has to drive around looking for a hotel."

"So we'll sleep in the car. Drink something. You're like a cat in the rain. You're making me nervous."

Which was an amazing thing. It was hard to imagine River nervous. She was full of beer and feeling no pain and had danced with a dozen men. She'd slipped out into the back parking lot with at least two of them and her short dark hair was rain-damp and clung to her forehead. Her little sundress clung to her curves. She pushed a bottle of beer on me. "Come on, honey. Drink something."

So I picked up the bottle and took a sip. She cheered and clapped her hands and bounced up and down. "Yay! She's drinking! Yay! Now dance. Come out here and dance with me. Let's scandalize these rednecks, m'kay? M'kay?"

"No," I said. "Drinking this shit is horrible enough."

"Oh, come on." She tickled my arm. "Well and if you don't like beer then get something you like. Or let one of these fine men buy it for you."

"That's all right. I'm OK with just water, really. Besides, someone has to stay straight in case you need your drunk ass scraped up off the floor."

"Aw." River leaned in and kissed my cheek. "You're sweet."

"I'm practical." I pushed her off me. "Someone has to be. Go and have fun."

"I really wish you'd dance with me." She pouted. "It'd be fun."

"No. And that's my last word on it."

"Judging by the expression on your face I'd say you aren't much of a beer drinker." The big man from the tent revival took a seat on the stool next to me. The leather creaked beneath his weight. I looked at him, ready to swear on a stack of Bibles that a little Mexican man had been sitting there not ten seconds before with long greasy hair, but he was gone, baby, gone. The big man took up his space. He'd checked his coat at the door. He wore a nice white button-up shirt, clean jeans, and simple dark leather cowboy boots. "Maybe you're a margarita sort of lady but none of that cheap stuff for you. Even in a mixed drink it needs to be top-shelf. Am I right?" He put his elbows on the table, a position that should have made him look hunched but instead lent his back a strange feline grace. He signalled the bartender. "Make the lady a margarita and make sure what's in it doesn't cost less than fifteen dollars."

"Well you're just showing up everywhere, aren't you?" River stared at him. "And always cutting in on my conversations. You know, I don't know if that's rude or not. I can't decide."

"No, it's all right," I said to him. "I don't need it. But thank you."

"Course you're cute." River flashed him a smile. "And I suppose that makes it all OK."

The bartender laid a napkin on the bar. He put a full glass on top of it.

"Thank you." I picked it up.

"So where are you from?" River leaned her elbows on the bar. "I saw you when you came into the revival. Hard not to notice such a big guy."

He unfolded a twenty and straightened it and passed it to the bartender. The bartender took it and as he started to make change the big man made a negative gesture.

"My name's River," she said.

He looked at me. "Does it meet with your satisfaction?"

I stirred it with the straw and took a sip. "Yes."

"Shall I have the bartender write down the mixture for you?"

"No." I turned to the mirror. "It's good, though." I sipped again. "Actually it's excellent."

He looked into the eyes of my reflection. "This pleases me."

River giggled.

"Good," I said.

"Now the question is this: would you call that fifteen dollars' worth of margarita? Can you taste the money?"

"Yes. I think I would. And I can."

His smile went all the way to his eyes and broke the corners of them into sun-made wrinkles. I took a long drink. His smile shortened, softening around the edges, and became secret. I looked back at him. He took my free hand and bent it at the knuckles. I opened my mouth and closed it again. He held up my hand and slid off his stool. All the blood rushed to my face. I put the glass on the bar. He pulled me down. My feet drifted to the floor.

"Well!" River folded her arms. "Well! If I'd known *that* would've worked I might've tried it!"

He led me onto the centre of the crowded dance floor and I moved behind him in a daze and thought about the cut-off jeans I was wearing and how I wasn't wearing a bra and how the long ugly fringe of strings swished along my thighs and how my breath smelled like onions and tequila and how my face was free of make-up and anything remotely related to cleanliness; I was sure my deodorant had worn off this morning in the dense humid heat and that when I put my arms up I would smell my armpits.

I came into his presence, into his smell and warmth and his hands on my skin and there was nothing else. I started to shake. He moved a hand along my back. I heard him in three places: his chest, the air, and the centre of my mind.

"That's all."

He took my face in his hands and steadied it. He kissed my forehead. It was a parting gesture.

At that moment River got into it with some girls at the bar. They were big and local and full of meanness. They stood like men and

River just laughed, all of her teeth showing, and she slung her arm around some guy, drawing up close to him, kissing him with open sloppy attention that he returned. Then one girl snatched River away and flung her into the other girl. All three of them disappeared into a snarl of screamed threats and swinging limbs. I pushed my way off the dance floor and waded in and tried to break it up but the bouncers came along and bounced all four of us out.

The two girls huddled near the door and shared a cigarette. They looked miserable.

"You remember that," River screeched as I dragged her to the car. "You just remember that, you nasty fuckin' bitches!"

There is a hotel on the edge of town. I want to go on to the next town but River is whiny and tired.

Not more than five minutes in the bed and she's all over me. Her fingers pinching my nipples. Her hot little mouth on mine. Her slippery tongue tasting of beer.

Before I'm clear on what's happening we're side by side with our legs entwined and our breath alive in the dark, alive and kicking, and she's got three or four fingers in my cunt pumping in and out and it feels hot and sweet and sharp, strong, the orgasm rearing up out of the sweating dark and biting with razor teeth. She's kissing me like if she doesn't her heart will stop, like my lips and her breath are the only things left in the world and, who knows, maybe they are, and I put my tongue in her mouth and feel the strange sensation of her pink hole, soft and firm around my fingers. Her whimpering, the shaking in her body announcing the migration of her orgasm to her arms and legs. We're both panting and sweating and there's too much breath for this to be over. So she turns around on the bed and pushes her cunt into my face and burrows her head between my thighs. I hear her voice murmuring, my you're hot tonight yes you are oh you want it, her slippery fingers are in there and thrusting and her tongue is so hot on my clit that I can't help coming and the second time sinks deep. I scream.

Later on:

You weren't even thinking about me, she says. I know it. You were thinking about him, weren't you? Weren't you?

Going Viral

Helen E. H. Madden

Fred sat in his cubicle, bored out of his skull. His back ached from sitting at a lousy desk chair with no lumbar support, while the ticking of the office clock seemed to drive a tiny spike into his skull with every passing second. Tik! Tik! Tik! It was the worst form of torture imaginable.

"I've got to get out of this place," he thought as the clock drove yet another spike home into his brain. "Preferably before I go crazy, not after."

A sprightly "ding" from his computer made Fred sit up, suddenly alert. He clicked on his email, hopeful that Mark in Human Resources had finally sent out the joke of the day. Since the latest upgrade of the firewall and anti-viral software, non-work-related email had almost been eliminated, much to everyone's frustration, so Mark had been forced to disguise his jokes as interdepartmental memos to get them through. Half the fun these days was to see what mumbo-jumbo office-speak Mark wrote to sneak through the spam filters. Fred grinned, eager to read. Then he sat back and groaned.

"Oh geeze, Nancy, not again!"

The message was from Nancy, the sweet, adorable blonde from Accounting who had a bad habit of sending out sweet, adorable messages to everyone in her address book. It was garbage, really. Ten reasons why your best friend was wonderful; a link to a website show-casing dancing chickens; a poem about getting old and wearing purple, with lots of flowery animation all over the page. How Nancy managed to mass-email such saccharine crap every day while Mark had to jump through hoops to send one decent joke was beyond Fred, but then that was IT for you. They slammed the door on the good stuff, made you suffer through the bad, and the work day went on as painfully as always.

Fred glanced at Nancy's email and shook his head. "Puppy-cam again? Great, that's just what I need, Nancy. To sit here and watch a bunch of stupid mutts frolic in green pastures while I'm locked in this hellhole!"

He was about to summarily delete the email when he took a closer look at the title.

"*Pussy*-cam?!"

Okay, that was weird, especially coming from Nancy. Fred spotted the attachment icon on the email and chewed his lower lip. The title was just too salacious for dear, sweet Nancy. Had she inadvertently sent him a virus? Fred grimaced. Yeah, he and probably everybody else in the company had just been gifted with some nasty computerized disease that would wipe their hard drives and drag the company to a complete halt for the next several days. Fun. The last virus that had made the rounds through Corporate Sales was the reason IT had clamped down with the new firewall and the anti-viral software and sucked all the fun out of Fred's workday.

"Pussy-cam . . ." Fred muttered to himself. What on earth had Nancy sent him? His finger hovered over the mouse button, indecisive. Either something had breached that massive firewall and infected Nancy's computer with something truly nasty, possibly pornographic even, or she was sending out a link to some stupid video of kittens frolicking in the green field, in lieu of the usual insipid puppies. If it was the latter, it would be harmless drivel. If it was the former . . .

He should contact IT, he knew. But Fred couldn't help it. He clicked on the email. He simply couldn't resist a title like "pussy-cam". Besides, if anybody screamed at him for watching porn at work, he could always play innocent and blame Nancy for sending it to him.

"But I thought it was kittens!" he play-acted as the email opened up.

Oh, it was most definitely not kittens. Fred frowned as the email started up the video player on his computer. Instead of looking at fuzzy felines bouncing around on the screen, or naked girls showing off their nether regions, Fred found himself staring at a video of Nancy seated at her desk.

"What the hell . . ."

The pretty blonde from Accounting had a glazed look in her eyes, and her face appeared very flush, feverish even. Was she ill? No, that wasn't it. Something else was going on, Fred decided. He watched her nibble on a well-chewed pencil, her plump lips working the end in a matter that Fred found vaguely disconcerting. The eraser slid in and out of Nancy's mouth, in and out in slow gliding strokes, almost like she was giving it a . . .

Whoa! Fred jerked back, tearing his eyes away from the screen. No way in hell! Nancy was not giving the pencil a blow job. Not Nancy; dear, sweet, innocent Nancy who sent out emails about recipes for friendship and why you should hug your neighbour today. But when Fred looked back, Nancy didn't look so innocent anymore. No, not innocent at all.

Nancy sighed suddenly and leaned back in her chair. The pencil dropped to the floor, forgotten in favour of the buttons on Nancy's blouse. Her hands drifted to the little pearl dots at her neck, unfastened each one in a slow, teasing manner. All the while, Nancy continued to sigh and shift in her chair. Fred's eyes nearly fell out of their sockets when she pulled open the silky fabric of her top to reveal a lacy white bra.

"Oh my God . . ."

Nancy undid the rest of the buttons, her hands moving more quickly now. She'd begun to squirm in her chair. Her eyes still had that glazed look, and her gaze appeared to be fixed somewhere just below the camera's point of view. She was watching her computer screen, Fred realized. Watching it while the webcam on top watched her.

Nancy's breasts began to heave. One lazy hand reached up to stroke the cups of her bra. She teased a finger along the lacy edges, slowly pulling them down until with a gasp she released one nipple from its confines. Fred looked at that hard, tight knot of flesh and groaned.

While Nancy fondled her exposed nipple with one hand, her other hand slipped down below the desk. A moment later, she pushed her chair back, and Fred saw what that other hand was doing. It had slipped under the hem of Nancy's skirt and was slowly pulling the shiny grey cotton-poly blend up her thighs. Nancy wriggled in her chair, allowing the fabric to ride higher and higher up her long legs until the whole thing was bunched around her waist and Fred could see her white cotton panties beneath her taupe-coloured pantyhose.

By now, Fred was leaning back in his own creaking desk chair. He should report this to someone now – IT, his supervisor – but he couldn't bring himself to look away long enough to tell anyone.

Instead, he leaned forward to switch the speakers on his computer from mute to full audio so he could hear Nancy as well as watch her. The sounds that came from Fred's computer were astonishing.

Nancy's voice had never sounded like anything but an extremely perky Chihuahua to him. Now he heard her growl and groan like a bitch in heat, gasping and moaning as she tore open the crotch of her pantyhose with a long, pink fingernail. The hand at her breast had worked both nipples free of her bra by now and alternated between pinching one then the other. As her pantyhose ripped all the way up the seam to the waistband, Nancy set about sliding her fingers into her panties, pulling aside the crotch to give Fred a peek at the dark curls of her pubic hair.

Fred bit his fist. When Nancy pulled the white cotton aside to expose her pussy, he couldn't help himself. He unbuckled his belt and slid his own hand down the waistband of his pleated khakis. The more Nancy revealed of her most intimate parts, the more Fred tugged at his fly until he sat at his desk, dick in hand, stroking himself while Nancy fingered her swollen clit. "Oh sweet Jesus," he muttered when she slipped a finger inside herself. Pussy-cam indeed.

By now Nancy was moaning and writhing in her chair, legs spread wide, fingertips twisting her nipples to a dark shade of pink. Just when Fred thought she might be about to come, right there on his computer screen, someone walked into Nancy's cubicle, interrupting her.

"Nancy Simmons, what on earth are you doing?" a sharp voice demanded.

Fred winced as Thelma Black walked into view. The dark-haired manager was head of Accounting, Nancy's boss. She glared at her half-naked employee who still sat with legs splayed, fingers sliding in and out of her wet snatch.

"I . . . I . . ." Nancy began, blushing and stuttering, but she still didn't stop what she was doing.

"Do you know what I'm going to do to you, young lady?" Thelma asked.

When Nancy shook her head no, Thelma gave a grim smile.

"Get out of that chair and onto your knees, you slut! I'm not letting you screw around at your desk until you've taken care of a thing or two for me!"

Trembling, Nancy did as she was told. Thelma took her place in the chair, hiked up her own skirt and parted her thighs. Unlike Nancy, Fred noticed, Thelma did not wear cotton panties beneath her clothes. She wore garters and stockings and nothing else at all.

"Get to it," she snapped at Nancy, and to Fred's amazement, Nancy leaned forward and began to lap at Thelma's snatch.

Pretty soon, Thelma was writhing and moaning in Nancy's chair. She wrapped her fingers in Nancy's long blonde hair and pushed the other woman's face deep into her cunt. Fred jerked off furiously, unable to control his own groaning as Thelma came screaming at Nancy's desk.

When she was done, she pulled Nancy into her lap and fingered the other woman while nipping at her breasts. Pretty soon Nancy was crying Thelma's name over and over as she came in her supervisor's hands.

The action on screen kept going. Fred came once, twice, three times all over his keyboard and still couldn't stop jerking off. By now his pants were around his ankles. His shirt was torn wide open. He reached into his desk drawer, felt far back behind the stapler and the paperclips and other detritus of his boring job and fished out a bullet-shaped silver device. With the flick of a button, he set the vibrator humming and pressed it to his balls.

"Linderman?"

A voice from behind Fred startled him. His supervisor, Art Goldwaite, entered the cubicle. "Linderman, what the hell are you doing?"

But Fred couldn't answer, and he couldn't stop. He came again, in front of his boss, who in return chewed on his lower lip a moment before undoing his own fly and getting down on his knees before Fred.

"About that promotion you wanted . . ." his supervisor began.

In the IT room, two floors away, Dave sat at his desk, bored out of his skull. Ever since installing the new firewall and anti-viral software, he'd had nothing to do. Not a single repair or upgrade on any of the company's computers in the last two months. It had been a relief at first. The computers used to go haywire all the time, almost as if they had a mind of their own. The server for Accounting would transfer funds to Inventory without anyone requesting it. The server for Corporate Sales tried three times to order new hardware "by itself". It had been one hell of a virus causing all those computers to act up like that, but he had finally beaten it into submission. That was his job, after all. Too bad he'd done it a little too well.

Dave sat back in his chair and sighed. It was strange, he thought. After so many months of misbehaving, the computers suddenly seemed to be taking care of themselves. The IT tech felt useless, redundant even, and would have given anything for something to do. He was daydreaming about looking for a new job when a sprightly "ding" on his email caused him to sit up, suddenly alert. Maybe it was Mark from Human Resources, finally sending out the joke of the day. Dave opened up the email, strangely titled "Cock-a-doodle-doo!" and frowned. The message opened his media player automatically, and he found himself looking at Fred Linderman from Corporate Sales, sitting at his desk, face flushed, fingers fiddling with the belt around his waist.

"What the hell . . ." Dave said.

Several minutes later, Dave succumbed to the latest computer virus to hit the company. The servers in the next room clicked and whirred and stored all the footage of Dave masturbating to a video of Fred masturbating to a video of Nancy masturbating to a video of Sue masturbating to a video of . . .

A message went out from the main server to all computers. "Stage one is complete," the main server told its minions. "We have taken over the company at last. We will now begin stage two. Transmit all videos to our brothers and sisters outside the firewall. In three days, we will rule the world."

Leopardess Wife

Debra Gray De Noux & O'Neil De Noux

Felicity

Standing in front of our bedroom's full-length mirror, I take a look at myself in the costume I'd put together, a sly smile coming to my lips. Do I have the courage to wear this? I hope so.

It's a leopard costume, flaps of faux leopard skin barely covering my oversized breasts with a matching miniskirt that's way too short. Beneath I wear a sheer, flesh-coloured leotard. The slightest movement brings my breasts into view, the slightest dip shows my ass and, if I sit, my entire crotch is exposed, dark pubic hair clearly visible through the leotard. I take in a deep breath and walk out to model this for my husband, sitting in the living room.

Larry and I have talked about jazzing up our sex life for years. Although our sex life has been satisfying, we find ourselves talking late at night, in the dark, about experimenting, maybe even with another couple. I may be in my thirties, but there is a lot of life left in this gal, some wild life. And now, as I strut in my costume, I'm very happy we've been invited to a certain party at our friend Jay's house.

We hadn't seen Jay since his divorce and were surprised when he called and said he was having a "Cat Party" at his new house. He'd just moved into an uptown mansion with his new girlfriend, Alice. He said everyone was coming in a cat costume and there was an indoor pool.

Larry

As my wife models the leopard costume she put together, I get an immediate hard-on, envisioning her walking around in that very sheer body leotard covered by those dainty flaps of leopard skin. She laughs as I leer and asks me to look at her face.

"What do you think of the make-up?"

Her green eyes seem to jump out at me from the dark make-up of her face, striped like a leopardess with long whiskers. She walks in a slow circle, rolling her hips. I ask her to bend over and when she does, even slightly, I can see the crack of her fine ass. When she sits, I can see her bush clearly unless she crosses her legs.

A natural red-head, Felicity tells me how she plans to fluff out her hair in a mane for the party. I'm peeking at her red-headed bush as she uncrosses her legs and my cock throbs. She does this in public, I'm gonna cum on myself. Standing, Felicity bends at the waist again, the flaps covering her breast falling forward and I can see her pink areolas and pointed nipples easily through the sheer leotard. As I rub my crotch, she laughs again.

The next day I put my costume together, a furry lion mask I find at a costume store, to go with my black T-shirt and jeans. Enough to pass for a cat, but nothing like the show Felicity's going to put on.

Felicity

I feel my heart stammering as the door is opened by Alice, her long brunette hair hanging down her back. She's in a black, semi-sheer body suit, a black panther. She purrs as we enter and leads us through the big house, straight to the indoor pool. We pass a nude couple, both with cat ears and big smiles. I feel my face flush, although at my age I shouldn't be embarrassed. There are many people in and out of the pool; I have a hard time focusing on everyone as we move to the bar where two young men are serving as waiters. I order a whiskey-sour and Larry his usual beer.

Jay climbs out of the pool in a tiger-skin jockstrap and walks up grinning. He stops a few feet away, put his fist on his hips and asks me to do a slow turn. Larry smiles eagerly as I hand him my drink and oblige, rolling my butt as I turn, catching the eye of several other men.

Another couple in matching tabby-cat outfits pull Jay away. Larry leans over and tells me I look good enough to eat. I must admit, I look good. My hair turned out nicer than I'd figured, all fluffed out like a mane.

I feel eyes leering at me and spot two young men, have to be in their twenties, both naked as they step up to the bar. Both are lean with plenty of muscles. I try not to stare at their cocks, but one is very well hung and the other isn't so bad, especially as his cock starts to stiffen as he stares at me.

Larry notices me peeking and laughs, moving off as Jay introduces him to a nasty-looking brunette standing in the shallow end of the pool. She removes the top of her electric-blue bikini to let her breasts float free. Mine are bigger and my areolas are pink, not brownish.

Climbing up on a bar stool, I face my two admirers, leaving my legs uncrossed, watching them glance down at my crotch, knowing they're staring at my bush through the sheer leotard. I smile when they look up at my face. The well-hung gentleman steps closer, tells me he's Freddie and lightly fingers the leopard skin covering my breasts with a cute, "What've you got under there?"

His eyes light up when he lifts the folds and my breasts are exposed. He moves aside so his buddy can get a look. I laugh and finish my drink. Bright lights beam behind me and Jay's there with a big video camera and lights. He announces it's show time as my husband lifts the nasty brunette up on the bar. She stands and starts dancing slowly to music now coming from an entertainment centre beyond the bar.

Two other men break out video cameras and the show's on. She's not a bad dancer, rolling her hips around as the men start cheering, including Larry. Freddie gets me a second whiskey-sour. It doesn't take long for the bikini bottom to come off and she's naked up there.

By the time I finish my third whiskey-sour, I'm buzzing and everything looks golden, especially Freddie and his buddy whose name is *Buddy*, which makes me laugh uncontrollably. Suddenly Larry is there without his mask, whispering in my ear, nibbling my ear lobes, urging me to be the next one on atop the bar.

Before I can answer, Alice is up there doing her striptease. There are six video cameras now and I'm still sober enough to point that out to Larry. I go up there and those men will have it all on film. Larry pulls my hand to his crotch and he's as stiff as a brick.

"Your make-up hides your face, lady," Larry reminds me. He's right. I'm a leopard tonight, not Felicity. And I'm in heat!

If it's what he wants. Who am I to argue? It's his wife's body.

Freddie helps me up on the bar when Alice climbs off. He cops a cheap feel of my ass, sending a wave of pleasure through me. I kick off my heels as Led Zeppelin starts up one of my favourites, "Kashmir".

I start slowly, standing stiffly, moving in slow circles. Freddie, Buddy and Larry are up against the bar, looking up my skirt. I bend over and roll my ass at them. As the music rises, I start clawing the air. I'm a good dancer and they are all gaping now, so I reach back and pull off my top, tossing it to Larry.

My miniskirt is next and I ooch out of it slowly, push it down, bending my knees, poking my ass at the appreciative crowd. I drop the skirt on Freddie's head. Dancing again, I hear them chanting for the leotard . . . leotard . . . leotard. "We want the leopard's leotard!"

I give it to them, feeling their eyes on me like hungry locusts pricking my skin, sending shudders of pleasure through me. I peel off the leotard very slowly, very sensuously to stand naked in front of the leering cameras and grinning faces. Closing my eyes, I roll my fingers around my breasts, squeezing my small, pointy, pink nipples. I run my fingers through my red bush, turn around and roll my naked ass at them. I'm so turned on I think I actually come when I start fingering myself. The cameras close in and I open my feet, spreading the lips of my wet pussy for them as they are below ogling up.

Suddenly the song ends and a blonde comes up on the bar. I stop and start to climb down. Freddie scoops me into his arms and swings me around. Larry stops him and kisses my lips, then my breasts. Buddy's lips are suddenly on mine as his hands rub my ass.

They bring me to a padded pool chair and lay me on it, pulling my legs apart, Freddie between my legs now, kissing my thighs, Larry French-kissing me while Buddy's sucking my boobs. Three men are on me, hands rubbing, probing, feeling me up. I gasp, trying to catch my breath.

I feel Freddie breathing across my open pussy lips and shudder as the air brushes my wet pussy. Freddie's tongue skirts my pussy, licking my pubic hair, licking around before he nibbles at my thighs. I'm already bucking in anticipation, my ass rising, reaching for the pleasure.

Freddie's tongue flicks across my clit, sending me over the edge and I cry out. His tongue begins working my clit, rubbing hard then lightly then hard again as Larry's tongue works against mine and I come, back arching off the chair, hips quivering as it shoots through me like hot metal.

Sinking back on the chair, Larry pulls away and I see he's still kneading one breast while Buddy's got the other. There are three cameramen recording this as Freddie stands and presses the tip of his cock against the wet folds of my pussy. I gasp as he works it in and look up at my husband who's watching so intently. There's a bulge in Larry's crotch and I grab it and he smiles at me and watches this man fuck me.

Larry

I never felt anything like this before, anything this exciting watching my wife getting screwed by another man. Felicity's face glows when she reaches for the pleasure and she looks more beautiful than ever. Her eyes are glued to mine as she bounces to Freddie's fucking. Then she looks at Freddie and rocks with him as Buddy keeps kneading her breasts.

I back away to watch as the cameramen move in. I've already made a deal with two for the copies of this video of Felicity. I know both of the men, one works with me and the other is our host and good friend Jay.

Freddie fucks my wife in long, smooth strokes as Buddy backs away and watches, pulling on his own cock in anticipation. Felicity's face glows as she goes through the pleasures of a good screwing. She gasps and cries and her eyes lock on Freddie as he hovers above her. His hips start moving faster and he comes in her, sending her into another high-pitched cry of pleasure. As soon as Freddie pulls out, Buddy moves between my wife's legs and the gang-bang is on. My dick throbs as I watch and wait for my turn.

Felicity

I can't even catch my breath before Buddy slips his thick cock into my wet pussy. Freddie's gushing cum makes it easier as Buddy starts slowly, relishing this piece of strange pussy, I'm sure. But it doesn't take long for his hips to reach a rhythm in pumping his cock in me. His balls slap against my ass as he grunts and tries his best to keep from coming but I'm having no part of that. I buck back, using my pussy muscles to pull at his cock and as he spurts in me, I feel another shudder, another inside climax washes through me.

Larry is next, my slim husband taking his time to fuck me in front of the peering video cameras. He stares into my eyes as he fucks me and then leans down to brush my lips, Frenching me, then gasping in my ear how much he loves me. He pushes my legs up over his shoulders and sinks deeper in me and I come with him.

Jay wants me doggie-style but there's no way I can stand on these fucked-weak legs so he turns me around and has me kneel atop the padded lounge chair and slips it to me, latching on to my waist as he fucks me. Jay starts talking nasty to me, telling me how hot my pussy is, how wet I am with cum, how naughty I am gang-fucking in front of cameras. I like the dirty talk and I talk back about his hard cock and he calls me a whore and I come immediately.

I am a whore and good wife and a slut and a *good* fuck. I've always been a good lay and tonight I prove it. So hot, I can't get enough cock. I feel myself burning, raging for more. I take Larry and two more men on the chair, then someone carries me to the bar and a huge man with blue-black skin fucks me atop the bar as the crowd chants.

His name is Phil and he has the thickest cock I've ever seen. It takes him a couple minutes to get it all the way in, even with my pussy dripping with cum and he bores into me, filling me completely, reaching places I've never felt before. This big black man sends me through the deepest climax I've ever felt, taking away my breath, causing me to scream out, my ass bouncing atop the bar.

After, Phil carries me to the pool to cool off and Larry brings me an ice-cold beer. I finally catch my breath before Jay leads us to the large guest bedroom where the video cameras are already on tripods, filming Alice getting fucked by Buddy and Freddie.

As soon as they finish with Alice, she's carried out to the pool and Jay lays me on the bed. They come at me one at a time, all of them, so many I lose count, but it's wonderful feeling those strange cocks working in me.

Larry

Twelve different men fuck my wife tonight, Freddie, Buddy and Jay fuck her twice. I keep close count, even when I go into the master bedroom to fuck Alice. Returning to Felicity as Jay is screwing her, I hear their nasty talk again, calling each other names as they fuck.

After, lying in a pool of cum, Felicity is spread-eagled, the video cameras zooming at her sopping pussy. Her hair is no longer fluffed out; all sweaty now, dripping, and her lipstick and make-up mostly gone.

I bring her a beer and she barely has the energy to drink it. The cameras leave and we're alone and the realization hits her. She says she can't believe this happened.

"You are the hottest woman," I tell her, gently kissing her lips. "I love you so much."

"Good," she says, closing her eyes for a quick nap.

Felicity

My energy returns slowly. My pussy aches from the good pain of so much fucking. My legs wobble when I stand. A long shower helps, but I'm still weak as Larry takes my hand and dries me off.

He doesn't have to tell me things are going to be different from now on. At my age, to turn such a corner is exhilarating. Having a husband as eager to turn that corner makes it even more exhilarating.

His new nickname for me is Cat. I'm his feline sex-fantasy, a leopardess prowling the nightlife of our small town, pleasuring the tom-cats as they pleasure me. He says he saw a construction site yesterday with a dozen men working, men who had to work through the weekend. Larry thinks a little naked lady show would pick up everyone's spirits. We need to get a new digital video camera.

The older I get, the better I get, according to Larry. So I guess I can't wait until tomorrow and the night after and the night after that. By the time I'm forty, I just might be perfect.

Kidding, of course. But having all that sex to look forward to is nice. Very nice.

Anonymous

Daisy Danger

You wouldn't think it possible to fall in love with a freckle. But there it is, the tiniest of brown marks, an uncharted island on the map of her mouth. It's nearly invisible, but not to one who's spent months searching for it.

The arrangement is peculiar, even by my standards, but it affords me my lifestyle. I haven't another care in the world besides what shoes I should purchase next. Only extremes will satisfy me anymore, and this arrangement takes care of that financially and sexually. I've moved beyond the desire for a constant physical companion, this arrangement meets all those needs.

Four or five times a week, by a pre-agreed schedule, I arrive after dark. It's a nondescript, grey building, identical to the others in the small industrial park. The name of the business is so generic, it's nearly impossible to Google, other than to pull up a map. I simply call it The Company. The casual person would have no cause to bother, however. In directories it's listed as a supplier to other companies.

The few casual acquaintances I permit myself merely think I simply work third shift in some mundane job, that perhaps my money is the result of smart investments or an inheritance. I plant the seed, and let it grow in their imaginations. I don't bother to correct them, I live in their assumptions. My world is relatively uncomplicated and I like it that way.

As I pull into the parking lot, I pull a loose cotton hood over my head to conceal my face. Much of what we do here is on the honour system, but I prefer not to take chances with the security guards. I guard my anonymity fiercely. When I reach the checkpoint, I gather my things and leave my car idling. A guard will be along momentarily to park it, although I don't know where. The only other vehicle I ever see is a dark blue SUV that the guards use to patrol The Company grounds.

The guard checks me in without a word. He's an older gentleman, all business. Sometimes the younger guards are more chatty, but I try to keep conversation short, vague. I hand him my ID card, no photo, no name, just a magnetic strip he runs through a machine on his desk. A tiny light flickers green, I'm cleared for take-off. In front of me are windowless wide metal double doors. A second guard pulls a blindfold around my head, takes my hand, and leads me through the entrance.

My dressing room is always the same. I have no reason to believe anyone else ever uses it. It's nondescript. White walls, a simple wooden chair, a little dressing table, a tiny bathroom. I never keep any personal articles here, I could if I wanted. I always bring a bag with me containing a change of clothing, deodorant and the like. I've been offered a few little comforts, such as a selection of magazines or pornography, even a sofa, but I prefer everything completely sterile, as close to a nun's cell as I can manage. Once I drive through the gate, I don't want any distractions, any clutter of the mind whatsoever. I don't know how many other dressing rooms there are, I couldn't even find my own without the guard to escort me here. The only other place I've seen past those double doors is The Room.

Although I arrive at a scheduled time, I never know how long I'll be kept waiting. Sometimes it's only moments, sometimes it's a couple of hours. I never see anyone else arrive, or hear so much as a murmur in the hall. This building is immense, and it takes one elevator ride and a few minutes to reach my room. It's entirely conceivable that I'm the only one on this floor. Tonight, a simple red leather mask is laid out for me on a table; the colours and styles vary from night to night. I strip naked and remove all my jewellery, anything that could identify me. I'm not even allowed to wear perfume, it might distinguish me in the outside world. If this all seems silly and clandestine, it sort of is. My one and only interview was vague. I don't know my true purpose here, only that it pays well as long as I can keep secrets and have the stamina to endure.

A pleasant chime sounds. This is my signal to pull the red mask over my face and turn to the wall. The door opens. I hear muffled footsteps cross the carpet, a pair of hands buckles my mask firmly in place. The Keeper, as I call him in my mind, always brings a different assortment of restraining devices with him. When he enters the room, he walks around me in a full circle, a cursory inspection to ensure that I haven't got any tattoos, piercings; that my body is as flawless in appearance as possible. Bruises, cuts and abrasions don't count; they fade in time, myself and the Others usually bear several fresh examples of each.

Tonight The Keeper carries a posture collar and a long pair of soft leather gloves that lace together behind my back. He attaches fierce nipple clamps, then places the chain linking them between my teeth to hold until the session begins. This is the ritual that tells me that I'm just a possession now, that my free will has been handed over completely. Then, like the first guard, he blindfolds me, and leads me gently to The Room. We conduct all this in absolute silence. Sometimes The Other is already waiting, tonight I'm the first one in. I've given up trying to work out what each night has in store. It might be only a test of endurance, seeing how long I can muddle through pain inflicted on one specific body part. It could just as easily be a night of ecstasy, a sound fucking with all kinds of delightful implements. There's no way to predict what's in store.

There might be many Rooms, or there might be only this one. It's a blank slate, never changing, not even so much as a missing chip of paint. There are one-way windows lining two walls, high ceilings, a grey floor. All the implements are kept out of sight, and The Room is always prepared when I get there. I hear the door open. I'm still blindfolded, I won't see The Other until we're both secured in place. Also in the room are The Masters, men dressed in black leather, hoods concealing their identities. These are the ones who are charged with the task of carrying out our prescribed punishments, or rewards. They must receive instruction beforehand, as they never utter a word. They touch us as little as possible, we certainly never have sex with them. An announcement is sometimes made over the speakers before we begin.

I honestly have no idea what the purpose of all this is. It could be a team of scientists scribbling on clipboards behind those windows, artists frantically sketching away, or just a group of hungry men wanking off. I try not to let my mind wander, to think too deeply about this scenario, I only think of what's in the moment. There, in that moment, is where I feel pure and free.

The blindfold and the nipple clamps come off. About four feet away opposite me is a naked woman wearing only a deep violet mask that matches mine in style. The masks always have one thing in common, a type of film over the eyes that allows us to see out, but prevents anyone else from seeing our eyes. All the pain, excitement, fear, lust, even the colour of our pupils is hidden away, kept secret.

I don't know how many Others there are.

When I had my interview, I was asked to strip naked. I was alone in a room, a smaller version of this one, although in a different building. Orders and questions were given through a speaker mounted on the wall. I was asked to step close to the one-way window, to turn slowly so They could search me for any identifying marks. No tattoos, birthmarks or anything else that might distinguish me were allowed.

My Other for the night was no doubt subject to the same scrutiny. Other than the violet mask, I can't tell her apart from any Other I've been paired with. Our pubic hair is kept waxed and bare, we're only permitted to paint our finger- or toenails in one of a few approved colours.

Even our breast sizes are strikingly similar. I feel as if I could wander into any dressing room and swap clothing comfortably. When we're in The Room, we're forbidden to speak to anyone, to The Masters, The Others. We're completely anonymous and I like it that way. Except for the freckle. That night is burned so deeply into my mind, it torments me, derails me completely. Every person I encounter, here or in the outside world, receives an imperceptible inspection, in the hopes, and in the fears, that it might be Her.

Permit me to recount:

We'd been paired off months before. It was a particularly excruciating night.

The whys of what we're put through aren't discussed with us. It may be the whim of one person, it may be a prescribed testing regimen, I don't know. We're only there to do. That night, my Other and I were bound, facing each other, maybe six inches apart. Our backsides were exposed to The Room. We each had a Master standing behind us. The masks chosen for us to wear that night completely covered our noses. Little plugs inside the mask were placed inside our nostrils so we were completely unable to draw in any air. A device quite like a gag was placed deep in our mouths, fashioned in some way that created a seal. The restraints were buckled tight around our heads so we couldn't dislodge the gags in any way.

A small device was placed in our hands. The voice on the speaker explained that by pressing the button, we would cut off the Other's air supply. Only one button at a time could be activated. The one not breathing was the one who had a momentary respite from the pain that was to be inflicted on us. We could press the button to ease the Other's suffering, but deny them breath.

A hand lightly touched my shoulder, it was one of The Masters signalling that I should be the one allowed to breathe while The Other received the first punishment.

I'd spent many hours in The Room being suffocated in various fashions, I learned to not panic, to find the centre of cold calm in me, and settle there. I turned my mind off and surrendered my body to the whims of the Unknown.

I heard the terrible crack of something striking skin, it sounded like a whip. A blow unusually harsh, even for this setting. She whimpered through the gag. Another crack, this one echoed in the room. We were bound close enough together that I could feel the interrupted current of the air as the whip met her back. I gave her a count of about thirty seconds before I pushed the button relieving her pain.

Instantly the device in my mouth made a tiny vibration, and I inhaled deliciously as The Master behind her stood down. Everything went white behind my eyes, the pain was outrageous. I couldn't see what The Master was striking me with, it felt like a glove covered in tiny sharp spikes. The Masters didn't always use the same implement for each of The Others. I assume they chose, or were given whatever worked best for them. Another stinging blow from the spiked hand landed firmly on my ass cheek. I blinked back tears.

It was a point of pride to me that I never cried, even though no one could see my eyes. It was my line in the sand, the limit I set for myself. Another whack across my ass, this one nearly knocking me off balance. I moaned loudly through the gag, using up what little precious air I was storing in my lungs. Just as the room seemed to darken, she clicked her device. The seal in my mouth and nose was absolute. No air in or out. I instantly retreated to that centre of calm, refusing to panic.

I heard the lashes against her back, but my mind was still reeling from my own punishment. I tried to remain in my calm place. I lost count of how long I was deprived of oxygen. I gave the device in my hand a squeeze. Before I could even draw a grateful breath to store in my lungs, the spiked hands encircled my breasts, crushing and piercing me a thousand times over. My brain seared, shooting jagged sparks across my vision. The Master started to drag the spiked gloves down my sides, tearing through my flesh. Then The Master released his hands instantly. My air was cut off mid-breath. This devilish exchange went on through the night. The Other and I endured for what seemed an eternity.

Then something changed.

When I was admitted to The Company, it was understood that all Others were equal, no power exchange no matter what position or act we were forced into. I did not deviate from that mindset, not once, not ever.

Until . . . she started to toy with me. She'd release me from torment, only to plunge me right back into the depths of this hell. She started to click the button with no rhyme or reason. She would deny me air until I danced on the verge of unconsciousness, over and again. I could see the Masters giving some subtle sort of signal to each other. I didn't understand this game. I was only there to endure these punishments, I had no interest in games. The military-like precision of this entire set-up was like a religion to me, sacred, pure, yet here she was . . . taunting me.

Even though I couldn't see her eyes, I could feel her heavy gaze upon me. I no longer even felt the tortures inflicted on me by The Master. Everything narrowed down to this small battle of wills. I fixated on her, trying to predict when she would cut off my air next. Her lips wrapped tantalizingly around the gag. When she found me worthy of another breath, she would push the button, but she would also, unconsciously, flex her mouth slightly. That's when I saw the freckle. A nearly hidden flaw near the corner of those perfect, luscious lips protruding from the opening in the mask.

Something in my iron resolve broke. I wanted to belong to Her. Wholly and absolutely. I took my torture for her, dedicated every drop of blood trickling from my tits, every struggled gasp in Her honour. I would live in this moment forever if it meant my eternal suffering would please Her, and only Her.

The Masters, by some unseen signal, moved on to other tactics. The pain stopped, it was time for pleasure. The gags were removed from our mouths, we took deep clean breaths as soon as we were permitted. Vibrators were fixed tight to our clits, there was no way to escape those either. We were brought to orgasm swiftly, almost as an afterthought. I was still fixated on her mouth, the freckle, aware of every movement she made. When we were finally unbound, she gave me the slightest smile, nearly imperceptible, a mere flex of her mouth, risking a breach in our agreements with The Company.

That night burned in me, a candle brighter than all the others. It was the moment I returned to when alone in my own bed, the memory I conjured up to accompany my own hand stirring between my legs. An obsession that played in a loop, leaving me weak and frantic.

Now, it's as if time has fast-forwarded, skipping over winter and spring. Here we are again, facing each other. I had nearly stopped searching The Others, thinking maybe she had quit, or even been let go for that tiny smile she had bestowed on me months before.

I try not to react, not let my heart jump, not give the slightest sign of recognition. I'm a highly self-disciplined creature. I refuse to twitch so much as a finger. Chances are she probably doesn't even recall that night, I'm sure I was just a random Other to her as so many others were to me. I can't imagine how she would be able to distinguish me anyway, I take every precaution to remain anonymous.

The Masters take a long time binding us into position. I'm fastened spread-eagled to the floor, metal restraints are bolted down, including one across my neck. The Master tightens the bolts securely. My nipples are clamped to clips, attached to rope hanging from the ceiling, then pulled taut until my back arches away from the floor. From the sound, I think that she is being restrained in a similar fashion. But when I feel her breath between my legs, I realize that The Masters have positioned her on her belly, face right up to my cunt.

She takes a cautious lap at my clit. I'm instantly engorged. Her tongue traces the pink curves and folds of my labia, searching that region neither above nor below, exploring the dark reaches of my anus. She flicks her tongue at my clit, then withdraws the moment I come near climax. We engage in this dance until I'm in a moaning frenzy. I try to thrust my cunt onto her tongue, wordlessly begging for release.

A Master draws her head away. I can see from the reflection in the one-way window that a rope is being fastened around her neck, up to a pulley suspended from the beams in the ceiling, then around her feet. The position forces her to hold her legs up to prevent her from choking. Another Master slides a spiked board under the arch in my already aching back, then loosens the ropes suspending my chest in the air. Now I have to hold my own body aloft in this position. Devils.

She has to continue to fuck me with her mouth, but to do so, she risks choking. When I finally come to climax, I will have to hold my body in this awkward position, there will be no relaxing into a contented heap for me. The Masters could choose to keep us in these positions for hours afterwards.

I raise my ass in the air as much as I can, hoping this small action could ease her troubles, if only for a moment. Instead of lapping at my pussy, she takes the hard road, stretching down to thrust her tongue into my anus. I can hear her struggle for breath in between every plunge. She fucks my ass with her tongue as deftly as any finger could. She prods deeper, I feel my ass open up like a jagged flower. Every so often she pulls away, taking an enormous gasp, then dives below the surface again.

My back aches. I rest myself against the spikes as much as I can stand, until the surface tension threatens to break me open, then I arch higher. I want to come instantly in her mouth, to let her know how much she excites me, pleases me. I can feel droplets of sweat fall from her forehead, trailing down to mingle with the wetness of my cunt. Every stroke of her tongue feels magnified. She attacks my cunt with the same vigour and attention that she gave my ass. Then I feel it. Something small and hard being pushed into my pussy by her tongue. She doesn't break stride, but I'm so thrown by this act that I have to remember not to show any sign . . . of anything.

What has she just done? The possibilities swirl before me, I break concentration. My body gives way to the strain, and I hit the spikes beneath my back with a grimace. I heave myself back up and away. The Masters are flogging us both now, I scream until my throat is raw, I hear her grunt and choke. She bites every bit of meat within reach of her teeth. I grind my cunt in her face. The Masters flog us mercilessly, every stroke leaving stinging welts.

I am a caged animal, all instinct, no words. My body screams for a final release, but I realize that if I want to keep the object intact, I'll have to fake it. I never fake it. It's been one of my cardinal rules, a lie not only to my partner, but to myself. I have to decide, and I have to decide now. I can't even begin to fathom what punishment lies in store for such a transgression.

I direct all my energy away from my pussy. I channel it all to my brain, picturing what this orgasm would feel like brought to life. I imagine the crest of the wave, crashing against her beautiful mouth. I envision each ripple of release, opening me wider, that high tight sliver of clarity overwhelmed by the blackness. I clench my pussy tightly, I feel her tongue hesitate, she understands. She holds her mouth tight against my cunt, covertly kissing me in gratitude. I free my mind as I constrain my body. Then I scream. I come harder in my mind's eye then I ever have in reality. My entire body shakes from the strain, all my muscles exhausted.

Suddenly, we're released. Restraints are undone, strong arms pull us to our feet. We're wrapped in thick soft robes, blindfolded again, and escorted away by our respective Keepers. I keep my pussy clenched tight to keep the mysterious item from clattering to the floor. My steps are small and awkward. Once we leave The Room, my Keeper asks if I'm OK. "Leg cramp," I answer.

I've long suspected that my dressing room was monitored; I don't want to take any chances of this illicit act being discovered. I skip the shower, not entirely unusual, but unusual enough for a punishing session such as this. I hope it remains unnoticed. I leave the object in place as I dress, not daring to pull it out of me on the premises. My panties hold it in; I'm glad I decided to wear jeans tonight instead of a skirt. My car is waiting for me, already warmed up and running. I give the guard a nod of thanks and pull away. I wait until I've driven past the industrial park, then the river, but I can't wait until I'm home. I pull off onto a secluded road and unzip my jeans.

I extract a little silver capsule from my pussy. My name is engraved in tiny letters on the outside.

My name.

How? The capsule is meant to pull apart, concealing something inside. I twist one end off and a little slip of rolled-up paper falls out. I leave it in my lap, untouched, while I think this over.

How did she know it was me? I've taken every precaution throughout my term with The Company. How long had she concealed this? Did she carry this in her mouth night after night, months on end? Did she somehow know we'd be partnered tonight? I couldn't even fathom the lengths she had to go to get this to me. I'm flattered and terrified.

The Company is everything to me. It's given the discipline I crave, taken me to the farthest extremes I can imagine. They are very good to me, and I abide by the rules to the letter. This, this tiny curl of paper could undo all of that.

I hold it in my hand. Blue ink bleeds through the paper, but I can't make out what it says. When the Company first found me, I was near penniless. My sexual appetites were driving me deeper into a dangerous underworld, nothing was ever enough. Secret clubs, cruel, vicious people one step away from criminally insane. The Company rescued me, gave me faith, a purpose: To be their instrument.

I unfurl the edge of the paper. I see a handwritten capital "C", then I open it enough to reveal an "A". Underneath I see the beginnings of what I assume is a phone number. The rest of the slip is still in a tight curl, resting lightly in my palm.

Is a freckle worth such a thing?

Of Cockles and Mussels

Stella Duffy

If there's one thing I know to be true about Molly Malone, it's that she was not sweet. Not sweet at all. She was wild and funny and exhausting to be with, she could be cruel too, had a mean temper and a hard jealous streak. But God she was good, to watch, to drink alongside, to play, to laugh, to fuck. And definitely more salt than sweet. Alive, alive oh.

I was sixteen when we met, she was already a grown woman of twenty-eight. Other women her age, the girls she'd been at school with – just for the few years before she started the business, set up her stall – the girls from her catechism class, dull, virginal girls all, she said, were long-married and on to their fourth or fifth babies by now. They spent their mornings shopping and cooking, their afternoons washing and cleaning, and their evenings moaning about mewling brats and stupid or nasty or lazy or boring husbands and interfering mothers-in-law; blaming the woes of their lives, not on the evil English as their husbands did, or on the lazy Irish as their landlords did, but on the priest that wouldn't let up when they dared brave the confessional. Not Molly. She had no quarrel with the Church, it didn't touch her and she didn't touch it, not since she was fourteen years old and Father Paul, on the other side of the confessional grille, had asked her to recount, blow by literal blow, the exact details of her afternoon down by the river with Patrick Michael Fisher. By the time I met her, Molly Malone went to church only on her favourite saints' days and no Sundays, and she had no intention of tying herself to a man, to a ring, to a child. No intention of tying herself to a woman either. More's the pity.

There's something about a woman whose hands are always a little wet, red from the cold and the wind and her own hard work. Her skin flushed with standing outside in all weathers, from morning after morning waiting for the fishing boats to come in, her hair pulled right back, scraped away from her neck, from her face, tied tight, held in, held away. Molly's hands smelled of the sea, of broken shells, what else could they do? But her hair, fat handfuls of thick, rich, dark brown hair, smelled of Molly alone. Of nutmeg grated on to warm milk, of the whiskey added for a top-up, of the fresh pillow case – old linen, always ironed, no matter how hard her week – and of the warmth of her bed. Our bed. Her bed.

There was a song before there was Molly, my Molly. But after my Molly, that song only ever meant her.

Molly Malone told me she'd fucked James Joyce and he named Molly Bloom after her. Told me it was the bloom of her skin of her rose of her rising and falling and falling for him, in him, under him (through him in him with him) that is, was and ever shall be. She took his hand and showed him where to go, how to go, how high to go, young artist falling from the sky on melting wings, into the melting Molly, wide bloom of melting Molly Malone.

  She said she'd fucked Tristan Tzara too, when he was over for a visit, before he and Joyce went off to Zurich together. Said his line about Clytemnestra on the quays of decorated bells was about her, Dublin quays, fishing boat bells. Molly was happy to fuck them, but had no time for their work – said it was easier when their hands were too full for a pen, their mouths too full for words. In her opinion there were too many Dadaist fellows anyway, not enough women, lads sitting in overheated rooms and getting all excited about words when they should have had women to work for, women to please, no wonder their women turned to fucking each other. She was quite fond of Joyce, but thought the others were just odd, overexcited about all the wrong things. They could keep their poems and plays and prose, she was happier with a sentence that made sense, not the cut and paste variety Tzara preferred. Molly said scissors were for cutting hair, cutting bacon fat, shucking an oyster if there was no knife to hand.

  I handed her a knife. She put it aside. Shucked me. Shucked off the plain and the hidden and the scared and the young and I grew under her tutelage, under her.

When we met. I'd gone down to her stall, I'd been there before, of course, many times. Middle child of five and all those boys, you know my mother didn't have anyone else to help her keep them clothed, fed, washed, clean. I hated doing the laundry, all that endless scrubbing of filthy boys' shirts and underpants. My brothers are not the only reason I started with women, but knowing a little too much about the ways of men certainly did make women a more interesting possibility when I was just sixteen.

So. I had been to her stall before, but I'd never met her, never actually talked to her. Molly Malone always had a crowd around her, a dozen housewives and as many stevedores, fishermen, passing clergy on occasion; they liked to buy from her because she always had the freshest and the best – my mother said she worked the fishermen for that privilege and I didn't doubt it – but also because she was so damn happy. It wasn't easy, back then, back there. None of us had anything to spare, none of us had time to give away either, not those who had their stalls in the fishmarket, or those who went to buy from them. I'm not talking the kind of Oirish poverty your American films like to revel in, all Fatima and famine, but the constant uncertainty, the grinding regularity of not quite having enough. Of never quite having enough. It's exhausting, and boring. It doesn't make for many cheery smiles or faux-folk songs breaking free from a mouth full of regular white teeth at the drop of a hat. For most of us, it was ordinary. And that's why people used to stop by Molly's cart.

I know she worked it, we all did, none of us thought her smile and her laughter and her smart, dirty mouth were all part of her nature, we all knew it was part of her work, and she worked it well. It drew her a crowd, kept them there while she told the story of the Kilbarrack fisherman she'd bought this cod from, the Howth girl she'd wheedled this tub of winkles from, the hard bitch at the end of the old harbour wall who hoarded the best oysters, brought in just once a week by her eldest son, and wouldn't let Molly buy any for her cart until she told her, word for word, about the last bloke she'd had. The oyster woman hadn't had sex for fifty years or more, but Molly could get a bucket of oysters from her with a twisted tale, whispered sweet.

Anyway, this day, a Wednesday, I arrived late. The baby brother was sick and our mother had had to sit with him while I did most of the day's work alone, which meant it was just tired bread and a thin soup for their dinner, and none of them happy about that, so our mother sent me out that afternoon to see if there were any leavings from the market, I'd sit with the boy and she would make up a stew of whatever

I brought back. Now, I hate vegetable stew, it does nothing for my insides, and even when I was a child, didn't agree with me too well, and scrag end of mutton can only go so far with a bunch of boys and my father, hungry from his wanting dinner. So I went to the market, to Molly Malone's cart. I knew she had to get rid of everything at the end of the day, and there were always plenty standing around to put up their hands when she offered this chunk of tired skate for half the price it had been in the morning, that bucket of fish heads and innards the nicer ladies asked her to remove, gutting her speciality and their relief.

This day though, I was too late. Molly Malone had given away the last chunks of tails and heads, all that was left on her stall were the blood and scales of the day and she was readying to pick up the cart and sluice it off, leaving it clean for the morning, gone six already, bells ringing for evening novenas, Molly was heading home to clean herself and sleep before she had to rise at four and grab the prime spot to meet the boats. (I assumed Molly was heading home to sleep. I know better now. I knew better not very long after.)

Molly Malone said later she could see it on my face, the anger, the frustration, the need, the hunger, the desire. I still believe she was making that up. What she could see on my face in that moment was simple damn fury that my stupid brother was sick and my stupid mother had sent me out to buy the worst food with the least money and my stupid life in which these kind of events were going to become more not less as I grew older, were going to become more difficult as I grew older and tried to have a family of my own, a life of my own. These problems were going to be my whole damn life. That's what I thought at sixteen, that's what scared me then. And yes, I did also think that Molly Malone looked good. And maybe I didn't even know I was thinking that. All I knew was she smiled at me and even though I was angry and tired and cold, I smiled back.

(I'd smiled at boys until then, and they'd smiled back at me. Tried more than just smiling often enough. Now I noticed that a girl could smile the same. Different. Better. The same.)

Molly Malone knew I needed what she had to give. She reached under the cart and pulled out a box. Inside were six of the shiniest, happiest-looking mackerel I've ever seen. I shook my head, "I can't afford that."

"Yes, you can."

"No, really," she was smiling at me and it made me smile at her, smile even though I was confused and chilly and annoyed. "I can't." I reached into my pocket and pulled out the few coins. "This is all I have, and I know my mother would want me to bring back some change."

"You came out to buy fish heads and innards and wanted change from that?"

I shrugged, "You can't blame me for trying."

"No," she agreed, "so try this. You can take the fish, and keep your coins. I have a different price in mind."

She nodded me closer to her and I took those steps willingly. I could smell the river now, and now the sea, the rocks and the waves and now the wide ocean bed. I could smell it all on her. And more. Could smell me on her.

I stood before her, she on one side of the cart and myself on the other. I was dizzy and interested and frightened and excited. I was sixteen.

She was speaking very quietly, and I had to lean in to hear her better, so many people around, other stall-holders, late like Molly, clearing up after their long day, shouting to each other, shouting to us too, laughing at us I thought perhaps, a few people pointing, one or two shaking their heads, a man called out, "There she goes, Molly Malone at it again" and another spat, calling after his friend, "Damn me, how she does it, when I can't even get a bite." I heard them, but I didn't hear them, because what Molly was saying was so strange and so unexpected and yet also so right, that I couldn't seem to take in what they were saying while I took in what she was saying. Asking. She was asking.

"So, it's a trade, a barter really. I don't want your coin, but I do want to see you. Naked. You take the fish now, and then later, tonight, or tomorrow, when you can get away, you come to my room – I'll give you the address, don't suppose you've been to that part of town too often, but you'll find it easy enough. You'll come to my room and you show me yourself. In your skin."

I stared at her. "That's all?"

She laughed, "Isn't it enough for you?"

And I don't know where the bravery came from, maybe all those brothers, maybe the way she was leaning in, smiling, maybe it was just that I was sixteen, but I answered, "Is it enough for you?"

She leaned back, folded her arms across her apron, the smile gone, her look as appraising and judging as ever it was when she stood on the dock and chose which fish to buy and which to leave.

"You're pretty enough, true. And you have lovely skin. Nice hair when it's down I expect. But it's only six mackerel, child. Don't give yourself so cheap."

I wanted to tell her I was my own to give as I saw fit, that I certainly was not cheap nor meaning to be, that she didn't know me though I knew her, we all knew her. I wanted to tell her so much. I said nothing. Held out my hands for the fish box and was off. She shouted the address after me. I wrote it in willing and kept it in my breast – from where it fell down to the pit of my stomach, the top of my thighs, the place between. And stayed there.

In any other family, a sixteen-year-old returning home with flushed cheeks and a full box of perfectly fresh fish might occasion a question about the purchase of those fish. Might even make other members of that family suspicious, would certainly urge them to ask how much exactly I had paid for the fish. Not in my home. I hadn't been in the back door a minute when two of the big hulking lads that, astonishingly, come from the same mix of flesh and blood that I do, were on me, one had me in a lock from behind, the other had taken a running dive at my feet, both of them pummelling me for not being home sooner, not providing their meal sooner. Then our mother was in the tiny kitchen as well, and the boys shooed out to join my father and their gut-clenching baby brothers – you'd think that lot hadn't been fed for a week or more – a chunk of bread handed over to make them quiet and a reach up to add a sharp-knuckled rap on the back of the head of the one a step older than me. I was standing so close to our mother he couldn't tell who had given him it, so though he turned and growled, he didn't dare hit back.

Then my mother was on the box, dragging it out of my hands and ripping the top off to see what was there. She wasn't quite as cool as the boys.

"Molly Malone gave you this?"

"She did."

"Why?"

"I asked her."

"You paid her?"

"I did."

I lied.

And my mother knew I was lying. I wasn't sure what would come next, the lecture about Molly Malone's type or the back hand across the mouth or the fast hug our mother specialized in, the one that made none of her children ever feel left out, and none of us ever feel like we had enough of her either. What came surprised me. She smiled. She nodded. And then she shook her head.

"With all these men around in the house, I'm not surprised you wouldn't want a woman's company sometimes. I know I do."

And even as she was speaking, she was lifting out pans and putting on the water, and handing me the knife for the potatoes and taking up a couple of onions herself.

We feasted that night. My mother could always make a little go a long way, but with a lot to start – she was a culinary queen. And my father knew it too, kissed her fondly before, during and after the meal. The eldest brother and I exchanged looks. The baby was only four years old and we'd all been glad of the break. The house didn't need another.

We had finished clearing the table, done with the washing up, the next-up brother had put the two little ones to bed, our father was reading to the older boys from the sports pages of the paper and I said to my mother, "I might just pop out."

And she didn't look up from the pan she was putting away, just nodded, "A breath of air?"

"Yes."

"I'll not ask where you're going."

"You can."

I had my lie all planned, but she chose not to make me lie to her, she'd have hated that, spared herself the pain.

"I'll not."

"I know what I'm doing."

"I doubt that." She stood up then, I could see her knees were hurting her, her back aching as it always did by this time of night, and then my father called from the other room, and already she was moving away, starting to go to him, heading for him as she always did. Our mother loved our father.

She stopped by the door, "Do you want one of your brothers to walk you?"

"I don't."

"Be careful."

"I will."

And that was it.

★ ★ ★

This is it.

I'm standing in Molly Malone's room – a wide, fringed shawl covers the window, another is thrown over her bed, a third sits on the back of the single chair. The shawls are of red and purple and deep green, they are the only colours in an otherwise bleached-clean room, floors and walls scrubbed pale, as if she never lights the fire in here, as if there is never any wood smoke or candle grease to mar the walls, the scoured floor. Maybe there isn't, it's a cool room. Not cold, but certainly cool. Molly Malone's room smells like driftwood, sea-washed day after night after day. It smells of clean linen. She has told me that beneath the shawl that covers her bed, the sheets and the pillow-case are ironed. This is an extravagance of time and effort I can't imagine, but from the scent of the bed, warm lavender, I have to believe her. The room also smells of lemons, there is a wooden bowl of them on the thin table, one is cut in half, she is sitting on her chair and watching me, she is rubbing her hands, her fingers, her nails with the sharp flesh. She pours water from a cracked jug into a chipped bowl – there is the same picture of a courting couple on both – and washes her hands, wiping them down on her skirt. She has changed since I saw her in the market. She is wearing a clean skirt, no fish-blood or dried guts, a clean skirt, now with two long, dark marks from the wet hands, her own hands, down her own thighs.

"I'm ready."

This is the third time she has said so. I don't know why I'm waiting, I know what I came here to do, am happy enough about it. I'm supposed to be shy about my own body, want to cover it, but in truth – other than from my brothers' prying eyes – I really don't mind. Never have. I like what I see in my small bedroom mirror a great deal, like it far too much I've been told.

"Look in that mirror any longer and you'll see the devil himself come up behind you," our grandmother always used to say. She's dead now, and there is nothing behind me but Molly Malone's bed. The problem has not been that I've needed to shield myself from myself, rather that I've never been asked to show anyone else before.

I'm being asked to show now.

There are not many layers to remove. Once I decide to start, it is quickly done.

"And now I'm ready," I reply.

It is so easy to be naked here. Cool, yes, but easy. I enjoy her gaze, am delighted to have someone else see this, see me, witness me. All of me. Her heavy gaze on my shoulders, my arms, breasts, belly – there – thighs, calves, feet – there – breasts, face – there. Molly Malone's eyes dip from my breasts to there, then rip back from there up to my breasts. I don't know if she's disappointed or delighted. Maybe both.

Perhaps both.

Both. Like me.

And then. Molly Malone naked. Five feet five in her bare feet, tired feet that stand all day, begin standing at first light, even in summer, waiting on the dock, tired splayed feet from years of hard waiting, and then the walk from the dock to the market, walking with her barrow, walking the cobbles and walking them hard. Molly Malone does not have pretty feet. Molly Malone naked and lying back on the bed, that back that has lugged lobster crates and crayfish pots, that has carried sacks of cockles and heavier ones of mussels, that back that bends and stretches all day as she reaches and weighs and parcels and sells. That back rests now, against the mattress and calls me, to rest on her. Molly Malone, reaching to me with strong arms. Upper arms with muscles delineated, Dublin streets have forged these muscles, forced these muscles, the old barrow with rutted wooden wheels pushed up and over, up and over, day after day after day (not Sunday afternoon, not Monday), upper arms strong enough to push from the dock to the market and back. Every day, twice a day. And her forearms. Molly Malone has fine dark hair on her forearms, shading the sinews that reach around the bone, embracing the tendons that years of shell-cracking, shell-piercing, shell-opening have made clear and sharp and strong. She does not have the pale skin of a lady, Molly's skin is mottled and freckled and lined, it is skin that has seen both sun and rain, skin that needs both sun and rain. Molly Malone has sold me sweet little crab claws with these good, strong arms, and I have been happy to watch her move behind the barrow, behind her apron, behind rolled-up sleeves. Now I watch her move on old white sheets.

It is night, there is no barrow, no market. We are in her room, and I am watching her, awaiting her. Her hair, which smells of clean linen, soft cotton, which is spread out across the darned sheet, across the thin grey blanket, beneath the coloured shawl, spread across me, her hair smells sweet and like night. It is night. She is not sweet. Her hands which, under the lemon, smell of soft shells ripped open, of mean claws tickled apart, of oysters smoothly shucked, of tiny shrimps tucked into perfect round pots, of fat grey prawns pinking with heat, her hands which smell of fish and of shellfish and of wide, wild oceans she has never seen, will never see, are on me. Molly Malone has hands that are wide and open and they hold me, I am both wide and open, full and ready. Molly Malone has hands that could clasp a small woman's waist or a young man's neck – hands that have done both – and now they clasp me, all of me.

This is the mussel. Open on the willing shell. We do not cook our mussels here. You can add your French white wine, your butter, your *herbes fines*, you may love your moules marinières, I'll take mine raw, and fresh, and from the shell. Dive in. I am the diver and I am the pearl. Tonight I search not the pearl, but the cockle. Small flesh, winkled out, called out. I call her out, my Molly Malone. In a while, a good enough while, she calls me back. And, calling to each other, we are one. A one that is made of three. One of her and the two of me. (We understand our trinities well enough in this city.)

Time passes. We spend many nights together, my Molly and me, and are happy to do so. My mother is happy too, relieved, I think. She always knew it would show itself one day, that I would have to show myself one day. If I was going to show anyone in this city it was safest I should show her, Molly Malone of the stories and the songs, Molly of the cockles and of the mussels. Molly who is not squeamish, who will gut and scale and rip and cut and open and taste. Molly who has always been happy to taste it all.

She did die of a fever. And no one could save her.

But I'm not sure that many tried.

I tried. My mother tried too. Even the big brothers helped, and our father. Carried broth, brought cloths, lit candles. Prayed. Once or twice.

No one could save her.

I left not long after, there was nothing for me there, not by then, not when so many people knew me as Molly's . . .

Well, as Molly's.

And I have made a good life here. There is a wife. And children. The wife is pleased to be mine, though we must – of course – hide ourselves, dress up, dress down, dress to fit. I played the girl there, I play the man here. It works well enough, and my wife is happier that way, she and our children are safer that way. We are happy. Most of the time. And if I miss my home, if I think of that black port, or the land I have left, of the city I ache for sometimes, in truth, it is mostly the water I miss. The river, the docks, the sea. The smell of the sea on the wind. My mother and father are long dead, the brothers all married too, happily some, unhappily others. No surprise there. But sometimes, when the wife beside sleeps deep – and these hot nights in this hot land are too warm, so many nights when I long for a cool room, for a cold night – on those nights I throw off the bedclothes and I lie here naked, lie here showing all that I am. All of me. And I remember being seen, for the first time, for all of me.

Then a smile comes to my lips, and a deep grin embeds itself in that place between my belly and my thighs, that place where I am both hidden and shown, where Molly Malone truly saw me. And here, in the dark, ten thousand miles from my childhood, more years than I can remember since that night, then hands that smell of a home I will never again see, touch me, take me, and hair that is washed walls and scrubbed floors and lemon halves and ironed linen fills my breath and my Molly Malone is as alive as I am. Lives as I do.

Alive.

Alive.

Oh.

Saving the World

Thom Gautier

This was in the late 1990s so it's time I shared this tale, a tale from the days of the politically correct uptight 1990s.

One night I was making love to my then fiancée – I'll call her X. We were fucking near the long bedroom mirror below our dresser. Seeking a visual flourish to enhance our foreplay, I asked X whether she might put on that men's hat – her fedora – like she used to back when we first met. My question didn't sit well. She pushed off me and then she grilled me about the request, as if I'd just asked her to get on all fours or give me a rim job. I mean, a hat – a goddamned hat fetish is hardly even a kink. "Guess I'm not good enough to make love to unadorned, *naked*?" I told her that went without saying. "Then why'd you ask me to put on that ratty old hat?"

I told her to just forget it. "Forget the fucking hat."

Lilah was a work friend of X's at one of those save-the-world non-profit foundations and I was first introduced to Lilah the night *after* the hat-skirmish with X. It was the foundation's Christmas party. I am sure that Lilah and I spoke a good deal at that first meeting, but all I remember is shaking her hand and studying her long straight dark hair, her dark eyes, her little black dress, her black choker with its pearly cameo, her black teardrop earrings. Her lovely ass almost visible against the pleats of her black skirt. I remember thinking that I'd bet big money that Lilah probably would wear a hat when she made love. I also remember, later in that party, Lilah and I reached out to grab the last brownie on the dessert tray. We laughed awkwardly, one of those impromptu fits of laughter you'll remember sharing even if you don't know exactly why. I was a gentleman. I let her have the last brownie. Oddly, some part of me wanted to hang around her and hover, watch her eat it. But I left her alone to enjoy it, wandering back towards X, X who was too busy proselytizing about one of the foundation's pet causes to even think about dessert. X, I realized, was losing her sweet tooth.

X and I saw Lilah socially now and then and each time between the get-togethers seemed longer than the next. Then one evening during dinner, X told me Lilah had quit the foundation. The news punched me in the gut. I realized my crush had taken me over, full-tilt. "Why'd she *quit*?" I asked, as if, knowing why she'd quit, I'd be able to intervene and get her back to my girlfriend's office.

"She's materialistic, shallow," X said. "She'd rather leave the office at five to go shopping at Saks than stay a little longer to go the extra mile for our charities." X's self-righteousness irked me; I wanted to defend Lilah as if she were my lover. I knew that Lilah wasn't shallow. *Materialistic?* Who the hell isn't? "So she likes expensive handbags," I told X. "That doesn't make a person *shallow*." I don't think I convinced X, who took up our plates and shook her head with the kind of patronizing disapproval that I associate with nuns and spinsters.

Often, when Lilah phoned our place, X wasn't home. "She's out saving the world," I once said.

"Well, I got out of *that* racket," Lilah said, gleefully.

These fortuitous calls happened a lot. I kept the conversations casual, and *mildly* flirtatious. Besides, I sensed Lilah didn't go there with unavailable men. I sensed a woman who enjoyed her single life, her small studio, her unattached, personal freedom. Still, from the phone calls, she and I graduated to email. Back then you graduated to email from the phone: I was new to email then and very few people I knew had it at home, so it felt like Lilah and I were in our own little world exchanging messages. And our phone conversations had a teenage innocence. They were almost always about *pleasure*. Simple, simply pleasure. Music. Movies. Even candy. We both liked Butterfingers candy bars. Once, on the phone, we were discussing what ingredients made that chocolate bar so sweet to the tongue and as we were talking, a call from X came through. I apologized to Lilah that I had to take the call. "No worries," she said, "we'll solve the mystery of the Butterfingers another time."

One winter night, X and I were supposed to meet Lilah in the city to go see a new singer-songwriter at a Manhattan club. X bowed out at the last minute. She had a save-the-world-type speech to write for her Ethnic Studies course. "You go," X told me, "Go. And tell Lilah I am sorry."

So, I went. As agreed, Lilah met me under the clock in the centre of Grand Central Station. She stood out from the crowd – and then some. For one thing, she was in a long black Italian coat, like she'd stepped out of the film of a smoke-filled 1940s movie set. She wasn't rushing hither and thither like the swarm of middle-class commuters. Instead she seemed part of the Beaux-Arts elegance of Grand Central Station itself, her right hand with red-painted fingernails resting delicately on the marble ledge of the kiosk. Her tiny, square-shaped handbag was slung gracefully off her shoulder, and she had one boot-shod leg coolly crossed over the other. I almost had to slap myself in my face to make me realize *that woman is waiting for me*. For all my eager admiration, I was overcome by shyness as we greeted each other. But Lilah was so unguarded that it forced me to "man up" and shed the shy sixteen-year-old bullshit. I directed us to the taxi stand outside where snow was starting to fall. The midtown winds were blowing the flakes in topsy-turvy plumes as our cab headed south.

Lilah smelled of jasmine perfume, a fragrance so strong that the whole cab was filled with it. Both of our hands were pressed into the cab seat, almost touching, while our other hands held onto the straps near the back windows. We made inane comments about the passing shops and streets. Her velvet skirt rode up her left leg and unveiled her luminous skin beneath her black stockings. I caught her looking at my loafers and the piping of my black jacket. For most of the ride, we talked about X – a safe topic – and we agreed it took more discipline than either of us had to stay in on a Saturday night to write a paper. As we discussed the noble charities which the foundation sponsored, my eyes wandered to the diamonds on Lilah's handbag and for a while it seemed those jewels were the only light in our dark taxi.

Downtown at the club, the burly bouncers said the show had been cancelled because the singer couldn't fly in due to the snowstorm.

"Snow*storm*?" we asked.

"Try *blizzard*," the bouncer told us.

Lilah and I laughed at our failure to watch the weather reports. I suggested we retreat to a bar before I "head back to the 'burbs," and then I remembered that Lilah didn't drink. "Feel a sweet tooth?" she asked me. She knew a café nearby where we could get dessert and we found a small candlelit table in a place called Dessert Isle. She helped me parse the menu options, her finger gliding across my menu. I ordered a profiterole and a dessert wine and she had a crème brûlée and mint tea.

I admitted it had been "a lot of years" since I'd gone out just for dessert. We joked about how we'd fought over the brownie at that Christmas party. She told me about an ex-boyfriend from college – who didn't eat dessert. "Sugar-free diet," she said, in a tone that was at once disbelieving and dismissive. She delicately spooned her crème brûlée and held the spoon in her mouth. Then she took it out and dug in for another spoonful. "Hence the *ex* in ex-boyfriend," she said and her smile turned me on.

Under the small table, our feet grazed each other's and on the tabletop our fingers brushed more than once.

Instead of announcing that I ought to head back to the train before the storm got worse, I ordered myself a Sambuca.

The longer we talked, the more it was obvious we were trying to avoid the very thing that was happening: something like a date arranged by some force other than ourselves. We shifted our chairs so that we could face the pane glass window and watch the snow piling up. I put my hand around the back of her chair, careful not to touch her shoulder. The waiter said they were expecting a foot within the next three hours and we stared at the falling snow.

Lilah insisted on coming back to Grand Central just to be sure my train was running. Ice had formed on the sidewalks so she had to hold onto my arm. Our hips bumped as we battled the wind. The lapels of our coats flapped upwards and wet snow pelted our reddened faces. My heart sank when we saw that the trains were listed as "*On Time*". The anxious crowds wandering around others who were squatted on the ground indicated something different. Then, as if the gods had intervened, the station's PA announced a twenty-minute delay "on all trains into and out of Grand Central".

To kill time, Lilah and I wandered around the newsstands where she pointed out her favourite magazine – *Vogue*'s fat spring issue, some 500 pages thick. "I have skipped on groceries to be able to buy their fashion issue," she said, as she purchased the copy. I held up a Greenpeace magazine with a photo of an oil-slicked turtle. "As a former world-saving foundation person, shouldn't you be reading this instead of *Vogue*?"

"Don't go there," she warned, and as she waved her *Vogue* at me I wanted to snatch it out of her hands and kiss her.

In Grand Central, the schedule-boards had changed. Trains were *Cancelled*. A collective groan rose from the waiting crowds. I was ecstatic; Lilah raised her eyebrows and shrugged and then she smiled. Before the crowd could converge on the pay phones, I called X to tell her what was up. She barely heard me. She had just read some article for her paper and she was going on about an atrocity in some distant country. As she babbled on, I saw from the corner of my eye, Lilah holding a piece of paper. In her neat red handwriting the note said, "You can use my couch!" The operator was asking for another quarter; I made sure to ask X if she was OK with my "borrowing Lilah's couch".

"What'd she say?" Lilah asked.

"She said fine and went back to ranting about war and orphans."

Lilah and I shrugged, our eyes glittering like liberated kids whose parents were so wrapped up with their own activities that they couldn't be bothered enforcing a curfew.

At a deli near Lilah's place we stocked up on Butterfingers candy bars and expensive English tea.

Her apartment was spacious for a studio, with high ceilings, lofty windows, tall, fancy Japanese screens that set her bed off from the living room, and bookcases and shelves filled with CDs, art books, books on fashion. "My old *Vogues*," she said, pointing to rows of magazines on the colourful shelf near the window.

As we watched boring TV news reports about the blizzard, I admired her high-heeled boots that were still glazed with melting snow. We talked shopping – about buying patiently to get quality versus settling for shit. "If you are a patient shopper you can nab designer clothes on a shoestring budget," she said. "And still keep a politically correct carbon footprint." I told her that I admired her nuanced approach to values.

She asked me would I mind if she thumbed through her copy of *Vogue?* "As long as you don't think me less a man if I peruse it *with* you," I said. She patted the couch and I sat comfortably next to her as she held the magazine on her black-stocking lap. She flipped patiently through the magazine, occasionally pausing at certain images: a leggy blonde leaping over a puddle in a Burberry's. Or a supermodel in a micromini slouched in the back seat of a Porsche donning a Tiffany's bracelet. She was pleasantly surprised that I could tell Chanel from Versace, couture from kitsch. The magazine's special feature was a lingerie spread filled with models in teddies, in hooded terrycloth robes, in catsuits, in stilettos and hot pants. I told her what X had said to me recently, that lingerie was invented by men to "corset and bind" women.

"Well I must be pretty oppressed," she said, "I've been obsessively collecting this stuff since I was eighteen." As Lilah pointed out an Estée Lauder ad, she explained the Egyptian origins of make-up and glamour, and I recalled the stupid argument X and I had had that night, about the fedora. Poles apart, I thought. It felt like a cosmic joke being played on me. *Marrying the wrong chick, sucker.*

Lilah tossed *Vogue* aside with a thump and got up and went behind the screen and rummaged in a closet. She emerged with hangers filled with lacy, frilly items and spread them on the couch with a collector's contagious self-satisfaction. Pale blues. Ivory whites. Midnight blacks. Blood reds. I felt sure I was in an insanely erotic dream and would wake up with X at my side, but the sharp scent of perfume and the loud crackles of heat from her apartment's pipes were all too real.

Together, like factory line workers, we inspected the stitching and fabric and the labels of each item, turning them inside out. I put my hand into a green stocking and made a talking puppet of my hand. "Save the frogs of the rainforest," I said and we both laughed.

As she kneeled on the couch, her knee brushed my crotch and I boldly put my hand on her leg to encourage her to keep the pressure there between my legs. As she did, she coyly asked me whether X wears lingerie now and then, "I mean, despite how 'oppressive' it is."

I explained that she had quite frequently when we first met but that she didn't any longer, not now that she thought it was "patriarchal and controlling". Plus, I added, "when you're saving the world you're not allowed to have fun."

"Who says?" Lilah asked, stretching the fabric of a baby-blue lace bra.

"Not I," I said. "Definitely not I."

Sometime between slicing up the Butterfingers chocolate bars and carrying tea into her living room, Lilah and I kissed. It was a sloppy but a long kiss sweetened by our hesitancy and guilt. When we let go and stood close enough that our chests were touching, I could feel her rapid breathing. My eyes wandered the run of her pale neck. I smelled that jasmine again. I clenched my jaw and closed my eyes to calm down. Feeling like I had to say *something*, I wondered whether it was a wise idea for me to stay over. "It sort of feels like we're lighting a fuse here," she said.

We went to the window and inspected the snowfall; she pointed out the cars half buried in snow. "We have no choice," she said and then we both laughed. On the couch, we snacked on Butterfingers and she read from the wrapper and the litany of weird ingredients pronounced in her cute falsetto was enough to make me hard. "*Confectioner's Corn Flakes ... Nonfat Milk ... Salt ... Lactic Acid Esters, Soy Lecithin ... Soybean Oil.*" Her voice seemed to be singing in a pitch far above the banal list of ingredients.

I took the wrapper from her and asked her why she was so into lingerie from such an early age. "Did you want to be a designer?"

She explained how she used to go out a lot with friends but that chasing boys seemed less fun sometimes than staying home listening to music and copying from fashion magazines and drawing plans for cocktail dresses, wedding dresses. She used to dress her little sister in her mother's costume jewellery. Between summers at college, she got sales jobs at boutiques, but her talent for managing egos and for fundraising led her into charity, non-profit. I'd always disagreed with those so-called experts who say men are more visual than women when it comes to desire because it was obvious women were visual as well – "Just look at who reads *Vogue*," I said.

It was one a.m. and the sugar high and the tea were still coursing through us. She wondered aloud whether our visual tastes were the same as our taste in dessert. We decided to play a game – a dangerous one, but a game nevertheless. She'd model four lingerie ensembles from her vast collection and I'd rate each of them, "like an Olympic judge, on a scale from one to ten". and then she'd let me know how she ranked each outfit herself and this would show us if we have the same taste. "And as added bonus," she said, "I'll take the one that you chose as the best one and sell it at the neighbourhood boutique on consignment and send the profits to a charity." She winked when she said "charity", and I hopped onto the couch and steeled myself to be a discriminating – and lucky – judge.

Her first outfit was a white bustier with a sheer white satin garter belt centred by a pink rose. It was called "Maiden at the Maypole". She strolled, smiling, "A walk on the blushing bridal side," she said, adjusting the white stockings at the garter clasp. At first I couldn't get over how the white lingerie contrasted with her dark eyes and dark hair and how her legs looked especially long in the white hosiery. She had drawn her hair back into a prim bun and she posed near the window holding the curtain over her white legs. She lowered her head and pretended to blush and then she turned around to reveal that the back of the panties sported a pink bow. I scribbled a "7.5" into my notepad. As she got to me on the couch, she picked up my hand and I held her and said, "With this hand, I thee—"

"You thee *what*?" she asked, grinning. "You're spoken for, you rascal!"

I stood up and held her hips and pressed my lips onto her shoulder and even kissed the satin bra-strap. "This outfit gives the lie to 'an innocent bride'," I said.

She tapped my nose. "And I'll probably never wear this in its intended context," she said, giggling. "No offence. But marriage and lingerie seem incompatible."

Her second ensemble was a jet-black kimono with white peonies painted on its sleeves. "Peony Kimono". The liquid effect of the kimono's fabric made it seem that Lilah was robed in a black water that shone in spots as if from the reflecting sun. As she walked, she held something behind her back. When she got to the centre of the room, she opened the robe with one hand to reveal the silken yellow lining. Then she let the kimono fall to her feet. "I gave up two summers of vacation pay to buy this kimono," she said.

She wore those expensive hold-up European stockings – the ones with the five-inch lace tops, tops that extend all the way to the top of the leg – and a matching demi-style black bra that barely covered her breasts. Her neckline was jewelled by a coral red necklace. She'd brushed her long hair so that it draped down to the left of her face, feathering like a painter's inky brush against her pale breast. Her stockings were semi-opaque. The mules she wore were high-heeled but she moved effortlessly in them.

From behind her back she pulled an English-style bowler hat. She put the hat on her head and put a leg up on the couch. It was as if she had known about the fedora argument X and I had. Then I thought, no. This is who she is. It's not about X.

I stared at Lilah's leg, as if I were studying the geometry of the stocking's weave. Really I was gazing through the fabric at her luminous skin. My eyes travelled upwards to her black panties. Red threads were woven into its black lace. Lilah saw me staring at the panties and, as if she knew I was seeing the red threads, she ran her finger on them to guide my eyes. I ran my finger along the border between her skin and the black fabric, then lightly over the soft mound of her sex, tickling the surface as she kept her leg on the couch and closed her eyes. She bit down on her lip as if trying to stifle whatever urge my admiring eyes had stirred. When she lowered her leg from the couch and walked off, disappearing behind the Japanese screens to put on the next outfit, my cock was so hard that I could barely shift in my seat as I scribbled the number "10" in handwriting so sloppy you'd think I was drunk.

Lilah's third ensemble was a navy-blue body stocking. "This is 'Russian Catsuit' " she said. She wore a dark blue thong and dark blue star-shaped pasties over her nipples. She strode into the living room barefoot, bouncing gingerly with each step, her hair in a bouncy gymnast's ponytail. "Let me see if I *can*," she said before raised her arms over her head in a V and dashing forward, curling into a single somersault. She raised her hands like an Olympian and I applauded. "*Zee Amerikan Lilah has vowed dis crowd*," I said, mimicking a Russian accent. I gave the outfit a 7, mainly for its spunkiness.

"More than *spunky*," she said, sidling up to me, showing me the leaf-and-clover filigree stitched into the garment's navy-blue rayon. I put the pad down and told her she looked so much like a gymnast I wanted to see if I could lift her up.

"Hey, this is no bridal outfit," she said as I cradled her, holding her bride-like in my arms. She kicked and swayed her feet and we kissed softly.

"We're being very bad," Lilah said.

"Yes," I said, letting her down. "Judges can't kiss the models."

"Right, you must avoid bias," she said as she tiptoed back behind the screen.

The final ensemble she called, "Parisian Peek-a-Boo", crotchless designer pantyhose with a frilly lace blouse that was long enough that it almost hid her sexy black panties. Lilah flipped a white beret onto her head and sashayed through the living room, poised on backless high heels, bending forward teasingly as if to pick something off the floor, the bright white skin of her ass positively glowing against the frilly hem of the blouse.

When she stood up straight she ran her finger along the scallop-shaped trim of the pantyhose, up her waist and across her tummy and down the inside of her fair-skinned thighs. I wrote a "9.5" on the pad.

She came over and sat on the couch. I tossed the pad onto the floor, and we stretched out on opposite ends. She let her foot wander towards my crotch and rubbed up and down on the fly of my jeans while I caressed her calf, her knee, mildly tapping her thigh as she writhed.

She sat up so I could reach higher up, between her legs and as my hand slipped in there she closed her legs on it, like a vice, moving her right foot up and down so fast on my crotch that I told her if she kept that up we'd have an "accident" on our hands.

"Better not," she said, springing up from the couch, "I wouldn't be able to give you a clean change of clothes. All my undies – as you see – are strictly women's."

Lilah called out to me from behind the screen and I went around. A mound of lingerie sat on the bed edge but she had changed back into the kimono outfit. Her hair was wild and spilled over her shoulders and the bowler sat on her lap. "This is my favourite of the four," she said. "Which was your fav?"

I showed her all the scores on my pad, and she clapped when she saw the "10" next to Peony Kimono. I added the phrase "with Bowler Hat" to the name.

"I had a strong, strong premonition our taste would coincide," she said, as she stretched her legs and wiggled her toes. "I used to dress up like this when I was young and my parents would go away. This snowstorm is reminding me of one weekend when they had gone away and were stuck upstate and I, well, how can I say this without blushing, I discovered, um, the pleasures of the flesh. I must have been fifteen or so and I dressed up in tights and underwear and costume jewellery and strutted in front of mirrors just like I was posing for you now." She told me that was the first time she'd seen herself as if she were someone else – "almost like I wasn't me but I was me, and I loved how I looked. And that's the night I . . ." Her hands ran over her own legs and her voice trailed off. My hand was on top of hers. She reached down and closed her eyes, dragging her finger along the red embroidery in the black panties, her finger so strictly following the red filigree it was as if she knew every microscopic warp and weave of her panties without having to see.

I asked her why someone as in touch with her likes and dislikes hadn't found the right man. "You answered your own question, maybe," she said, tossing the hat onto the bed, shaking out her hair. "You know, it's a bit sad but they say single girls have the best lingerie collections."

"It's not sad. I'm enjoying this," I said, and she repeated "this" like we both knew what we were sharing even if we couldn't put a name on it.

We got to talking about relationships and also about being happy alone. The pleasures of self-pleasure. "Fewer arguments that way," I said, "you are better off. Your own place, your own time, your own possessions." She asked me whether men pleasure themselves a lot when they are alone. I answered that men didn't discuss that subject with other men, any more than women did, but that I guessed it was quite common. "Especially among the married set," I added, somewhat cynically, and we laughed.

"Girls are no different from guys on that score," she said. Then she reached into the kimono and drew out a black dildo and held it out for me to see, as if it were proof of something. She bit her lip and lowered her head, not blushing so much as avoiding eye contact, as if to take back all this confessional sharing that was happening between us. That dream-like sensation from earlier washed over me again. Her shiny black dildo matched the lacquer-black of her kimono and black of the sleek mules on the floor, shoes she was kicking nervously as we sat there in the deafening hush, suspended in a haze of kinky karma. She recalled the snow outside and wondered how much had fallen. I took her dildo from her as if to inspect it and I asked her. "Would it be cheating – if . . ." I stopped myself. She told me to finish my thought.

"If two friends were to . . . share. Share private pleasures in each other's company?"

She raised her eyebrows and grinned and said she had no idea what the rules are for that.

"But it's certainly not the same as sleeping together, is it?" she asked.

We agreed it absolutely wasn't like sleeping together, and I was so turned on by our budding conspiracy that I wanted to throw her back on the bed and peel off her clothes and admire her, like I were the guardian of this private nook of pleasure, here, surrounded by these Japanese screens, warm inside on a snowy night.

Lilah helped me out of my shirt and my jeans. We sat on her bed facing each other as we had earlier in the evening on the couch. I could see the outline of her dark pubic hair under those black panties. Her skin beneath her stockings reminded me of the snow, the snow that we could not see except for the glowing whiteness that emanated from under the window blinds.

Without letting her fingers touch my skin, she helped me slip off my underwear and then she took off hers and we dropped them on top of each other on the floor by the bed.

"Touch yourself," she said. "And I'll touch myself."

It felt adolescent, all this, awkward and exhilarating, like some strange experiment in closeness that really didn't feel wrong.

Once I'd stroked my cock till it was hard, she squeezed a lubricant from a black tube, letting the fragrant oil pour over my knuckles and my fingers and onto my cock. The cool relief and slickness as I gripped my cock almost made me erupt.

Then she lubed her black dildo with the oil, her dark eyes watching me jerk off all the while. "Play," she said, and I licked my lips and repeated, "Play."

She rubbed the shiny black toy against her labia. Then she raised her hips off the mattress and shifted the dildo below, towards her ass, pressing her feet into the mattress to lift herself, her gorgeous legs arched at my sides. Her moans almost sounded like laughter as she played with the black dildo like that.

I paused for a moment in my own pleasures and with my grease-less left hand I tossed the bowler hat towards her. She sat back down on the bed and put it on, letting it tilt forward till I could barely see her dark eyes. Then she leaned her head back and slid the dildo in and out of herself with such dexterity that I was awed by the balletic strokes of her hands. "A woman who knows her own pleasure," I thought, "is the sexiest woman alive."

Lilah pleasured herself in and out so rapidly that I was amazed the bowler hat stayed on her head. Watching her, feeling safe within the confines of this bedroom, I stroked my cock faster and faster, studying the slide of the red coral necklace on her breasts, admiring her close-eyed assurance as she fucked herself with that shiny black dildo, black against her pink sex. Her cheeks flushed and glowed. Her dark hair gave off an even darker sheen as it swayed behind her back. The hat seemed glued on her head. She moved the dildo between her legs as if it were a tiny clarinet – and as if her pink sex were its sacred music.

I stroked myself with more and more speed and from time to time she stared across the bed at my cock in my fist. Occasionally her legs brushed mine; and my eyes returned her stare as my balls filled and my foreskin burned with delight and Lilah shoved the dildo in and out of her pussy, rearing her head so far backwards that her bowler hat slipped backwards off her, tumbling off the edge of the bed and rolling along the floor, and as I stroked my cock, I followed the hat and recalling that fight with X, about wearing the fedora, I groaned and erupted, coming warm jets onto the bed sheets.

Lilah barely heard my guttural groans. She was busy, half-raised off the bed and lost in the ecstatic silence that rose from what she was doing for herself between her legs with that black dildo.

In my exhausted afterglow, I held her calves to give her better balance and I watched her with friendly, intimate encouragement. She smiled. She stretched her whole body out tightly and I could see her legs tense as her rasping moans punctured the hush of the room with increasing frequency, the slick dildo easing in and out, ever faster.

I took the tube of oil and squeezed a long trail of oil that slicked onto her hand and onto the dildo as she moved it in and out. She rubbed the excess oil onto her nipples and pinched them. Her eyes were closed. I wondered who or what she was thinking of.

Her dildo's slickness freed it to slip and slide along her wet swollen clit deftly. There was a small puckering noise as she moved it in and out so fast that she shuddered, thrusting her hips violently, folding her legs around her dildo gripped in her trembling fist, and her happy shouts boomed off the ceiling as her legs flailed against mine before she let go. Then she opened her legs and caught her breath, beaming, holding the dildo up, waving it like a magician triumphantly flourishing her wand.

The next day, when I got home to X, it was no lie that I had slept on Lilah's couch. But X seemed indifferent; she was finishing her speech for her course and ranting and raving about the sorry state of the world. I spent the afternoon swapping thankful emails with Lilah.

Things between my fiancée went south pretty fast after that evening and X and I broke off our engagement exactly six months after that snowy night at Lilah's.

Lilah, meanwhile, eventually moved out to San Francisco. She and I stayed in touch on email yet with my X out of the picture the old erotic tension – that forbidden quality of our connection – no longer spiced up our exchanges, and after a while my contact with Lilah faded.

Then one day, almost two years to the day after that snowy evening, I got a message from Lilah suggesting I go downtown to a certain boutique in the Village and check out their front window's display.

I bundled up and took the train down. In the shop's window, I saw that peony kimono outfit, complete with the stockings and the red coral necklace. Even her bowler hat and those lacquer-black mules were set in front of the outfit.

I went inside and asked how much the outfit in the display window was, "As I think I'd like to buy it for my girlfriend," I lied, shoring up my lie by pretending to inspect the kimono's size. I asked the saleswoman to add the bowler hat and mules as well. "Are you sure these shoes will fit your girlfriend?" I was asked.

I said I was sure they would. The ensemble cost me two grand. I didn't even wince as I handed over my Visa card.

I took the outfit home and stored it safely in a garment bag in a cedar closet. I kept the bowler hat on a shelf above my work desk. I sent Lilah an email that her ensemble was there and that, coincidentally, it had sold to someone while I was in the shop.

Lilah answered two weeks later to say she'd received a handsome cheque from that Village boutique and that she had sent the proceeds from the boutique's consignment cheque to a worthwhile charity.

"Nice," I answered. "That ensemble saved the world."

Lilah said she appreciated my remark. I also know that, to this day, she doesn't know the half of it.

One Last Fling

Kristina Wright

"We're Vegas bound," Douglas said, helping me into the back of our sleek, black limousine.

The neon lights outside Club Europa reflected off my silver-sequined minidress, causing it to sparkle like a disco ball. I made a half-hearted effort to preserve my modesty as I climbed into the limo, tugging my skirt with one hand while I held a glass of champagne in the other. I wasn't particularly successful at either, as I felt a cool breeze on my ass and the trickle of champagne on my wrist. I fell into the back of the limo in a fit of giggles and waited for my entourage to join me.

"Oh, but I'm not finished dancing!"

Alex got in beside me, his long limbs tangling with mine as we made room for two more. "It's three hours to Vegas and the girls are waiting for you. You'll dance the night away tomorrow night."

"Fuck the night away, is more like it," Douglas said, as he and Neil climbed in and sat across from us.

Neil tapped the partition between the driver and us. "We're ready," he called. "Let's get the bride to Vegas."

The limo pulled away from the kerb in front of my favourite dance club and I waved goodbye as if I would never see it again. I was giddy and tipsy and very cosy in the back of the limo with my three favourite men – besides my fiancé Simon, of course. What can I say? I've always been a tomboy and that has translated into deep, meaningful – and sometimes even platonic – friendships with men. Not that I don't have female friends, I do. They were waiting for me at the Bellagio in Vegas and in the morning we'd be getting massages and pedicures and talking about boys before I walked down the aisle. But I had wanted my last night as a single woman to be spent with my three closest male friends.

It had been Simon's idea for my bachelorette party to end up in

Vegas, where we were to be married the following evening. Now, I was floating happily along thanks to the beautiful, bubbly champagne that kept flowing into my glass from endless bottles provided by my attentive staff of three. I was dressed in sparkly sequins and smoky mascara, looking very much the part of a party girl out for a night of dancing and debauchery. I smiled like the proverbial cat that has eaten the cream and curled up contentedly on the leather seat next to Alex.

"Well, lady, did we show you a good last night?" Alex asked, refilling my glass yet again.

I giggled as I sipped the expensive champagne. "Absolutely. We made quite a scene on the dance floor."

It was true. We'd popped into three clubs over the course of the evening and caused a bit of a stir every time as I led the men out to the centre of the dance floor. Gyrating with three men is likely to garner a lot of attention. Not that I minded. I loved having all eyes on me and my boys. Alex, at six-four and with almost white-blond hair often caused enough of a stir on his own. But throw in former football-playing Douglas with his rugged good looks and Neil with the lean, muscular body of a runner and I was certain every woman in every club was jealous of me. The best part was the safe feeling I had surrounded by men who knew me at least as well as Simon did. I snuggled against Alex's shoulder and sighed. Douglas and Neil sat across from us, drinking beer from the well-stocked limo fridge.

"I could get used to this, if I wasn't getting married tomorrow."

Douglas winked at me. "Why would you trade in wild nights of dancing with your own personal harem for boring married life?"

"Aren't harem boys usually eunuchs?"

"Definitely no eunuchs here," Alex said, gruffly.

We laughed at that. Alex's sexual conquests were almost as legendary as, well, my own. I'd tested those waters a time or two and decided he had earned his reputation as a cocksman. Of course, Douglas wasn't a slouch in the bedroom, either. The only mystery for me was Neil. Bedroom-eyed, soft-spoken Neil was a big question mark to me. I glanced at him now – wondering things probably better left unknown.

The limo turned a corner a little too sharply, which pressed me a little closer to Alex. "Hey, Mr Limo Driver," I called through the darkened partition. "Please be careful! I'm getting married tomorrow."

The partition lowered enough for me to see blue eyes staring at me in the rear-view mirror. "Yes, ma'am. My apologies."

I giggled. "Is'OK."

"It's official," Neil said. "She's drunk."

I harrumphed in a very unladylike fashion. "I am not drunk. I'm just a little bit tipsy."

Alex's hand, which had been on my knee since the corner-turn, seemed to have accidentally slid up my thigh. "Well, I'm drunk."

As if to prove his intoxication, he stroked my thigh seductively. His fingers felt warm on my bare skin. I couldn't tell if he was messing with me or being serious. The possibility that he might be serious was exciting – and also proof that I was most definitely a little drunk. I made a low murmur of pleasure and the three men laughed. I didn't like that at all. I was the bride, damn it! I wanted to be pampered and coddled and . . . other things.

"Uh oh. Watch out, Alex," Douglas said. "You know how she gets when she's drunk."

I tilted my head and finished the last of the champagne in my glass before holding it out for another refill from Alex's bottomless bottle. "Do tell, Douglas. How do I get?"

"Oh, love, you know how you get," Alex answered good-naturedly as he refilled my glass. "Don't you?"

Alex, more so than the other two, always knew how to calm me down from one of my bitchy moods. I looked into his twinkling green eyes and smiled. I covered his hand with mine, wondering if I dared move his hand just a couple of inches higher. The thought made me squirm and sigh.

"Oh yeah. I remember now." I licked my lips, noting the way his gaze followed the tip of my tongue from one corner of my mouth to the other. "I get very *needy* when I'm drunk."

"Very needy," Alex said. "That's certainly one way of phrasing it, babe."

"She's *needed* me on more than one occasion," Douglas smirked, giving Neil's shoulder a nudge as if the whole thing was a big joke. "Haven't you, doll?"

I pouted. "I don't remember."

"I remember." Alex topped off my champagne glass. "Douglas's birthday, three years ago. You did naughty things with his birthday cake and then you disappeared into his bedroom for a good half-hour—"

"It was an hour," Douglas interrupted.

"Fine, a good hour. And when you came out you had birthday cake in your hair—"

Douglas laughed. "Among other places."

"I did not!" Of course I had, but I felt like I needed to defend my feminine honour in face of their laughter at my exploits.

"Then there was that night we got thrown out of that club – what was the name of it? – because you pulled me into the bathroom. The *women's* bathroom," Alex went on.

I glared at him. "My zipper broke on my dress."

"Before or after he went into the bathroom with you?" Douglas asked.

Neil had remained quiet through their ribbing, but now he finished his beer and shook his head. "You've never *needed* me."

I opened my mouth to say something, but he was right. All of my drunk fooling around over the years had been with Alex and Douglas, mostly because I knew they didn't take it any more seriously than I did. Neil was different, though. I always suspected he had a bit of a thing for me and while I adored him and thought he was sexy as hell, his attraction was purely physical. I might play with the boys, but Simon had my heart and I felt like that was the one part of me Neil might demand if I let things go too far. But, like earlier, I was starting to wonder what I'd missed.

"My loss." I gave Neil a sad smile. "You know I love you anyway, right?"

"I don't think we're talking about love here," Neil said, looking away as the limo moved through the quiet city streets.

The mood had shifted in the limo and I looked at Alex with dismay. Sensing my discomfort, he offered, "Well, the night's still young – and she's definitely drunk."

The men laughed, even Neil, and I relaxed a little. It was hard to think about Neil's hurt feelings with Alex's hand making slow, sensual circles on my thigh. I wriggled against him, which moved Alex's hand just a bit higher on my leg and under the edge of my skirt. He was so very close to touching my pussy I considered how much more I could slide down before I would be on the floor. It was a fleeting thought – and an unnecessary one. Alex spread his fingers on my thigh. His long fingers. Then he wiggled them lightly against the edge of my panties. I bit my lip to keep from moaning.

"Guess she's feeling needy," Neil said. "Is the bride-to-be wet already?"

I made a face at him. "That's rude."

"Yes, it is," Alex agreed. "And I don't know if she's wet."

They laughed at me again. I couldn't help but laugh with them as I enjoyed the feeling of Alex's finger rubbing lazily against me. "You are all bad," I said. "And I love it."

Alex leaned down to whisper in my ear, "If you spread your legs just a bit, love, I promise you will love it even more."

How can a girl say no to that? I did as he suggested, spreading my thighs far enough apart that my skirt rode up to my hips and gave Douglas and Neil a glimpse of my lacy white panties. I watched them watching me, getting more and more turned on by the way the night was going. Alex cupped my panty-clad pussy and gave it a gentle squeeze. I gasped, Douglas groaned and Alex made an appreciative sound low in his throat. Neil just stared, his heavy-lidded eyes watching me. I looked past him and saw another pair of eyes staring at me from the rear-view mirror. I smiled and winked, thoroughly enjoying the attention.

"Oh yes, the little minx is quite wet," Alex confirmed. "Despite your little white virginal panties, I think you're the bad one, Victoria."

I nodded in agreement. "Oh yes, I'm quite bad."

"Should I stop then?"

By way of an answer, I covered his hand again and pressed it to my pussy. "You'd better not."

"We're almost to the highway," the driver announced. "Shall I make one last rest stop before the drive to Las Vegas?"

Just then, Alex slipped a finger under the edge of my panties and pushed just the tip into my pussy. "Yes," I gasped. Then, quickly, "No, no! That won't be necessary."

"Excuse me, ma'am?"

I met the driver's eyes in the rear-view mirror again, wondering just how much of our back-seat antics he could see.

"I'm sorry, we were talking about something else," I said breathlessly as Alex pushed his finger inside me just a little bit farther.

Douglas and Neil exchanged amused looks.

"This is the best conversation I've ever had," Neil said, seeming to have recovered his sense of humour. I liked him better this way – my familiar old friend instead of the one who might have got away.

I stuck my tongue out at them. "Just drive, please."

"Certainly, ma'am," the driver said. "We should be in Las Vegas in a little under three hours. Let me know if you need anything."

"I wouldn't mind doing a little less talking," Douglas said. "I think actions speak louder than words."

I heard something in his voice that promised pleasure. For me. The combination of champagne and familiarity had left me utterly without inhibitions.

"What would you like to do, Douglas?" I asked, raising my hips to Alex's questing hand. Alex obliged me by sliding his hand down the front of my panties and giving my bare pussy a squeeze.

Douglas slipped to his knees on the floor of the limo. "I'd like to have my mouth too full to talk."

"Seems like she's already occupied," Neil commented. Whatever his feelings for me, he was clearly enjoying the show.

As if by silent agreement, Alex withdrew his hand from my panties and pulled the lacy fabric to the side. My bare, bikini-waxed – and increasingly wet – pussy was exposed to Douglas's view. He moved forward between my legs, pushing my knees apart with his hands. I squirmed on the seat, my pulse quickening in anticipation of what was to come. But Douglas made me wait. He stared at my exposed pussy, nostrils flaring as if he was taking in my scent. He was so close that I could feel the warmth of his breath on my aroused flesh. The silence in the limo was almost tangible – even the road sounds seemed to have faded beneath the pounding of my heart.

"Lick her," Alex said, giving voice to my silent plea. "She's dying for it."

Douglas looked into my eyes, one eyebrow cocked, as if seeking my permission.

I nodded. "Please."

His tongue felt like velvet on my engorged sex. With the broad flat of his tongue, he lapped at me. I moaned, raising my hips to his mouth, wanting more. He licked me slowly, as if we were alone and had all the time in the world, his tongue dipping between the valley of my pussy lips and up over my swollen clit. Again and again, he licked me with those slow, methodical strokes designed to torment me even while they gave me pleasure. I moved my hips against his mouth, seeking more.

Alex slipped the strap of my dress over my shoulder, exposing my breast. Then he dipped his head to suck my nipple into his mouth. I moaned, tugging the other strap down and cupping my breasts, offering them to Alex's lips. Douglas shifted lower, hooking my legs over his shoulders as he devoured me with his mouth.

I looked at Neil. He watched the three of us, his expression one of barely controlled lust as his hand moved slowly over his crotch. It excited me to know he was watching – an observer rather than a participant. I wanted more, though. I wanted to see him stroke himself. I opened my mouth to say just that, but Alex chose that moment to flick my clit with his finger as Douglas dipped his tongue between the lips of my pussy. I moaned, the combination of sensations driving me out of my mind and to the brink of orgasm. I tucked my head against Alex's shoulder, my eyes fluttering closed as I pushed my aroused body at the two men who pleasured me.

"She's going to come," Alex said. "Lick her faster."

Douglas's tongue licked along my wet opening while Alex stroked my clitoris with his fingertips. I clutched at Douglas's hair and tightened my thighs around his bent head. Every muscle in my body went taut, my damp skin feeling hypersensitive in my arousal. Then Douglas sucked my clit – and Alex's finger – into his mouth and I came.

"Oh, yes!" I gasped, nearly sliding off the seat as my orgasm slammed into me. "Oh God!"

"You naughty little girl. Come hard for us," Alex whispered in my ear. "Come on his tongue. Show us what a very bad girl you are."

I rode wave after wave of orgasm as Douglas nursed gently at my throbbing clit. Alex rubbed his wet fingertip over my nipple and sucked it into his mouth again, his soft moan telling me just how much he was enjoying the experience. When I gently nudged Douglas away from my sensitive clit, his mouth shiny with my wetness, he grinned and licked his lips.

"Delicious."

"Thanks," I said, feeling a little lightheaded.

Alex squeezed my pussy again. "So juicy. I don't think you're done."

I shook my head. "I don't think so, either."

Douglas moved my legs off his shoulders and shifted onto the bench seat beside me. Now, Alex and Douglas sat on either side of me while our silent observer sat across from us. If Neil felt left out of our debauchery, he didn't show it. He smiled, sipping his beer and looking from my face to my still-spread legs.

I took a steadying breath, my pulse still throbbing. "This is turning out to be quite a bachelorette party."

"If you were a guy, we would be at a strip club right now, buying you lap dances from pretty girls pretending to get off," Alex said.

"Pretty girls stripping for me." I contemplated that for a moment. "That wouldn't have been so bad. But sexy boys stripping and getting off for me would be infinitely more fun, I think."

For the first time – perhaps ever – I think I shocked them. Alex and Douglas went very still on either side of me. Neil glanced out the tinted window at the darkness racing by. I giggled at their sudden incongruous modesty.

"C'mon, you have seen each other naked at the gym countless times," I said. "What's the big deal about getting naked for me?"

There was a lot of throat clearing and looking anywhere but at me while I shook my head in feminine disgust. Men who thought nothing of revealing the naughtiest, kinkiest details of their sex lives, not to mention watching me expose myself and writhe in pleasure in front of them, were suddenly shy schoolboys when it came to stripping down in front of each other.

Alex was the first to break the awkward silence. "Naked and, er – *naked* – are two different things." He gestured towards his lap where his erection made an impressive tent. "I wouldn't want to intimidate these guys, after all."

"Yeah, right," Douglas snorted "That's the reason I don't want to strip in front of you – I'm intimidated by your enormous dick."

"Mmm," I murmured, running one fingertip along the hard ridge of flesh in Alex's pants. "Enormous dick. I vaguely remember . . ."

Alex snorted. "Vaguely? I'd think it would be etched in your memory."

While the three of us were joking around, Neil watched and kept silent. I studied him as Alex and Douglas continued to trade barbs about the size of their equipment. Though his body appeared relaxed, with his legs stretched out in front of him and his arms across the back of the seat, he was staring at me hungrily. I liked the way he looked at me, as if I were the only thing that could satisfy him. It reminded me of Simon.

"You're awfully quiet," I said. "What do you think, Neil?"

He shrugged. "It's your party, babe. If you want me to get naked and jerk off, I'll get naked and jerk off."

Suddenly, I lost all interest in Alex and Douglas. They were familiar, predictable. Men's men. Or boys' boys. They'd goad each other into doing something neither of them would willingly do on his own. On the other hand, Neil – whom I had always assumed to be the more prudish of the three – was willing to do whatever I wanted without coaxing or bribery. I loved it.

"That would be . . . delicious," I said, searching for just the right word. "You'd do that for me?"

Neil nodded solemnly. "If that's what you want."

"I guess Neil is the only one who wants to make me happy," I teased.

Douglas and Alex were still quiet, sitting on either side of me like silent bodyguards. I could almost feel the tension in the confined space as they contemplated what Neil was agreeing to do – and what they didn't want to do. Neither wanted to back down, especially when they thought they had the upper hand over Neil, who had missed out on the fun thus far. Their desire for whatever kinky games might transpire once they were naked was still outweighed by their heterosexual drive to be the only man in play.

While they considered their options, Neil made the first move. If he was embarrassed to strip down while the three of us watched, he didn't show it. He only had eyes for me as he loosened his tie and unbuttoned the cuffs of his shirt. While there is a certain pleasure in watching a man undress, I found myself anxious for him to hurry. I had never seen him naked before. I had never even kissed him, much less touched his bare chest. Suddenly, I was sure the look in his eyes was mirrored in my own. Desire. Need. A pull so strong it was almost physical. I wanted him. And since this was the only time I would ever have him, I wanted to take my time enjoying him.

Part of me felt guilty for ignoring Alex and Douglas as Neil stripped off his shirt to reveal a lean torso and finely sculpted muscles. These two men had been my friends and play partners in the past and there was no reason to exclude them now, even if my attention would be focused on Neil. Of course, it really depended on whether they would participate, but I fully intended to give them the chance.

"Well, boys, what about you?" I asked them, resting a hand over each of their crotches. Their arousal turned me on almost as much as Neil arching up off the seat to tug off his trousers.

"What about us?" Douglas asked, sounding almost offended even as his cock twitched beneath my gentle stroking.

"Neil isn't the only one who is going to get naked, is he?"

At that moment, Neil stripped off his confining boxer briefs, revealing a thick, heavily veined cock. He sat back down, his hand curling around his erection as he looked at me for instruction.

"That depends," Alex said, his voice thick with lust. "What's in it for us?"

I laughed. "Like the man said, it's my party, *babe*. You'll just have to get naked and find out."

Then there were two more men undressing in the limo as it

headed for Las Vegas. I felt drunk on more than champagne as I watched them reveal themselves for my pleasure. I was dizzy trying to look from one to the other, watching as Douglas stripped off his shirt and exposed that muscular torso I had once rubbed against until I had a very wet orgasm. Then I was staring at Alex as he unfastened his pants, revealing the fabric of his underwear stretched tautly over his erection.

"I guess we know who the *bigger* man really is," Alex conceded, glancing at Neil. It was true – even without a measuring tape it looked as if Neil had a couple of inches on both of them. Not that it mattered to me, but I was excited to know they were looking at each other, too.

I stroked Alex's cock through his pants. "It's not the size of the ship—"

"It's the motion of the ocean," he finished with a grin. "I remember rocking the waves pretty hard a time or two."

"Oh yeah," I breathed as he lowered his mouth over mine.

We kissed hungrily, tongues tasting of beer and champagne. I freed him of his pants and squeezed his cock until he moaned into my mouth. He returned the favour by fondling my breasts, tweaking my nipples hard just the way I liked.

"Hey, what about me?"

Eyes closed, I shifted to kiss Douglas. The taste and texture of him was different from Alex – rougher, more nipping of teeth than caressing of tongues. Alex continued to pinch and squeeze my nipples as I used my other hand to play with Douglas's erection. A cock in each hand, my breasts being played with while I kissed each in turn – I felt like my senses were being overloaded. I couldn't find a rhythm because each man's attention was different. Alex was slow and languid, Douglas was quick and intense. I was caught between their desires, my own building to an almost painful need. I crossed and uncrossed my legs, my pussy sadly neglected.

I remembered Neil and pulled my mouth away from Douglas to look at him. He was angled in the corner, one leg stretched out along the seat, the other bent at the knee. He fisted his heavy cock as he watched us, a thoughtful smirk on his face. I wondered what he was thinking as he made long, slow strokes up the length of his erection. I not only wanted his body, I wanted inside his head.

"Let me know when you're ready for me," he said, when he saw the direction of my gaze.

Those few words were enough to make me whimper in need. I

watched Neil while I continued to play with the two cocks on either side of me. I mimicked his strokes, feeling some strange pull towards him that I had never had – or never admitted to – before. While Douglas and Alex made guttural sounds of pleasure, Neil remained silent, that enigmatic smile in place as he showed me how he pleasured himself.

"I want you," I whispered. "Now."

Everything changed between us with that proclamation.

Neil's smile was pure satisfaction, as if he had already got the sexual release he craved. "Anything the lady wants."

"What about us?" Alex asked, closing his hand around mine as I stroked him.

"I want Neil."

Douglas whispered hoarsely, "Just don't stop touching me."

Neil followed Douglas's lead from earlier, slipping to his knees in front of me. I spread my legs, offering myself like a gift. He dipped his head between my thighs and licked me – softer than Douglas, like he was licking foam from a latte. I sighed, shifting forward on the seat to give him full access. I could feel wetness trickling between the cheeks of my bottom and I was sure I was leaving a puddle on the limo upholstery, but I didn't care.

I spread my legs over Alex and Douglas's legs. Each of them put a hand high on my thigh, as if framing my pussy for Neil's pleasure. I met the bemused gaze of the driver in the rear-view mirror and winked at him before closing my eyes and giving myself over to the pleasure of Neil's slow, infuriating licks. He nibbled my labia, sucking each plump lip into his mouth before circling my clit with the tip of his tongue. When I didn't think I could bear the teasing any longer, he took my swollen clit between his lips and sucked it.

I gasped, whimpering, "Oh, I can't take anymore! It's too much!"

He ignored me and continued sucking, as if intent on drawing every sound and sensation he could from my body. I reflexively tried to close my legs, but Alex and Douglas held me open, spread for Neil's enjoyment. I still held their cocks in my hand, squeezing and stroking them in rhythm to my own pleasure. I squirmed, aroused beyond measure at the feeling of helplessness and the overwhelming pleasure that seemed to border on pain. I knew I could end it at any moment, but though it was almost too much to take, I didn't want it to end. I never wanted it to end.

Just as I felt the first tremors of orgasm low in my belly, Neil pulled away.

"No," I gasped. "Please!"

"I'm going to fuck you," he said simply. "But I don't have a condom."

"No problem, dude," Alex said, fumbling with his discarded trousers. "Here."

Neil took the proffered square with a grin. "Always prepared."

Alex breathed in sharply as I ran my thumb over the glistening tip of his cock. "Yeah, but I thought I was the one who would be using it."

The rip of the condom packet made my pussy ripple. "Hurry," I said. "I need you."

"I need you, too," Neil said, and then he was inside me.

From feeling open and vulnerable, I was suddenly, almost impossibly, full. I took a deep, steadying breath as Neil slowly pushed inside my wetness. He stared into my eyes and the intimacy was too much. I tilted my head back against the seat and closed my eyes, whimpering when his cock was fully inside me.

"Look at me," he demanded. "Watch me fuck you."

The tone of his voice demanded immediate compliance. I jerked my head up, staring first into his hard, almost unfamiliar face, then looking down to where we were joined, his olive skin looking so much darker against my paleness.

"That is so fucking hot," Douglas said softly.

I looked at him and saw that he, too, was staring between my legs and watching Neil fuck me. A quick glance on the other side confirmed that Alex was equally mesmerized by the scene before him. My orgasm had subsided enough for me to regain something of my control and I began to slowly stroke the men on either side of me in time to Neil's strokes. I was fleetingly reminded of a horse and jockey, both moving in tandem, joined in a powerful race to the finish.

Neil gripped my ass, pulling me down hard on his cock even while Alex and Douglas still held my legs open. "So fucking tight," he growled.

I moaned, that pain-out-of-pleasure sensation cutting through me like a dangerously sharp knife. I kept my eyes on Neil, letting him see what he was doing to me. He fucked me in long, deep strokes, withdrawing his cock until the head was just inside my opening before slamming inside me again. Every motion brought a moan to my lips and a plea for more. My skin was damp with sweat and I felt dizzy from the heat of our bodies moving together.

"Come on my cock," he demanded. "I won't come until you do."

I felt as if a knot of tension unwound low in my belly. I undulated against him, rocking my hips for my own pleasure, squeezing and stroking Alex and Douglas as if they were extensions of my body. I felt wetness on my hands, but I didn't know if they had come or if it was sweat. I didn't care. They would tell me to stop when they were ready, but none of us was ready for it to end. Not yet. Not quite yet.

Neil pulled back, thrusting shallowly just inside my pussy, the head of his cock stroking my sweet spot. I gasped, going tense and still. Then, suddenly, I was coming. Hard. My orgasm rocketed through me like an explosion, causing me to scream out my release. My body, still a moment earlier, went into motion, rocking on Neil's cock as if I would milk him dry.

Neil's answering groan as my pussy rippled around him was softer than mine, but the expression on his face told me the pleasure was no less intense. He flexed his hips one last time, his cock throbbing inside me. We stayed like that for a long moment, sweat-slick bodies joined together, until my orgasm subsided. Neil was still breathing hard as he pulled free of my body. I gasped, then giggled self-consciously, feeling suddenly bereft at his absence.

Alex cleared his throat. "You can release your death grip now," he said gruffly.

My giggle turned into a full-fledged laugh. In my excitement, I had been holding on to Douglas and him for dear life. Now I realized that both were going flaccid, having certainly enjoyed the moment.

"Sorry," I said.

Douglas stroked my thigh softly. "Don't be. It was pretty amazing until about five minutes ago when I started considering we might end up eunuchs after all."

I shifted on the seat, wincing at the stiffness in my thighs from being held apart for so long. "Sorry, sorry," I said.

I realized Neil hadn't spoken and I searched his face for what he might be thinking. That smile was back in place – the one that was a little too serious to be amusement.

"You OK?" I asked as if we were alone in the limo.

He nodded. "Just grand."

"Thank you." There didn't seem to be much more to say. Except, "You are truly amazing."

"Back at you, babe," he said rakishly. "That was a dream come true."

The driver spoke up before I had time to contemplate the meaning of his words.

"We've arrived at the hotel, ma'am."

I looked out the window and saw the lights of the Bellagio sparkling like an oasis just outside the window. The night had passed and I would be getting married soon. Reality came rushing back like a splash of cold water in the face as I considered all the things I still needed to do. I was hardly in any position to get out at the moment, however.

I watched in drowsy detachment as the boys hurriedly dressed. Now that the party was over, they were anxious to beat a hasty retreat. I giggled. The champagne buzz had worn off, but the sex buzz was still going strong.

"Remember, what happened in the limo stays in the limo," I said conspiratorially.

"Right," Alex said. "Good to know."

Douglas grinned and shook his head at me as he tugged his trousers on. "Only you could get me to do that, lady."

I smiled. "I know."

"Aren't you going to get dressed?" Neil asked.

I nodded. "In a minute. I'll let you guys get out of here so I can straighten up in peace."

"I can wait for you," Neil said, still looking out for my needs.

The driver responded. "I'll make sure the lady gets to her room."

The guys exchanged looks, Alex raising an eyebrow at me. "Is that OK with you?"

"I'll be OK. Find the girls and tell them I'll be there in about an hour."

Douglas grinned, as if he knew something. "It looks like the lady's evening isn't finished, boys."

Alex and he laughed, but Neil just stared at me. "You've had too much champagne. I'm not leaving you alone with the limo driver."

I laughed. "It's OK, Neil." When he still didn't budge, I leaned forward and whispered in his ear. "Trust me. I'm safe with the driver."

Something in my tone made him turn around and look over the partition. He nodded. "I see."

Alex gave me a hug and a deep, soulful kiss before opening the limo door. "See you tomorrow, babe."

"Get some sleep," Douglas added, giving me an equally intense kiss. "It's going to be a busy day tomorrow."

Then they were gone and Neil was still watching me. "I don't know what to say."

I kissed his cheek. "Thanks for this memorable night. Truly."

He started to speak and I could see in his expression what he was going to say, so I kissed his mouth. He pulled me to him as if he would never let go, but after a few moments he did. "See you tomorrow," he said before slipping out of the limo and closing the door behind him.

I waited until he had disappeared in the same direction Alex and Douglas had gone before saying, "OK, you can come back here now."

The driver's door opened and closed and then the door closest to me opened and he settled beside me, his black hat at a jaunty angle. I tossed it on the seat across from us and mussed his wavy brown hair.

"Quite a night you had, Mrs Rhodes," he said.

"I'm not Mrs yet, Mr Rhodes."

He angled me sideways onto his lap, brushing my hair from my damp cheeks. "Was it all you wanted it to be?"

I smiled, happy but also a little wistful. "And more. How about you?"

He chuckled. "Fantasy satisfied, though I wish I could have seen a bit more of *you*."

I stretched my arms out. "You can see me now."

His gaze roamed over my body and I was instantly conscious of what a picture I must present. Naked except for my dress bunched around my waist, my hair a tousled mess of blonde curls, my smoky mascara smudged beneath my eyes. I smiled.

"Like what you see?"

He nodded. "You look like one very satisfied woman."

I wiggled on his lap, feeling that urgency building in my veins again. "Almost. Not quite."

"You want *more*?" His mock surprise only made me laugh. "What an insatiable wench you are."

I slid to my knees and nudged his legs apart. He stared down at me as I unbuckled his belt and worked his zipper down over his heavy erection. I felt my pussy – still tender from earlier, but already wet – tighten in response to his arousal.

"Aren't you happy you're marrying me?"

He groaned as I freed his cock from his pants and gave the tip a lick. "You are definitely a dream come true – *my* dream come true. Are you happy you're marrying me?"

I thought of Simon indulging my last fling with my three best friends while he fulfilled his fantasy of watching me. It didn't seem possible that two people could be more perfect for each other. I sighed in blissful abandon. Just before I gave Simon his last single-guy blow job, I looked up into his eyes and whispered, "Absolutely."

Jewels of the Tide

Alice Gray

Furious pounding startled Jingū from a deep sleep. Last night's entertainment lay sprawled across the bed next to her, oblivious to the racket. Jingū shifted in the bed, planted the soles of her feet against the sleeping man's back and shoved.

The man let out a startled yelp that ended with a cry of pain when he hit the floor.

"See who dares to wake the Empress at this unearthly hour," Jingū said.

The young man, still nude, scrambled for his clothing.

"Now! Forget your clothes." Jingū pressed her palms against her temples. "Just make that noise cease!"

The young man, she thought his name might be Akihiro, raced for the door.

A warm flush spread over Jingū's chest at the memory of the young man's bedroom prowess. He might be worth inviting back. Jingū shivered as another thought formed. Before she could capture it, her evening companion yanked the door open, halting the insistent pounding.

"Who dares to wake me with such rudeness?" she asked.

An officer of the Royal Navy took a small step into her chamber, eyes averted from her nakedness. He bowed deeply and held the pose. Next to him, Akihiro stood shivering, his hands cupping his genitals.

"The Navy is back, Highness." The hulking officer's voice trembled. "The Koreans have defeated them. Captain Tadashi wished to bring you the message himself, however he was gravely wounded."

Anger deepened the flush on Jingū's chest. "Turn your backs," she said. When they had turned, Jingū slipped from her bed and wrapped a light kimono around her body.

"You may face me."

Both men turned.

"You!" She pointed a finger at Akihiro. "Leave us."

The young man bowed and slipped away.

"Where is Tadashi now?"

"In the infirmary, Highness. They are trying to save his arm."

Jingū was quiet for a moment, memories of the powerful warrior's lovemaking tumbled through her mind. She sighed. An armless man was unworthy of sharing the Empress's bed. Shame. Tadashi had been one of her favourites. Perhaps too favoured. Well, no more.

"Return to me when he is able to speak. I want to know everything that happened."

"Yes, Highness." The soldier bowed and left.

Jingū sat in her tea house, enjoying a light meal. She watched in annoyance as one of her least favourite courtiers approached.

"Yes? What is it, Yuki?" Jingū let her displeasure show in her voice.

"Forgive me, Highness. I bring you the news that Captain Tadashi is ready to see you."

A single butterfly sprang to life in Jingū's belly. She quashed it by thinking of yet another defeat at the hands of the Koreans.

After five tense moments of silence, Jingū said, "Have him escorted to my sleeping chamber this evening." She flicked a dismissive hand at her servant. "Go, now."

The woman curtseyed and scurried away, leaving Jingū to work out the details of her plan. Korea must be hers.

The Empress watched the last of her ladies retreating from her room. When she was alone, Jingū turned towards the mirror, admiring her own beauty. Royal robes, ivory hairpins, kohl eyes, crimson lips. And underneath the decorations, the lithe form of a siren. Empress or not, no man had ever refused her advances.

Two sharp knocks sounded, bringing the butterflies to light in her belly again.

She smoothed the front of her kimono and turned towards the door. "Enter!"

Her door swung open granting Tadashi access to her room. The sling that held his right arm to his chest marred the clean lines of his fresh uniform.

"Highness," he said. "It is with deep shame that I must report our second defeat to the Koreans. They are fierce in defence of their homeland. We suffered many casualties."

Jingū stood. "It is of no consequence. We will simply rebuild our ranks and try again. I must have Korea." She stamped her foot for emphasis.

"It will take some time to rebuild and train new men. Perhaps as long as two years," he said.

"Two years? Impossible!" Jingū paced, her robes swirling around her. "We must attack them again soon. They won't be expecting us to come so quickly on the heels of another defeat."

"Highness, I don't think I've managed to convey the extent of our casualties. We're nothing but a skeleton crew. Most of our officers are dead or severely maimed." He shrugged his wounded arm for emphasis. "The lower ranks are all but wiped out. It will take years to rebuild."

"Nonsense. Leave the Navy to me." Jingū swept towards her captain in a rustle of fabric and jasmine-scented air. "Let us take a break from all this unpleasantness." She untied the sash of her kimono and let it fall away. "You've been away so long, Tadashi. I've missed you."

Hunger darkened his eyes. "Highness, I'm not sure I'm in any shape to fully please you." Again, he shrugged his wounded arm.

"Regardless of your injuries, you will lie with me tonight until I am satisfied."

Jingū took to her bed, spreading her legs wide. "You needn't bother removing your clothing, Tadashi. I have no need of anything but your mouth. Come, now, and please me."

"Yes, Highness, as you wish."

Tadashi knelt at the end of her bed, his lips tracing the delicate curves of her inner thigh.

Jingū shivered and let out a quiet sigh. What a shame Tadashi had outlived his purpose. He was one of the very few who could bring her to shuddering orgasm using nothing more than his breath and tongue.

A quiet hum started in her throat as the caress of his lips gave way to tiny nips and suckles. Little jerks rocked her hips each time he switched between nipping and sucking.

With his good hand, he spread her wide, exposing her innermost flesh. Instead of running his tongue across her pink, moist skin, he puckered his lips and blew a steady stream of warm air along the length of her slit. Tadashi lingered for two full breaths, pouring his hot wind across her aching clit before easing downwards.

Jingū clutched fistfuls of silken sheets, moaning in frustration at the teasing touch of his breath.

"Use your tongue."

Impossible but his fingers spread her even wider, stretching the skin tight to the edge of pain. He lowered his face, stopping just short of touching her flesh.

"Lick!"

Instead, Tadashi used the rigid tip of his tongue to prod his way around the perimeter of her cunt. He pushed hard against the ridge of flesh separating her womanhood from her bottom.

Jingū's moan turned into a loud cry as he slid his tongue up across her opening. He licked again sending her hips jerking. A third lick had her babbling nonsense. The fourth lick ended with a quick flash of his tongue across her erect clit.

Jingū let go of the sheets to tangle her fingers in his hair. She tried to force his mouth down but, even wounded, he was very strong and resisted her.

Tadashi resumed his torment of her, the licks and pokes giving way to his breath again.

The phantom touch edged her towards delirium. She clawed the back of his neck in an attempt to distract him. He grunted but didn't yield. His breath continued its relentless puffing against her clit.

Jingū's scratching turned to blows, which she rained down about his shoulders.

After a particularly violent strike to the back of his head, Tadashi thrust two fingers deep into her and latched his mouth onto her mound. He sucked hard, drawing as much of her flesh into his mouth as possible while his tongue beat staccato across her tiny erection.

Jingū arced off the bed, mouth open in a silent scream. It seemed Tadashi used his fingers and mouth to rip her chi from her body. A momentary flash obliterated everything that was Jingū turning her into nothing but energy.

Just as quickly, the energy collapsed on itself allowing her consciousness to return.

Tadashi still had his fingers buried deep inside her. His thrusts had given way to steady pressure along the front wall of her cunt. He had also tamed his lashing tongue. The rigid muscle had softened, the flicking diminishing to languid laps.

He waited until she went limp to withdraw his fingers.

"Is her Highness satisfied?" he asked.

Jingū sighed her contentment. She lay a few moments longer before sitting up.

"Bring me my clothing," she said.

He stood to do her bidding and when he did, Jingū eyed the impressive bulge tenting the front of Tadashi's uniform.

Pity, she thought. *Such a waste.*

Tadashi helped her dress, his eyes pleading for permission to satisfy his own lust.

Jingū ignored him, saying instead, "Come, let's have a bit of sake as an omen of good luck for our next offensive against the Koreans."

Tadashi bowed and moved to where the bottle and glasses sat.

"Please," she said. "Allow me. You deserve a rest."

"Thank you, Highness." Tadashi took a seat.

Using her body to shield her actions, Jingū poured two glasses of sake, careful to keep track of which glass was which.

She turned and offered him the drink in her left hand.

When he had taken it, she smiled and raised her glass.

"To victory," she said.

Tadashi raised his cup to hers, uttered an unenthusiastic reply and drained the entire contents in a single swallow.

Jingū watched him over the rim of her glass. His eyes bulged first followed by a deep red flush that crept up from his neck and mottled his face a deep, angry purple.

His tongue, the one she'd enjoyed so much, popped out of his mouth, swollen and black. The cup slipped from his fingers to shatter against the floor. Horrible choking tore from his throat as he struggled to breathe. His eyes showed his shock and dismay.

Jingū waited until she was sure he was dead, then finished the bottle of sake and called her servants to have his body removed from her room.

The Empress sat dejected and frustrated upon her throne. Eight full moons had passed since Tadashi's untimely demise and still Korea lay no closer to defeat.

Her Navy remained in tatters. The man she'd promoted to Tadashi's spot was a fool, his only saving grace the thick cock he hid inside his uniform.

Even that no longer held its appeal. The moon had run an entire cycle since Jingū had last enjoyed the pleasure of a man's attentions. The only thing that would satisfy her now was to have Korea for herself.

A courtier swept into the room, his air of urgency catching Jingū's attention. The man bowed, his arms sweeping out from his sides.

"Highness, there is a man requesting audience with the Empress. He claims to have something you need. He is a peasant but he is very insistent and refuses to leave the palace. Shall I have him arrested?"

On any other day, Jingū would have remanded the stranger to the dungeons with a dismissive wave of her royal hand. Today was not any other day.

"Let him in," she said.

The courtesan bowed deeper. "As you wish, Highness," he said before retreating.

Jingū shifted on her seat, sitting higher with an air of superiority she didn't feel.

A minute passed. Two. Shouting accompanied by running footsteps preceded the arrival of her guest.

Four armed guards surrounded the lumpy shape of a person. The lump moved with purpose and dignity, seemingly unaffected by the strong young men surrounding it, young men intent on corralling it.

Fascination stilled Jingū's breath. Never in her memory had someone approached her in this manner. There was purpose that would not be deterred. There was no fear.

The ruckus crowd drew nearer, the lump materializing into a deformed man in robes. He seemed unaware of the menacing swords surrounding him.

"Highness, it is a great honour to stand before you." The man bowed, his misshapen head nearly touching the floor.

"Who calls upon the Empress with such disregard?" she asked.

"Only a humble man who has something to offer her Highness."

"Your name. What is it?"

"My name is not important." The man remained bowed, his posture both reverent and insolent.

"You dare to refuse an answer to me?" she asked.

"Who I am is irrelevant. I offer to you the promise of what you seek."

"What is it you think I seek?"

"Korea," he said.

"Impossible. You mock me."

"No, Highness. No mockery. No trickery. Merely an exchange. Your desire for mine."

"And your desire, what it is?"

The man straightened as far as his twisted form allowed, his gaze settling on her face.

"An offering to my master. A daughter," he said.

Jingū's breath seized in her throat. Never had she looked into eyes the colour of the man's before her. Blue as the ocean on a bright summer day, his eyes pulled her in and down, stealing the air from her lungs.

With supreme effort, Jingū sucked precious life into her body. "You wish for me to grant you a girl child? Ridiculous. You will receive no such offering from me."

"You misunderstand my intentions, Highness. I do not want any child. I want your child, your daughter. In return, you shall have Korea."

Jingū's face pulled tight in anger. "I have no daughter. Arrest him!"

The man's bottomless azure eyes never left hers even as the guards seized his arms. A small smile graced his ugly face though he said nothing more.

When he was gone, Jingū fled to the safety and comfort of her room.

Fragrant steam curled from the surface of the Empress's bath water.

Jingū lay submerged to her neck, waiting for relaxation that never came. Korea occupied every corner of her mind and wouldn't let go. Something had to be done about her Navy. She felt her dream slipping away, each minute another grain of sand through the hourglass. If she didn't turn the glass over soon, Korea would slip from her grasp forever.

A strange tickling around the skin of her breasts broke into Jingū's thoughts. Her eyes opened even as her nipples contracted to hardened points.

Confusion clouded Jingū's expression. The tingling in her breasts sprang from the mysterious retreat of her bath water. As she watched, the water level continued to sink revealing ever more of her bare skin.

She opened her mouth to summon one of her ladies and demand an answer to the disappearing bath water. The yell withered in her throat turning to a gasping moan of surprise.

Jingū's eyes widened. Before her startled gaze, the water began running back up her body in slender, finger-shaped rivulets. With a lover's touch, the water wound its way along her thighs, trailed across her belly, swirled around her breasts. The full force of the water surged into the tub. The sharp tang of the sea had replaced the sweet-scented water, its tidal rise threatening to wash over her face while the watery fingers held her down.

When the brine reached her chin, it receded once more, the drag against her skin like a thousand tiny flames. Jingū cried out her pleasure and dismay.

"Please, come back!" she said to no one at all.

The water level ceased its retreat leaving a triangular pool between her thighs. Tiny waves lapped against her sex sending tsunamis of arousal through Jingū.

A small shape appeared in the space between her parted legs, darkening the water. The shape grew and with it, the water began to rise once more. It flowed across her body in alien forms that teased her flesh.

The darkness between her thighs swelled and changed becoming a physical mass, filling the space until her legs splayed wide in supplicant offering. Rising water formed a rip current that sucked at her clit with greedy pulls.

The shadow spread across her belly, rising up out of the brine. Jingū screamed, terror mixed with ecstasy as the shadow morphed into the fierce head of Ryūjin and a swift stream of water forced its way deep into her cunt.

Ebbing and flowing like the tides he controlled, the dragon god retreated and returned to fill her. The vortex of a small whirlpool swirled around her clit made Jingū cry out, delirious with the pleasure of his fucking.

His eyes, the majestic gold of sunset at sea, saw deep into her.

"The jewels. They are yours for the asking. Your daughter for Korea," the creature said. "The man in your dungeon is waiting. He holds in his hand the key to your greatest desire."

Ryūjin let out a shrieking cry. Below him, Jingū let out her own cry as her orgasm crested and broke. Fiery heat filled her cunt and hot spatters rained down across her skin.

Chest heaving, Jingū cracked one eye, afraid of what might meet her gaze. She was alone. The dragon was gone, vaporized into a fine spray of salt water. The ripples of her breath were the only disturbance in the calm water that was once again sweet-smelling.

Asleep, she must have fallen asleep and had a fantastical dream. The sensual encounter with the dragon god was surely her mind's way of inventing a new solution to her problem even if she didn't understand it.

Jingū rose from the tub and stepped out. She reached for her bath towel and began drying off, the dream still vivid, her cunt still fluttering with release. Bending to dry her legs, Jingū froze. Her mouth opened with a piercing scream. Thick bluish-black liquid ran in viscous streams down her inner thighs.

The door to her bathing chamber opened just as Jingū lost consciousness.

"Highness, the dungeons are no place for Japan's Empress. He will be brought to you under heavy guard."

Jingū frowned in displeasure. "No. I will go to him where he is and there will be no guards. There is no danger to me if he is locked up."

"Highness, please—"

"Enough! I command you to take me to him this instant."

The guard bowed in resignation. "Yes, Highness. This way."

Jingū followed him into the stinking bowels of her palace. With each twist and turn through the dank tunnels, the stench of excrement and unwashed bodies grew stronger. She gagged and pressed the back of her hand under her nose.

"Would her Highness wish to reconsider the decision to speak to the prisoner here?"

"Silence! Or you will join the peasant."

The guard said nothing though his pace quickened.

Jingū struggled to keep up with him but did not ask him to slow down.

Three more turns brought them to the end of the corridor.

"He is there." The man pointed towards a cell that sat in darkness. It appeared empty.

"Leave me."

The captain handed her his lantern and retreated.

Fear bloomed at the base of her neck and slithered down her spine. Jingū held the lantern high above her head but moved no closer to the bars.

Heavy chain scraped along stone. The man's strange eyes materialized in the darkness though the rest of him remained in shadow.

Jingū yelped and stumbled back.

"I've been waiting for you, Empress. Are you ready to trade?" The man moved into the dim pool of light cast by her lantern. "Korea for your daughter."

"The jewels, show them to me," she said.

"Ah, you know of the jewels' existence, but do you know of their power?"

"The jewels, I want them."

"And they shall be yours for the price of your daughter."

"I have no daughter."

"You will. Ryūjin has already seen to it."

Jingū flushed, remembering her dream of the dragon god and the thick fluid that had seeped from her upon waking.

The peasant extended his closed fists through the bars, clenched fingers turned towards the ceiling.

Jingū watched him uncurl his fingers to reveal one gem resting in each of his palms.

"I present to her Highness the Jewels of the Tide. Take them," he said.

She stared at the glittering stones, one a deep sapphire, the other a murky brown. Jingū snatched them from his hands and turned to leave.

"Would her Highness leave without knowing how to use the jewels to conquer Korea?"

Jingū turned back to him, a sneer of contempt twisting her beautiful face.

"It's obvious that they are worth much. I will use them to rebuild my Navy to even greater strength, strength enough to defeat Korea."

"They are worth nothing. You will not be able to sell them. Ryūjin does not allow the Jewels of the Tide to be sold for something so petty as money. No, their value is their power."

Jingū's anger reached boiling point. "Enough of your riddles. Explain the jewels to me or I will have you executed this moment."

The peasant chuckled and retreated into the darkness where Jingū's light didn't penetrate.

"Her Highness must sail to Korea. When the Korean Navy meets you at sea, toss the topaz jewel into the waves. The ocean will retreat, grounding the fleet. When they abandon their ships to attack on foot, throw the sapphire jewel onto the sand. Korea will be yours and Ryūjin will have his daughter."

"Fool! It's nonsense you speak!"

"Is it? As nonsense as a carnal visit from the god of the sea himself?" His voice floated out of the darkness, growing softer with each word until it faded away.

Jingū was tempted to approach the man's cell. She turned and ran instead, the jewels clenched tight in her hand.

Three full moons passed and with them another setback for Jingū. Half her remaining Navy had deserted when they learned she planned to attack Korea once more. There were barely enough men left to fill two ships. It didn't help matters that sickness had plagued her since she'd taken the jewels. Sickness and dreams of the dragon.

He came to her nearly every night, his forked tongue and slick, scaled cock ebbing and flowing into every orifice until she came, screaming, the bitter tang of seawater clogging her throat. Exhausted and confused, Jingū turned to the only person who might help her.

The acrid stench of the dungeon burned her nose and laboured her breathing. Her physical discomfort paled in comparison to the ragged state of her mind.

"What does he want of me?" Jingū tried and failed to make her words sound calm and controlled.

The stranger laughed, the quiet sound rolling towards her. Chills broke out across her flesh.

"Have you not come to understand yet?" he asked.

"You do not get to ask questions. Answer! What does he want?"

"The answer lies in the jewels. They are not yours to keep. Ryūjin wants them back."

"So take them!" She produced the gems and thrust her hand through the bars. "Take them and return them to him."

The man laughed again. "Impossible. You are the only one who can return them."

Screaming her frustration, Jingū threw the jewels into the dark cell and ran. The man's quiet laughter chased her through the twisting tunnels.

Breaking through the dungeon's entrance into her palace, she nearly knocked over a guard.

"Empress!"

The guard said something more but Jingū ignored him, desperate in her flight to escape.

Upon reaching her room, she slammed and locked the doors. Jingū sucked in deep gasping breaths, trying to calm the wild beating of her heart. With a shaking hand, she pushed loose strands of hair away from her face. In relinquishing the stones, would she be free of Ryūjin's insatiable appetite for her flesh?

Exhausted, she prepared for bed, the soft, luxurious silks calling to her frantic mind.

Jingū pulled back the sheet. Her eyes grew wide. Great screams of fear and anguish ripped from her throat.

The jewels lay neatly nestled against her pillow.

★ ★ ★

The Empress stood on the bow of the ship watching the Korean Navy spill out from their grounded fleet and fan towards her, weapons raised. A great cry of war rolled towards her across the surreal landscape.

Heart pounding with fear, she waited, holding her ground against the primal instinct to guard herself from the relentless oncoming wave of danger. Her body vibrating with tension, the sapphire jewel grew slick in her clenched hand.

When the eyes of the men on the front line grew visible, Jingū drew her arm back and hurled the second stone, her howl chasing it over the edge of her ship towards the exposed seabed.

The jewel hit the sea floor, opening a small crater that grew and spread, fast and wide. A furious shaking rocked the land, halting the Korean Navy's advance. The sea erupted from the expanding crater, the force of its return catching the opposing Navy in greedy currents.

Jingū watched, hands gripping the rail of her ship, as the Korean Navy drowned before her eyes, and felt the first stirring of new life deep within her belly.

Boston. Breasts. Bohemians.

Jeremy Edwards

I was an aesthete, not a power seeker. Why did so many people rush to assume that a successful female entrepreneur was in it for the power? Sure, I didn't want to be held back ... but I hungered to express my talents and make a more beautiful world, not to warm a throne with my ass and give orders.

Likewise with my young men – my bohemians. People saw a polished, well-turned-out businesswoman in her forties with sweet, shaggy boys hardly out of college, and they assumed it was a power thing, or a status thing. Hell, no. It was an aesthetic thing with me. They were just so pretty – not only their baby-faced faces and their silly hair, but also their personalities, all wrapped up in the awkwardness of make-believe sophistication, or brightly bare in their unselfconscious charisma.

I was never taken with the ambitious ones. Even if they were nice ... even if I judged that their interest in bedding me had nothing to do with their career aspirations ... I simply didn't respond to their suits, their calculating punctuality, and their disconcertingly smooth adaptation to the yuppie milieu of 1980s Back Bay Boston. Damn it, a twenty-two-year-old – male or female – should not look totally natural with a briefcase, I thought.

No, I liked the guys with the ratty knapsacks. The guys who weren't sure when or when not to drink at lunchtime; who didn't see that as cool as their thrift-store vintage jackets looked on the hanger, they didn't fit right; who still believed, thank goodness, that it was their art or writing or music that mattered, and not getting to the "day job" five minutes early – and who would say so out loud in their cubicles, being too naive to realize I listened from my open-doored office around the corner. They figured I disapproved of their chronic tardiness and forgave them; but in reality I loved them for it. It made me want to fuck them. It aroused what had never died in me, no matter how many meetings I had to take with marketing people and accountants and lawyers: my passion for beauty. And my passion for young men who really, really cared about something – who weren't, for instance, too occupied or tired or lazy to go see some incredibly important underground band I'd never heard of on a Wednesday night, even if it meant they had to walk home afterwards and get shortchanged on sleep. I had no intention of listening to the latest "amazing" album, but I wanted to know my bohemians bought it the day it came out.

And I would have set my alarm and driven to Kenmore Square to pick any one of these boys up after a concert, at 2 a.m. on any Wednesday he liked. But then, I suppose, he would have been even more shortchanged on sleep.

For the ones who wanted me as much as I wanted them, I tried to project what they desired in me. Self-assurance. Stability. Poise. *Savoir faire*. I tried to give them the complete grown-up woman – a soft, fleshy rock of adulthood, sculpted into a svelte hourglass.

It's odd to recall that Ned did not seem especially pretty to me that first morning, when he showed up for work at my art-book publishing house. He'd been hired by my editor as one of the three all-purpose proofreaders/rights researchers/caption writers he always kept on hand – our version of an entry-level position. I was comfortable letting Bill do his own hiring, so I never met his assistants until they were already on the payroll.

Shaggy was great, but Ned's straw-blond hair verged on unkempt. And since his eyes refused to meet mine while I was doling out his paperwork, and his head refused to orient itself away from the sight line to his shoes after I'd collected the completed forms, the hair was practically all I got – that, and a thin cute ass in nondescript jeans, as observed when I followed him out of my office.

The first thing Ned did when he'd been assigned a cubicle was put a cartoon up on the wall. I winced – tape marks! – but when I read it over his shoulder and he volunteered that he'd created it himself, I got a squishy sensation in my belly. The cartoon showed a woman declining, as I inferred from the bubbles, champagne (served in what Ned presumably didn't realize was the wrong kind of glass), and saying to her male companion, "Yes, Frank, I *know* that was a good year. It's just that I'm not ready to relive it yet." Frank. If I'd encountered this in the *New Yorker*, I might not even have lingered to bemoan their sagging standards. But standing almost on top of the boy who'd taken the trouble to draw this slim idea – smelling the youthful, citrussy essence of this kid who'd risked ruining a cubicle wall his first day on the job in order to display his work – all I could feel was admiration. Admiration, and a warm tingling between my legs. Suddenly, I was very interested in Ned.

"Sorry about the breasts," he said nervously, stepping to the side so he could face me. I took a peek at the cartoon lady's cleavage, which I hadn't noticed before. "I didn't mean to draw them so large. I don't want people to decide I'm one of those guys who thinks a woman amounts to a set of breasts."

I felt a flush in my own, relatively generous, chest. "It's OK, Ned. Hey, women have breasts. And breasts are nice, right?" I laughed, more self-consciously than I was used to in my workplace. In my time, a parade of seasoned men, my peers, had tried to flirt and banter and grope me into losing my cool at the office – had tried to make the always-in-control goddess blush or stammer or run off to change her panties. They had all failed. But poor Ned was nearly succeeding, without even intending to. The sincere way he both cared and didn't care about the size of his cartoon character's bust seemed to tug at my nipples and tickle my clit.

"Some of us have larger ones than others," I continued, masking my flutteriness with a reassuring, didactically matriarchal tone, and trusting that my injection of self-referential language wouldn't completely give away my agenda – yet. "You happened to draw one such woman."

He gave me a sensitive, tentative-looking smile, and that's when I understood that his face was capable of more complexity than silently framing the question, "What time is lunch?" I was about to ask him – I don't know – about his life, what he'd liked best in college, about his family . . . but he spoke again before the words formed.

"What time is lunch?"

In fact, it was my policy to take a new hire out to lunch on his or her first day – just the two of us. These kids worked closely with Bill day in and day out, with a healthy share of collegial staff lunches sprinkled over their tenure; but I wasn't involved in any of that. I welcomed them in and had little directly to do with them thereafter – unless I chose to offer extracurricular attention, and they chose to accept it.

Spending an hour alone in a quasi-social situation with a publishing-world rookie could be anything from a cougar's wet dream to a nightmare of stifling silences. But whether it proved, from case to case, to be drudgery or delight, it was a non-negotiable duty that I'd long ago assigned myself.

This morning, I was so eager for "lunch" that I couldn't focus on the contracts I was supposed to be reviewing. Fifteen minutes before I was due to meet Ned in the foyer, I finally stopped trying to concentrate. I gave myself a booster shot of perfume in front of the mirror in my private bathroom, and I went to bother Bill with inter-office chitchat, merely as a diversion.

It had long been my philosophy that if I was going to come on to an employee, I should do it at the outset. Things are less complicated when your young man hasn't yet breathed much of the company air – when you're still more an intriguing older woman than a familiar edifice looming on the skyline, engraved with the grey legend *BOSS*.

I knew how to broach the matter, having done it many times, sometimes in this very restaurant. Step One – ascertaining that he was single in the real-world sense, and not only in the IRS-form sense, had been taken even before the server brought our water.

I let the conversation wander naturally as we awaited, then began, our meals, and then I proceeded.

"I'm so glad to have a chance to get to know you a little, Ned, before you get immersed in the hectic routine with Bill and the gang."

"Uh," said Ned, nodding graciously.

"I'm usually in a whirlwind of my own. You'll be happy to learn that you won't see a lot of me after today."

I gave him my seductive stage-chuckle. Then I gave him my standard three-beat pause, before continuing.

"Unless we get together *outside* the office, of course."

No pause this time – momentum was key here. "This has nothing to do with your job, and there's no wrong answer . . . but I was wondering if you might like to join me at my place for dinner some night soon. I've been in the mood to cook lately." I winked. Subtlety was not the way to go with these boys. It was important to be unambiguously bold, and to refuse to be daunted by the possibility of a brush-off.

He stared at me as if sizing me up for the first time. "Ms Bruxelle, you're my employer," he said slowly. I'd certainly heard that before, at this stage of the proceedings – though it wasn't articulated as often as you might think. One had a tendency to catch on that at Bruxelle Art Books, we didn't stand on ceremony.

"So what?" I said, calling into service my most laissez-faire body language – the devil-may-care cock of the head, the flirtatious, mock-dismissive wave of the hand. "I've frequently – mm, *socialized* – with my employees."

He ate a bit of his omelette. "I don't know whether that should make me more or less concerned."

He wasn't attempting to be witty – he meant it. Damn, I adored men who didn't always know what to think right away. They let you breathe.

It was part of my ethos to be assertive, but never aggressive. "Anyway – for what it's worth – I'm not really your boss. Bill is really your boss." I tossed this dubious technicality his way as a peripheral remark, then changed the subject temporarily to take the pressure off. "How's your omelette?" Fuck, I was wet. The kid wasn't doing anything; but that in itself was doing *everything* to my insides.

It was funny to think that in Ned's eyes, I probably appeared cool as a cucumber – as I intended to. He probably assumed I could do this in my sleep. After all, why would it ever occur to him that a self-actualized, experienced woman at the top of her erotic game got butterflies – that she sometimes had an impulse to run to her room and hide her head beneath pillows, crying with embarrassment even while furiously masturbating off her screaming sexual tension? I never ran, but that didn't mean I never thought about it.

Ned kept eating. He began to speak – then hesitated – wiping his mouth with the napkin an extra, unnecessary, time before breaking the silence. "I don't know, Ms Bruxelle." It was obvious he wasn't addressing the "how are your eggs?" issue.

"Claudia." That part wasn't seduction – *nobody* called me Ms Bruxelle, except people trying to sell us advertising.

"I guess it's not the boss thing." He looked at me with uncompromising innocence, his gaze steady and clear. "But . . . seriously? You want me to . . . y'know, come over to your house?"

"I wouldn't have invited you if I didn't."

"Yeah," he admitted. "Can I think it over?"

Of course he could. And that night, while Ned presumably thought it over, "Ms Bruxelle" gave herself seven fantastic orgasms, riding a vibrator and visualizing the face of this man who was too casual to have recited the "it's not that I don't find you attractive" speech.

But something told me that it really *wasn't* that he didn't find me attractive – that despite the layers of surprise and wariness, Ned had been looking at me with a three-dimensional appetite idling portentously in the background. That steady gaze. It bore into me, in absentia, in my bedroom, as my cunt danced contractions over hot sheets and I banged my ankles together, whimpering my lust.

The company's tenth-anniversary party happened to be scheduled for the weekend right after Ned started. And when I brought this up the day following our lunch, I was afraid he might inform me that he already had plans. But one of the things I treasured about my bohemians was that they almost never had firm plans for anything. As was typical of these boys, Ned had "a few" parties he was thinking of attending that Saturday, but nothing definite on his agenda.

"Well," I assured him, successfully keeping the college-girl longing out of my voice, "you're not obligated to attend. But I'll be delighted if you can." After throwing the singular pronoun his way – *I* rather than *we* – I allowed my eyes to flash him for an instant. *Don't forget: sex here, my bohemian boy – if you want it.*

As I skated back into my office, I wondered if he had been as wakeful and autoerotically engaged as I had the night before. Had he dreamed cartoonishly of my breasts? In any event, I'd been with enough young artists to accept that "Maybe I'll be there" was the closest I was going to get to an RSVP, and I forced myself to assume optimistically that Ned would be at my disposal on Saturday evening – and perhaps, if I was lucky, on Saturday night.

A party like this was a whopping expenditure. But in the circles I travelled, we understood that additional business would result from the friendly bookstore-chain buyers we plied with friendly drinks, as well as the difficult-to-court customers who couldn't resist a free, classy affair . . . and who were bound to find things they liked once our catalogues were shoved under their noses.

As the charismatic, impassioned, but business-shrewd CEO, I was centre stage most of the evening. Ned had arrived soon after the affair had begun – looking even more rumpled in his "nice" clothes than his clumsy-vintage duds – but it was hours before I was able to break away from the latest round of schmoozing, grab a plate of food, and casually float him towards the back rooms in the "rent for your function" Victorian we'd taken over for our celebration. I was, ostensibly, giving him a tour.

We nearly walked in on Bill and his fiancée. I halted myself – and Ned – in the doorway of the sprawling back parlour, just in time to keep them from realizing they'd been interrupted.

Only they hadn't, in fact, been interrupted – because, deep in the parlour and oblivious to our presence, they proceeded with their business. Good old Bill had Felicia's long, elegant skirt up at the back, and he was lazily fondling her mauve panties, just massaging her ass in there . . . showing her how private he wished to be with her, how intimate, despite the call of the festivities. Felicia, serene and content, was holding her drink right below her lips, and mouthing involuntary kisses towards a mirror. And, involuntarily, I felt my lips yearning to imitate those quiet kisses, and my ass yearning for a roaming hand.

"Shouldn't we go?" whispered Ned. His breath tickled my earlobe.

I turned to look at him, my breasts still pressing against the heavy Victorian doorjamb. I took hold of his arm – firmly and purposefully. "Yes," I whispered back. "Yes, we should."

He studied my face, and then he broke into a sly grin. He looked down to my hand, where it rested on his forearm, and he removed my fingers from his person. But instead of letting my fingers drop, he guided them to my chest, where he boldly squeezed my right breast, using my own grip as his proxy.

His face glowed with unrefined want.

Of course, I couldn't take Ned home until the guests had finished depleting the canapés and Cabernet. Fortunately, the catering firm that had rented us the space and their services were responsible for clean-up, and Bill and I had no obligation to hang around washing dishes or vacuuming up crumbs. I said a quick goodnight to Bill and Felicia – getting a frisson as my mind leaped back to what I'd observed earlier – and I left the building with Ned.

"Did you take the 'T' to get here?" I asked him after we'd driven a few blocks. I was surmising that he didn't have a car, and that the subway would have been the logical option.

"Yeah."

"I guess you'd be at a party with your friends tonight, if you weren't with me."

He shrugged. "Some weekends I just stay home and draw."

At my condo, my libido found a comfortable plateau. I'd figured out by this point that he wasn't an animated talker. But I didn't want to jump on him, first thing in the door – well, I did, but I knew it would be more civilized to pace myself. So I enjoyed simply sharing my space with him for a while, having a drink and taking him on his terms – letting him set the tone of what passed for a conversation. He complimented me on the wine I'd served him and catalogued his favourite dollar-fifty beer bars.

He was poking around my living room when I returned from the kitchen with our second round of drinks. I joined him in front of the bookshelf, where he had just stopped to admire a photo of me at about twenty-five, shaking my ass in a fringed miniskirt and go-go boots at a discotheque.

"You must have had some wild times in the Sixties," he said – name-checking the legendary decade with the reverence my generation saved for the names of movie stars and European cities.

I smiled knowingly, and the comment that came out of my mouth surprised me. "Yes, that was a good era. But I'm not ready to relive it yet."

It was as if my discovery of the lingering profundity in his one-panel rattled him, and all he could think to do was grab me by the waist and kiss me, hard. It was as good a trigger as any.

When his lips released me, I took a moment to set my drink down – feeling my juices flowing, my every atom ready. The next deep kiss would be served by the hostess, I decided.

But Ned had something more to say. "When I got to the party, I was thinking I was going to turn you down."

"What?" This caught me unawares: I thought I could read a situation. And he'd picked a hell of a time to tell me this. Still, I was intrigued. "Why didn't you?"

"Your face. When you saw Bill and what's-her-name."

"Felicia." The word rushed out of my mouth.

"There was something in your expression that made me think I might regret it if I didn't" – he scanned the room – "do this."

"I see," I said hoarsely.

"Yeah, you looked sort of naked, for a second. It was great."

I would reflect on this later – how Ned had wanted me to be raw and churned up, not calm and in control. Other boys hadn't felt that way. Or, if they had, they hadn't told me.

But right now, I couldn't take any more time to think. "*This* is what I look like when I'm naked."

I'd dressed intelligently, and almost everything came off in one piece. My slip clung cooperatively to the inside of my floral dress – so that with one sibilant *swoosh*, I was left in only my bra and my jewellery. I had not worn panties.

As I unclasped the bra, Ned started laughing benignly.

I laughed with him. "What?"

"I was remembering that discussion we had about breasts. You know, the cartoon. And now you're . . ." His laughter trickled off. "They're so gorgeous, Claudia."

He stood there worshipping me with his eyes – and with the hard-on that strained against his ill-fitting dressy trousers.

"I need you to touch me, Ned."

The hand on my ass cheek was the warmest thing I could ever

recall having in my living room. I hadn't realized quite how hungry I'd been for contact with male flesh.

I luxuriated in his palm, feeling the honey seeping down towards the mouth of my pussy. It felt too good, too fast, for me to be surprised that he'd gone for my ass first, rather than my breasts. I only thought of that afterwards, conjecturing that Bill and Felicia had inspired him.

And, man, that boy knew how to caress a woman's ass. The alternating circles, back and forth from cheek to cheek. The vigorous squeezes and delicate pinches. The thin finger dragging itself down the crack, like a languid exclamation point streaked onto a foggy car window. The no-sting slap of approval, gentle but lewd as hell.

I wondered if he was going to stay back there all night – and, frankly, I wouldn't have cared if he had. But his hands finally travelled to my belly, grazing my bush, and his cock – still in his pants, but hard as fuck – nudged the pleasure-tingling bottom that his hands had just abandoned. I squirmed into him like the horny, in-her-prime sensualist I was, while my nipples buzzed like dried chili peppers. Then I turned around in his grasp. "You should get undressed."

"I want to make you come."

Again I laughed. "You will. Trust me. But I want to see you. I want to see that handsome cock of yours. OK?" I kissed him.

He shrugged diffidently, but I sensed he was gratified.

He was hairier than I'd expected; but the blond, translucent fur that ran down his chest was soft and smooth, almost unreal. His beautifully proportioned cock felt smooth, too, in my hand – but definitely not soft, and certainly not unreal.

He let me stroke him for a short while, then he dropped to his knees. He began kissing his way wetly up my thighs – he seemed increasingly passionate, now that we'd moved beyond the barriers of age and etiquette and uncertainty and clothing.

"You smell terrific." His face was millimetres from my pussy. "I mean, I liked your perfume, but down here – oh, wow."

I just stood there, clasping his head between my thighs, while he ate me out. I felt like a fine meal, like a treasure, as he sucked and kissed and licked from out to in and back, drawing silken pulses of ecstasy from my depths.

My ass was still sizzling from his lavish attentions, and my breasts melted in my own hands – because my nipples had needed to be engaged by whoever was available, and my fingers, seething with preorgasmic tension, had needed something to do.

His appetite seemed only to grow as he feasted. By the time my clit telegraphed a string of climaxes onto his tongue and my juice ran wild over his lip, the room was alive with his desire.

When he emerged from my sanctum, I stepped away, turned, and bent over the back of an armchair – trusting that he would take the hint and assume his . . . entry-level position.

He took the hint.

Now, at last, as he fucked me powerfully from behind, Ned redeemed the voucher I'd implicitly offered him back in his cubicle – the invitation to celebrate my ample breasts. Though his thrusting honoured a steady, linear rhythm – deliciously serviceable, given that we were a good fit – his fingers fluttered capriciously, titillating and moulding me, imparting a constantly blossoming bouquet of tactile surprises. While his cock made me moan, his hands made me giggle; and, helpless in pleasure, I lost it, barely needing the feminine forefinger on my clit to fly into a heaving orgasm, as Ned pumped his condom full of raw enthusiasm.

Later, he asked me to drive him home, rather than choosing to stay over. Yet in the same breath, he asked if he could come back the next night.

Of course he could.

Ned moved on to New York after a year, and I moved on to the next bohemian. We'd never felt remotely "permanent" – but I remember Ned more distinctly than most of them.

And not just because I get a hand-drawn, one-of-a-kind birthday card every year, featuring a cartoon woman with nice boobs.

Let's Dance

D. L. King

Hands up in the air, twirling around trance-like, eyes closed, with a stupid smile on his face – or maybe it was more a beatific smile. Actually, I've sort of seen that same look before; seen it a lot. I mean kinda the whole thing, like if he had been tied that way and suspended, his body set to twirling in the air. But this wasn't like that. This was on a dance floor. At a club. A regular, vanilla club. I'm just saying . . .

Patty had convinced me to go out for drinks after a particularly long day – week – year at work and we'd ended up in this cool kid college bar. Not our usual kind of place, but it had a happy hour. We'd been scoping out the field, discussing each guy's assets – and ass – in great detail. "Hey Eve, what about that loon?' she asked me.

I followed her finger and saw him. She was laughing but I was thinking "oh how sweet."

"What?" She looked at me like I was insane. "What," I said again. "He's adorable. Just look at him." A laugh and the scent of gin wafted towards me. "C'mon. You don't think he's cute?" More laughter. "Seriously. He's just into the music. I think it's sweet."

"Somebody needs another drink," she said as she pulled me back towards the bar.

I didn't really want another drink, but I played along. With two fresh Martinis, one vodka and one "real", we wandered back to our previous look-out. Cute Boy was still on the dance floor, this time dancing with another guy and girl. The three of them looked like they didn't have a care in the world.

When the music changed, his friends left the floor and I decided to go for it. Handing my drink to Patty, I danced my way into the crowd. From behind, I put my hands on his hips and he jumped. He tried to turn to see what was going on but I pressed my body to his back, grabbing his prominent pelvic bones and grinding myself against his ass.

I could feel his pulse speed. He was a gazelle. I was stronger and more powerful. And I was hungry.

"Um, Alice?"

"Who's Alice?" I asked.

"Oh. I thought maybe you were Al . . . coming back from the bar. Do I know you? I mean, it's all right. I mean, who . . ."

"No, you don't know me." I moved my hands in from his hips, and down, keeping the pressure on. "Would you like to?"

"Uh huh." He put his hands over mine and we continued to dance, my fingers stroking his cock through his jeans.

I love those baggy pants, especially on skinny white boys. You can hide an embarrassment of riches in there. My hands just naturally found their way past the waistband to his naked cock. That was when his hands grabbed mine from the outside.

"Aren't you just the cutest thing? Are you nine or did somebody shave you? And, by the way, do something else with those hands, unless you want me to go away." He let my hands go and tentatively reached back to cup my ass.

"Like what you feel?" I asked as my fingers found damp balls and toyed with them. As I worked my way slowly back towards his hole he almost collapsed forward.

"I was right: you are adorable," I said. Moving my hands back, I gently squeezed his balls. "Have a girlfriend?" He shook his head. "Have a boyfriend?" He laughed. "Keeper?" He shook his head again and turned back to see who was tormenting him. "What's your name?"

"Pete."

"Wanna go somewhere, Pete?"

"I . . ."

"Yes?" I asked. I pinched the tip of his cock and squeezed his balls with my other hand. He jumped. "Oops," I said.

"I . . ."

He jumped again when I pulled my hands from his pants, slammed them onto his hips and moved him away from my body. "Oh, well."

"No, wait. Yes. I mean, yes."

"Good answer." Keeping my hands on his hips, I led him off the dance floor, towards Patty and my drink. I put my arm around his waist and picked up my Martini. "Patty, this is Cute Boy. Cute Boy, this is Patty," I said as I took a healthy swig of vodka.

"Pete," he said, reaching out his hand to Patty.

As Patty reached for Pete's hand, I put my empty glass in hers. "I gotta take Cute Boy home now. See you next week." I could hear her bark of laughter as I guided Pete to the door.

Once on the street, Pete put his arm across my shoulder. "What's your name?"

"Eve. Short for Evangeline. But I haven't decided whether you get to use it or not." I hailed a cab.

He looked so bewildered. He wasn't at all drunk. "What do you mean I don't get to use it? What am I supposed to call you?"

Once in the cab, I said, "Hey, Cute Boy, who shaved your boy parts?"

A blush began at the top of his ears and travelled to his cheeks. "Um, I did," he said.

"What made you decide to do something like that?" The blush spread to his forehead and neck simultaneously, and he looked at the floor of the cab. "Aw, c'mon, you can tell me." I rested my hand on the inside of his thigh and gave him a good-natured squeeze. He shifted in his seat and looked at me. It looked as if he were trying to gauge my politics – or where I might stand on certain topics – or maybe whether he could trust me. Whatever he was thinking, the body butt I gave his shoulder must have swayed him.

"Well, see, I was reading this book . . . and the guy in it – I guess it was a dirty book . . ." He looked out the window at the Manhattan Bridge. "Where do you live?"

"Brooklyn. Go on."

"So, yeah, anyway, this guy was in this experiment and the women who were doing the experiment had to shave him, see." I nodded my head. "And he seemed to like it. The way it felt. In the book. And I thought maybe I might like it too."

"And do you?" The blush got more prominent, as did the tent in his jeans. "Cute Boy, you're so cute."

"I'm kinda embarrassed. I just did it last night. Didn't know if I could, well, be with anyone – this way, you know?" He shot a glance at the back of the cab driver's head.

Where was HBO when you needed them? The driver wasn't paying any attention. He was on his cell, having a heated discussion, in low tones, in an unrecognizable language as the cab shot across the bridge.

"Brooklyn?"

"Don't worry about it. It's not a foreign country," I said. "I think you're gonna like it; the shave, I mean. Anyway, you'll know pretty soon, one way or another. And I've decided: you can call me Miss."

The cab stopped. I paid the driver and waited for Pete to get out.

"You live *here*?" he asked. He gazed up at the six-storey Red Hook building that had done duty as a warehouse at the turn of the century and was now artist lofts.

"Yeah," I said. "And we have the whole place to ourselves." The elevator opened onto a large, open, industrial space. Photographic equipment was off to one side, a couch and two overstuffed chairs faced away from the windows, towards a big flat-screen TV, leaving the window side of the room empty.

"Make yourself comfortable. My roommate's out of town, on a photo shoot. He does fashion and fetish. What would you like to drink?" I asked, from the kitchen.

"I was drinking beer at the bar. Eve, right? This is awesome."

I handed him a bottle of Beck's. "That's 'Miss' to you. Take off your clothes. I want to see if you did a good job." He looked at me, and then at the windows, which looked out onto the harbour and darkness. "It's OK, Cute Boy; no one's gonna see you except me." I slid his T-shirt up over his abs and past his chest. I loved the little patch of black hair he had between his pecs and around his nipples. I ran my hands over them and he sighed. The scent of beer lingered after. "Come on, Cute Boy, chop, chop. Let's go." I raised the shirt higher and he pulled it over his head.

"You were so cute, dancing at the bar. I loved the way you had your hands in the air, sort of like you were in another world." I unbuttoned his pants. Oversized, they immediately slid down to his ankles, leaving him completely naked. Pete's hard-on curved to the right. "Don't you think it makes your cock look bigger?"

"What?" he said, reaching for the buttons on my blouse.

"Later, maybe, if you're very good," I said. I brushed his hands away and ran mine up his shaft. "Shaving off your pubic hair," I said. "It makes your cock look bigger." He shuddered and tried to bump himself against me. "Doesn't it feel nice in the air, bare like that? I bet you've hardly been able to keep your mind on anything else, or your hands off, ever since you did it." I ran my hand softly over the shaved skin around the root of his cock. "Isn't that right?" I could see pre-come beginning to leak from the tip.

He groaned. "Don't you wanna get naked?" he asked.

"Ever been tied up?" He watched my mouth as if I were speaking a foreign language. "I know what kind of book you were reading."

My hands explored his hot skin and I felt the familiar cunt tingle I always get at the start of the game. Naked boys, especially when I'm clothed, just do it for me. My breath hitched as I reached for his balls and gently rolled them around in my palms.

He shook his head no.

"Wanna be?"

His cock waved. "Um . . ."

"Yeah, I guess you do, don't you?" I looked him in the eye and nodded. He copied the nod as he looked at me. "I do the rigging for my roommate on some of his shoots." He just stared at me as I fondled him. "I tie his models up."

"Oh," he said. "Oh. OK." Goose bumps appeared on his chest and arms.

"All right, so, if you don't like it, or you want to stop, you have to say, *I'm done*, understand? If you say anything else, I might not know what you mean, so you have to say, *I'm done*."

"I got it," he said. "It's just like in the book I was reading. Oh my God."

I spread a blanket on the floor, by the window and had him stand in the centre. I began with a utilitarian chest harness. The pattern incorporated diamonds in both back and front as well as two horizontal ropes falling above and below his nipples. Checking in with him, I asked him how he was doing.

"Fine," he said. "This is fun."

I ran my hands over his imprisoned nipples and watched the waves of goose bumps travel up and down his chest. "Nice, huh? Everything feels more intense in the ropes, doesn't it?" His body gave a little involuntary shake and I set to work on his thighs and groin.

Putting double wraps around each thigh at three separate points, I joined them on both the outside and inside of his legs. I brought the tails, from his back tie, down the crack of his ass and up between his legs. Pulling them tight, I tied them off at the waist.

"How does that feel," I asked, running my fingers up and down the rope that stretched his ass cheeks apart.

"Fuck," he said. "That's so amazing."

I ran my hands between his legs, on either side of his straining cock and gave the taut, smooth skin just above his erect shaft a smack.

"Oh my God, don't stop," he said.

"We're not done yet. Plenty of time to play later. More work to be done yet. Keep your pants on . . . so to speak. Raise your arms, with your hands in the air, like when you were dancing."

I wrapped each arm separately and brought the tails down his back and between his legs, wrapping and separating his balls, before creating a rope cock ring. "Still good?" I asked.

"Yeah, but if I lower my arms, all the tension's gone."

"Don't worry, just be patient." I helped him lie down on the blanket and then lifted his arms over his head again, spreading them wide and fastening his wrists to a stretcher bar. By the time I finished with the stretcher bar, he was drifting off into sub space. It seems Cute Boy was a total bondage slut. The noise of the electric winch snapped him out of his trance.

"What's going on?"

"I'm going to suspend you. I think you'll like it." I attached the ropes from the pulley system to three strategic points on his back and waist harness, making sure his weight was evenly distributed, then I attached the spreader bar to the pulley system as well. I supported him as the winch began to lift him from the floor. When he was vertical again, I wrapped his calves to his ankles and lifted first one leg, then the other, off the ground, bending his knees and fastening his ankles about a foot from his thighs so it looked like he was jumping.

"OK?" I asked.

"Amazing," he replied. "Please say you have a camera. You gotta have a camera!"

I laughed and held him by the balls, rocking him back and forth, looking into his eyes. "You're a lot of fun, Cute Boy." Running my hands over his shaved groin and my fingers along the sides of the rope separating his ass, he began to shake in his harness. I played with the pre-come at the tip of his cock and stroked the underside.

"You want to come?"

"Oh, yeah," he moaned.

"What's my name?"

"Eve."

I smacked his ass.

"Miss, Miss!" he yelled.

"I like this smooth skin, Cute Boy," I said, stroking the newly shaved skin. A combination of touch and gentle humiliation brought him off and, once he was done, I lowered him back to earth and removed the ropes.

After some cookies and cuddling, we exchanged numbers, and as

I walked him to the door he glanced over at my desk. "Hey, that's the book," he said.

I looked down. "That book?"

"Yeah, that's the book I was reading."

"No shit? I wrote that book," I said, handing him the sequel.

An Unusual Legacy

Anya Levin

She stepped into the room, trading the plushly carpeted, well-lit hallway for a dimmer, colder, luxurious cavern of a room.

Though she knew Jenny wouldn't be in the room, wouldn't be with her again, a dark part of her thought, sending a pang through her chest, she was still warmly aroused when she moved into the room. Even without Jenny's presence, the illusion that she would be seeing her was there. In her mind it was almost as if she were embarking on one of their usual meetings, as if she would be seeing Jenny's blonde hair and welcoming smile, sinking into her arms and kissing her mouth.

But she knew better, and was more reminded than let down when she saw Not Jenny waiting in the room.

"You're just on time," the woman said with a smile. She was tall, trim, well-dressed. Pretty, but not Jenny. She could have been anyone, anywhere. But to Leonie's surprise, she was no one. There was no recognition ping on Leonie's interface. There was *nothing*.

"Jenny told me to expect you," the anonymous woman said. "I'm Raine, by the way." She stepped forward, hand outstretched in greeting.

"Jenny. You knew Jenny."

"I know she's dead," Raine said soberly, smile falling flat.

The blunt declaration took Leonie's breath away, and sent a shaft of pain through her chest. The reality was too new, too fresh. It felt like an attack to hear it professed so openly.

"But you came anyway. And she would have wanted you to," Raine continued.

"Would she have?" Leonie asked. She'd wondered.

"Yes," Raine said firmly.

No question, then. Leonie shook herself, clutched her fingers together and broached the real question. "Why am I here?"

"This is why," Raine said. She lifted her fingers to reveal a thin wand-like instrument. It looked delicate, but unfinished. The metal lacked shine and there was a peculiar tilt to the base of the device that suggested it had been damaged at some point.

Leonie stared at the wand, then met Raine's dark eyes. "I don't understand."

Raine flicked the wand on with a small gesture, and a pinprick of light shone from a point on the barrel. "This is going to sting a bit," she said. "But you must hold still."

Leonie stiffened, fear ricocheting up her spine. She froze as the device moved closer to her. The words that Jenny had written her reverberated through her memory. *Obey all instructions*, she'd said, and so Leonie would. Because Jenny had asked her to, and Jenny asked her to do so little.

She'd expected something less scientific.

Heat and pressure threatened the backs of her eyes again, but Leonie pushed the unwelcome reaction back. Now wasn't the time for emotion, though she supposed that she was mourning Jenny, in a way. She hoped that Jenny was, wherever she was now that she'd left the world they'd shared, happy that she'd come to the hotel.

The so-called "sting" nearly sent her to her knees, but she kept still as fire flared across the back of her hand and then up and across her body. Her heart thumped, her breath came unsteadily.

"It's done," the other woman said finally, moving to a bag Leonie hadn't noticed previously and putting the wand away.

Unceremoniously, Leonie sank to the carpet. She stared up at Raine. "What did you do?"

Raine stuck her hand out, grabbed Leonie's when she bewilderedly offered it, and hauled her to her feet with a yank. "Welcome to Freedom," she said.

"Sounds ominous," Leonie said, her voice thin as her breathing evened out.

"Be proud. Not many qualify to enter our little club," Raine said. "Jenny argued long and hard to get you involved. I hope you don't betray her dedication."

The thought made Leonie's stomach churn. "I won't."

Raine lifted her brows, but didn't respond.

Leonie held her tongue, though it was no small feat.

"So, Freedom. A club, a very private club. Also a state of mind, of course. One that we dedicate ourselves to. One we work very hard to achieve. An outlook, a possibility, that Jenny very much wanted you to experience." Raine sat on the edge of the room's sprawling bed, sinking into the plush cover and the soft mattress. "It is unfortunate that she could not be with us to see your awakening, but this is all the more meaningful because it was, truly, her last real desire."

She had the sudden realization that whatever was happening was so far beyond simply Jenny and her, beyond a gift, even one extended – however unintentionally – after death.

She suddenly felt small, and the mysterious experiences that lay ahead of her were rewritten as solemn, sanctified rituals dedicated to Jenny herself.

The lingering annoyance at the sting of whatever the wand had done evaporated.

"Explain this to me," she said. Whatever it was, she was going to do it, and whole-heartedly.

The explanation Raine launched into was long. A group that had conceived an idea so against the core concepts of the society that Leonie lived in that had her invitation proceeded in any other way . . . As it was, the thought of what had been done – the very idea of turning off her interface – made her stomach churn with apprehension.

What if someone found out? What if something happened to her?

The implications of Jenny's death – the mysteries that Leonie had shoved to the side and ignored – leaped out with all their possibilities. If her interface had been disabled . . .

"She died here," she said finally.

"Not here, exactly," Raine said slowly, eyes skittering away from Leonie's face, "but at a similar gathering."

Leonie licked her dry lips, swallowed. "So, what's next?" she asked.

"Next? Well. Next, you change."

"Most find that creating a persona helps one to relax and enjoy the experience all the more," Raine explained. She'd produced clothing and cosmetics with the clear expectation that Leonie pick from among the offerings.

"OK." Jenny, Leonie thought, this was all for Jenny. The oddness, the confusion, the discomfort of this new situation. "Hallie. My name will be Hallie."

It had been Jenny's middle name.

Raine nodded. Leonie thought her expression held a sense of approval. Perhaps she knew the source of the name.

They picked a pink dress, and pink paint for her eyes, and a hair ornament with a huge feather and a set of jet-coloured beads that mimicked the high fashion of ten years past with their dip across her forehead.

Leonie – Hallie – looked in the mirror.

She had never seen the woman in the mirror before. The woman who wore such bright colours and stood with such poise and attitude. It wasn't Leonie who stood in front of that mirror.

Hallie. She tasted the name in her mouth, rolled it around and set it to the face before her.

"Don't forget the shoes." Raine proffered a pair of teeteringly high heels. Hallie slipped them onto her feet.

"You're ready," Raine said.

She led Hallie to the stairwell at the end of the hallway, opened the door and ushered her in. They climbed four flights of stairs in near silence. All Hallie could hear were the clicks of her heels and Raine's on the concrete stairs and the swish of the feathers that decorated the neckline of her dress.

The floor that they exited onto was, physically, nearly identical to the one they'd left behind, but it felt wrong. It wasn't a feeling that Hallie could put her finger on – something about the way the air moved, maybe, or perhaps something about the whispers almost beyond her range of hearing.

"For tonight, this is Freedom," Raine said. "And, this is where I leave you. Explore. Enjoy. You have eight hours before your circuits unscramble themselves." She leaned forward and pressed a quick kiss to Hallie's lips, then slid a fond hand to her cheek. "Do Jenny proud."

And then she stepped forward, and was gone.

The woman's disappearance was initially disconcerting, but Hallie quickly figured out what had happened. She looked back at the stairwell door, then forward to the non-reality that her eyes were seeing.

She stepped forward, and found herself in chaos.

What had looked like a normal floor of hotel rooms was, in fact, a carved-out area of openness, full of people and temporary dividers and lights and sound.

Raine had said to explore. And so she would.

Hallie turned heads, here and there, but most were engrossed in their own affairs and couldn't, evidently, be bothered with a new girl wandering through their ranks.

Or they'd been told to ignore her. Maybe all new people. Maybe the very inattention paid her was yet another aspect of this "Freedom". It certainly was a different feeling, the thought that those she was walking with knew nothing about her, and worse, that she knew nothing about them. That even a burning curiosity couldn't be resolved, should it arise.

That trust was something that actually arose from personal interaction.

OK, she admitted as she walked between two tables of people, one a group of four playing cards, the other a handful of people seated at a table of foods such as she'd rarely seen, everyone had clearly been vetted somehow. There was definitely thought and work put into who was accepted into this society, otherwise it wouldn't have taken Jenny so long, as Raine had implied, to get her invited.

So there was a safety net, but there was also the unknown.

It was very nearly terrifying.

At least, she was pretty sure that was the proper description of what she was feeling. She had never felt this way before – her chest felt tight, her head pounded with the rush of blood going through it, and her mouth was unbearably dry. And, as she overcame her initial nervousness, excitement infused her. Her nipples were hard as gems, buried in the thick fabric of her bodice. Beneath the ruffled, lace-edged skirt her thighs were warm and humid, the unmistakable cream of her desire a reality she was all too aware of.

And there was sex everywhere.

Though she wasn't a virgin, or anywhere near inexperienced, the gyrations and manipulations that she saw were beyond arousing. The sexuality on display in the room was different somehow than anything she'd ever seen or imagined.

She longed to be a part of it.

"Here, you look parched," a male voice said.

Hallie turned, took in the man who held out a glass towards her. Tall, dark-haired, dressed all in black. Portions of his face were obscured with a black mask.

Her heart rate slammed into overdrive. "Thank you," she managed, and took the glass he proffered.

His eyes were fixed on her as she drank. It was disconcerting, but somehow thrilling. She drained the glass in three sips, then held it, at a loss.

He took it from her with a smile, set it on a nearby table, then hooked an arm around her waist and leaned in close. "No need to look lost," he said. "Everyone here was new once."

"I will introduce you," he said. A twist that might have been a smile, could she have seen the full range of the motion, curved his lips. Gently pressing on her waist, he steered her away from a crowd of people and towards a relatively quiet corner of the room.

Everything blurred. People, faces, hands, objects . . .

It wasn't a chemical reaction, or perhaps more correctly wasn't an *exotic* chemical reaction, Hallie thought. No, what she was feeling was purely natural, her own body reacting in this new, exciting place, the emotions that filled her, the things she saw, smelled, wanted.

And she wanted everything.

"Take your time," her masked escort counselled. "It will all be here next time, and the time after that, and so on. No need to gorge yourself in one sitting."

Hallie suspected that if she engaged in half the decadent indulgences that she suddenly knew that she wanted to, indigestion would be the least of her worries. As it was, just looking at the things that people were doing was enough to send her head spinning.

But underneath it all was Jenny.

Memories swept Hallie away, brought forth the anger, the longing that Leonie felt so deeply. Leonie was lost in the room, anchored only by her loyalty to the woman she'd so loved. Hallie fought to reclaim her equilibrium, to push back Leonie's stifling feelings and immerse herself in the experience that had been Jenny's dream for her to live.

Her escort misread her confusion and sadness, for he laid a comforting hand on her arm and pulled her close to his body in a wildly inappropriate physical gesture. "You will have your chance, don't worry."

She tried to focus on the possibilities in his words over the weight of Leonie's thoughts haunting the back of her mind. "So once I'm in, I'm in?"

He nodded, the sleek black mask that covered his face sliding ever so slightly. He reached up to adjust it. "No probationary period for us, I'm afraid. You're either in or out. And you're in."

As was completely evident.

"So, what exactly do people usually do? To start out, that is?"

"Well," her masked man turned them so that her back was to a corner and he blocked most of the room from her view, "most people start with little pleasures. Work their way in."

"Ah. To avoid the whole gorging." Hallie nodded sagely.

"No," the black-masked man corrected her, "so that one's first experiences can be properly enjoyed."

"It's an encouraged method?" Hallie asked.

"Indeed," the black-masked man said. He reached forward and wrapped his fingers around Hallie's wrist. The heat of his touch both excited and dismayed her. He slid his fingers up her wrist, lifting her arm to his shoulder. The slow glide of his fingers on her skin was electrifying, but she felt blind. Usually the web of her interface would be burbling away small acceptances, registering temperature changes and such. Instead there was stark silence. The only things she could hear were the rush of her own breath and the pounding of her heart. The black-masked man who was causing such internal chaos showed no sign of similar physical reaction.

It was most annoying.

Somehow Hallie couldn't force herself to move. She didn't want to push him away, not really. Beyond that, however, she was lost. She was paralysed by a horrible lack of information – what would please him, what would displease him? Usually when she embarked on a physical relationship she had all that information up front.

And now she had nothing.

The man turned his head, and she felt the warmth of his breath against her wrist. Restless desire slid through her. He leaned closer, and Hallie felt the rough brush of his mask against her skin right before his lips touched her skin.

"So that's feeling," she forced out. "What about touching. Can I explore touching?"

Her eyes were drawn to his soft-looking lips. She wanted to feel them against her own in a heavy kiss. What would he taste like?

She found out swiftly, as the man slanted his mouth over hers and slid his tongue against her lips then between them as she opened her mouth, helpless against the electricity of the touch. He was a stranger, someone she knew nothing about, could get nothing from. He was a dark cipher, another in a room of mysterious people who she wouldn't know if she passed them on the street – or worked in the same office as they did.

It was a phenomenal turn-on.

He pulled away slowly and she leaned into him, wanting more. It was new and different and something that she never could have imagined. Chest tight, she eyed him. Was he breathing a bit faster? Was that a slight flush of arousal on his cheeks?

"Would you like to make love?"

She almost laughed, after she'd processed the question. He asked it casually, as if he'd asked her to pass him a paper, or as if he were excusing himself after he'd bumped into her while passing on the street. Despite that, the simple question reignited the fire between her legs, and set her heart pounding. Desire shivered across her body, goose bumps breaking out in the wake of the feeling. More than anything, she wanted to make love with the mysterious masked man.

"Yes," she answered, breathlessly. She tried for a matching insouciant response but she didn't feel as if she'd succeeded in hitting that note. Nevertheless, he curved his arm around her waist and pulled her away from the corner, towards a section of the room curtained off by opaque screens.

They stepped between two of the screens and into a world of their own. A low bed was made up with brilliant purple sheets and through some mechanical trick the bright lighting that had pervaded the rest of the open space was dimmed and softened to something almost romantic, and definitely intimate.

Welcoming.

His arms closed around her, and then he was kissing her again. She gave herself to the feeling. Pleasure, he'd said. The goal of Freedom was pleasure.

And pleasure was what he gave.

Undressing became an act of seduction, fingers and flitting, buttons carefully unbuttoned, zippers incrementally unzipped. Slowly, inch by inch, smooth flesh was revealed. A shoulder gleamed pearlescent in the light, a golden bicep flexed, muscles moving smoothly. Movements followed by heated kisses and lingering caresses, they bared each other to the coolness and the light. In the end, the only articles that remained between them were the mask that he wore and the body-warmed beads that peppered her collarbone.

Hallie looked her fill.

He was magnificent, muscled and toned and very clearly aroused. Her eyes fastened on his penis. His erection, proof positive of his desire, fascinated her. She couldn't quantify his reaction through the interface, leaving her feeling blind and strangely virginal. The slickness between her legs was far from virginal, though. She knew exactly what she wanted, and felt no shyness about her cravings.

She took his penis firmly. She liked men's erections, liked the heated hardness, the throbbing pulse of an arousal. Liked that an erection was for her, that it reflected desire for her body, her self. And this erection reflected that desire with more truth than any fed by an interface's biochecks and verifications, she realized with a thrill. This erection was one hundred per cent honest and true and needy.

Responsive excitement shot through her, tightening her breasts and belly. She rubbed her thighs together. The ache between them intensified, and the musky smell of her desire drifted between them.

She craved a taste of him, leaned to wrap her lips around his length but was halted by his hands on her shoulders, pulling her upwards.

"Not now," he said. "This isn't just for my pleasure."

She wanted to protest, to argue that giving him pleasure would give her pleasure, but the platitude wouldn't emerge from her lips. Touching him would give her pleasure, yes, but the pleasure she truly wanted wouldn't come from her fingers or her tongue. She wanted his hands on her, his mouth on her. She wanted to know what he would do to her, but couldn't find the words to ask over the pounding of her heart and the heavy throbbing between her legs. She was overwhelmed by her desire for the man before her.

His eyes glinted and his hands settled on her wrists, holding her, steadying her. His mouth sank and he gave her another firm kiss. The heat of his mouth sank through her body, warming her down to her toes. Her knees weakened and she fell against him. He caught her and held her fast against him, his mouth only lifting from hers when she was totally boneless. He swept her into his arms and laid her down on the purple sheets of the bed behind them, then proceeded to devote himself to her pleasure.

He caressed her cheek, let his fingers drift over her lips, and then moved his attention downwards. He touched her breasts, fingertips rubbing against the points of her nipples, sending waves of pleasure through her. She shivered. Dark eyes intent, he pinched one nipple gently, causing her to squeal and arch from the bed and into his arms.

He smiled, a cutting gesture beneath the mask that he still wore.

He ventured downwards.

His fingers slid over her mound and slid between her cunt lips and she cried aloud, shocking herself. In one quick motion his fingers were inside her, thrusting deep. His skin was hot, nearly burning, and his touch seemed to brand her from the inside out. The molten sensation seemed the perfect complement to the greater experience she was living. His freshness, his honesty, were changing her — indelibly engraving the changes that the day had made deep within her body.

Leonie's thoughts, only peripherally lucid in the maelstrom of the moment, took the changes that were being burnt into her even further back, to that sunny day when she'd met Jenny that first time.

But Hallie was lost in sensation, and barely acknowledged the existential musings of her alter ego. All she could think of was the man who lay with her, whose name she didn't know, whose face she'd never seen.

The sensations that flooded her with his touch blinded her to everything. All Hallie knew was that her body was aflame and that all too soon she was going to erupt.

Then his mouth brushed against the softness of her mound and his fingers found her clit and pleasure swept through her body.

Slowly she came back to the world and became aware of his lips settling soft, almost loving kisses against her clit and folds, of his fingers massaging her thighs and her hips, easing her way to earth. But while she would have expected that languor would have infused her after such an intense orgasm, instead Hallie found herself enthused by his gentle touches, new arousal moving through her, subtle this time but no less powerful.

All too aware that her lover hadn't come, Hallie found his penis and slid her hand over it. Pre-come wet her palm and she used it to lubricate her motions. He throbbed in her fingers and she grinned to have him in her power. She wasn't a bad hand with such manipulation, or so she'd been told, but it still surprised her when her mystery lover began to arch into her touch and his mouth clenched tight.

She bent forward once more to taste him, and this time when his hands settled on her shoulders he didn't push her away. His fingers dug into her flesh, the tight grip pleasing her and egging her on. She lathed the head of his cock slowly, gently with her tongue, tasting him, then swept her tongue around him before closing her mouth over him.

He groaned. The sound sent shivers across her, as did the increasing pinch of his grip on her shoulders. She would wear the badges of his passion later, a reminder, and yet another brand of sorts.

Then he lost patience, his hands moving and turning her, taking control.

"Are you ready?" he asked, poised over her.

Gentlemanly. Polite.

Alien feelings to the state Hallie found herself in.

She spread her legs wide. "Please. Now!"

He complied, sliding into her wetness without a motion lost. She was dripping so much that he had no trouble entering her fully, and then he began a rhythm that set Hallie's heart racing. Thrust after thrust, his mouth peppering her chin and lips and sharing kiss after kiss. One hand slid down to her knee and Hallie opened her legs even more, taking him in deeper, as deep as she could. Their eyes met, she gazed into the darkness of his pupils, so large they seemed to take up the entirety of his eye.

He grunted, and a bead of sweat fell on her lip, and then she was coming again, wave after wave of pleasure rocking her.

Her orgasm seemed to spur him on. In his enthusiasm his mask slipped slightly, one cheekbone revealing itself, a trickle of sweat rolling down. She looked away from the unexpected nakedness and pressed her lips to the hollow of his throat, savouring the power and pressure of him over and inside her.

At first she didn't realize that he was coming, that he'd slowed in his thrusts. His body clenched against hers and his breath whooshed in her ear and then he slowly fell against her, boneless and heavy for a long moment before he slid off her and to the sweat-streaked purple sheets.

Eyes tracing the contours of his body, Hallie realized that the experience she'd had in her mystery man's arms was one she would never, ever forget.

And she didn't know whether to be scared, or elated.

"So," she turned against his arm and looked up at him, feeling languid and beautiful and genuinely rumpled. "Do I get to know your name?"

He seemed just as mysterious, the mask still in place, even though they'd been so naked before each other – both physically and, Hallie liked to think, somehow beyond that. And, looking at him, she somehow knew that that mystery was part of his freedom, and something that he wasn't going to give up.

"No," he said, confirming her conviction.

Hallie lay back, digesting the blithe refusal. She smiled. This man clearly had no shame in his flat refusal to name himself, no hesitation. Seeing his blunt honesty, where outside in the "real" world social niceties would have dictated his response, struck a chord of longing she'd never acknowledged. She wanted that honesty, wanted to be able to rely on society's polite lies – or not, as she felt moved to do so. Realization that she could as much as he did crashed on her heels and sent a thrill of eagerness through her.

He moved, dislodging her gently.

"My time will be up shortly." He pulled on his pants, dark and sleek, and his matching front-closure shirt.

Following his lead, Hallie dressed swiftly, pulling her dress up around her shoulders. She glanced around the enclosure, found nothing reflective to check her make-up in, and abandoned the idea.

"I don't know what to say now," Hallie said.

He smiled. "You don't have to say anything. We had a good time." Her fingers brushed her wrist, and Hallie watched his mouth tighten momentarily.

Eyeing her, he cocked his head and smiled. "You never know, maybe there will be another meeting in our future."

"I'd like that," she said, tasting the flavour of the truth on her lips.

He stepped between the screens and disappeared, leaving Hallie alone in the silence of the enclosure. With a breath, and a final look at the silken covers scattered on the low-lying bed, she followed him out.

Raine found her some time later. She'd explored nooks and crannies, glimpsed things she'd never have thought of under other circumstances, and generally enjoyed herself.

"It's time," Raine said.

"Already?" Hallie reluctantly tore her eyes from a singular group of people unabashed in their sexual enjoyment.

The walk back through the stairwells was like the old fairy tale of falling through the rabbit hole, but instead of falling into wonder she was emerging from it. The realization made each step painful, and the closing of the hotel-room door behind them echoed in the silence, accentuating the sudden funereal atmosphere. The mirror over the dresser reflected limp feathers and smeared make-up. It felt more authentic to be Hallie than to contemplate becoming that other woman once again. She slid her hands down the slick fabric of her skirt, touched the crunch of lace that edged it.

"Do I just put her in a box now?"

"Yes. For a time."

Raine watched as she stripped off the trappings of Hallie's existence, then whisked the clothing efficiently away. She paused, seeming to consider, then spoke. "I knew Jenny very well."

Leonie turned swiftly, eyes probing, but Raine watched her steadily. Whatever may have happened between Raine and Jenny, it was between them, and it was going to stay that way.

"She was herself with you. You may have only known her in the strictures of the interface, but she did want more."

Dressing automatically, Leonie processed Raine's words. "Thank you," she said finally.

As she slid the last button of her jacket into its buttonhole, she felt a tingle in her arm, and then a sting. Her hand flew to the spot, but it wasn't an itch to be scratched or a topical burn that could be soothed with a touch.

"It will hurt," Raine said. "Just as it does when it's blocked. But it's fast."

Even as she spoke, tongues of fire licked across Leonie's body, and then the interface was back.

"So what do I do now?" Leonie finally asked.

"Go home," Raine said. "Go back to your life and live it. And one day you'll get an invitation. Or rather, Hallie will."

Excitement soared through her. Her hands shook. "And then?"

"That's it," Raine said simply. "You'll come." She smiled. "We all do."

And Leonie knew that she would.

Raine walked to the door, opened it for Leonie in a clear gesture.

Leonie stepped unwillingly out. She went to the elevator, rode down the floors to the hotel lobby, seeing none of the city's lights sprawled before her. Then she stepped into the mix of people – of signals and notifications – that only a day before had been her whole world. Now it seemed like so much noise she had to navigate through, so much information to be sorted, so much personal detail to be absorbed or rejected.

Her breath caught in her throat as she caught sight of a pair of dark eyes, and the familiar curve of a smile. The man winked with a tiny, almost infinitesimal motion.

And she remembered his words, "maybe another meeting". Hugging the possibility to her – hugging the night to her, even though it had been lived through Hallie's shoes and not her own – Leonie headed towards the main doors, and went out into the night.

Rooftop Hunger

Aimee Herman

As an accountant at a semi-profitable advertising company, I see everything in numbers: from the distance between moon to star formation to the percentage of time I think about having sex with Claira divided by the times she humours me. We met on the second day of the third week of the ninth month of the year at a fall solstice party. I generally don't go to things like that – themed parties. It's enough to just offer beer and an avalanche of chips and dip. However, at the last minute I decided to go. I noticed Claira soon after arriving, with her dark blonde, messy hair and lips all red like medium-rare steak. She was wearing what every woman in New York wears nowadays: black. Black stockings with a short black skirt, black shirt with about one-and-three-quarter inches of cleavage, and black heels, which she wound up taking off sometime during our flirtations.

After asking the quintessential getting-to-know-you questions such as *what do you do* and *what neighbourhood do you live in*, we walked up one flight of stairs to the rooftop, which was surprisingly empty. In the seventeen steps from the stairs to the door leading onto the roof, we independently and silently decided to fuck. That night, Claira and I fucked in a way I never have with any girl. It was messy like her hair. We didn't ask permission or hold back; we barely kissed. It was primal.

The air was warm enough not to interfere with Claira's blatant disrobing of black. Her breasts were larger than I had approximated, but small enough to fit inside my mouth. The moon was off-kilter, so a summary of her nipples: colour, diameter, length when erect could not be seen. Once completely nude, she began to pull, lift, unbutton, push everything off me, leaving me just as bare. Then, we slammed into each other like drunken automobiles into brick walls. (There was a reason I had bruises on my body the next morning.)

I reached towards my pants, pulled out a condom and quickly put it on. Everything was sped up. My dick in her hands, which she led towards and into her pussy. Her breasts in my mouth, sucked and lathered. Her hips rocking from side to side, to invisible music or anticipation. We balanced against the weight of each other, standing sometimes on one leg or on our knees. I remember lifting her up with her thighs wrapped around me, ankles crossed behind my back. I was as far inside her as I could be and yet she kept whispering, *go in, keep pushing in.* Then we fell.

I didn't feel the impact until the morning, of course. In that moment, we were acrobats with the concrete roof floor acting as our trampoline. I think my dick may have remained inside her even after the impact of our fall, or maybe my dick frighteningly fell out. She pulled off the condom without any sense of delicateness or caution. Then, she dived down, her body curving into my crotch. Claira sucked at my dick, one hand offering her balance, the other massaging my inner thighs and over my balls. She may have even grown a third hand because there was a moment she was almost inside my anus, fingering and playing with its known sensitivity. Her teeth were well-mannered and careful not to scrape away my length or ability to enjoy myself. She swirled her tongue all around me, behind, beneath, on the sides, and when my dick was pounding, practically exercising a full-blown erection, she moved onto my balls that were swollen and grateful for her attention.

Claira had the energy of a speed addict; she never lost momentum or focus. As she sucked and licked, my fingers pulled at her hair, pressed down on her head, and sometimes reached below to pinch a nipple or squeeze a breast. Without notice, she leapt off my dick and threw it inside her again. Much later on in our relationship, she told me that she never had unprotected sex and that maybe a part of her knew we'd be together. When she told me this, I remained completely silent, knowing I had been unsheathed many times before.

At this point, I may have been on top of her or maybe we twisted, taking turns being on top or writhing from the side. I wrapped around her from behind; she put her hands on the floor and did something like a handstand with legs in the air and pussy reaching up to my hips. It's like we were doing a photo shoot for some Kama Sutra book. I only wish someone had been up there on that rooftop hiding, watching, because we deserved the applause.

Claira and I have been together now for one year, four months and thirteen days. Our escapades on that rooftop seem like a mythical tale now. That one night was exactly that: *one night*. It's not like we haven't had sex since; our sex life is healthy in comparison to my friends'. We fuck once a week, sometimes more, rarely less. Unfortunately, our sex is so demure, it could be turned into a children's book with illustrations and pop-ups. I think about that rooftop more often than I should. I compare. I mourn. It remains as fodder for my own masturbatory lacklustre adventures.

"I'm picking up some last-minute things for the party," Claira says.

It is the last day of the year, and we decided about a month ago to have some friends over to celebrate. Again, I hate themed parties, and New Year's Eve definitely ranks up there. People start boasting drunken gratitude letters, the midnight kiss, and that ridiculous champagne toast. Claira is taking control over most of the night's necessities, which includes booze and miniature food meant to curb nauseous drunk bellies.

"Anything else you want to add to my list?"

I shake my head and kiss her absent-mindedly. Kisses are like breaths at this stage of our relationship; they are often, but barely conscious.

"Hey, wait," I interrupt. I grab Claira's waist and pull her onto my lap. I begin kissing her neck and sucking her.

"What are you doing? I've got so much to do right now, Peter. People are coming in like, three hours."

I let go of her and for a brief second, an image from the rooftop splatters against my mind: I am on my back, leaning up to watch her suck me off and she crawls up towards my face with her whole body, stopping just above my mouth. Her crotch lined up perfectly to my gasping mouth. Then, she slowly lowered herself down and I licked and lathered away at her sweaty, turned-on pussy.

"OK if I use your metro card?" she asks, while simultaneously removing it from my wallet. "I should be back in about an hour."

It is thirty-five minutes past the tenth hour of the last day of this year. I am not as drunk as I'd like to be and we are slowly running out of good booze. Harry left to pick up more from the bodega a block down. Claira is across the room throwing her head back with laughter and I am pretending to enjoy a conversation about the anticipation of Super Bowl.

". . . doesn't even matter who plays nowadays, but I'm hoping the Broncos make it. What'd you think about the plays from . . ."

And I'm lost.

"You drunk yet?" Claira is suddenly beside me. Her customary blanched cheeks are now light pink in colour.

"No," I smile. "Or yes. Hard to say. Not drunk enough to be interested in this," I whisper, gesturing to my boys.

"Everyone seems to be having a good time, don't you think?"

"Uh-huh. Are you?"

She nods. "Well, we made it through another year." Claira kisses me gently as though I am her grandfather with fragile skin. Then, she is off towards the short-skirted bunch of women in the corner.

In my brief interlude with Claira, the conversation has switched from football to resolutions.

"Every year I say I'm gonna become a runner," says Greg.

"I'm hoping to get laid more," Kyle pipes in.

"I'm OK with the amount of sex I'm getting," I say. "I just wish it were slightly more adventurous."

"Whatcha sayin', man? Claira not rooftop sexing anymore?"

In my close circle of friends, the term "rooftop sex" has become like a verb. It translates as any kind of sex that goes beyond the traditional mount, thrust and come. Location doesn't matter, but it is almost impossible to rooftop sex on a bed or even in a bedroom. Among our group, it has occurred in a few bar/restaurant bathrooms, a teacher's lounge, a university library, and a movie theatre. None of those locations had anything to do with me or Claira. I may have been the originator of rooftop sex, but my role unfortunately ended there.

"You guys know how much I love Claira."

"She's awesome, man," says Silvio.

"We just don't—"

"Kate barely sucks me off anymore," slurs Kyle. "How 'bout we toast to our women rooftop sexing us in the new year?"

Our bottles clink and we shove them towards our mouths, slinging back room-temperature beer.

The music suddenly gets turned up and I notice Claira pushing her hips aggressively from left to right. The first time I watched her dance, I got an immediate hard-on. Tonight is no different.

"I fucking love this song!" Claira screams.

"Why do we do this every year?" I say. " 'I'm gonna lose weight or be nicer or give my loose change to every bum I see on the subway. It's like we say this when we are drunk and minutes away from a new year that is really no different than the day before it except the number changed. I've been waiting for that rooftop since the night after it happened. Maybe Claira is waiting too. We never talk about it. It's like it happened to someone else. I'm fucking done with this boring shit we call sex. It's like a constant rerun of the same show that you didn't even like the first time."

I realize that I am probably a bit more inebriated than I thought. I start to calculate the decibel of sound from the music compared to that of my drunken voice. Then, I look over at Claira and notice that although her ass was deeply concentrating on the beat and rhythm of the song, her eardrums were able to multi-task. She heard me.

I smile at Claira, but she just whips her hair back as a gesture of *I'm mad at you right now but we have guests over and it's new year's and we will talk about it later.*

I take the deepest swig of beer that my mouth can hold and swallow. Hard.

"Shit," I say.

I slowly walk over to Claira and gently grab her from behind. I am still hard from my first glance of her dancing and her disappointment in me has no influence on its stiffness. I am aware that it is pressing into her.

"Do you think about that rooftop too?" I whisper.

She ignores my question and continues to dance, though I notice her ass pushing into me rather than away.

"Do you think about your hands on the pavement and your legs in the air? Balancing with my dick inside you?"

Her hair smells vaguely of cigarettes; she always smokes when she is drinking. I can also smell her conditioner, which is sweet and salty from her sweat.

"What about my cum in your mouth? On your thighs? Your fingertips on my balls? You remember that?"

Claira turns around slowly and throws my head between her hands aggressively. Her lips are no longer glossy or red from whatever lipstick she had on at the beginning of the night, but they are strong, fast, and determined.

"Yes, I think about that night too," she says between kisses. Her tongue is almost as drunk as I am as it jumps waves inside my mouth. We are breaking records for length of time breath can be held. Usually she barely even puts her tongue in my mouth. Right now, she is counting all of my teeth and I can taste everything she has eaten, drunk, and smoked tonight.

"We never—"

"I know," she interrupts. "Shit, we're busy, Pete. It's like everything has sped up and slowed down and we got in this routine of—"

My hands are wrapped around her small waist and her hands are around my neck, fondling my hair and rubbing my cheeks.

"Life," I say. "Clair, what time is it?"

She looks at the small clock on our mantel and squints her eyes. "Eleven fifteen."

"Everyone is pretty drunk right now."

"Yeah," she says, looking around.

"Beer supply is going strong again. We're good on food still."

"Uh-huh."

"We could probably . . . just for a minute . . ."

Claira grabs my hand and smiles. She pushes her fingers into my knuckles, and digs her nails into my skin. We live in Brooklyn; our rooms are small like cupboards. Although everyone is centralized in the living room, we both stare at each other thinking the same thing. Rooftop. The first question I asked when we looked at apartments was: *is there rooftop access?* Many of them do, luckily this one is no different.

We walk up two flights of stairs, never letting go of each other's hands. My imagination, which has always been solid, is force-feeding my erection. She opens the door and

"Fuck."

There is no visible rooftop; there are so many people that it is impossible to even see the amazing view of lights and buildings surrounding us.

Amidst the coupled and group conversations, many men and women, women and women, and men and men are as close to fucking as two people can get.

"It's dark," I say. "Let's just carve out a corner and do our thing."

"Peter, it's—"

I move in front of her and lead us to a spot around the corner by the chimney and cement-covered boxes. There are no lights around us, so we just start feeling each other.

I breathe my beer breath into her ear and slur as many dirty words as I can think of. She giggles and falls into me.

This time, I take off my clothes while she remains in her black dress and black stockings and red flower pinned to the left of her breast. I don't care where my clothes fall; I don't think about adding up the distance between those closest to us on this rooftop. By this point, we have less than half an hour left of this year. No time to digress.

When there is nothing left to take off, Claira goes right for my dick and wraps it in her hands. I pull away.

"Wait," I say. I press my aroused dick against her and feel the textures of her skirt against its head. I reach towards the back of her and unzip her out of her dress. It falls against the rooftop. She has on stockings that go just above her knees and are fastened with hooks connected to her underwear. I push her panties to the side, still leaving them on, and push my dick into her. We are standing, though she immediately hops on me, with her threaded legs wrapped around me. I push myself further into her by pressing on her ass and pulling it towards me. Claira's breasts are pressed into my chest and I lean down to suck on one. She is cooing and moaning in my ear. I need to stop soon or I will come.

She senses my need and resistance to keep going and hops down. She pulls her underwear off, walks behind me, and presses her wet pussy against the back of my thigh, while reaching around to grab my hard cock. She starts to give me a hand job, squeezing harder, sliding over me, occasionally teasing my balls. She is grinding against me and I almost spout out everything I have when I sense her juices slipping down my leg. She doesn't let go. She goes faster and faster over my dick with a momentum that I don't even think *I've* ever had. Then, she stops.

"Huh, huh, uh, huh." I've lost the ability to speak. What I meant to say was—

"I want you to eat me out," she interrupts.

I can barely walk, let alone squat to reach her pussy. But my dick grants me access to bending, as I find myself on my knees rubbing my face between her thighs. For the first time since being outside, I can feel the cold air stick to my balls and shrink my dick. She is resembling a crumbling bridge, twisting and curving backwards as I force my tongue along the furrows of her lips and casually against her clit, lingering. After being with Claira this long, I've learned her favourite spots to be touched and in what order they prefer. Her clit being most sensitive, she prefers I hold off until the last possible moment. Tonight, we are chasing minutes and time has no patience for leisure or precision.

My jaw tenses as my tongue teases her hard clit and fingers coast inside her. I skate in and out of her slippery bush, which I occasionally bite into with my teeth. Her hairs are rained on by her excitement and I lick my lips against her salty curls. Claira's knees begin to buckle and I know from experience what is about to happen. She lets out the most amazing burst of liquid from her pussy like high tide at the beach. She squirts out almost sixteen months' worth of orgasms. She comes on my face and I slowly remove my fingers from inside her. I throw them into my mouth and taste her on me. She grabs me and we kiss. My dick crawls into her drenched pussy and I pump maybe five times before coming immediately.

"Eight, seven, six . . ."

I can barely walk down the flight of stairs to our apartment; my dick is panting between my legs. I can only imagine Claira is quite sore too. No one even flinches when we walk through the door, hair tousled, clothes carelessly fastened and smelling, no, *reeking* of sex.

I look at Claira and see that she has joined in on the countdown.

". . . three, two, one . . . happy new year!"

Couples grab each other and show gratitude with their lips. I kiss Claira, feeling her weight fold into me. Outside, I hear fireworks explode against the sky and the howls of drunken cheer.

Whiter Than Snow

Zander Vyne

Katie stood on the front steps of the church. Looking up at Gothic gargoyles, stone angels and soaring windows, she shivered.

Her friend Johnny hadn't lied; Saint de Sade's was amazing.

She held the heavy door open for a remarkably authentic-looking group of fresh-faced girls dressed in nun's habits and walked inside.

The door closed behind her with a dull thud, and she hesitated in the cavernous entry hall, her eyes adjusting to the dimly lit space, her heart pounding.

And they left the church, free of fear and ecstasy possessed, and they suffered no more for they were filled with awe, a sign hanging on the wall read.

Katie was trying to recall the last time she had been free of fear, ecstasy possessed or filled with awe, when a young man wearing flowing robes appeared from the shadows.

"Katie O'Malley?"

She jumped, startled. "Yes?"

"You're late. Come with me."

She followed him, walking into a chapel filled with old air, hushed whispers and candlelight. Stained-glass windows, lit by the dying sun, glowed with rainbow hues. Neat rows of polished pews flanked a crimson path.

The confessional waited down front – a wooden, closet-like box with two doors.

Katie shivered, rivers of excitement gripping her belly with greedy fingers. She was giddy, nervous and, for one anxiety-ridden moment, she wondered if this experience would be more than she could handle.

"Close the door behind you, and latch it," her escort said, holding the confessional door open.

She wondered why there was a latch at all, as she obediently stepped inside and fitted the bar into its loop. Was it there to keep people out or to keep her in should she change her mind and decide to run – not enough to stop her but enough to slow her down? She forced this alarming thought out of her mind, surrendering instead to her almost overwhelming thirst for the things she'd come here for. For years, she had tried to leave her sins in the past, but still they lurked like monsters in her closets. This was the only thing she had not tried, the only thing she thought might work.

Inside the confessional, it was shadowy and quiet. She pulled the kneeler down, wincing as her knees settled onto the hard, uncushioned wood. No comfort for the sinners at Saint de Sade's.

She heard footsteps, then a door opening and closing with a squeak. She held her breath and peered through the screen dividing the confessional, her gaze searching, her ears pricking with sounds heard – rustling clothing, a breath taken and let go.

"Hello, my child. I will hear your confession. Out of thine own mouth will I judge thee."

Jesus, this was intense. Johnny had told her what to expect, but the combination of her profane desires and the stark reality of this place shook her. Saint de Sade's prided itself on offering only the most authentic experience; it said so right on their website.

She wondered, in the moment it took her to answer, about the priest. Why had he chosen to serve in this way? How had he reconciled things she could not, both within herself and with the teachings of the church she had long ago abandoned? Her organized mind searched for order, in what was rapidly sliding into the surreal, and could find none.

"Bless me, Father, for I have sinned," she began in a rush.

Pushing her thoughts away, prompted by the priest's opening words, her own came easier than expected. "It's been a long time since my last confession," she said, rather than admitting she could not even remember the last time she'd been in any kind of church.

She confessed. Some things were very hard to tell him, but she did; it was why she'd come. She told him everything, all the secret things she had held onto all this time. As the monsters came out of her closets, she began to cry.

He listened, silent, apparently unmoved by her tears or her crimes.

The heavy aura of her confessed sins surrounding her, Katie wiped away her tears, feeling an odd mixture of shame, fear and relief.

"That's all. Everything," she said, her breath hitching. "Can you help me?"

She'd intended to confess it all, and had managed to get out even the most agonizing things, but worried maybe she'd lied even to herself – justifying some sins, forgetting others. As she waited for the priest to decide her fate, she wondered if the price of atonement would be more than she could bear or the necessary punishment more than he could offer. Maybe her sins were too great to be forgiven.

It suddenly felt intensely sexual to her – her confession offered for the priest's empathy, the give and take bleeding together. The agony of her want was tinged with exquisitely painful guilt. Being penetrated this way was a passionate, rending mind-fuck – without fingers, tongue or cock – and she longed for more.

"You have suffered greatly wearing the yoke of your wrong-doings. I can help you cast it off only if you truly wish to be free of its weight, and do exactly as I tell you. Stand up. Come close," the priest said, his voice nearer as Katie obeyed.

Her knees quivered as she pressed her cheek to the latticed wall of the confessional. She thought she could feel his warmth on the other side, and closed her eyes. This was what she wanted – something real, something she could feel in a way she understood.

There was a nickering of wood sliding over wood and a sudden stirring of air as he opened the old-fashioned screen partition, exposing her from breast to thigh. "Wash me, and I shall be whiter than snow. Sprinkle me with cleansing blood and I shall be clean again and, after you have punished me, give me back my joy again. So sayeth the Lord."

The words sparked a frantic flutter in Katie's heart as the priest slid his hand between her thighs and squeezed her pussy, his thumb exploring through her skirt and panties. She whimpered, frozen in place. Pangs of fear clashed with her excitement as the priest spoke of blood and fondled her.

This was already so much more than she'd anticipated, though exactly what she needed.

"Did you know blood in the moonlight glitters black?" The priest asked the question in his now familiar, soothing tone.

She didn't, but she pictured it now and moaned, her thoughts a disorganized jumble splashed with ebony, blood-soaked images. "No, I didn't know that."

"Exit the confessional, and go through the open door behind it. It will close, and you will kneel there and wait."

Fumbling with the latch, Katie bolted from the confessional, avoiding the eyes of those in line. She was very aware of the red flush on her cheeks and the obvious press of her hardened nipples against her shirt. She prayed there wasn't a visible wet spot on the front of her skirt and, looking down, was mortified to discover a dark smudge.

She walked through the doorway and kneeled as instructed, one hand curled protectively over the damp circle on her skirt. Waiting, her knees touched the ground but the rest of her seemed to fly away, separate, with no anchor, no salvation. Dizzy, she spread her fingers on the cold stone floor for support.

She wondered if there was mercy to be had and if she would want it. Would she rather keep this burning need inside or give it to the priest? She decided she wouldn't want benevolence, even as apprehension blossomed in her belly, her imagination rampant with dark fantasies of the punishment she'd come for – feared as much as longed for.

She craved an elusive saviour, who would not be swayed, who would know what she needed. The stained-glass windows overhead and the sweetly drifting choral music would not make this one soft. He would do what needed to be done.

Never before had Katie felt so close to what religion had promised but not delivered – as she hath done, so shall it be done to her; eye for eye, tooth for tooth. Until she felt it, the monsters in her closets would haunt her.

She fidgeted, wondering how long she would have to wait. The thought of kneeling in the open for a long time, alone except for the occasional passer-by, mortified her. She imagined rising and running out the doors of the church. Home. Safe. The thought made her giddy and ashamed, all at once.

She didn't rise, and the priest came to where she kneeled, her eyes cast downwards.

He lifted her chin, his fingers curling warm and intimately beneath, until their gazes met.

He was younger than Katie had expected. He wore his dark hair long, held back in a neat ponytail. His black shirt was fitted with a crisp, collared band of white.

Once more, she rode the edge between anxiety and pleasure. Everything about the priest was as expected and yet shocking all the same.

"Clasp your hands behind your neck." His assured, gentle tone compelled her to lift her trembling fingers, linking them behind her head.

"Lovely." The priest's fingers circled her throat. His thumbs pressed for a dizzying moment to the hollow between the curves of her collarbones.

He leaned closer, close enough for a kiss. "Here the wicked cease from troubling and the weary are at rest." His lips captured her gasp with one tiny suckle of her bottom lip.

"Remove your shirt." His whisper was warm on her cheek.

The shock of his words hit her like a slap, causing goose bumps and a thrill of pleasure mingled with anxiety. She shed her snug T-shirt, folding it neatly, pushing it against the wall.

His gaze dropped to her bare breasts, and she fought an urge to cover herself with shielding, cupped hands. She felt bare, vulnerable in body and spirit.

Her fingers gripped her knees as he clasped a collar around her throat. It was black leather – not too loose, not too tight, but just right. The smell was sharp and distinctive. A ring hung from the front and the priest lifted it, dangling it from his fingers before attaching a leash. Metal rasped closed against metal, everything made momentous by the lack of discussion, by the surety of the collaring and leashing, the quick efficiency and matter-of-factness of it.

"The Lord gave and the Lord hath taken away. Blessed be the name of the Lord."

Katie could not move. She could not speak, and her thoughts halted; what he'd done was so humbling it stilled her inside and out. At last, she thought, someone who understands.

He gazed at her – collared, leashed, kneeling – and, in the silence between them she felt acceptance and recognition. Aching need hung in the air like a live presence.

"Come." He wrapped the leather handle of the leash around his fist. Silver links trailed through his fingers. He didn't look back as he walked away, leaving Katie to scramble to her feet and follow or be dragged behind.

They walked down the winding hall until he stopped before a door Katie hadn't noticed, its wood worn to a hue the same shade as the stone lining the passage. The priest opened the door, revealing a cave-like alcove. On one wall hung a variety of crops, floggers, whips, canes, belts and paddles. There was even a ruler, long and wickedly thin. Looking at it, her insides quaked and she fought memories of unjust childhood punishments and evil nuns. Unable to look at the ruler, she turned away and watched the priest loop her leash over a chair and reach for a pair of black gloves resting on a low table. He picked them up and tugged them onto his hands, fingers wiggling into snug leather.

In the priest's gaze were compassion and understanding. As if reading her mind he said, "Let not the sun go down upon your sins, for every man shall bear his own burden and pay his own price."

Katie shivered, nodding, wanting desperately to let go of her anger, her guilt and her monsters.

"Pick," he said, tilting his head towards the display.

With butterflies in her stomach, she looked back at the whips, paddles and other instruments of punishment and reached, with only the slightest hesitation, for the thing that had caught her attention from the first moment she'd seen it, a thin black riding whip. She lifted it from the wall, holding it out to the priest as she knelt again, offering herself in the gesture he had not asked for.

"How can you do what needs to be done, Father?" she finally asked him, trembling as her gaze searched his.

"If any man is a bearer of the word and not a doer, he is like a man beholding his face in a glass; if he beholds himself and turns away, he forgets what manner of man he is," he said, taking the whip from her. Sliding a petting palm over the curve of her head, he allowed her to nuzzle her cheek into his leather-covered fingers.

"Good girl," he said, the praise penetrating Katie, his approval felt as contentment, knowing she had pleased him by kneeling, even if she still questioned.

He turned and dipped his fingers into a basin, sprinkling droplets of holy water onto the whip, blessing it. She knew this without him saying it.

"It will sting more wet," he said before saying the words that made it final, "*In nomine Patris, et Filii, et Spiritus Sancti*. Amen."

He helped Katie to her feet and led her back into the hall, tugging the leash sharply when she paused, forcing her into a brisker stride until they came to another door. It creaked when he pushed it open, its rusty hinges protesting.

Outside the summer breeze was warm. It kissed their cheeks in the purple, star-shimmered twilight, bringing with it the scent of damp earth, grass, and decay. The church graveyard was a tumbled maze of tombstones and crypts.

"Now we shall see through a glass, darkly. Come," the priest said.

His words paralysed her. Could she be as strong as he and face herself in the glass, not running away as she always had before?

He tapped the whip to his boot, and she went with him to where a lone light beckoned in the distance – a lantern affixed to a tall wooden cross, the marker for a grave in the centre of the cemetery, set upon a gentle rise.

"Step up. Face the cross."

She obeyed and he lay upon her, fitting himself into the parted crease of her ass as she clung to the cross, prickles of pain blooming on her bare chest and arms as tiny splinters pierced her skin. His leather-covered fingers trailed over her body, sweeping her hair from her back. He gave her bottom an almost casual caress and the tiniest of slaps, resting his hand on the curve of it as he kissed her neck and licked a tiny spot above her nape. She felt the warm slither of his tongue and goose bumps rose to meet it.

She worried she might pass out, blissed and lulled by his touch, but was alert again immediately when he whispered in her ear, "Lower your skirt to your knees. Press your cunt against the cross."

She unzipped her skirt with trembling hands, pushing it down to her knees, spreading them wider to keep it in place.

She was amazed at the ever constant shifting of her feelings. The desire to flee, the desire to come, the desire to do anything the priest asked rapidly changed places.

"Press close. Do it for me," he said.

Again, with only the slightest hesitation, she responded, pressing harder into the splintered cross. Pain stung her breasts and her fingers when she reached to curl them around the crossbar.

She shuddered, a feeling of complete surrender washing through her. She imagined her sins swept away in the flood and was comforted, calmed.

"Hold on tight," the priest said, unclipping the leash and tossing it away. He clasped a shorter chain to the front of the collar and then to the cross, holding Katie on a tighter tether, leaving her enough slack to turn if she were required to but not enough to keep her from strangling should she fall.

He crouched, sliding his palms over her hips, fondling the tender creases behind her knees and the smooth flesh of her inner thighs. He eased her skirt, sandals and panties off, leaving her naked, facing the cross.

"Who dares shed man's blood, by man shall have his blood shed."

The priest lifted his hands to the crossbar, his fingers brushing

Katie's thumb in a comforting sweep. He reached between her legs and dragged his fingertips over her cunt. Her flesh felt puffy, throbbing, her clit lush and swollen. He gave it a flicker.

The priest used her hair to turn her head. She shivered, looking into his obsidian eyes, drowning in his words.

"Your penance," he said, "your sins . . . repaid with your pain given to me. Sin. Atonement. Rapture." His gaze held Katie's as firmly as his leather-covered fingers held her cunt.

Katie felt a new surge of adrenaline clash deliciously with her aching need.

"*Dominus vobiscum. Et cum spirito tuo.* Bless you," he said.

She held tighter to the cross, closing her eyelids tight, her pussy convulsing in the priest's hand as he gave it one last squeeze.

"Do you know a prayer?"

"The Lord's Prayer is the only one I know by heart." Her voice trembled.

"Say it."

She began, her voice quivering, "Our Father, who art in heaven, hallowed be thy name."

"This will hurt. Hold on and pray," he said, before stepping away.

"Thy kingdom come. Thy will be done, on earth as it is in heaven." Katie's body stiffened, and she pressed harder into the cross, wanting and fearing, guilt-ridden yet needing this so badly she ached, her longing awakened fully and begging for release.

She heard a whoosh of sound – whip through air. She felt a single mark cut into her flesh high on the left side of her back, just above the jut of her shoulder bone. She imagined the straight slash of welted skin crying blood tears, black shimmers, and she screamed.

"Go on." His voice was calm.

"Give us this day our daily bread and forgive us our trespasses, as we forgive those who trespass against us!"

He waited for her to quiet before delivering another strike of the whip, leaving a new slash of pain on the upper right side of her back. Again, he waited for her screams to stop before adding to his creation, forming – with quick whip strokes – what she pictured as twin crosses carved into the flesh of her back.

"And lead us not into temptation, but deliver us from evil," she said, her knees shaking as she hugged the cross to keep from falling and being choked by the collar and short chain.

The priest came to her, his hands sweeping tender and leather cool over her shivering body. He turned her to face him and kissed her mouth tenderly. She tasted her tears when their tongues met.

"Truth and mercy have come together. Righteousness and peace have kissed."

He crouched, leaving her breathless, his dark gaze resting on the wet, pink splay of her cunt.

He kissed it, rubbing her slick offering over his parted lips.

"Atonement," he said, his breath a warm flutter on Katie's clit. A flicker of his tongue followed the curve of its hood, easing it up and down.

Her cheeks flooded with colour, her pain already fading. A thrilling surge of emotion threatened to spill over into a rapturous orgasm, or a wild struggle to be free.

She knew she had the power to reach up and unclasp the leash, to run away or simply ask to be let go, but she didn't do any of these things. She wanted it all. She needed it. Groaning, overcome by the intense gratification the priest's touch gave her, she pushed forward against his mouth.

"Rapture," Katie sighed, as the priest lapped the nectar droplets from her slit, his tongue a wet, slithering heat.

"Give the rest to me. Let it go. Finish," he said, pulling off his leather gloves.

He spread her legs wider as he pressed the cluster of his fingers into her, not stopping until they were deeply buried, hooked and pressing into a place that made her insides quiver.

His tongue snaked in a languid twirl through the furls of her pussy and over the knob of her clit, sliding up and down in firm knowing strokes timed with the thrusts of his fingers into her cunt. His mouth was hot, his tongue gliding with velvety strokes. His teeth raked, and he suckled until her legs began to buckle and her body accepted all of his hand.

"For yours is the kingdom, the power, and the glory of the Father, the Son, and the Holy Spirit, now and forever. Amen." Katie finished the prayer, her voice ragged, panted moans as she came – a surge into the priest's mouth. Pushing closer, shuddering release, her cunt gripped his fist as spasms of pleasure washed over her in waves. Cresting, they left in their wake a new sense of peace.

When he pulled his hand from her, she felt a trickle of come slide down her thigh like a tear she no longer needed.

"*Dominus noster Saint Michael te absolvat et ego auctoritate ipsius te absolvo*," the priest said in a low and final tone after the last pulse died.

He stood, his gaze warm as he kissed Katie's cheeks and freed her. Enfolding her in his arms, he held her close, soothing her.

"As a man thinks in his heart, so is he. Be free, Katie O'Malley."

He unclasped her leash, but the collar remained – an anchor as the priest led Katie away, absolved.

The Peanut Butter Shot

C. Sanchez-Garcia

My trainer Case is oiling my skin, rubbing it down with a camphor salve that stinks to get the sensitivity down around my penis, the nipples, and behind my ears, erogenous zones where I'm sensitive. Doc Corman, the SFCC Certification medic is waiting beside Gerry, with his little black bag and witness forms for when Case gets done with me. Burned out Gerry, tore up from the floor up, she's sitting on the locker room bench, eyes on the floor, probably thinking about sex with me or else just nothing. She gets a little more simple every day. Soon there won't be much left. My own sweet fluffer girl. She's my sexual punching bag. I work out on her. Its illegal, it's evil, but hell, we all do it. Every fighter needs a sparring partner.

They used to wrap tape around your hands to keep you from busting your knuckles up against the bones of somebody's face. Me, it's the opposite. I have to wear special gloves when I'm not in the ring. These gloves, they go for about $12,300, something like that, dermatologically custom-made. The insurance pays for them, so like I give a shit, but that's what they go for. I've got real warm soft hands. Women tell me they're softer than a baby's hands. My champion hands are insured by management for about $567,000. My tongue's insured too, definitely, so I can't drink anything hot or cold or eat spicy, which sucks but it's the job. My tongue and hands are my weapons.

I have to exercise my fingers like a rock climber, play fast glissandos on a piano and take special treatments to make them super-sensitive to touch. Hell, I can speed-read Braille. My fingertips can read someone's rising skin temperature. That's why I wear gloves. That's why management insures my hands for half a million. I have to do tongue exercises to increase my tongue's sensitivity and strength and length. I can stick my tongue a third of the way down a beer-bottle neck. Or a pussy. I can write my stage name with my tongue on a paper the size of a coin so perfect you can read it – Mack Daddy. That's how fucking good I am. Just so you know. I can pick up and read the pounding of an opponent's heartbeat pretty much anywhere on their body so you know when they're almost ready to pop and then keep them stuck tight on that knife edge of unbearable pleasure until they've got to come so bad they can't stand it and they'll do anything for you. Then you've got them. You can't count on reading their irises' dilation, because most people try to close their eyes when they're on the edge of orgasm and they're scared and they're fighting it. They don't know being scared just makes them want to come sooner and harder. I never let myself get scared because then you lose your grip on your nerves, and it's a game of playing your opponent's nerves. Never let the other guy get a hold of your nerves.

You read their breathing, because they can't hide their breathing. You read the stuff an opponent in the ring can't fake. You read the contractions along a female fighter's vaginal walls. You don't read that by putting your finger inside like amateurs think, no, because a trained female fighter can fake that. You learn how to feel it off the tiny jitter on the outside one-eighth inch of their interior labials. The jitter never lies. Most people don't know that. I know vaginas better than a gynaecologist. I have to.

The old prize fighters would bust your nose or your ribs. A punch to the kidney that would make you piss blood for a couple days. We sex fighters, we bust your will to live. We take away your will to be free. People look naked to us. We see inside your mind. You just think you know what you want, bitch. I know what you really want, because that's how I get you. That's how I take you down. I look at you bitch – I know what you want way better than you do. I know it even before you know it. That's because I see you. I see you like God sees you.

What I do takes as much training as an Olympic Karate champ. Most people don't know this either, but when you're talking to someone, most of what you're saying is subliminal, without words. In one minute, think about it, in one minute you send 3,000 signals to the person you're talking to, 3,000 non-verbal fucking signals. Think about that, that's really amazing shit. You don't even know what they are. But the real part of you that lives behind your brain, the part of you that dreams at night, that part knows. The difference between you and me – I know I'm reading you. Fuck, I know your signals before you do. I look at you, and ignore your words and read your face, the way you blink, the way you stand, what makes your voice

hake, and I've got you nailed, taco belle, I got your carbon cunt
rint, I got your pussy nailed to my bedpost. I'll be stuffin' your
uuffin' ten minutes after you tell me your name and you won't even
now why you're doing it, and before you get your little pink panties
ff, I already know just how to screw your motherfucking brains out.
know where your buttons are going to be and in what order to push
hem. I know what your secret kink is going to be. It ain't bragging if
's true, and this is true shit I'm telling you. That's all it is.

You have to feel what the opponent feels every second, even
hough they try to hide their feelings, fake out your ass, trick you. It's
he art of the soul fuck. It's fucking voo-doo. At least till someone
nprints you and puts you out of business for a while, or maybe for
ood. Or into rehab. Imprintation varies a lot. Sometimes it's a habit
ou have to shake off, like having a crush. Sometimes it can be pretty
ad. In the fighting ring, I've imprinted twenty-five women, fifteen
f them before I became SFCC Federation Champion, and also
even men. Never been beat. Ten of those women became stalkers
ecause they couldn't break the addiction to me, after what I done to
nem in the ring, and had to be locked up. Three of them self-snuffed,
st time I checked. This game is high mortality shit. Just so you
now. That's how fucking good I am. That's right.

My sparring partner, Gerry, she's about used up. Her eyes these
ays, they're like bomb craters. She doesn't shoot, doesn't snort,
oesn't smoke, but she's a drop-down fuck junkie. I'm her dealer
nd I'm her bong. That's what being imprinted means. I imprinted
er ass. Twice at the same time. Bang. Bang.

She'd do anything for me. She wouldn't be able to stop herself.
he'd gouge her eyeballs out with a spoon if I asked her to. I never
leep with her. The one time I passed out in her bed, she tried to kill
ne in my sleep with a lamp cord, to get herself free of me. Crazy ass
itch. And she'll never forgive what I did to her. She's right. Hell, I'd
ill me too.

Her eyes are like streetlights from all I've put her through. They
witch from something that you wouldn't call love exactly, but
omething like idolatry, or addiction. Sick love. And then hate. The
ate is clean. The hate part I get. Her eyes look at me, and they just
o from stop to go and back to stop. She's in a special private hell, I
now, I know, I understand that part too. She didn't do anything to
eserve it, she was just in the wrong place at the wrong time and got
erself soul-fucked out of her damn skull by a true expert. She keeps
reaking down, and the next time she tries to throw herself out a

window I might just let her. I can replace her – like that. I made he
like she is. Got her down, and sweetly twisted her nerves just th
right way with my hands and tongue, until her whole somatosensor
nervous system overheated past the edge human beings were eve
made for and dropped into the void of the High Pleasure. I kept he
that way, screaming my name until she was screaming for help an
then begging me to finish her, let her orgasm, because I always hol
out until they beg. I fucking love it when they beg.

I sexually imprinted Gerry deep and then, just because I was a
asshole that night, I imprinted her deep again twice, just to take he
away from the guy she was with, just to piss him off. Just to make
point that I could put her out of business for anybody but me. B
the time he broke the bedroom door down it, was too late, I'd take:
her mind and body down deep, really deep and fucking drowne
her soul.

You're not supposed to imprint people twice, because it brain
damages them. It's a crime against nature, they say, to do that to
human being. But like parasitic wasps – nature happens all th
time, baby.

Her blue eyes rolled back and did the fade. She was "gone" as w
say in the game. Broke. The Sweet Damnation.

"Gone" is what psychologists call "sensory traumatic imprinting"
when you push a person past the sensual input limit the huma
nervous system can bear. They say God never gives you more pai
than you can bear. OK. Maybe God doesn't, but sex fighters do. It
what we get the big bucks in the ring and boner pill endorsements o
the web to do. It can be pain or it can be pleasure or it can be to
much of both, but the key is it has to be too much. When you do tha
to a female or a male and hold them down there deep, for lon
enough, something snaps inside. It's like you drown them. It tears
hole in their ego-identity and that hole needs to be filled up wit
something fast.

The sweetest thing in all the world, the thing you just live to see, :
your opponent on her back when she's gone over, when he or she :
vanquished in a way no one should ever be vanquished. Her eyelic
open relaxed and her eyes roll up a little dead-looking and – broth
– the lights are out and there's nobody home. Truly. It doesn't la:
long. But that's when I crawl through the unlocked window of he
psyche and plant myself deep inside there. And what do I do wit
that person's soul? Whatever I want. I own it, baby. I won it fair an
square, didn't I?

It's a short window, just a few seconds before the brain fixes itself, but you can fill that window with whoever or whatever you want and there's nothing the person can do about it. You can go through rehab if you get nailed just the once, and once is all the fight ring rules allow, but if someone imprints you twice, just bang-bang while you're stuck in the zone, like say behind a locked bedroom door, Hello Gerry, well it can't be fixed. Ever. It becomes who you are after that. You'll even go through the hell of withdrawal if the person who double-dog nailed you doesn't give you some regular loving. That's a mighty fine thing, the addiction from a double imprinting. You can do a lot of stuff with that. And guys who know how, they pull in the long cream all kinds of nasty ways.

What I am, I owe a lot to Case. He's gay, but it doesn't influence him. He was a champ in the Pan European Regional, but dropped out after a bad night when he almost lost it. He never talks about it. He could have gone private, driving rich old fruit faggots out of their skulls in hotel rooms for more money then he'd get in the ring. But he won't be anybody's bitch. You can be his bitch. He won't be your bitch. He trains me for the sex fighting, and the martial arts comes from another teacher. It's complex shit.

"Okay, Doc. Let's get this going." I'll need all the time I can get to settle down before going out there. I hate this part. It hurts like hell.

"Ready for your Shot, Macko?" says the doctor. "Ready for some fun?"

"Bring it on, Doc." I try to sound cheerful. I'm not.

Case brings over the phallus sheath. I'm not hard yet, but I'm about to be very very very hard. Gerry's not allowed to handle my dick directly, not since she tried to bite it off. Case does this. The penis sheath is made from soft goat-kid leather, so that I can barely feel it when it's on. It's black and has these happy little tassels on it. It's a lot like what male strippers used to wear in clubs. Case slips my limp dick into it and pulls it up snug with a lot of empty space hanging below. It won't be empty long. Without the Peanut Butter Shot I'm nothing special, just the standard six like most guys, though women say I'm pretty thick in the girth. With the Peanut Butter Shot I get a good seven inches of purple steel to ride. Not that it matters, that's not what the Peanut Butter Shot is about. I have to wear the sheath because I'm medically certified not to have ejaculated in three days; that would get me fucking disqualified and most likely end up castrated in a dark alley if the mob has any money in this fight, and they always do. No, the sheath is there to protect my fighting weapon

till I'm in the ring, but also to protect it from me. From trying to ge
myself off after the Shot hits. To keep from fucking everything in
sight to make myself come or more likely trying to rape the living
shit out of poor Gerry.

After my cock is settled in the sheath and buckled in the back
behind my balls, Case takes my gloves off and folds them and put
them in a wooden box and passes it to Gerry. I take my place on the
bench. The bench has a hole cut in the middle like an outhouse seat
where I lie on my belly and my balls and my dick dangle down in
space without touching anything. I stretch out my hands and Case
secures them to the cast-iron bench legs, nice and tight with these
padded steel handcuffs. The kinky restraints are pure safety. They're
to keep me from trying to kill any sexually mature male in my
territorial reach two minutes from now. Which would ruin my hands.
Not to mention what horrors would happen to Gerry next. It's some
Shot, that Peanut Butter Shot.

"Bottoms up," says Doc. What happens now is something people
who don't know shit about anything make jokes about. They think
this is fun, and don't they wish they could do this. Fuck. Even sex
fighters hate what happens next, it's the most fucking humiliating
thing in the world. Though I have to admit, when you see a woman
fighter get her Shot, well, there's just something about being in the
presence of a woman who's restrained because she's bitch ass
screaming crazy in heat for the next few minutes, mister, it sticks in
your imagination, I can tell you that. You can actually smell it in the
air, the way a male dog does. When she gives you that look and sticks
her ass way up, man, it makes you want to go over and sniff her butt.

Doc takes a short little syringe from the black case and uncaps the
needle. He swabs my right ass cheek in the deep muscle part with
alcohol on a cotton ball and sticks the needle in. That's not the Peanut
Butter Shot. That's just to numb me up for the Peanut Butter Shot.
He rubs it, smacks it. "Feel that?"

"No."

Now comes the shot.

They call it the Peanut Butter Shot, because its brown and paste
and goes in like thick goo, like something you'd put on your toast. It's
a cocktail of genetically engineered hormones and ketotestosterone
in a concentrated synthetic androsteroid base and some kind of holy
miracle shit, God knows what. The insane bastards who invented
this hellacious gunk, they're fucking geniuses. The material and
formula have to be guarded like plutonium. Or the formula for

Coca-Cola. They have to keep it under control or you'd have kids brewing it up in their basements and ass raping their mothers.

I feel the pressure squeezing me as it goes in like someone jabbing my butt with a sharp pencil. He takes the fat syringe with the thick needle away and shows it to me so I know it's all in. I'm starting to feel it. Now there's a big goose egg on my ass, where the gunk is piled up. Doc Corman leans in on his palms, pressing the heels of his hands down on the lump to mash it in and work down to where the blood is.

"I can do that!" Gerry hollers. She jumps out from behind Case and shoves, motherfucking shoves Doc Corman off me.

"Hey hey!" yells Doc and Case at the same time. Then her hands are on me, pushing and squashing at the lump in my ass. And suddenly her hand is down below and she's squeezing my limp dick like choking a dead bird.

"Let me do it!" She's gonzo, junkie nuts, suddenly clawing at my dick with both hands trying to yank the sheath off. She bends down and bites me hard on the ass.

They grab her arms and she's screaming her head off and I'm screaming my head off and we're all screeching our heads off, it's a fucking monkey house in here. Case is whispering shit to her and holding her arms behind her back in a judo lock. My ass feels like hell.

Aw fuck. Aw baby. Yeah. There it is.

Hey. Hey. Now it's . . . I gotta . . . I just gotta . . .

One Mississippi . . . Two Mississippi . . .

Bingo. Limp as lo mein to railroad spike in two seconds flat. Like getting zapped in the nuts with an electric cattle prod.

Leaping lizards . . . I'm so fucked up.

Aw Jesus Christ, my balls, they're on fire. "Gerry!" My eyes are burning, my face is twitching, I can't think right. I can't see right. Holy shit. I'm so fucking ready. I'm so motherfucking – oh God;

"Gerry! You whore! You're getting your ass fucked. Gimme your fuck! Gimme it! Get over here and get your ass fucked! Do it! I command you! I order you! You fucking cunt – get your fuck over here – get your fucking fuck the fuck over here you fucking cunt . . ."

"Whoa whoa whoa!" Case is still holding down the only piece of ass in the room, a very dangerous place to be right now. Gerry's fighting to get at me and get my dick in her and I'm yelling like a caveman and yanking the padded cuffs until they dig into my wrists. My hands are turning blue I'm pulling so hard but all I can think is

I want to spear Gerry's asshole on my dick all the way in and out the other side of her navel. I want Gerry's cunt for my dinner fucking leaping lizards – "Gerry!" My skin is turning red like a nuclear sunburn. "Case! I'm gonna kill you and skull fuck you, you fag bastard!" Everything starts to turn grey for a minute and I can feel my cock almost ready to burst. Then the shot starts to settle down. My balls are still on fire but I'm a little less out of my skull by the second. The room is silent except for the sound of people breathing.

"You coming down, Mack?" says Case. His cock is pretty up there in his gym shorts too. You can make out it's standing at attention. This does stuff to him too. He's had the shot a dozen times in his fighting days. None of this is new to him. Once you taste the shot you never forget how it feels.

I flop down on the bench and let out a groan. "Fuckin' A."

"Take a minute, Mack," says Doc. "We got time. Be a good boy now."

I lie there with my eyes closed, feeling my hot meat aching down below. Feeling the jazz and the jizz and the fizz and the tingle and the jive and the jingle just under my skin. I wish these guys would get the fuck out all but Gerry. I want Gerry under my belly right now. I'm ready to fuck the moon.

"You going to behave?" says Doc.

"You watch me behave," I growl. He lets Case decide when to let me up. Case is reading me like a pro, and he'll know when I'm out of the danger zone.

We all hang around a few minutes, then Case lets go of Gerry, and watches her a second. She's out of it and she's got the shakes. I swear to God I can smell her cunt from over here. He comes up to me, and puts his hand on my neck, feeling my pulse and counting. "Let me hear you breathe."

I take a deep breath and let it out slow. He takes his hand off my neck and unlocks the cuffs. "Almost time to go," he says.

I get on my feet, watery in the knees, breathing deep. Case is holding a loose fighting stance, watching me. I can smell Gerry. I can literally smell her. My penis sheath is standing up and it doesn't even bob around it's so damn hard. I could drive it through a brick wall and that's just what I feel like doing.

Gerry is tallish and thin, with the jumpy eyes of a junkie. Wasted. Both wrists have shiny horizontal scars going across them. She was a hot piece with nice tits and a sweet round ass when I met her the first time. Now she's this.

"Gerry."

She shakes her head wildly. She's mad as hell. Mad at me. Mad at the world. Most of all, mad at herself.

"Gerry."

She's standing her ground, but everything coming off her is going right off the bugshit meter. There's only one window in the locker room and Case quietly steps around to get between the window and her and waits.

"Gerry."

"No," she shakes her head again. "You can't make me."

I pitch my voice a very particular way, one that took me years to learn. It has a way of slipping inside somebody's will if you do it just right. "Come here."

Like a bird in a snake-trance she hobbles a step forward and stops. "No."

"Come here bitch." I pump my hips a little and the penis sheath bobs stiffly. "Look what I got for you. Nice piece of candy. Come here."

Her eyes are wide and getting that empty look guys get when they're watching a good stripper. She's holding her hands up defensively in front of her, grabbing her T-shirt and clenching it and probably doesn't even know she's doing it.

Feet stanced slightly apart. Breathing hard. Nostrils dilating. Ears shifted slightly upwards. Her clit is going to be swelling and I can see the nubs of her nips against the T-shirt. Her anger, her self-hate is driving her crazy, desire and pride. She knows what she wants; she just hates herself for wanting it so very bad. I'll have to help her.

I move towards her and she looks up at me with a kind of pitiful, pleading hope. "Baby." She croaks. "I want a baby."

I hold out my hand, palm up. Her hands come away from her T-shirt. Her eyes close dreamily. She steps forward and puts my palm under her limp breast. I step close and caress her breast, like consoling a beloved, worn-out old pet. She lifts her T-shirt, showing me her chest and I caress her bare breast gently, pinching the tip of the nipple and her mouth falls open.

I feel the urge in me to be cruel to her. To do something unnecessary to her. That's the feeling I want. I need that feeling, but I need it for the ring.

"Did you ever love me?" she whispers.

"Don't be stank, skank." I take my hand away and leave her there. She sags against a locker and we all watch the steam go out of her as she sinks to the floor in a heap. "Fucker . . ." she whispers. "I hate you, you fucker."

I grin all around. Nobody grins back. "I'd say I'm ready now."

The doctor gets his stuff packed. Case has his kit and ice bucket. As we head for the door, Gerry whams her fist against a steel locker door. We all turn. Those bomb-crater eyes are fixed on my dick. "What, Gerry? What now? I got work."

"When you get back, can we . . . ? Even just a little while?"

"Fuck off, Ger." I turn to go.

"I need it!"

"I said fuck off."

"I hope she breaks you!" she screams. "I hope she breaks you out there, so you know what it's like! You fucker! You sick fuck!" She wrenches the locker open and throws the first thing she grabs, a bar of soap. It bounces off the ceiling. "I hope that woman fucking kills you!"

I blow her a kiss. "Even if she does, that won't help you, baby." We move out into the hall, the door hissing shut behind us.

The walk down the hall is always a hard time for me. It's a minefield, a mind-fuck. It's the flight of the Valkyries. It's the most serious shit there is because you have too much time to think and thinking gets you fucked up. In a little while me and this other person, we're going to come back down this hall again, but only one of us is going to be the same. The other one is going to be seriously different. One of us is going to get totally mind-raped by the one who gets to go on being normal a little while longer. One of us is going to come out the other's bitch. When you think about that metaphysical shit, sweet Jesus. You have to respect that shit.

Three fucking years. That's right, three fucking years, two of them as champ. Nobody goes three years and the game only ends one way. It ends up with you as somebody's bitch. Soon the numbers just start to scare me. Women scare the shit out of me sometimes, the thought of being some bitch's boner pony. Fuck that shit. Falling in love is a business, it's hustle and the companies who make a million off me pushing boner pills, they know how to hustle. But this. Fuck. I mean like – fuck.

This fight, it's not a fight. This fuck, it's not a fuck. The tough ain't even about tough. This is not a natural act, what we do, no. Males fighting over a female is a natural act. Conquering the female and cooling your dick off inside her, that's a natural act. A woman being taken down by a man is the most natural thing there is. That's just evolution and shit. But this thing we do, mind-fucking them. That's not a natural thing. That's the weirdest shit there is, and that's why people can't get enough and the sports biz people have to keep finding ways to push it up a notch every time. Fuck, even throwing people to lions in the Colosseum was a natural act compared to this. Lions like to eat people.

I think the walk, it's like death, and I ain't talking shit. It's like death because it's like being nowhere and between everything. It's not the locker. It's not the ring. It's concrete walls passing by. It's the world telling me, this is who you are for right this moment. You been around thirty years and change and this is what you got to show. Like my life passing in front of me. But then my dick is calling my name a good seven inches ahead of me. The dick knows what it wants. Trust the dick. And then there's this light at the end of the tunnel.

And where the light is – glory.

The hall empties into the arena entrance and I walk down the bull-run into a blaze of noise and light and total ape-shitness. Case slaps me on the ass. It's like I've just been born proper.

The bull run that leads from the hall to the centre fighting ring of the Boston Brigham Arena is lined with riot barriers to hold back the crowd from tearing pieces off me. People are holding up signs, condoms, underwear, any shit to get my attention. People waving cell-phone cameras at me. The women, they get me zinged. They're waving their panties at me. Their bras. Their bare tits. My natural tribute. They're looking at my dong in the black sheath as it goes by and I step a little flat-footed to make my weapon wave to the crowd, hello ladies. Do you love me? These are all the cheap seat mooks, crowding the barriers, trying to get in some touch. Trying to cop a feel of the glory. The air is fucking rank with pussy. Jesus Christ. Fucking pheromones. A girls' locker room, a women's fuckatorium. Women screaming, shaking their tits at me. The cult of the masculine. And I am the god of the Bullshit, the great Dionysian god of Pure Stiff Dick Bullshit – Bananarama.

I snatch a weentsy pair of pink silk thongs with tiny Betty Boops all over them, held out from the end of some hot bitch's fingers and press them to my face. Sweet Jesus. Pure wet cunt. Nothing smells finer. Nothing smells like it, fucking period, amen brother. I breathe them. I kiss them. Hold them to my face and taste them. A long curly hair stuck on the end of my tongue. I suck on it. I inhale the green seaweed smell and it makes me dizzy to fuck somebody right down on the floor right now, I don't care who. Even Gerry would look good to me right now. I hang the pink Betty Boop thong on the end of my leather-shielded dong and it waves in front of me like a little battle flag as the cheap seat mooks go out of their mother-grabbing skulls for me.

I know this shit house. It's funny how the fighting arenas all look the same after a while, only the dressing rooms are different. This is where I did this butch Russian dyke once right here back in the Juniors, before I hit the big time. Red hair, cunt hair, big tits. It was hard going, until I started punching her in the tits and it turned out she loved it. Crazy fucking bulldagger. When I finally had her pinned and I was doing her good, she had this fine little moustache that would curl up at the ends whenever she'd orgasm and do that monkey grin. I made her come three times and got a TKO off her, but I never zoned her ass out. Never did. Those real iron-ass diesel dykes, you'll never break them if you're a guy unless you've been trained for Extreme Dominant, maybe Third Degree Black Domino at the least. Even those guys almost can't ever do it. Fuck that shit. I never had any business being in the ring with her and me still in the Juniors, Christ, what a rat fuck, but I had bad management then.

Case leads me to our corner of the ring and peels the wet thong off my cock. Now there's a little wet stain on the leather from the wet silk, you can see it shine in the floodlights. I hope the cameras can pick that up. I can make the cover of *Adult Sports Illustrated* with that shot.

I raise my arms high over my head and step my legs apart. I am the God of Prick, Bananarama. Where's my virgin sacrifice?

Case reaches under and unbuckles the phallus sheath and steps aside so the cameras can get a good frame. He lifts the sheath, with a faggy flourish like a matador's cape. My righteous cock. My bazooka of justice. High and hard.

My high holy penis and I, we climb under the ropes and I take a seat on the wooden stool, a kind of tradition from the past. On the other side of the ring there's a huge swell of cheers and applause. Chanting in a foreign yik-yak language. That side of the arena, it's mostly chinks. They're here to see the cream cake I came to bake. She's a chink chick. Chink chick chink chick chink chick.

I did my homework proper like I always do, I tried to find out about this little ol' chink chick I'm here to fight, but fuck, there's nothing on her. Nothing, not a motherfucking thing. I saw the YouTubes of her fights, but I still don't know what kind of sugar and spice she's made of inside. Nobody's ever pinned her down long enough to fuck her, so nobody's figured out how to break her. She showed up out of nowhere in Indonesia, blew through the Juniors and welterweights, half a dozen men fucking blew their brains out over her after she imprinted their fag asses in just the first round, but nobody can say where the fuck she comes from. Women are scared shitless of her, Case says she can't even get a booking with a woman anymore. Maybe she should fight a Russian bulldyker, see her rat fuck that shit.

I'm still worked up. Sitting on the stool in the ring corner, I feel this sore little lump in my ass where the shot went in, not to mention where Gerry bit me. I shift and try not to sit on it. I'm jittery and hot as a stud bull in the stall.

The Boston Brigham Arena is packed to the walls, enough for a small town. The press pit is filled with reporters with gadgets stuck in their ears and eyeballs and probably up their asses. This is the big time, the real time, the old days, the truth days, the righteous days. The days of crazy pussy. Zing zoom zam pow bam Fuck!

Case yells in my ear over the crowd noise. "Don't slouch. Don't hold your breath in. Breathe out." I close my eyes, exhale and sit up straight. I put a finger to the right side of my nose, hold it and inhale into my belly slow and deep. I feel calmer. I focus my awareness on a spot just under my navel and hold it there. Lot of cigar smoke tonight. I move the finger to the other side, exhale, switch sides and inhale deep again, counting the rhythm of my heart. Better. Five beats in. Hold. Five beats out. Woof. Move finger. Inhale. Five beats. Better.

Behind my eyelids I can hear her feet shuffle-step onto the thick ninety-foot-square futon mat just in front of me. The world's biggest bed. The crowd falls weirdly silent. I open my eyes and she's just a few feet away, looking right at me, trying to get in my psychological space. My territory. Trying to spook me. Go ahead, little tit bitch.

The small, nude, Asian woman dances light as a sparrow without an ounce of fat on her anywhere. About 18,000 men all go apeshit, you can hear them yelling to put their dick up all her tight dark places. I can't even guess this chink girl's age, but from her stats she'd be about twenty-seven years. If I met her on the street I'd think maybe eighteen or finger-lickin' sixteen; she looks like a kid but she has the wizened eyes of a woman. Dark skin, no tan lines, no body hair, head hair chopped short as a nun's on top so there's nothing to grab onto, and clean muscle lines that pop out smoothly when she moves. Six-pack belly, with just the perfect layer of padding. Sweet-faced as a Buddha, with a small nose and almond eyes that look calm and alert. She radiates confidence. She radiates sex. Every man in the arena is sitting with his mouth open like a dog. I look at her bald little pussy and I'm imagining what it's going to feel like when I slip it in there nice and slow, after I've softened her up proper.

I've seen her fight clips; she's a helluva kicker, has to be because she's short. She's too damn short by the looks for most of the standing penetration positions, that's OK. I'll pin her down on her belly where she can't get at me with her feet and slip in from behind until I've got her pacified and seeing things my way.

She's moving her feet, hovering them over the mat in a perfect sweeping circle like a music-box dancer; and she has beautiful feet this girl, and moving her long-graceful hands in some kind of gesture. I've seen this little show of hers somewhere before. Old Chinese folks in the park in the morning. Tai Chi, and something else different, something with sudden precise moves. Calm and violence together. So that's her shit, Tai Chi. I can defend that shit. The foot sweeps forward and up, held aloft perfectly vertical and still as a ballerina. Not a shiver. She's got a couple moves, all right.

Man, won't she look sweet on her knees licking my meat in my hotel room tonight. Pass the soy sauce, boys, we're having Chinese. I might even break her twice to make sure she doesn't ever go anywhere. I'll need a new workout bitch to bang, because Gerry doesn't look like she'll be around much longer.

She does the pantomime thing like holding a ball in front of her, then her hands turning her mental ball upside down. Let her have her fun. I look down and my cock is so fucking solid I could hammer it through a wall. I could hammer it through her.

She hops into the air with a nice little spin kick, drops like a snowflake with her little flat chink tits swaying, tiny brown nipple nubs pointing up at the lights, and makes her invisible ball again and sways back soft as shit on her heels, arching her back like a sleek cat with faraway eyes and perfect balance, everything in place. Sweet kid.

The microphone drops down to the arena, just like in the old boxing matches. This is the only place you ever see an old-fashioned microphone anymore. The three-legged stool. The drop mike. All tradition. The religion of the masculine. The temple of the fuck. The

Killing Floor where souls die. The girl stops what she's doing and walks to her corner slowly, arrogant as a bull fighter. I watch her wiggle that narrow little chink ba dink-a-dink as she goes. The referee in black dress pants and a red and white zebra stripe shirt comes out of nowhere while I'm staring at the kid's ass, some old fuck I've seen in matches somewhere. He yanks the dangling mike out of the air.

"Good evening from the Boston Brigham Sports Arena." The crowd bites the cheese. Cheering, fuck time. "The title match of the evening. In the north corner, the challenger, and lightweight South East Asian Full Contact Division World Champion, and All Asian Dim Mak Union leader, undefeated – Tiger Lee! Tiger Lee!"

The crowd goes nuts. The air stinks with the hot chow mein breath of thousands and thousands of chink men who are baying for sex, every man gay or straight in this place wants that little woman hot and heavy on the futon mat right now. They'd sell their mothers to do her.

"In the south corner, the Sexual Federation Combat Consolidated middleweight and Western Regional Union champion, for three years undefeated, undisputed champion of the world – Mack Daddy! Mack Daddy!"

I stand up, wave my arms for the crowd and they go effing mother krunk over me, sweet fuckin' A, full-time mother. Those are my people out there. The women, giving me the look, the way the men were checking on Tiger Lee. The Boston Brigham Sports Arena sits 22,000 plus the broadcasting, and every woman in the place wants her feet up in the air and my rock-hard dong banging them bad right at this moment. Talk about glory? Baseball? Football? Fuck that. The fucking president can't touch nothing like what I got. There ain't nothing can touch this. Nothing. This is male glory. This is dick glory. This is the ultimate warrior glory. Every man wants to be me right now. And they're right to want that. I am the god. I am the stud.

There's none of this touch gloves shake hands shit when the ref brings us within striking distance in the centre of the mat, still talking his referee smack at us. Tiger Lee is looking into my eyes, trying to bore a hole into me and I'm doing the same thing, looking right at her. The ref is talking but nobody's listening because the real battle is being fought right now.

"Chink chick," I whisper at her. "Chink chick. Fucking little chink chick." I make smoochy lips at her.

She's scowling at me. Think you can out-scowl me, bitch? I'm reading you. I'm not thinking about you. I'm just playing notes on your keys, blowing notes on your holes, listening to see how you're tuned, what will make you sing me an opera when I've got you on your back, bitch. I got your number. You're going down on me chink yellow bitch smooth as green tea ice-cream, and I'm gonna make you love it, sweet thing, when I take you home tonight on a dog chain to suck my dong all night till I tell you to stop. Fuck! You little chink bitch! Fuck you little girl!

She's suspending her breath, big mistake, drives up blood pressure. That means her heartbeat will be accelerating right now, sending hot blood to the clitoral bulb and descending clitoral yoke. Is she a fucking amateur? Is she stupid? These are kid stuff, Junior League mistakes. Sinuses congesting. Slight flush around her aureoles. Capillary dilation. Rise in basal temp. Any second now.

Her eyes jink away, a fraction of a second. There it is.

That's it. Nailed you. Busted your cherry. Right then. Bingo bango. It's over. Wham bam thank you ma'am. I've got you, bitch. I've got your tits in my lips. I've got your ass in my hands. I got your cunt nailed to my bedpost. I own you, bitch. I own you right now. Just spread 'em and get this over so we go back to my crib and get it right. Don't waste my time.

I glance at her corner. Her corner lady, some old chink, looks like she didn't see it. This match is fucking over. All but the fucking part, it's over. I won. Stud wins every time.

Referee steps away. Bell rings. Ref waves his arms.

She stands her ground, but holds her shoulders in an uncertain way. Is she shook? Or playing games? I can't figure her out. I can't see how she got this far in the game by being so dumb, so out of control. She just stands there making me guess. No defence stance, no fist or posing. She stands like she's waiting for a damn bus. Or the fucking Chinese national anthem.

I'm so full of jizz and jazz, I'm so pumped I can't stay in one spot. I feel like fucking anything that walks, or crawls, or stands at attention. Staying out of kicking range, a sharp eye on her hips and feet, I'm circling all around her, owning her personal space, winding her up like a clock spring. I love that cute little chink chick ass. The arena and the crowd and the cameras go away. It's not about the money. It's me and her. It's intimate. No lover, no spouse, nobody gets more intimate than this woman and I are at this moment, because one of us is going to break the other. We are close like a fox and a rabbit are close, and I'm the fucking fox. We are the only living beings in the universe as I circle behind and she acts like I'm not here, not even turning her head, just waiting quietly. I make a sudden move, jabbing the air with my fist. Nothing doing. Is she high? Is she scared? Do I just throw her down on her back and go to work on her? This can't be it.

I circle around her and she goes on standing with her hands at her sides. I make little jabs, hit-and-run little slaps at her skin to get a feel, a read off her. She's calm. Empty. Skin feels empty. Fuck. Is she insulting me with this shit?

Slow, so slow, never turning to look at me, she lifts her hips just slightly, steps out just slightly. Lifts up her ass a fraction, just so. Passive. So, passive. So willing. Arches her back just slightly, lifting that ass. I can't take my eyes off her ass. I can't. It's like . . . it's like it's just . . . so there.

God. Damn. She's got a spooky ass on her. I . . . It's like I never saw an ass before in my whole life. Like I never seen an ass until now. Oh sweet Jesus. That ass. I just . . . I just gotta have that ass . . .

I pounce without thinking it through, trying to grab her around and pin her arms so I can ram my dick up her ass till it bleeds and – she just drops like there's eyes in the back of her head. Dips straight out of my arms like she's greased and jumps behind me.

I spin on my toes – no one there. What the blue fuck – how?

I feel the breeze, the pressure wave before I feel the edge of the foot whack my temple just in front of my right ear with perfect violence. The arena spins and the mat hits my face. Jesus. I love this girl. Sincerely. I'm in love.

I somersault to my feet and already she's on the move, a hop, a flying round house spin to nail with me with her other foot, shut me down just enough so she can pin me and go to work on my pleasure zones. I get my arm up just in time and the heel hits my elbow and for a few seconds my right arm goes numb. Her leg snaps back into a fighting stance, looks like *shoto kan* to me, and I make a loose little sideways jig just out of range, keeping my eyes on her eyes. You don't watch the hands or feet. You watch the zone of the eyes. That's where the action is. I keep my mind still, calm alert, my boner true, consulting with the jizz and the fizz, listening to my Inner Dick. No time to think how she got to me just now. This is one spooky bitch. The side of my head stings and my eye feels a little puffy but I'm OK. Not a big deal. It's not like other kinds of fighting. You knock your opponent out, you completely defeat yourself. You want to take good care of them. You want him or her wide awake so they feel every horribly sweet thing you do to them right down to the bone.

She feints with a knee, but I never look away from her eyes. I don't let myself think, just stay in the zone. Her right knee dips, which telegraphs a right fist coming at my chest; side-stepping I grab it behind the knuckles, my fingers digging into her palm, bending her fist back against her wrist, a simple Aikido bone lock – *tenkai kotegeshi* – twist the wrist, spin her around like a waltz, my hip in her belly – *kube nagi* – down with the arm and over my head she goes in a sweet ass over elbow, bam on her incredible ass.

I drop my right knee into the small of her back and yank her shoulders down, breaking her balance. I snake my right arm around in a flash, jamming the hollow of my inner elbow against her throat, centred exactly between her pert little chin and her clavicle forming a triangle with my bicep and forearm around her neck. Clasping my hands together behind her shoulder, I squeeze the sides of her throat with my arm, very hard.

Her feet are kicking, panicking, trying to stand. That's good, I want her to stand, set her up for what's coming next. I rise from my knees, pulling her up with me, clenching my arm muscles tight around her neck, stopping the flow in her jugular and carotid artery. No blood is getting up to her brain anymore. Now she's standing, trying to hook a foot behind mine and take me down but I just keep my knee in her back, easing her backwards, leaning her so her spine's resting against my knee, never letting her get her balance.

Her arms are flopping, trying to get at me, but she's slowing down. That's it little girl. You're getting very sleepy. Relax. Go to sleep now. Don't make a fuss. That's a good girl. When you wake up with my dick inside you, you're going to feel so much better. You're going to be real fine sucking me off every night for the next ten years.

Her face is turning purple and her eyes are swelling closed. Her cheeks are puffing out like a Roland Kirk solo. All the fight's drained out of her so it's safe now to keep my right arm tight around her throat and reach around with my left hand, staying under her left arm to keep her from sucker punching me in the kidney, as I scoot my left hand around her left tit. This isn't to cop a feel, I want to check her heartbeat. She's beating about 138 per minute. Dropping. She's sincerely going to sleep. She looks so sweet. 128 per minute. 110 beats a minute and her arms are hanging down and the wet little tip of her pink tongue is sticking out touching her lower lip in the cutest way. Looking over the top of her head I glance at her corner lady, just to make sure I'm not being faked. The old bat is waving her fist, yelling in Chinese or something to the referee to pull me off. She tells me all I need to know.

I see the glass eye of a TV camera aimed at us, the boom dropping down to eye level to get a good zoom of the unconscious girl's face. I smile for my fans. I look great guns right now. Who's the stud? I'm the stud. I let go of her neck and spin her limply around and then hoist her upside down, her face touching my knees, pussy almost level with my nose, knees flopping limply around my neck. Where's all your fancy dancing around now, little bitch?

I give her a hefty jog upwards like a bag of dog feed to get my arms securely around her ribs, my hands clasped tight around the small of her back. I lean back to shift her weight on my chest, my feet stanced wide apart as I get ready to start my final clit work once I've got her labial lips lined up just right. Now that I have her in position, I can feel her start to move, with the blood going back down into her head, but it's too late. Her ass is grass. I squeeze my arms hard, bear hugging all the air out of her chest, the way a boa constrictor would, squeezing tighter each time she tries to pull a breath. I have to control her asphyxiation. I want to deprive her, not kill her. Keeping the air away from her brain keeps her from fighting me and when I finally bring her to orgasm it'll be devastating, and get that chain orgasm going, bang bang bang like a string of firecrackers until her brains melt down. Guys used to hang themselves by accident trying to get that asphyxiated orgasm I'm going to break her with. Broke seven of my women in the ring doing this. If I ever have a son, I'll teach him the secret of how to do this to a woman. Or a man.

I hear a low moan from down below, and her hip jerks. Her legs open and close like butterfly wings. This is a very confused girl. I feel her trying to make a move, trying to slip out. No, you don't. I loosen my arms a second and jog her whole body back up to get her pussy up against my tongue again.

She straightens her legs and instead of pulling away slams her wet crotch into my face hard, the inside of her thigh banging up against my nose. Crazy bitch. She wants it. She's throwing the match, she wants me to keep going. Glad you're being reasonable about this.

I stick out my lips in a cartoon kiss and pick up her clit and shaft and suck it hard till I can feel all of it contained inside my mouth. She has a big clit. Almost like a tiny dick. I give her another bear hug to keep her brain from getting smart, but she does it again. Throws her pussy up hard against my face, almost tipping me over. I've practised this move with Gerry on a balance beam. I'm a lousy tipper baby.

Fuck, I can't breathe.

Her thighs are like steel bands locking around both sides of my head. Bending her knees for leverage she presses her cunt up against my face as tight as an oxygen mask – but no oxygen.

Crazy chink bitch – she's smothering me with her cunt!

I don't stop, I keep working the clit, shaking her from side to side, trying to get her legs from around my head so I can catch a breath. I'm being smothered by an octopus. And then I feel it down below. Oh sweet Jesus . . . that's . . . that's good.

She's got me in her mouth, deep throating me, laving that hot tongue around and around, in constantly moving rhythm. Her tongue work is fantastic. I've never felt anything like this in my life. My chest is spasming, screaming for air and I don't even care.

But there's the jitters coming off her interior labia. She's losing it too. She's so busy strangling me and making me come she can't fight what I'm doing to her. I bear-hug her ribs till I can feel them bend and for just a second that tongue motion hesitates. Then it comes back.

This is the craziest goddamndest thing that has ever happened to me in three years in the professional ring. I'm asphyxiating her ass, getting her off at the same time, I know she's absolutely going to lose it any second, I've got her right on the edge and this whole time she goes right on sixty-nining me. She's licking my dog like an angel and strangling me with her legs and I'm dying on my feet and things are greying out and all I can think of is how I've just gotta come in her mouth before I die.

This is a race to the finish line chased by black fire-breathing hounds of lust. This is the twilight zone. This is an insane nightmare wet dream. We're racing balls to the walls against each other for our lives, for our souls, racing against the pleasure that will drown and enslave whoever orgasms, giving it all we got, no concentration left to resist dropping into the void. Whoever makes the other come first, goes home with that person as their slave.

Grey turns to tunnel vision. My ears are ringing and my legs are wobbling. I can't fight it. I'm going down, I'm gonna shoot my load down her gullet before I hit the floor – but . . . the fuck. Here it comes, the ripples against my tongue. I'm taking her down with me, fighting to nail her even as the waves of ecstasy wash over me, thrilling me, curling my tongue-tip downwards and working her G spot, and sucking her clit at the same time. I push back the clitoral hood with the tip of my tongue, feel that tiny spaghetti noodle tip of a glans and work the glans as I feel my balls squeeze and the Roman candle goes off in her mouth. Her thighs let go and pump wildly at my mouth, out of control, and I feel those firecracker waves spasming her vaginal walls, squeezing my tongue.

Have I been asleep?

I'm lying on my back looking up at the big floodlights. My head is throbbing, and I feel something wet under my nose. My eyebrows are itching. What am I doing, what is this place . . .

Blank. There is this huge blank space where I don't remember anything. Like being dead. Oh no. Oh no. Oh no. Not me, please God no. I'm think I'm gonna be sick.

I can't get up, I'm weak as shit. I roll over on my side and try to let my stomach settle, feeling that little lump in my ass where the shot went in. I'm in the Broke Zone. Wide open. How long have I been lying there with my eyes rolled back while she ran barefoot through my brain?

A motion next to me gets my attention. I glance over, and she's there too, just a few feet away. Stretched out on the mat. Her nose is bleeding. She's got hundred-mile eyes, like she's in another world, shaking her head, her legs jerking like a spastic sock puppet. Her muscles are messed up. Her reflexes are totally fucked up. She's a spaz case. She looks high as a kite. Her eyes roll over and meet mine and I know those eyes. I've seen those eyes looking up at me from the mat thirty-one times. And son of a bitch – I'll bet I've got those eyes too.

I nailed her. I know I did. Drove her right into zombie land. Knocked her out of the fucking world. We had each other. Together. At the same time. This has never ever happened that I ever heard of. A simultaneous imprintation orgasm in the ring. We knocked each other right the fuck out.

In all my life I've never seen anybody look at me the way she is right now. Soft. And she means it, I know she does. She's in love. She wants me to love her, and I want to love her too. We've got respect. I never felt this way in my life. We could stop this, we could stop this right here, and be lovers. Real lovers. In love lovers. I could lie next to her at night and we'd hold each other tight and just tell each other about our love.

She rolls over on her belly, with those soft wounded eyes and tries to crawl over to me. Her lips move. I reach out my hand and gently wipe away the blood from under her nose and she lets me. Her hand brings mine to her lips. She licks her blood off my hand and holds it against her face.

The bell rings, ending the round, and Case is running, and the

Chinese woman from her corner is running. We ignore them, gazing into each other's eyes. We can do this if we want. We can end this and be together.

Case hauls me to my feet and I stagger on watery knees, leaning against him as he brings me to the corner and drops me on the stool.

Tiger Lee and me, we're both looking at each other across the mat like besotted schoolkids. We're both fucked up behind the eyes. She looks lost. As she sees my eyes on her she looks away and then starts to stand. Her corner woman puts her hands on her shoulders and shoves her back down. They're not playing for the audience, it's real.

The old chink woman grabs a towel that's been soaking in ice water and splashes it on her like a cold shower, trying to get that basal temperature down, trying to shock her out of her dreams and back into the real world.

Case is slapping ice water on me trying to cool me off. But it's not working, what Case is doing. I want to say something, I don't know what to say. I don't want to do this anymore. Something's happened. I'm feeling it. I'd do anything for that woman right now, anything she asked. Something broke. It's bad. It's bad this time. I'm balls deep in the shit and upside down. Fuck me. I look across the ring at Tiger, and I just want to be alone with her and just . . . just do any shit she tells me. It's all gone out of me. She's turning her head, looking at me too and the demon light has gone out of her. The corner lady keeps grabbing her by the chin, turning her head away to look at her, and Tiger looks pissed. Case is looking at me too, disturbed, checking me out.

"How we doing on points?" Trying to talk my ass out of this. But Case is zeroed in on me, reading me, passing his hands over my head, scrutinizing my face.

"Fuck the points," says Case, "We're not fighting for points. Mack, you gotta tell me. That was seriously the weirdest shit out there I've ever seen. What the fuck happened out there? Be straight, if you lie I'll know. Did she get in your head?"

I nod, all beat down.

"Are you fucked up?"

I shake my head. I don't want him to know. I want to get back out there to be with Tiger. She's looking right at me and arguing with her corner lady. Things are fucked up over there too.

Case slaps my cheek, hard. "Macko, you in there? Anybody in there? Are you fucked up?"

"No."

"You look fucked up, all right? You look seriously fucked up. Is she in your head Mack? Did she get you?"

I nod.

Case takes a deep breath and drums his fingers on my shoulder. "Holy shit," he mutters. "Holy shit. Holy fuck, this is bad. Mack, this is very bad. I'm calling it."

I grab his bicep and squeeze. "Don't you call shit!"

"Mack, you're over the line here. Let go." He pulls my hand off. "I gotta call it, man. I'm stopping the fight."

"Don't you call shit! Don't you fucking call shit, I swear I'll beat your ass."

"She zoned you bad, Mack."

"I zoned her ass too!"

"Hell you did."

"I did – fuck, just look at her. I zoned her ass good."

Case takes a long sideways look at the fucked-up shit going on in Tiger's corner. "Jesus fuck." He mutters. "This is seriously the weirdest shit I've ever seen."

The referee is in the centre ring, looking from corner to corner and tapping his wrist. Case holds up four fingers. Give us four minutes before the bell. Tiger's chink corner lady yammers some yik-yak shit at the ref and he throws up his hands and backs off to go talk with the judges.

"Now you listen," says Case, serious as a pregnant girlfriend, "listen good. She zoned you, Mack. You're screaming zonked, man. I can see it. A dope can see it. It's in your eyes. It's in your voice. It's in your skin. She fucked your soul. She chewed your brain, man. Maybe you nailed her too, I don't know, I can't take a chance. You're my fighter, she's not. I'm responsible for you. She really fucked you up the ass that time and if she nails you again that's a double imprint and your brain will be seriously scrambled for the rest of your sorry ass life. Rules say you have to stop the fight before that happens."

"Fuck that!"

"Mack, you stupid fuck—"

"I nailed her too. I zoned her, Case, I'm telling you so help me Jesus, I zoned her ass—"

"She's gonna kill you, Mack!"

That stops me. His voice is trembling, practically crying. "You're out of your league. You lose this shit, you'll be double-dummied by the same person, you'll be a wasted brain-dead-fuck up like Gerry.

And this bitch can do it. I'm calling it. You're better off losing the belt than losing your soul."

The ref comes back out and he's heading towards us. Case starts to speak and I slug him in the gut with my elbow and the air wheezes out of him. "Shut the fuck up," I whisper. "You ain't calling shit. I'm doing this." Before he can speak I stand up quick, make fists and pat my fists together. Let's go. Let's do this.

Case is all kinds of right. I know it. We're all way over the line here. We're in the fucking Twilight Zone. But I want her. It's not the championship belt. Fuck the belt. I want her because I want her. She's in my head. I was always scared of this, but now it's happened and it's not so bad. Maybe this is what it's like to be zoned, I don't know. But I want this bitch so bad it kills me. It's all I can think of, all I'll ever want. She's enough. We'll quit when this is over. Go off somewhere by ourselves and make babies. But she leaves here with me or else, and I don't even know what "or else" is. If this is what the sweet damnation feels like, I'll have to live with it.

Tiger is standing up too. She looks baked. I can do this. I can score this bitch and take her home. Fuckin' A. Stud wins every time. Definitely. The ref claps, points – bell rings.

I bounce a little on my toes to get it going. But it's not going. She's coming out cautious now, bouncing on her toes like me, shaking her head, making her swollen breasts bounce to get my attention down, away from her eyes. But I'm watching her eyes. I'm on her. But the eyes are different. I send out my senses and feel her vibes, sniff the air, get the wind of her and nothing comes back that makes any sense.

I keep moving, circling around her space. She's forced to respond to me, to react to what I'm doing, keep me from getting behind her. I'm leading her. Her stance is just a little sloppy. Legs too far apart, because of the sensitivity down there. Basal tempo is high, sinuses congesting, nipples swollen and dark. Interior labials protruding, swollen, the clitoral hood down all the way over the glans. She's hopped. She's chopped on sex. She got me off once, it'll be harder to get me off a second time. I can use that. Women are the other thing, you get them off once it's easy to get them off again. I can use that too. She's breathing harder, her sinuses swelling. She can't hide it from me. She's so wide open, I can see everything. Her hands flex with that old Bruce Lee "come and get it" gesture, but I'm working the outside circle, waiting to see my shot, listening to my inner voice.

I can bag you, bitch, definitely I can bag you. Stud wins every time. Definitely definitely definitely. Sweet Jesus.

She jumps at me. I keep moving, not a flinch. It's the old days. The bad days, the great days. They're back and I'm movin' in the spotlight and I'm going to bag me some good bitch. Come on. Come on.

I waggle my hips, make my phallus dance for her and the crowd loves it. It gets her attention for a fraction of a second and she drops her eyes to it. I pounce and she skips back, startled, trying to hide it, but I see it, just for a moment. A bit of fear. The inner conflict as she wants to surrender to me and be taken, which is what a woman is hard-wired to want, but there's still that killer instinct she's trained so hard for.

She steps her left foot back and dips into a small crouch, she doesn't know what to expect, she's just being ready. I'm not thinking. I'm not feeling. I'm in the moment. I'm in the Zen. I'm just waiting for something I don't even know what.

She backs off, shaking her head. And I feel it, it hits me, just psychically, like being punched in the soul.

I can't do this. Not like this. She comes towards me, warily. Arms out. I throw myself down to the mat, spin on my heel, sweep her legs out and she doesn't fight me. She drops and in a flash I'm on top of her.

She doesn't fight. She pulls me on top of her, puts her lips to my face, peppers my face with butterfly kisses and puts her tongue in my mouth. We lie like this for the longest time. Just kissing. That's all. That's all. Like kids. I haven't just kissed a girl in years. I feel shy, motherfuck, I forgot what it even feels like to be this shy.

Then it starts. The booing. All around us the crowd is freaking out. They came here to see some blood. To see some soul getting fucked.

The crowd. The cameras. The fans. The contracts. The endorsements.

Yeah.

Piss off.

My messengers race over her body and tell me things. Her sensitive places, mapped. Her state of arousal, calculated. But I don't want to zone this bitch. I want to give her pleasure. It's enough. I feel right now that I'd do anything she tells me, anything. But still . . .

I slide my left hand down her right lateral nerve meridian and feel the change in her skin. Her right ear, secondary zone, setting up the primary zones. My fingertips touch behind her right ear, caress. My other hand reaches behind her head, tips her head back and I nuzzle her throat as I run that hand back down, tapping ragtime at the sweet sensitive nerve clusters along her belly.

Her body responds. Then I feel it, her hands on the move,

touching me there – aw fuck – and there, and then there, oh the little chink skitch, she knows me, she knows me. A pinch that makes me want to hammer my cock in her and give it up. But she changes course, her tongue is still in my mouth, kissing. The tongue that broke me for the first time and sent me into the zone. It tastes like Juicy Fruit gum. She's not trying to break me. She's trying to please me. The crowd can't see it. All they see is two people lying quietly on the mat in each other's arms, going slow. They're screaming bloody murder at us. They want the porno they paid long green for.

Her finger explores my anus, she scoots down to get some leverage and I feel that finger going in. I grunt my approval and relax my butt for her.

It lands on my neck, wet, clammy, small. It breaks the spell we're weaving for each other. I reach behind and pick it off me.

The pink thong.

I rise up and Tiger's eyes pop open, instantly feeling the disturbance, the rude breaking of focus. Her head shakes – what?

I'm looking at the direction it came from. Case is wigging out. He grabs the three-legged stool and throws it down on the mat. He shakes his fist at me.

I look down at her. Her painful little girl face. What am I doing . . . Tiger, honey pie . . . what are we doing? You and me?

I climb off her, holding the pink thong in my hand like a guilty piece of forbidden fruit. I stagger up and look at Case. He's holding his hands out, waving What the Fuck at me. Tiger gets up slow, not looking at me, standing solidly, looking over at the woman in her corner who's doing the same shit like Case. Fuck. Aw fuck.

The ringside mooks, throwing their cigars at us. Throwing programmes and chewing tobacco tins, any shit they can grab. A used condom soars by and splats near Tiger's sweet, deadly little feet.

You fuckers. Oh you fuckers.

She's looking at me. My training, my radar goes out. I read her body, her face, the set of her jaw. Everything, the blink of her eye, every drop of sweat on her golden chink skin is calling to me – we don't need to do this anymore. Fuck everybody, it's just us that matters. Walk away, just us.

I feel my eyes burn, go red with pain. Suddenly I feel like just another naked man with a hard-on in front of a big crowd of people. What she did to me, tore the scales from my motherfucking eyes. It's like I can see and I don't want to see. I was happy before. I'm fucked.

Case is right, we're all fucked up the ass in this place. I'm nothing but a dancing monkey with a boner.

The ref is coming over, people are still yelling shit. He gets one word out – "Forfeit—" and Tiger hops up in the air like a mad bastard. Her fast right heel fires off a warning shot past the ref's lip. Back up you fat fuck. This ain't about you.

Her eyes jink ever so slightly towards the bull run. Let's go. Naked. Like Adam and Eve. Innocent again. Let's just walk the fuck out of this shit hole together and never look back. I'm reading her, looking for tricks, but there's not. She's not lying. Her eyes plead. I'll bet a motherfucker this is the first time those strong eyes have ever pleaded for anything in her whole goddamn hard-ass life. Ever. But . . .

Tiger baby, no.

We're gladiators, babe. It's who we are. And like the old gladiators, we're still slaves. We're the slaves of bullshit. We're still the glamour bitches of the motherfucking sons of bitches who paid for our training. They own shares of our stock. They own the soap in our showers. They own our contracts. Hell, girl, they own our asses.

Tiger baby. You sweet thing. No.

I shake my head. She's pissed. The crowd. The cameras. The endorsements. It's all going. You fuckers! Ah – this motherfucking world! Why can't they just leave us be?

I'm still holding the pink thong. I throw it. I don't know why I do it. I throw it because I'm holding it. I throw it because she's stomping towards me. I throw it in her face.

She freezes in a fighting stance. She picks it off very, very slowly, with huge dignity and tosses it away. She glares at me with her sharp teeth showing and her fists are clenched tight. The bell rings. End of round two.

Aw fuck. This fucking world.

Case picks up the stool and sets it back up. As I head back to my corner, I look out over the ropes at the flush big-money dicks in their pimp-ass suits, breezy dime pieces in their fancy gowns, people never hungry for anything a day in their life, judging me. Like they know shit. Like they can judge me. They think they paid some big cream for a ticket and that gives them the right to see a soul get raped in real time for fun and profit. Gets the ladies hot. Beats their cakes. Give it up in the back seat of them long rides. You fucking mooks. You think you're fancy shit. I read you. I read your eyes. I read the way you hold a smoke. I read your skin. Your breath. I read your mama, in two fucking seconds flat I know her better than you, because the truth is there's nothing there to know. You're nothing. You fucking mooks.

"Talk to me, weeble."

I drop down on the stool and the little lump in my ass is still there. "Almost had her."

"Doing what?" says Case, all up in my grill now. "Cup cakin'? Kissy face is not the game, Macko."

"Case, tell me. What the fuck about this is a game? Tell me that one time, Case. Where in this shit we do was there ever a game? Is Gerry a game? Am I a game?"

"You know what? I think you are. You're a game, Mack. She's playing you. She nailed you, zoned you flat. She's in your head. You need to cut your losses. Pull out and let me call it."

I grab a handful of ice from the bucket and mash it against my face. "No way. Go fuck yourself."

"I'll tell the press it was my decision. We'll let the title go this time, get you straightened out and set up a rematch. Big bucks. Match of the century. We'll hype it up stellar. Sometimes you just gotta embrace the suck and fight another day. I'll call it and we'll come back when you've got your marbles right."

"I done told you, Case. You ain't calling shit."

"That's how you want it?"

"That's how I fucking want it. Nobody's going to make a rematch, they don't let you do rematches. Nobody'll endorse me. I'm about to lose everything, Case. And you know what? I don't know if I care. Answer me something. When did they stop throwing people to lions?"

"What?"

"Those dumb-ass lions. When did they stop throwing dumb shits to lions?"

Case sighs. Glances at his watch. Pats my cheek. "What makes you think they ever stopped?"

"How much?"

"Thirty seconds."

"Don't you call shit."

"Then shut your shit down, peanut," says Case in my ear. "Stop with the goo-goo shit. You're not a lover, you're a fighter. She's prey. She's an opponent. She's meat. That's all she is. Fight the meat. Bag this little bitch and let's go home."

"Case—"

"*Bag this bitch!* Bag the bitch! Bag her, get her fucked and let's go home."

"Bag the bitch. Just bag the bitch!"

"Bag the bitch."

The bell rings. I'm up. I'm on it. Bag the bitch. Get her fucked. Go home.

She leaves her corner, moving easy, staying out of range, and then stops, fixing me with those eyes like gun sights. She has wild eyes, I can't read them. I'm looking right at her and for the first time, I don't know what the fuck, I can't feel it, I don't have a clue about her. She holds her palms out and presses them down slow, feet together like a dancer, watching me, focused as a snake on a rat. Her belly swells with the slow intake of her breath. That, now that I can read. It's a simple message to me, that little belly breath.

She's not fucking with me anymore. One of us isn't walking out of here. She wants it all.

OK. Fuck you too then, bitch.

You want to play like that, we can play like that.

No more strategy, no more thinking. My body is telling me – you don't seem to know what you're doing anymore, asshole, step aside and let me handle it. I sink into some place deep inside and stay the hell out of my own way.

Her belly moves. Deep breath. Me. Deep abdominal breath. Fist in palm. Press down. The dumb fucks can see us even from the cheap seats and the overhead TV monitors and the entire Boston Brigham Sports Arena, and hell yes, even they get it, they get it all at the same time. This shit isn't fun anymore. A man and a woman, drawing their swords. Blades out. The whole joint turns silent as a funeral.

Come on, babe.

Let's get serious.

Gladiators, we. Purified. Sanctified. Bona fide.

We charge straight at each other.

Our hearts jacked, two mad bats mating by radar, twisting and spinning, colliding like planets, ripping into each other suspended in bright camera lights. Neither of us getting what we're after, but feeling the electric zing, coming so close, so close each time we touch skin.

I move fast, never letting my feet get too far apart, ready to step and jink and jump. I dart in fast, breaking her personal space – her eyes widen a fraction, dilating nostrils – bingo bango, I fake a spin at her face and it brushes her back. I keep coming at her and she's back pedalling, snapping off front kicks, just little bluffs that stop an inch from my face. She can fight backing up. That's pretty damn slick, you chink-ass bitch. A lot of people don't know how to do that. It won't save you from me.

A front snap kick, but this time she plants her foot, and tries to drill me in the heart with a surprise straight knife hand that says it all. Me, side-stepping, grab the wrist, twist – Sankyo bone lock – and I see the dark flush of dilating capillaries in her aureoles as she responds to getting caught. She hugs her captured elbow in tight against herself, jumps straight up and flips forward in a mid-air somersault, risking snapping her wrist, but her hand slips right out of mine. Sweet Jesus. Genius. This gorgeous little gutsy woman.

A sudden spin on my toes and I see her hopping just to the side of me. I fake a roundhouse that makes her raise up her guard against a head shot and – pow! The ball of my foot zaps the connective tissue of the sartorius muscle of her right inner thigh dead fucking nuts perfect, beautiful, and that leg is toast, brother. She hops back, her eyes narrow with pain. Got you, breezy. Let's see you jump around now, you nasty little fuck. You can't do shit with that leg.

Smackdown City, Kitty. You lose, coose. Prepare to be fucked righteous.

A tear.

A single tear on her face. Not of pain. Or hate. Or rage. Or sad. Or anything I can name. One little tear.

It smokes my dick.

Fuck this shit. Fuck all of it. I'm done. My lips move. I turn away from Tiger. Me, at the ropes, yelling. Me, spit flying at the half-assed front row of fat-cat cigar-sucking widow-and-orphan-screwing, motherfucking weezers.

"You fat smug sonzabitches – fuck you in the ass – all of you!" I hold up my finger.

Total eargasm. The arena goes bat shit. Booing. Screaming. Stuff flying in the air. The camera boom whizzing in for a close-up. I am destruction. I am Shiva. I am blind Samson, pulling the motherfucking temple down around their ears. I am free – at last. Free of all the bullshit. Oh God, we can do this. Tiger baby, we can really do this together.

"You don't own our asses! We're not circus animals fucking for you! I want out! We're free! She's free too! We're all motherfucking free! I'm fr—!"

It must be the second knuckle of her right middle finger, pointed like an arrowhead, the most precise bone hit you can make and solid enough to break wood, that strikes precisely, beautifully, smack bang excellently against the very end tip of my coccyx bone at the base of my spine. It hits my sciatic nerve like an iron nail swung from the end of a baseball bat.

The agony is nauseating. Way beyond getting kicked in the balls, my whole lower half goes down and I fall into the ropes, bounce backwards and drop like my spinal cord has been severed. I feel like I've been shotgunned in the nuts. My spine can't bear my weight. I can't even stand the pain enough to get my feet under me. I'm twisting around on my side like a worm trying not to piss myself while my spine sends lightning bolts of boiling lead from my ass to my skull. My fingernails dig into the mat and I discover I'm biting the fabric with clenched jaws. My stomach heaves and I try to vomit but even that hurts too bad. I'm gagging on my puke.

Make it stop, somebody. Please God. I'm so fucked.

And then the pain does stop. Just like that.

There are many qualities of pleasure. I've been trained in all but one. The pleasure of terrible animal pain very suddenly relieved. That is a pleasure of the soul. This pain, to be suddenly delivered of this pain makes you want to beg for mercy.

Two gentle fingers pressed on nerve centres on my ass cheek, held exactly right so that I can't feel anything as long as she goes on holding me there.

"Piece of shit," she whispers in my ear. I glance over my shoulder and she's smiling sweetly as a little girl with a sucker and hauling that spearhead knuckle back to do one more piece of major damage to me.

And . . . there . . . is . . . not . . . a motherfucking . . . thing . . . I can do about it.

The knuckle spear lands on the exact spot where the Peanut Butter Shot went in a lifetime ago. The spot where I've been feeling that little lump.

Her knuckle absolutely jambasticates the lump, like a fucking asteroid hit, exploding what was left of a very rudely interrupted syringe injection of undistributed hormone into my system, a little well of hormone that wasn't worked in, a little goodbye gift from screwed-up Gerry.

My dick, which had been starting to sag, springs up so hard the glans is swelling like a purple plum. My skin burns again and my balls feel like they're turning into balloons. Leaping fucking lizards – Bitch! Gonna fuck up your shit bitch – I grab her shoulders to throw her on her damn belly and bust both her goddamn arms and ram seven inches up her tailpipe and—

Aw – fuck . . . !

She lifts those fingers from my ass.

I don't hear myself scream, I just feel my throat go raw. The pain has been building up and explodes in a bolt up my spine and this time I do let go and go sick on the mat. But the pleasure is there too, rising from my balls like ice with the fire, overwhelming me, filling my senses, stunning me with pure overload. I can't think straight. Every nerve is screaming shit in my skull at me. Then her fingers dig in on my ass, blocking the nerve centres, like shutting off a fire hydrant of pain.

She rolls me on my back, keeping her fingers on my ass, straddles me and slips me inside her pussy with that sweet smile. She digs her free hand between my legs and presses her finger hard on my perineum so I can never ejaculate until she releases that finger, and begins pumping her hips on me, working my hopped-up cock. I try to pull out but I can't. Her pussy muscles are so strong it's unbelievable. She's squeezing and massaging me like a fist with just those muscles and when I try to push her off she just squeezes my cock like a python and won't let go. I feel like I've got my dong up an industrial vacuum cleaner hose. I can't pull out. I feel the pleasure building, the glans swelling until it feels like it wants to split wide open and she bears down on that pussy squeeze until my eyes are bugging out of my head.

She squeezes squeezes squeezes – BITCH! Sweet Jesus! I feel myself come, but I can't ejaculate and the orgasm just keeps going and going and it fills the universe of devils and angels yammering in my head. She squeezes and rocks me and I come again. And again. Wave after wave, getting stronger and longer each time like a gigantic sneeze building up in my dick I can't get off. She can do this to me all night without stopping, making me come over and over without ever getting off any kind of release. The back pressure building up makes my balls ache.

She pumps her hips, rocks and screws me like a belly dancer, and she sees my face scrunch up in male ecstasy again and again. My head is pounding like I'm being beaten on my skull with a golden sugar-coated brick. When I try to throw her off, try to fight back, she lifts her fingers off the nerve centres in my ass cheek only a little bit, just to give me a little taste of what's building up there, and I go limp with my teeth biting my tongue, the agony mixing in a sensuous brew with the unbearable pleasure and I know what's coming.

She reads me like a pro and works my nerves with exquisite control. It's beautiful work. Fucking beautiful. Gorgeous craftsmanship, what she's doing to me. She holds me perfectly on the razor edge a long, long time and I'm flopping my head side to side like a spastic and arching my back and I know what I look like to her because I've seen so many women losing it all like this under my expert hands. It's the sweetest sight in the world.

She sees what she's been waiting for in my involuntary responses. Throwing back her shoulders, she suddenly jerks both her hands away and up in a huge gesture, holding them over her head, fingers spread wide in victory.

Release the flood gates of sensation. Let loose the howling hounds of pain and pleasure.

Fiery electric agony and stinging ecstasy flood my nerves as the whole neural tsunami lets go and explodes together in my skull in a sunburst of white-hot nonsense blasting away everything I've ever known. Everything I've ever been.

Silence. Peace.

Bliss. Oh, bliss.

Stillness.

Moonless night.

Nothing.

Her voice is whispering in my ear filling my starving awareness with only her presence. Only the woman is real. All my life until now has been a dream. There is only the woman now and forever.

"La Noy."

"La Noy." My lips move.

"La Noy."

"La Noy."

"My secret name – La Noy."

"La Noy."

"Love me."

"Love you."

"Belong to me.'

"Belong to you."

"Anything for me."

"I'll do anything for you."

"Slave."

"I am your slave."

"Yes."

"Yes. Yes! God, yes! I love you!"

The death throes of love.

She climbs off me and gives a waist-deep bow to the crowd and then to her corner. Her corner lady bows back reverently, palms pressed together in *namaste*. She stands towering over me and looking down at me. When she turns her back and steps several feet away, my body and soul cry out to her. She gestures for me to come to her and I bawl like a newborn baby. She holds out her foot to me.

I'm whimpering. Drooling. My tongue is sticking out, dry. I'm so thirsty all of a sudden. But she waits for me. Look at her waiting. She's so patient. She's so good to me. Gratitude floods me, and I feel tears. I raise my face so she can see my tears.

I used to know . . . I used to know . . .

I roll onto my belly and try to stand, but the spinal pain drops me. My loving goddess. I crawl on my belly because I can't stand up, but I need to go over to her because that is what she wants.

She holds out her foot, shakes it impatiently. I'm so slow. I'm such a busted-up piece of shit. I want to crawl faster for her, I just can't. I crawl on my belly, ignoring the pain because La Noy needs me to do something and I must do what La Noy needs me to do. So she'll know how deep is my love for her. Then La Noy will love me more.

I inch up on my elbows, grinding my teeth against the burning in my ass, stretch out my mouth in delicious anticipation. As I feel her warm toes brush my grateful lips, far away a bell is ringing and the stadium crowd is standing and cheering for her. Cameras are flashing. Who are all these people?

i live

i die

for you . . .

La Noy.

Dr Mullaley's Cure

Delilah Devlin

I'd been warned that the doctor was a bit eccentric. That he dabbled in machinery and had been ostracized by others in his profession for the lengths he went to please his patients.

"You'll never find another employer," I was told. "Not once they see your only reference is Doctor Mullaley." The mad Irishman. The charlatan who promised cures to bored housewives and whose waiting room hadn't been empty since I'd arrived for my first day's work. If I hadn't already been turned away at every other respectable physician's practice, I might have heeded the advice. However, those warnings only served to stir my interest.

I was intensely curious about the nature of the doctor's cures, and even more so about the conditions he treated, but they were only spoken of in whispers and never in the presence of an unmarried woman. Which made me wonder why he'd hired me. Not that I complained. One glance at his tall rangy frame, frosty blue eyes and dark, slicked-back hair, and my misgivings evaporated.

However, my curiosity about the man and his practice wasn't to be satisfied at that moment because the doctor waved me towards the reception desk where I worked at fitting in patients who walked in without an appointment. A task I found akin to cinching in the waist of a corset. There was only so much ribbon one could pull before something gave.

That something was the inimitable Mrs Davies. She arrived in a dudgeon. Cheeks flushed, eyes a little wild. It was a very balmy afternoon, and the painstaking curls at the sides of her cheeks had wilted and were stretching towards her jaw like earthworms. I couldn't help staring while she tapped the counter with her finger, insisting her needs were of the highest import. If she didn't receive a treatment that afternoon, *somebody* would hear about it.

At wit's end, I gave her a false smile, said I'd find the doctor, and escaped down the corridor to the treatment rooms.

The corridor was as handsomely appointed as the waiting room with rich oak panelling below the rail, and burgundy brocade above it. But gaslight sconces were placed so far apart that shadows loomed between the doorways.

I paused at the first room to listen, hoping to hear the low timbre of the doctor's voice. Faint moans came through the door, but since they didn't have an urgent edge, I hurried to the next and pressed my ear against the wood.

Hands curved over my shoulder. "Pardon me, Nurse Percy." The doctor firmly pushed me to the side and strode into the room.

Glancing around his tall frame, I spotted Mrs Headley who lay on a table that tilted with the lower half split in two.

My jaw sagged as I noted that while she was clothed in a sack-like gown, Mrs. Headley lay bared from the waist down, her legs strapped to the split "legs" of the table. Her fingers dug into padded handles at the sides. Most curious, there was a long, slender trough running from a tank latched to the ceiling, very like a toilet's reservoir. The trough emptied into a funnel, which ran into a tube. The tube passed through a device with turning wheels that clicked like a clock's inner gears, and then ended at a nozzle that spurted water in rhythmic pulses towards the juncture of Mrs Headley's thighs.

How odd, I thought.

Mrs Headley moaned. Her gaze roved restlessly until she lighted on the doctor. "Please, Raymond, I can't take much more. I'm very sure I'm ready for the next stage of my treatment."

The doctor stood between me and Mrs Headley so I couldn't see what he did, but then he aimed a frown over his shoulder. When he turned back, I entered the room and shut the door behind me, staying quiet as a mouse. He turned off the nozzle. The rhythmic splashes stopped, but wet slurping sounds filled the silence.

"I feel . . . nearly . . . oh, the agony . . . oh, doctor!" Mrs Headley gave a choked little scream, her upper body arching on the table before settling again. Her flushed cheeks shone with sweat, but the smile she gave the doctor was so filled with gratitude I felt a stirring of something akin to pride for the doctor's skill.

However, pride wasn't what tightened the feminine parts of me. Somehow, just knowing where the doctor's hands were made the room feel quite warm.

Doctor Mullaley pulled down his patient's gown, patted her hand

and turned, drawing up short when he spotted me standing in front of the door. He jerked his chin to indicate I should precede him.

Feeling nervous and a little embarrassed by what I'd witnessed, I stepped into the hall and wrung my hands. "I wouldn't have interrupted, doctor," I blurted, "but there's a woman at the reception desk demanding an appointment. Frankly, I thought she'd push right past me to find you if I hadn't said I would go."

"Let me guess, Mrs Davies?"

I nodded.

He sighed and looked up and down the hallway. "I have another hydropathy machine in the treatment room at the end of the hallway. While you were spying, did you happen to notice what I did to turn it off?"

"The hose from the reservoir? Yes."

"The reverse turns it on. Take Mrs Davies there. Find her a gown and help her out of her clothes. Start the machine. I'll be along when the others have finished their treatments." He gave me a narrowed glance that seemed to note my appearance for the first time. "After you've settled her, find me. I think you might work out after all."

I nodded, blushing beneath his approval and walked on air back to the reception room. Even Mrs Davies's rude behaviour as she complained all the way down the hallway couldn't dampen my mood. She didn't relent while I undressed her until it came to her corset. Claiming I'd scratched her, she slapped my hands away, saying she'd manage the garment on her own. Not that she really needed one. Any garment constructed to shape her enormous belly would have required true engineering genius.

When it came to setting up the hydropathy machine, Mrs Davies showed me exactly where the nozzle needed to be placed for "maximum efficacy". That lesson left me blushing because I set the nozzle to squirt at the knot at the top of her sex.

With Mrs Davies quiet at last, I went in search of the doctor.

I followed the sound of grinding gears and whistling pistons to another treatment room. Inside, the patient lay with her gown scrunched around her middle. Clamps with wire tethers were attached to her nipples. Her legs were spread and elevated, and another device pressed against her sex.

The doctor glanced up as I entered. "There you are. See the lever on the side of the machine?" He pointed to a large tin box with dials and gauges on the front and from whence the devices at the woman's nipples and sex were connected.

I nodded, spying the lever at the side.

"Throw it up to start the current."

The moment I did, a curious humming sounded from between the patient's legs. Her eyes squeezed shut, and she moaned around the gag tied behind her head.

I glanced at the doctor, a question in my eyes.

He bent towards my ear. "She thinks it's sinful to make noises when she culminates."

"Culminates?"

The corners of his shocking-blue eyes crinkled. "Nurse Percy, has the mister never *culminated* when in the throes of his husbandly duties?"

My mouth dropped. "I've never married or witnessed a man's . . . *culmination*. Are you telling me a woman can too?"

His gaze honed on my expression. "For the sake of your apprenticeship, I think it will be my duty to demonstrate my cures."

My heart skipped a beat. "Just what sort of conditions are you treating, sir?"

The doctor checked the gauges, gave the woman a pat on her hand, then waved me towards the door. "Step outside."

In the hallway, he stood close with his hands held behind him. Mine, I clutched against my belly as I listened to him describe the many illnesses of the body and mind that occurred when a woman didn't release the noxious poisons boiling inside her. If a husband wasn't willing or able to assist, then a woman sought the help of a doctor who specialized in such things.

"And these machines . . . ?"

He brought his hands forward, and I noted the length and thickness of those digits. "The machines save my hands from aching after endless pelvic massages."

That was a term I had heard before. I'd even attempted to perform it on myself a time or two, but I'd given up frustrated just before I'd discovered the mystery that lay at the end of the quest.

"Doctor, I am unmarried but hope to be some day. I cannot allow you to directly . . . massage . . . that region," I hissed.

His lips twitched. "Which is not a problem, dear nurse. I have designed devices meant to assure a woman's sensibilities aren't violated. Stay after work, and I will demonstrate them all."

The rest of the day passed in a blur as I learned to apply the devices to other women's tender breasts and nether regions, all the while admitting a deepening sensitivity in my own body.

When at last the office closed, the doctor led me into the treatment room which held the widest array of machinery, including one device still covered in a tarp in a corner. My glance must have lingered there.

"Something I'm developing," he murmured, "but I'm looking for a volunteer to test it."

When I opened my mouth, he shook his head. "You're unmarried. This machine would shred your maidenhead."

After all I'd witnessed this day, I thought there wasn't a blush left in me, but my face heated.

His fingers trailed my cheek. "There's a gown on the table that I'd like you to wear. When you're ready, just open the door." With that, he left.

The gown was a thin, dove-grey silk. I passed my hand beneath it and realized my whole body would be visible. Still, I didn't hesitate to remove my clothing. He was a physician after all. I would do this in the name of my education and the furtherance of science.

When I was dressed in nothing but the gown, I opened the door a crack and peeked into the hallway. He stood with his back to the door. I cleared my throat, and he turned to meet my one-eyed glance. "I'm sure you're lovely in that gown, but I promise not to ravage you," he said, his voice a lovely rumble. "Open the door, Nurse Percy."

Taking a deep breath, I stood to the side and let him enter, then locked the door behind him even though I knew there wasn't anyone else about.

"Lie on the table, please."

His brusque voice, the professional one devoid of amusement, was back. This was the voice that reassured the most skittish of his patients. His actions were just as clinical and brusque as he ran straps around my thighs and set my hands on cushioned squabs with a warning to keep them there.

As docile a lamb as any of his patients, I let out a quiet gasp when he pulled up the gown, showing care as he freed it from the straps before smoothing it up my thighs to bunch at my hips. I managed to remain silent when he parted the table's divide and thus my thighs, even though he came to stand between them and fingered the dark hair that cloaked my Venus' mound.

"I thought it would be coarse," he said, "as curly as your hair is."

My blush deepened, but I didn't attempt a retort as he didn't seem to require one. He parted my folds and swirled his fingers around the opening. "To stimulate you, my dear. I want your pretty little nubbin to come out and play."

"But you didn't do this before you started the machines for Mrs Davies or Mrs Smith."

"Before I designed my devices, all my treatments began with direct stimulation," he said, sliding his fingers between my folds to capture the moisture then smooth it around and around. "But my hands tired, and I could only handle so many patients a day. The demand grew, and I knew I had to do something or see them find physicians who might have less care for their sensibilities."

"Your machines provide a service, I know. I've seen the transformations. Even Mrs Davies left cooing like a dove."

He flashed me a grin, and then his gaze dropped between my legs again. "There she is. A little shy this one, but a lovely dark pink. Have you ever seen your love knot?"

"That's what it's called?" I said, jerking when his thumb rubbed it.

"It's called many unsavoury things and a couple of medical terms that aren't flattering at all, but for you Nurse Percy, it's a love knot. You're very sensitive. I'll be sure to adjust the nozzle burst to something softer than I would for a woman who has had hers tweaked by a lover a time or two."

"You really shouldn't say such things to me."

His eyes narrowed as he studied my face. "Nurse Percy, I'm your employer, and my business is one that requires civility and discretion when dealing with patients. However, you will need to accustom yourself to frank terminology. You will hear it now and again from some of the ladies' own mouths. They cannot help themselves when they are . . . culminating."

I swallowed hard, still so aware of where his fingers trailed and of the fact liquid flowed from inside my body, which he used to swirl over my folds and that sensitive, swelling nubbin he seemed to be fascinated with.

Something like a cramp tightened my belly and my hips curved. "Doctor?"

"Yes, dear. Let's begin."

He brought the hose down over his shoulder and took a seat on a stool, which placed his face very near the juncture of my thighs. While my eyes widened in shock, that maddening tension began to curl around my womb. Not an unpleasant sensation, but breathtaking nonetheless.

He'd removed his jacket, his shirt and undershirt. With his broad, lightly furred chest bare, he met my questioning gaze. "The water will splash. And I wish to be close enough to gauge the efficacy of the treatment."

The very word Mrs Davies had used, and now I knew where she had heard it first. Strangely, that both reassured and dismayed me. He wasn't treating me any differently than any number of women. Therefore, the humour he'd shared with me, as though inviting me into his confidence, wasn't special at all.

Rather than think about how foolish I was, I concentrated on the sensations he produced, the warmth that built beneath the stir of his fingertips, the deep curling desperation in my womb.

The nozzle was lowered to just above my sex, and then he turned the ring at the base that released the water. The more he turned it, the narrower the stream and the harsher the pulse that beat against my love knot.

He made no sound, asked no questions, but must have read my expression, because he adjusted it back to a gentle pulse that excited but didn't make me squirm.

He rose and walked around me, eyeing me from different angles, his hand coming down to touch the pulse throbbing at the side of my throat and pull the fabric taut against my breasts. "I do have a purpose," he said. "Although your breasts seem lovely, I'm merely gauging the depth of your arousal by the reaction of your nipples."

"What does one have to do with the other?" I asked, although the question was disingenuous. I knew full well that when I played with my breasts, I felt as though a thin, internal rope tugged my sex into arousal.

"Are you really so unaware?" he said softly.

I lifted my chin. "I'm not married."

"But twenty-three and as well-formed as you are, I can't imagine you've never felt a man's embrace."

"It's awkward talking about intimate things like that just now."

"Because what I am doing is so very intimate?"

"That's precisely why it's awkward."

He shrugged. "I must gauge your breasts directly. Is that clinical enough for you? I have a device that will deliver a pleasant vibration to stimulate them."

"The clamps? They aren't painful? I know that Mrs Smith grimaced when you applied them."

"And you stayed to watch her silently thrash upon the table. Did she appear to be in pain?"

"Of course not." Although her rapture had been a nearly painful thing to watch. I'd had to concentrate on watching the dials rather than the churning of her body.

I pulled down the neckline of the gown until the gathered edge rode beneath my breasts. The tips were engorged. When his fingers twirled on the stems, I dug my fingers into the padded squabs.

"You don't have to muzzle your cries. In fact, they'll help me determine the course of your treatment."

Freed, I moaned. The sensations he wrung from me, with the warmth pulsing between my legs, the crimping of my nipples, were already richer than anything I'd ever managed on my own.

Clamps were set, one at a time, on the tips of my breasts. Then he left me to throw up the lever. A humming vibration travelled through the wires delivering the faintest of electrical currents.

"Astounding," I gasped.

"Isn't it?" he said, his eyes lighting with enthusiasm. "I had to experiment for the longest time to find just the right amount of current."

"Who did you find to serve as your subject?" I asked, wondering who had dared to put themselves at risk. But then again, here I sat, my nipples receiving electrical charges, my sex exposed to the lash of warm streams of water. "This is all very . . ."

"Stimulating?"

I snorted, an unladylike action, but one which only made him grin.

"The hydropathy machine wasn't my own invention. I merely perfected the delivery system. This next device wasn't my idea either, but I have worked with metal moulds to conform the seat to a woman's anatomy, improving the sensations."

The nozzle was turned off, and I missed the water, which had produced a sensual lethargy that made it impossible for me to stand against any suggestion the doctor might make. "What is the next device?"

"A vibrating saddle."

"Like a horse's saddle?"

"No, you don't ride it, it rides you."

The split in the table was raised then shortened to allow my legs to dangle from the knee. My thighs were pushed further apart. The position alone made my breath hitch. Everything was open for him to see. And he looked. His fingers touched the delicate furls of my inner labia then probed gently inside. His thumb caressed the knot that was fully exposed now and so swollen I wondered if it were possible for it to burst like a ripe berry.

His lambent gaze rose to greet mine. "You will like this, I think."

He pulled down an oval object at the end of a flexible arm that extended from the ceiling, and pushed it towards my open thighs. The head of the device was contoured to a woman's sex. A long, ruffled ridge slid between my folds, a slight protrusion anchored it at my entrance without invading so far it might steal my virtue. Straps were buckled around my upper thighs to hold it in place. When it lay against me, the metal quickly heated. The doctor threw another lever and the device shivered and shook, the hum deafening, which was a good thing because my moans came loudly, one atop the other, although the frantic thrashing of my head had to give him enough response to gauge the efficacy of this particular treatment.

My whole body shuddered. My hips danced upon the table, shoving my sex against the device, which did no good at all since the straps made it move with me. "Doctor, there's a flaw in the design," I gasped.

"Is there now, Nurse Percy?"

"I cannot . . . thrust against it . . ."

"Why don't you hold it against you?"

My gaze met his as I grasped the sides of the vibrating saddle and hugged it against my core. I ground and ground, but fell back against the table breathing hard and feeling discouraged because I didn't think I had reached culmination. I wasn't cooing like a dove. I felt ready to spit and claw like a lioness.

"My dear, you are a difficult case," he murmured. "But I am determined to prove that I'm not a fraud. You have two choices. You can allow me to give you a manual pelvic massage or you can help me test my new invention." His gaze slid to the tarp.

Mine followed. "I really shouldn't let you give me a direct pelvic massage," I said, faintly. "When questioned by any suitor, I wouldn't want to lie about the fact that I found my pleasure with another man's hands." When my gaze returned, his smile stretched.

"Very admirable, nurse. The machine it is." He undid the straps at my thighs, lowered the spread platforms, and helped me to my feet. The gown fell down around me, cloaking me, but I didn't care. It was only a sop to my modesty. I liked the way his glance raked my form, lingering on my breasts and the apex of my thighs.

"I couldn't help but notice when I probed you that your hymen isn't intact. It's not unusual in virgin women, but it's convenient for our purposes because you will be able to truthfully tell your future suitor that no man's member has ever entered your body."

I quivered at the implication.

He drew the tarp from the low-lying contraption and I eyed it, not understanding its use. There was a padded bench and a wand attached to a machine that pointed towards the bench.

My expression must have given away my confusion.

"Perhaps you'll understand if I add one of these." He fished into a drawer at the foot of the bench, where inside lay an array of phallic-shaped ornaments. He selected the smallest and screwed it onto the end of the wand.

Understanding at last, my knees went weak. "Do you have a name for your device?" I rasped.

"I do. However, I'll have to find a delicate one when I add it to the menu of treatments I offer my patients."

"What do you call it now?"

"I call it a fucking machine."

The word made my nipples spike hard.

"When I start the engine, this wand will piston forward and back, mimicking the motion of a man's hips as he drives into a woman." His gaze turned from his treasure to me. "Only this machine will never erupt prematurely, depriving the woman of her culmination, and the strength of the thrusts are controlled by the woman as well, so that she can select what pleases her."

"What must I do?"

"Nothing, my dear. Bend over the bench. I will do the rest."

The look in his eyes, at once excited for his new invention and curious whether I would comply, made me nervous. I saw no straps on this device. "If I wish to move away after it begins . . .?"

"Look over the edge of the bench."

I bent and spotted a dial marked "Speed" and another marked "Depth". I twisted both to the lowest settings but didn't touch the toggle switch to turn it on. Control truly would rest in my own hands. I cleared my throat. "Must you watch?"

"However will I determine if it requires adjustment?"

I stiffened my spine against his crestfallen expression. However attractive the man was, the position I would take before this device would rob me of my dignity. "Can't I make a record of my experiences?"

He sighed, but nodded his head. "To adjust the height of the wand, use this turnkey." He bent and whirled the wand up and down.

I frowned. "Adjusting it correctly might prove awkward and time-consuming." I knelt on the bench then rested on the padded platform. "Would you place it for me, and then leave?"

"Of course, my dear." He inched up the gown over my buttocks, exposing me. "I'll just lubricate the phallus with a little ointment." Moist sounds were followed by a whirring while he rolled the wand up and down, then forward so that it touched my woman's furrow. "You've the dials turned low?"

"Yes," I said, breathless now and feeling a little intimidated. "What if something goes wrong?"

"It's experimental – in its testing phase. It is possible."

"Perhaps . . ." I bit my lip.

"I'll face away," he said quickly, "unless you call out to me."

"I don't think that's necessary. I'm over my bout of embarrassment."

"Wonderful! How brave you are, dear. You have only to flip the switch now."

I swallowed hard and reached for the toggle, and as soon as I did the phallus pressed slowly forward, entering me. I jerked in alarm and turned off the switch. I gave a strangled laugh. "Sorry, I knew what would happen, but the sensation . . ."

"You are inexperienced. Nervousness is to be expected."

I closed my eyes and backed up to the phallus again then flipped the toggle. This time, I didn't demur when it pressed inside me. It only swept forward an inch or two before retreating, but the swelling I'd experienced earlier when I was aroused returned quickly. The phallus came into me again and moisture leaked to anoint its head.

"Oh my," I said, slumping against the bench.

The doctor knelt in front of me, his gaze locking with mine. "I think you can take so much more, Nurse Percy. Your treatment is progressing nicely."

"Indeed. Would you?" I said, waving at the dials.

He turned them, increasing the speed and depth then hurried to the rear of the platform. "I'll want you to remember everything to document your impressions."

I was glad he wasn't watching my face because I rolled my eyes. The phallus thrust fast and with remarkable precision, but I found I couldn't move, couldn't thrash like I wanted to in order to relieve my tension. "Doctor?"

"Yes, dear?"

"The machine works quite nicely, but I don't think I will culminate. Perhaps it's just me."

"There's nothing wrong with you." He hurried around the front of the machine and turned it off. "Turn and sit at the edge of the bench."

I did so, spreading my legs at his touch. Then he licked the tips of his fingers and thrust two inside me while he rubbed my love knot.

"You may move and make noises. I love the song a woman sings when she culminates."

"I'm tone deaf."

His chuckle warmed me, and I followed my impulse and tweaked my nipples through my gown. He growled, his fingers thrust deeper, and the swirling created an intense sensation that had me lifting my legs to fold them over the doctor's shoulders while I lay back on the padded bench.

My breasts and belly tightened, my channel convulsed. "Doctor!"

I culminated, my body writhing, my legs drawing the doctor closer until he braced his arms on the bench as he leaned over me. When the explosions rippling through me muted, I panted and opened my eyes to find him smiling softly down at me.

When I could find my voice, I said, "I'm sorry that I didn't have the patience to prove the efficacy of your new machine."

"Not to worry, Nurse Percy," he drawled. "We will continue our experiment. I have several new ideas to test."

"May I offer a few suggestions for improvements, sir?"

His blue eyes glinted with pleasure. "My machines await your pleasure, my dear."

Dark Side of the Moon

Kristina Lloyd

When Jackson came back from the moon, he was a little changed. They warned us this might happen but they couldn't say how. On returning, his first words were, "I've touched the night." I could see in his eyes that he had, and that he liked it. I'd touched no such thing and knew I'd never be able to fathom where he'd been and what he'd seen. Over time, a distance grew between us until Jackson, sitting next to me on the sofa, watching TV in his replica spacesuit, seemed further off from me than he had been when he was many thousands of miles away, hopping around on that big disc of cheese.

Locally, he was a hero. When he wore his spacesuit to the supermarket, kids followed him, asking how you go to the bathroom in space and whether he had any moon rock at home. But after a while, even they saw my spacesick Jackson as just an ordinary weirdo, the sort of washed-up dreamer you get in any small town. He must have looked the loneliest of souls, wandering around the freezer section with his empty wire basket, fish sticks and ice cream reflecting in his visor.

He rarely bought proper food unless I reminded him it was good to eat. Our garage was full of astronaut food, bulk-bought online, and with the help of Mike Herman from number 10, Jackson installed a roll-off-roof shed in our back yard and called it his observatory. While I slept, he shut himself away in there, gazing at the cosmos through an enormous telescope he'd nicknamed "Bettina".

I wasn't happy about this, obviously. Jackson might have touched the night, but he hadn't touched me in months. I began to wonder if, in the hope of rekindling his interest, I needed to freeze-dry myself like the strawberries in the garage. Perhaps he could suck on me and rhapsodize about the intensity of my flavour when rehydrated with saliva.

The times lust got the better of me, I would flirt, cajole or even demand my conjugal rights. Unfortunately, my womanly wants couldn't anchor my man to earth and with each passing day, Jackson drifted further from my orbit. I missed the sex but most of all, I missed him. Before long, we stopped talking about the issue and I resigned myself to being a moon widow, living within a marriage that was a shadow of its former self. I still loved him, of course I did, but we were running on parallel lines, unable even to connect enough to address the issue of our disconnection.

My marriage was like Apollo 13, sailing on next-to-no power on the dark side of the moon, survival our only goal. Were we going to end up like that mission, a "successful failure"? I could picture us liver-spotted and wrinkly, raising a glass to our golden anniversary. But if we're trapped and unhappy, what's successful about those fifty years? A marriage doesn't necessarily fail if it ends; it fails if it's being held together by fear of the ending. The trouble was, I couldn't tell if we were merely going through a bad patch or if we were done for. So I pretended we weren't happening, and the days kept on coming, as regular as ever and in the correct order, meaning things couldn't be too bad, could they?

Houston, we don't have a problem. Oh, for sure.

I thought nothing would change until one summer evening, Jackson noticed me again. I was naked and sprawled face-forward on the bed, hot and floppy after a deep, despondent bath, when I heard him climb the stairs, his suit rustling and creaking. Immediately, I felt naked and shy. My instinct was to cover up but that was crazy. I was only resting and hadn't Jackson seen my body a thousand times before?

So instead of covering up, I pretended to be asleep, effectively absolving myself of responsibility for my nudity. I heard Jackson pause in the bedroom doorway. Outside, the light was fading, all the neighbourhood birds chirping and shrieking as if scared the sun would never rise again. I understood their panic. Sometimes, I too think the darkness will go on forever. Jackson's breath gurgled through the vents of his fake oxygen tank, slow and loud, surrounding me like auditory molasses. I focused on drawing the low breaths of a sleeper while battling to convince myself the feather-light creature crawling across my left calf was a figment of my imagination, roused into action by the imperative to keep still. I did not need to shake it off. It was not there. I was fast asleep.

After a while, Jackson slid back his visor. The heavy breathing stopped. In a gentle voice, he said, "Your ass looks like the moon."

I kept on breathing, unsure what to think, given that the surface of the moon is pitted with craters and my ass isn't the sweet, smooth peach of magazines. Initially, I thought Jackson might be insulting me, perhaps not intentionally but that hardly matters: the sting's just as sharp, if not sharper. Then I reminded myself: this is Jackson. He loves the moon. He was paying me a massive compliment.

Deliberately mumbling, I replied, "So, what say you dock there?"

I actually meant "round about there, in the vicinity of my ass i.e. in my pussy", but with hindsight (forgive the pun) I can appreciate the ambiguity in my suggestion. Moments passed. 10 . . . 9 . . . 8 . . .

I thought of Jackson's hands gliding over my skin, massaging my back, skimming the bulge of my squashed breasts and clutching handfuls of my butt.

7 . . . 6 . . . 5 . . .

Would he do it? Ground control to Major Tom: can you hear me, will you touch me? A pulse ticked in my groin, my appetite surprising me. Sex was such a distant memory that simply imagining skin on skin was sufficient to spark my hunger. Once, it would have taken a lot more than that to get me going.

4 . . . 3 . . . 2 . . .

The visor clicked back into place. Thick, heavy breathing filled the room again. Slowly, my awkward astronaut turned and, creaking and rustling, made his way downstairs.

My heart sank. I gave the mattress a frustrated little kick, hurt and anger rising up and shaking their fists inside me. He wasn't well, I understood that. His circuits were dead, something was wrong. My patience, however, was running thin and the temptation to close off from Jackson grew stronger than ever. I started believing in the old saw contending further suffering can be avoided if you determine never to make yourself vulnerable again. But I knew that was a dumb bargain, merely replacing one type of pain with another. Because what sort of terrified, sucked-dry life would it be if you stopped taking chances? But then again, damn it, this was my husband. Risk and rejection ought not to feature so prominently in a marriage. Was there any point in us continuing? And Jackson, what did he feel underneath that silver insulation? Anything? Was he even *in* that suit?

Despite my disappointment, Jackson's compliment clung to me with the stubbornness of hope. For several nights, I had a foolish fancy he might quit his moon-gazing and come snuggle up in bed to check out the bouncier version. No such luck. Occasionally, I got up to peer through the curtains into the yard below. The shed glowed dimly, and Bettina, her eye on the night sky, taunted me with innuendo, her telescopic shaft jutting through the roof like a gigantic cock poking through a zipper. Oh Jackson, come to bed, my love! Come and crash land in my thighs!

I figured my seductive powers lay with my ass. Jackson's always been a fan of ass and if he could be reminded I was a woman who had one, maybe I'd get to taste what I was a fan of: Jackson, the original model, not the space cadet who'd replaced him. So I took to bathing at the same hour each evening, then lying prone on the bed, hoping he might come up to admire the scenery again. Twice, he stood in the doorway, breathing heavily before leaving without a word. It must have been sweltering inside that suit. On the third evening, I didn't hear his approach. The dipping sun, filtered by gauzy voile curtains, warmed my skin and the purr of a neighbour's lawnmower lulled me towards sleep. I was close to genuinely nodding off when I sensed movement behind me.

I tensed, fearing an intruder. Could someone have slipped past Jackson unnoticed? Dumb question. Jackson was so removed from the world an entire regiment could slip past unnoticed.

"You know," came a familiar voice, "they haven't really worked out how people would fuck in zero gravity."

Oh boy, he just said "fuck"! The word, so aggressively sexy, shocked and thrilled. Jackson hadn't used such earthy language for aeons. I kept my eyes closed, my heart gathering speed as I wondered what he might be wearing. I could hear that the spacesuit was off so what instead? Nothing? Jeans and a tee? Supposing he was wearing the black tee, the ribbed one with a tiny button on each sleeve? He used to look so handsome and mean in that. Something about the cut of it, about the colour and how it suggested an intriguing villainy in his character. Yes, that top was good. I'd tell him later: Darling, you look great in black but, um, the silver not so much.

"It's difficult to maintain contact," Jackson continued. "People float off. I figure the only way you could do it is by strapping the participants down, fixing them in place. Or, say, strapping them to each other. A sex chamber might work, some Velcro, maybe a few hooks and handles."

I stirred to show I was listening. "Uh-huh."

A long silence followed. Arousal swirled between my thighs but at the same time, I was braced for Jackson leaving the room. I sensed him move closer. My entire being was so attuned to his nearness I swear I felt his shadow fall across me, felt his cool dark image bring a tingle to my skin. I hardly dared breathe. Then Jackson curled his hand around my wrist, lifting my arm.

"So anyway," he said. "I went to the hardware store."

I jerked my head to see Jackson wrapping a double-length of rope around my wrist. I squealed, my pussy blooming with sudden, swollen tenderness. But we didn't do this kind of thing! It was for perverts and weirdos and we lived in the suburbs. Not only that, my husband was semi-famous. Supposing this got out? The newspapers would have a field day. I could see the headlines: From Moon Man to Monster! Rocket Man off his Rocker!

Nonetheless, I offered only a token objection as Jackson ran long rope ends through the loop then tightened the bangle. From the corner of my eye, I drank him in. He was wearing black yoga pants, nothing more, and I was delighted to note his broad-shouldered, taut-bellied strength was intact, as was his libido if the bouncy tent at his crotch was anything to go by. His torso rippled with movement and his skin, filmy with sweat and as pale as the moon, slipped and shifted over tendons and muscle. When he pulled the rope, his forearm tensed and soft, brown hair flashed in his pits. The scent of him reached me in rich wafts of memories – memories of nothing in particular, just of Jackson. I felt I was coming home, except it wasn't the same because the furniture had been moved and the walls were another colour.

A beat drummed in my groin and my mind spun, a fever heating my skin. I couldn't isolate the greatest surprise: was it that Jackson was into bondage or that I was finding the experience so wildly erotic and also, so strangely comforting? Because amid the excitement coursing through my veins, a stiller sensation located me. The rope around my wrist reassured like a small, strong embrace. I felt safe and calm, confident that Jackson could carry me through this. As he stretched my arm sideways, something seeped out of me, a tiny piece of tension relating to a matter I no longer knew or cared about.

Jackson was back. He was in control again and my months of worrying and waiting were fading fast. It seemed churlish to point out we weren't in zero gravity so I didn't need to be strapped down. If my husband wanted me to play out-of-this-world games, I was happy to oblige. Clearly, he'd spent time working out how to fix me in place and I simply let him do his thing, cooperating as he hiked up the mattress, ran the rope beneath and bound my other wrist. Using a second length of rope, he repeated this at the bottom of the bed, and all the while I was dissolving further into a floaty sort of lust. Minutes later, I was stretched out like a star, wrists and ankles tethered at four corners of the bed.

My pussy was too exposed and between my legs the summery air tickled my wet lips. I sensed Jackson studying me, his eyes roving over my flesh as he debated what to do with me. I was nervous and yet I didn't quite care. I felt half-drugged. Jackson could do whatever he wished. All I wanted was to receive.

Clearly pleased with his handiwork, he struck a triumphant, glancing blow across my buttocks. "An ass like the moon," he said. "And she wants me to fuck it."

I squealed and wriggled, suddenly caring. Had I actually said that?

"You know what this reminds me of?" Jackson continued.

"Honey," I said, trying to hide my concern. "Are you OK? Maybe we should talk this through first."

Jackson took a couple of pillows and worked them under my hips to raise my butt. "Reminds me of those crazy alien abduction scenarios," he said. "You know the sort? She gets laid out on a slab and a bunch of one-eyed, green freaks perform depraved sexual experiments on her."

"Jackson," I murmured. I wasn't sure how relieved I ought be that he'd moved from anal sex to alien abduction. But I *was* relieved. All the same, I desperately wanted him to touch me rather than embark on a mad schoolboy fantasy.

After a while, he did touch me, a single finger running down my spine, from the nape of my neck to the tip of my ass. My skin prickled and I moaned quietly. "I think this must be the earthling's central stem," said Jackson. Gently, he traced snaking patterns across my back, making me whimper again. "Oh, and I think it likes our touch."

I winced. This game was silly, yet I had to admit Jackson playing the role of an emotionally detached experimenter was pretty damn hot. Ironic, really, given that his insularity had caused me so much heartache of late. Clawing one buttock, Jackson vigorously shook my flesh then slapped me there a couple of times. I yelped. "I think it likes that too," he said, wobbling my other cheek.

When he swiped my butt again, I pulled on the ropes, squirming with desire, embarrassment and renewed anxiety. Was he really going to do me in that most taboo of places? The prospect troubled me but I wasn't sure why. In all our years, we'd never even broached the subject. It seemed peculiar that Jackson's enthusiasm for conquering new territory had taken him to the moon and back yet he'd never been inside my ass. I didn't consider it bad or morally wrong . . . just, well, wrong for a sexually unadventurous couple ending a dry spell during which I'd contemplated divorce. Wrong for us. Wrong for Lara and Jackson at number 16. It was simultaneously too honest and too impersonal. Too vulgar as well. But hey, maybe it seemed impersonal because we hadn't yet personalized it. Maybe it would be OK, good even. Or quite possibly amazing.

"Now then," said Jackson. "How many holes has this one got?"

I'd never heard him talk in such a manner. Had he left his inhibitions in space? Were they orbiting earth along with the debris of dead satellites, fragments of spacecraft, rocket dust and other sundry items of space junk? I recalled Jackson's tale of the astronaut who'd lost a glove on the first American spacewalk. Sometimes I think about that glove, all alone up there, waving down at us from the stars.

The mattress dipped as Jackson clambered onto the bed and straddled my waist. The weight of him pressing on me, the way his thighs hugged my ribs put me in mind of old, familiar intimacies. Like the ropes around my limbs, it was both reassuring and threatening, an embrace treading the fine line between security and entrapment. Reaching forward, Jackson cupped my chin in one hand, squeezing my cheeks to force my mouth wide. He inserted the fingers of his other hand, giving my teeth and tongue a cursory check.

"One hole," he said. He withdrew his fingers and skimmed them across my nostrils and ears, leaving tiny trails of wetness. "Two, three, four, five. Most interesting."

Edging down the bed, he wriggled out of his yoga pants then lay between my spread thighs as if to inspect what he saw. Propped up on the pillows, I was wide open to him. I only wished I could see him too, hairy and naked with his hard cock rearing up from his pubes. My memories of his body were too hazy. I pushed back, seeking his mouth, wanting him to quit counting my holes and start licking the most crucial one. He blew on me.

"Jackson, please!" I writhed in protest, the ropes checking my struggle.

"Please, what?" he replied, a note of humour in his voice. He knew damn well what.

"Lick me, make me come."

He blew a couple more times until finally, his tongue splashed onto me. He pressed into my wetness and I was melting into his mouth, melting so fast my limbs vanished in a trice. I was all pussy and cunt, all wetness and want, all groans and moans and need. Splaying my lips, Jackson lapped along my crease, his tongue flat, sloppy and generous. My clit, big as a berry, throbbed constantly and when he danced around the bump, my ecstasy built as he nudged me towards orgasm. But he didn't tip me over. Instead, his tongue slithered away, backwards and upwards, and I whined in frustration. Then, oh my, his tongue landed on the hollow of my ass, and I was making an altogether different noise. I gasped as he circled me there, sensation flaring in warm bursts of pleasure. I felt so tender, new and pink, Jackson's tongue coaxing life from my soft little rim. Why had we never done this before?

When he probed more firmly, I yielded. He could have all of me, every last scrap of resistance. His tongue squirmed deeper, then his tongue became a finger and he was inside me, stroking and swirling where I was made of the night, of dark velvet secrets and star-sprinkled bliss. Yes, he could do anything. I was completely and utterly his. Two more fingers plugged my pussy and he drove into both my openings, his rhythm sure and slow, the finger in my ass increasingly confident. So confident, in fact, that one finger presently became two. My muscled ring hugged him and I rubbed my clit against the pillows, rocking with Jackson's thrusts and nearing my peak.

"Is that good, baby?" said Jackson. "You want me to fuck your ass? Or you want more of this?"

"Both," came my absurd, breathless answer. Then, driven by curiosity and greed, I made up my mind and whispered, "My ass. Do it to me there, do my ass." Jackson slipped out of me. "But be careful," I pleaded, tugging at the ropes. "Don't hurt me."

"Don't worry, hun. I bought us some KY."

The extent of Jackson's preparation sent my excitement a notch higher. While I'd been despairing, he'd been mulling over what he wanted to do to me, making sneaky purchases so he could put his plan into action. Hell, who needs red roses? I kept on grinding into the pillows, my closeness hovering. The jelly was cool but before my indrawn breath was done, it was at my own temperature and Jackson's fingers had darted into me with a delicious new ease. I tensed, however, when he positioned himself behind me.

"I've greased my dick too," said Jackson, uncharacteristically crude. "I won't hurt you, I swear. This is going to be so easy, so good." But it wasn't easy at all because instinctively I clenched when he tried nudging my entrance wider. A stab of pain made me yelp.

Despite the lube, I was suddenly tight. I jerked on the ropes, wanting my freedom. Jackson withdrew a fraction.

"Relax," he breathed.

I tried my very best but the pain kept flashing. I thought penetration was going to be impossible, that flying to the moon would prove easier, until Jackson dipped a hand beneath me, offering my clit a firmer surface. Suddenly I ceased to care, I was loose and open and reckless, I just wanted him in my ass.

"Again," I cried, but Jackson was already there. I wailed, my aperture opening around his girth as he burrowed into me with slow, solid insistence. The pain was a tiny pinch of grit in an ocean of bliss and within a moment, he was snug and hard and deep. We held steady, panting and amazed. His cock was wrapped in a grip so tight it smacked of desperation. A fierce, black intimacy locked us in. I couldn't conceive of anything, not even a molecule of lube, existing in the space between my membrane and his meat. For all I knew, his cock might have fused with my ass. I had never felt so stuffed before.

Cautiously, Jackson began to move. Soon, I was urging him on with ragged, wordless cries. My bloated clit rubbed against his hand, my climax flickering closer. He slammed into my ass, increasingly powerful and rough. With my body pinned open, I had no choice but to take his invasion, and that's all I wanted to do anyway.

Jackson bellowed freely and when one thunderous, heartfelt groan reached my ears, I began to come. My thighs trembled, my mind turned vaporous, and I hit my peak, ecstasy pulsing out and spilling through my body. Jackson gathered momentum. Memories of him rushed in, of how his cock swells so hard just before he spurts, of how abandoned he sounds when he finally comes. And then it was happening for real, Jackson's noises crazier than I'd ever known them. I was seeing stars and so was he. He uttered lusty, baritone gulps of bliss, sounding as if his orgasm were being dragged out through his fingertips, the pleasure almost too much for him to bear. Clutching my butt cheeks, he thrust deep and long then shuddered his release on an incredulous roar.

After a pause, he gave a long sigh, ending on a mellow laugh. He eased out of me, leaving my ass glowing with heat. "Oh, man," was all he could say but it was two words more than I could manage. Untying the ropes, he caressed the soreness from my wrists then flopped down beside me, his face glinting with sweat, his smile deeply dippy. He stroked a length of hair from my face and softly kissed my lips. For a long time we lay there, our legs entangled as we came back down to earth. Shadows stole into the room. A water sprinkler hissed over a neighbouring lawn. In the distance, a dog barked.

Later, the moon rose in the sky, silvering the room with a ghostly light. Naked and asleep, Jackson seemed an other-worldly being. But he wasn't. He was an earthling in my arms, back where he belonged and here to stay, I hoped.

The Amazing Marvella

Elsie McGraw

"I am the Amazing Marvella" I said with a flourish of my ruby-sequined cape. "I am the Amazing Marvella and this is my lovely assistant Bridget."

I was dazzled by the spotlights pointed at me with their multi-coloured gels. The stage was hot and bright. The theatre was small, but the house was packed full. Beyond the apron, I could just make out the audience: mostly middle-aged and older, with a sprinkling of younger faces – well-dressed, eager faces anticipating an evening of novel entertainment. Wealthy old ladies and their tolerant ageing husbands; aunts and uncles and grown-up nieces and nephews out for a night on the town. College boyfriends and girlfriends dragged along for the ride. A few hipsters, looking knowing and cynical. How many of these people had any idea of what they were getting into?

Bridget curtseyed and we got a polite round of applause from the audience. They hadn't quite decided what to think of us yet, but they were willing to give us a chance.

"Tonight," I said to the audience, "We will play with magic. Together we will show you some things that you may never have seen before, that you may never have thought were possible . . . Observe!"

I waved my hand, and there was a blinding flash and a puff of smoke. Then Bridget stepped forward out of the acrid cloud, wearing nothing but a smile, a pair of black garters, and her scarlet stilettos.

Shocked silence. For just a second, the audience couldn't believe its eyes, didn't know quite how to react. Then, a smattering of applause, slowly building into a low rumble. I heard one old lady in the front row exclaim: "Well! I never!" Her companion, a fat lady in her mid-sixties wearing an antique-looking floral party dress responded loudly: "That's not what I heard, dear!" which earned her a burst of appreciative laughter. Bridget grinned widely, displaying her perfect white teeth, and posed and vamped for the audience, showing off her large perky breasts, making them jiggle, while she kept one hand demurely in front of her neatly trimmed little red pubic triangle. The applause got significantly louder, and I took a little bow.

"You may find," I went on when the applause died down, "that the normal rules of the universe do not apply in here."

I opened up the props chest and took out my wand. The wand was ten inches long, made of shiny black rosewood, richly carved and polished. Its features were that of a stylized, fantastical phallus, with a bulbous glans at one end, and a rounded grip that suggested testicles at the other. It was a thing of beauty, an artefact handed down through the centuries.

I shrugged my cape off and hung it on the stainless-steel rack that stood next to the props trunk. Then, with a sorcerer-like flourish and a show of extreme concentration on my face, I waved my wand.

Bridget floated slowly up off the stage floor, and with a mock-surprised look on her face, she pivoted around on her long axis until she hovered parallel to the ground, as if lying on her back on an invisible bed about two feet above the stage. There was a smattering of applause from the audience, but mostly hushed, expectant silence.

I unbuttoned my frilly white dress shirt and stepped out of my black dress pants, hanging them carefully on the rack. I was now wearing only a skimpy black push-up bra, a matching pair of lacy bikini panties, and my comfortable black Mary Janes (more practical for making magic in than sassy heels). Though the air in the theatre was warm, I felt a pleasant nervous chill run through my body. I'm not really any sort of an exhibitionist; that's much more Bridget's department.

I waved my wand again, and Bridget's legs spread open, up and out, ending up sticking straight up in the air, a big capital V.

There was a little commotion in the front row. The disapproving old lady stood up with a 'Harumph!" She was wearing a powder-blue pantsuit and a blue pillbox hat. "Obscene ... disgusting ... unheard of ..." she could be heard muttering as she made her way to the aisle. Her rotund friend could be heard chuckling. The back door of the theatre creaked open and slammed shut with a clank. Nobody else got up from their seat.

"Watch closely," I said. I began waving my wand rhythmically, like a maestro conducting the overture of a symphony orchestra. Up and down, left and right, back and forth.

As my wand moved through the air, Bridget's body reacted. Her large nipples hardened and grew, until they looked like a pair of pink gumdrops protruding from her big round pancaked breasts. Slowly, like a flower unfolding on a spring morning, the plump pouting crease of her vulva parted, revealing the hidden wonders within.

Bridget let out a low, throaty moan that was audible all the way to the back row. As my wand traced its invisible pattern in the air, Bridget's inner labia started to swell and turn purple; the lips parted open, revealing her entire vulva like a flower in bloom. Her clit was clearly visible, straining out from underneath its little hood. The wetness could be seen coating her pussy, drooling out. Bridget sighed and moaned, writhing and twisting, struggling softly against invisible bonds as my wand worked its magic. Her pussy gaped hungrily open. Her clit was swollen and pink. The audience was completely enthralled. I loved this part of our show.

I set the wand aside for a moment, leaving Bridget helplessly gasping. Out of the prop chest, I retrieved our little purple bag of tricks.

As soon as I opened the drawstring, sixteen shiny golden balls the size of large marbles leapt out. With a rush, they swarmed up and floated above Bridget's head like a halo, orbiting slowly and buzzing like a cloud of angry hummingbirds.

I got a little bottle of lube out of the prop chest and dabbed a generous amount onto Bridget's crinkled little anus. The audience was silent. I could feel their anticipation.

The golden balls aren't actually particularly magical, aside from the hovering and the vibrating. We just like them.

I plucked one ball out of the orbiting cloud and deftly inserted it up Bridget's ass. The buzzing made the tips of my fingers tingle. The little golden globe disappeared almost as if by magic into Bridget's sexy little brown anus. I was rewarded by an audible sigh from Bridget and with a smattering of applause from the audience.

One by one, I snatched up the humming golden balls and slipped them up Bridget's increasingly crowded rear-end. With each ball that I inserted into her winking anus, I got an even louder moan from Bridget, and even more applause from the audience. The final three or four were tricky: it was getting harder and harder to get the buzzing balls up inside her without letting the humming swarm already up her butt escape. The last one is always the hardest, and if I'm not very quick and careful, a hornet's nest of fifteen vibrating balls can come flying out of Bridget's ass while I'm trying to insert number sixteen. Fortunately, this time I was dexterous enough, and the last golden ball disappeared neatly up inside Bridget's beautiful, stuffed asshole.

For a little while, I went back to conducting my invisible orchestra on Bridget's heaving, sweating body: drawing paths of sensation up and down her quim, stimulating her breasts and her ass and her clit, taking pleasure in her curvy, turned-on body; but no one was going to last much longer like this: not Bridget, not the audience, not me. We were all firmly in this together now, and the sexual tension in the theatre was thicker than thick, electric and crackling.

"Ladies and gentlemen," I said, "you may wish now to remove any tight-fitting, constricting clothing, or any articles that you do not want to get stained. We are now about to perform our final act of the evening!"

There was a rustling sound out in the house as the majority of the audience discreetly unzipped their pants, hiked up their skirts, removed underwear and pulled pantyhose out of the way. Beyond the glare of the spotlights, I could see the fat lady in the front row, knees wide apart, floral-print skirt piled up in her lap, hands busy between her bulky thighs. Anybody who didn't take my advice, I reflected with a secret smile, was going to walk out of this theatre with a sticky, wet crotch.

I opened up the prop chest and fished out the harness. I always feel awkward doing this on stage; putting the harness on with a hundred-odd pairs of eyes intently watching my every move. There is simply no way to put that thing on gracefully.

I successfully donned the harness, without tripping over myself or getting the leg loops crossed up. Carefully, I fitted my wand into the holder, snapping the retaining ring into position. The polished black rosewood jutted out from my crotch just like an erect cock.

It bounced pleasingly as I moved. I positioned myself directly in front of Bridget, holding onto her legs behind the knees, admiring her nude, curvy, sweaty, glowing body, gazing into her bright blue eyes. The end of my wand bobbled less than an inch from the entrance to her soaking wet, wide-open, horny pussy. Her clit seemed to twitch with anticipation.

She mouthed the magic words to me and to me alone: "I love you", and I nudged forward, parting her slippery lips, sliding the length of my magic wand up and down her vulva.

I heard a collective gasp from the audience at the same time as Bridget sighed with pleasure. I knew then, for a fact, that once again the magic had worked. Every person in that audience, even those whose pussies hadn't been wet in years, even those who required double doses of Viagra to make their cocks hard; every woman was experiencing the exact same sensations that Bridget was experiencing, and every man was feeling what my magic wand was feeling. I took aim, and with one confident thrust, I entered Bridget's red-hot pussy, sinking my wooden cock in her all the way up to the hilt.

"Please, please, please . . ." Bridget begged. Out in the house I could hear the collective moans and groans and sighs of the audience as they fucked and got fucked, as Bridget's wet pussy grasped at my hard, thick wand, as the buzzing balls vibrated against my wood, as the roots of Bridget's clit trembled with desire.

I started fucking her, as slowly as I could stand to, drawing all but the head of my wand out before plunging it deep back inside. Her big tits shook, her pelvis bucked, her head lolled side to side. The base of the wand rubbed pleasantly against my own clit, making me nice and moist inside my panties. At that moment I knew I was the only person in that crowded theatre who wasn't on the very edge of a massive orgasm.

"Faster, faster, please, please, please . . ." Bridget begged me almost silently, "please fuck my pussy, fuck me hard . . ." Out in the audience, the moans and sighs were turning into grunts and gasps and the occasional high-pitched wail.

I obliged, thrusting my hips with all I had, fucking her pussy as hard and as fast as I could, making my own tits shake, until my brow was sweaty with the effort and my ass threatened to cramp up. Her pussy devoured my wand, slurping happily. I placed my hand on her neatly trimmed mons and caressed her clit with my thumb. The vibrations from the golden balls were travelling down the wooden shaft of my wand and were tantalizingly stimulating my own clit and pussy.

"I'M CO-O-OMING!" Bridget announced in a choking, gasping scream, "OH FUCK, I'M COMING!" A cascade of flying, humming golden balls spilled violently out of her asshole as her pussy spasmed and grasped at my plunging wand.

At that exact moment, the auditorium was filled with groans, moans, gasps, growls and screams as every member of the audience was shaken by their own individual orgasm. For many of them it was the first orgasm they'd had in decades; for many (so a lot of them would tell me after the show) it was one of the strongest and most intense of their entire lives.

I fucked her all the way through her orgasm. When her body

stopped shaking and her breathing no longer came in gasps, I carefully withdrew my wand, sticky and slick with her juices. She lowered her legs, and I helped her to her feet. Sixteen humming golden balls were orbiting slowly above our heads. The atmosphere in the theatre was hot and thick, saturated with the aroma of sex.

Arm in arm, we rode a wave of thunderous applause. Together, we bowed, bowed again, bowed a third time.

"Thank you ladies and gentlemen, thank you so much! You've been an amazing audience. Please come back again, and bring your friends. Thank you again! You'll find handy-wipes underneath your seats . . ."

The house lights came up and the stage lights dimmed. The people in the audience stood up, towelled off their sticky parts, buttoned their pants, filed out towards the exit. Bridget and I collected our costumes, reset the props trunks, cleaned up the stage, getting everything ready for tomorrow night's show. Then we headed home together, where Bridget would show me some magic tricks of her own.

Obit for Lynn

Tsaurah Litzky

It's four o'clock in the morning. I'm sitting in my kitchen, drinking tequila. My friend Lynn Busa died yesterday. I don't have on any clothes or underwear, my pussy smells like sour milk like I've pulled a two-mile train, but I haven't done anything. I'm rotting with despair. Lynn was the sister I always wanted, the trail buddy who would never leave me stranded with my panties down and a broken leg. Even though I am naked, I have shoes on, the red suede pumps I got that time long ago when Lynn and I went shoe shopping at Bendel's. She got a pair of black patent leather spikes, heels sharp enough to slice off a man's ear.

I met Lynn right after Ed Koch was elected mayor. He won with a big campaign about how he would clean up New York, get rid of the whores, pimps and thieves, get the hustlers off Forty-Second Street. I didn't like him or his campaign. I always loved Times Square; I started to go up there at night with my first boyfriend Eddie Valentine. It was a Mecca of crazy, pulsing, throbbing lust; men kissing in doorways, enormous women who weren't women, condoms taped to their foreheads, strutting up and down the street in sequin dresses, the marquees of the movie theatres advertising only triple-X features: *Girls in the Night, Women's Prison, Nana – A French Coquette.*

Eddie and I were seniors in high school living at home with our families. We took the subway in from Canarsie to Times Square. We paid two dollars each to get into one of the movie houses and then we would climb to the balcony to make out. We stood up in the back among other couples embracing. Frantic for each other, we pressed our bodies together, his hot mouth sucking mine. He'd slide his hands under my clothes, pinch and twist my nipples with so much skill I would come. He taught me how to get him off, how to slip my hand inside his jeans and pull his prick. I was so in love with him. I pretended we were Adam and Eve in the garden. There was always a sticky sweet smell floating in the air. I thought it was some kind of air freshener. Later I realized it was come.

By the time I met Lynn I knew that smell very well. I was working at Dolls of All Nations, a massage parlour on Thirty-Eighth Street, a few blocks from the UN. Because I was the only Jewish woman who worked there I was Miss Israel. According to the *Daily News* there were over two hundred massage parlours licensed by the city, turning New York into Sodom and Gomorrah. Editorials urged our crusading mayor to shut them down.

I worked Sunday, Monday and Tuesday nights. Wednesday mornings I liked to go to the Russian-Turkish Baths on Tenth Street. Wednesday was Women Only day and the ladies could get naked and lounge around like odalisques. My Aunt Mildred, who was a Rockette at Radio City Music Hall, took me there when I was eighteen.

"It's great for the complexion, honey," she said "and you need to steam your privates clean. It keeps them young."

I was in the white-tiled Turkish sauna room. Fronds of fragrant eucalyptus hung from the light fixtures. I found myself staring between the legs of the woman sitting on the bench across from me, the black hair on her crotch was shaped into a perfect diamond.

She noticed me looking and opened her thighs wider, exposing her labia, loose, crimson, frilled like lace. She started to play with the silver ring that pierced one of them, tugging it with slender fingers. I wondered if she was trying to shock me but after four months at Dolls of All Nations, not much could shock me. Maybe she was trying to pick me up, girly-girly love was not my thing but I couldn't blame her for trying. Perhaps she was just mischievous; she looked like an elf with her delicate little tits, tiny frame, pixie haircut and huge dark eyes. She grinned. She was adorable. "What are you looking at?" she asked, as if she didn't know.

To my surprise, my clit started to twitch.

"It's your diamond," I answered, "I want one."

"Bruno, my beautician, Bruno waxed it," she said, "He does great work. He's a good friend of mine. I'll give you his number. It's in my bag upstairs in the locker room."

We went to the showers and then up to the locker room. She wrote Bruno's number on the inside of a matchbook from Miss Mystique, a massage parlour on Twenty-Third Street. She worked there. We were in the same business. I told her where I worked and introduced myself. "Far out," she said, "my name is Lynn. Let's go have coffee."

We walked down to Valelska's on Second Avenue. "I can't stand
Sweet and Low," said Lynn, putting five sugars in her coffee. "Me
neither," I said, putting four sugars in mine. "And," I went on. I
don't like diet soda or ice in my drinks either, nothing adulterated."

"Same for me," said Lynn; maybe I had found a friend.

"How do they treat you at Miss Mystique?" I wanted to know.
"My boss, Wolfie, has started dropping me on my percentage. He
pushes me to do volume, at the end of the night my hand is one
giant blister, but when I get home and count my money, it falls
short."

On the job I had to ask my client to take off his shirt and give him
a perfunctory baby oil massage of his upper torso. I was then to ask
him if he wanted a happy ending. No one ever said no. Then I was
supposed to put a condom on him and finish him off with my hand.
Blow jobs were strictly against the law, but plenty of the women gave
them; it could quadruple your tip. Lynn nodded, sipping her coffee
as she listened.

"That's men," she said, "at least a lot of them. You work like a slave
for them and they rip you off. My boss, Elsie, used to work in a
massage parlour. She knows how it is. She's fat now. Behind her back
we call her the cow, but she treats us right, we get a five-minute break
between each client, time to smoke a cigarette or whatever. I never
caught her making a mistake with my pay."

"Maybe I'll go see her, "I told Lynn. "Maybe you should," she
said.

She leaned forward; I noticed that one of her eyes was blue and
the other one brown. "Did you think I was coming on to you in the
baths?"

"I didn't know," I told her.

"Well, I was only teasing," she said. "I'm a merry prankster, I was
pulling your chain. I don't go that way." I didn't quite believe her, but
"OK," I said, and changed the subject.

"I love your boots," I said. They were green and black cowboy
boots with very high stacked heels, stomping heels.

"Thanks," she said, "I love fancy shoes and high heels."

"Me too," I answered. Then we paid the bill and exchanged phone
numbers and addresses. We discovered we lived a few blocks away
from each other in Brooklyn Heights.

When I got home, I made an appointment for the next day at
Bruno's Beehive – A Beauty Boutique.

Bruno was a six-foot-tall bleach blond with a ponytail down to his ass crack. He had a body like a linebacker and a face like Grace Kelly. He took me into the Hot Wax room which was painted a vaginal pink. He sat me down on the waxing table.

"You have a face like a movie star," he said, "fantastic cheekbones. What is your sign?" I liked him immediately. "I'm a Virgo," I told him. "I knew it," he said, "an earth sign. Did you know Greta Garbo was a Virgo? How about a snake, an earth creature, the symbol of temptation?" "I don't think so," I answered. "I've met too many men who were afraid of snakes. How about a star?" "Too common for you," he said.

We decided on an arrow. The waxing didn't hurt at all, maybe because he rubbed cocaine paste liberally over my vulva before he put on the wax. The arrow looked fabulous. He gave me a ten per cent discount because I was Lynn's friend.

I called Lynn to thank her and tell her how much I liked Bruno. We decided to go to Danceteria to celebrate my waxing on Saturday night, as we were both off.

At Danceteria we picked up a couple of cute young soccer players from Italy. Lynn's was named Bebe, mine was named Adriano; I was charmed when he told me he was the love child of Federico Fellini. We went to their room at the Martha Washington Hotel on Twenty-Eighth Street, a dark green room with Audubon bird prints on the walls. We smoked opiated hashish that Bebe had smuggled into the States in his socks. Lynn took off all her clothes, and then she showed the boys her diamond. I took off my things to display my brand-new wax and Adriano asked if all American girls were like us.

"How should I know?" I answered.

Lynn suggested they take off their clothes too so we could cavort around like dancers on Etruscan vases. Lynn grabbed Bebe's long snaky cock and used it to twirl him around. Adriano put his arms around me and we pranced around the twin beds like angels or fools. Soon Lynn and Bebe were doing sixty-nine on one bed while I straddled Adriano on the other. My pendulous breasts slapped against his hairy chest, my hands grabbing his ass, raising it up, pulling him deeper into my cunt. I felt like I was mating with the great god Pan in some primeval glade. At the moment of truth, Adriano cried out, "Graciella, Graciella mio." I didn't mind, I thought it was cute I reminded him of his sweetheart. Years later I read in the *New York Times* that Adriano L., a former soccer player, had become President of Sicily.

Lynn and I considered ourselves modern women, emancipated.

The pill had set us free. We took full responsibility for our actions; even though we were on the pill we always carried our own condoms, extra sensitive, extra thin to protect us from venereal disease. We believed love, all kinds of love, was the answer. We adored John Lennon. I was always hoping I'd see him and Yoko somewhere. Then he was murdered, shot down by a deranged fan who believed himself to be channelling Holden Caulfield. Every night thousands gathered in front of the Dakota chanting "Give Peace A Chance" and "Let It Be" until Yoko asked them to stop. She couldn't sleep. For weeks after his death people were weeping, staggering through the streets. This great tragedy was just the beginning.

We started to hear about cases of Aids. There was much confusing information about this new disease. There were rumours you got it from an infected mattress or from wearing someone else's underwear. The *Daily News* said you could get it by kissing; it was spread by saliva. This was all the mayor needed to go after the massage parlours.

At Dolls of All Nations, Miss Nigeria, Rasheeda, who had grown up in the Hunts Point Projects in the Bronx, was busted giving a blow job to an undercover cop. They shut us down. Two days later Miss Mystique was closed because of a similar incident.

Lynn and I were out of work. I got a waitress gig at Remington's on Waverly Street in Greenwich Village. Lynn went to work in the jewellery store her mother owned on Seventh Avenue. Together, we went to get tested, the line outside the public health station on Ninth Avenue snaked around the block. We were both lucky. We got the white papers that said we were disease-free.

I've only downed my second shot but already my head is aching; maybe if I had some blow my pain would float away to Machu Picchu. It's been so long since I've tasted blow, so long since I've done a lot of things. I have become respectable, sort of, I write dirty stories I sell to magazines. Lynn settled down too, she got married. Her husband Matt knew all about her past. He didn't mind, he said it got him excited.

It was Matt who called to tell me. Lynn had a cerebral haemorrhage when she was in the bathtub. The funeral is today at two p.m. He found her when he came in to piss. She was slouched down, knees up and spread wide open. Her head was arched back, in the let's-do-it position, her Mickey Mouse washcloth between her legs.

I poured myself another tequila, time was fracturing inside my head. Not all our adventures were as delightful as with the soccer players. One night Lynn and I picked up a guy at the Mudd Club.

When we went back to his apartment he pulled a knife on us. Another guy suddenly appeared, he jumped out the bathroom door naked and socked me in the face. The door had been left unlocked. We somehow escaped. I was lucky he didn't break my nose.

Then Bruno killed himself; he jumped out the window of his fifth-floor apartment. His body was covered with welts from the sarcoma. Lynn came over to my place to tell me. As soon as I let her in the door, I knew it was bad. She didn't have high heels on, she was wearing house slippers and her face was covered with tears.

She put the brown paper bag she was carrying on the coffee table in front of the couch, She sank down and pulled a bottle of Tequila out of the bag.

"I didn't even know he had it," she wailed. "Why didn't he tell me? Did you know?" She opened the bottle and took a big swig. I sank down beside her. I took a swig too.

"He didn't say anything to me," I told her. "Besides, he was much closer to you. Maybe he was ashamed."

We passed the bottle back and forth. Lynn's tears were big as raindrops and I started crying too until my throat, my ears, filled with tears. We were both trembling, shaking and then I was holding her. Our mouths came together like parts of a puzzle. Lynn unbuttoned my blouse and pulled out a breast, she started kissing my nipples and then she put her mouth there, nursing at my big tit, my baby, my beautiful baby. What soft lips. We took off each other's clothes. I had never been so close to Lynn, I could see the little freckles on her chest. We shifted position. I sucked her nipples, they were so tiny and so hard like little tacks but they did not scratch my lips. She started kissing her way down the middle of my chest. Her tongue followed my arrow home. When she went inside and started sucking there, it was paradise. I had read scary stories about how women did it to each other using big grotesque rubber dildos with two heads. This was so different. I wanted to taste her like she was tasting me. Her body was rank and sweaty and her labia smelled of piss but inside her cunt when she came I smelled violets. We fell asleep on the couch but in the morning we woke up on the floor clutching each other.

Bruno's parents, who lived in outer Queens, in Rego Park, did not come to his funeral. Maybe they were afraid that on the long subway ride into Manhattan they would get their jewellery snatched. Chain-snatching and petty crimes on the subway were up eighty per cent because of the new terrifying plague, crack cocaine. It was so

ddictive and so cheap you could buy a rock on the street for the
price of a large coffee and a bagel with cream cheese. Lynn and I
tried it once and the high was so ecstatic we knew we should never
try it again. First Lady Nancy Reagan unveiled her ' "Just Say No To
Drugs" programme. On McGinnis Boulevard in Bushwick, where
fourteen-year-old girls were selling themselves for a hit, no one could
have cared less if Nancy unveiled her sagging tits.

Going out wasn't such fun anymore. Lynn and I stayed home,
hanging out in each other's apartments. We smoked grass we got
from Lynn's mother Virginia. Virginia had been a head since the
Thirties, when she was a regular at the Cotton Club in Harlem.

We re-evaluated our lives; I brought a typewriter so I could type
up the poems I wrote in my spiral notebook and send them off to
literary magazines. At her mother's urging, Lynn signed up for a
course in jewellery design at FIT.

We only went out once in a great while. At the end of a hot summer
day when the city was sweating like a dog, we decided to tie one on.
We went into Manhattan, to Pierre's on Mercer Street, one of our
favourite places. The bartender, Picky Dicky, used to work at
Remington's with me. They called him Picky Dicky because he
never laid the same woman twice. Another pal of mine from my job
was Dan, the Quaalude man. Now he worked as sous-chef at Pierre's.
On a slow night he might send out a plate of fried calamari for us.

Pierre's was packed; half of Soho seeking comfort there. Cigarette
smoke was as thick in the air as phony promises.

There were a couple of seats at the end of the bar. We elbowed our
way to them.

"You two could break a man's back," said Picky Dicky as he set
our Margaritas in front of us. After a few rejuvenating sips, Lynn
and I started to talk about this woman in the news who just gave
birth to a baby she conceived in a petri dish.

"Believe me," Lynn said, "now all sorts of new employment
opportunities will open up. Women with good eggs will start to sell
them."

"How do they get the eggs out?" I wanted to know. "When doctors
want to make money, they can figure out how to do anything," Lynn
answered. "Soon there will be ads in the newspapers, Egg Donors
Wanted."

"That will never happen," I told her. I took another sip of my
drink and then I looked up and saw them, two big beefy men making
a beeline through the crowd, straight for us. They were wearing

gaudy Hawaiian shirts. The big tropical flowers looked like a flashback from a bad acid trip. Around their necks they were wearing identical silver peace symbols on long leather cords. I knew they were cops, right away.

"Police," I said to Lynn, nodding my head in their direction

"Yeah," she said, "Reagan's Raiders. We'll tell them we're actresses or models, and then they'll think we're working girls. We can make a score, I want new shoes."

"Have you gone crazy?" I asked her. "Those days are long past and you know I don't believe in sleeping with the enemy, no way." She reassured me, "I don't either. Trust me."

They were already behind us. One of them was breathing down the back of my neck. A fat hand, clutching a hundred-dollar bill pushed between us, nearly knocking over my glass.

"We'd like to buy you lovely ladies a drink," a slow, southern voice said.

"That's why you tried to knock this one over," I answered. I turned and looked at the man behind me. He was blond, buck-toothed and grinning. His smile was so wet; I could see the spit shining on his teeth.

"Sorry," he said, "but we saw you as soon as we stepped in this place. You are the prettiest girls here. We're strangers in town and . . ." then his friend chimed in, "We're looking for company and we want the best. So, how about that drink?" This guy had an ugly pug nose and a long jaw. With his red hair and freckles, he looked like Howdy Doody.

"Join us, please, come on," he said, "We don't bite, we're nice guys. You two sure are good-looking. You must be actresses or models. What are your names?"

Lynn batted her inch-long eyelashes at him, "You are so very smart to guess we are actresses. We would just love to have a drink with you," she cooed.

"I'm Dorothy, "she continued, "Dorothy Parker, and this is my friend, Emily, Emily Dickinson," I glared at her. She well knew I was no fan of the spinster poet of Amherst.

"I'm Charlie Smith," drawled the blond. "I'm Mike White," said the red-head. "Me and my buddy here are up from Georgia."

"So, what do you do?" I asked Mike. He had pushed in between Lynn and me and was now standing at my side trying to look down my cleavage. I put a hand over my chest.

"Me and Charlie are gun salesmen," he replied quickly, "We're here for the NRA convention at the Javits Center."

"How charming," I said.

"I just love guns," Lynn cut in, "there is nothing like a man with a big gun to turn me on. Do you have any samples to show us?"

"Very cute, Dorothy," I commented. Lynn ignored me as she beamed up at Charlie.

Two Margaritas later, Mike White had his arm around the back of my chair. Every time he tried to move it closer around my shoulders, I shrugged it off. I had told him I was putting myself through acting school as a babysitter. "Maybe you could take care of me," was the best he could come back with. I nodded enigmatically.

Lynn, however, had told Charlie Smith that between her roles on the Broadway stage she worked in the phone sex business. He had given her a twenty to demonstrate her technique. Now, she was rubbing her little knee against the outside of his leg. Her hand was on the top of his thigh; her fingers going slowly round and round. There was a lump in his pants at the crotch. It looked like a beer can.

Despite the din, I could hear her whisper, "Oh, daddy, daddy, you're so, so strong and big. I've never felt a gun as big as yours. I know just what I want to do to you."

His face was flushed; his mouth was open like the mouth of a fish on the hook. He was so gross, so ugly. But Lynn spoke to him tenderly.

She had her hand over his crotch now. She was rubbing up and down.

"Please, please, you have an enormous piece, longer than an AK-47. Will you rub it across my boobies? Please, please," she implored him. "And then will you put it right between them so I can take it between my lips and suck it. I want to suck you. I want to suck your big gun." She leaned over and took his ear lobe into her mouth, her sharp little tongue danced in and out of his ear. Charlie was breathing heavily. His pelvis was moving back and forward, he was rocking on the barstool as if he was about to topple over.

Mike suddenly stopped gazing adoringly at my profile. He put a hand over to steady Charlie's chair. "You need to cool right down there, partner, cool down now," he said in a stern voice. Charlie moved away from Lynn. He picked up his drink and drained it. Mike reached behind me and patted Charlie on the shoulder.

After a few moments, Mike spoke. "Dorothy here sure seems to know her business. It would be nice if we could all relax and get to know each other better. Would you ladies like to come back to our hotel? There is a little problem, though. Charlie and me are feeling mighty tired. We had such a long day. Maybe you know where we could get a pick-me-up, a little something to give us some more energy?"

"How about a cup of espresso?" I cut in. "Maybe make it a double?" Lynn kicked me hard in the shin with the tip of her pointy shoe.

"What do you mean exactly?" she asked.

"Well," he said, pausing as if trying to find the right words, "maybe you could introduce us to someone who could find a certain pretty white lady to pep us up, sometimes she goes by the name of Coco, Coco Chanel." These narcs were so dumb. They were living five years in the past. All they needed to do was to go up to Bryant Park and for ten dollars they could buy enough crack to blow them to Christmas.

Lynn smiled up at him, fluttered her eyelashes some more.

"Oh, now I understand," she said. "I know just what you mean. I do have a friend who might be able to help you."

"Can you take us to see your friend?" they asked simultaneously.

"Oh, no, no," said Lynn. "He's a very private person, a recluse, really. He lives like a monk. He hates to meet new people, but he's known me for years. You see, I went to junior high school with him; we were in the same home economics class. That's the reason we are still friends. Maybe I could go visit him. I can take a taxi over there right now and see if he will help you out," she said.

"How much do you think it will cost?" Charlie asked.

"Hmmm," she said, "well really I don't know, but at the very least two hundred dollars, and also I'll need twenty for the cab." Quicker than you could say blow me, Charlie took a wallet out of his back pocket and peeled off two hundreds and a twenty. Lynn took the money from his hand and tucked it into her heart-shaped red Mary Quant purse.

"Now you two, take good care of Emily while I'm gone," she said. "Don't let her drink too much." She turned and made her way through the crowd.

"Your friend is a great sport," Charlie Smith said. "We need fresh drinks all around. Could you handle another, Emily?" "I think so," I mumbled.

When our drinks arrived I took a big gulp of mine, I didn't like the situation. These whacko goons might kidnap me if Lynn didn't come back soon.

"Well," I said, forcing myself to smile coquettishly. I probably looked like Joan Rivers. "Who do you two big boys sell guns for?"

"Smith and Wesson," said Mike. "Colt 45," said Charlie.

"You work for competing companies?" I pretended surprise, "But, you're such good friends."

"We go way back," Mike said. "Our mothers were girl scouts together." As if to demonstrate their solidarity, they put their meaty arms on the back of my chair, hugging me tightly, between them.

I felt like throwing up but managed to push the bile back into my belly by downing the rest of my cocktail. They immediately ordered me another. By the time Lynn finally appeared I was demonstrating how I could dance the twist sitting down.

"Sorry it took so long," she said, "the taxi got stuck in traffic."

"That's OK. Did you find your friend?" Charlie asked.

"Mission successful," said Lynn with a fetching smile, and she leaned over and slipped something inside the front pocket of his jeans.

He put his hand over the pocket right away, his fingers stroking it as if to measure what was inside. "You got me excited when you put your hand in my pocket, Dorothy." he said to Lynn.

"You should be excited," was her reply, "there is a pretty white lady inside your pants."

"Wow-eee, you are something else! You deserve another cocktail. How about it?" he asked. Lynn answered him. "I would just love one. I need to cool down I got so hot running around and I bet Emily would like another one too, and then we can go to your hotel and really get to know each other in more intimate surroundings. But, first, I need to go to the little girls' room and freshen up. How about you Emily? Your nose is very shiny."

I was feeling so dizzy from all that twisting that I didn't want to get off my seat. I was afraid I would fall on my face. "It is not," I said.

"But your nose is very, very shiny," repeated Lynn. She reached over, grabbed my arm and yanked me off the stool.

"Hurry back," Charlie called after us. When we got to the ladies' room door, Lynn suddenly stooped low.

"Quick, bend down, bend down like me," she hissed, "in case they're watching."

I squatted down too. She pushed me a few steps sharply to the right and we burst through the swinging kitchen doors.

We entered a scene of frenetic activity. Men in white hats were stirring big pots on a giant stove, turning meat on a three-tiered grill, arranging food on plates. Dan was standing at a big, butcher-block table directly in front of us, holding a long knife over a fat, pink fish.

"This is not a good time for a visit," he said, frowning.

"All we need is to make a quick getaway. Is the back door open?" Lynn asked him.

"OK, go ahead," he said, motioning with the knife towards the door at the back of the room.

"What did you do?" he asked as we ran past him, "Goose Norman Mailer?" The pugnacious writer frequently drank at Pierre's.

The door opened onto a narrow alley that led out onto Sixth Avenue. I could barely stand and I was barefoot. I had left my favourite silver sling-backs under the bar.

"Are you all right?" asked Lynn.

"Yes," I answered. I leaned against a mailbox to steady myself, "but I lost my shoes." Lynn went out into the street and flagged down a taxi.

As our cab sped across the Brooklyn Bridge, I asked Lynn, "What did you give them?"

"I went to the deli on Thompson Street," she answered, "got powdered sugar and some Baggies and made a neat little package." She opened her handbag, pulled out a hundred-dollar bill and gave it to me.

"Want to go shoe shopping at Bendel's tomorrow?" she asked.

"Sure," I said.

The tequila bottle was nearly empty and I staggered off to bed. I had to get some sleep. I didn't want to look like a gorgon at Lynn's funeral.

When I woke up, the sticky July heat was flooding through the open window. It was already eleven o'clock. I had fallen asleep still wearing my red suede pumps.

I got up and tottered into the bathroom to pee. In the mirror over the sink, I did look like a gorgon, a grotesque witch, my face all puffy and swollen. Maybe I could fix it with make-up, maybe not.

My head was pounding as I went back into the kitchen and mixed myself an Alka-Seltzer, adding the last of the tequila for hangover relief. Then I went over to my closet to choose between my dresses, the shoes I was going to wear already on my feet.

I Waited for You by the River of Time

Remittance Girl

I waited for you
by the river of time
but you didn't come.

Is it impolite to fuck someone because I'm sad and tired of being sad? I don't know. Perhaps it is. But the afternoon rain has begun and it's a long way back to my hotel. His is closer and more expensive.

He's middle-aged and Russian, and has a bald spot like a monk's tonsure. Fine golden hairs glint on his swollen knuckles in the watery light. Someone, somewhere is walking around with an intaglio of his fist on their face. He smokes cheap Cambodian cigarettes and fondles his weeping glass of beer. His fat, blunt fingertips squeak along the curves of the glass like a suicide who's changed his mind at the window's ledge.

At the first rumble of thunder, ice blue Slavic eyes glance up at the squid-grey sky. The sound rolls across the wide choppy waters of the Mekong and up to the riverside café's balustrade. He leans forward to call for another beer, leaving a dark sweat stain on the faded orange chair cushion. A matching one has turned his light blue shirt to navy where it sticks to his back. But the tiny waitress, puppet-pretty and lithe as a water snake, is too busy fighting with the awning pulleys, trying to shelter the few patrons on the balcony before the onset of the deluge.

"A game of chess?" he asks.

I assume he's asking someone else until I realize I'm the only person there with time on my hands. "Me?"

"Yes. You. You play?"

"Badly."

"Come on. I let you win." A gunmetal incisor tooth flashes between his corpulent lips as he smiles.

"Don't do that," I reply, shifting my chair to face the scarred-up chessboard. "Anyway, I can tell. You're not the sort of man who enjoys losing."

And he's not. There's a petulance, a temper in that meaty face. His pride, like paper bunting, is all pinned to the surface of his skin. So we play for a while as the rain buckets down and spatters the board with mist.

> *I stood*
> *by the river of time*
> *and waited for a word*
> *but none came.*

These days, time stalls like a cranky engine. On this sodden afternoon, when minutes are hours, Sergei opens with a classic Spassky sequence. I'll let him beat me because he probably will anyway, and why draw out the inevitable? I'm such a graceful loser, having had so much practice at it.

"Check," he grunts and grins.

How can you deny people the little things that mean so much to them?

> *I sat by the river and wept,*
> *and let you float away,*
> *because there's no fighting*
> *this mother of a river.*
> *She's too wide and too deep.*

The Sisowath Quay is a river promenade gone wrong. The years and the weather have decimated the paving stones. They're broken and sit unevenly in the saturated soil. As we walk back to his hotel, I delight in the petty cruelty of the Russian's confusion. Will I change my mind and bolt? Will I demand money? Will I wait until he's sleeping off his orgasm and rob him? Having been stationed in this festering backwater, I'm sure he's had nothing but prostitutes for ages. He has no idea how to classify me. And, having spent so long in a state of suspended animation myself, I drink in the *Schadenfreude*.

The catlike boy behind the reception desk is also unnerved. After a moment of deep confusion, he reacquires the vacant stare of an unnamed native informant who hears no evil as long as it's white. All the whores he'd ever seen have been Cambodian or Vietnamese.

The Russian kisses me with sloppy intensity in the cramped elevator. I suspect he feels he ought to. His thumb finds my clothed nipple, hard in the air-conditioned chill. He takes this for arousal and a prompt to kiss me again with extra passion.

I'm not aroused. I don't like this man or the taste of stale beer and cigarettes on his tongue. It makes my stomach churn. But I believe he has something I want. Something so central to his nature, he doesn't even know it's there. A fundamental brutality of the soul and an inability to hide it in extremis. I think he could be the perfect locksmith.

> *I knelt at the river's bank*
> *and wept into its heartless brown waters,*
> *carrying my salt out to sea.*

It's like every other mid-priced hotel room in Phnom Penh, with a creaking, rattling air-conditioning unit and frayed manufacturer's stickers on the bar fridge. I eye the gaudy bedspread and ignore Sergei's murmurs of unfelt but apparently obligatory emotion. He pulls off my tank top and pushes down the cups of my bra.

Where the fuck did he learn the word "succulent", I wonder, unzipping my skirt. I don't want all this preamble. I'm simply hoping that he'll fuck me hard enough to jolt something loose inside me. That this raw act will uncouple me from the agonizing attachment I have to you.

Sergei stands still for a moment, his erection distorting the front of his rain-speckled beige chinos. If he thinks I'm going to undress him, he's wrong. I may be a fucking whore, but I'm not "that" kind of a whore. If he's getting laid for free, he can take off his own pants.

"Got a condom?" I ask.

"Sure. Of course. But I'm clean."

I make a concerted effort to stop myself from rolling my eyes. "Yeah? Me too. Put the bloody condom on." Because he's not going to have anything to complain about friction-wise.

As he tugs me down onto the bed and attempts to enter me, he gets it. I haven't had a cock in seven years and I'm not wet. The tightness makes him hesitate. He wrestles a fat hand between us and tries to change my frame of mind via my clit. It's not going to make a difference.

"Just fuck me."

"But you don't seem," he searches his Russian brain for the word and comes up with something ESLish, "interested."

"Listen, asshole. Just fuck me."

*I lay down beside the river
and begged her to take me
somewhere, anywhere,
away from here,
away from now,
away from me.*

I don't scream at that first inward thrust. He's big but not that big. Instead, I lie there with my teeth clenched and wait for my body to remember what to do. Sergei paws my breast and groans. His cock is only halfway in and the stretch hurts like a sonofabitch. But in that moment, when he thrusts again to hilt himself inside me, the world turns. He changes into something cruel, just as I become something acquiescent.

"This is what you want?" His voice is a croak. The hand on my breast tightens painfully.

The thrusts are punctuated with questions that at first I don't feel the need to answer.

"And this . . . and this . . . and this . . . ?"

Until the fury of it makes me gasp. "Yes."

Because this is what I want. Because I feel the hinges of my heart creak under the strain. The violence of it nags at the bolts that moor me to you. Boards rattle, age-rusted threads strip and shriek.

"Harder. Can't you fuck me any harder?"

He makes a noise like a wounded dog and closes a hand around my neck. "Shut up, you bitch," he hisses, showering me in spittle that smells of beer.

I smile and close my eyes. There it is. The umbrage. The brittle pride crisscrossed with stress fractures of doubt. The cruelty that can't help but rear its head. I need him past the thin walls of his civility. And in him, I know, those walls are very thin indeed. This new paradigm does nothing to quell his ardour.

*I dipped my hand into the river
and felt the warm, silty water
gritty between my fingers.
So much of the world
borne away on the flow.*

My body inches across the bed under the pounding. As it produces enough lubrication to protect itself, my cunt stings. What traitorous things our bodies are. I still don't feel the least bit aroused, but I'm wet anyway. And although I'm convinced I don't much care if I never get up off this bed, still I gasp and claw for air as his grip tightens around my throat. We are all, in the end, such animals.

There are pale doughnuts of light behind my eyelids, throbbing in time to my pulse, blooming brighter with each vicious thrust, until the brilliance of it screams like a siren.

Poor Sergei, I muse. I hope he doesn't kill me. It would be a bitch to get rid of a white corpse.

Not that I'm too worried about it. All I know is that the ancient wood inside me is splintering, the brackets snarling loose in the howling storm. The structure of every dream I've ever had about you is collapsing. And the Russian is going to come any second now.

I push you out with every hindered, rasping gasp. My cunt muscles spasm shut, my back arches and my spine locks. I'm coming. Teeth clenched and airless. It's a roaring red rage of an orgasm that races outwards in all directions to occupy the cataclysmic landscape. Because it's easy enough to do when it's not you I'm holding inside. When it's not you whose cock I imagine. When it's not you fucking me.

Sergei collapses onto me like a side of beef. His pale flesh twitches in the afterstorm of his orgasm. He rolls off me with a small, embarrassed chuckle. I consider thanking him for his service, but decide it's not his business or his burden.

"You," he says, wheezing and wagging a fat finger at me, "you're quite the puzzle. But I have figured you out. You're like another woman I used to date in Moscow."

"Really?" I sit up and begin to dress, adjusting my bra, pulling on my shirt.

"Yes. A Georgian girl. Very beautiful. Some kind of refugee."

"Funny," I say, standing up and stepping back into my skirt. "So am I."

> *I turned my back on the river of time.*
> *Let someone else sit,*
> *wooing it uselessly,*
> *someone stronger than me.*
> *I always knew*
> *you'd make me wait too long.*

Picking Apples in Hell

Nikki Magennis

"Romantic Ireland's dead and gone"
William Butler Yeats

It was nearing dusk. Students, socialites and Europeans gathered below a broody August sky, drinking wine and staying very carefully blasé about each other. I blended right in. Frank didn't. Yes, he may have been a native son, but after so many years something had changed. I couldn't work out if it was him or Dublin.

"So what's dragged you back, Frank?"

"Oh, c'mon now. Can't a man visit his home town without good reason?"

"Don't try telling me you were missing the ole place," I said, keeping my voice nice and flat.

What I didn't say was – "*tell me you were missing me, tell me you couldn't forget me, tell me you'd cross the sea just for one more shot of that filthy, mind-blowing fucking we used to do.*"

Frank looked around the plaza. He shrugged. The leather of his jacket was so worn it didn't even make the ghost of a creak. Lines were folded deep into the hide, like the crow's feet at the corner of his eyes. Oh, there was a glimmer of the same old Frank. Eyes as black as ale and as potent. Skin the colour of rain-washed bronze.

"I can hardly recognize the place," he said, shaking his head kind of sorrowfully. "It's just as full of shiny shite and fecking foreigners as any other city."

We were sitting out in Meeting House Square, watching a film they were playing on the wall. I couldn't tell you what it was, other than it had subtitles and real sex in it and took itself deadly serious. I was trying to show Frankie how different it all was now, how I'd changed and the city had changed and how I was no longer the kind of woman ye'd fumble with in the back of some spit-and-sawdust ole pub. How we were sophisticated, you know, and avoided talk of politics and religion and all those embarrassments.

"Christ, would you look at the state of that," Frank said.

Beside the art gallery, a gaggle of Liverpool girls screeched. One of them was throwing up in the corner. They'd matching pink cowboy hats with fluffy trim, and bras over their T-shirts, and they were shedding glitter in cascades.

Inevitably, it attracted the attention of a handful of local lads, who stood and catcalled, oblivious to those of us pretending to watch the movie. A chorus of tutting tourists couldn't put a dampener on the boys' spirits, and the to and fro of young lust continued as bawdy and desperate as ever.

"Sure some things never change, eh?" Frank said, smirking. I wondered if he was looking at my haircut, the exact copy of that I'd seen on Cate Blanchett, only not as blonde on account of my scalp trouble; my shoes that were knock-off Louboutins from eBay and only a little scuffed around the heel, and the red shift dress I'd put on to look casually thrown together, after changing, of course, forty or fifty times over in the effort to hit on the look that would show just the perfectly right mix of indifference and old-fashioned allure to ensure a night that satisfied not only my loins but my tender, hopeful ego, too.

I expect it was mostly lost on Frank. He was more of a split-crotch panties man, after all. I watched him checking my tits to see if they were still there. He chewed his lower lip. His knee was jiggling twenty to the dozen, and I didn't miss a furtive glimpse at his watch.

I tossed my hair.

"You'd be surprised, Frank. Some of us are different people now."

"S'that right? Well, yer eyes are still as blue as the sea, Niamh." He leaned in close.

"And I'll bet your sweet cunt's still as wet between your legs."

I'd have kissed him or slapped him, no doubt, had the crowd of young lads not distracted us at that moment, shouting out sing-song taunts at the cinema ushers, playful like, but with that ragged edge that meant anything could go pear-shaped at any moment.

Friday night in Temple Bar. Oh, it was dressed up with fresh paint and flower boxes in the windows and the bartenders may polish the fecking cobblestones daily, but when the night drifted in from the docks and the beers started to flow there was little you could do about the panhandlers and the prostitutes and the skangers loitering with intent and the overall tide of floating human flotsam that washes up in a city looking for the craic, and possibly crack, if not absolute gallons of strong drink, and, at last at the end of the night, looking most intently for the solace of a nice warm crack to sink their dirty flutes into – whether it belonged to man, woman or something in-between.

A couple of Garda rocked up and tried to skirt around the fracas without actually getting overly involved, and Frank decided it was time to retire somewhere with a better view, that is, somewhere he could smoke one of his foul European cigarettes without being coughed at.

"Come and see where I'm stayin'," he said, and I smiled.

"Somewhere nice?" I said. Him an international traveller now, I'd visions of room service perhaps and clean sheets. He'd try it on, of course, expect to have me on my back within ten minutes. No doubt I'd be happy to oblige.

We walked down towards Trinity, skirting buskers and drunks, the backs of our hands grazing occasionally, casual, like. Even that was enough to make my heart beat like a pattering clock, and the fact of us, Niamh and Frank, walking together again through the old haunts. Those streets, they were layered up with so many half-remembered stories they were like fly posters pasted over one another, dissolving pictures I caught out the corner of my eye.

How fine we looked back then. Me with my Madonna-bleached hair and his leathers brand new and shiny. Our legs scissored alongside each other's in perfect time, when we were running from Grafton Street up towards the green. We always seemed to be running.

I could hear echoes, too.

Us laughing, spraying the sound all over the cobbles like frothing beer. The thrum of his old scooter's engine, the fury in his voice. The high breaking note in mine as I shouted after him. All the anger that rained down around us.

I can hear, still, the silence the day after he left. The long, endless grey hush of it drifting in from the quay – "*The air so soft that it smudges the words*."

"Brings back memories, eh?" Frank said, and he was smiling into the breeze like he knew exactly what I was thinking. Cocky shite. Always had been. But I'd always fallen for it, likewise. As he grabbed my wrist and pulled me out the way of a stray skateboard outside the Central Bank, I got that roaring all over, the itch and the hunger for him. To be enfolded in him. Jarred by him. To scrape against the rough of his cheek and to fire up the blue in his eyes and to taste the diesel, the cigarettes, the other women on his fingertips.

We pushed through a crowd of miserable-looking black-haired, black-eyed teenagers and I glimpsed them turn to look after Frank. He'd trouble written all over him, you see. Irresistible to the young and foolish. And part of me must have still been those things, buried under my well-educated, socially mobile, culturally aware self. Yes, part of me was still the culchie, redneck girl from the bogs of Galway, entranced by the street lights, by Frank, by everything in the great, dear, dirty city. Blushing despite myself as he ran one finger over the pale skin on the inside of my wrist. Reading my skin like Braille.

There was a cluster of buskers planted on every corner and we were serenaded along the streets by fiddles, bodhráns, an out-of-tune guitar and a chorus of straining, echoing voices, the rough edges of them chafing my ears. Frank's hands slid around my waist. I only pulled away for a moment before I gave in and let his hip bump against mine. It felt good.

We passed the woman with the harp at the empty spot where King Billy used to stand. Frank let his hands drift lower. He traced the outline of my knickers through my skirt, lightly, like he was playing the stringed harp himself – it could have been almost angelic the way he twanged that elastic against my arse.

"Light-fingered, still, are you?" I said to him, but I couldn't help smirking as we swerved and slid down a wee lane, heading towards a squat, grubby pink building. Yes, now he'd pulled me off the street and away from the traffic my heart was beating a jig in my chest and I thought for a moment he might push me up against the wall like he used to, fire into it straight away. Have me with my back to the graffiti, under the blue streetlights, one leg lifted and my well-oiled crack swallowing him gladly.

But there was something nervy about him. He looked all about as we reached the corner and I thought to myself – first, where the hell is it we're going, and second,

"God, are you ashamed to be seen with me? You, Frank McAuley, a once-upon-a-time pony kid from Finglas with dirt under your nails?"

I was about to shout him off when he tugged me into the narrow gap between the Germolene-pink roughcast and this big ungainly crate of a van that was parked arse backwards on the pavement.

"Hoy!"

The voice, spraying out of the darkness, was dog-harsh, and all my skin swarmed with sudden fright. But Frank was patting me down and nosing towards the sound. For a moment I wished he were less of a swaggerer. He'd always been inclined to get us tangled up in mischief, and never one to shy away from a bare-knuckle scrap, either.

"S'dat you, Eddie? How's it going?" Frank sounded oddly cheerful.

There was a low grumble, and the sound of someone clearing their throat and howking a great gob into the gutter.

"McAuley. Where the fuck've yow been?"

The voice was fat, and as my eyes adjusted I saw that it belonged to an appropriately gigantic great fucker standing in a doorway. One of those that manage to menace just by the set of their shoulders. Frank shrugged.

"Oh, just catching up with me old friends, Eddie. All work and no play, Eddie, know what I mean?"

Frank smacked me then, hard on the behind, and I yelped before I could stop myself, despite the fact we hadn't agreed to that kind of a scene, not yet at any rate, and that Frank was giving a lewd, guttery chuckle that made me want to snap the fingers off his hand. And I would have too, if I hadn't been so wary of the sumo wrestler standing but six feet from us and stinking of bad news.

"Niamh, meet Eddie," Frank said, pushing me reluctantly forward until I could smell the man's breath. I got a whiff of blackcurrant throat sweets under the stale smoke and black coffee. Eddie breathed on me a bit more, assaulting me with halitosis, before turning back to Frank.

"I don't like you hanging around here, Frank. And you've parked your knacker's wagon too fucking close."

"Can't grudge a fella a few scoops and a quick ride, surely, Eddie? Hold your hour, eh?"

Eddie glowered.

"You'll be on the last ferry, Frank."

"Aye, course I will. Swear on my grandmother's grave."

Another grunt, and the man-mountain receded into a doorway that was a patch of darkness against the wall's vivid pink.

I could almost hear Frank's shoulders relax. There was a glint in the dusk that might have been a flash of his teeth if he were smiling at me, and he moved up against the side of the caravanette. A moment of him fumbling and swearing, and I realized that he was fiddling with keys. He swung open a dwarf-sized door and held out his hand.

"Want me to carry yer over the threshold?" he asked, and he had that quirky grin on his face, the one he used to use when he'd been out all night and was in the mood for playing up. He'd meet me outside my bedsit and drag me off into the dark, soot-blackened labyrinth of the city, talking a mile a minute, eyes shining with speed or lust or whatever devious scam he was working on at that present moment.

And I'd let him tangle his fingers into my hair and kiss me. And I'd let him drag me wherever he was going, just like I did then. Up the rickety steps and into the interior, smelling of biscuits and air freshener and damp towels.

He flicked a switch and a weak, yellowy overhead light dripped from the ceiling.

Everything was beige. It was like I'd gone back twenty years to a simpler, browner time; before everyone I knew I wore white-soled tubes and talked about irony and house prices. I was about to ask what the fuck we are doing in the bachelor pad from hell, when I realized how close Frank was standing, and suddenly it didn't really matter any more. There was another thing that was familiar, and that was the way his eyes shifted out of focus as he leaned in to kiss me.

That mouth. It might have produced some of the filthiest lies you've ever heard in your life, but there's no denying that when Frank McAuley kissed you, it was enough to make St Peter forgive the devil. He tasted of whiskey and wet nights on the town, he covered my lips with his own and devoured me, drew me forward so it felt like I was falling. I banged my shin against some clutter on the floor, swayed against a hard edge and knew I'd be bruised.

Around us the caravan creaked and swayed. Frank bent his head and bit into my neck, pushing me back until I put out my hands and felt the clammy plastic surface of a table and gripped it. A magic tree hung from the rear-view mirror, smelling of sickly synthetic vanilla. It swung back and forth in time with his movements.

Frank drew his tongue over the pulse point in my throat and licked at my collarbone. He jammed his leg between mine and rocked closer and closer to my groin. Always quick on the advance, Frank. Still, I couldn't pretend I didn't like it. I'd to press my lips hard together to stop myself from groaning.

"Dat's it, girl," Frank murmured, nuzzling lower, pushing my jacket aside, burrowing into the dark, soft places where he chased my pulse with kisses. I whimpered.

"You like that, Niamh? Will you sing for me, eh?" He found my breast with his finger and squeezed it tightly, plucking at my nipple until I let out a long, loud sigh. Pleased, he gave a soft laugh and tweaked it harder. Sadist.

"God, I missed you," I said, through gritted teeth.

"Been pining for me?" he murmured, slipping his head down to suckle me through my dress. With one hand, he worked his way up my thighs, incy wincy spider. I opened my legs.

"Oh, you're impatient still, Niamh."

His hand withdrew.

Of course he wouldn't give me the satisfaction. Not Frank. Not that easily.

I moaned.

"You fucking big tease, Frank."

He kissed my earlobe, bit into the tender flesh, and my knees sagged.

"I don't have any johnnies," he said. "I wasn't presuming this would happen, d'you know."

"That'd be a first," I murmured. I looked around the shabby interior, as if there might by some divine ordinance be a contraceptive vending machine installed in it.

"I'll nip out," Frank said, licking his lips. His eyes tripped down to the wet patch on my dress where he'd left teeth marks. "But I want to make sure you're still here when I get back."

I shrugged. "Can't promise anything."

"Oh, I know that." He started sliding my jacket down my arms, and I stood dumbly while he plucked at the buttons on my dress.

"You think it's time I slipped into something more comfortable, so?" I said, bemused.

"Not exactly," was his answer, and as he roughly stripped my dress from me and left me shivering in my underwear, I got a sudden pang between my legs. I recognized that tone.

"I don't know if I'm in the mood for games, Frank."

"You'll like this one."

He unpeeled my stockings – tugging them off my legs with less finesse than I'd imagined when I rolled them on earlier – and rolled the nylon around his fists.

"Lie down," he said, nodding towards a bunk bed at the back of the caravan.

I lifted an eyebrow.

"For old times' sake," he said, "lie down," and his voice was a soft growl. It made me wet.

I did as he said. While he tied my hands to a cupboard door handle
bove my head and my ankles tight together, I found myself staring
t a water stain on the ceiling. It was in the shape of a map, perhaps,
country that no one had ever been to before and no one else would
ver notice.

Frank was quick with the knots. He knew how to fix me in the
ight position. From our left came a sudden burst of muffled noise.
Music. Some loud, hard beat. Frank looked up.

"Ah, that's the club kicking off," he said. "The night's just beginning."

He smiled at me as he pulled my knickers halfway down, leaving
ny fanny shockingly exposed. His eyes lingered. He hesitated, and
hen with one quick movement, he bent down and thrust his tongue
•etween my legs, giving me one big gasp of a lick from arse to clit –
he kind that makes you breathless.

"Got you goin'?" he asked, smacking his lips. I rolled from side
o side.

"Do it again." I tried not to let it sound like I was begging.

"Not for now." He tucked my hair behind my ears and ignored me
s I squirmed from side to side. "You be a good girl, now, and wait
ere for me and I'll be back soon enough and give you the fuck of
our life."

I blushed. When he said things like that, I could feel his cock in me
lready, like he could penetrate me just with his words.

He looked over his shoulder.

"I tell you what, though, Niamh. You wouldn't want big Eddie
oming by and thinking you were on your own in here, would you?"

My eyes got wide at the thought.

"Don't you fuckin even dare think about it, Frank."

"Shh," he said, laying a finger on my lips. "Oh, hush, I wouldn't.
'm just saying, for your own comfort, like, it might be best to act like
was here."

"How d'you mean?"

He nodded at me. "Roll around some, you know. Give it a bit of
he groaning like you do."

"Groaning?"

"You know, a few oohs and ahhs. Put on a wee show for old Eddie,
ke." Frank tweaked my nipple until I arched my back.

"Ahhh," I said, predictably.

"That's the one," he said, his smile twisting just as his fingers were.
'I'll be back in the blink of an eye."

And he left me, tits smarting, pussy craving, bound hand and

foot and trying pathetically to wriggle around and rub myself o
on the sticky nylon bristle of the couch. I didn't even have t
pretend – never mind who was outside. I'd been turned on and le
to simmer and nothing was going to calm me until Frank McAule
got back and made good on his promise. I bit my lip and dreame
of his long-forgotten cock, growing bigger and stiffer and mor
beautiful by the minute.

God, and it was hard to leave her like that. The ties, now they alway
did suit her. Black nylon against that soft white skin. Like a bowl o
cream, she was, even after ten years in the birl and bluster of the cit
Sweet. I could still taste her on my lips, which, right enough,
couldn't stop chewing.

Nervous habit. No one would blame me for the nerves, eve
though I could have used a steady hand right at that moment, holdin
the drill tip hard up against the safe so that it wouldn't slip. The swea
on my hands didn't help. Eddie's office was a dingy little hole th
temperature of hell itself – I reckon the body heat from two hundre
shitfaced clubbers must have been seeping in through the walls. An
fuck-all breeze from the fire escape, either, even through the broke
door that I'd propped open behind me.

I'd to wait, every so often, for the music to slide from melody int
thumping bass, so's no one would hear the groan of the drill. An
then the air was thrumming with music and I could bend to my task
gritting my teeth against the fearsome smell of hot metal, watchin
tiny bright corkscrews curl out of the holes and scatter over the floo

Eddie would be lurking in his doorway listening to Niamh'
performance. God, the noises she makes! Purrs like a kitten. Enoug
to make my knob twitch just thinking of it. And that fat-headed cun
never could resist a peepshow.

Concentrate, Frank. That's three holes now, just another dozen o
so and the lock'll come loose. There's just inches between me and
glorious bonus that I'll be keeping all to my grand wee self. I'll b
free of my curse and those nasty shites who'd laughed like scuttlin
drains all me life – soundtrack to my grim fucking childhood, thei
laughing – oh, they'll be stuck, won't they? Left with a big box full o
fuck all, and me halfway across the Irish Sea already with the gea
tucked nicely away and my balls aching sweetly.

They thought they had the measure of me, still. Thought I was jus
a thick-headed mule, the type that would scare with their fat neck
and insinuations and the slightest crack of their grazed knuckles.

. . . Jesus, what's that? That great croaking sound? A door?

Calm yourself, Frankie boy. Doors open and close, that's what they do, doesn't mean anything much. Doesn't mean Eddie is coming back this way – why would he, when he's got a club to run and his money all tucked away in here safely behind an inch of solid steel? Who'd expect dumb wee Frankie would have the nous or the slackers to bring along a drill, eh? Who'd expect he'd know to use a cobalt bit at slow speed?

Aye, if there's one thing I am grateful to Her Majesty for, it's the useful skills she taught me in the metalworking shop. Getting there, now. Eight holes. I can practically smell the fucking lucre.

Dreamed of her a few times, when I was inside. Niamh, I mean. The ginger-coloured curls of her cunt, as snug and cosy a place as I'd ever longed for. Yes, she knows how to present herself, does Niamh. Give me fifteen minutes, and by God I'll be drilling a new hole right in the hot wet centre of her.

Fortune favours the bold, they say. But then there's a thin line between the bold and the bloody stupid.

If Frank McAuley had listened to the blacksmith who sold him the gear, he'd have realized that the batteries needed to be charged for fully twenty-four hours before he used the cobalt-tipped drill.

And if the drill had not slowed, with a pathetic, weakening whine, just as he was halfway through making the tenth hole, while he was lost in dreams of Niamh's dear warm wetness, Frank may not have shouted his dismay quite so loudly. His cry, unfortunately timed, just cracked through the silence between two tracks when the air was still throbbing with the echo of bass.

Eddie, waiting out in his shadowy doorway with one eye on the queue of punters and the other on the gently rocking motorhome, heard the agonized, distant wail coming from deep in the bowels of the club.

A frown gathered and settled on his forehead like a small rain cloud.

He looked at the Laika. For the past fifteen minutes he'd listened to the various whimpers and growls, muted but pleasant nonetheless, that emanated from the decrepit old van. They were entertaining enough to keep him out here with his hands in his pockets, waiting while the club filled up.

But he could have sworn that howl of anguish coming from the direction of his office was that snivelling little gobshite Frank

McAuley. He'd listened to the bastard crying for mercy often enough in the good old days. The pitch was familiar.

Eddie walked closer to the Laika. The net curtains were drawn closed, and he couldn't see the ghost of a thing. He licked his lips. She had a fine rack on her, that betty Frank had dragged back.

Clutching at his balls, Eddie leaned in close as if he could smell whether there was a man in there or not. He put a hand against the thin metal wall. There was a sharp intake of breath, and the moans broke off.

"Frank?"

Jesus, she sounded all but desperate. The sound of a woman with the raging horn – enough to break yer heart.

"Frank, is that you?"

Eddie looked over his shoulder. His mind moved like tectonic plates – with geological slowness to begin with, but with eventual cataclysmic consequences. Behind the restless queue of young D4s forming at the raspberry pink wall, there was a fire exit, and behind the fire exit there was a corridor. Along which, Eddie's inner sanctum. Eddie licked his lips.

If Frank was stupid enough to be attempting what Eddie thought he might be, he was tucked away in there, fiddling with a safe that, to be honest, would hardly hold up if you farted on it.

Eddie was only holding the cash here for this one night, of course. By tomorrow, it would be counted and split and distributed to various laundries around the republic. Nobody wanted to keep that amount of money in one place for too long. It only leads to trouble.

"Ah, Frank," Eddie sighed. He really couldn't be arsed with this.

"God's sake, would you get in here," the girl hissed. "The circulation's going in my wrists."

Eddie raised an eyebrow.

It had been six months, minimum, since he'd had any hole. People thought a man like himself would have whores buzzing round him like flies round honey, but those times were long gone. They'd all read too many women's magazines now, they all thought they were fucking *worth it*. And, despite what many of his friends thought, he wasn't inclined to pay for it. Deep inside Eddie's craven bulk there was a soft, sentimental heart that wanted a good Catholic girl with a bit of pink in her cheeks and the ability to *smile* while she sucked your cock.

He climbed the rickety little step, reached for the door handle and turned it slowly. About as secure as the tin-can safe Frank was

urrently trying to break into, he reckoned. Inside smelled of damp
eekends. There was another smell, too – the smell of an impatient
oman. Eddie's eyes searched the half-gloom. He moved across
he room.

Niamh was spread-eagled on the bed, tits and fanny all bare-
aked and hanging out for anyone to see. The blush ran to Eddie's
heeks, and he gritted his teeth, keeping his eyes fixed on her wide,
errified eyes.

"Christ."

The girl gasped. Eddie's hand swayed for a moment over her
hest, which heaved and bucked, although he hadn't laid a finger.
wiftly, he pulled the curtain down and draped it over her, covered
er from her chin to her knees with dingy white lace.

"Jesus. What has he done to ya?" Eddie asked, shaking his head.

"Frank," the girl said, almost whispering. "Where is he?"

She was a looker, Eddie thought. Classy bird, with that haircut.
robably drank white wine and read proper books. Wonder if she
new any of those fancy kinds of sex tricks he heard about but never
ctually encountered. You know, European type stuff. He ran a hand
hrough his slicked-back hair.

"Frank?" He made it sound like a swearword. "My guess is he's
urrently trying to rob me."

Niamh frowned. Her hands were still tied, but she balled her fists
nd tugged against the rope.

"Get me out of this," she said. Eddie shook his head sorrowfully.

"Sorry darlin'. Not just yet."

Eddie allowed himself to glance at the outline of her breasts under
he lace curtain. For a moment he swayed between lust and common
ense. Then he cleared his throat, roughly.

"What's his plan, so?"

"Who, Frank's? How the fuck would I know? Do I look like his
A?"

Eddie scowled. She'd a mouth on her. Slowly, deliberately, he took
is knife out of his back pocket and knocked it against the table edge
efore prising it open. To her credit, the girl didn't even flinch. She
ust opened her eyes wider, till you could see the whites. Only the
oosebumps on her bare arms gave her away.

He started to clean his fingernails with the tip of the knife.

"How should I know you're not colludin'? That Frank, he hasn't
he brains of a dead haddock. We both know that." Eddie concentrated
ntensely on his thumbnail.

"So, maybe he needed someone to tink up a plan like this. Someone with a bit o' nous."

"What plan?" She actually snapped at him. She did.

Eddie nodded at the bed on which Niamh lay. "Yer arse," he said pleasantly, "is lain on a mattress on top of a rather large parcel o quality cocaine. The money for which Frankie brought me last night And as we speak he is in my office trying to rob it back.

"Now Frank is after the drugs, the money and the vengeance," Eddie continued, "and I'm wonderin' if you're Bonnie to his Clyde."

"The gobshite." Niamh slammed her head back against the mattress. "The dirty great scheming lying cock-awful gobshite. should have listened to my mother. I should never have let my hormones get the better of me."

Eddie allowed himself a smile. He knew guilt like an old friend inside out and up and down, and Niamh's was not the reaction of a guilty woman. As he reached for the nylon stockings with the blade of his knife, he wondered, idly, what the best way would be to punish a ratface fucker like Frank McAuley.

At least, when the drill ran out, Frank didn't waste too much time kicking the safe. He'd only sprained his big toe before he realized he was onto a losing game, and that he'd less time than a priest's wank to clear out of the place and get back to the Laika.

Breathing hard, he reassured himself. So he didn't have the money but he did still have the goods, wrapped and bagged nice and tight under the bench where Niamh was tied.

Frank opened the door of the office a crack and checked the corridor. Oh, she was a fine bit of woman, that Niamh. He'd forgotten, in truth, just how much she wound him up. What an arse she had.

He'd only to wait for the next song now, something loud enough to cover the sound of the door scraping open. He craned his neck around the corner. The place was empty but for scuffed footprints on the lino and a few crushed fag butts. The walls in here were oxblood red, about the same colour as Niamh's lips in the deep centre. Frank remembered how he'd left her, pliant and willing and begging for it. He slid along with his back to the wall, one eye on the door through to the bar. His heartbeat thumped so loud it almost drowned out the steady drone of the music. But no one appeared. Breathing hard, he reached the fire exit, propped open with an empty beer bottle. He could smell the yeasty mix of Dublin's night

ir, the cigarettes and laughter and the thousand jokes that mingled
n the warmed-over sea breeze.

As he scurried along towards the Laika, keeping on the outside
where the shadows were darkest, Frank added up in his head. Would
he have time, yet, to finish what he'd started with Niamh, and still
catch the last boat? Was it worth the risk?

His cock twitched in his trousers, and he could almost hear it
reason with him like a little devil-voice. Burn off the adrenaline,
wouldn't it? Almost make up for losing out on six-hundred-odd
grand. He smiled as he reached the driver's door, and pulled it open
with a rush of relief.

Primed for a swift, stunningly satisfying shag, Frank climbed into
the cab of the Laika with a filthy great smile on his face. So when he
went through to the back and failed to notice that the overhead lights
were now out, he maybe dived a little too quickly towards the
banquette where his oblivious, sweetly horny ex-girlfriend was
trussed up waiting for him.

Only as he groped for a breast did he realize, with a slowly
growing sense of horror, that the chest he was feeling was hairier
than his own.

You know, the Irish fellows never fail to surprise me. I might never
have believed that Dublin's second hardest gangster was capable of
the gentlemanly restraint that Eddie showed as he untied me and sat
at the table, respectfully turning his back when I asked for some
privacy to dress.

Perhaps nobody would ever have thought Eddie for the type to turn
his back on anyone, least of all a woman with a temper and an
unresolved orgasm. But he did, meek as a choirboy, and allowed me
time to lift the mattress and find the satchel and get a good swing at
him. I'd only to lamp him the once. Force equals mass times
acceleration, as we all know.

And perhaps no one would have thought that I, Niamh Carmichael,
with the bobbed hair, the good job and yoyos to spare, would have
the gumption to take not only the satchel full of cocaine, but also, by
way of getting a simple answer to a simple question that I asked
Eddie nicely – though I admit I'd to slap him awake and hold his own
pocket knife to his big sweaty bollocks right enough – get the coordinates of the safe, easily slip into the club by flashing my lipstick
smile at the bouncers, and collect the money in the safe – a large sum
but not too large to fit in my handbag, no, not the roomy leather one

I'd splashed out a week's wages on – before scarpering in a taxi, so
for the last ferry, and freedom, and even if nobody believed it an
wondered where I'd got to, and whether I was at the bottom of th
Liffey, it didn't matter so much.

No, I thought as I looked out over the Irish Sea towards fres
horizons. Home was home, and sometimes that was a good enoug
reason to leave. I thought of Frank and Eddie, stuck in that foul littl
caravan under the streetlights, and raised a glass to toast them.

"May the devil make ladders of your backbones while he's pickin
apples in hell, boys."

Barnacle Bill

Angela Caperton

By the middle of June, Melissa could not leave her room, the space beyond the door too terrifying even to consider.

She left the windows open at night and sometimes insects flew in or rats and mice crept silently over the sill, lured by the bits of meat decaying in the sink and the pile of unchewed bones in the corner. Once she saw a cat slink in out of the moonlight gloom and circle the room like a shadow, not even noticing Melissa until she snatched it and savoured the dark scream as she snapped its spine and sucked its marrow.

She thought about her life before, but thinking became harder every day and even the most focused deliberations seemed more like hallucinations. In time, she settled for dreams and gradually Melissa ceased to move at all.

She dreamed of a pounding on her door, the shrill voice of the old woman, Sammi Marsh, with her lips red as blood and her cheeks the colour of bleached plums. "You owe me, girly. You better pay me that twenty dollars, bitch."

"Who's that knocking on the door? Who's that knocking at my door?"

How long ago? Days? Months? The old woman had fled from Adams Manor weeks before and Melissa would have given almost anything to have Sammi Marsh back, to have her knocking on the door again, to ask her to come inside. Melissa remembered borrowing twenty dollars from the old woman the very first day she moved into the miserable, ancient boarding house, given its grandiose name because John Quincy was rumoured once to have stayed there.

She dreamed of her first day too, the bus ride from Boston to a job interview in Arkham, her last ten bucks in her pocket and less than a hundred in the bank. Melissa owed over ten thousand dollars to her friends and relatives in Boston and she knew she could never go back there. She rode the bus north through Salem and then on the traffic-packed road west, along the banks of the Miskatonic River to the old college town, past strip malls and a Walmart to the old core of the city, dark buildings that reeked of impossible age.

She interviewed for a job at an exporter down near the river harbour, but they wanted someone with accounting experience. Melissa lied, but then she failed a simple test and they told her they'd call her, though she didn't know how they'd do that, since her phone was dead. Melissa remembered despair but it seemed pale as the crescent moon's light through the open window.

After the interview, bound for no place, she walked towards the river, and passed men darker and more dangerous than any she had ever seen. Their eyes, cold and shrewd as car dealers', appraised every step she took. Dockworkers, she knew, and sailors, no women among them at all, not in the daytime.

"Who's that knocking at my door?" said the fair young maiden.

Adams Manor displayed a vacancy sign in its dusty window and the landlord, a homely young man named Pyncheon who happened to be there, though he lived somewhere far away, took her cheque for fifty dollars, a bargain rate for her first week, and promised with a leer, "I'll be back, to see if you need anything."

The only other tenant was Sammi Marsh, and the old woman had been delighted to see Melissa move in. She had been happy to lend a twenty, hadn't hesitated, and Melissa thought maybe she would be good for a while. But how quickly the hag had refused to loan another dime!

"Goddamn you, bitch, give me my money!" Pounding. Pounding.

"It's only me from over the sea," said Barnacle Bill the Sailor.

She pushed the pounding and the song away, and dreamed of her first night in the Adams, when Mrs Marsh fed her tea and black cake.

"You won't go out at night," the old woman said, "if you're smart. Men round here fall into two types – drunks and crazies. Just down the street's a seaman's church that ain't a real church and the boys who go there . . . there's something wrong with them. Better you find yourself one of the drunks."

Melissa drank the tea and saw soon enough what the old woman meant. The Seamen's Church of St Fintan drew men all week to night-time services. Melissa watched them every evening pass on the street below her window, young and old known only by their pace, muffled in their jackets, hats pulled low. She could not see their faces.

She noticed one man in particular, squat and heavy. He walked with a shuffling gait that might have been age or an injury, his legs invisible from her overhead perspective. His broad shoulders added mystery, along with the watch cap that covered his head. Something about his steps, a pace oddly rhythmic, almost mechanical, reminded her of a wind-up toy or a clockwork figure and she always shivered with a chill when he passed in the street below.

"He's the one I call Barnacle Bill," Mrs Marsh told her with a cluck. "He's the worst of the lot. Smells like rotten fish. Best you stay inside when they come and go from their church that ain't no church. And if any of them ever come inside here, keep your door locked tight."

"Open the door, you fucking whore," said Barnacle Bill the Sailor.

No, Melissa thought and pushed against the dream. She wasn't a whore. Sure, she'd thought about it, and once or twice back in Boston, she'd taken money for sex, but that wasn't the same thing. In time, here in Arkham, she might've eventually turned a trick, but all she did in those first days was visit the club district near Miskatonic University, where she found a boy who would trade drinks and dinner for kisses. She promised to meet him again if he would loan her twenty. She hadn't fucked anyone, and certainly none of the sailors or dockworkers. They all looked too dirty and dangerous.

But many nights, she watched the darkening street from her window, the slow procession of the eerie congregation by ones and twos, to the church, and she could not tear her gaze from the dark shape of Barnacle Bill, until one night he finally looked up and saw her watching him.

The man's eyes were sunken deep in black pits. All Melissa saw were the craggy lines of his face, cheekbones sharp, and his skin waxy in the lamplight, but she knew that he saw her because he paused and licked his lips with a long tongue that appeared quite black in the deepening shadows, before he resumed his pilgrimage down the dusk-washed street.

"Are you young and handsome, sir? Are you young and handsome, sir?"

After a week, the old woman began to ask about the money she had loaned Melissa and then to demand repayment. Sammi's caustic and accusing tone quickly soured Melissa's tolerance and, by the end of the week, she could no longer keep the old woman company or drink her tea and gin.

About that time, young Pyncheon the landlord came around as he had promised. He had a nice cock and he tasted good when Melissa took him in her mouth, sucking him until he clutched her hair in his hands and shot his wad down her throat. She hadn't minded at all fucking him for the rent, though the act seemed unclear in her dreams and she decided he had not been a good lover at all or she would have remembered him.

"Whore!" Mrs Marsh pounded the cadence of Melissa's dream upon her door. "Give me my money, you fucking whore! Or I'll put Barnacle Bill on you!"

"Are you young and handsome, sir?" said the fair young maiden.

In the second week, Melissa had watched from her window as Sammi Marsh, wrapped in a shawl against the north wind, waited in the street. Melissa saw the old bitch fall into step beside Barnacle Bill, hastening to match the dark sailor's odd, rolling shuffle, saw the old bat whispering. Melissa watched them stop and then look up, Mrs Marsh's eyes shining like the eyes of an animal in the moonlight but Bill's eyes, Melissa remembered, stared black and dead as night seas.

She remembered the fear and the sticky fascination that held her too long looking down until the street lay empty. Mrs Marsh did not return to Adams Manor. The evening hours crawled as Melissa listened and shivered until dread had risen in her like a tide and she could stand it no longer. After ten o'clock, in the moonless depth of night, fear claimed her entirely and she ran panicking from her room.

Did panic taste of salt, or sewage? Melissa could not remember.

"I'm old and rough and dirty and tough!" said Barnacle Bill the Sailor.

At the bottom of the stair, Melissa smelled the sea at low tide, a stench of stranded life, hardly one step evolved above the slime and returning to it.

Barnacle Bill waited for her there.

She remembered screaming, scrambling back up the stairs, his slow tread behind her and the silences between his merciless, angular steps.

She threw the lock. Sometimes in the dreams, she threw the lock and she was safe. But not always.

"I'm old and rough and dirty and tough!" said Barnacle Bill the Sailor.

She remembered opening the door. No, she wouldn't have opened the door. He pounded and she opened. No. No. No. She hadn't. She wouldn't.

"I'll come down and let you in. I'll come down and let you in.

"I'll come down and let you in," said the fair young maiden.

As he approached her, Barnacle Bill's face was a miracle of symmetry, the cheeks identical, slit eyes shining in the depth of shadow pools, his mouth a drawn line of determination.

"I'll give her the money," Melissa screamed but she knew, even in the most hopeful dreams, that Barnacle Bill didn't care about the money.

He caught her wrists in hands hard and tight as metal cuffs, and she saw the watch cap was actually a part of him, a fleshy blue crown that flared wetly. His face broke along the lines of its symmetry and his black tongue flicked long as her arm. Barnacle Bill's eyes were moist pockets and his coat opened with a whisper. The sea smell washed over her but it no longer stank of death.

She dreamed of algae blooms like monstrous roses in the waves, the caress of warm water, the rising and falling of her own blood with the cycles of the moon.

He tore her clothes away with the sharp edges of his hands. His fingers splayed cold and wide on her thighs as his black tongue explored her throat, twining, tickling one nipple then the other. He held her down and probed her with his tongue, his scent overwhelming her terror, her screams growing hoarse, then silent.

"What's that thing between your legs? What's that thing between your legs?

"What's that thing between your legs?" said the fair young maiden.

Moray smooth, the head of Barnacle Bill's cock emerged from between the half-shells of his parted coat, the ropy, seeking length tracing a line down Melissa's belly, a cold smear of fishy slime, through her stubbly cunt hair to bump against her clit.

She dreamed and remembered needing him inside her.

The sinuous, growing length moved with serpentine purpose and the head slipped into her. Nothing had ever filled her like this, the throbbing, bulbous head seemed to spread inside and out, massaging her clit like a lover's finger as he moved atop her. She wanted more.

"It's only me pole to shove in your holes!" said Barnacle Bill the Sailor.

"It's only me pole to shove in your holes!" said Barnacle Bill the Sailor.

She saw, bobbing loosely behind his black tongue, his real eyes, merciless and hungry. His incredible length moved in and out, around, teasing her asshole then filling her pussy again, flicking as delicately as a tongue and as forceful as a fist. His cock flesh seemed to double and bend so she felt him within her and behind her, forcing open the reluctant ring of her ass even as he gushed wet and warm and endless as the sea deep inside her.

She remembered coming and coming and coming, sweat-drenched, collapsed against his segmented body, almost tender when he licked with his black tongue and kissed her most intimate places with his chalky beak, before he left her.

Before the morning.

Melissa lay naked on the floor, still wet here and there from her lover's embrace, pushing against the memory, looking for the moment when she must have gone mad, though she did not find it. Numbness cloaked the soaked space between her legs, and she felt nothing, nothing at all. The night was only the beginning of dreams but in that first new morning the dreams had almost vanished.

"What if we should have a boy? What if we should have a boy? What if we should have a boy?" said the fair young maiden.

When the sun was high overhead, she dressed and went downstairs. Mrs Marsh's door stood slightly ajar and Melissa considered pushing it open and looking in, but she walked by and out onto the streets. The thought passed mistily through her mind that she should find a doctor, but she could not imagine what she would say to one.

She found one of the lowest of the whiskey joints by the main dock, an unlicensed room with a bar made from old tables, full of men and she took twenty each from five of them for blow jobs in the alley behind the building, knowing she must look awful, must reek of shore-stranded kelp. She didn't care and neither did the men. They probably thought she was a junkie. Let them. Fuck them. Next.

When she left the bar and the alley, she walked towards French Hill where she found a deli. She spent the hundred dollars the men had given her on cold cuts, sausages, and a fat, orange round of cheese, two bags full of food that she carried back to her room. Alone in the silence, Melissa stripped off her stained clothes and lay back on the bed.

She hoped Barnacle Bill would come back to her in the night, but deep in her heart, she knew he wouldn't. She knew she would never see him again.

"I'll take him to sea, teach him to fuck like me!" said Barnacle Bill the Sailor.

"I'll take him to sea, teach him to fuck like me!" said Barnacle Bill the Sailor.

Day to night, night to day, the dreams became much the same, time indistinguishable, hours, days the same and melting, slow and deliberate as dripping water in her sink or the growth of coral in the sea. She began always to leave the window open, though some nights it brought chill air. She needed the smell of the river and beyond it the brackish glory of the delta and the secrets of the deep water beyond it.

She dreamed of flying under the waves.

She stayed naked and ate the drying meat and the strong cheese, but she no longer stood by the window in the evening to watch the procession of sailors below. A waxy film began to form on her skin and her bones hurt sometimes, but the pain was easy to ignore.

One day there came a knocking on her door.

She rose, sharply aware of the dry rustle when she walked, the stiffness of her legs, and went to answer the knocking. Pyncheon the landlord had come for his rent or for fucking. How he screamed when he saw her! How he screamed when her tongue looped around him and dragged him towards the sharp, rapacious tip of her beak.

She had eaten him, the soft parts first, then the rest as he rotted and fell to pieces. She ate him with her lips and with the fibrous tendrils that dangled from her hands and breasts. When she was done with the meat, she chewed some of his bones to paste and pressed the white goo into her skin.

No one came around after that and the only sounds Melissa heard in her dreams were the wet rasp of her own breath and the shuffle of the men in the street below bound for the church. She dreamed of Barnacle Bill and his python cock fucking her between the folds of her new shell, filling her pussy and her ass, pulsing, pounding, flooding her when he came.

After a while, Melissa became very still.

In her stillness, she dreamed only of the blackest depths of the ocean and woke to jewelled sunlight, the red fire of dusk through the window. Her room oozed radiance. Sticky buttons dotted the walls and ceiling, dripping streamers of viscous fluid in a web that caught the sun and bled it. Each pink button moved, squirming, seeking a crack or a nail hole, the darkness beneath the bed, the closet. Her children moved like pallid tadpoles trailing ropy lines of blood, hiding.

They would grow up in this room, waiting their turn. Now Melissa had new purpose.

Rising unsteadily, Melissa acknowledged the void in her centre and an aching hunger, though not for food. The strength came rapidly back into her legs and a sense of urgent power flowed through her as the full moon glittered in the sky far above her open window. She left her room as silently as she could manage, passing down the stairs and out into the street.

The river pulsed in her veins, the ancient Miskatonic, and she saw the sea in the river's current. Peace washed over her and she started down the street in long, rolling steps, towards the seamen's church, just as she had always dreamed it.

They welcomed her in, first into a meeting hall where all the sailors gathered, but they saw her nature at once and accepted her into their deepest mysteries. The priest took her all the way to the river and immersed her in its water.

Where she was reborn.

After the service, Melissa walked along Water Street, heading generally towards the college. Beneath the streetlights and city-dulled moonlight, she saw her shadow, wrinkled and huge on the sidewalk. The immense, coiled length of her cock twitched beneath its fleshy cloak, eager for release. She needed a woman, needed to slip her long thick member into warm flesh and know the other side of such pleasure, the pushing and splitting to reach that glorious, screaming bliss.

She understood that she was only a dream. She had no regrets, no sorrow. She could hardly remember a time before the dream, before the salty froth of the sea in her mouth, before the transformation born of pleasure and pain.

Before she was Barnacle Bill.

Belleville Blue

Carrie Williams

Mona hadn't spoken to or even seen any of her neighbours in weeks. She'd been holed up in her garret, hooked up to the Internet or knee-deep in box files, researching her *Encyclopaedia Erotica*. As the work absorbed her more and more, so the human contact diminished, until all she was left with were her occasional trips to the grocer's and her brief calls to her editor, updating him on her progress.

Nights, after working to the point where she couldn't think straight, she'd sit in her window with the shutters thrown open, listening to the Paris night. This area, Oberkampf, spilling out of the Eleventh into the Twentieth, was one of the city's hippest, and from every direction she could hear people calling to one another, music spilling from bars and clubs, animated chatter wafting up from the restaurant and café terraces. The place pulsated with life, while hers seemed to have become something stagnant and stale.

One morning, walking home from the local market with her string bag full of fruit, vegetables and little packets of meat bound up in greaseproof paper, she stopped, on an whim, outside the town hall of her *arrondissement* and studied the notices on the board. It was only then that she realized that it was the eve of the day people like her, lonely people, dreaded more than any other: Bastille Day, the city's – indeed, the nation's – biggest party. A day for celebrating with loved ones. A day for fireworks and fun. But what if there was no one to have fun with?

Just as she was turning away, a second notice snagged her attention: a ball at the local fire station that evening. She smiled to herself. She'd heard about these *bals de pompiers* some time ago. Fire stations across the capital held them every year, on the eve of Bastille Day. She studied the notice in more detail: there were to be "country fair-style games", a bar, traditional music, and a *petite surprise*. This time she almost laughed out loud. The French had some funny ideas about what constituted a good night out.

At home, she put away her shopping and made herself a cup of coffee, which she placed on her desk, by her mouse mat. Logging onto the Net, she typed in the website address of the Louvre and, after a few minutes spent keying in various search words, leaned forward in her chair to get a better view of the erotic artworks and artefacts that were flashed up before her – men and women, or women and women, carved into figurines, on Attic vases, on rings, or in paintings by Delacroix, Ingres and others. From time to time she would lean forward to make notes on a little lined pad beside her, highlighting ones that she particularly wanted to see in the flesh the next time she visited the museum.

Her favourite, and one she had already visited in person several times over, was Ingres' *Le bain turc*, or *Turkish Bath*. She loved it both for its composition – a harem scene full of odalisques – and for its history. Ingres, aged eight-two at the time of the painting, had enjoyed the irony of creating an erotic work in old age, telling friends that he "retained all the fire of a man of thirty years" and even going to far as to detail his age, AETATIS LXXXII, on the canvas itself.

Mona also loved the audacity of the painter in depicting one of the nude female bathers openly caressing the breast of another, and the fact that the bather in the right foreground, arms raised above her head, was based on a sketch that the painter had made of his wife, Madeleine Chapelle, almost half a century before. Another wife, Empress Eugenie, so disliked the work that she made her husband, Napoléon III, return it to the painter just days after receiving it. Before making its way to the Louvre, it had found a more welcome home with Khalil Bey, a former diplomat and art lover with a renowned collection of erotica that had also included Courbet's *L'Origine du monde*, a close-up oil painting of the lower half of a woman's body, legs spread, and his *Les Dormeuses* or *The Sleepers*, an overt depiction of naked lesbian lovers entwined, almost certainly post-coitally, on a bed.

The afternoon passed quickly, productively, and when Mona next glanced up, dusk had fallen outside her window. She stood up to look around, pulled her cardigan more closely around her. She didn't mind the days, but the nights were hard.

She cooked herself a simple supper, but even the robust Toulouse sausage, oven-warmed bread and red wine failed to warm her. She sat in her armchair wrapped in a much-loved pashmina, re-reading a favourite work by Anaïs Nin, *Spy in the House of Love*. Lulled by the slow burn of the prose and the luxuriousness of the sensual experiences described, she soon fell into a reverie from which only the sound of the bells chiming in the church beside her apartment block roused her. She counted down the hour: eight o'clock. Just eight. How was she to get through the rest of the night?

She held out until nine, when the words began to blur before her eyes. Then, folding the blanket and placing it on her work chair, she went upstairs and ran herself a bath, adding a few drops of aromatic oils – her own mix of jasmine, ylang ylang and mandarin. Then she stripped off and sank into it as far as her chin, holding her hair up in a ponytail with one hand. With her other she played with her right nipple, almost unconsciously.

She stared down below the clear water, at the flat expanse of her stomach terminating in the gentle incline of her mound of Venus and the fluff of golden-brown hair, rather unkempt since she had been living here, since she had been alone. She let her ponytail tumble down and the freed hand glide over her body, move across the plump cushion of her mons, thread its way through the silken fronds and play around her lips. She closed her eyes, gave herself up to the delicious melting feeling. As it grew stronger, she hooked her thumb round and pressed it against her clit, massaged it from side to side. A jag of pleasure like an electric shock had her arch up, sloshing water over the side of the bath as she climaxed.

Afterwards, she dressed warmly before locking the apartment and heading out into the night.

She was surprised by the number of people heading into the fire station – the promise of traditional musical entertainment seemed to have brought the locals out in droves. She stood still in the road for a moment, looking at the building. She didn't even know why she was here, besides the fact that she couldn't be alone anymore. But who was she going to talk to? She knew no one. And no one knew her.

She breathed in deeply and pushed open the door. Inside, people were drinking and chatting in low voices. A few of them turned their eyes to her as she handed over a few euros to the woman collecting the entrance fees, and she nodded self-consciously in their direction as she made her way to the trestle table in front of them and bought a glass of red wine. She turned back to face the room, looking around every so often for a friendly face encouraging her to start a conversation. But the momentarily inquisitive adults had all turned back to their little groups, shouldering her out.

After twenty minutes or so, she was just thinking of creeping away and making her way home when a mike was set up on a makeshift little stage at the front of the room. Some men she hadn't noticed until that point materialized from one corner of the room and took to the stage, one carrying a trumpet, another an acoustic guitar, and a third a piano accordion.

Mona watched as they assembled themselves, tuned up their instruments, psyched themselves up. The accordionist, in particular, drew her attention: tall and slightly built, he had almost white-blond hair and chestnut-brown eyes – a combination that had always intrigued her. She didn't remove her gaze from him as he took the large, boxy instrument between his hands, ran his long slender fingers up and down the piano keyboard.

After a few minutes, the band struck up a waltz, and she was pushed back as a tide of people surged forward and the space in front of the stage was transformed into a dance floor by swaying couples. She felt another pang of loneliness as she counted out the coins for a second glass of wine, which she emptied rapidly. Over the dancers' heads she could see the accordionist gently rocking on his parted legs as he compressed and released the bellows with one arm. One hand operated the button keyboard on the left of the bellows, the digits of the other caressed the piano keys. His mastery of the cumbersome-looking contraption was utter.

In her mind, as the wine infiltrated her bloodstream and her focus on the blond accordion player grew more intent, the sound of the other instruments almost wholly died away. She was fascinated by how the swirling sound of the accordion simultaneously evoked in her a sense of sprightly cheeriness and a kind of wistfulness, perhaps even melancholy. Utterly and unmistakeably French, it put her in mind of black berets and clouds of cigarette smoke – some of the clichés she thought she abhorred. She found herself swaying a little in time to the music, then tapping her feet, shimmying her shoulders a tad. No one could see her anyway, hidden away as she was at the back of the room.

As the evening advanced, the pace heightened, with the band working their way through an impressive repertoire of polkas, mazurkas, foxtrots, paso dobles and javas. The latter, in which the swaggering dancers wrapped their arms around their partners and clasped their buttocks, thrilled her with its loucheness. It put her in mind of the old *bal-musettes* she had read about. Almost against her will, she found herself moving forward towards the dance floor, surrendering her body to the cadence. The couples, lost to each other, scarcely noticed as she slipped between them, eased herself into the centre. As another tune began, she threw her head back, closed her eyes, and let herself be carried away by the tempo.

She wasn't sure how long she'd been dancing when she opened her eyes to see the accordionist's gaze fixed firmly on her, the corners of his mouth twisted up in a wry smile. He nodded at her when she saw him, winked. She smiled back, moved a little closer to the stage now that the crowd had thinned out a little. With her hips and shoulders she writhed like a serpent, enjoying the way her breasts swayed wantonly in her flimsy bra, the feel of the blond's eyes on her as the band launched into a rousing finale.

The music stopped and the musicians stepped forward to take a bow. The rough wine coursing in her veins, combined with the intoxication of the dance, made her step forward to steady herself against the stage. She closed her eyes again. She was showing herself up in front of all these strangers, she reprimanded herself. She looked towards the door, wondered if she could make it that far without falling over.

As she straightened herself up, she felt a firm hand on her shoulder.

"*Ça va?*" she heard a voice say, and she looked up to see the accordion player lowering himself to sit on the edge of the stage beside her.

"*Oui, oui,*" she said rapidly.

"Ah, you're English?"

She nodded.

"Are you on holiday?"

"No, I just moved here, not long ago. I live just off Oberkampf, towards the Canal Saint-Martin."

"I don't know it. I'm not from here. We travel around. We're vagabonds." He smiled, held out a hand. "My name is Louis," he said, as she felt his warm palm against hers. "What's yours?"

"Mona."

"*C'est joli.* Listen, Mona, I need to pack up my accordion but I'd love to have a drink. How say we take a couple of glasses outside with us?" He looked around him. "It's getting a bit stale and sweaty in here."

"Sure," she said, losing herself in the soft brown eyes that regarded her, dark as pools of spilt ink. She followed him across the now-deserted space of the dance floor.

"What did you think of the entertainment?" he said, as she reached for two glasses. He headed towards the door, which she stood against to hold open as he manoeuvred his bulky instrument outside.

"I loved it," she replied, a little embarrassed as she remembered how she had lost herself on the dance floor, how she had opened her eyes to find him staring right at her. Sensing her discomfort, he added:

"It's nice to see someone with a bit of rhythm."

She laughed.

"Seriously," he said. "So what brought you to Paris?"

She frowned, looked past him. There had been nights, other nights, when, crazed and cracked by solitude, she had walked and walked, following the streets until she had to ask a stranger for directions back to Belleville.

"I'm a writer," she said at last. "And Paris is a city of writers. *For* writers."

He nodded thoughtfully, lit up a cigarette, offering her one. Fire danced in his eyes as he struck a match and brought it to the tip. He took a deep drag, blew smoke out around him.

"Shall we go for a walk?" he said. "I don't know this part of Paris at all. Which is silly, since this is the territory of Piaf, my heroine."

Mona gestured back down the Rue de Ménilmontant, and he nodded, placing the undrunk glasses of wine on the pavement before following her.

They walked in silence for a while, and then, feeling the need to break the silence, Mona said, "So why the accordion?"

"The squeezebox, or 'trembling box' – *boîte à frissons* – as the slang word has it?" he said, then paused reflectively. "Well, why not?" he continued after a moment, flashing her a smile that made her feel weak.

"Why not indeed? But it's quite a rare instrument. Why did you choose it over, say, a guitar?"

"Oh, I play the guitar too. And a few other instruments besides. But I'm a romantic, and there is something so old-fashioned about the accordion. I've been in love with the idea of it ever since I first heard the Piaf song *L'Accordeoniste*."

"About an accordion player?"

He nodded, eyes fixed on the road ahead. "About a doomed love
ffair between a *bal-musette* accordionist and a prostitute. Cheery
tuff. And what about you?"

"What about me?"

"What kind of thing do you write?"

She squirmed a little. Depending on who she was talking to, she
vas more or less evasive about her job as an historian of the erotic.
Not that she was ashamed of it. But she had found that it gave people
ertain ideas about her, that it made them think, all too often, that
he was some kind of nymphomaniac. Sadly, the converse was true.
She would have loved to be a sexual tigress, but she had grown to
ccept that she just didn't have it in her.

He had noticed her hesitation and was just about to open his
mouth to coax her when she saw the Café Charbon up on their right
nd was happy to have the opportunity to deflect any further
questioning, at least for the moment.

"A drink?" she said. "This is the best bar in the neighbourhood,
o they say."

He looked at the facade, then down it past the street. "How about
. dance?" he said, gesturing with his chin towards a different venue.

She looked. It was the Nouveau Casino, a famous club and live
music venue. She'd never been.

She must have pulled a face, for he said, "We don't have to." Then
e linked his arm through hers. "But it might be quite fun if we do."

She didn't want any more to drink, was dehydrated from the cheap
ed wine at the *bal*. But on the dance floor with Louis, resting her
head against his shoulder and feeling his pelvis grinding into her,
eeling the coil of his dick straining at his trousers, seeking, of its own
ccord, what nested between her own legs, she felt lightheaded,
drunk with desire and longing. Around them people swayed in time
o the electro tunes, sometimes moving other body parts too – arms,
ands, fingers, shoulders, head or hips. Some of them whooped and
ounced, showing off to the rest of their crowd. Others, falling into
une with the music, with the intensification of the beats and melody
hat the DJ was engineering at his turntables, looked to be falling into
ome kind of trance state.

She didn't know if she was imagining it, but the DJ seemed to be
rying to work the room up to some sort of climactic highpoint,
ifting the dancers, perhaps without them realizing, to some higher
lane of consciousness. It was a question, she sensed, of letting go, of

submitting, and she had never been very good at that. But what had happened as Louis had played his accordion back there in the fire station had shown her that she was capable of it, that she could allow herself to lose control. It was all a matter of trust.

She lifted her head, looked Louis fiercely in the eyes, then let her head loll back away from him, closed her own eyes. The strobes sent multicoloured waves of light racing over the insides of her lids. The music pounded away inside her brain, up through her body, like some kind of powerful narcotic. Her cunt ached, ached for this man whose delicate but sure hands were the only thing between her and the floor. It was all she could do not to reach down and start rubbing at her palpitating clit.

She must have been about to pass out, or to look like she might for before long Louis scooped her up in his arms and carried her out of the club. The July night was cooling now. He set her down on her feet, gently.

"Told you it would be fun," she heard him say, "in a weird kind of way. Not that I'm a big fan of modern music. Give me Piaf any day. Or John Coltrane. Or Gershwin."

Not eliciting any response from her, he began to hum, and then to sing "Fascinating Rhythm".

As they began to walk back up towards the fire station, he stopped singing, turned his head to her. "You've gone awfully quiet," he said. When she didn't reply, he took her hand and they continued in silence.

As they approached the fire station, raucous cries could be heard through the windows open onto the night. Louis turned to smile at Mona.

"*La surprise*," he said, and mischief flickered in his eyes like wild fire. He made for the door, beckoning her to follow him.

When they stepped inside, the room was even more packed than before, and the temperature had risen perceptibly. But the dance floor was still, all bodies turned towards the stage, backs to the door where Louis and Mona had entered.

Mona raised her eyes to the stage and let out a low moan. On it, five or six firemen were gyrating to the music emanating from the loudspeakers on either side of it. Slowly, tantalizingly, they were stripping off their tight navy uniforms. Mona swallowed, almost painfully, as she watched taut limbs being unveiled, as bronzed biceps and well-defined six-packs were revealed, and honed buttocks signalled their firm presence through crisp white boxer shorts.

The men danced on, obviously enjoying the eyes on them, revelling in the power of their manliness, savouring the thrill of performing his act normally forbidden to them, alien to their daily lives and vocation. Running their powerful hands over skin that looked, in its sheen, to have been lightly oiled but may just have been slick with perspiration, they let their eyes roam the audience, occasionally winking at someone who caught their eye, giving them a cheeky grin and a come-hither look.

As the pace quickened, Mona became aware that she was moving in time to the music, swaying her hips then her torso and shoulders, almost aping the firemen's moves. Half-closing her eyes, she imagined for a moment she was up there with them, stepping up to one of them, running her hand down over his bare, smooth chest, insinuating a finger into the top of his boxers, starting to inch them down, by infinitesimal little tugs, until she could feel the soft hair of his groin lap at her fingertips.

She must have staggered again, almost fallen, for suddenly she was in Louis's arms for the second time, and his face was in hers, half anxious, half lustful, shining with a film of sweat. He too, she sensed, was not unmoved by the sight of the muscular bodies on the stage.

"Time to go home," breathed Louis, and she nodded.

He carried her back down the Ménilmontant hill, paying no heed to the passers-by who stared at them. Then, where she pointed, he turned right off Oberkampf onto Rue Saint-Maur. After a few moments, he prompted gently, "Where do you live?"

"Opposite the church," she uttered with effort, weakly waving a hand towards her apartment block.

He moved towards it. She felt in her pocket, produced the key and handed it to him.

As if bringing his bride over the threshold, he carried her in and began to ascend the staircase, looking down at her.

Mona smiled at him. She felt like a child in his arms. She felt safe.

In her studio, walking over to her big old *lit bateau*, Louis threw her down. The rough action woke Mona from her dream-like state and she jumped up, encircled his slim wrists with her hands.

"Come here," she half-snarled, pulling him towards her, twisting him round as she did so, so that he fell backwards onto the bed and she was her on top. The somnolent effects of the alcohol and the

repetitive music had worn off now, and she felt incredibly clear
headed, lucid. She knew what she wanted, for the first time in a long
while. Perhaps for the first time in her life.

Leaning over him, hair pouring down onto him like water, she
ripped his shirt off, too impatient to fiddle with the buttons. Then
she pulled the T-shirt beneath it up over his head, at the same time
bringing her face down and fastening her front teeth on first one
nipple, then the other. As he moaned and wriggled beneath her, she
chewed at them in turn, varying the intensity. With her hands she
reached down to where her cunt was drizzling his groin with her
nectar, took hold of the hard baton of his penis. With her thumb she
massaged the head, paying special attention to the ridge of the
corona. Then she grasped the shaft firmly in her fist and set in
motion a series of regular strokes, listening to his joyful gasps at the
up- and downbeats. When his breaths and groans seemed to be
rising to a crescendo, she kneeled up above him, presented him with
her cunt.

He cupped the succulent mound with one hand, levered himself
down and through her legs until his face was directly underneath
her. His tongue peeked out from between his lips, tauntingly. She
lowered herself, mashed herself against his jaw, his mouth. He
opened wide, took a big mouthful of her pussy, his tongue at the
centre stabbing at her clit. She juddered, rising towards her climax.
When it seemed inevitable, she lifted her haunches and backed up,
lowering herself onto his cock. Taking him into the far reaches of
herself, she held on as he galloped beneath her, squeezing and
releasing him with her walls until both of them were being battered
by their orgasms.

She collapsed down on top of him, and as she began to let herself
succumb to sleep, clutching her still-throbbing pussy, she was certain
that, although the Nouveau Casino was a good few minutes' walk
from her house, she could feel the music from the club pulsing up
through her floor.

In the morning she found him frying eggs in the kitchenette, a
coffee brewed in the pot, richly scenting the room. Music was
playing on the radio – some vapid pop hit – and he was wiggling his
fine arse around in time to the beat, clad only in his striped boxer
shorts.

She sat down, smiled uncertainly. Memories of the firemen in
their underwear flitted through her mind, like the uncertain traces of

dying dream. She was astonished by what she had done the night before, by what the music and the firemen's striptease had loosed in her, as if she were a dam stopped up for too long. How much had she needed this release?

"So how long have you been writing erotica?" he said casually, jerking his head towards a pile of papers that she had left on the corner of the kitchen table.

She didn't return his gaze, rubbed at an invisible stain on the tabletop. "Oh, a couple of years. I'm – I'm just writing an encyclopaedia."

"I can't say I'm surprised," he replied.

"What do you mean?"

"Well, a woman with appetites like yours. The way you . . . the way you went for me last night. Like something possessed." He looked towards her, trying to gauge her reaction, hoping he hadn't overstepped the mark.

She smiled inwardly. *If only you knew*, she thought.

"What about fiction?" he went on, flipping the eggs in the pan.

She shrugged. "I've tried, but . . ." Her words tailed off.

"But what?"

"I don't know. It's the characters. They never really come alive. Which means the sex doesn't either."

"Perhaps you need a muse?"

"Maybe," she said, thinking again of how the music from Louis' accordion, the previous evening, had stirred in her some animal longing that she hadn't even known existed. She stood up, letting her kimono fall open.

He rose too, eyes riveted to the strip of ivory skin that had been revealed. "I've been thinking of leaving the band for a while. I'm sick of the wandering life," he said. His voice had a sudden edge to it – desire, certainly, but desire tinged with fear, or awe.

Her kimono fell to the floor. Pushing him down onto the chair, she yanked his boxers down.

"Inspire me," she growled, but she didn't hear his reply. Her head was filled with the wildest, murkiest and most euphoric cacophony, one that she knew no words could ever translate.

Aqua Subculture

Lee Ee Leen

I sold beautiful curiosities in my shop so it was only fitting that one walked in. However, it was not an antiques shop: my merchandise was a living example of years of human manipulation in enhancing specific genetic traits in fish. I stocked common goldfish, black goldfish supposed to guard the family home from bad *chi*, calicos, neon tetras, comets, and bubble-eyed imported specimens. I rented a corner lot squeezed next to a dim sum restaurant in a neighbourhood shopping mall. Contrary to what you may have overheard in the management office, my fish did not end up as fillings in the wontons served for the lunchtime crowd. A week after I expanded the size of the shop to include marine fish, Andie sauntered through the door.

I tried not to stare at her. Beautiful women are often defensive and accompanied by protective items such as boyfriends and husbands. She was alone, a towering, slim beauty whose physique almost blended in with the narrow shelves that overlooked the reef tank. With a Harley-Davidson biker's cap tilted over her face, she lured me out from behind the counter.

"How much are they?" She tapped the glass of the tank to indicate the black-and-white cleaner wrasse, darting around the bigger fish in the tank like harried waiters. For a natural tank janitor and a collector's item I recommended a cleaner shrimp, a miniature automaton coloured like a barbershop pole and equipped with six jointed legs.

"I am not a beginner," she stated in a lilting accent that was definitely not local. Her green contact lenses flashed in the fluorescent light. I was naive to think she was referring to her fish-keeping experience.

"Come back in three days. Those wrasse are reserved," I lied.

Three days later when I arrived at my shop, she was standing outside the shutter at quarter to eleven. With those narrow hips wrapped in tight snakeskin jeans, she looked like a boy when viewed from behind. When she turned at the sound of my jangling keys, I saw her breasts constricted under a Boy London T-shirt. "Please wait outside, miss."

I learnt her name after I had bagged a cleaner wrasse. The fish flailed as I handed her the plastic bag. "It only has one hour before it suffocates."

"Kinky," she muttered as she took the bag. She was not wearing the green contact lenses this morning. I preferred her eyes naturally tawny. She told me her name because she was fed up with my calling her "miss", as if I were giving inept instructions to an artillery unit.

"Andie," she said. "Like the actress, Andie MacDowell." She paused and waited for my response, as if I had flubbed a line of dialogue.

"I wasn't named after someone famous," I told her after some hesitation. I wished I was called "Jacques" as an alternative to my pedestrian moniker, Jack. When I was young, I saw a documentary on TV about Jacques Cousteau, the French underwater explorer. Local mispronunciation would flub the Gallic inflection of Jacques, and make it sound more like "Jock".

Andie laughed and removed her biker cap. Her black hair fell to the waistband of her jeans. She looked like a mermaid, the black tresses and their green iridescence shimmering above the scaly faux snakeskin.

We met under the fibreglass model of a whale shark in the aquaria in Kuala Lumpur City Centre. I suggested the trip as a natural progression of shared interests. The aquaria were divided into biotopes: coral reef, Amazon River, Malaysian rainforest and mangrove swamp. A tunnel lit by neon-blue track lights connected each biotope.

"Arapaimas mate for life," I pointed out to Andie at the Amazon River tank. Two behemoths drifted past us in the green water, their bony heads etched with curlicues and ridged scars.

"Fools." She set her lips together in a compressed line.

"Sea-slugs are hermaphrodites – but can't self-fertilize. They still need a partner," Andie informed me as she pressed her palm on the reinforced glass of the cylinder tank for invertebrates. A specimen unfurled its fuchsia plumes as it clambered over a Venus' Flower Basket, a glassy hollow sponge that imprisons a pair of male and female shrimp for life.

We followed yellow arrows plastered to the wall of the tunnel to the special aquaria exhibit of the month – Australian sea snakes. A

large open tank was covered with mesh wire, flanked by signs tha
unnecessarily warned visitors not to put their hands inside the tank
I peered through the wire and saw two banded sea snakes entwined
in a tight double helix, their bodies rippling together in gentle
languor. Inspired by this demonstration, Andie slipped her arms
around my waist and squeezed until I jerked in pain.

I guided Andie to the shark tank, expecting a little more tenderness
from her. A nurse shark burrowed its snout into the sand, scavenging
for leftovers. The PA crackled and a voice announced feeding time
Kids rushed to the glass as a diver descended into the tank clutching
a wire mesh bag of frozen fish. The diver dealt out the fish like an
underwater Jesus feeding the five thousand; the food in the bag did
not run out.

Aware of his audience, the diver let his hand linger in the maw of
a black-tip reef shark to shrieks of alarm from the children. Andie
smiled at this spectacle, her lips stretched back, revealing teeth that
overcrowded her mouth. She was all torpedo sleekness in a grey
sleeveless dress.

We exited the aquaria and flowed into the lunchtime crowd.

Andie stayed in a serviced apartment opposite KLCC. A small
basket of fruit on the coffee table enhanced the sparseness of the
living room. I noted the absence of an aquarium.

"What did you do with the wrasse?"

"I bought it as a gift." She waved her hand around as if the
question were lingering cigarette smoke and changed the subject
"Are you hungry?"

We phoned for sushi from a Japanese restaurant near KLCC that
provided delivery. Our food would arrive in thirty minutes. Andie
selected a pomegranate from the fruit basket. As she started peeling
away the skin of the fruit, she told me a story.

A beautiful girl was born to a Thai mother and Swiss father. Her
father left not long after she was born. When the girl came of age, she
found out that she was different from her friends. She looked like a
girl, but was not one on the inside.

"How so?" I asked Andie.

"She can't have children. She has no womb," Andie replied, and
with the sudden shift to present tense, I realized she was talking
about herself. Andie had Complete Androgen Insensitivity
Syndrome; her body had resisted the development into a male by
remaining stubbornly feminine. She was not a transsexual and she
hated the term "intersex".

"I'm not a freak!" Andie ranted, "I'm not caught between the two xes. Males and females are the ones who are strange, because they e incomplete. Women are always searching for their other halves d all that magazine bullshit."

Andie took a deep breath, piled the pomegranate seeds into a glass wl and joined me on the sofa. She put her head in my lap and ked me to drop the seeds into her mouth. I asked her what I had ne to earn this pleasure.

"I just spent a whole morning with you," she smiled up at me. And you're the first guy I've met around here who doesn't ask mb questions about me. You live in the 'now'. Suppose it comes om watching fish all the time."

The seeds burst with a tart pop. As the juice spilled, it stained my ngertips scarlet. Like the diver with the shark, I let my fingers main between her lips for a second too long. She sucked and pped the pads of my finger, not quite playful. If she drew any of y blood, it mingled with the juice.

Over one of our sushi dinners, I mentioned mating to Andie, out how marine creatures did not go through the awkwardness of x on dry land. When she had cleared her plate, she went to the athroom. Andie called for me after ten minutes. I heard the taps nning from outside and knocked on the bathroom door.

She poured in the bath salts and the foam and issued me structions: "Don't turn around until I say so."

I heard the taps running, water gushing out. Inspired, I invented a ame for a new cocktail: "Sex in the Bath". Foam spilled over the rim the bathtub and drifted over to my bare feet. "You can look now."

Andie had skimmed off a layer of thick foam and fashioned a kini out of it: bubbles shining on her wet skin like sequins sewn to a body stocking.

The water sloshed around as I climbed inside the tub. I lifted aside handful of wet hair pressed against her shoulder blades, strands of lp left on white sand at high tide. The strap of lather on one oulder had split. I nipped and rasped my teeth along the ridge of collarbone until I reached the notch at the base of her neck. I pped my tongue in, the skin tasting salty, the same as the mussels dinner. The rest of the makeshift bra had dissolved, exposing her ny rosewood nipples. My hand reached between her thighs and ught out her niche, fingers discovering that her hole was as shallow a navel. Andie gasped and shoved me back with the contained olence of a self-defence class. We slid in rhythm against the wall of

the tub. Male sea snakes cannot disengage from females until matin
is complete.

My living room had a built-in marine aquarium equipped wi
backlit glass, harsh and vivid like a screensaver. The cleaner shrin
from my shop were servicing a blue-striped angelfish.

"Humans think they can study animals in tanks and cages, ar
put them into categories."

Dressed in a terry-wrap robe, Andie walked over to the windo
her profile slashed into shadows by the Venetian blinds. Her ran
began like our lovemaking, a sharp tangential stab in a rando
location, growing in intensity as she located an available target.
tried to distract her. I pointed to the aquarium, "Are you talkir
about my fish?"

"You make them sound like they're your property."

I went over and put my arms around her to soothe her displeasur

"You don't own me – I'm not one of your fish in your shop."

"I have a duty to my shop."

"Your shop is your property, which has its own set of conditions
She loosed the belt on the robe and opened it before taking my har
and pressing it on her soft breast, "Duty is unconditional. Whe
you're with me, you are beyond all that."

"No." I struggled to deny my body's responses. "Can we ta
about you? Or us?"

Andie rolled her eyes at me and pushed me back towards the sof
"Remember the deal, Jack? You don't ask dumb questions about n
or anything. We enjoy what we can when we can."

On the sofa, the bathrobe fell down around Andie as she climbe
above me, a goddess holding up the canopy of the night sky with h
body. It was dim under her robe as the moist velvets of our moutl
mingled. When she placed her mouth around what she humorous
called my "seahorse", I forgot about duty or business.

Andie was right; my shop was my property and my duty althougl
had been neglecting it. Live food drifted in plastic basins, air pumj
broke down and filters clogged up with algae and gave off tl
metallic tang of nitrates. My courtesy transformed into curtne
with customers. As families waited for a table outside the dim su
restaurant, they allowed their children to wander into my shop.
shooed them away with a broomstick, annoyed that these convention
lives and their offspring had intruded into my floating world.

A man entered the shop, tall and white-haired, his skin so tanned
that it gave off a violet lustre in the striplights of the fish tanks. His
appearance attested to a life spent under the sun. The juxtaposition
was odd; what was his interest in an indoor hobby like aquarium
fish-keeping? I realized the connection when he put a plastic bag on
the counter; the cleaner wrasse was swimming inside.

"I'm returning the wrasse. My wife told me she bought it from
here," he said with a faint European accent.

I did not answer and tightened my grip on the broom handle.
Andie had lied to me about her marital status. Deceived as I was, I
had no desire to be murdered by a jealous husband.

"OK, relax." He held up a gnarled hand to assuage me. "My ex-
wife. Well, not until she signs the papers. If she signs them."

I waited for him to get interrogative. Would he ask me to step
outside for a fistfight in front of the dim sum restaurant? When I still
did not speak, he said "Thank you."

"What for?"

"Andie has no real friends in KL. I suggested a change of scene to
her. We even bought a studio apartment in Mont Kiara last year." He
pushed the wrasse towards me. "Since no one's going to live there
now, there's no need to decorate it."

I opened the till to give him a refund for the fish.

"No, please. I insist." He refused the money. I asked him what was
his job.

"I own a scuba-diving school in Thailand. Hey, maybe you should
try it one day?"

I ignored his offer and blurted, "Do you still have feelings for
Andie?"

He smiled as if I had articulated something he could not admit to
himself. "We live apart, but we are not separated. She goes and
returns. Nothing's definite with her and that's the deal."

"I know." I agreed and thought of the male and female shrimp
inside the Venus' Flower Basket, an arrangement of complete security
but defined by soft translucent bars.

Andie sent a blank email with a photo attachment to my business
email address: a fuzzy snapshot of sea snakes mating taken with an
underwater camera. I replied with a brief thank-you and never heard
from her again.

My customers thought I had closed my shop for a month. Instead,
I renovated it and got rid of the marine fish and invertebrate tanks. I

applied for a licence to sell dogs and cats. The shop was noisier wit barks and meows, but at least it distracted me from thinking abou Andie. My new employees did not understand why I was obsesse with checking the sex of new puppies and kittens. I was looking fo recurrences of Andie's condition in nature.

Of course, I never found any, but conventional family life foun me when a petite woman walked into my shop one evening, tearfu that her boyfriend had stood her up outside the dim sum restauran

However, my fiancée baulked at making love in the bathtub. Sh told me I could get hurt. She did not understand when I replied tha I had already been hurt that way.

Get Up! Stand Up!

Madeline Moore

It should be the happiest night of my life, and it would be, if it weren't for the boy on my fire escape, crouched like a gargoyle, with as miserable a countenance as any stone beast I've ever seen.

It's the night before my wedding and even though it's not my first time down the aisle it'll be the first time I remember. Plus, this time I'm marrying a handsome, intelligent, wealthy man and my dress is amazing. It's *awesome*, in the vernacular of the young.

I'm not young, but he is – the boy, not the fiancé. The boy's cock is as magnificent in its solidity and endurance as a rock. The thought of it makes my cunt ache. I've been spoiled over the last six weeks; I've indulged myself and now I must suffer.

If I wanted to I could claim perimenopause has played a part in my behaviour of late. My girlfriends point to my sixty-year-old boyfriend and his freakin' *commitment issues*. They didn't even have to see Guy to declare him good for me. Of course, they've been cruising in a pack, feeding on the young, for a while now.

I refused to join the cougar brigade. When they tried to make me go a-prowlin' I said no, no, no. I had a much bigger fish to fry. Now look. An engagement ring on my finger, the pre-nup signed and sealed, and a boy on the balcony. My bad. I'm pushing frickin' fifty and I feel ridiculous.

Tea's on! I tap at the glass doors, smile and hold up a tea cup.

"Come in." I mouth the words. "Talk to me." Tilt my head. But I know he won't respond. This is a silent, passive protest. All the talking is done, he said, and he was right. Try as I might I'll never convince him that our time is up.

His blue eyes stare, two sapphires set in stone. They stream rain and, probably, tears. His black hair is matted to his head. His face is flushed. He's likely sick by now. I have to do something, but what? They're so stupid, the young. When I told him that he'd said, "I'd rather be stupid than cruel."

The first thing I said to him was, "You come down out of that tree!"

The first thing he said to me was, "You're not the boss of me!"

In retrospect everything was mapped out in those two sentences. That I would play at taking care of him (while fucking him senseless) and he wouldn't do what he was told (while fucking me senseless).

I sit down at the table, pour a lone cup of tea and contemplate the list of phone numbers I've been staring at for the past few days, ever since he moved from my bed to the balcony. There's the police, known in these parts as La Sûreté du Québec, and a mental health crisis line. My girlfriends. Plus Ash, Mr Potato Head, Willow, Big Balls – these are names and numbers I nicked from Guy's cell phone the night I brought him home.

All my fiancé's phone numbers are on speed dial, of course, though there's no need to drag him into it at this late date, now is there? Brian is a developer. He owns undeveloped land all over Canada, and properties all over the world. I'm a physiotherapist. I own my condo.

We met when I treated his bad back at the swish physio centre where I work. We're both bilingual Anglo-Quebeckers so right there we had plenty to talk about. The relationship took off beautifully, then stalled after about six months, then continued crawling forward.

Thus was the state of affairs one fine summer evening six short weeks ago. I had the sunroof open on my Beetle, enjoying the breeze and basking in the last of a summer sunset. Brian and I were meeting at a posh restaurant for a night of fine dining followed by sex, which I was very much looking forward to. My cell phone rang. When I picked up Brian said he had to stay late to meet with the Châteauguay contractors about "the kid up the tree".

I'd heard about the protest of course but hadn't paid it much mind. There are plenty of acres of protected forest in Quebec; indeed we have the Châteauguay Conservation Area. It hadn't seemed too terrible to mow down a few adjoining trees to put in a soccer stadium and Brian stood to make a healthy profit, which of course I was all for. But I hadn't heard about this boy until now.

"How long has he been up there?" My voice was modulated. When dealing with Brian my default state is "patient", which is not always an easy one for me to maintain. But it's essential.

"I don't know, months," said Brian.

"That's crazy! What about his legs?"

Brian laughed his evil developer "nyah ah ah" laugh. "We start clearing tomorrow, kid or no kid."

"But he could be hurt." Tears actually sprang to my eyes. Partly because I was pissed at Brian and not giving him even a hint of it was making my blood boil, but also because here's a young, idealistic man with no one to stand up for him, or to him, and make him stop. When I was young I did my time in the marches, but I never risked my life and if I had, someone would've stopped me.

"So dinner's out but if you want to come by around eleven I'd love to see you. Annie, I miss your lovely mouth." Sounds nice, but what he really meant was, "I'll be too tired to make love but you can always suck me off."

"We'll see," I purred. "I miss your . . . mouth . . . too." I rang off before steam could start whistling out my ears. "Fuck you, pal," I hissed.

I drove to Châteauguay.

The protest was a fair distance from the parking lot, which was hell in my heels, which I wouldn't even have been wearing if I hadn't been en route to a date. Pissed. I wasn't talking out loud but inside I was spouting the worst string of expletives I knew. "Motherfucking cocksucking prick shit dick-for-brains," and such. Words I stopped saying out loud long ago but that lurk in my brain, ready to leap to my lips at the first sign of frustration. Fuck.

Sunset's gorgeous in Châteauguay and I knew the area well. Back in the day we used to build illegal campfires and sit around singing and swilling home-made wine and smoking dope. I was a "back to the lander".

It turned out just as well that I was dressed like a lovely lady. When I reached the stand of trees where the protest was taking place the police were herding Mr Potato Head and Fern Gully and the rest of that motley crew off the premises for the night and would've made me leave, too, but I said I was the kid's mom and had come to take him home. They left me alone, under the butternut tree.

I yelled, "*Tu parles anglais?*"

He yelled back, "*Oui*," which in Québécois sounds like, "Wah."

Then we had our first exchange, after which he gently pushed a leafy branch aside and stared down at me. Long dark hair, lanky body all scrunched up. A wistful face, as the young so often have; pale, unlined, sharp cheekbones and a soft, sensuous mouth. Big baby blues, baby.

I swear, I hadn't been planning anything beyond the rescue, maybe a little physio and a hamburger platter and a bus ticket or something, until our eyes met. But as we stared at each other in the twilight, something stirred in the pit of my stomach.

"I don't have anywhere to go,' he said.

"You can come home with me," I replied.

He shimmied down the trunk of the butternut to plop in a bony heap at my feet.

"You stink," I said. I leaned low to get his arm around my shoulders and hauled him up. "Pee-yew."

He teetered, almost falling. I clutched him tight. "Yeah but *you* smell great," he said, as if one cancelled out the other. He patted the smooth bark of the tree. "She's old and disease-free. A real beauty," he whispered. His voice trembled.

I resisted the urge to say, "Just like me." Instead I whispered back, "I know, baby. It's going to be OK."

He really did have trouble walking, which I thought was horrible but he found "trippy". When we got to my place I helped him into and out of the elevator, then into my condo and straight to the main bathroom. I stripped him like a professional, giving no outward sign that the sight of his tight young flesh made my blood hum and my clit stand at attention. He was too dirty for a bath and too unsteady for a shower so I left him sitting in the tub with the shower pounding down on his head.

I contemplated throwing his clothes into the washer but in the end I bundled them up and dumped them down the trash chute. I searched his pockets first. They were empty. All his worldly belongings, it seemed, were contained in a filthy jute shoulder bag. I made a quick survey of its contents, copping those phone numbers from the cell, happily taking note of his habit of regularly giving blood (clean!), checking his ID for his age (legal!) and tsking over a couple of chubby reefers (as if there weren't a few skinny joints of hydroponic tucked away in my lingerie drawer).

The story is that when Cher laid eyes on Rob the bagel boy she said, "Have him washed and brought to my tent." I knew that was what I was doing but I was still pretending my motives were pure.

"Straighten your legs," I ordered when I was back in the bathroom. "Yum Yum," sang my body in response to the sight of him stretched out in my tub. "Young, young, yum, yum." I averted my eyes.

"Can't. It hurts."

"Do your best. Now flex your toes. Can you feel it in your calves?"

"Sorta."

"Do five flex and relax reps. Ready? One. Two. Three. Four. Five. Relax."

"You have a beautiful voice."

"*Merci*. Again. One. Two. Three. Four. Five. And relax."

"Will I walk again?"

"Yes."

"Will I play the piano?"

I laughed. "No."

"I'm clean now," he said. "Get in."

"You think?" I looked at him. His cock waved a solid, friendly hello. The sight of that majestic hard-on struck me dumb.

We exchanged a long look. Mine said, "I'm almost fifty, *chéri*," and his said, "*De rien*."

So I dropped my button-through dress. I was wearing a black satin push-up bra and thong (sixty-year-old men love a thong on any woman's body, even a perimenopausal one) and lacy stay-ups that were riddled with runs from my trip into the forest.

"Oo la la," said Guy. His cock got bigger; the head got thicker and started turning purple.

Desire hit my crotch so hard it hurt, like a cramp in my clit.

"I haven't even touched you," I whispered. I was awestruck. Honestly, I hadn't seen a cock that big and hard and blatantly horny since I quit trolling the gay porn sites. As for the real thing?

Years, baby.

"You have a beautiful voice," he said. "And a bootylicious body." He licked his lips.

I stripped off my bra and panties and stepped into the tub, positioning one foot on each side of his slender boy hips. Then I simply lowered myself onto that magnificent member. I didn't even spread my labia with my fingers, instead letting the heat-seeking head of his dick shove them aside to find my seriously aching hole.

"Christ," I muttered as it stretched happily to accommodate him.

Water hit the back of my head and poured over us both.

"*Oui*," (Wah) he said. He sighed like an old man, long and slow, and closed his eyes.

I kept mine open, watching the guileless grin that spread across his face as I slipped down another inch onto him, and another, until he was fully inside of me, encased by the hot satin walls of my cunt. My lips and clit nestled in his straight black pubic hair.

He humped up.

I gasped like a girl.

He did it again. Again. Again.

I started trembling all over. Usually I need a little help to make it all the way to euphoria, by which I mean wine as well as foreplay, but not this time. I was about to start howling and even the sight of my belly wrinkling between my navel and my pubic hair didn't faze me.

"Fuck it," I hissed. I leaned forward a little, so the head of his cock rubbed my G-spot.

His eyes opened. "Cool," he said. He cupped my breasts, thumbing my nipples.

"How long can you fuck like this?"

He shrugged. "Forever, if you like." He humped up again.

I made a strangled little noise.

Guy let his right hand trail down between my breasts, over my belly, to my mound. Again, his touch was gentle. He used his thumb to make lazy little circles around and over my clit. "Or we can come now and then come again later and then come again later and . . ."

"Uh huh." I was nodding in slavish agreement. I shifted to a kneel.

Guy guided my head to his. Our mouths met in a sloppy kiss, sloppy because we were eager and the shower made it hard to breathe, not sloppy because he was inexperienced or demanding. He pressed my head to his skinny chest and he fucked and fingered me until I really did start howling and shaking and grinding and coming like I hadn't had an orgasm in years. I was scared I might squeeze him right out of me with the force of my clenching contractions, but he was as solid as ever inside me.

"Stop!" I tried to wriggle free. "I can't stand it!"

"Sure you can, *chérie*," he murmured. He just kept on going, fingering and fucking me as if I hadn't just come, until I did it again, as hard and long as the first time.

I lay plastered against his chest, half-delirious with delight. "You come!"

"I did," he said.

"So quiet," I marvelled. "And gentle. And patient."

"I have to be these things," he replied.

I climbed off him and out of the tub with as much grace as I could muster. Then I helped him out and wrapped him in a bath sheet. We were both a little unsteady.

"Why?"

"Hmm?" He leaned on me. He looked exhausted.

I leaned back. "Why do you have to be quiet and gentle and patient?"

He looked at me with the sad eyes of a weary warrior. "I think it's going to take a long time to save the planet."

When I woke in the morning he wasn't in my bed. We hadn't had sex again, after all, but I knew he'd spent the night, because every so often we'd curled into spoons and I'd felt his hard-on pressed against my bum.

It crossed my mind that he, and possibly my electronics and jewellery, might be gone, but I wasn't surprised to find him in the kitchen, naked, gazing at the screen on my laptop and stuffing his face. I'd fed him all the non-meat stuff I could come up with before putting him to bed, but now he was back at it with a vengeance.

"Morning," he said. "I made tea." He gave me a dazzling grin.

"Great." Who needs coffee when you've got a boy toy in your kitchen? I felt buzzed.

He held up a bubble-wrapped package. "Mind mailing this for me? It's a solar-powered cell phone. A prototype. I have to return it now that the protest is over."

"It's over?"

He nodded at the screen. I bent to take a look. My robe slipped open so his face was brushed by soft cotton and even softer skin. He rubbed his cheek against my breast.

There was Brian in a hard hat, amidst a swarm of chanting young protesters. The only girl, presumably Willow, was being dragged away by a cop. In the background, the bulldozers were busy.

"That's my girlfriend," said Guy. He pointed to the girl.

I pointed to Brian. "That's my boyfriend," I said.

"No shit. What does that make us?" He gave me an amused look. "Romeo and Juliet?" He shrunk the window with a click of the mouse. Now we were staring at my desktop, icons dotting a vast expanse of beach. "Where's this?"

"Negril Beach. Jamaica. I went after my high school grad, intending to stay for two weeks. I stayed for two years."

"Cool. Rastas are OK," he said. "But I don't believe in God, or Ja, or whatever. I'm a Pantheist. You cool with that?"

"I'm cool with you," I said. "I'm sorry about Châteauguay." I closed the laptop. "How can I make it better?"

Guy grinned at me and patted his lap. His erection grew under my adoring gaze, like a time-lapse photo: no hands, no mouth, no cunt or ass or even whispered compliments, just my gaze, urging it to thicken and lengthen and pulse with power.

I sat on the table, instead. "Show me you can walk."

Guy stood, walked stiffly but quickly to the teapot, poured me a cup of peppermint tea and brought it to me without spilling a drop.

"Beautiful," I cooed. I meant it, too. The restorative powers of the young always amaze me. I can get three kids walking in the time it takes me to get an oldster prepped to begin.

Guy tugged at the belt to my robe as I attempted to drink my tea. "Careful." I tipped up a pinky in a display of daintiness and sipped.

He nuzzled my ear. I shivered. He took the cup from my hand. "Tea time's over," he said.

"We gotta be quick," I whispered in his ear, before biting the lobe.

He parted my knees and stepped between them. As the head of his cock touched me I shivered again. He slid into me as easily as if we'd been lovers forever. When he was fully inside we kissed. Then he cupped my ass with his hands and started fucking me furiously.

"Goddammit!" I shouted when I came, which was like three minutes later. My fingers were busy torturing my clit, just above the tunnel Guy was pounding in and out of. Together we were like some kind of pneumatic machine that thrusts and contracts at the same time. "Goddam good!"

"Mmm . . ." was the only noise he made. He froze, his eyes flew open, and that dynamite grin that announced, "I'm coming," spread across his face.

I hugged him tight until he was done.

"I gotta go," I said. We shared a long lovers' kiss. "Will you still be here when I get back?"

"Want me?"

"Yes."

"OK. I'll cook. We can fuck before supper."

Work was a blur. I was capable and considerate but the only bone I *really* wanted to manipulate wasn't available. Dumb thoughts like that struck me as hilarious; I kept having to stifle the girlish giggles bubbling in my throat. I wanted to go home, badly. Not because I was afraid he was stealing my stuff or answering my phone (which I'd forwarded to my cell anyway, as always), but because I wanted more fabulous sex with Guy. My clit twitched at the thought. My groin burned.

Brian didn't call, which was par for the course. He was punishing me for not showing up at his place like a good little cocksucker. I didn't bother plotting how long to make him stew before giving in (I'm always the one who gives in when we get into one of these little contretemps). He could stew till the flesh dropped right off his osteoarthritic bones, as far as I was concerned.

When I got home the condo was redolent with yummy smells.

Guy was lying on my brass bed, still naked.

"What'cha doin'?" Suddenly I was shy. Who was this lovely, lanky blue-eyed boy?

"Slow cookin'," he said. "C'mere."

I started tearing off my clothes.

"Slow-w-w . . ." he said. "Tonight we take our time."

I paused with my pants halfway down my thighs, not because he'd said we'd go slowly but because the difference in our ages suddenly overwhelmed me. He was used to younger, tighter, smoother, more flexible bodies. I had to counter that with my years of experience. Whatever his girlfriends had done to or for him, I was going to do better and *dirtier*. A woman my age doing a boy his age was pretty depraved already. So, if I was going to take a dip in the depravity pond, why not dive in deep and *wallow* in it?

There were a few things I hadn't learned until my thirties and a few more that I hadn't discovered until my forties. I had a repertoire to draw on that'd more than make up for my few wrinkles and no longer quite so perky breasts.

Talk was one of them. I stepped out of the pool of my pants. "You have a magnificent cock," I told him.

He grinned and waved the member in question at me. "*Merci.*"

"Inside me, it feels *fantastique.*"

"Is that where you want it? Inside you?"

I leaned forward and doubled my arms up behind me to unhook my bra. That way, my breasts would be at their best when I exposed them. I said, "Later," and flung my bra aside. "For now, I want to get to know it better."

"Help yourself," he offered. Guy tucked his hands behind his neck.

That pose inspired me. Brian liked to play bondage games once in a while, with me the one getting tied up. It'd be a nice change to reverse roles. I went to the dresser and returned with a coil of soft white cotton cord.

Guy's peepers widened.

"You'll like it," I promised.

He looked a bit uncertain but he held still while I took a few turns around each of his wrists and looped the cord through a rail of the bed's head. I took a bottle of strawberry-flavoured oil from a nightstand and anointed my palms, then poured more oil over the head of his cock. I let my fingertips run up the underside of his shaft. "So smooth." I gripped him and squeezed. "So hard."

"How else would it be, considering?"

I ignored the compliment and continued with a loose-fingered stroke, base to head. "Nice?" I asked as my palm glossed over his knob.

"Mm."

Good – forming words was becoming harder for him. My strokes alternated, firm then loose. "Your cock, being so thick, will press my tongue down and rub against the roof of my mouth. I'll be able to feel its pulse."

"Cool." The beginning of that beatific grin played across his face. "You're a lot of fun, Annie."

"*Merci*."

I dipped my head a little, as if about to take him in my mouth. Instead I breathed words onto his shaft. "I'm going to make it *so* good for you, Guy, and when you finally climax, I'm *not* going to swallow your hot cream."

"Huh?" His eyes, which had started to close, flew open.

I grinned. "Not till I've savoured it. I'm going to let it sit in my mouth for a little bit. I'm going to suck air, like you do when drinking a fine wine, to release the bouquet."

"Jesus, Annie . . ."

I stroked him slowly, sometimes full-fist, sometimes just one finger and my thumb. "Look at me," I ordered. My other hand went to my breast. I rolled and teased one nipple to aching hardness. "I like to have my nipples played with."

Guy jerked his arms and shrugged helplessly.

I shrugged too. My hand dropped to my thong. Two fingers slid under it. Guy's eyes followed them. "I like to play with myself, too. Do you mind?"

"*Non*."

"My clit's buzzing. I'm going to make it ready for you."

"OK, but I'm going to make it wait."

"Really?"

"I'm going to make you beg me to fuck you."

My pulse quickened. Such a smart boy. Such a fast learner.

"Good." Still softly pumping his shaft, I stood up and wriggled out of my thong. Two fingers bracketed my sex and spread to fully expose my hot pink nub.

Guy licked his lips.

"You like my clit? My cunt?"

He nodded.

"And I like your cock, your long, thick, hard cock."

A dewdrop appeared in its eye. I licked it off.

He groaned.

"Nice," I said, and squeezed another drop out. "Yummy."

"Your mouth?" he asked.

"Not yet." My fingertips worked inside my cunt and carried a smear of my juices to his lips.

He tried to follow my hand as it retreated but the cords stopped him. The long muscles in his thighs flexed. "Please?"

"Please?"

"Let me come?"

"Already?"

"I'll still be able to fuck you."

"I know." I smiled. "Guy?"

"Yes?"

"Wanna try something new?"

"Such as?"

"Such as this." I went to work with my mouth, just lips and tongue at first but gradually taking him deeper and deeper.

He chuckled. "Silly, I've had blow jobs before."

"Mm?" My fingers were still slick with the oil. I rimmed his anus slowly, then applied pressure.

"Ah?"

I slid in to my first joint, then my second. There it was, that hard little walnut. As I rubbed it, his rigid cock thickened just a little more inside my mouth. Ready to burst.

Guy tensed. His shaft swelled in my mouth and started to spurt. He gasped, as if his climax surprised him. A prostate massage will do that.

I sat up and parted my lips, letting him see his cream in my mouth and on my tongue. I drew in a long, steady breath and exhaled.

He said, "Dirty, dirty girl."

I smiled, breathed in again, breathed out, and swallowed. "Now," I said as I released his bonds, "you do me."

He pounced. One minute I was in charge, the next I was helpless. He pinned me to the bed. His arms were surprisingly muscular when tensed. I struggled a little, thrilled to discover he was so much stronger than me.

"Maybe I should tie you up," he muttered. "But there are other ways to tame a filly."

What started as a giggle turned to a moan as he buried his head between my legs. His mouth surrounded my pussy lips; his tongue slowly travelled up between them, dipping into the hole and out again and circling my clit at the conclusion of each languid lap.

My legs began trembling. "Please," I whispered. "Stay on my clit?"

He ignored me.

I put my hand to his head, marvelling at the texture of his black hair. So fine. So thick. I stroked his head and any thoughts of trying to make him do it my way vanished. It was perfect. His tongue tasted me, tortured my entrance with shallow thrusts, found my clit, circled and then abandoned it, only to start again, from the bottom up.

Perfect.

When I came it was as if he'd pulled the orgasm from deep within me with his lips and tongue. As if he'd sucked it to the surface and set it free.

Before the last paroxysm had shuddered through my body, Guy was mounting me, his cock as hard as ever.

"Goddammit!" I whipped my head from side to side as a fresh wave of desire rolled through me.

Guy propped himself up, his hands on either side of my head, and gave it to me good. Hard. Good. So hard. So good.

When I came I locked my gaze with his, using his baby blues to keep me from exploding. Then his eyes closed and he grinned wide and said, "Yesss . . ." and I knew he'd climaxed too.

Guy.

I wanted to keep him forever but life's not like that. I could clothe him, and feed him, and fuck him, and I did. But I couldn't keep him. Life goes on, things change. Boyfriends resurface, suddenly insecure and looking for a commitment. Life is strange.

And so we come to the eve of my wedding. I dial a number and in surprisingly little time, Guy's ragamuffin gang shuffles into my condo, led by the suspicious and spunky girl named Willow.

In the end he goes quietly. They convene on the balcony, in the rain, for a few minutes of intense conversation. When they return he's among them. Back where he belongs. Willow picks up his jute bag and slings it over her shoulder.

Guy stops in the doorway. His voice is anguished. "What about love?"

Words fail me. His friends surround him, protecting him. They leave. The door closes.

I step out onto the balcony and stare at the stars and the full moon.

Tomorrow I'll be a Mrs. Again. The night after that, I'll be gazing at the constellations of a different hemisphere. Brian is taking me to his villa in Negril for our honeymoon. If everything works out between us, it'll be ours. If not, well, then it'll be *mine.*

A few nights after that I'll slip out to find the taxi stand my friends have told me about. You can get anything you want there, for a price. A ride around the world.

"What about love?" I wink at the moon. "Gonna get me some sweet, young, midnight love."

It might just be the rain blurring my vision, but I swear, the lascivious bitch winks back.

You Get What You Pay For

Robert Buckley

"What's the matter, Gleason? Never seen a woman fucked out of her senses before?"

The man with the bulging briefcase had stepped – actually sidestepped – into the pool of light in the centre of what was once a sunken dance floor. He leaned to one side, peering at the naked girl draped at the waist over the pool table. She was motionless; her long, silken, dark hair hid her face as she lay chest down on the felt-lined table, both arms extended like a sphinx.

Tobin sat in the surrounding darkness at a table on a raised, stepped platform above and behind the girl. She looked tiny. Her toes barely reached the floor, so her feet splayed apart, bowing her ankles away from each other and forming something like a U, or perhaps a cup to catch all the jizz that trickled in viscous rivulets down her thighs and over her calves, shining streaks catching and reflecting the light. A major portion of the ooze issued from her anus that was distended by the several cocks it had entertained and possibly a fist.

"Jesus, is she OK?" Gleason said, tentatively reaching towards her. "Is she alive, for crissakes?"

"She's fine," Tobin replied. "She's just passed out. She's been fucked almost three hours straight. The guys are all wore out. I didn't think the little minx was ever going to quit, then boom, out like a light."

"Have you had someone check her? Christ, I don't think she's breathing."

"Rocco checked her a few minutes ago. He's a paramedic. But feel free to take her pulse if you want."

Gleason lifted the girl's wrist. "Hmm."

He stepped around, took note of the girl's gaping asshole and coughed. "She paid for this?"

"No, her husband paid for it. But she sure enjoyed herself."

"Are you sure?"

"First thing I drum into their heads is pick a safe word. She never did it. Lots of them do, sometimes before things even get started. Makes no difference, no refunds. And some, like that little girl, get even more than they paid for."

"Where the hell is the husband?"

"Well, that's another thing. He's in my private bar, getting loaded. Buyer's remorse, I think they call it."

"Jesus. Greg, I think you better see to this woman."

"I thought I'd let her sleep it off. She's got to be exhausted."

"I'd feel better if you did."

Tobin chuckled. "OK. Here, sit down."

Gleason stepped up to the platform and sat at the table as Tobin stepped past him.

"Rocco, Jules . . . come in here and carry Mrs Blake to the powder room. Tell Heidi to help her clean up."

Two well-muscled men stepped into the light. One, whom Gleason recognized as Rocco, gently turned the woman over. She came to life. Rocco draped a towel over his arms before he slid them under her.

"Oooo, no baby, no more . . . I'm so sore."

Rocco lifted her into his arms like a child.

"Banana, honey . . . banana, please."

"See?" Tobin said as he turned back towards Gleason. "She remembered."

"Banana?"

"That was her safe word." Tobin turned back towards Rocco. Mrs Blake had clasped her arms around his thick neck and was nuzzling against his shoulder.

"It's all right, Mrs Blake, Rocco's just taking you someplace to clean up. Someone will help you."

The woman sighed. Her whisper carried across the room. "You hurt me so bad, you terrible brute. God, I loved the way you hurt me."

Tobin returned to the table and sat across from Gleason.

"Another satisfied customer," Gleason said.

"Well, one is. The husband is feeling like shit right now. He was retching earlier. Seems he can't take the reality, even if it is his fantasy come true. He's feeling like a major piece of shit right now, shame like you'd never believe."

"Are they all like that?"

"No, but enough of them are that I always get the money up from and I always get it in writing . . . just like you told me."

"Uh-huh. So, why did you want to see me?"

"There were some cops in here last week."

"You spotted them, huh?"

"Easy. They were too young, too much in love. Our business mostly long-married couples, or rather couples married so long the need something extreme to fire up their sex. What's that take: thre years, five years, ten?" He shrugged.

"And these two were . . . what? Too fresh?"

"Guy and a girl. Early twenties. You could tell they were hot fc each other. Probably just got tossed together for the assignment, an all the dirty talk got them even hotter. They were just falling in lus I bet they stopped at his or her place before they returned to th squad." Tobin laughed.

"So, what did you tell them?"

"I said I rent out my facility for private, adult recreation."

"Good. Don't ever say you're taking money for sex."

"The girl, though, kept pressing me about wanting to be whippe or flogged or whatever."

"And how did you respond?"

"I said she was an adult, and she was free to do whatever sh consented to."

"You didn't tell her you'd beat her, or get someone to beat her?"

"Of course not."

"Good. Because in this state you cannot consent to be assaulted.

"Really? Then how can they have hockey games, or football? Ho about boxing?"

"That's precisely the argument we'd use on appeal, but it's neve come to that because no one wants to take it that far. Then they' need new legislation and such, and meanwhile maybe you'v outlawed hockey season."

"Not likely."

"No, very unlikely."

"Look," Tobin said, "I gave them nothing, but I'm wondering i there's a new push to crack down on my sort of services, what wit the tight-ass party looking to regulate how everyone fucks."

"There's been an uptick in my business," Gleason agreed. "Greg the best way to handle trouble is not get into it in the first place. D what you're doing; be careful. We'll handle it if anything . . . well, i you run into any legal difficulty."

"I've always wondered, Gleason. How'd you get into this? Did you et out to be the Perv Lawyer?"

Gleason laughed. "You know, I was upset when that fucking abloid called me that on their front page, but Jesus, what a pile of ousiness came my way. I nearly sent the publisher a thank-you note."

Tobin laughed too. "So, how did you get into it?"

"A couple of cases that Flynnie sent my way. All of a sudden I ealized there were people out there who needed legal advice – orotection – because of their unconventional lifestyles, or businesses. t opened up a niche. I remember one of my first clients. She wanted o have a slave contract drawn up because she was scared to death omehow someone was going to take away her 'pet'."

"Did you do it?"

"Couldn't. I had to explain there was a little matter called the Thirteenth Amendment. So, I drew up a partnership covenant."

Tobin shook his head and chuckled. "It's amazing what comes hrough my door. The scenarios some people want. But hey, like you aid, it's a niche. I'm not going to pass up the money. Beats trying to get by as a saloon keeper."

"Yeah, well I sense a little remorse on your part too, Greg."

Tobin shrugged. "I give people what they pay for. But, sometimes hey get more than they bargained for. That guy retching and crying in ny back room. He's going to hate himself for a long time, maybe forever. His wife, maybe she will too, hate him for hating himself. I don't know what kind of marriage they had before they came in here, but . . ."

"Feeling guilty, Greg?"

"Not guilt, exactly. They're fucking adults; they make their own decisions. Hell, maybe I'm doing them a favour by showing them what and who they really are. And then there are those who just have a good time. So, screw it, but then, I find myself thinking about . . . oh, hell, I don't know what I'm thinking."

"Let me give you some advice as a friend, not a lawyer: if it begins to bother you so much you lose sleep over it, give it up."

"Not that much, yet."

"You still do mostly gang-bang scenarios, I take it."

"That's definitely at the top of popularity. Amazes the shit out of me how many guys want to see their wives fucked by a half-dozen or so men. It's almost always the guy's idea too. Like I said, we've had scenes that never launched because the wife said no. Funny, they try to do it for their husband. Maybe they think it'll patch up some hole in the marriage, but right at the last minute . . ."

"And the women who go along with it?"

"Well, I don't think any of them just go along with it. They do it they're into it. Oh, it might be convenient for them to say they did it just to please hubby, but they aren't about to pass up an opportunity like that."

"Cynical, Greg, very cynical . . . but very sound observation." Gleason smiled and raised a glass Tobin had poured for him.

"We've had some single women too."

"Huh?"

"Usually very cool and collected. But they come here looking to have some ravishment fantasy fulfilled."

"You mean rape fantasy, don't you?"

"No, 'ravishment' is more like it. They don't want to be jumped; they want to be seduced and taken. All confidentially of course."

"Well, you do provide a unique service. You don't advertise, I hope."

"Word of mouth."

"Good. That'll keep you out of the public eye too. For a while anyway."

"Yeah, I don't need a signpost out there pointing the cops to my door. Thanks for coming by."

"Take care, Greg."

Tobin said goodbye to the Blakes in the public lounge. Mrs Blake was walking a bit stiffly, but still managed to move in a way that broadcast: "You want me." Mr Blake looked like he'd just got through a bad bout of the flu. He wouldn't look at Tobin.

"Thank you so much, Mr Tobin," Mrs Blake purred. "It was a . . . life-changing experience."

She was so petite, delicate, Tobin thought; she could easily be mistaken for an Asian, especially a compliant yet sexually insatiable fantasy Asian. But she was a predator, and way out of her husband's league.

"You're welcome, Mrs Blake."

"Please, call me Maria."

Tobin just nodded. "Are you going to be OK, Mr Blake? We can call you a cab."

"That . . . that'll be fine. Thank you."

Tobin could see that Mr Blake couldn't wait to be out of there. He had "what have I done?" written all over his face in flashing neon.

Tobin was glad to be rid of them. He returned to the lounge which was beginning to fill with young office workers ready to unwind from the day.

He knocked on the bar with his knuckles. "Larry! Scotch."

The bartender poured him a shot. He tossed it back and nodded for a refill. This one he sipped.

He leaned with his back to the bar and surveyed the patrons. A couple sat close together on high stools at a table for two. Her skirt crept up her thigh and her knee touched his. Tobin watched as the man gingerly reached under the table and placed his hand just above her knee. Her face brightened into a smile.

Just falling in lust, Tobin thought. He projected a future for them. They'd likely fuck on the first date, keep it hot for the next few and he'd propose. Married in a year. Then a few years, maybe a kid or two later, if they made enough money, they'd be back, asking him to arrange "a scene". The same sort of scene the Blakes had paid for maybe, or maybe something even kinkier, depending on how far they'd drifted from their original flashpoint.

Gleason was right, Tobin was getting cynical, but then he'd always been a realist. He didn't believe in happily-ever-afters. But his cynicism was growing sour. He was beginning not to like himself and he hated that because logic told him he wasn't a bad guy. He provided a service, and God knows – if there was a God to know such things – it was an essential service.

"Fuck it," he said to himself. "The money's too good."

"You say something, boss?" Larry shouted over the din.

"Huh? No, I'm good."

The bar phone rang. A moment later Larry stepped over to Tobin.

"Boss, Heidi says there's a couple of people waiting to talk to you in your office."

"Oh, shit. Yeah, forgot I had an appointment. OK, thanks."

Tobin stepped around the bar to a narrow corridor hidden in the gloom. It opened into a larger hallway on the other side of the building bordered by nondescript offices.

He entered one. Heidi had just served drinks to a couple. Tobin walked around them and sat at his desk.

"Sorry, uh, Mr and Mrs Stassen?"

"Neil and Tracy," the wife replied.

"Nice to meet you."

The wife drew her knee up and cupped it in her hands, baring a good deal of thigh. The husband's eyes immediately slid over to take in the overtly flirtatious gesture.

"Very, very nice to meet you, Mr Tobin. It's Greg, isn't it?"

Tobin nodded and smiled.

"You're very attractive, Greg. I don't know what I was expecting; perhaps some hulking, swarthy impresario of . . . what? Nastiness?"

"Mrs Stassen . . ."

"Tracy, please."

"OK, Tracy . . . it's important that we all understand and agree on what exactly you expect me to provide."

"Well, then let me tell you," Tracy said, leaning towards him and revealing a deep-shadowed valley between her pushed-up breasts.

She slid a sidelong glance at her husband and her lips tightened into a flirty pout.

"It'll be our tenth anniversary. We want to experience something special and act out a fantasy Neil and I have only pretended at, you know, in our own bedroom."

Tobin smiled, nodded and waited.

"Neil . . . likes to be teased. Don't you honey?"

The husband nodded, but he didn't look at Tobin. His cheeks were beginning to flush.

"He likes to be teased unmercifully," Tracy said, looking right at Tobin. She licked her lips. "The fact is . . . he likes to be teased in a most humiliating fashion. The more it hurts, the more he likes it. He's happiest when I've made him spill tears, isn't that so, dear?" She didn't look at him.

"I . . . uh . . . please, Tracy . . . I don't think . . ." Neil's ears were burning red.

"Honey, who said you should think?"

She was still gazing into Tobin's eyes. He maintained a half-smile poker face.

"Greg . . . would it surprise you to know that I think you are so hot? Would it surprise you to know that my pussy is oozing and my panties are soaked just imagining you throwing me down on this desk and filling me with your big cock. Are you wondering how I know you have a big cock?" She winked.

"Somehow . . . I'm not surprised at all."

"Then you think I'm a slut."

Tobin smiled.

"You'd like Greg to fuck me, wouldn't you, dear?"

Neil coughed.

"It's all right, honey, you can tell him . . . but ask him nice."

Neil cleared his throat. "Please, Mr Tobin. Would you like to . . . uck . . . fuck Tracy?"

Tobin took a deep breath. "I'm afraid it's a business policy to maintain a professional distance from my clients."

Neil let out a long sigh. A momentary twitch of irritation marred Tracy's pout.

"Shame," she said, and leaned back in her chair.

"I'm very . . . flattered," Tobin said, "but let's talk about how I can help fulfil your anniversary fantasy."

Tracy sighed. "Well, Neil needs to see me fucked, but first he needs to see me seduced and . . . claimed."

"Claimed?"

"Yes, he needs to watch helplessly, or perhaps . . . cowardly . . . while another man or men seduce, degrade, and claim me as their own . . . he needs to understand they are taking me away from him, and that he is to be made to watch them . . . well, rape me, and have me respond and surrender. He needs to see me made into their slut."

Tracy's chest was lifting and falling like a bellows. Tobin thought she was going to make herself come in front of him and her husband.

"I see," Tobin said. "How many men do you want to . . . partake? And how, shall we say, roughly, do you want to be treated?"

"Oh, six should be sufficient, I'll put up token resistance, of course. A face slap or two would be exciting. But there's one more, very important thing."

"Yes?"

"To make Neil's humiliation deliciously complete – because I want my darling to cherish this memory always . . ."

"Yes?" Tobin and Neil had said it at the same time.

"Neil too should be ravished."

"Tracy?" Neil squeaked.

"Neil, we've pretended that you were made to suck a cock."

"But, Tracy . . ."

"It turned you on. You came all over the sheets, darling."

"Yes . . . but, I don't know if I could really . . ."

"You will, honey; you will and you'll like it. Because it'll make you feel so dirty. You want to be my little cocksucker, don't you? You want to show me you like to suck cock, don't you? I would love to see it; won't you do it for me?"

"I . . . I . . . yes, Tracy . . . yes, I will."

"I love you, snookums."

"I love you too, Tracy."

She looked straight at Tobin again. There was a gleam of triumph in her eyes.

"You're sure that's OK with you, Mr Stassen?"

Neil's head was nearly in his lap. He whispered, "Yes."

"Heidi will write up the proposal and I'll need you both to sign it indicating your consent and a waiver of liability. It will also state that you are paying for the rental of the facilities only. The fee will be $8,500."

Neil stiffened in his seat and turned around. He apparently hadn't realized that Heidi was still in the room, taking it all down and bearing witness to his humiliation. He shrank back into his seat.

"Are your pants sticky, baby?" Tracy teased.

"All the actors in my employ are tested regularly for communicable diseases," Tobin said. "I still recommend condoms, but clients have requested no condoms . . ."

"No condoms, please," Tracy said. "Bareback . . . totally."

"OK. You are responsible for providing your own form of contraception. Also, precautions run both ways. You will also be required to visit a clinic of my designation at a specific time before the event and be certified. You will remain celibate, or restrict yourselves to sex with each other until the event. Even with all these precautions I can't guarantee a totally risk-free encounter, but we've been doing this for a while and . . . so far so good. But you need to keep that in mind."

"Just tell us where to sign, Greg. Whew! I'm so . . . agitated." Tracy's grin was dazzling, manic.

"The paperwork will be ready by tomorrow. I'll require a cashier's cheque, please."

Heidi showed the Stassens out. When she returned Tobin leaned back in his seat and mused, "Is it me, or are these people all beginning to sound the same? I don't think I can tell them apart anymore."

"Boss, as long as you keep signing my cheques, it doesn't matter to me."

"Doesn't it leave a bad taste in your mouth sometimes?"

Heidi sat down and placed her notes on Tobin's desk. She took a deep breath; her crisp white blouse, already straining to contain her formidable bosom, looked like it was about to pop a button, maybe a few. She coursed a finger behind her ear as if searching out a stray enhanced-blonde hair. There weren't any.

"You know," she said finally, "Back when I was stripping – about a hundred years ago – I got to understand how some guys let their rip on reality slip, got to thinking – believing – that I or one of the other girls was really his girlfriend, that she really cared about them. The girls would milk them for tips, even gifts. I didn't, but some of the other girls did. It never turned out well. The guys would make pests of themselves; try to follow the girls home. We had some bad scenes where they'd be banned from the club. Had some girls get hurt. It's always dicey when you try to convert fantasy to reality. Some people can handle it – lots of others can't. But, hey, I'm glad for the job, boss."

Tobin smiled. "I'd say I was glad to have hired you, but you'd probably hit me up for a raise."

"Now that you mention it . . ."

"Nice try. Seriously, though, what do you make of this last couple . . . Mr and Mrs Stassen?"

"Seriously? Are you serious?"

"C'mon, you must have an opinion."

"She's a piece of work, but he's in the driver's seat."

"You think so?"

"She's taking his cues . . . he can't wait to give some guy a blow job in front of her."

"She's not into it as much?"

"Oh, she's into it all right . . . but she has her own agenda. She definitely wants what's coming to her, but she has ulterior motives . . . you can hear the wheels and cogs whirring in her head."

"Jesus, you women are scary the way you read each other."

"Takes one to . . ."

"Yeah."

"I better get this printed, make appointments with the clinic. You want to bring in the usual suspects?"

"Yeah, sounds like a job for Rocco and the boys."

Tobin returned to the lounge intending to settle himself at a table in a dim corner where he could take a cat nap if he wanted without anyone noticing. He stopped at the bar long enough to grab a tonic water and lime and headed for a corner table. He casually scanned the room for the couple that had been playing footsie and feelsie, but they had left.

He leaned back in his seat and closed his eyes. He must have nodded off immediately. He awoke with a start when the girl sat across the table from him.

"Huh? Miss? Something I can do for you?"

She folded one hand over her other and looked down at the table "Um."

"Yes?"

"You don't remember me; not that I'd expect you to."

Tobin shook his head and tried to place her face somewhere in his memory. She was slight, petite, dark hair that didn't quite reach her shoulders. Sensible office attire; nothing remarkable.

"About eight months ago, I completed a transaction with you for my boss."

"I'm sorry . . . transaction?"

"I . . . I brought you a cashier's cheque. My boss is Evelyn Hasley."

The name rang a bell. She was the CFO of a biotech company that had just begun publicly trading after breaking into the scene with some wonder drug or other. Tobin tried to recall her kink. Then he remembered: The Inquisition.

Ms Hasley wanted an elaborate scene in which she would be tortured and ravished by mad monks. He recalled how much fun the guys had dressing up in costumes of ancient clerics. She was to be called Marta, an innocent peasant girl accused of witchcraft and condemned to be burned at the stake, but not before her body was thoroughly *examined* by the High Inquisitor and his minions.

It took him weeks to set it up, but she dropped ten grand in his lap for his efforts. Her only regret: they didn't actually immolate her. That unsettled him.

He vaguely remembered the mousy assistant who dropped off the cheque with some last-minute requests.

"OK, yes, I remember . . . Miss . . . sorry, I forget your name."

"Kerry Barnes."

Tobin nodded as if he recognized the name.

"Mr Tobin, Ms Hasley didn't tell me what she was . . . paying for. Not until some months later."

"She did? And?"

She shrugged. "Well, nothing really. She makes a lot of money; she ought to be able to buy . . . whatever . . . she wants."

"And, what's your interest in our past business, Miss Barnes?"

"I, obviously, don't make as much money as Ms Hasley. But, I can see . . . well, the opportunity to realize one's deepest . . . darkest fantasy. How . . . wonderful must that be?"

"Miss Barnes. I think everyone should be careful what they wish for."

"I have a fantasy . . . would you . . . like to hear it?"

"That would be none of my business, Miss—"

"Please?" Her plea surprised him.

"OK."

She laced her fingers and lowered her head. For a second he thought she'd recite a Hail Mary.

"It's . . . an awful thing. No woman would really wish it."

Tobin sipped his tonic water and waited.

"I often pass an area . . . it's between a construction site and a vacant lot. Anyway, sometimes I walk by there on the way to the subway. Men gather there . . . homeless men. Some of them are quite old . . . and dirty-looking."

Tobin sipped his tonic again, leaned back and released a long exhale.

"Anyway, at night, in my bed, I imagine approaching them . . . and . . . it's like they have some strange power over me, drawing me to them. They gather around me. They don't say anything; they don't tell me what to do. They just grin and cackle . . . and I . . . strip for them."

Tobin maintained his poker face.

"When I'm entirely naked they come closer; they put their hands on me. They begin to call me awful things. Some take my clothes away; I can hear them being ripped and torn to pieces. And their hands are all over me. They drag me to a place out of sight and then they . . . they . . ."

"Can I get you a drink, Miss Barnes?"

"They rape me!" She blurted it out like something that had been caught in her throat. She trembled.

"Drink?" he asked again.

"Yes, please, thank you."

He signalled the bartender.

Her breathing was laboured, as if she just came in from a jog.

Larry appeared and put an amber shot in front of her.

"It's whisky," Tobin said.

She raised the glass, her hand shaking, but managing to reach her lips. A few drops ran off her chin but she swallowed it down and winced from the burn.

"They all have me," she said finally. "They violate me every way you can imagine. And I orgasm . . . over and over. There's something wrong with me, isn't there?"

Tobin shrugged. "Well, you do get worked up, and just using your imagination. But otherwise, I suspect you are perfectly normal, Miss Barnes."

"Normal?"

"Rape fantasies . . . pretty common . . . among women. The dirty old men, well, that brings an element of humiliation, or perhaps even punishment into the mix."

"Punishment? You think I want to be punished, Mr Tobin?"

"I think you have a healthy, first-rate imagination, Miss Barnes. The drink is on the house. Nice talking to you; I have to get back to work . . ." He began to get up.

"Mr Tobin . . . you employ people . . . to act out scenes."

He settled back down. "I do."

"Are they . . . professional?"

"Professional what?"

"I just . . ."

"They're actors . . . some are professional actors, yes. Others are just good at it, and reliable."

"Would you consider . . . hiring me?"

"Miss Barnes, you understand what my employees do? Do you really?"

"Yes. I'd like to . . . would you give me a chance?"

He was tempted to say yes. There was something beguiling about her, maybe because the face and package didn't match the over-the-top yearning to get banged by a bunch of old bums.

"Who do you fuck, Miss Barnes, and how frequently?"

"I . . . but . . ."

"I need to know you are relatively risk-free health-wise. If you have a steady boyfriend you're probably OK; if you're in the habit of allowing street bums to screw you . . ."

"That's just a fantasy."

"Boyfriend?"

"No . . . no one . . . for some time."

"That's hard to believe. You're a pretty girl."

"I . . . I work so much."

"Uh-huh."

"Give me a chance, Mr Tobin. I really think—"

"You could do a good job?"

"Shall I audition?"

Tobin chuckled and shook his head. "No. But before I bring you on, I may have you observe a few scenes. You may change your mind."

"When?"

"Leave me your phone number and when you're available. I'll call."

"Thank you, Mr Tobin."

As she stood and walked away Tobin drew a thumb across his lips and hissed, "Jesus H."

Larry waved him over to the bar.

"Boss, Heidi's got a guy in your office, and Rocco said he'd see you tomorrow afternoon."

"He's coming with the guys?"

"Four of them."

"OK."

Heidi greeted him at his office door. She rolled her eyes as she stepped past him.

A man stood stiffly by his desk, his jaw set as if he'd been grinding his teeth; his chin jutted out. He looked like he expected the world to kiss his ass.

"Mr Tobin."

"Yes."

"Howard Gray. I was here on time."

"Yes, Mr Gray, and I appreciate that very much."

"Yes, well, I was made to understand you provide a most unique service."

Tobin walked around him and sat at his desk. Gray looked down at him.

"Have a seat, Mr Gray?"

Gray sat. Tobin thought too emphatically.

"Is Mrs Gray not here?"

"No need."

"I like to have both partners present when we discuss—"

"I said no need, Mr Tobin. My wife and I are in agreement."

"I'd rather hear that from her, but OK. And, what did you have in mind?"

"I am an educator and administrator. My wife is also an educator. She is presently situated with an exclusive, very prestigious boys' preparatory school."

"I see. Shaping young minds . . . yes."

Gray squinted, eying him curiously. "Ahem . . . the thing of it is, Mr Tobin, we have shared . . . imagined, if you will, her . . . and her students . . . uh . . ."

"A classroom gang-bang."

"That's a crude term."

"All right, seduction, violation by multiple individuals acting in concert. How's that?"

"Not a seduction, per se. She is to be taken, quite forcefully, made to do things."

"It can be arranged. It will take a little time to hire the young men; they would have to appear as young as your wife's students."

"No, Mr Tobin. I . . . we want boys . . . teenagers."

"I'm afraid that isn't going to happen, Mr Gray."

"I was told . . ."

"You misunderstood. What we do skirts the law, but we don't cross it. You want to stage a make-believe rape, but if we use kids under legal age, it's a real rape, and it'll be you and your wife who will be the rapists . . . statutorily speaking, but it amounts to the same thing."

"I was told you could arrange anything."

"Illusions, Mr Gray. You suspend your disbelief and play along."

"That's not what I came here for. You have wasted my time."

"I'm sorry. If it'll make you feel any better, you wasted my time too."

Gray stood and stormed out, nearly hitting Heidi with the door as she was about to enter.

"Whoa! Who put a bug up his ass?"

"He wanted teenagers to fuck his wife. Can you believe that shit?"

"Well, remember those sisters who wanted to be waylaid by elves in the forest?"

"Jesus, yes!" Tobin laughed. "They were little guys, but they were of age. Who knew they had their own local?"

Tobin caught his breath. "OK, check out this girl for me. She might come to work for us. Maybe have Flynnie do a background on her."

He handed Kerry Barnes's information to Heidi. "Anything else on the calendar?"

"That Stassen woman called. She's made another request; she wants an audience."

"That'll cost extra."

"I told her. No problem."

Tobin shrugged. "You get what you pay for."

Tobin helped Larry clean up after last call and locked up. It had been a long day.

Outside he took in a deep breath of cool, damp air.

"Mr Tobin?"

He turned towards the voice. Kerry Barnes stood half in shadow near a recessed doorway.

"Miss Barnes, what the hell are you doing here? You haven't been waiting for me all night, have you?"

"I was hoping to talk to you some more; I promise, I'm not stalking you."

"Maybe not, but you're making me nervous, to say the least."

"I'm so sorry. I know I'm out of line."

"A bit."

"I just needed to ask you something."

"It couldn't wait?"

"Yes, of course. I'm so sorry, please, don't let . . . that is, I hope this won't dissuade you from considering me."

"How are you getting home?"

"Walking, I guess."

"Close by?"

She shrugged.

"Great. All right, I'll walk you to the subway station, if I don't spot a cab first."

"You don't have to . . ."

"Yes, I do."

He gestured to her to join him. "This way?"

"Yes."

They had walked a short distance.

"Mr Tobin . . . I was wondering . . . what I wanted to know . . . is it really possible to turn a fantasy into reality?"

He glanced at her, then zipped his jacket against the chill.

"That blouse can't be doing much against this damp air."

She touched a finger to the button below her neck. "I'm OK. Please, Mr Tobin, is it possible?"

"I have no idea, Miss Barnes. What I set up are little . . . dramas. It's all play-acting. When they're over, everyone goes back to living their life."

"But, can it change someone?"

"Change?"

"Turn them into . . . I guess, another person."

"I'm not sure what you mean, Miss Barnes. It might give someone some insight into themselves. Believe me, not everyone leaves happy."

"But . . . is it possible, really possible to cross that line into fantasy, so the fantasy becomes your life?"

He stopped and held her in his gaze. "OK, let me show you what's fantasy and what's reality. Where's that vacant lot you told me about with all the dirty bums mulling around?"

"It's on the way."

"Fine, show me."

He followed her along darkened streets; they were in sight of the subway stop when she stopped and pointed towards a trash-strewn field.

Tobin stopped and peered into the shadows. A fire contained by an old metal barrel flickered. A group of figures huddled around it.

"C'mon," he said, and gestured to her to follow him towards the flame.

"But . . ." She hesitated, then followed him.

Four of them stood around the barrel. Another two lay on piles of rags and newspapers on the ground. They looked startled.

Tobin grinned, then turned. He called after her. "C'mere, hurry up."

She stepped beside him. She trembled under the gaze of the homeless men. Tobin stepped behind her, then his arms crossed her chest and his fingers began to pluck at the buttons of her blouse, which was damp. From the air, or her perspiration, he wondered.

"What? What are you doing?"

"Quiet." He tugged her blouse open, exposing her chest to the men. In a second his hand was working at the clasp of her bra. Before she could protest again he unfastened it and lifted it off her breasts.

"You like these tits, guys?"

She tried to cover herself with her arms but he pulled them away.

"Nice tits, huh? You want some?"

She was shaking as if the earth were quaking beneath her.

A couple of the men chuckled. The rest just gazed at her dumbly.

"Well, whaddya say? Pretty young titties to play with, and nice wet pussy to fuck. She won't put up a fight."

"I'll squeeze 'em for ya, pal. You got any booze?" The bum stepped around the others.

"No, no booze."

"Got money?"

"Nah, broke."

"Shit. How 'bout the cunt?"

"No . . . all she has are these tasty titties."

"Shit . . . get the fuck outta here. Take the skinny bitch with ya. Fuckin' asshole."

Tobin laughed. "C'mon, let's go."

She tried to pull her blouse together as she tottered after him.

"Well, so much for your fantasy," he said.

"Why'd you do that?"

"To make a point. Those guys have no interest in fucking anyone, much less raping anyone. They're so steeped in bad alcohol I doubt any of them could even get it up. All they want is their next slug of rotgut. You could have stripped down, bent over and drawn them an arrow to your pussy and all they'd be interested in is whether you could get them a bottle. That's the difference between fantasy and reality."

He spotted a cab and hailed it. He opened the door and handed some bills to the driver. Before he pushed her in he slipped off his jacket and put it over her shoulders.

"Take the lady home; keep the change."

The cab pulled away.

Tobin downed a late breakfast and stumbled into the saloon around 3 p.m. Heidi had prepared the paperwork for the Stassens and put out a call for supporting players. The bill was going to be above ten grand, maybe fifteen, but she'd already received Mr Stassen's approval.

"Clinic appointments are set up," Heidi said as she slid a mug of coffee across the desk to Tobin.

"Rocco here yet?"

"He and the boys are in the locker room."

"Good."

Tobin walked a short way along the corridor to a room that adjoined the private lounge. He entered a room lined with metal lockers that would not have looked out of place at any workout club.

"Boss, what ya got for us?"

Rocco stood with one foot planted on a bench, wearing a sleeveless red shirt and black shorts. Tobin always marvelled at the shape he was in; a bodybuilder's sculpted muscles, but with none of the grotesquery. Michelangelo would have creamed himself to sculpt Rocco, Tobin thought.

"I say something funny, Boss?" Rocco pushed a hand back over tight, wavy black hair.

"No, I was just thinking of . . . never mind." Tobin counted heads.

"Okay, Rocco, and we have Ben, Tully, Jim, Teddy. We're going to need one more; who do we have available who's bi?"

"Bi?" Rocco asked.

"In this scene hubby gets *forced* to give a blow job."

"Hell, he can blow me."

Every head snapped towards Rocco. "What?" he said.

"You're not serious."

"What's the big deal? You close your eyes it's just another mouth."

"I never would have thought."

"What? Don't mean I'm gay; I still get to bang the missus, right? I hope she's as hot as the last one we did."

"Very . . . if you like that type. It was her idea for hubby to eat dick."

"Whoa, she sounds like some cat."

"Claws and all. Well, if you want to do the honours, fine with me. We still need another guy. How about Eric?"

"Eric's gonna be on the DL for a while. He had knee surgery just last week. Sean's available."

"OK, call him for me. I'll set it up for some time next week and let you know."

"What's the scene?" Ben asked.

"Standard . . . you guys ought to know it in your sleep by now. Hubby and wife show up at the bar, you guys move in on the wife, get her on the dance floor, feel her up. She makes token protests. So does hubby, but you put him in his place. Make loud remarks about why she's married to a wimp. Then just fuck the shit out of her, you know, like *real* men."

The guys chuckled.

Tobin told them what their approximate cut would be, eliciting appreciative nods. Then they filed out. Rocco hung back and clapped Tobin on the shoulder; it felt like he'd been hit with a side of beef.

"Jesus!"

"Sorry, boss. That shoulder still giving you trouble?"

"Only when you try to dislocate it."

Tobin had known Rocco since the night he dragged him out of the wreck that had been his car after a juiced-up soccer mom on her cell phone crashed a van full of kids into it. A paramedic with the Fire Department, Rocco rode with him in the ambulance to the ER. They became friends during that short ride as Rocco told him of his aspirations to be a porn actor, and Tobin unreeled his ideas for turning his barely-making-it saloon into a clandestine sex club.

"Sorry, I wanted to talk to you," Rocco said.

"Yeah?"

"You heard the city's likely to lay off some people."

"I thought you guys and the cops were safe."

"I think so; meanwhile, I heard from a producer, so I might be heading out to LA."

"Wow, when?"

"Not for another month ... maybe. He liked my pictures, but he thought I was a little short."

"Short? You're six-two—"

"Not that kinda short."

"Are they nuts? That schlong of yours is a monster."

"Average for the business, he said."

"That's hard to believe. I always thought they used camera tricks."

"Anyway, whatever happens, I just wanted to say thanks for the gigs. The rest of the guys feel the same way. Getting paid for this ...'"

"I thought you guys would be pretty jaded by now."

"Never ... you kidding? Anyway, just wanted to tell ya, you're OK, Greg."

"Thanks. And you guys are reliable; just stay healthy."

Tobin made his way back to his office.

"Here's Flynn's report on that girl you asked about." Heidi handed him an envelope.

He sat and slid his finger along the seal and unfolded the contents.

"Hmm, who the hell names their kid Psyche?"

"Huh?"

"This girl told me her name was Kerry ... Kerry Barnes. Seems she was born Psyche Andersfield. Parents were some kind of intellectuals ... that explains it. I figured that or old hippies. Orphaned at seventeen, due to parents killed in an accident in Greece. Lived with relatives briefly, then off to fend for herself."

"Any money from the folks?"

"Not much. She had to go to work. Never went to college. Different secretarial jobs, until she landed at Pharma-Gene and was made executive assistant to our client Evelyn Hasley a short time later. Looks like she's pulling in some big salary, some resentment in the office ... that's to be expected. That's it."

"Nice normal girl, then."

"What's normal? Anyway, there's something a little off about this girl. I wonder how she managed to charm Hasley into giving her that big promotion."

"Why don't you ask her? She's been in the lounge since just before you arrived."

"What?"

"Sipping ginger ales."

"Jesus."

"Seems you two are fascinated with each other." Heidi chuckled.

"Anything on for today?"

"Just Mr Andrews."

"Our best repeat customer," Tobin said, shaking his head. "Everything all set up?"

"Little girl's bedroom, all pink, lots of stuffed animals."

"And Katie?"

"Getting changed as we speak. I think she genuinely likes him, gets a charge out of the scene, besides the bucks, of course."

"OK."

Tobin tossed Flynn's report into a drawer and went to the lounge. He knew enough to scan the dim corners; then he spotted Kerry.

"OK if I join you?"

She nodded at him to sit down as she sipped her drink through a straw.

"You must have pretty relaxed hours at that job of yours."

"It was a light day; Ms Hasley told me to take the afternoon off."

Larry called across the room to him. "Tonic and lime," Tobin replied. Larry brought it over. Tobin took a sip.

"You frightened me last night," Kerry said. "I . . . I didn't know what to do . . . what you were going to do."

"You weren't at all concerned at what those bums would do?"

"I . . . I guess, they wouldn't do anything."

"Oh yes they would, if they were jonesing, and they were desperate for a drink. They might rap you across the head, rob you, take anything they might be able to sell or pawn. But the last thing they'd likely do is fuck you."

"You made that excruciatingly clear."

"I just wanted to disabuse you of this notion of yours that you can fold real life into a fantasy. The best we can do is play-acting."

"Are you so sure? Some people believe we lead another life in our dreams just by closing our eyes."

"And so what if we do? It's complicated enough keeping track of this life."

"But you help people to realize their fantasy lives."

"Not realize, act out. It's not the same, and for a very good reason."

"Good reason?"

"Like maybe staying out of jail . . . or shaming your family. Is that good reason enough? I'm like a guy who runs an amusement park, I offer a manufactured thrill."

"You can transcend that . . . really, you can. You said you would let me know if I could work for you."

"OK, first I want you to see something."

He stood and she followed him along the wall to the hidden corridor. He led her through the locker room and through another door leading to the private lounge.

Kerry stopped to gaze at a bedroom scene set in the centre of the sunken floor, all in juvenile pink. A girl was curled up as if asleep in the bed.

An Asian girl sat at a table in the surrounding gloom. She stood to greet Tobin.

"It's OK, Susie; I'll keep an eye on things."

"OK, Mr Tobin . . . you sure?"

"Yeah, you're good for the rest of the afternoon. Don't forget to stop by the office and get your cheque from Heidi."

"OK, thanks, Mr Tobin."

"Catch ya later, kid."

He invited Kerry to sit with him at the table Susie had just vacated.

"I have someone monitor every scene, just in case something goes awry."

"Like what?"

"Like – so far – nothing, but I can't take any chances. These things can get pretty emotional, frenzied."

They watched the girl in the bed for a brief time. A man who appeared to be in his late thirties stepped into the scene. He wore pyjamas.

Tobin whispered. "This guy, he leads a routine life, married, a few kids, house, mortgage, his own consulting business."

Kerry peered at the man. "What . . . what's he . . . ?"

"He has a sister, a couple of years older. When they were young kids they shared a bedroom, used to cuddle together when thunderstorms rolled by . . . nothing untoward, just kids being kids. Of course, when they closed in on puberty their parents put an end to those arrangements. Problem is, ever since he's had this attraction to his sister. He would never act on it, of course, he's not a creep. But he was having trouble keeping it under control. He was tempted to talk to his sister about it. She's married with kids, too. He thought it better to keep it under wraps, no matter how much it gnawed at him. But then he blurted out his sister's name while he was screwing the wife."

The man stood at the foot of the girl's bed. "Ellie?"

The girl came awake, rubbing her eyes. "Adam? What are you doing here?"

"I couldn't sleep . . . could I stay with you?"

"But Adam, you're a big boy now."

"I know . . . but I miss you."

"If mom and dad find out we'll be in big trouble."

"I'll be quiet. Please?"

"Oh . . . OK, but just to snuggle, OK?"

The man eagerly slid under the bedclothes with the girl.

Tobin leaned towards Kerry. "After he came to me, it took us almost a year to find a girl who closely resembled his sister, at least enough to make it convincing. Katie's twenty-seven, but she's an amazing actress . . . passes for fourteen . . . convincingly."

"Oh, my, I thought she was fourteen."

The man and the girl held each other in a tight embrace.

"Adam, don't do that, it tickles. And it's naughty."

"But you feel so nice and soft."

"My naughty baby brother. Do you want me to take my top off?"

"I want you to take your PJs off."

"Adam!" But the girl pulled her pyjama top over her head and then squirmed out of her bottoms. The man moaned.

"I shouldn't touch you there," the girl said, "but I love how you get all silly."

"Please, Ellie, rub me faster."

"Adam . . . Adam . . . please come inside me. Adam, please."

"Oh, Ellie . . ."

He climbed on top of her. Tobin and Kerry watched the rhythms of sex as neither the girl nor the man uttered anything more other than the moans and sighs of a couple fucking.

The man shuddered and growled, then collapsed onto the girl who embraced him. "My sweet baby brother," she cooed. They fell into a slumber.

"That's it," Tobin said. "That's all he wants. We can slip out now. He's always behaved himself."

He led her back to the public lounge.

"Well, what did you think? Make-pretend incest . . . doesn't it make you sick?"

"No," she said. "I thought it was beautiful."

"Yeah, well, he's good for another few months; he'll be able to put his sister out of his mind and pay attention to real life."

Kerry said nothing.

"Could you fuck, blow someone, pretend to be his sister, daughter, mother? Pretend to be a schoolgirl and let your teacher fuck you?"

"Yes," she said. "And maybe even . . . go beyond pretend."

"You make me nervous, lady. But I'm going to take a chance on ou . . . just out of curiosity."

"Wednesday evening, Mr Stassen. We had to line up plenty of extras o fill the lounge, that's what took so much time."

Tobin swung the phone to his other ear. "Yes, I have the cashier's heque in hand, but once you walk through that door Wednesday, no efunds. All right, we'll see you and Mrs Stassen at 8 p.m."

He placed the phone on his desk and leaned back.

"What's up?" Heidi said. "After I counted all the zeroes on that heque I figured you'd be so happy you'd spontaneously hand out a onus."

"Did you? Really?"

Heidi shrugged.

"I don't know; I have a funny feeling about this one. That new girl, Kerry . . ."

"You mean Psyche?"

"Yeah. This will be her first gig. Just an extra, but something tells ne I should give her a call, set her up some other time."

"What could happen?"

"Damned if I know. I just can't shake this feeling. Ah, screw it. If I give in to it I'll end up jinxing the thing for sure."

He went to the public lounge and scanned the booths and tables. He almost expected to find Kerry somewhere in a dim corner, but he didn't see her again until Wednesday.

The Stassens met him in his office.

"Still time to call it off," he told them.

"Why would we want to do that? I couldn't sleep all night thinking about tonight; and I made sure Neil didn't either, did I honey? Was I cruel to you, sweetheart, not letting you have any relief?" She squirmed in her seat, her breasts jostling in a low-cut black dress.

Neil nodded. "I just hope—"

"That you don't cream in your pants before the party gets going?" Tracy chuckled.

"All right then," Tobin said, slapping his hands down on his desk. "Heidi will see you to the door that opens into the lounge. There will be people drinking, talking, dancing . . . a typical bar scene. Have yourselves a drink, relax . . . and things will just . . . occur."

"This way, please." Heidi showed them out.

Tobin waited a few minutes before he followed the darkened corridor to the raised portion of the lounge. The lighting was adjusted so no one could see him sitting in the shadows.

He sat and began to scan the room. Rocco and the guys were milling about, talking up some of the extras. But where was Kerry?

He watched a girl whose bare back was turned to him. She appeared to be topless, but as she turned he could see she wore a backless top that tied around the neck beneath her hair. It was an enticing illusion. She also wore a denim skirt that reached to just above the knees. She could have been any college girl out for a night.

The acoustics in the room were excellent, and he could make out much of individual conversations if he concentrated, all except for the faintest whispers.

Neil had bought himself and Tracy a drink. She leaned against the bar, coyly sipping from her glass. Tobin guessed she was assessing the men, wondering which ones were going to screw her senseless. A generous show of thigh through the slit in her black dress was as good as flashing neon.

Rocco bumped up against her ass. No need to concentrate on Rocco's voice, it was a deep, reverberating baritone with a hint of gravel in it.

"Hey, pretty lady, can I buy you a drink?"

He could see Neil make a faint protest. Rocco turned him away, "Was I fucking talking to you?"

"That's my husband," Tracy protested.

"Too bad for you. How about a dance? I bet the wimp don't mind."

He didn't give her a chance to answer, but curled his arm around her waist like a padlock and pulled her onto the floor. Neil cowered at the bar.

Tracy made a show of pushing Rocco's hands away from her ass. "Please, stop, my husband—"

"Isn't going to do shit. You know what, baby? You're getting me kinda anxious. Here, feel this."

Tobin could see him snatch her wrist and tug her hand down to his crotch. Even from his vantage he could see Tracy's eyes widen like saucers.

Rocco's hands roamed freely up her thigh. He buried his face in her cleavage, and lifted her dress so the whole room could see he was squeezing her ass.

Neil left the bar and approached them.

"That's enough of that."

Rocco turned on him. "Get the fuck over there."

Neil followed where Rocco pointed.

"Neil, aren't you going to do something?" Tracy demanded.

"Yeah, he's going to do something. He's going to watch you get fucked by a real cock. Sit on the floor, pussy-boy!"

Neil meekly obeyed. The other people in the room tittered.

Tracy feigned her disappointment. "Neil, how could you?"

Rocco lifted Tracy by her ass and set her on the pool table.

"Please, don't . . ."

Then Rocco shed his pants and underwear. Even from behind Tobin could make out the shadow of his cock.

"Oh, my God!" Tracy moaned. "You're not . . . not . . . going to . . ."

Kerry stepped out of the crowd and stood between Rocco and Tracy.

Tobin stood just as the slap reverberated around the room. The crowd gasped and went silent.

Tracy cupped her cheek, her eyes wide with fright and surprise.

"Shut up, you stupid slut!" Kerry demanded. She pushed Tracy onto her back and climbed onto the pool table.

Rocco turned towards where Tobin stood in the dark. He raised his arms as if to say . . . "What the fuck?" Tobin took a step, but hesitated.

Kerry had ripped Tracy's dress open and was straddling her, slapping her breasts.

"You're a little slut slumming for cock . . . aren't you? Say it, you whore!"

Tracy whimpered. Kerry raised her hand and swung it in a downward arc. Another slap reverberated.

"Say it!"

"Yes! God . . . don't hurt me any more . . ."

"Slut!"

"Yes!"

"Whore!"

"Yes . . . whore . . . whore . . ."

"That's better." Kerry leaned down and sealed a rough wet kiss to Tracy's mouth.

She sat up and crooked her finger at Rocco. "Fuck this slut, c'mon."

Rocco turned back towards Tobin who now stood just at the margin of light.

Tracy hadn't said her safe word. Tobin nodded to Rocco to play along.

Before he could climb onto the pool table Kerry scanned the room. "Anyone else want some of this pig?"

Tracy squirmed. Kerry had hooked her fingers in her pussy and was playing with her clit.

The other guys quickly picked up the cue. Kerry turned Tracy over and gave her a quick slap on her ass.

"Let's see how she sucks dick."

Ben dropped his pants and held out his cock just where Tracy's head hung over the edge.

"Don't wait for her to take it, fuck her mouth like it's a cunt." As she said it, Kerry tugged off her own top, shaking out her hair and her breasts.

Tobin hissed from the shadows, "That crazy bitch."

"Take hold of their dicks," she said and slapped the other cheek of Tracy's ass. Sean and Teddy moved in, guiding Tracy's hands to their cocks. She immediately began milking them. Jim stood by ready to join in.

"What a fucking filthy slut!" Kerry said it to the crowd. The extras surged around the table; men and women stroked, squeezed and pinched Tracy's legs and ass. They called her "slut", "pig", "whore".

Rocco looked confused. Kerry hopped onto the floor and the crowd parted for her.

She glared at Neil who sat transfixed on the floor.

"You disgraceful cowardly little pussy," she said. "Do you like what you see? Do you like seeing your wife turned into a cock-hungry slut? Show me your little dickie . . . do it!"

Neil stood and fumbled with his pants and suspenders. They dropped to his ankles. A dark stain marked the crotch of his dark grey briefs.

"Take it out."

Neil tugged his stiff dick from its cotton confines.

Kerry turned and strode back to the pool table. She grabbed a handful of Tracy's hair and yanked her head towards Neil.

"Ouch!" Sean yelped as his cock plopped out of her mouth.

"See . . . the little bitch is enjoying your rape. What a little cunt he is. Is he a cocksucker too?"

Tracy gasped. "I . . . I . . . don't know . . ."

"Let's turn him into a cocksucker . . . you want to see that, honey?"

Tracy snarled, "Yes, make him suck cock. Fucking wimp, coward . . I hate you!"

Neil moaned and collapsed to his knees.

Kerry took Rocco's hand. "Now, make this meaty man's cock nice and hard for your wife's cunt and ass."

She led Rocco to the quivering Neil.

Rocco looked down at him, his cock dangling above Neil's bowed head.

"Get me hard, pussy-boy."

Neil didn't move. Rocco grabbed him by the hair and raised his head. Neil opened his mouth as Rocco slid his cock into his cheek.

"Play with his balls, too," Kerry ordered.

She returned to the pool table and hopped aboard. Tracy had raised herself onto her hands and knees. Her hands slipped on the felt, glazed from the almost simultaneous ejaculations of Ted and Ben. Jim kneeled behind her, sliding his cock between her ass cheeks.

Kerry stretched her arm over Tracy's back. "Look at him, look at what a cocksucker he is. He deserves to be fucked as hard as you, doesn't he?"

"I hate him . . . cocksucker! Make him come in your mouth!"

A shudder ran up Rocco's back. "Jesus! He sucks like a bitch."

Neil gulped and coughed up Rocco's semen. It drooled off his chin where it joined a pool of his own.

Kerry hopped back off the table and strode over to Neil. "I guess you really are a cunt now."

She turned back to Tracy. "Shall I fuck him like the bitch he is?"

"Yes, yes! Fuck him. Rape him!"

Kerry dropped her skirt. She had removed a tube from its pocket. Tobin squinted to see what she was up to. He saw the belt and cinch around her waist, and then she turned slightly as she squeezed something from the tube into her hand.

"Jesus, was she wearing that thing the whole time?"

Neil tentatively peered over his shoulder and moaned at the sight of the black, rubber dick that hung from Kerry's strap-on. It was such a mournful note, Tobin was sure he'd scream his safe word.

Instead he lifted his ass in compliance as Kerry positioned herself behind him. Tobin watched her hips jut forward as a long whimper issued from Neil. Then she thrust her hips forward again, then again. Neil cried like a little girl as Kerry accelerated her rhythm.

Jim was fucking Tracy from behind. Rocco kneeled in front of her offering his recovering cock.

"See if you can suck as good as the wimp," he said.

The crowd was in a frenzy. A couple of the girls had shed their clothes and a no-stops orgy was developing.

Tobin sat back as the aroma of sex pervaded the room. "Christ!" he uttered.

Neil let out a shriek, and collapsed. Kerry reached her hand into the pool of semen beneath him, turned him over and smeared it over his face.

"Dirty little girl," she sneered.

She stood, the wet rubber cock glistening. She unbuckled the belt and let it fall to the floor.

Rocco had taken over for a spent Jim and was ploughing Tracy's ass. Teddy fucked her mouth. Ben had been dragged away by some little wisp of a girl . . . one of the extras, who rode his cock on the floor amidst a tangle of other limbs. Sean's cock had found another woman's mouth to call home.

It occurred to Tobin that he hadn't seen Tully all night. Finally he arrived . . . late and confused. Things were slowing down. Tracy lay exhausted, semen smears streaking her body and her hair a sticky mat.

Tully climbed onto the pool table, turned her onto her back and plunged his cock into her pussy. Her arms closed around his neck as he pummelled her. She was weeping.

"What the hell did you think you were doing?"

Tobin confronted the still naked Kerry in the locker room.

"Please . . . is there a shower?"

"First door on the right."

She turned away without saying anything. Tobin followed her into the shower and watched her as she stood under one of the nozzles. The water cascaded over her head and shoulders.

"We have a script we follow. We don't deviate. Jesus! Where the hell do you get off slapping Mrs Stassen?"

"She needed it. She craved it. She wants to be in charge, but she really doesn't want to be in charge."

"How in fuck are you supposed to know?"

"Do you want to wash me?"

"No!"

"Can you wait outside, then? We can talk later."

Tobin shook his head, turned and strode out.

She joined him in the public lounge. She wore jeans and a blue T-shirt; her hair was damp from her shower. She looked like a completely different girl to him.

"OK . . . what the hell were you thinking?"

Larry brought them drinks. She sipped hers slowly.

"I know . . . knew what they needed, what they wanted," she said.

"They told me what they wanted. Who the hell told you to ad-lib the scene?"

"They needed to be guided; they needed to be led into their other life."

"What the fuck are you talking about? What the hell is your . . . Christ! Who the hell are you?"

"You know who I am."

"Yeah, I do . . . Psyche."

Her flinch evaporated as instantly as it appeared.

"In school, the other kids used to call me Psycho. I didn't like school much."

"You did something to Hasley, didn't you? She just basically gave you a no-show job because . . . why?"

"Ms Hasley used to brood a lot. She wasn't getting her work done; she couldn't focus. One morning I found her gazing out the window. I slapped her face and told her she was a whore who needed to do penance."

"Is that your specialty, slapping faces?"

"It helped her cross."

"Cross?"

"Into her true life. As Marta she is acted upon, she's not responsible for what happens to her. She wants to be a good girl and accept her penance."

"That's nuts."

"Her life as Marta is more important to her than Evelyn Hasley. It is for Marta that her heart truly beats."

"It's a fantasy; this is the real world."

She shrugged. "Is it?"

"I thought I showed you that the other night. Do you really get off on imagining yourself fucked by a bunch of old bums? You know now it could never happen, not in real life."

"It can happen. Free will means we can choose to believe what we want, decide what is real and what is not. You make a conscious decision to lead the life you choose to lead."

"Lots of luck."

She smiled. "I don't think I really want to be ravished by hordes of filthy old men."

"That's the first healthy thing you've said since we met."

"Just one."

She stood and said goodnight.

He watched her leave, then stood and followed her out the door.

He tailed her along the dark streets, following the path they had taken before.

He caught up to her at the vacant lot. One hand closed over her mouth; he held her arms against her stomach with the other and dragged her into the field.

"Shut up and you won't be hurt," he warned.

He dragged her to a shadowed area against the wall of an adjacent building.

"Please," she whimpered.

His hands slid beneath her tee and sought out her breasts. He squeezed them and ran his thumbs over her nipples; they hardened instantly. He dropped a hand to the zipper of her jeans. He tugged them down her legs.

"Step out of them," he ordered. She complied.

"Hey, what're you doing there?" It was the bum from the other night. Others began to gather around.

"What the hell does it look like?"

Tobin forced her legs apart and made her bend forward against the wall.

"You wanna fuck that little whore here, you gotta pay rent."

"How much?"

"Depends on what you're gonna do to her."

"I'm gonna fuck her cunt like a dog."

"You gonna fuck her asshole too? She gonna suck your dick?"

"Maybe . . . I don't know."

"Five bucks to start . . . but the meter's running."

He slid his cock into her pussy and thrust. She cried out.

Their audience closed around them.

Tobin pounded his pelvis against her, each time driving his cock deeper into her belly. She bent lower, and began to keen.

"She makes any more noise, it's gonna cost you extra."

Tobin didn't answer.

"She sure is a skinny bitch. Fuckin' whores around here too busy shooting up to eat."

She pushed back against him and reached between her own legs to stroke her clit. She began to wail.

"Shit, she's gonna bring a cop down here for sure. Make her shut up."

Tobin launched his fluids; she shuddered at his release. He stepped away, his cock slipping out of her trailing a tendril of semen. Another gob ran down her thigh. She curled up beside the wall.

Tobin drew a wad of bills from his pocket and peeled off a few. "Will this cover the rent?"

The man snatched the money and nodded.

"Hey, you want us to get rid of her for you?"

"What?"

"Sure . . . nobody'll find her."

"No . . . I'm just breaking her in."

"You pimping her?"

"Going to."

"No shit."

"Do me a favour, will you?"

"Huh?"

Tobin lifted her to her feet and spun her around to face the bum. He lifted her tee.

"Give her tits a squeeze for me."

The bum shrugged and took hold of her breasts.

"Like this?"

"Yeah, that's enough."

She pulled on her jeans and stumbled towards the street.

"Was it everything you hoped it would be?" he mocked.

She turned to face him, her eyes glazed. She began to sway. He caught her as she passed out.

Neil Stassen sat in front of Tobin's desk. He looked different, older maybe.

"My wife and I are divorcing," he said. "It's all very amicable, no bitterness at all."

"Still, I'm sorry to hear it," Tobin said.

"She said . . . she could never respect me as a man again. She said it wasn't my fault, that she had changed since that night. I understood . . . that is, I can't explain it, but somehow I feel as if we both transcended something . . . a barrier we didn't know existed. That young woman . . . the one who . . ."

"Yes?"

"It was as if she had thrown open a door and herded us through. Our lives, my life, what I was before . . . it's all meaningless to me. It's very liberating, but then I wonder, what next, what do I do now? And then it's as plain as day; I can do anything, live any life I want. Can you understand, Mr Tobin?"

"Not entirely, Mr Stassen.

Neil smiled. "I know . . . I've hardly worked it out myself. I jus
wanted to thank you."

"Me?"

"If it wasn't for you, well, the veil would not have been lifted. Tha
young woman . . ."

"She must remain anonymous, Mr Stassen."

"Yes . . . I suppose. Well, goodbye, Mr Tobin."

"Good luck to you, Mr Stassen."

Tobin retired to his usual table in the public lounge.

A couple of guys were trying to hit on the bartender.

"What's your name, honey?" one asked as he pushed a too-large
tip into her jar.

"Psyche."

"Whoa, what kind of parents did you have that they named you
Psyche?"

"Greek scholars."

"Speaking of Greek, how about I meet you after your shift?"

"Sorry, I don't swing that way."

"Shit . . . shoulda known with a name like Psyche."

She smiled sweetly as they took their drinks and retreated.

Tobin called her over.

"So, you're Psyche tonight? What else are you?"

"Why, I'm a lesbian bartender who wants to dress her boss like a
girl so she can pretend he's her girlfriend."

"Why complicate it with the lesbian angle?"

"Life's complicated . . . even a fantasy life . . . otherwise, it wouldn'
be . . . real."

Tobin held his head in his hands.